SIEGE OF SHADOWS

LYNN ABBEY

ACE BOOKS, NEW YORK

This book is an Ace original edition,
and has never been previously published.

SIEGE OF SHADOWS

An Ace Book / published by arrangement with
the author

PRINTING HISTORY
Ace edition / February 1996

Cover art by Jeff Barson.

For information address: The Berkley Publishing Group,
200 Madison Avenue, New York, NY 10016.

The Putnam Berkley World Wide Web site address is
http://www.berkley.com

ISBN: 0-441-00306-0

ACE®
Ace Books are published by The Berkley Publishing Group,
200 Madison Avenue, New York, NY 10016.
ACE and the "A" design are trademarks
belonging to Charter Communications, Inc.

PRINTED IN THE UNITED STATES OF AMERICA

10 9 8 7 6 5 4 3 2 1

Prologue

Weary of heaven's endless strife, the Hesse had vowed to put that timeless place behind them. They were an immortal folk with magic in their blood. There was no limit to their searching, their journeying, but of all the lands beneath heaven, the Hesse chose a peninsula jutting into a deep, inland sea. The Hesse named the sea Prayse, which was also the name they gave to their new world. They named the peninsula Alberon, their word for the white-blooming trees that greeted them in the springtime of their arrival.

A range of black-rock mountains separated Alberon from the other lands around the Sea of Prayse. The Hesse called those fierce, forbidding peaks the Eigela, after the equally fierce king who'd led them safely from heaven to their new and peaceful home. Another mountain range, not so high or rugged, ran the length of the peninsula. Those mountains were green, not black, and teemed with life of every sort. The Hesse named them after their beloved queen, Spure, the mother of them all.

Between the mountains of Spure and the sea, Alberon was divided into countless river-drained valleys where the forty-seven kindred of Spure and Eigela settled. They gave their names to their valleys and set about learning the secrets of agriculture and architecture. Throughout those first years of their new lives the Hesse labored as they'd never labored in heaven. They built and named, named and built. From Sandrisan in the northeast, to Ulver on the southernmost spit, to Bercelen in the far northwest, the Hesse used magic and the black stones of the Eigela to construct the fortress-homes they called rocs; not because they were warlike folk, but because they remembered war and preferred peace.

The world was wondrous to the Hesse, who'd dwelt in heaven's unchanging eternity. They walked lightly on their land, taking only what they needed—and they needed little beyond their magic. The Hesse traveled freely between their rocs, especially King Eigela and Queen Spure, who built nothing for themselves, but lent their greater magic and wisdom to their children instead. Life in Alberon became a celebration of the seasons: springtime's burgeoning life, summer's first fruits, autumn's harvest, and the dark, snowy nights of deepest winter.

For a millennium the Hesse dwelt in bliss and peace, defended by their magic, their king, and their rocs. Their heavenly enemies did not pursue them, but they were not alone beside the Sea of Prayse. Mortal folk had lived and died in Alberon long before the Hesse gave it a name.

These mortal folk made crude shelters deep in the forests. They knew little of clothing, nothing of fire. They hunted in packs, like wolves, or with solitary stealth, like long-fanged cats. When the Hesse ventured into the Spure mountains to harvest stone and timber, food, fur, and other needful, precious things, they traveled in groups. Hesse magic—and the steel weapons they'd learned to forge—were more than enough to intimidate mortal hunters throughout the first millennium.

But in the second millennium relentless cold came to Alberon. The Eigela was sheathed in thick, icy shrouds. Snow lingered in the Spure mountains from one winter to the next. The Hesse adapted; the Hesse endured. They had fire and magic. They made boots from tanned leather, blankets from plush pelts, and wove fine cloaks from the fleece of the sheep they first hunted, then tamed.

Life was not so snug or warm in the deep forests. Mortal folk had neither Hesse magic nor Hesse lore. Their leather was untanned, their pelts uncured, their garments unseamed. Hiding in caves and in the lee of fallen trees, they shivered through the icy storms. They died in droves, but those who survived sniffed the wind and caught the scent of fire rising from the Hesse valleys.

After that, nothing in Alberon was safe from mortal hunger, mortal hunters. They crept up to the very walls of the black rocs. They fell upon the sheep and horses, feasting on the spot, leaving the carcasses for the horrified Hesse to find. They fell upon the Hesse, too, slaughtering them, devouring them, taking their fine, warm garments as prized trophies.

The Hesse turned to their king. Alberon was their home now, they protested, and they feared it would become another bloody heaven if Eigela didn't unleash his fierce power. King Eigela listened and vowed to rid Alberon of the troublesome mortals. He led great hunts into the Spure and gave handsome bounties to any kindred leader who kept his valley mortal-free. For a time the mortals retreated, and it seemed that Alberon was safe for Hesse celebrations, though winter still gripped the land and mortal folk still died in shivering misery.

But mortal folk were as clever as the Hesse, and far more numerous. In their bitter, highland retreats, they shared such knowledge as they'd stolen from the valleys. Using wood and stone instead of steel, they made deadly weapons and formed themselves into huge, howling hordes that swept out of the forests, into the valleys. The mortals burnt the neat fields and trapped the Hesse in their rocs. They never breached the bleak, black walls but, once again, they slaughtered travelers.

Faced with the outrage of death among his immortal subjects, his kin whom he'd delivered from heaven's strife, King Eigela renewed his vow:

What was the worth of trees or deer, birds or wildflowers, he asked his queen, if mortals could be consumed in waves of flame? The king answered his own question: The wonders of Alberon had no worth while immortal Hesse lives were in jeopardy. King Eigela called the storms of his namesake mountains. He harnessed their lightning and set the forests ablaze. All Alberon was lost in smoke-darkened days and flame-lit nights, until Queen Spure protested the destruction of the green mountains named for her.

Queen Spure made her own vows: Peace could not be bought with the annihilation of mortal kind. Mortal kind was not evil, not like the enemies the Hesse had left in heaven. Mortal kind was simply cold, starving, and desperate. If the Hesse would shelter mortal folk, as they sheltered their king and queen, then Alberon would know true peace.

Eigela, who feared his queen as he feared no enemy in Alberon or in heaven, let the storms extinguish his lightning fires. He made peace with the sooty folk who'd survived his wrath and invited them to live in the valleys, since their forest homes were charred and desolate.

None of the mortal folk would have accepted the king's invitation were it not for Queen Spure, who walked among them, tending their wounded, teaching them the mysteries of the hearth, the loom, the plow, and the shepherd's crook. Because she assured them with her honor, mortal men and women washed themselves in valley rivers and covered their bodies with clothes the Hesse gave them. By day they learned to farm and fish, to weave and build. By night their Hesse lords taught them to sing and write, to paint with bright colors and—in the peaceful passage of time—to work wizardry with lightning held captive in iron-and-crystal talismans. Talismans, because mortal folk could not swallow a storm's might as the immortal Hesse did.

The second millennium, the cold millennium, became Alberon's golden age, when Hesse and mortal folk alike learned from their mistakes and lived in passionate harmony. Children whose lineage was both Hesse and mortal danced with their parents at the season celebrations. Flowering vines grew up the black walls of rocs used only for storage and ceremony, because the mortals elsewhere around the Sea of Prayse offered no threat to Alberon, and the Alberonese did not fight among themselves.

At least, they didn't fight until King Eigela grew careless with Alberon's peace. The Hesse's ancient enemies slipped down from heaven and skulked through the shadows of the undefended land. Such folk, no different in appearance from Hesse or mortal folk, hinted that the Hesse had not shared *all* their secrets and how, despite generations of harmony, the Hesse still plotted mortal annihilation. Most mortal folk were unseduced, but Alberon's enemies needed only a few malcontents—Nezzaran and Gandrel foremost among them—and a few wizards—Alaria above all others—to start a terrible war of blood and lightning.

First causes were soon forgotten. Hatred flourished.

The mighty rocs where mortal and immortal together sought shelter were besieged with fire from the sky. Loyal Alberonese fought back; King Eigela summoned his mountain storms. His lightning was terrible to behold, impossible to withstand. Alberon was smoking and barren again, but the war continued, as the war in heaven had always continued.

Realizing at last that the Hesse faced their old, immortal enemies, King Eigela went to his black mountains. He swore that he wouldn't return until he'd forged a weapon that would annihilate the treacherous immortals who'd trespassed his kingdom. He promised to burn the clothes from ungrateful and mortal shoulders, to drive them back into the forests on naked hands and knees. The Hesse would grow fat on flesh, drunk on blood.

This time, Queen Spure did not gainsay her husband.

But King Eigela lost his way in his mountains. The war persisted; the scent of Hesse defeat gathered in the air. Wearing mourning clothes, Queen Spure entered the Eigela. She climbed the summit of the highest peak and looked near, in Alberon, and far, along the edge of the world; her king was gone, her enemies were waiting. Wrapped in a cloak darker than the mountains, she wove a bridge from her tears. She surrendered and returned to heaven. The last of the Hesse followed, leaving their mortal companions and children behind forever.

Alberon's golden age ended with Spure's tears. Its iron age began with the chaos she left behind.

Abandoned and disheartened, the mortals who had stood loyally beside the Hesse offered little resistance to their mortal enemies, who told similar tales: Alaria had betrayed them. She and Nezzaran and Gandrel had disappeared days after King Eigela climbed the black mountains. Mortal enemies made peace, but after so many generations of peaceful reliance on their Hesse lords, the mortal Alberonese were ill-equipped to replace them. Each of the forty-seven rocs became home to a mortal warlord whose ambition grew larger than his valley.

Those folk who did not wield a sword lived beneath the weight of a gauntleted fist. Wizards sold their lightning where they willed. A valley might know peace, after a fashion, while its warlord ruled supreme. But all Alberonese were mortal in the age of iron. All warlords died enfeebled and aged, if they didn't die sooner. Succession meant war—endless wars that rippled around the peninsula as warlords probed for opportunity and weakness. But no matter which warlord won, or lost, it was the common folk who suffered most. Huddled together in hovels and huts, scarcely better off than their ragged forest ancestors, they lived without hope and remembered the Hesse with curses, or with nostalgic prayer.

The chains of the iron age remained tight across Alberon's

valleys when a miller's son of Sandrisan had a dream on the eve of his seventeenth birthday.

Enough! an awesome voice said to him as he slept that night. *Enough war. Enough blood. Enough killing. Enough suffering. Put an end to this, Eigela*—which was a common name in the black mountains' shadow—*Forge peace among your neighbors, your enemies.* And before young Eigela could awaken from his nightmare, the voice filled his head with not only battle lore, but treaty talk and statecraft, too.

Eigela said nothing the next morning, not wishing to be taken for a fool, but the dream stayed with him and the grist mill, where he labored with his father and brothers, no longer filled his life. He asked Sandrisan's infrequent strangers for news of the other valleys. He carved a sword from the limb of an Alberon tree and feinted at shadows. Talking to himself on long, solitary walks, he mastered the rhetorical arts.

Young Eigela was accounted a fool by all those valley folk who'd watched him grow from boyhood, but not by other youths who slowly, steadily, made their way to Sandrisan. They were searching for the new king they'd seen in the dreams each of them had dreamt on the last night of their sixteenth year.

A single man with a dream-born vision might well be a fool. A handful of men, even twenty men, who claimed to share that vision might be dismissed as fools and safely ignored. But a hundred men practicing together under the miller's son's command—and the son of a southern warlord with them—was nothing to ignore.

Moreover, visionary dreams had become as frequent as seventeenth birthdays. Rich youths and poor youths, lords and commoners, women and men alike, all of them dreamt on the verge of seventeen. Folk—especially the folk of Sandrisan—began to hope for peace and think about *gods*.

Never before had the Alberonese thought of gods, though gods were known in the other lands around the Sea of Prayse. The Hesse admitted no gods, nor were they gods themselves, and the heaven of their legends was a horrible realm where immortality begat violent death. When the golden age began, the Hesse politely scorned the fetishes that mortal folk had carried with them, and after mortals mastered wizardry, the fetishes were buried, abandoned, finally forgotten.

When mortal men and women could command lightning, what need did anyone have for gods?

Even after the Hesse were a fading memory, the mortal folk of the valleys did not turn to altars, priests, or prayers. They buried their dead with respect, not expectation. They continued to celebrate the seasons because seasons were joyous certainties in years of war. They turned to their wizards if the weather soured. Their wizards turned to lightning, not gods.

Alberon's magister wizards, with their brilliant, lightning-filled talismans, didn't flock to the young Eigela of Sandrisan. They mocked the apprentices who, after a birthday dream, set off for Sandrisan with a few firefly sparks glowing in the crystals hung from their belts.

It was madness, the old wizards said: mortal foolishness of the worst sort, childish foolishness, *adolescent* foolishness—until the miller's son of Sandrisan began his march down Alberon's east coast and up its western one.

Young, they were at the start, but no ragtag children's mob. Eigela the miller's son was no more than twenty-five when came the dawn that he stood below Sandrisan's roc, demanding its warlord's surrender. The miller's son's poorest adherents had come to him with no more than a dream and the clothes on their backs—but not all his adherents were poor. Some came with their parents' blessing and as much treasure as their families could provide.

The Sandrisan warlord looked down on ranks of disciplined, well-equipped warriors and a cohort of young wizards who, working together, were mightier than their elders. He looked past the miller's son and his glistening army to the black mountains which glowed like fire in the day's first sunlight. A man didn't need dreams to read the omen in *that*. Old King Eigela had gone into those mountains—his mountains—looking for a weapon.

Two centuries had passed, but the old king had found what he'd been looking for.

Sandrisan was the first of the forty-seven rocs to open its gates to the miller's son, the new King Eigela. Not all of them succumbed so easily. There were sieges; there was bloodshed, but the outcome was never in doubt. Long before Bercelen in the northwest, long before southern Ulver, farsighted warlords staked their banners before the new king's tent.

Alberon's sad iron age ended in the spring of the 2,030th

year after the coming of the Hesse. Midway up the western coast, Eigela, the miller's son, accepted the surrender of the last valley warlord. He accepted a plain golden crown that the first King Eigela was said to have left behind. The truth of that legend, as with so much of the 2,029 years before the second King Eigela began his reign, could never be proven. But it was beyond legend that the new king ruled from the place where he'd been crowned. By his command a new roc, Chegnon, rose on Alberon's west coast. Mortal royalty might wander through the Alberon's valleys, but it would always have a place to call its own.

Chegnon was not the only change in Alberon. A priest anointed King Eigela with bitter oils before setting the gold crown on his brow. God had come to Alberon. Not gods in profusion as were worshipped in other mortal realms around the Sea of Prayse, but a solitary god who bestowed a singular gift on each Alberonese child on the verge of maturity: a Rapture dream, such as the one that had inspired their new king.

Early on, the Alberonese were minded to call their new god Eigela, after their new king; but King Eigela put a quick stop to that. Alberon had a god who doled out dreams to everyone born on the peninsula, but by the king's decree, Alberon's god had no name.

Alberon's nameless god, its Hidden God of Rapture, manifested no objections. Indeed, aside from the dreams, the Hidden God evidenced no concern for any Alberonese. But the dreams were enough. For some youths on the verge of seventeen, Rapture was as detailed and specific as it had been for King Eigela. For others—for most Alberonese—it was as simple as a perfect memory. Rapture visited wizards and laborers alike, in rocs and in hovels. It came to the flower-hung chambers of the nobility where eager, hopeful children slept childhood's last sleep. It found children who hid in corners or caves, or fled Alberon altogether.

In the twenty-fifth year of King Eigela's reign, Rapture came to the king's youngest son bearing a dream like no other. Prince Ganelon's sleep was filled with visions of shrieking women, lightning, bloody hands, and bloody knives. The royal priests—the same priests who'd crowned the king—scratched their collective heads. They consulted the oracles of other lands, other gods. They devised their own oracular rites. They prayed to a god who had never seemed to listen. All to no avail. The kingdom was serene, with a prince, Melkonor, able and ready to inherit the throne when the time came. Ganelon himself was a personable youth who got on well with his family, a paragon of rectitude. No one had foreseen Ganelon coming to a bad end or was comfortable with Rapture's foretelling.

Throughout Alberon there were whispers that Rapture was failing, fading, that the Hidden God was no more than the first King Eigela's weapon that was no longer needed.

But if Rapture was fading, what need had Alberon, for priests, who, in a mere quarter century, had insinuated themselves into every valley, every aspect of ordinary life? In the years that followed Ganelon's Rapture dream, wizards and warriors, the mainstays of the displaced but not quite forgotten warlords, called on King Eigela to disenfranchise the priests. The king would not hear them.

Alberon's priests had transformed Hesse magic. They built steepled monasteries that lured lightning into crystal-lined chambers. They mediated the weather, healed the sick, educated the young. They were loyal to the crown. And, besides, Rapture had not faded. Dreams still came, and only the priests could interpret them.

Every year, every season for five years, the wizards and warriors petitioned their king to restore Alberon to its godlessness. In the sixth year, the wizards and warriors revolted. They took possession of the east coast roc at Lanbellis; they proclaimed Prince Ganelon the rightful king.

King Eigela moved swiftly and without remorse. The Lanbellis roc was retaken. The traitors were thrown down from the ramparts. Prince Ganelon cut his own throat rather than submit to his father's mercy. Ganelon's hands and his knife were slick with his blood when the king's men found him.

What Rapture had foreseen had come to pass.

Measured by lives or damage, Ganelon's rebellion was a paltry thing, but it resonated deep in the Alberonese soul. Men and women who'd never told their Rapture dreams, confessed visions of violence and grief. King Eigela himself admitted that his own bright dream had contained a bloody shadow: a son who would betray his vision. All his adult life, King Eigela had prayed that his dream be proved wrong, but what his Rapture had foreseen had also come to pass.

If the Hidden God would not heed the entreaties of the king

to whom He'd sent His first dream, what hope did ordinary folk have that their smaller prayers would be heard?

Rapture was neither failing nor fading. It was relentless, inevitable—as much a curse as a gift, for although most Alberonese found contentment in their visions, there were always those who suffered.

In the aftermath of Ganelon's rebellion, priests strengthened their numbers and stature. They couldn't capture the Hidden God's unhearing ear, but they offered solace, explanation, expiation when guilt or despair weighed too heavily on mortal shoulders. By contrast, the kingdom's wizards, disgraced by their rebellion, declined in number. All but a few were denounced as charlatans or worse. They likely would have become extinct, but King Eigela was a truly wise ruler who understood that his realm needed a loyal opposition. A few freelance wizards who'd stood aloof from Prince Ganelon's ill-fated rebellion found welcome at Chegnon, where they mentored a handful of talented students.

By the day of King Eigela's death in the waning years of his seventh decade, the structures of mortal Alberonese society seemed solid. A new aristocracy, oathbound to the king, was settled in the Hesse rocs. Priests—bolstered by their manifest piety and the equally manifest power latent in their huge, steeple-crowned talismans—had divided themselves into three orders: eremitic Mellians who dwelt apart from the world, scholarly Ultramontaines who stood firm against the king's wizards, and pastoral Bydians who filled the valley monasteries and the daily needs of Alberon's folk.

Market towns and trade ports throve as Alberon took its place among the other lands around the Sea of Prayse. No town or port grew faster than the city that sprang up in Chegnon's shadow. Most Alberonese, though, lived as they had in the golden age of the Hesse, in valleys restored to fertility by a mortal king's wisdom and peace.

Such was the Alberon that King Melkonor inherited from his father. Such was the Alberon recorded in the oldest surviving chronicles, which were written at Melkonor's order. But by then, the events of his father's youth were disappearing from living memory; few written accounts remained from the iron age of anarchy, and the reign of the Hesse King Eigela was shrouded in legend. Indeed, by the year 2,535 the Hesse would have faded completely into legend were it not for the rocs that still stood in forty-seven valleys. Their mortarless black walls remained as smooth and solid as they were the day when the Hesse had raised them with magic no contemporary priest or wizard could hope to match. While royal Chegnon, mortal-built Chegnon, needed repairs every year, renovations in every reign.

Like the Hidden God who sent Rapture dreams, the existence of the Hesse couldn't be doubted, but, also like the Hidden God, neither the Hesse nor their legends had much effect on daily life. Alberon took her place among the other lands around the Sea of Prayse. Trade with Kol, Jiverne, Bardisk, and even Stercia at the opposite end of the sea was more important than any obscure entry on a moldering scrap of parchment.

Then, in the winter of 2,535, a fireball appeared high above the Sea of Prayse. For a month it blazed red-gold in the night sky. From Stercia to Alberon, it could be seen moving against the sun in the noontime sky. It lengthened until it was a bloody gash extending from the zenith to the western horizon, then, slowly it descended and disappeared below the eastern horizon.

Folk turned to their priests, who, in turn, prayed for revelation, consulted oracles, and generally prophesied doom. In Alberon, where it seemed that the fireball had disappeared into the Eigela mountains rather than below the eastern horizon, folk were afraid to venture outside their homes. The name of the first King Eigela, the Hesse King Eigela of the black mountains, was whispered in the shadows, especially when, day or night, an ember glow hovered around the highest peaks.

While the priests and wizards of Alberon contemplated the ominous wonder glowing in the Eigela, an obscure sect in far-off Stercia knew exactly what had happened: Their prophecies had been fulfilled. The Siege of Shadows was open. The age of Veshkai—the god who had governed the world for the last millennium—was coming to an end. Whoever made his way to the Siege of Shadows and looked unflinchingly upon Veshkai's face would become the god of the next millennium. They had Veshkai's word in the matter: a mountainside inscription in a language only members of the sect could read.

Veshkai described how, as a mortal man, he had found a golden throne atop a glowing mountain. He'd seen terrible sights when he first sat on the throne, but eventually Veshkai looked upon the face of the god who'd governed the world for a millennium. That old, tired, and forgotten god passed his awesome power to Veshkai. With his last breaths the old god bestowed his divinity on Veshkai and commanded him to recreate the world in his image. The old god had a warning for his successor, a warning which had become a prophecy: after a millennium, Veshkai would grow weary, and then Veshkai would send a fiery Harbinger across the heavens to tell mortalkind that the Siege of Shadows, the throne upon which Veshkai had seated himself, was open. And another brave, bold, and worthy mortal would sit on his golden throne.

The Stercian sect didn't worship Veshkai; they intended to replace him. When they heard of a glowing peak deep in Alberon's Eigela mountains, they sold their lands and possessions and set out across the Sea of Prayse. Their theology rang hollow in Alberonese ears. However inconsistent their chronicles had become regarding the Hesse, the Alberonese were confident there'd never been a mortal named Veshkai wandering *their* mountains. They were equally certain there was no improbably glowing golden throne in the Eigela right then because no Alberonese boy or girl had dreamt of Veshkai or his Siege of Shadows.

But Stercian gold was another matter. It trickled into Alberon with the first shipload of Veshkait pilgrims and it flowed freely thereafter as the Veshkait prophecy spread throughout Stercia and the other Praysean lands. Some pilgrims came with simple devotion, some with gargantuan ambition, and some believed only in the treasure of the supposed golden throne itself. Mostly, though, pilgrims came to Alberon and kept coming so long as a sunset glow clung to the Eigela. That no one returned from the quest—except for Alberonese guides who'd declined to enter the mountains—fueled the pilgrim fire rather than quenching it.

Throughout the lands of Prayse, priests and wizards of every stripe gave advice to the hopeful and the foolish. It was not enough to find the Siege of Shadows. Clearly, said the continuously reinterpreted oracles, there were other conditions, new and additional conditions, that the pilgrims had to fulfill.

Three years after the Eigela began to glow, the crown prince of Pelipulay came to Bercelen with a retinue of a hundred armed men, three avowed virgins—the Pelipulasean priests had opined that a virgin sacrifice might assure a successful quest—and a ballista that could throw a stone the size of a horse—in case the oracles of Pelipulay's celibate and martial wizards were better informed. The merchants of Bercelen needed a month to assemble the journey fare for the entire retinue. The baggage train, when the oxen and horses finally began to move it toward the Eigela, took a full day to clear the walls of Bercelen town.

If ever there were a pilgrim likely to ascend the Siege of Shadows—and put a stop to the steady stream of pilgrims—it should have been the crown prince of Pelipulay.

But neither he nor any of those who traveled north with him was ever seen again. There was shock and grief in Pelipulay, and war with neighbors who sought to exploit its loss. For the remainder of that autumn and through that winter, too, Bercelen harbored no foreign vessels. But the Eigela still glowed. The pilgrim ships returned the following spring and every season thereafter until it was five years to the day since the Harbinger had appeared.

The unnatural glow vanished in a single sunset. Those pilgrims who'd been in the Eigela reported hearing an awesome *thud*, as of a great door closing, and those pilgrims were the only ones who ever directly reported anything about the Siege of Shadows. They were the only ones who survived their quest.

By the reckoning of the verge-lord of Bercelen, who collected the king's tariffs on the foreign ships in his harbor and levied his own duties on the baggage trains as they crossed his bridges, more than a thousand pilgrim cohorts had braved the Eigela. That was nearly one ill-fated party for every two days the golden throne had supposedly cast its glow across the black peaks. The verge-lord counted cohorts, not men. Some cohorts were a handful of mounted men and another handful afoot; others were as large as the crown prince of Pelipulay's had been. On average, perhaps twenty-five men; twenty-five times a thousand, and all but the last few were never seen again.

Veshkai's Siege of Shadows had wrought a madness on the lands of Prayse, a madness worse than any war and one not unmasked until the mountains were funereal black again. Folk all around the sea shook themselves awake after a very long night with too much wine. From one end of the sea around to the other and back again, every town, every village, every farmstead had bled, not in battle, but from twenty-five times a thousand self-inflicted wounds. Except in Alberon, where the

Harbinger had landed, where the Eigela glowed with a five-year sunset, and no Rapture vision had ever shown a golden throne.

Belated protests were lodged with Alberon's King Euben III, a hot-tempered man who turned misfortune into disaster when he declared, before the assembled emissaries of his brother monarchs, that the Siege of Shadows had been nothing more than a Stercian fraud from the beginning and that every missing pilgrim was a thrice-damned fool.

With empty graves to tend, folk around the Sea of Prayse needed to blame someone, something, somewhere—but not themselves or the kin they'd lost. The cults of Stercia *were* a likely target. But Stercia itself was the mightiest of the Praysean lands and the one that had bled the most during the pilgrimage years.

Rumors of King Euben's remarks crossed the sea as fast as rumor could, reshaping itself in wind and wave. When the rumors reached the Stercian shore, folk whispered that Alberon's Hidden God had fanned the fire in the Eigela, and Alberon's king had filled his treasure house with the gold and goods of slaughtered Stercian pilgrims.

What sailed back to Alberon was war, not rumor: a mighty fleet flying the banners of Stercia, Pelipulay, and all the other grieving lands that craved vengeance for their lost children. They sailed the coast of Alberon, looking for a fight, finding Chegnon, instead, and the forty-seven impregnable Hesse rocs—one for every fertile valley, every deepwater harbor, every river mouth or marsh. Invasion by land was equally impossible: The damned black Eigela stood between any army and any hope of conquest.

The fleet tried to lure King Euben into open water. It fired a few wooden harborsides, a few isolated fishing villages. It returned, every spring, for another five years.

Alberon suffered, but it was not invaded, not conquered. The Alberonese inflicted no direct losses on their assembled enemies; they didn't need to. Their king was hotheaded, but not foolish. The sea itself was no land's ally. Storms took their toll of the ships; woodrot, fire, and disease also. Year after year, the blockading fleet grew smaller as Stercia's allies cut their losses and stayed home.

It was written in the chronicles that in the years immediately following the Debacle—as Alberon called the decade-long madness of Veshkai's Siege of Shadows and the ensuing blockade—that the Stercians were hated and despised above all other folk; but the Stercians still had a fleet and the will to use it. The other lands found it safer—more expedient—to turn their hatred and despite on the Alberonese who hadn't fought, hadn't won or lost, and who seemed content in their isolation.

The Stercians forged themselves an empire to salve their national pride. At their empire's height, the Stercians ruled all the lands around the Sea of Prayse—except Alberon, which they scorned to conquer. And when the Stercian empire slipped into its inevitable decline, those warlords who would replace it looked across the sea to Alberon and the hated, despised Alberonese, the poor Alberonese who'd been excluded from imperial trade, the invincible Alberonese who'd never paid a tin *fent* coin to the imperial tax collectors, much less a silver *crettig* or a rare golden *deya*.

In its own truth, Alberon had no wisdom for the would-be warlords, no secrets to sell at any price. After generations of isolation, Alberon *was* poor. She had too many sons trying to raise families on too many tiny plots of land. After generations of isolation, Alberon's king couldn't be tempted into alliance with any petty tyrant. Instead, Alberon offered up its excess sons in tight-knit mercenary cohorts that were unswervingly loyal, so long as their wages were paid in advance.

The Alberonese hadn't fought since the days of King Eigela II. They were unskilled with their weapons, untutored in battlefield tactics. At first, they were employed as shock troops and thrown against an enemy's strongest position. The sons of Alberon died in droves, as their ancestors had died fighting the Hesse. And, like those forgotten ancestors, they learned fast.

Nearly a millennium after the Debacle, there were still Alberonese cohorts scattered though the Praysean kingdoms. Hate and despite had become fear and grudging respect. And when a mercenary's fighting days were over, like as not, he returned home to Alberon, where ancient black rocs still guarded fertile valleys and peaceful forests.

Chapter One

It was a warm, high-summer day in the Renzi Valley. The springtime's crop of foals, calves, and lambs grew strong in the meadows. Lush fields of grain ripened in long, sun-filled afternoons. On any other golden afternoon, Kyle Dainis wouldn't have been sitting on a rooftop looking across the valley. He would have saddled Rawne, his favorite horse—his only horse—and gone exploring.

The whole valley was Kyle's to explore. The Dainis had been verge-lords of Renzi for five generations. That which wasn't theirs outright still fell under their protection and purview: fields, orchards, vineyards patchworked along the valley slopes, fishweirs in the estuary mud, mills and forges, a Bydian monastery on the headland, another in the forested foothills where the valley ended. There was no place in the valley where the verge-lord's youngest son couldn't go, if he chose. No one in the thousand or so valley households—freehold, tenant, yeoman, or gentry—who would deny him hospitality.

If the verge-lord's youngest son had dared to impose himself on anyone.

Kyle knew that what Alberon's king gave to his verge-lords could just as easily be taken back. The ungrateful sons of many an unlucky verge-lord had destroyed what their fathers had carefully built, and brought down their entire clans. How else had the Dainis themselves come to live in a black-walled roc?

Among Kyle's earliest memories was a cold winter morning when his father led him down to the black-stone crypt far below the roc's north tower. While he shivered, his father had told him the cautionary tale of Renzi's prior verge-lords, the Sodal.

The last Lord Sodal had raised an ungrateful son who abused the trust of the good folk of Renzi. King Otanazar I had stripped the Sodal of their wealth and privilege. The king had locked the Sodal women in convents. Then the king had chained the unlucky lord and his ungrateful sons to a greenwood raft that was towed up and down the peninsula—as a warning to the other vergers—before it was cut loose in open water. Now the Sodal were reduced to a handful of names on the crypt's lead-sealed niches.

Understand this, my son, Father had said in a soft, but very hard, voice, *the Dainis will not be brought down by our sons. Honor your family and we will shelter you. Dishonor your family or disgrace us, and I will judge you myself. Is that clear?*

It had been so clear that Kyle's voice had hidden in his stomach and Father had had to shake his shoulders hard before he could swear his understanding and obedience. Even now, on a warm summer day years later, the memory sent a chill down Kyle's spine. He was the youngest son, the fourth son: a superfluous hart-lord in the Dainis lineage, forever dependent on family charity. A sunny rooftop or a by-himself ride on his one horse was the best life would ever offer him, and that could always, *always*, be taken away.

A few months after Father had lectured him in the crypt, Kyle had left the roc and Renzi: Verge-lord's sons—even their superfluous hart-lord sons—spent ten years in fosterage, living in other rocs, migrating from one valley to the next, like the legendary Hesse king and queen, and sternly kept apart from their families except for short vacations.

I haven't forgotten. Those were the words Kyle said to his father as he left Renzi to dwell for the first time in another verge-lord's roc, and every time thereafter. *You don't have to remind me. I'll be careful, very careful. I won't disgrace the Dainis.*

And wherever he was for the next ten years, Kyle had been careful, so careful that he earned a reputation for clumsiness. He thought carefully and deeply about everything he did. His fellow fosterlings called him Dreamer and the men charged with his education despaired of teaching him anything. But Kyle survived his fosterage, and shortly after his sixteenth birthday—almost a year ago—he'd returned to Renzi, which he expected never to leave again.

This warm summer day was the eve of Kyle's seventeenth birthday: his Rapture night, the most important night in his life, the night he left childhood behind to become a man. With all the festivities the family had planned, Kyle was being especially careful, staying on the roof, out of trouble.

Festivities . . . Kyle dreaded festivities of any sort, dreaded them most of all when he'd be at their center. He truly wished he could stay here, on the roof, until evening, then slip unheralded into the room he'd chosen for his Rapture dream: the roc crypt. And he would have wished, if it weren't so unthinkable, to skip Rapture entirely. He already knew his fate.

But a hart-lord's wishes were never heeded. His mother had been planning these festivities since winter: lengths and lengths of flower garlands, musicians hidden in the galleries, fish-shaped fountains that spurted sparkling wine . . . and a thousand other unnecessary wonders. After three sons, he'd have thought she'd be tired of Rapture nights.

And perhaps Lady Irina would have been, if the event had been entirely in Kyle's honor. Lord and Lady Dainis had been blessed with an embarrassing abundance of sons, but only one daughter: Kyle's twin, Kiera. Kiera loved attention. Kiera loved festivities.

And Kyle loved Kiera.

Their mother couldn't skimp on her only daughter's Rapture, and wouldn't exclude her last-born son who happened to be born at the same time. Everything Lady Irina planned for Kiera, she planned for Kyle, and he'd never think of objecting.

There was real reason for the festivities. Rapture notwithstanding, tomorrow morning Kiera would be a woman and tomorrow evening Flennon Houle, a young man who cheerfully admitted that he worshipped Kiera and would cut his own throat if she asked him to, would ask Lord Dainis for Kiera's hand in marriage.

Kiera and Flen—a part of Kyle resisted the combination, though the marriage had been planned for years. Flen was the praverge of Lanbellis, eldest son of the verge-lord of Lanbellis. He had a future, and he'd share it with Kiera. It wasn't the first time the Houles and the Dainis had allied themselves through marriage and it wouldn't be the last. But Kiera and Flen . . . Flen, who could belch louder and prouder than anyone else in fosterage and bring down a charging boar with no more than a flanged spear and his own strength, that Flen would take Kiera into his bed . . .

Alone, on the sunlit roof, Kyle shook his head. Until they were six, he and Kiera had been inseparable. Then he went off to fosterage and she stayed home, surrounded by the folk who knew and loved her, and the passel of Renzi boys, who owed everything to the Dainis, spent their fosterage years at the Dainis roc. Kiera had learned everything she'd need to know as a wife and mother without ever leaving the Renzi Valley.

But she hadn't learned everything she wanted to know.

Wherever fosterage took Kyle, Kiera's long, rambling letters were waiting for him when he arrived. She expected prompt, equally long replies, but she didn't want to hear about the loneliness, the bullies, the beatings, and the boredom that were the lot of every fosterling. Kiera wanted to hear about the excitement and—as they grew older—the gossip.

He tried to please his twin sister, and though she complained endlessly about his inadequacies as a correspondent, he knew she was grateful. It wasn't her fault that she wanted his life, or what she imagined his life to be, and he wanted hers. But for all her complaints, for all that they dreamt of trading places, whenever Kyle came home for one of his infrequent visits, Kiera's face was always the first truly friendly face he saw. She'd be on the docks when his ship sailed in or waiting astride her pony at the boundary stone where the Inland Road entered Renzi. They'd pick up where they'd left off, sharing the laughter and secrets no ink could delineate.

And when the visit was over, she'd follow him to the docks or the boundary stone, promising to count the days until his next letter arrived, the days until his next visit.

She'd never failed him, and he wouldn't fail her. For her happiness, Kyle would endure a score of Rapture nights. He'd even pretend that he *liked* Flennon Houle, who was three years older than he and had never, in all their mutual years of fosterage, missed an opportunity to make his life miserable. But as the last-moment preparations at the roc reached a battlefield frenzy, with every member of the vast Dainis household rushing and shouting, he'd had to escape—or burst.

Literally.

On his rooftop retreat, Kyle would have preferred to stretch out on his back and stare at the clouds, but he didn't dare risk getting his shirt dirty. He'd have liked to stretch out the kinks a sleepless night had left in his back, but he was afraid he'd split the seams.

The cut of a young man's Rapture shirt was as old as Rapture itself. Tradition decreed that a mother made the shirt herself, before the birth of her first son. Lady Irina had done more than make the shirt Kyle wore; she'd harvested the flax, retted it, bleached it to snowy brilliance, spun it into linen thread, woven the thread into cloth. Then she'd embroidered the cloth with lustrous white silk before cutting the shirt pieces and sewing them together.

Lady Irina's Rapture shirt was a beautiful garment, full of her skill and her love. Kyle was very proud to be wearing it—as his elder brothers had worn it before him. He only wished it didn't pull quite so much when he moved. The sleeves fit him, but the sleeves of a traditional Rapture shirt were supposed to be long enough to reach the wearer's knees and loose enough to circle his thigh. Everywhere else, Kyle was simply too big for the shirt. His shoulders were too broad for the yoke, his neck too thick for the collar band, and the hem fringes, which should have touched his knees, stopped a hand span above them.

His mother had gasped and turned as white as the shirt when he presented himself for her approval not an hour ago.

"When did you get so big?" she'd muttered while tugging on the too-short yoke. "I'd have sworn both Muredoch and Angrist were bigger when their time came, and Varos was surely taller. Well, there's no altering it now. You'll just have to be careful."

Careful.

So, here he was, on the north tower roof, where the only eyes that could see him belonged either to the birds or the watchmen in the taller, western tower. The birds didn't care and the watchmen were looking for storms that weren't in the offing. As the sounds of a watchman's reed pipes floated over the northern tower, Kyle eased himself carefully against the cold stones of a chimney and tried to remember when he'd stopped being little.

He'd been little when he'd started his fosterage—littler than the other six-year-old boys. And he'd remained small until he was thirteen, maybe fourteen, because bullies only tormented smaller boys and he was somewhere around fourteen when they stopped tormenting him—which was the only reason he could pretend now to like his sister's suitor.

But bigger than Muredoch or Angrist? Taller than Varos? Kyle hadn't come home for Angrist's Rapture night and what he remembered about Varos' Rapture had nothing to do with this shirt. He hadn't seen his brothers Angrist and Varos in several years. They'd both joined the Gray Wolves mercenary cohort right after they turned seventeen. But he remembered them as big, man-sized brothers who had a lot in common with the other bullies he knew.

Kyle was only five when Muredoch wore this shirt for the first time. In memory, Muredoch was as big as a mountain. Muredoch was the oldest, the heir. He lived at Roc Dainis with his wife and children, waiting for the day when their father died and he became verge-lord of Renzi. Since Kyle's fosterage ended, he'd seen Muredoch every day, just as he saw his father every day. But he didn't truly look at either man. When Kyle thought of Muredoch, he thought of someone as big as a mountain and when he thought of his father—

Well, Father was bigger still.

With his fingers laced to together, Kyle lifted his hands carefully toward the sun, yawning and stretching until his knuckles popped. He carefully hadn't gone to bed last night; hadn't let himself sleep at all. The priests said Rapture couldn't fail: A boy dreamt and became a man. But what if the boy couldn't fall asleep? Kyle was determined not to discover the answer to that question.

Not that it would matter if Rapture passed him by. The simple truth was that he was a hart-lord, a fourth son. There weren't any titles in his future, no fortune or glory, not even a wife to share his bed or children to comfort him in his old age . . . unless his brothers died, and Kyle never wished for that.

Never.

Besides, Father and Muredoch had already made all the decisions. They hadn't consulted him, but then, Kyle hadn't expected them to. They were verge-lord and praverge. If they'd wished, they could have disavowed him completely. His father could have disavowed him the day he was born.

But Father hadn't. Father had waited until Muredoch was old enough to participate in the decision-making, and then they'd both waited until Kyle was out of fosterage. If he'd shown any aptitude whatsoever for magic or theology, they'd have sent him to a neophyte's cell in the valley's Bydian monastery. But the priests had tested him one last time when he got home and, one last time, they'd found him lacking.

Kyle's prospects as a warrior were similarly bleak. The various armsmasters who'd trained him praised his diligence. He'd mastered the sword, the lance, and the bow to their collective satisfaction; but each and every master declared that Lord Dainis' youngest son lacked a warrior's spirit. With a single voice they'd advised Father and Muredoch against endowing him to the Gray Wolves cohort. Not only would it be a waste of Dainis gold, but his placid temperament and dreamy carelessness might risk the lives of those who served with him.

So, last winter Muredoch had offered Kyle a lifelong place at the family table if he'd become the family steward. Kyle hadn't known Muredoch well at the time, but Kiera had assured him that their eldest brother, though stiff, stuffy, and utterly without imagination or humor, was a fair man whose word was his honor. Kyle had trusted Kiera's judgment, and at midwinter, some nine months ago and the traditional season for binding oaths, Kyle had knelt before his brother and formally dedicated his life to serving the Dainis estate.

Given a choice, Kyle would have eagerly refused tonight's Rapture. He could be happy with his fate—he *was* happy. He didn't need Rapture. Didn't want Rapture. He could only pray that Rapture wouldn't reveal a worse fate.

Let me not become Uncle, Kyle whispered to the sun.

Grandfather and Grandmother Dainis had produced two sons and two daughters. Nustrum, their eldest son, had become Lord Dainis and Kyle's father. His aunts were both dead: one in childbed and the other in a pestilence that had swept through her household faster than magic or medicine. Both aunts had, however, produced the sons their marriages had been meant to produce; both were reckoned with respect and honor in the family chronicle.

And then there was Uncle. Uncle was so soft and round that his very name, Balwin, disappeared in the buttery folds of his face.

As a young man, Balwin had served in the Gray Wolves. His freelance exploits were lovingly recounted in the chronicle. He'd won respect and a chest of gold from Jiverne's king, but when Kyle's father needed a steward, Balwin had come home. He'd set aside his sword in favor of a pen and abacus and served his brother as he'd served the mercenaries.

Then Muredoch had turned seventeen and Muredoch became the Dainis steward.

Ever since then Uncle had dwelt in a wine-sotted haze. Kyle couldn't remember Uncle completely sober, but Uncle was careful never to get so drunk that he misplaced his perpetual smile. Uncle was careful. Uncle never forgot that his life—what remained of it—depended on his brother's charity.

As Kyle's would depend on Muredoch.

Let me not become Uncle.

Kyle dreaded dreaming of himself with a bulbous red nose and a great sagging chin, nodding at table with a grin and a goblet.

But if that were his fate, if that were his Rapture, there'd be no escaping it. God would find him no matter how hard he strove to remain awake. God found every Alberonese youth and God delivered Rapture, bright and shiny or dark and doomful.

Four years ago, Varos had seen blood flowing in his Rapture. The Bydians had prayed for ten nights, seeking the inspiration that would reassure the valley and the roc. On the eleventh morning they'd announced that all was well . . . probably. The blood had flowed across the middle of Varos' dream. It probably wasn't his, and it certainly didn't prefigure his death, since the dream had continued and—quoting a proverb almost as old as Rapture itself—death was rarely the most significant moment in a man's life.

Varos had been satisfied. He'd left to join Angrist in the Gray Wolves the next day; but Kyle wouldn't ever forget the way his mother had collapsed while listening to Varos describe his dream on the morning of his seventeenth birthday. Even Father's face had paled.

Now, as Father's last son waited for the last midnight of his childhood, he bargained with his god. He'd face doom with noble grace and courage, but—

"For my family: please leave my fate as they've planned it. Please don't make them suffer for my foolishness." He cupped his hands, one against the other, in the Hollow Sphere token of prayer all Alberonese used to entreat a god who seldom listened.

"Kyle Dainis, who *are* you talking to?"

The voice rising from the stairwell behind him was cheerful and feminine. Kyle caught his breath with a gasp and smiled as Kiera joined him on the roof.

"No one," he answered, which wasn't quite a lie. God never paid attention to prayers. "Just thinking out loud."

Kiera wore a faded, comfortable gown; unlike him, she wasn't already dressed for the festivities. Her hair, on the other hand, had been primped for the impending event. Lacquered, golden curls glistened in the sunlight as she shook her head.

"Dreamer," she chided him gently with the eke-name his foster-brothers had given him. "You'd better do your thinking quietly and downstairs. Mother's got half the household looking for you."

"Looking for me?" Kyle raked hair that was darker and drabber than his twin's but wouldn't—thank God for small mercies—require lacquer or pins this evening. "Why? All I've got to do is pull on my trousers. How long does she think that's going to take?"

"Mother doesn't waste time *thinking*; that's what we've got you for." Kiera tucked her skirt around her legs and settled down on the gravel-covered roof beside him. "Well, what were you thinking?"

Kyle stared past her to the sun that was sinking toward the western tower. He couldn't tell Kiera he'd been thinking about Uncle, about becoming Uncle. She'd laugh and tell him he was foolish, which he didn't mind, but sometimes, in a misguided effort to reassure him, she'd share his confidences with everyone else, including Flennon Houle, and that was an unbearable prospect.

"I was thinking," he began slowly, because Kiera expected an answer and Kiera never forgot a question—at least not a question she herself had asked. "What happens to the sun after it sets? Does it get blown out like a candle? Or does it shine someplace else? Is there another world where our sun shines when it's not shining on us?"

Kiera laughed. "Oh, no, you weren't, Dreamer. I know you. You were thinking: Is there another broody Kyle Dainis somewhere, wondering what's to become of him. Well, I certainly hope not!" She mussed his hair. "One little brother like you is enough."

Little brother. She was the elder twin—by a few moments—

but she took great pride in her seniority. And she used it now to tease him out of his melancholy.

"If there were two of me," he said with a half-smile, "there'd be two of you, and that would be *more* than enough!"

Kiera poked him hard between the ribs and Kyle defended himself, grappling for her slender wrists, then raising her arms above her head. As the only girl-child among brothers and an assortment of boisterous fosterlings, Kiera knew her wrestling. Normally she was quite capable of defending herself.

But not today. Not after three women had labored over her hair.

And not with him in this shirt.

Within one heartbeat the shirt had torn, Kiera had screeched, and he'd let her go.

It had had to happen. Kyle had known it would happen from the moment he slipped the shirt over his head. No matter how careful he set out to be, he'd ruin something. Flexing his arm cautiously, he tried to measure the damage.

Kiera went from screeching to inspecting the tear. She declared that the seam had split without tearing the cloth. "A moment and a needle and it'll be fixed. Honestly, Kyle—don't worry about it. I'll sew it up myself, if you'd like, and no one will be the wiser." She mussed his hair again and gave him a quick hug. "I'm sorry. I shouldn't have prodded you like that."

He couldn't think of anything to say and, with a sad, gentle smile, Kiera smoothed the hair she'd just ruffled.

"You'd rather be anywhere but here, wouldn't you?" she asked. "Even a place where the sun shone at night."

Turning away, toward the sun, he pulled free of her hand. "Not truly. It wouldn't be different . . . better. This is home; where I belong. I like Muredoch—he's not *that* stuffy. We'll work well together . . ." His mind filled with grape arbors, Uncle's buttery face, and Muredoch's already two-year-old son who'd replace him . . . in fifteen years. "It's a long time."

"But you'd rather be that other Kyle, sitting on that other roof, because maybe he's not a hart-lord."

She put her hand on his shoulder; he shrugged it off.

"If there were another Kyle, he wouldn't be sitting on the roof. His sun wouldn't rise until ours set. He'd still be in bed."

"Would it be the morning before his Rapture, or the morning after?"

They'd played question games like this for as long as Kyle

could remember. He'd always had ready answers, make-believe or true, but not today.

"I don't know—after, I guess. I think I'd like the other Kyle to have it all behind him."

To have it all behind him.

Kiera studied her twin's face, confident that he was lost in his thoughts again. There was much about Kyle that remained resolutely boyish—his cheeks, his nose, the way his fine, honey-colored hair fell loosely around his face—but much that was changing as well.

Lately there'd been a steadiness in those dark eyes as they scanned the horizon, replacing the dreamy look that had earned him his eke-name, Dreamer. His chin was strong and manly, despite the still-soft whiskers that blurred his profile. And his hands were the hands of a powerful man; her wrists still throbbed, for all she knew that he'd held back. Kyle wouldn't ever hurt her. He wouldn't *hurt* anything.

Poor Kyle. It really wasn't fair that he was the youngest of four. Of her brothers, her twin was by far the best. He was shy, unassuming. He never overshadowed her or took offense at the attention she received from the family. He never asked or expected more than life offered him.

And he deserved better.

She closed her eyes on her brother's image and made an oath. Soon—very soon—she'd be married. After that Kyle would have a place where he wasn't last in line, a place at her table . . . *and* a place for his family. Kyle *should* have a wife and children—God knew he was easy on the eyes and could be quite charming when he wasn't being hopelessly shy. He shouldn't have to live alone.

Flen would have to agree, or there'd be no marriage; it was that simple. But she wasn't concerned about Flennon Houle; he'd agree. Flen *always* agreed with whatever she wanted. Besides, Flen and Kyle were already good friends.

The sun came out from behind a cloud. She blinked and saw a different Kyle in a harsher light: Kyle with scars and hardened features.

Her breath caught in her throat. If this were an omen of

Rapture— But the clouds closed again, the light softened, and Kyle was just Kyle again. The rugged stranger had been a trick of sunlight playing with her twin's worried expression, nothing more.

Kyle was worried about tonight. He hadn't said anything, but Kiera had known, in the way she always knew the secret things twins didn't bother to put into words. She wasn't worried, of course. This night was the culmination of *years* of waiting. She'd made her own gown, had finished it before she was fifteen. The Rapture chamber at the center of the roc was as familiar to her as her own bedchamber. She'd been sneaking in to sleep in the huge, old bed—a legacy from the Sodal—for months. Her sleep would be easy and tomorrow morning she'd wake up having seen the faces of her children. That's what Mother said she'd seen, and Kiera expected nothing less.

She *had* been worried when Kyle came home last year and Mother started making plans. They couldn't very well share the Rapture bed. Kiera was the oldest; but Kyle would be the man. Father said Kyle should have the Rapture bed; she could sleep in her own bed. *That* wouldn't do. She hadn't exactly pressured her twin, but she had sighed her best sigh whenever the subject was raised and he'd gotten the hint.

Still, Kiera hadn't expected Kyle to announce that he wanted to spend the night in the creepy crypt. She'd expected him to choose the roof right here. But he said he wanted to be at the roc's heart when God found him. Kyle could be very persuasive when he chose to be, which, fortunately, wasn't very often. Mother and Father were shocked, and just a bit embarrassed: word of Kyle's choice had spread quickly and folk thought . . . well, folk thought Kyle was *odd*. They'd discussed their concern with Kiera, which made her feel quite grown-up, and asked her to persuade her twin to dream in a wiser place.

She hadn't succeeded; Kyle could be stubborn, too. But it wasn't too late; Mother had said so just before Kiera came up to the roof. He was still sitting quietly with his hands folded in a flattened version of God's Hollow Sphere. Maybe he was praying . . . maybe he was having second thoughts . . .

"I get shivers just thinking about you tonight, sleeping in the crypt and all," she said gently, persuasively. "I'm sure you could sleep up here on the roof, if you wanted—"

His head snapped around. "I made my choice, Ki, and I'm

happy with it," he snapped in a tone that didn't sound happy, didn't sound like him at all. "It doesn't matter where we sleep, does it? You're going to marry Flennon Houle and become the Lady of Lanbellis. And I'm going to wind up *drunk*, like Uncle. Right? Right, Kiera?"

There was anger, and a hint of desperation, in her brother's voice and, for a moment, the scarred stranger was looking at her. She pulled away, but before she could say anything, do anything—

"Kiera! Kyle! Your mother's looking for you. Come down at once!"

"Father," Kiera whispered and the scarred stranger was gone again, leaving her beloved, wide-eyed brother behind. She gathered her skirts. Kyle bounded to his feet and hauled her up beside him.

"He sounds angry," he said, stating the obvious. "I'll go down first. Any idea where he is?"

"The atrium. I'm sorry, Kyle, I truly am. I was supposed to bring you right down."

"This is not an auspicious beginning." Father's voice was deep and measured, its usual tone when Father was annoyed, or talking to his youngest son.

Kyle shifted uneasily in his tight shirt. They were alone beside the atrium wellhead where Roc Dainis would draw its water in the very unlikely event that the roc was besieged—as Kyle was besieged right now. If only Father would raise his hand and get it over with— but, no, Father wanted Kyle to understand *why* he was angry.

"Your lady mother's worried sick that you won't present yourself properly. I thought you were going to do better on this, above all other days."

"Yes, Sire, I was . . . ," Kyle murmured, although an explanation, preferably with an apology, would have been wiser, if he could have come up with one.

"Speak up, Kyle!" Father commanded. "Look at people when you talk to them. No wonder your masters called you devious. You give the impression you have something to hide."

With visions of a torn shirt flashing behind his eyes, Kyle raised his head a fraction.

"Well, do you? *Do* you have something to hide, boy?"

"No, Sire," Kyle lied.

Father's arm rose, his fist clenched, and Kyle braced himself for a blow that didn't fall. Father's dark frown eased into mere puzzlement, and when he spoke again, his voice was as gentle as Kyle had ever heard it.

"Are you still determined to dream in the crypt, son? Rapture's no time for false bravery."

Kyle could practically hear his father thinking: The boy—Kyle didn't imagine that he'd ever be a man in his father's eyes—is soft. Soft: the greatest frailty that could be weighed against a man's character—the precise opposite of the martial spirit the masters already said he lacked.

"I'm sure you know," Father continued, "Rapture will come to you anywhere, even in your own familiar bed. Or not in a bed at all but under the stars, on a roof. The night will be warm, I think, should you wish for a starry roof."

Kyle's ribs contracted. Father knew about the northern tower. Someone had told him. One of the watchmen, possibly, or Kiera, which was more likely. Kiera didn't tell tales out of turn, but her idea of helpful was different from his. His eyes drifted downward again.

"I stand by my choice, Sire. I want a bed made up in the crypt."

Father sighed and clapped him between the shoulders. "As you wish. You'll be a man this time to tomorrow. High time to start making your own decisions. Now, head inside and let your varlets get you ready. Your lady mother's seen to everything. Josaf has all he'll need to get you presentable."

"Yes, Sire. Thank you, Sire."

Effectively dismissed, Kyle backed out of the atrium, keeping the telltale rip in his shirt from his father's eagle eyes until he could make a run for the stairs and the safety of his own room.

Josaf and two young men—Kyle's varlets and supposedly his to command since his return from fosterage, but sworn to his father— were waiting in his room. There was an unseasonable fire laid in the hearth and a wooden tub full of steaming, herb-scented water between him and his bed.

Your lady mother's seen to everything . . . How could anyone talk about his decisions when his mother was still telling his varlets how to dress him for dinner? What difference did manhood make when either Father or Muredoch would have the ordering of his life forever?

Josaf, the eldest of his varlets, was a man who'd served the Dainis for six decades. He commanded the other two varlets as a shepherd commanded sheep and appraised Kyle from the far side of the tub much the same way. Without a word, Kyle spread his arms and pivoted, displaying the wreckage on his back. A grunt, which might have been humor but was more likely disgust, confirmed his worst fears.

"At least it's still clean."

Josaf's voice held a dry resignation. Kyle lowered his arms and turned around.

"How bad?" he asked in a low, abashed voice, and Josaf laughed.

"Easily mended, lad, easily mended. Let's have it off." As Kyle loosened the laces at his wrists, Josaf said: "When you turned up missing, we all feared the worst."

The worst. Kyle wondered what constituted "the worst" today. He wasn't mischievous, but he did have a history of accidents—spectacular accidents—both here and in his fosterage homes.

Or, rather, small accidents with spectacular consequences.

Just last month he'd gotten a sleeve caught on the brackets of the hawk-mews door. Anyone else would have simply torn the shirt, but he—trying to be careful—had somehow knocked the heavy door off its hinge posts. And the door, rather than crashing to the ground outside the mews like a sensible door, had rotated backward and fallen against the perches, killing two of the goshawks and freeing Father's prized kestrel.

But he hadn't torn the shirt.

They didn't bother to punish him anymore. They just rolled their eyes and repaired the damage. It was no wonder that everyone wanted to know where he was and what he was doing.

"But I *am* careful," Kyle muttered in his own defense. "Sometimes I manage. And I *did* lure the kestrel back."

Josaf's eyes widened. He unhanded Kyle's shirt, letting it drape snugly across his shoulders again, and swirled his fingers like someone stirring tea. Kyle, realizing his imagination had spoken out loud—again—refused to spin around.

"No, I haven't been to the mews," he said and started to claw the shirt off by himself. "I haven't been anywhere."

Josaf inspected the seam at close range, then set the shirt aside. He muttered something about shirts and mothers who didn't notice when their sons had grown to be men.

Blaming his mother—that made Kyle feel more guilty than ever. He only had one way to deal with guilt: belittle himself a bit more. "I'm surprised anyone trusts me to wear white trousers."

"I have my orders," Josaf said, as drily as before.

Kyle doubted Josaf had taken a direct order since Kyle's grandfather, Lord Pancel Dainis, died, and that was years before he and Kiera were born. In his heart of hearts, Kyle suspected his own father was intimidated by Josaf.

"Lady Irina said you were to be kept here, dressed and ready, until the music started."

That explained it: No one, not God Himself, intimidated Kyle's mother. He sighed and faced the steaming tub. "Must I take *another* bath? I'm not dirty."

Josaf made a dismissing gesture with his knobby, long-fingered hand. "Take it away now," he said to his sheep. "Use it yourselves, if you wish, but the young lord has no need of it."

The other two varlets, Renard, who was a little older than Kyle, and Enobred, who was a little younger, grumbled, but not too loudly. Varletry was easy work compared to the work most Renzi valley boys returned to after their seasons of fosterage at Roc Dainis.

When Enobred and Renard had gone, hauling the heavy tub between them, Josaf kicked the door shut and produced a bowl of berries and cheese from a shelf the open door had concealed. He raised a brow at Kyle, who nodded eagerly, paused, then shook his head.

"The Rapture feast . . . I can't. I'll spoil my appetite."

"What appetite? If I know you, lad, you won't be eating at this grand feast they're giving in your honor. Sit by the window and eat while you've the stomach for it."

More grateful than was strictly proper for an elderly varlet's bullying, Kyle took the bowl in his hands and settled himself on the ledge of his bedroom's solitary window.

"Kiera's honor, too," he reminded Josaf around a mouthful of berries. "She'll enjoy it enough for both of us."

"That one enjoys anything when the young men are about. She'll spoil her marriage, not her appetite," Josaf retorted before he plucked a needle and thread out of the inside lid of

Kyle's wardrobe chest—this was not the first mending emergency the elderly varlet had faced—and went to work on the torn seam.

In truth, Kyle could have sewn it up himself. No one hovered over the verger fosterlings, that passel of high born sons and brothers who wandered from roc to roc, learning the lay of their country and the habits of their peers. They took care of themselves, sometimes of one another, and learned skills their mothers would never think to teach them, skills their wives might never suspect they possessed. Kyle preferred to take care of himself.

Growing up, coming home between fosterages, Kyle had been terrified of this stern, gray-haired man. Last year when he'd come home for good, he'd swallowed horror when his father told him that Josaf would be his body servant; "warden" had seemed a more apt title. But he'd quickly come to like and trust Josaf, and more importantly, Kyle suspected that Josaf liked him, even approved of him: a gift he rarely received.

But for all that, Josaf was wrong about Kiera. She could give an impression of self-centered frivolity to those who didn't know her as well as he did. And she was impetuous, impetuous to a fault, but she was good-natured, loving, and fiercely devoted to those she loved.

Kyle didn't argue with Josaf, though; he stuffed his mouth with cheese, because Josaf was absolutely right about Kyle's stomach. He was hungry now; tonight he'd be too anxious to look at a feast platter without getting sick. With Josaf's approval, Kyle happily spoiled his appetite with every berry, every crumb of cheese clinging to the side of the bowl. He listened while he ate to the stories Josaf told about his years with the Gray Wolves. Familiar, comforting—distracting—stories.

He set the empty bowl on the floor and leaned back against the window jamb with his eyes closed, letting his mind drift among the images Josaf conjured. The door opened. Enobred and Renard shuffled inside and leaned against the wall, as entranced as he was by tales of far-off places and almost-forgotten battles.

The evening gong struck, startling Kyle back to the present. It was time. He jumped off the window ledge and his stomach began to churn acid. Pressing his hand against the hard, flat muscle below his ribs, he gazed blindly out the east-facing window. Sunrise came boldly to his bedroom, but the afternoon shadows were deep by noon, and sunset could slip past without anyone noticing.

"You'll do fine, lad," Josaf said, offering him the white shirt. "There's naught to worry over. This is your night. You can spill black-grape wine all over yourself and no one will gainsay you."

That was hardly the reassuring image Josaf intended it to be. Kyle's gut shifted beneath his fingers and he leaned far out the window, not caring whether he vomited or fell to certain death on the rocks below.

Then Josaf's hand reeled him back, to his room and the snow-white shirt.

A sea of faces, mostly familiar and some already crimson from Dainis largesse and Dainis ale, greeted Kyle when, wearing his fine, white clothes, he entered the roc's lower bailey. Every soul in Renzi had been invited to the roc for this feast, and a good many from other valleys up and down the coast. They'd come to wish him and Kiera well—and to eat the food the roc's kitchen had prepared in such abundance.

Lady Irina had created a wonderland in the bailey, all in the tri-blue colors of the Dainis: sky blue, ocean blue, and midnight. Blue paper lanterns swayed in the twilight breeze, spilling exotic scents that kept the insects at bay. Garlands of naturally and improbably blue flowers marked Kiera's path from the bailey to the Rapture chamber. Braided tri-blue ribbons (more easily rerouted, Kyle supposed, in the event he changed his mind at the last moment) led from the bailey to the yawning black-stone gate of the crypt.

Men from the valley communities vied against each other with their reed pipes from atop a broken wall. A drummer sat near the fire, tapping a come-hither on a shallow drum that was as wide as his arm was long.

Kiera's laughter, musical and full-spirited, echoed everywhere. As always, Kyle had no difficulty finding her. His twin gathered attention like a bee among flowers. Flennon Houle was at her side, holding her gown above the dust. By his stance and grin, he proclaimed she was already his wife.

Kyle would have been content to linger in the shadows, but obscurity was impossible in his all-too-distinct attire—and with Kiera waiting for him. She spotted him almost at once and, with a wave of her hand, summoned him to the thick of lanterns and guests. He could no more disobey her than his mother.

Kiera was in her element, blooming at the center of everyone's attention. Her gown was a testament to her skills with her needle as well as a perfect complement to her natural beauty. Moonlight pearls shone softly in her golden hair. Kyle approached her, feeling more drab and dull than ever, and stood awkwardly beside her wearing a shirt that didn't fit and blinking through vagrant strands of limp, brown hair.

She didn't notice how out of place he was; she wouldn't, that wasn't her way. Her way was to put her arm around his waist, drawing him closer while she bragged about the places he'd been in fosterage.

"My little brother was at Chegnon for a year. He knows *all* the court dances!"

He could have died; all her friends were staring at him. He ducked his head and stared at the lantern shadows dancing around his feet.

"Couldn't find a shirt that fit, Dreamer?" Flen jibed behind Kiera's back, and Kyle's shoulder—the one covered by the mended seam—flinched.

Recovering his nerve, Kyle met Flen's goading gaze. "It was my brother's." He noted, with some relief, that his voice was firm and proud.

"What *are* you two talking about?" Kiera's curls bounced brightly when she looked from Flen to Kyle and back again.

"I was complimenting his shirt," Flen said with an adoring, artless grin.

"Mother made it years ago, for Muredoch," Kiera explained blithely. "But Kyle's too big."

Flen's grin broadened; he looked at Kyle, not Kiera, and bared his teeth. "And here I thought nothing grew in the shade."

Kyle forced an equally broad grin and, mumbling that he hadn't yet paid his respects to his parents, made his escape. But rather than seek them out, he sought shadows where he could watch the dancing without being a part of it. Such foolish notions were quickly shattered.

Guests were obligated, by tradition and true compassion, to distract the Rapture dreamer's family and, especially, the Rapture dreamer himself on this evening that was as portentous as it was festive. The folk of Renzi took their obligations seriously. The moment Kyle thought he'd found a shadow deep enough to hide his white shirt, a young lady would find him and drag him back to the light and the music. He was hugged and kissed and hugged again, until the magic of the evening spun itself around him.

Sometime during the haze of chaste affection and the scents of blue flowers and ladies' perfumes, a harp joined the pipes and drum, and dancing began in earnest. Kyle's companions, recalling Kiera's boasts about his courtly knowledge, begged him for a dance, or two, or several. He blushed furiously, but he did know all the steps—once the armsmasters were done with a fosterling, the dancemasters had an easy time and willing students. The ladies shared him, dance after dance, until he was dizzy and exhausted and more than amenable when one young woman proposed that they go for a little walk.

They found a quiet spot. He pulled off the telltale white shirt; she folded it neatly and set it aside before suggesting that he lie down with his head in her lap. Her name was Pandrita and she was—God help him—Flen's younger sister. (Father was more protective of Kiera than most verge-lords were with their daughters, but, then again, Pandrita's marriage hadn't been arranged before she was born.) Pandrita walked her fingers down Kyle's sweat-moistened chest and kissed him sweetly, full on the mouth.

He was telling her the names of the stars when Josaf appeared at his feet.

"Look lively now, lad," Josaf advised, granting Pandrita an indulgent smile that restored her ease and roused Kyle's deepest envy. "The priests are nearing the gate."

There were six of them waiting outside the roc's iron gate. They were Bydians robed in nighttime colors. Their hands and faces were wrapped in gauze, making them a ghostly presence that dispelled the gaiety between one breath and the next. Kyle's tongue stuck to the roof of his mouth and he was more than willing to cede the honor of opening the gate to his older sister beside him. But she nudged him in the ribs and he reached for the great latch instead.

After that, everything was ritual, which was just as well, because Kyle's heart pounded too loudly for him to hear the sermon. His vision was blurred until his parents stepped forward and, with three of the priests, escorted Kiera along the garland path to the Rapture chamber. Kyle watched them go, too numb to care that they'd left him behind, alone. What did it matter, truly? He didn't need anyone to lead him to the crypt—other than the priests, of course. He'd been on his own since he'd turned six. Wasn't that why he'd been sent away? Why should tonight be different?

One of the remaining priests called Kyle's name and he fell in step behind them, following the blue ribbons. His feet were slow and heavy, as if he walked through springtime mud. His eyes were blurred again, and burning; he had to remember how to blink, how to walk—slowly, one foot after the other.

A hand circled his elbow. He flinched and staggered.

"Nervous?" Muredoch whispered, not loud enough for his wife—a plain-faced, kindly woman who now walked at Kyle's other elbow—to hear. "Don't be. What happens tonight is between you and God. What happens tomorrow morning is between you and your family. And God knows, you've got more imagination than the rest of us together."

Kyle shot his brother a slack-jawed, questioning stare.

"I expect a rousing good tale, little brother," Muredoch said with a smile.

Kyle tried to stay calm. What Muredoch had proposed—stiff, stuffy, straitlaced Muredoch—was heresy, although the thought had crossed Kyle's mind more than once.

"Varos was a fool—" Muredoch continued without the smile and would have said more if they hadn't arrived at the narrow crypt stairs.

A priest thrust a staff between them. Muredoch stood aside and Kyle descended ahead of the priests.

Lady Irina Dainis might not have approved of her youngest son's choice for his Rapture chamber, but that hadn't deterred her from preparing it properly. Cobwebs, dust, and leaves had been thoroughly banished. The floor had been scrubbed until the black stones shone in the priests' torchlight. The engraved lead seals had been polished until they were more mirrors than registries of death. There were bouquets in the empty niches and enough lanterns to conquer every shadow. A thick pallet of fresh straw and blankets had been laid on a makeshift platform where the priest told Kyle to sit.

"Sleep well, my child," the priest said as she crumbled herbs into two of the lanterns. "God will find you. We will wait with your family in the great hall. Come to us after dawn, when you awaken."

She left, then. The other two priests followed her up the narrow stairs. Kyle heard Muredoch's voice, but couldn't make out the words. Finally there was silence, broken only by the sound of music from the bailey, softer now, and very sober.

Chapter Two

Kyle filled his lungs with the unfamiliar, but not unpleasant, aroma of the priest's herbs. His eyes closed and he hung on the cusp of sleep, unmindful of his surroundings, faintly aware of half-formed thoughts dissipating within his mind. Everything was dark, quiet, comfortable . . .

Fading to black velvet sleep.

Then, from nowhere, a body-wrenching shudder.

He was awake again.

Despite the fair-weather clouds of the afternoon sky, gusty storm winds swept across the crypt's open stairs, leaving the air empty, expectant. The flickering lanterns cast wild shadows on the black walls.

Momentarily disoriented, Kyle asked himself: where? and why? and when? Once the answers came to him, there was no chance he'd rediscover the path to sleep. His pallet had become uncomfortable. The view—looking up at sealed or yawning niches—was worse.

The unthinkable had happened: Rapture had failed. God wouldn't find Kyle Dainis, couldn't—or didn't want to.

Outside the crypt, the bailey was quiet; the wind had driven everyone inside. Kyle considered joining them. It might be easier to make his confession now, rather than in the morning when everyone was weary from waiting. He could imagine their reaction: Priests would scurry for their augeries. Despair and disappointment would carve his parents' faces. And he would have done what his father warned him long against doing: He would have disgraced the Dainis name.

For their sakes—and his—Kyle decided to stay put, to take Muredoch's advice and concoct a tale to tell at dawn. He knew just what he should have dreamt: The Dainis prospering. Muredoch's son replacing him as steward. Everyone living healthy. It wouldn't be a difficult piece of tale spinning, and everyone would be happy.

Everyone except him, but no one noticed him anyway.

Kyle knew the tale he'd tell as soon as he'd convinced himself it was permissible to invent it. Contrary to Muredoch's expectation, it wouldn't require much imagination at all. Once he had the necessary tale fixed in his mind, the enemy was boredom. He began to examine the niches around him. The lead seals were clean and polished as he'd never seen them before. Every inscription was legible—or it would have been, if Alberon's alphabet and script hadn't altered over the centuries. The oldest names were cluttered with undecipherable marks, but the dates were clear enough. Alberon's numerals hadn't changed much at all.

The earliest date on the uppermost seal of the first column of the northern wall was 342, ancient history, if one truly believed that the Hesse king had come down from heaven 3,528 years ago. Kyle believed in the Hesse; he'd been born in a black-stone roc no mortal workmen could have built. But that didn't mean he believed there were Hesse bones behind the seal, or the bones of men, either.

Kyle had learned Alberon's history and other such rarified subjects from a score of rainy-day tutors, each affiliated with a different verger family and reading from a different chronicle. When his wandering took him to Chegnon, he'd learned the royal version of events, and—of course—there were always the Ultramontaine priests whose chronicles had God's approval.

There was broad agreement among the chronicles, but Kyle—who'd told more than his share of believable tales and intended to tell another when the sun came up—knew better than to trust a merely agreeable, believable tale. He also knew that the Dainis chronicle was a not-quite-perfect copy of the Sodal chronicle—which Kiera had found for him in a musty storeroom above the stable, along with another, even older leather-bound tome with the name Chellen burned into its binding.

Still, Kyle believed there were bones behind the old seal. However old the roc really was, its crypt had been collecting the dead since the beginning and there were only four black-stone walls, each with twenty niches—excepting the eastern wall, which only had twelve because of the stairs. Dainis, Sodal, Chellen, or the legendary Renzi of the Hesse—once seventy-two honored kinfolk died, a family ran out of niches.

When Kyle was nine and away in fosterage, his grandmother had died a sudden, painful death. The Bydians saw omens when they prepared her corpse. They pronounced it time to open all the niches for a thorough reinterment that all the Dainis must witness. In the dead of winter, he and Varos and Angrist were summoned out of their separate fosterages. Kyle recalled little of the grueling journey; he'd been seasick the entire time, but the reinterment ritual was etched deep in his memory.

On a raw, miserable day, Kyle and the rest of his family had stood on the cold, black-stone floor, wearing nothing but their mourning rags, while the priests shuttled bundles of disarticulated bones, stiff scraps of cloth, and varicolored tangles of hair from one niche to another. Ten niches were left completely empty. Grandmother rested by herself in an eleventh niche. Everyone else had been moved and their name added to columns on another lead seal.

By the end of the long, aching day the incense had been so thick, so bitter, that eight years later, Kyle would have sworn he could still smell it.

The sky had been as black as the crypt when Kyle had followed his kin up the stairs to a cold, funeral supper. Varos had pulled him aside and offered him a long, yellowed tooth—one of several Varos swore he'd swiped during the endless ritual. Kyle hadn't wanted to take the ghastly lump from his brother's hand, but twelve-year-old Varos would have teased him mercilessly if he'd hesitated. And, though they were far apart, in different fosterage rocs, the tale of his cowardice would have somehow followed him wherever he went. So he'd taken the rare fraternal gift, tucked it in his trousers, promptly lost it, and suffered nightmares *and* teasing for a year.

No wonder the family thought it strange that he'd chosen the crypt as his Rapture chamber. Kyle didn't honestly know why he'd chosen it himself, especially now that he'd refreshed those nightmare memories. In an attempt to steady his own nerves, Kyle returned his attention to the oldest seal and noticed that, after the undecipherable fourth-century inscription, there was an out-of-order cluster of names linked with a single date: 2,540.

That was a date included in every chronicle: midway through the Debacle, when foreigners still flocked to Alberon and died in the Eigela. To this day—at least according to Josaf and the other family members who'd served with the Gray Wolves—all around the Sea of Prayse, *He went to Alberon* was a polite way of saying a man had killed himself. A millennium later—almost exactly a millennium later, Kyle realized with a start—the Alberonese still fought prejudice and slander. Why else were the cohorts so prickly about their reputations? Why else had they been founded in the first place?

But Kyle had always heard, always believed, that no Alberonese had lost their lives searching for the elusive golden throne of Veshkai. No Alberonese was foolish enough to think that God would plunk Himself down in the middle of the Eigela.

"Coincidence," he said aloud. "Plague."

Plague could certainly sweep through a valley to slay five verger kin in a single year. But the inscriptions occurred only once, only on the first seal. Whoever they were, priests hadn't shuffled their bones in later reinterments, and that could only be true if their bones weren't here in the crypt.

Kyle considered the ways men could die away from the roc: "A ship lost at sea. A hunting accident in the Spure. Murdered and their bodies fed to wild beasts . . ."

His imagination got the better of him, again, and his heart started pounding anxiously. He calmed himself by concentrating on the names themselves. The grouped together script wasn't as archaic as the line above it. The third name of the series was the shortest and contained mostly recognizable letters: Tash-ell-*something*-em. And the inscription was framed with a solid line which, these days, meant the deceased was either a priest or, more rarely, a wizard.

No Bydian or Mellian priest would have been tempted to trek into the Eigela; Kyle was certain of that. But an Ultramontaine might, just for curiosity's sake, and a wizard . . . Wizards were rogues or heretics—sometimes both—who stood on hilltops, collecting thunderbolts in the wildest storms. Surely if any man of Alberon had gone searching for the Siege of Shadows, that man had been a wizard. And that man had gotten what he deserved. The only tragedy Kyle could see was that he'd doomed three other men to his fool's quest.

Kyle rubbed his eyes. He was tired again. The storm had blown over and he could hear a piper in the bailey again. He'd be seen if he tried to sneak up to his own room, so he curled up on the pallet and never felt his eyes close.

The rock beneath his feet and to his right was midnight-black granite, flecked with starlit mica. Jagged crystals rasped the soles of his boots and the sleeve of his shirt. His knuckles were battered and bloody, but the granite was solid, safe compared to the fog on his left.

His lungs burned with each breath of cold, dry air. His heart throbbed and his ribs felt bruised from the inside. A dull ache along the back of his legs told him he'd been climbing too long, but sitting down was impossible. The only rest a man could risk was leaning, eyes open and panting, against the granite until his heart steadied.

"Keep in step there!"

His head jerked up. He'd forgotten the others: the hunched shoulders of the man ahead, the weary voice of the one behind. For his life, he couldn't remember their names or faces. He started climbing again.

"Easy. Easy. Slow and steady wins through."

The same familiar, but unnameable voice. He slowed, wondering where he was, with whom, and—most important—why? The man ahead dislodged a stone. Habit said to dodge aside; habit could get a man killed up here. He gritted his teeth as sharp granite bounced against his ankle.

"Sorry," the front man said without turning. His voice, like the other voice, was familiar, but drew no name out of Kyle's memory.

Time had no more meaning here than the sky had color. He climbed until a harsh, two-note cry resounded off the black cliffs above them.

Dragon!

He didn't know the names of the men with him, but he

knew a dragon's call, though dragons belonged to Hesse legend, not his own life.

Didn't they?

And if not legend or life, then certainly to Rapture—

Rapture.

Kyle shivered and, half-aware of his sleeping self back in the crypt, nearly stumbled off the cliff. He strained his dreaming eyes, looking for color or movement in the fog. There were both: the color of fire and the movement of man shapes tumbling into oblivion. He couldn't see the dragon, and then he couldn't see anything at all.

Rapture restored him elsewhere in the dark mountains. Elsewhere because now the black granite was streaked with ice and the black cliffs didn't rise forever in the fog. They ended in a cavern's even blacker maw. Kyle was crouched on knuckles and knees; he started to rise to get a better look—

"Stay down, fool!" someone hissed angrily. "Do you want to give us away?"

Shamed, he hid himself again. He was in a stone-rubble ravine. There was a gap in the left-side cliff he and his companions faced from behind their rocky cover. He'd just deduced that he was part of an ambush when he heard the ambush's quarry approach. A nearby archer launched an arrow and a scream echoed back from the left-side gap. After that, the ambush became a skirmish which blurred before Kyle's dreaming eyes until the mountain quaked around him.

Chunks of ice and granite crashed down on friend and foe alike. He put his hand to his left hip, where the hilt of his sword reassured him, though steel was no protection against a falling mountain. Abandoning his position, Kyle headed toward the gap, where the enemy, and not the mountain, was the greatest danger. He drew his sword—or tried to. The weapon was bound tight in its scabbard and Kyle struggled to free it until a sword tip quite unlike his own pierced his vision.

He followed the alien sword to his enemy's arm, the arm to an immobile face swirled with narrow black-and-white bands. The eyes were gaping holes, without pupils or irises. The lips were deep red; they sneered fiercely over stained and protruding fangs. Grizzled silver hair stood like a boar's bristles on the crest of the creature's narrow head, but fell, thick and shaggy, over its shoulders.

With his own weapon still useless in its scabbard, Kyle beat the unfamiliar sword aside with the back of his off-weapon hand. Between his own fear and the mountain crashing down around him, he couldn't hear himself scream for help.

Then the mountain became his ally. Granite crashed down upon his enemy. The swirling bands across its face were shattered. Bright blood welled up between broken fangs and flowed like tears from empty eyes.

In the way of all dreams, Kyle's sword was suddenly, inexplicably free and he pressed its tip against his enemy's breast, where its heart should be, if it had a heart. He leaned on the hilt. Tempered Alberonese steel plunged through unarmored flesh, through a beating heart which spat blood upward onto his hands, onto his face. The strange creature writhed in agony, but its expression never changed, even in death.

An enemy had died; Kyle had not. He should have rejoiced at this demonstration of his warrior's spirit, but it sickened him instead. Ignoring the clash around him, the mountain crumbling above him, Kyle closed his eyes. The shattered black-and-white face remained as vivid in his mind's eye as it was on the rock at his feet.

Mighty pounding shook the mountain apart. Kyle's spirit became separated from his body. It was lost and drifting until cold raindrops struck his cheeks.

Opening his eyes, Kyle looked up at a maze of shadows on smooth walls as black as the mountain. His mind had barely begun to sort dream from reality when he was engulfed in blinding light and the air erupted with a deafening roar. The ground beneath him shuddered. Terrified, Kyle squeezed his eyes shut again and curled up in a ball.

The crypt. A storm. Thunder and lightning. *Rapture*. It all came clear to Kyle as he lay with his back against the western wall and wind-driven rain pelted his face. Or almost all became clear. He'd dreamt, he was sure of that. God had found him. But the only image he could remember was a strange, shattered face—black, white, and red—hovering in darkness.

Another thunderbolt—white light and heavy sound together. Another sheet of rain sweeping down the stairs, drenching him and his pallet. The last two lanterns gave up their fight, and though Kyle knew he was safer where he was, the only place he wanted to be was behind the curtains of his own bed.

Kyle was soaked to the skin and shivering before he pulled a door shut behind him. There was light at the end of the corridor immediately ahead of him: the roc's great hall, where his parents and the priests were waiting. But he wasn't ready to face them and headed for the spiral stairs instead, where lightning shot through arrow-slit windows to guide him to his chamber.

When that door was shut and the window, too, Kyle peeled off his soggy clothes in familiar darkness. He paused when he heard someone whimpering nearby. For one embarrassed moment he feared Renard or Enobred had gone to ground in his bed, possibly with a lover. He called the varlets by name and got more whimpering for an answer. Gritting his teeth, Kyle parted the lightweight summer curtains with his arms. A dog, half-grown and more frightened than he, thrust its moist nose under his hand. Climbing onto the mattress himself, Kyle wrapped his arms around the quivering hound, borrowing warmth, donating security.

"We'll wait it out together," he assured the dog, and got his nose licked in reply.

Time passed, taking the storm with it. Kyle dozed and reawakened at daybreak. Gentle light seeped through the wooden shutter and the curtain, not bright enough to see by, but not dark, either. With the hound still sleeping atop his feet, Kyle tried to eke his Rapture out of his memory but, except for the one horrific image that he couldn't forget, the dream had vanished. And as for that shattered face, it certainly resembled no one Kyle knew or could imagine knowing, either in life or legend.

Worse than the memory itself was the thought of describing it in the great hall. Alberon had the Hesse who, according to the chronicles, looked exactly like mortal men and women. And the Hesse had dragons: vengeful, flying monsters, one of whom was said to be entombed in the walls of the king's privy chamber. For generations, of course, mercenary sons had brought home the more colorful legends of Alberon's neighbors around the Sea of Prayse: epic tales about meddling gods, magical beasts, malicious demons, and exotic creatures that lived in the mists at the world's tales. But, according to the priests, such monsters shouldn't crop up in Rapture and, anyway, Kyle hadn't ever heard a bard sing about the face he remembered.

"Muredoch's advice is still the best," he said aloud. "I'll tell them I dreamt of my life just as it is, just as it's supposed to be."

The dog awoke and crawled up his leg to lick his hand. Kyle scratched between its ears. He could invent a believable Rapture to reassure his family, but the shattered face would always be a part of his memory. Smothering a sob in the dog's fur, he wondered what Varos *had* dreamt four years ago, then wondered if Varos' determination to join the Gray Wolves as quickly as possible hadn't stemmed from a need to meet his fate where his family wouldn't see it.

"Maybe I should go somewhere else, too," he whispered to the dog and to hear how the idea sounded to his ears.

"That *is* you in there, Kyle, isn't it? The storm was so awful. I went outside and called your name from the top of the crypt stairs. You didn't answer and I was afraid you'd drowned, but I was more afraid to go down those stairs, so I came here. You're all right?"

Kiera.

Kyle wasn't ready to talk to anyone, including his twin, whose silhouette was dimly visible through the bedcurtains. He said nothing, hoping she'd give up, knowing it was a fool's hope. She flung the curtains apart, letting light in.

"Answer me, Kyle, when I talk to you!"

Kyle lunged for the bedcurtains; she giggled and held them just beyond his grasp. He grabbed a handful of linen instead, but the dog lay on the cloth and wouldn't budge. She appraised his rain-matted hair and the half-grown dog sprawled across his half-covered thighs.

"God's pockets, little brother, look at you!"

Noblewomen weren't supposed to swear or stare, but growing amid brothers and fosterlings, Kiera knew all the curses and knew as well that Kyle couldn't keep from blushing when she used them.

When Kiera was satisfied that he was on fire from forehead to feet, she draped the curtains over bedpost hooks meant for that purpose and turned her attention to the Rapture garments he vaguely recalled leaving in a sopping heap on the floor.

"How could you?" she laughed.

She took the abused white shirt by its collar and gave it a

vigorous shake. Water splattered him and the hound, who leapt off the bed, leaving Kyle completely exposed to his twin's scrutiny. Embarrassment had its limits, and he'd finally passed beyond them.

"Because I'm not a varlet or a woman. I'm a man—if you didn't notice—and I don't *care*. Pass me my trousers."

Laughing, she held the white pair where he couldn't reach them. Kyle wouldn't play her games any longer. He swung his legs over the edge and headed for the rack where yesterday's clothes still hung.

"You're too old for this, Kiera." For an instant, he sounded so much like Father that they both hesitated, then he grabbed his trousers and pulled them on. "You shouldn't be here at all. You should be downstairs."

Kiera landed on the now vacant mattress with a heavy sigh. "It was a sunset, Kyle. My whole, entire Rapture was standing in front of an open window—freezing, mind you, because it was the very middle of winter—waiting for the sun to set! No husband. No children. No idea where I'll be or whether I'll be happy. I've been *cheated*, Kyle. That's what comes of listening to you talk about suns that shine at night. What kind of Rapture is a sunset?"

Kyle cinched his trousers and reached for a shirt. He was tempted to say it was a damned sight better than his Rapture, but he rarely swore and already felt a twinge of guilt. Had his tale spinning affected his sister's dreams? But, of course, that was impossible. Rapture was Rapture. The shattered face flitted in his mind's eye.

"I suppose you'll find out when you see the sunset," he said gently, trying not to think about the moment when, in life, he'd see that red, white, and black face. "Where were you? Did you recognize the window or the view?"

"I never thought— I was right to look for you first. You're so clever, Kyle," she said, without a hint of sarcasm, and closed her eyes. Her smooth forehead wrinkled with effort. "The lodge. Grandmother's lodge in the Spure. How odd. We *never* go to the lodge in winter. I wonder . . ." Her eyes popped open. "What did you dream? Did you dream about the lodge—is that how you knew? Are we going together? Did you dream in the crypt, or after? God's pockets! It must have been awful. But you dreamt of a sunset, too, didn't you?"

"No."

He unlatched the shutter. Spent storm clouds lingered, pale golds above the sunrise. Leaves and puddles littered the view. They'd be blown away, forgotten, by sundown. Would that the same could be said for his Rapture.

"Well . . . don't just stand there. Tell me what you did dream, if it wasn't a silly sunset at the lodge."

Kyle stared out the window. He could remember Muredoch's advice and his own resolution to follow it, but the words for a believable Rapture had fled his mind. All that remained was a naked lie: "Nothing. I dreamt nothing, nothing I can remember, anyway. The storm scared me out of my wits and Rapture both when it woke me up."

"Oh, Kyle . . ."

Watching her face dissolve into compassion, he realized he'd told the most believable lie and that his conscience didn't prickle at all.

"Nothing, Ki. Not even a winter's sunset at the lodge. Just thunder, lightning, and getting soaked in the rain."

"Oh, Kyle. You don't remember *anything*? Not one little, tiny thing?"

He took a deep breath, drawing deception into his heart forever. "Nothing at all. I've managed to forget my Rapture—if there was one." God didn't strike him dead. He relaxed a little while Kiera got up from his bed. "Just like me, isn't it? Never do anything right."

Kiera put her arms around him. "Oh, my poor little brother. It's just not *fair*. Can't you spin a tale? You're so good with stories; everyone says so. I'd believe anything—"

"It's Rapture, Kiera." He returned the embrace, then held her at arm's length. "I can't pretend about Rapture."

As if that weren't exactly what he was doing.

"You could, if you wanted to. I'd never tell."

Kyle shivered at the thought of Kiera keeping a secret for a lifetime. "I don't want to. We know what my destiny is: Muredoch's steward until his son's grown. What was God supposed to show me: quills, ink, an abacus? A goblet of wine?"

Kiera tried to free herself. Strength against strength, she was outmatched until she managed to get her fingers on the ticklish spot inside his elbow. His grip melted and she threw herself around his ribs, never considering for a moment that she could squeeze hard enough to hurt.

"Give yourself an adventure, Kyle," she suggested, looking up at him.

"I don't want an adventure."

"Then take my measly sunset and spin a tale for me. I *want* an adventure!"

"Getting to the lodge in the middle of winter should be adventure enough—"

He saw mischief in Kiera's amber eyes. He knew her thoughts before her lips parted.

"That's it, Kyle! We're twins. We *could* have the same Rapture. You could be my escort. We could go off, just the two of us, to the lodge, to anywhere—even *Chegnon*!"

Kyle shook his head. The lodge was on Dainis land, but not in the Renzi Valley. It was their grandmother's dowry and it lay four good day's journey away. Eight bad days and, in winter, the days would almost certainly be bad. But he'd go with her to the lodge. Chegnon, where King Otanazar IV kept his winter court, was another matter entirely and no place where he'd want to escort his beautiful, headstrong sister.

"Maybe I was wrong about the window, Kyle. In fact, I'm sure I was. I'm sure I was in Chegnon . . . in the chambers of the Gray Prince himself!"

"Don't even think about it, Ki. Father might let you go to the lodge, surrounded by himself, twenty men-at-arms, and twice that many varlets—and that only if Mother says yes. But you'll get no closer to Chegnon than you are right now, unless you can persuade Flen to take you there after you're married."

Kiera gave a high-pitched, exasperated trill. "Maybe I'll *marry* Prince Gravais instead of Flen. Maybe the Gray Prince will swoon at my feet the moment he sees me, forswearing all others. Maybe—"

"Not. I've been at Chegnon, Ki. I've met our crown prince. He's not for you. You should listen to Father—"

"I didn't *see* Father in my Rapture. He can't come if I didn't see him."

"You didn't see me, either."

"That's different. I'm inviting you. I'll let you share my Rapture and my adventure. And if *we* say we're going alone, neither Mother nor Father nor all the priests can gainsay us. And if I suddenly realize, after we're on the road, that I was mistaken, that I was in Chegnon, not the lodge, watching the sun set over the harbor—"

"Then I'd say you were *very* confused. Chegnon has a harbor, all right, but it's a bay to the *east* of the roc. You can't look west from Chegnon; it's built into the headland."

She twisted her mouth into an unattractive pout. Kiera didn't like to be wrong and Kyle didn't like to see her upset.

"Forget Chegnon," he said as mildly as he could. "Forget the Gray Prince. Even if you could turn his head and hold him, he can't marry you without the king's permission, and that's not going to happen while Ezrae Baldescare is Alberon's queen. At the very best, you'd be miserable. At the very worst—I don't want to think about it, Kiera, and you shouldn't either."

Kiera turned quickly away from him. "Father always said I'd be his princess," she whispered hoarsely.

Prince Gravais was an upright man. Truth to tell, Kyle would rather the prince, than Flennon Houle, as a brother-in-law. But not while Ezrae Baldescare was Alberon's queen, not while the Baldescare dominated the royal court. And if he, a lowly hart-lord, knew how treacherous the court had become, surely Father knew it, too.

Of course, Father did know it. That was one reason he wouldn't let Kiera go to court. Another was the prince's reputation with the ladies, and the last was Kiera, herself. But that didn't stop Father from calling Kiera "his princess" or telling her she was the most beautiful young woman in the kingdom.

"Flen will take good care of you, Ki," Kyle said lamely. "You'll be happier with him than you'd ever be at Chegnon."

She sniffled and blotted her eyes with her sleeve, all with her back toward him. "I want an adventure. One adventure. That's all: *one* adventure."

Kyle took two steps forward and draped his arms over her shoulders while she sat. "I'm sorry, Ki. It's not fair. You said it yourself."

Kiera leaned against him and they both stared out the open window until she broke the silence:

"You could escort me to the lodge. Just you and me—for adventure? The only adventure either of us is likely to get. Please, Kyle? Nothing can go wrong: I did dream about the lodge. I was there; I will be there. It's Rapture; it has to happen. We can go this winter. Please?"

He could think of objections by the handful, but his twin's tears were warm on his arm. "We can try. I wouldn't count on it. Mother and Father will have objections—to me, if not to you."

"*I'll* take care of Mother and Father. You stand with me, whatever I say, and we'll ride out of here with their blessing."

"Kiera—"

"Swear it, Kyle. *Please* swear you won't counter me. Swear you'll stand by what I say."

Kyle wasn't sure he could get himself safely to the lodge in the middle of winter, let alone his sister, but he couldn't say no to Kiera. Mother could and Father, sometimes, but not him.

"I swear it."

"On your honor and your sword."

"I swear it on my honor and my sword."

"Good!" She wriggled free and dried her tears as she stood. "It will be a great adventure, Kyle, just you wait! Leave everything to me!"

They left his room together, with Kiera—as usual—in the lead.

Chapter Three

That morning Kyle stood back while Kiera worked her particular magic on the rest of the Dainis household. It was fascinating to watch, and disillusioning, too, because it wasn't magic. Kiera wielded her voice, her face, her entire self no differently from the way an armsmaster wielded his weapons: a teardrop for a thrust, a sigh for a parry, a winsome smile to make Father drop his guard.

Kyle was grateful he didn't have to face her, horrified to realize that he already had, many times before. The gestures and phrases that had persuaded him to do some ill-considered thing, such as agreeing to escort her to the lodge, or to the pretense that, as twins, they'd shared a single Rapture vision, weren't acts of the moment. Suddenly, everything Kiera did seemed rehearsed—which also reminded him of an armsmaster with his roster of thrusts, parries, and guard stances.

And, whether it was on the sand of a practice arena or in the great hall of Roc Dainis, Kyle was not a warrior. He'd succumbed before Kiera joined her battle. Flen fell almost as quickly, seduced—that was the only word for what Kiera did with her voice and her eyelashes together—by Kiera's promise that they'd marry in the spring, "when this is over." Thus assured, Flennon Houle was the ally Kiera needed to persuade her father and her eldest brother: Nothing, not even a wild goose trek to the Spure in winter, could come between her and a marriage alliance with the Houle.

Lady Irina held out the longest. She insisted that a betrothed young woman—especially her only daughter—simply couldn't flaunt custom so boldly, regardless of Rapture, despite a twin brother as her escort. Had he been the one facing their mother's disdain, Kyle would have hidden in his room for a week, maybe a month.

But Kiera merely warmed to the challenge.

It was Rapture, she said, until Kyle lost count of the times she said it that day and the days thereafter. It was *ordained*, which was a priestly sort of word and very effective with their mother, who came from a more pious family than the Dainis. Kiera, of course, had been lectured and sermoned by the Bydians. But Kyle couldn't imagine the dour men and women of the nearby monastery teaching her the outrageous, but scholarly sounding, arguments with which she pursued their mother from one end of the roc to other.

He wondered where his twin had learned her disarming skills and asked her about them a week after their birthday, as they rode through the ripening orchards.

"I learned everything from you!" she replied with a laugh that made Kyle feel foolish for asking.

"From me?" he sputtered. "Ki, I'd never do or say the things you're saying. The words you use. I don't talk that way."

"Of course not, but you weren't here at Roc Dainis all those years. It hasn't been easy; Mother and Father would have me living in my rooms doing needlework day and night—for my own good, of course. God's pockets! I'd have died from boredom and pricked fingers! I had to do something."

Kyle nodded. "But what did I have to do with it? I wasn't here."

"But I had your letters, those wonderful, too short letters about the places you were staying. And when you *were* here . . . the stories you'd tell to get yourself out of trouble. After you left, Father would say it didn't matter whether you told the truth or not, your excuses were so *droll* that he didn't care."

God help him. Hearing Kiera's words, eleven years of mortification struck all at once. "Thank you," he muttered, very droll, he supposed, because she laughed again.

"You just didn't see the possibilities, the *advantages* you could have taken if you put your skills to proper use, little brother. But I did. I used them to get Mother and Father to let me do what I wanted to do—not simply to avoid getting thrashed for what I'd already done." She reached from her horse to his and patted him lightly on the forearm, very much the elder sister. "You wait and see: We're going to the lodge for the solstice. We're going to have an adventure."

After nine days of relentless persuasion, pouting, and sulking, broken periodically by floods of hollow-eyed, achingly silent tears, Kiera accepted a truce. She didn't get everything she wanted. The two of them would not—should not—travel by themselves; they'd rely on a cohort of seasoned men and varlets to get them to the lodge and back. Still, Kiera had wrung a victory of sorts from her defeat: Father and Muredoch agreed to let Kyle pick their escort and agreed as well that he would be the man to command it.

It would be Kyle's first command, perhaps his only one, and a gift he had not imagined receiving. Two months to the day after Rapture night, he set out for the lodge with Josaf and a few others. Flennon Houle rode with them, because it was high time for Flen to return to his own home and the inland road that connected the Renzi Valley and the Dainis lodge crossed the headlands of Lanbellis Valley along the way.

Riding side-by-side with Kiera's intended didn't make friendship bloom between him and Kyle. Kyle wouldn't believe there was anything on either side of the Eigela that could accomplish that miracle, but they had a few things in common: several years of fosterage and an affection for Kiera that stopped just short of awe.

The journey to Lanbellis was not as unpleasant as it could have been, and after a night at Roc Houle, Kyle and the Dainismen continued toward the lodge, taking care to introduce themselves at the inns and monasteries along the roads, to pay their respects to other verge-lords in the valleys they crossed, and make preparations for anything that might go wrong when they made the trek again before the solstice.

Returning to Renzi, Kyle had no time for autumn rides along gold-leaved lanes, or harvest dances. He made himself a list of what he had to do and studied it carefully every day. Kiera complained that he'd wring the adventure out of their Rapture with all his planning, but Father praised his diligence.

"Father wants you to do well," Muredoch explained one late autumn night when frost crackled on the hayricks outside the stable. "We'd both like you to do well," he added, picking up an oil cloth and a bit of horse harness as he sat down beside his youngest brother. "You need confidence, Kyle. You don't trust your own judgment. This wild notion of Kiera's will serve you better than her."

"It's not a notion," Kyle muttered without looking at Muredoch. "It's Rapture. It's *ordained*." The word had been burned on the back of his eyelids. He couldn't resist repeating it.

Muredoch chuckled as he rubbed musky oil into already supple leather. "As may be, Kyle, but it's also what she wants, though only God knows why. A solstice sunset in Chegnon, that I could understand, never mind that she's put her hand in Flen's. We couldn't permit it, of course; but I could understand it. Maybe the lodge is what she dreamt on Rapture night. She had you persuaded by the time you came down the next morning. Still keeping your dream to yourself?"

There was no accusation in Muredoch's words, or an elder brother's authority, either, just a canniness Kyle hadn't expected, and sympathy, too. He'd not likely get a better moment to share his own secret, but: "We're twins. We only had one dream between us. You can't understand."

"Not if it's twin stuff." Muredoch laid the leather strap between them as he stood. "But if it's got to do with the family, you can tell me. You're not one for friendship, Kyle. I know you kept to yourself all through fosterage; here, too. Maybe it is twin stuff. You and Kiera are closer to each other than either of you are to us. But I want you to remember, I'm your brother first, not your lord. I don't want to look up one morning and see you in the grape arbor like Uncle Balwin."

Suddenly Kyle did want to confide his deepest secret to this man, this brother, who already knew his greatest fear, but the broken demon face stared out of memory, demanding silence. "It's not family," he whispered. "I swear it's not."

"Then I'll believe you." Muredoch laid his hand on Kyle's slumped shoulder. "When the time comes—if it comes—you can tell me. I haven't broken Varos' confidence, and I won't break yours."

"It's nothing for anyone else to worry about. Nothing, truly, at all."

Kyle waited for Muredoch's footfalls to fade into the night, half-hoping that his eldest brother would return. Both the footfalls and the hopes faded. His attention fell to the harness straps in his lap.

"I'll be careful," he said fiercely to the straps whose stitching he examined by lantern light. "Rapture or no Rapture, I'll get this right. No one's going to whisper: There goes Kyle Dainis. He got his sister killed."

He'd heard similar whispers all his life, at Roc Dainis and his foster homes. Kiera's persistence had persuaded Father and Muredoch to let him escort their sister rather than be escorted himself. What his twin had won for him was more important than any dream. It was respect, if he weren't careless.

If he could avoid being himself.

The winter solstice marked the beginning of its season. In a typical year the Renzi Valley didn't see snow until a week or two after solstice, by which time Kyle should have brought his sister safely home again. But this year the season changed early. There were bright gold leaves clinging to the trees when a white blanket fell on the black roc.

Although that snow melted by noon of the next day, the Bydian weather-wards warned that the early snow meant heavy snow throughout a long, hard winter. There was a chance, they said, that the inland road through the Spure foothills was already snow-clogged, and a greater chance that anyone in the lodge for solstice would be there until the spring equinox. They advised Lord Dainis to put a stop to his children's foolishness, but the verge-lord, noting that Kyle had ordered the lodge lardered for winter-long guests, complimented his son's foresight.

Kiera was the family member with objections. If the adventure might last months rather than weeks, she wanted to bring one of her maids and she wanted to travel in a closed carriage rather than astride.

"The journey will take twice as long that way," Kyle countered. "Everything's planned for a four-day *ride.* You said you were game. You said you wanted adventure. Padded down inside a carriage isn't adventure, Ki."

"I said it would be an adventure if we were alone. We'll hardly be alone, and now we may be up in the Spure until spring. Surely you don't begrudge me a maid; you're bringing Josaf and two varlets."

True enough: Josaf was the first man he'd selected for the

cohort and Josaf had insisted on Renard and Enobred, but: "That's different. We need men's strength if anything goes wrong. And things are more likely to go wrong with a carriage than with horses alone."

"I could be stranded there with the caretaker's wife, Kyle. God's pockets! She's got no teeth and her nose is covered with warts! You can't expect me to entrust myself to her. I'll come back looking like the bottom of someone's shoe."

Sometimes Kyle didn't understand his sister—ugliness wasn't contagious—but he understood when he wouldn't win an argument. "You'll never look like an old shoe, Ki, but if it's important to you, you'll have your maid and your carriage. We'll have to leave sooner, though, if we're going to be there by solstice."

"It is important." Kiera flung her arms around him and kissed him on the cheek. "My face is my dowry. Beautiful girls marry whom they wish. Girls with leather faces get sold to whoever wants them."

"Kiera—"

"Kiera what?" She released him with a teasing smile. "It's very simple: Flen worships me because I'm beautiful. He'd be impossible to control if he didn't."

Kyle felt his face getting warm and turned away to hide the rising flush.

"God's pockets, Kyle Dainis—you're such an innocent. If I didn't know better, I'd swear you were *still* a virgin."

He stood mute and gaping as she walked away, her skirt swirling around her ankles.

The trek from Roc Dainis to the lodge was as uneventful as it could be. The weather was raw, with a fine rain on the second day, sleet on the third, and snow squalls each day thereafter. Everyone suffered chilblains, but there was no great danger as they followed roads deeper and higher into the forests of the Spure.

Wood swelled, axle grease froze, leather split, and the carriage horses threw off their cleated shoes—but these were the disasters Kyle had prepared for. It seemed to him that Kiera and her maid, Lille, spent as much time huddled on the side of the road waiting for the carriage to be repaired as they did inside it, but Kiera was wise enough not to complain.

Hot food and soft beds with fresh linen awaited them each night, courtesy of the riders Kyle sent ahead of them each afternoon, and his autumn preparations. On the sixth night, and several days before they were expected, they stayed the night at Roc Houle. They didn't see Flen, who was in the Spure himself, hunting something magnificent for his betrothed's supper in what would be her home after their marriage.

Kyle was relieved; Kiera was polite.

Eight days out of Renzi, shortly after noon and a full day before the solstice, they came to the carved stone pillar that marked their return to the Dainis-held land around the lodge. A collective sigh escaped the cohort; even the horses blew steam as they started up the narrow track. No one sighed louder than Kyle himself, who'd expected to be the inadvertent cause of at least one catastrophe.

There were smiles all around when he sent Enobred and Renard ahead with word of their imminent arrival. Fresh hands were waiting to unload the carriage and stable the tired horses. The savory promise of dinner spilled from the kitchen chimneys. Three red-faced children took Kyle's cloak as he crossed the threshold. The caretaker's wife, who was as hideous as Kiera had described, but a friendly soul for all that, pressed a mug of steaming cider into his hand while the caretaker dropped to one knee on the flagstones.

"Welcome, Lord Dainis," he said through his thick, black beard. "Welcome home."

Kyle caught himself before he looked over his shoulder. By strictest protocol—and wherever verger fosterlings gathered, the protocols were invariably strict— he was never *Lord* Dainis. Properly, he was Kyle Dainis, Hart-lord: the fourth son of a living verge-lord. Alberon's protocols defined the verger cadency down to a ninth-son rose-lord, though Kyle had never met a nobleman of lesser rank than himself. When he served supper at the king's court, he marched in front of the pot boys who carried the soup.

He'd lose the small title he had when his father died. Once Muredoch was verge-lord, Kyle would be simply a nobleman of Dainis and a part of the audience.

"Welcome, Lord Dainis," the caretaker repeated.

But on family land, in the absence of his father and brothers, Kyle was the Dainis lord.

"And thanks be to you," he stammered, taking a key ring from the caretaker's hand. He made a show of counting the keys before returning the ring. "All is as it should be."

The caretaker arose. A bearlike giant of a man, he stood a head taller than Kyle. "Be ye cold or hungry, my lord? There's food laid out and water heating in the solar chamber."

With her eyes looking upward, toward the solar, Kiera made a silent plea for the first hot bath. Kyle's numb feet burned pleasantly at the thought of hot water. He hadn't had the carriage's shelter and for once he had the rank. Even a rose-lord outranked any sister.

Kiera must have sensed his wavering thoughts. She shivered and raised her eyes again.

"The women of the house may attend my sister in the solar. I'll wait until later . . . until it's convenient . . ." Lordly phrases came awkwardly to Kyle's tongue. He'd had little opportunity and less need to practice them.

"No need to wait, my lord," the caretaker assured him. "There's a fire in the steam house. Your two young men went out straightaway to ready it for you."

There was only one thing better than a hot bath on a cold day and that was a working steam house. Every verger residence worthy of its lord had such a little house—for its men's enjoyment. Kyle saw his sister staring at him, pleading for an invitation: another adventure, but there were some traditions he didn't intend to challenge. She'd asked for the bath and he'd given it to her.

With Josaf and the other weary men of his cohort trailing after him, Kyle stomped across the snow-packed stableyard. He peeled off his clothes in the steam house's vestibule and hung them on pegs beside the fleecy blanket he'd wrap around himself when he'd concluded this very pleasant ordeal. Steam hit him like a wall when he opened the door. It was like breathing moist fire for a moment, then he relaxed and groped through the cloud to a bench near the rock-filled pit. Belly-down on the wooden planks, he closed his eyes and relaxed.

He heard men milling about, the opening and closing of the vestibule door. But those were expected sounds and he gave them no thought. He heard the clanking of buckets and water sloshing on the floor. That was expected, too. One didn't get steam without throwing water on the stones sitting on the firebox.

There was nothing to worry about—until hands clamped over his wrists and ankles. Then Kyle knew instantly what the men had been doing, what the buckets were for. He struggled to free himself before they doused him with slush. One arm got freed, but that wasn't nearly enough. They released him when the last bucket was empty.

Dripping and cursing, Kyle sprang to his feet, ready for another assault, which never came. The Dainismen were all grins and mirth, even the man sitting on the floor, the one who'd lost hold of Kyle's one arm. Deeper in the steam, well out of sight, Renard laughed so hard it must have hurt.

"Yer first command and ye got us here safe and sound," one of the older men said. "Ye be a right-good man now."

In Alberon, where the one god mostly ignored his worshippers, a young man's passage from boyhood to maturity was littered with initiations and commemorations. Kyle should have guessed he wouldn't escape his first command unscathed. Half-melted snow was far from the worst he'd endured in fosterage—far from the worst he'd dealt out, for that matter—but he'd truly hoped he'd left the pranks behind when he'd returned to Renzi. He unclenched his fists and swiped the damp hair from his eyes.

Wearing only a hint of a grin, Josaf strode out of the mist. "If I was a younger man, I'd find myself a switch and chase these curs to the nearest brook. If I was a fresh and right-good young man."

"The brook?" Kyle whispered in disbelief. Josaf nodded and jerked a thumb toward a braided-bark switch atop the hot stones. Some men got themselves switched in the steam house; they said it got the heat to their bones faster. Kyle thought the whole idea was silly, but he reached for the switch, hoping that Josaf's suggestion wasn't a prelude to some greater indignity. He flicked his wrist and made the frayed bark sing through the steam.

"Damn every man of you," he shouted, "to a cold-water grave!"

Someone opened the vestibule door and the chase was on. Kyle screamed and stumbled as he pursued them, but he wasn't truly cold until he hit the brook himself and thought he'd collapse from the shock. The caretaker and the men from the lodge stood ready with blankets and boots. They pulled Kyle out first and shoved a mug of hot cider into his hands as they bundled him up. Someone helped him stamp into a pair of warmed boots.

It had all been arranged by Enobred and Renard, who wouldn't have done it without Josaf's permission, without Josaf's suggestion. And Josaf, who *hadn't* run naked to the brook, undoubtedly expected to be thanked for masterminding the ordeal.

"I'm a damned goose," Kyle swore with cloudy breath.

A fist came out of nowhere to pound between his shoulder. "Nay, yer a right-good man now."

The blanket gaped; Kyle caught a blast of bitter air. "Then to be a right-good man is to be a goddamned goose!"

No one wasted time arguing with him. They were all hurrying toward the kitchen. Forsaking modesty, dignity, and all semblance of warmth, Kyle outran them all. He spotted the cook's hourglass on the sideboard and upended it.

"I'll have my supper in the master's hall before the sand runs out, or I'll chase you and yours next!"

His blanket had slipped from his shoulder. It covered his back, his other shoulder, and very little else. The cook dropped her jaw and her ladle. She nodded once then turned back to her stew pot. Blushing belatedly, but spectacularly—he could feel the blood rushing to his skin—Kyle bounded up the stairs to the quarters his parents would occupy when they were here, and where, God willing, a fire had been kindled.

God willed.

Flames crackled in the hearth and clothing awaited on the bed. With his teeth still clattering, Kyle grabbed the shirt and stood before the fire. He was still there, wearing the shirt and blanket, enjoying a moment of privacy, when a loud knock came on the chamber's other door.

"Will you be needing assistance, my lord?" an unfamiliar voice inquired. The latch lifted.

"No. None at all. Go away!" he ordered, tightening the sleeve strings with his teeth. He wondered how long he'd been daydreaming and he kicked the fleece boots across the chamber in a rush to don his trousers before his orders were ignored.

Kyle had always worn whatever was available, whatever was leftover from his brothers' wardrobes. Piled together, the garments specifically made for him wouldn't fill a small chest. He was accustomed to tight shirts and binding trousers, but the ill-fitting clothes laid out here in the lodge were his father's clothes, kept here for the verge-lord's pleasure and worn by him earlier this very year. The shirtsleeves were long enough, but the trousers weren't.

Had he unwittingly—unwillingly—outgrown his father?

His own boots were by the hearth. They were long enough in the shank to make up the difference between his ankles and the trousers. He tried to remember if he'd looked up or down when they'd said good-bye at Roc Dainis. Habit said Father was as tall as the caretaker, but careful memory said Kyle had looked down.

Strange, no one seemed to have noticed that he'd grown taller than his lord and sire. Or, perhaps, not so strange at all.

"Kyle? Kyle, are you dressed yet?"

Grabbing his father's padded surcoat from the bed, Kyle opened the door before Kiera tried the latch.

"Everything *does* take you forever. I told Cook she didn't have to hurry, that you'd never be dressed in time. They're bringing it up now."

"Thank you." Kyle yanked the surcoat shut. He might be taller than Father, but there was a fistful of empty space between his ribs and the surcoat clasps. "I got—" A rippling reflection in the spherical mirror above the hall hearth caught his eyes. He scarcely recognized himself.

"You got what, Kyle? As if I can't guess."

"Lost in my thoughts."

"You missed the sunset."

Kyle hung his head. "Sorry."

"Don't be. I watched from my window. Nothing happened. It was a wasted sunset, viewed from the wrong window. This" —she waved her hand toward a casement on the hall's short wall—"is the proper window."

"Good. We can have supper here for your Rapture's solstice tomorrow."

Kitchen drudges had brought up enough food to feed six men. Kyle's stomach growled; he wondered if they'd need more.

"Come over here and choose your meat," he suggested. It would be impolite to pile everything on his own platter first. "Supper smells delicious."

"Come over here instead. Pay attention when I talk to you, Kyle. This is important."

Fosterlings were accustomed to obedience, especially to noblewomen, but, wearing Father's clothes, Kyle bridled at being ordered about like a varlet. He spun around on one heel, ready to snarl at her, but Kiera had wandered into the bedchamber, where she clearly expected him to follow her. After swallowing anger, he did. Kiera closed the door and leaned against it.

"First," she lectured softly. "It's always *our* Rapture, never mine alone. I dreamt of the sunset; you dreamt of watching me. Never forget. Second, since the window I dreamt about is in the hall adjoining this chamber, I should be sleeping here. Josaf can have your things taken somewhere else."

Most likely Kyle would have made the suggestions himself—if she'd given him the opportunity. As he'd been taught at home and in fosterage, men were supposed to keep their women happy, safe, and under close guard; but happy first. In truth, he didn't know many women. There was his mother and there were the household girls who didn't shun a hart-lord's fumbling advances. And then there was Kiera, who gave orders where Mother never would and wheedled as no common girl would dare. Yet Kiera's methods were effective. His first impulse was always to agree with her, but this time—maybe for the first time— she'd pushed too hard.

"No. The hall isn't a bedchamber. A sunset isn't in the middle of the night. I'm settled here; you're settled elsewhere. There's no need to change."

Kiera wilted. "What's wrong? Are you angry with me?"

"No," he insisted. Kiera was nigh irresistible when her lips trembled and her eyes were half-closed, half-brimming with tears. "No!" he repeated, denying the denial. "I *am* angry. I'm not Flennon Houle and I won't be treated as you treat him. Ask me forthright, if you want something. Treat me as you'd have me treat you."

A great tear flowed majestically down Kiera's cheek. "It's me who's wrong. I apologize. I'm not hungry. I won't bother you. I'll return to my room; Lille can take care of me." Her voice broke. A second tear followed the first. She put a trembling hand on the latch, but didn't lift it.

Kyle didn't know any longer where his sister's drama ended and where her honest self began. He didn't think anyone did, maybe including her. This was surely drama, but old habits died hard. He couldn't let Kiera leave in tears. She had him hooked, treed, and cornered, exactly as she'd intended, but his sense of manly honor left him no choices. He called her back, gave her a hug, and asked her to sit with him while he ate, since she wasn't hungry.

Her lips parted.

"Don't ask again; not now," he advised. "We can talk about it tomorrow, for the solstice. But not tonight. Not another word, promise? Just sit with me before the fire."

"Promise."

Kiera wiped her tears and opened the door. A pot boy stood behind a trestle table holding a plate already piled high with food. She took it eagerly from his hands.

Kyle sighed and shook his head as the boy and other varlets scurried about the hall, providing his sister with an upholstered chair near the hearth, a fire screen to protect her face from heat, a linen cloth to protect her gown, a table for her plate, a goblet of sparkling wine, and a delicate but sharp knife. He'd been left to serve himself, which he preferred to do anyway. After dragging the remaining chair closer to the fire, he dismissed all the servants and balanced his plate in his lap.

"We don't need all that fuss," he explained when he noticed Kiera staring at him. "This is the lodge, not Chegnon, not home. We don't have to pretend that we're lords and ladies."

"I wouldn't know; I've never been to Chegnon. I've never been anywhere but Dainis land. Three nights past, at Houle, that was the first supper I've ever eaten where Mother and Father weren't at the table, watching me like hawks. The only time Father took in verger fosterlings, we were still in the nursery and I don't remember any of it. How would you like to be a daughter instead of a son, trapped on your lord father's land, your virtue carefully protected until you could be married off and you were trapped on your husband's land? Your whole life would be laid out for you: marriage, children, and more children. I *want* to pretend, Kyle. All I have is pretend. I thought you'd understand. You're always pretending."

And all this time Kyle had thought marriage, children, and the life of a verge-lord's wife was what *she* wanted! "I'll call them back," he said quickly, not wanting to rekindle their argument or compare destinies . . . again.

Kiera shook her head. "It's too late." She took a lock of her hair and began to twist it into her braids, then stopped.

"What's gone is gone. We'll sit alone here in front of the fire. I'll pretend we're a pair of common-born farmers, waiting to die."

They ate in silence, which, for all Kyle knew, was how farmers ate. It certainly wasn't like any other meal he'd eaten, without a horde of servers hovering and a babble of competing conversation trapped beneath the rafters. Kyle enjoyed the difference, but, as Kiera said, he'd been to court; he'd lived too long at Chegnon. He was glad Father maintained the smallest household verger honor permitted, taking in fosterlings from the Renzi Valley only.

Perhaps it was different for Kiera; different for anyone who'd grown up without leaving home.

He tried to make amends, talking about Chegnon and the other way stations of his fosterage, much as he'd done in his letters. But tonight his stories only sharpened Kiera's mood and turned it bitter. Finally he sat staring at the flames, until unseasonable thunder jolted him upright.

Glass panes rattled in their leaded casements. A swirl of cinders rode a downdraft out of the hearth. Kyle sprang to his feet and stomped the cinders, one by one, but the greater part of his mind was distracted by the persistent thunder. A handful of cinders still glowed on the planks when the peal ended. While Kyle ground them beneath his boot, Kiera flung the casement open.

"Kyle—come! The stars are falling! Come quick!"

Cinders were more important than anything Kiera had to say. When folk lived by hearths in wood-beamed houses, folk had to be careful first.

"Oh . . . Kyle . . ." Her voice filled with awe. "They're *moving*."

His twin's drama proved irresistible. Going to the window, Kyle stared over her head at a perfect winter night: moonless, cloudless, and studded with stars. A brilliant streak crossed the Warrior. Kyle squinted, counted; none of the stars he knew were missing. But the constellations were drawn with their brightest stars, not with the myriad pinpricks within them, any one of which could have vanished. Then there was another streak on the flank of Darr, the Warrior's horse. He squinted again, counted again. Before he was half-finished, a third streak sliced through the Warrior's spear.

The streaks came fast, a new one appearing before the last

was extinguished, until there were several in the sky at once. Such star showers happened in spring or late summer, but never near the winter solstice and never with so many colors. There were white streaks and fire-colored streaks and streaks of shimmering blue or green.

Thunder knelled again, hammering the ground. The lodge walls shuddered. More cinders swirled out of the hearth. Kyle thought of the danger, took a retreating stride toward the hearth, then stopped. The whole sky glowed as from a distant fire. The stars, both fixed and falling, disappeared in the ruddy light.

"Not a sunset," Kyle whispered as the glow intensified.

Kiera's icy fingers locked over his. There was neither drama nor pretense in the gesture, but he freed himself anyway. The broken face of his own Rapture had risen from his memory.

"It's yours, Kiera—all yours. I cannot share it." He studied the cinders on the floor. "I dare not share it." He knelt down, hiding from the light, and crushed the cinders with his hands, not lifting his sight from the floor, not even when the hall filled with bloody light.

Chapter Four

Red shadows danced around Kyle, turning the hearth dark by comparison. He heard the source of the bloody light: powerful as thunder, but shaped like the roar of softwood flame. With all his soul, Kyle longed to see what Kiera saw above the snow-capped Spure forest, but so long as Rapture's broken face loomed in his mind's eye, he constrained himself, defeating curiosity as easily as he crushed another cinder beneath his thumb.

His diligence wasn't wasted. A cold wind back-drafted down the chimney. Smoke, ash, and cinders showered the wood planks. Kyle decided the safest course was to break the fire apart and bank it with sand. An iron poker rose out of the sand bucket that sat beside every hearth in Alberon. He reached for it, but his muscles froze partway there.

Smoke and ashes swirled themselves into a tall, opaque pillar. Kyle skittered backward until he struck one of the upholstered chairs. He beseeched the Hidden God's protection and, blasphemy though it was, invoked the names of every foreign god his addled memory could recall.

The pillar swelled higher than the hearth lintel. It swallowed cinders and manifested them again as eyes glowing above a perfectly black mouth. The pillar thickened at its base, then divided into legs that strode toward Kyle as he sprawled speechless on the floor.

Wizards said the right eye was *nagah'bei*, the semblance of vision. Bracing himself against the chair, Kyle squeezed his left eye shut. Nagah'bei revealed tendrils of smoke and ash rising toward the rafters. Their shape wasn't manlike. But looking with his left eye, with *nasen'bei*, the vision of truth and summoning—the eye for seeing spooks or casting spells—Kyle saw a haunting apparition.

Where his right eye saw smoke, his left saw another young man. His face was pale, with dark hair wreathed around it like a storm cloud. A conical gold cap with red tassels sat in the midst of the wild hair. Golden wings rose behind the haunt's shoulders. His eyes were dark beneath heavy brows, yet they sparkled like firelight in the darkness.

The haunt was either a demon or a wizard of some sort, and Kyle, even in abject panic, preferred to dread a wizard rather than a demon. So it was the sparks in a *wizard's* eyes that congealed into two red-glowing eyes. It was a wizard's hand that reached through the tangled mass of hair, revealing a dark red sleeve and a jeweled ring on every knuckle. And, at the last, it was a wizard's finger that reached and stretched toward him.

Kyle couldn't move: not to rise, not to run. He couldn't turn away when the wizard's finger touched his forehead and his skull exploded in fire and pain. His screams echoed through the hall, then, mercifully, he heard nothing.

"Kyle? Kyle—can you hear me? Say something. Do something. Open your eyes. Please?"

The pain and fire were gone; the anguish had faded. Kyle opened his eyes and saw his sister. She sobbed with relief and curled herself around him. Her hands slid beneath his spine. Her cheek was warm against his.

He was alive.

Kyle found his arm extended flat and still on the floor. Willing his elbow to bend, he lifted his hand high enough to see it. The effort exhausted him. His hand fell, limp and heavy, against Kiera's back. He tried to say, *I'm all right.* The words were clear enough in his mind, but mewling sounds came from his mouth.

Kiera stroked his hair. There was a tender lump at the back of his skull and other aches in his back. He must have fallen, must have hit the floor hard enough to lose consciousness. How long ago? And why? The answers, if he knew them, were buried.

"Please don't die. I don't want you to die."

He found his voice: "I'm not going to die," he said, and knew he told the truth.

When Kiera sat up, smiling through tears, her gown was streaked with ashes. Ashes. He remembered ashes before—Before what?

With a blink and a shudder, Kyle's consciousness restored itself, like beads snapping on a string. There was a bead for him, another for Kiera as they'd finished their supper; another bead for thunder pealing and a fourth for Kiera standing beside the window. The next bead was missing.

The missing bead was ashes.

"What happened?" Kiera asked. "What's happening now?"

He tried a shrug and a lopsided grin. Both were bad ideas that left him dizzy. Kiera took his hand and helped him sit up. A wave of nausea crashed over him. When it had ebbed, the crisis was over. There was a little hole in his memory, one of many such dark spots: A fosterling didn't learn his trade without landing hard on his head at least once a season. Kyle reckoned he'd be dizzy for a day or so, maybe a bit nauseous until morning, but the little hole was no cause for alarm.

At least he hoped it wasn't.

"What did *you* see?" he asked, hoping to divert Kiera's attention. "Was it Rapture, large and clear?"

Kiera pursed her lips. "A ball of fire fell from the stars. It screamed my name and told me secrets that only I could hear. It was bigger, brighter than any sunset—" She held her fingers over her mouth. "Oh, God have mercy! The sun's fallen out of the sky. My Rapture was the sun dying. We're all doomed because of my Rapture."

"Stop babbling, goose-girl. That was the Harbinger, not the sun. God has returned. He's opened the Siege of Shadows. He calls upon the worthiest of His worshippers to look upon His face. He seeks a successor."

Kyle scarcely recognized his own voice. Worse, he didn't know what he was talking about and wouldn't have used those words, if he had.

"How do you know?" Kiera whispered. "I heard God's voice: 'Come, my child,' He said. 'I charge you to follow my Harbinger. I call you to face me in the Siege of Shadows.' Did you hear the same thing, Kyle? Did you? *Did you?* What does it mean, Kyle? What's a Siege of Shadows? What is a Harbinger?"

"I don't—" Kyle began, and stopped. His head hurt—no, not his head but his mind; it hurt to think. "I don't know . . ."

He shook his head and moaned in agony. No one was pounding a red-hot spike into his skull, but that was the sensation he had. Fosterlings were taught to rise above pain or battle through it. Sucking air like a diver, Kyle fought back and the missing bead slid down the strand.

"Tash— Ta-esh . . . ell-em."

<<Taslim.>>

A simple, smooth pronunciation sounded between Kyle's ears, banishing the hot pain as if it had never been.

"Taslim?"

Another haunt emerged from the aether where Kyle's thoughts were born: a dark-eyed face framed by a precisely trimmed beard, long purple robes with red-lined sleeves, a gold conical cap and golden rings on every finger—a memory, yet not a memory.

Kyle set his mind's strength against the haunt and it stared upward, where the sun might have shone, if the sun could shine inside a man's skull.

It said, <<I perceive we have a problem.>>

"We?"

<<Yes, we. I am here, you are here; that is we, is it not? Has language changed so much in a millennium, or are you addle-pated?>>

"Millennium?"

Kyle's own thoughts became words in his mind, then his tongue shaped them, and his ears, when they heard his voice, returned them to his thoughts: a simple cycle and a familiar one. But suddenly there were other words in his mind that did not touch his tongue or ears and were not formed from his own thoughts.

"Kyle—who are you talking to?" Kiera asked anxiously. "Kyle?"

<<Kyle? Is that you? Are you called Kyle?>> The elegant haunt stared again at a sun that did not exist. <<Yes. I perceive that you are called Kyle and that you are not addled, merely confused. I, too, am a bit confused. Very well, Kyle. We'll start at the beginning and see where that takes us. *We* have a problem because *I* am here, and you, obviously, are surprised. I am Taslim. Wizard—>>

The self-described wizard produced an iron-wrapped crystal

that immediately loomed large in the aether. There were symbols wrought in the iron. Kyle recognized the symbols as runes, the object itself as a talisman. The talisman shrank and the wizard's worried face filled the aether in its place.

<<Are you *not* a wizard? An apprentice? Lightning strike! Don't tell me you're a priest!>>

"I am Kyle Dainis, Hart-lord. I know reading, writing, ciphering, and the crafts of war. I stand ready to serve whenever my honor, my kin, or my king command."

Taslim uttered an incomprehensible oath, then added, <<I've been sucked into the night-dark soul of a whoreson nobleman.>>

"On your honor, unsay that!"

"Oh, Kyle," Kiera interrupted Kyle's half-spoken conversation. "There's no one here but me, and I said nothing. Who are you talking to?"

He raised his head. With his right eye he saw Kiera, frantic and weeping. Her gown was streaked with ashes. Through his left eye, he saw the haunt, but no longer hovering in the aether of his mind. Man-sized now, and opaque, Taslim stood precisely where his right eye saw Kiera sitting. Fearfully, Kyle opened both eyes. Nausea wrenched his gut. He closed both eyes, but the image of Taslim and Kiera together, mingled and shimmering, wouldn't be quickly forgotten.

"What are you?" Kyle demanded. He pressed his fist against his gut, mastering the nausea, and reopened his eyes.

"I'm your sister, your twin—Kiera!" She seized his shoulders and shook them.

<<I'll be damned,>> the wizard swore. <<Twins. *She's* the wizard. Tell me this woman knows wizardry. Take her hand between yours and tell me—>>

But Kyle was fully occupied keeping his supper inside his stomach. He sagged against the chair, unwilling to say another word. His will didn't affect the wizard.

<<Lightning strike. I'm undone. Trapped. Twins. *Twins!* I never reckoned for twins. I reckoned a single birth, a single seed, a single Rapture. Damn. A millennium waiting between life and death, waiting for the Harbinger and my heir. *Heirs.* Who would reckon twins? And neither of them with enough talent to make grass grow in springtime. You! You said you're a hart-lord. What, by the almighty bolt, is a hart-lord?>>

Kyle knew, of course. The words "fourth son of a living

verge-lord" rolled through his mind, but he had no intention of answering the wizard's questions.

<<Fourth son, eh? Well, you won't be missed. That rune spell came through straight.>>

The wizard could hear his thoughts. Very well, he'd think about nothing . . . about a blade of grass growing in spring.

Taslim swore another lengthy oath about lightning and vermin. He shook his talisman until the crystal glowed with that painful, white light.

Without thinking—exactly as he'd been taught in the sand-filled arenas of his foster homes—Kyle reached for the wizard's arm. The talisman continued to rain agony on every nerve, but he'd felt *something* when his hand passed through the purple robe.

<<You can't touch me, Kyle. You're no wizard. You're a hart-lord: last of the least.>>

Narrowing his left eye until the nasen'bei haunt was as solid-seeming as he could imagine it, Kyle reached a second time, directly through the robe's front. His fingers found a beating heart, and squeezed shut around it. The brilliant talisman fell from Taslim's fingers; it vanished from nasen'bei's sight. Fear filled Kyle's mind, but it wasn't his own fear and, smiling with grim satisfaction, he squeezed tighter. Taslim doubled over and writhed like a speared snake. The conical hat followed the talisman into oblivion.

"Taslim." Kyle made the name a curse. His nausea was gone. He could stand up, with his arm outstretched and his fist clenched. Through nasen'bei, the wizard dangled, helpless, before him. "That's the name I saw on the crypt wall while I waited for my Rapture. Whoever held the roc then thought you'd died in the year twenty-five forty. You're nothing but a dead man, Taslim. A dead wizard. You died on a fool's quest in the Eigela—"

<<I saw the Siege of Shadows. I saw its power. I know its secrets—>>

Kyle rotated his wrist as a warrior might twist a knife's hilt to enlarge a wound.

"There is no Siege of Shadows. I don't know what hell spat you out, but I'll see you back where you came—" He'd never felt such rage; it inspired him to eloquence. "You spoke to my sister; you pretended you were God. But God doesn't speak with your voice and I won't let you seduce her!"

Kiera screamed. She ran from the hall as he swiveled his wrist sunwise and back again. With her gone, and no other image to interfere with his nasen'bei vision, Kyle could squeeze tighter still.

"Be gone before she comes back," he advised. "Go back to your hell."

The iron-wrapped talisman reappeared in the wizard's trembling hand. White pain seared Kyle's eyes. Biting down on a scream, he kept his grip on whatever he held. The standoff lasted a few heartbeats.

Or an eternity.

<<Enough.>>

Fosterlings were taught that when a man conceded defeat, honorable men stood down. A year out of fosterage, there was nothing more sacred to Kyle Dainis than his honor. He unclenched his fist and lowered his arm. The nasen'bei wizard crouched on the wooden planks, bare-headed, empty-handed, and moaning quietly.

"Well," Kyle said after a moment had passed and the wizard hadn't vanished. "Begone. You yielded, now, *begone*!"

Taslim rose to one knee. He clutched the front of his robe, though there was no tear in the purple cloth, no blood welling between his fingers.

<<It's not so easy, my friend.>>

"I'm not your friend."

<<I don't wish to be your enemy, Kyle Dainis, Hart-lord. You're no wizard, perhaps, but I may have been wrong to call you a fool. I offer peace and friendship between us. That is all I *can* offer, Hart-lord. I wrought my spells a millennium ago. They sustained me in nasen'bei and now they trap me here. You don't have the skill to summon me out and you don't have the strength to drive me out, either.>>

"We'll see about that." Kyle lunged forward. His arm passed through the wizard's chest, catching nothing.

<<Don't mistake me for a fool, Hart-lord. You'd do well to listen. I've been to the Siege of Shadows. I know why no one returned. With me to guide you, you'll not succumb to old mistakes. You are bloodied, are you? You weren't supposed to be, but so much has gone wrong.>>

"Bloodied?"

<<Have you killed another man, Hart-lord?>>

"God have mercy, no. Not a living man. I meant to kill you

just now, but you're dead. I know the sword, the lance, and the bow, but my masters said I lack a warrior's spirit."

Taslim stood. <<Bitter, Hart-lord? Fourth son, last son, least son, son too meek to make trouble.>> The wizard's image shimmered. <<I can change that, Hart-lord.>> The words whirled seductively between Kyle's ears. <<The Siege can change that.>>

Kyle shook his head, as if that would rid him of his nasen'-bei vision. It didn't. He couldn't get Taslim out of his sight or thoughts. "Kyle. Call me Kyle, if you must talk to me."

<<Friends, Kyle?>>

He considered the reasons to turn his back on the wizard's offer—if it were possible to turn his back on a nasen'bei wizard, if it were wise at all. The wizard seemed real enough standing on the floor, but he cast no shadow, and by simply tilting his head, Kyle could see him over the mantel or floating amid the rafters.

"Where are you, that I see you in the same place no matter where I look?"

<<A good question, a very good question, but you already know the answer: I'm in nasen'bei.>>

"Where— No, *what* is nasen'bei? It's more than just what a wizard sees through his left eye, isn't it?"

<<Much more, much more indeed. Look around, Hart-lord. Nasen'bei is the between place, the behind place where the sun shines at night and the wind always blows. It's a wizard's sanctuary, his shortcut between here and there.>>

Taslim surely meant to dazzle and befuddle him, but the attempt failed. He knew exactly where the sun shone at night. It shone in his imagination. Strange, though, that wizards would call imagination nasen'bei: the vision of truth . . .

<<You're no fool,>> Taslim said softly and—Kyle thought—no more for his knowing than his own private thoughts were for the wizard's. <<Lightning strike. What went wrong with you, Hart-lord? If you were the wizard you could be, by the almighty bolt, we'd storm the Siege.>>

"Now who's bitter?"

Kyle surprised himself with his offhand question. Moments ago he'd tried to send this nasen'bei wizard back to the hell he'd come from. He still wanted to, but his blind rage was gone. How many lonely nights in fosterage had he gone to sleep wishing for a friend only he could see? A friend who could share his thoughts, his imagination? Kiera had been that friend when he wrote his letters, but he hardly knew his sister these days. Loneliness was worse in the midst of his family. He still went to sleep wishing for a confidant.

Be careful what you wish for: That was the moral of Kyle's favorite fables. He hadn't been careful. The sparks of friendship flashed between himself and a dark-haired wizard who'd been dead for almost a thousand years.

<<Friends, Kyle?>>

And the wizard knew it.

Kyle knew the wizard's hand would be warm and solid, if he clasped it. And he was tempted. Of course, he'd be chided for talking to himself—which he was used to—and, with his imaginary wizard standing between him and the world, he'd walk into things other folk could plainly see.

<<That's not a problem.>> Taslim shook a rune out of his talisman. It glowed bright, but not painfully bright. Then the glowing rune, the talisman, and Taslim all disappeared. <<You can see through me. I have power for small things.>>

"Aye, you have power." Kyle hooked his thumb over his belt. Temptation had vanished with the wizard. "You can disappear and you can pluck my thoughts. What else can you do? Can you plant your own thoughts, like weeds in the wheat fields? What will I wish for next? Will I wish myself on a fool's quest? Your friendship is a dangerous thing, Wizard. Too dangerous for me."

He picked up the poker and began reassembling the fire. "Tell me, Wizard, what happens to you if I die?"

Taslim appeared in the hearth, a scowl on his even-featured face. <<Oblivion, eventually, after maggots reduced your rotting corpse to dust and bone.>>

Kyle flinched as crunching and chomping filled his skull. Every nerve prickled.

<<Or were you thinking of jumping into the fire, Hart-lord? Do you have the courage to stand in the flames until your flesh chars?>>

Chomping became crackling, and the scent in Kyle's nostrils was that of meat roasting too long on the spit. His resolve faltered; the wizard's scowl reversed into a smug grin. Kyle understood he'd have to find a way to keep his thoughts to himself.

"I'm accident-prone," he said, as convincingly as he could

with the reek of burnt offal growing stronger. "Everyone says my carelessness will be the death of me. They're amazed I've survived this long."

Kyle knew that wizards said nasen'bei was the eye of summoning, as well as the eye of truth, so Kyle tried summoning a steady rain of mishaps, great and small, from his memory. Taslim retaliated with stifling heat and the sizzle of fat hitting the fire. Sweat stung Kyle's eyes, blurring his vision, but he continued with a litany of his stumbles, tumbles, collisions, and pure bad luck.

Taslim cringed as an eight-year-old Kyle climbed the pantry shelves in search of sweetmeats and brought the entire larder down on top of himself, ending with the sticky treats that landed—one, two, and three—on the tip of his nose.

<<You're quick—in a primitive, clumsy way,>> the wizard conceded. <<You made that last bit about the sweet meats up, didn't you?>>

Kyle caught himself smiling, caught himself wanting a friend. The wizard was also quick, and very dangerous.

"Look at him—he's transfixed!"

Caught between incompetence and imagination, Kyle hadn't heard Kiera return to the hall. She'd brought Josaf and a handful of others with her. They'd all stopped halfway between the door and the hearth, most of them with their hands cupped in the hollow spheres of prayer. Josaf put on his battle face and strode closer.

"This is no time for pranks," the old varlet scolded when he was close enough to speak in a hoarse whisper. "We've all had our nerves rattled by that omen in the sky. Your sister's addled: talking about Rapture one moment and you the next. She thinks a haunt's stolen your soul. Your father expected better of you. *I* expected better."

Kyle didn't know where to begin his apologies, his lame explanations. He stared out the nearest window, as he'd done countless times before, waiting for inspiration. Instead of inspiration, he found Taslim, and beyond Taslim there was only the dark, cold nothing of a winter's night and the rosy glow of the Harbinger on the horizon. It did look like a sunset—if the sun ever set in the north.

<<The Siege is open.>> The wizard's voice was hushed. <<God awaits.>>

With Taslim for inspiration, Kyle fell back on the wizard's first words: "We have a problem, Josaf."

"What sort of problem, lad?"

"A wizard sort. The haunt of a wizard whose name I read on the crypt wall on Rapture night. He died on a failed quest for the Siege of Shadows in the year twenty-five, forty."

<<I'm no haunt, Hart-lord, and most certainly did not *die* on a failed quest.>>

Kyle shook his head violently.

"Kyle, lad. What's happened to you?"

"He says his name's Taslim and he says he cast spells and waited a millennium for the Harbinger to open the Siege again. That's what we saw: the Harbinger." The sweet nectar of imagination—so useful when he had to explain how the butter got in the straw or why the chickens were loose—finally began to flow. "He was after Kiera, but I got in his way." The notion didn't seem so far-fetched; he almost believed it himself. "He wasn't expecting twins. I outwitted him, but he says he's trapped and has to stay in nasen'bei—"

"Nasen'bei!" Josaf interrupted. "What sort of nonsense is this? I'm telling you for the second and last time: none of your pranks. If you got frightened and knocked yourself silly by tripping over your feet, so be it. I was frightened myself when that thing roared overhead; there's no shame in it. But don't be making it worse with tales, and don't be telling them to your sister!"

Josaf glanced across the hall; Kyle copied the gesture. The doorway gathering had grown. Kiera had wandered closer, her hands cupped in prayer.

"You've got her thinking God spoke to her from that firey ball. She's frighted. Tell her the truth, lad. Put a stop to this, before it gets worse."

Kyle looked at his sister. The expression on her face was hard to read, but it wasn't fright or prayer. She looked more like a cat about to pounce.

And he was the hapless mouse.

<<Need assistance?>> a smooth voice inquired: another cat looking for supper.

"No!"

"No?" Josaf put his hand along Kyle's jaw and forcibly turned his head around. "Kyle, this isn't like you. Look at me. Let me see your eyes opened wide. God have mercy—you must have fallen hard enough to crack your wits. Listen to me: Set your sister's mind at ease, then we'll put you to bed."

Kyle twisted free. His head *was* throbbing. Maybe he was delirious. That could happen if a man took an unlucky blow. Taslim might be a dream; this all might be a dream—

<<And I thought you were clever, Hart-lord.>>

"Leave me alone!"

Josaf caught Kyle's chin again. "I tell you, I don't like this at all. If you're hurt, that's one thing, if you're not . . . You may be wearing the lord's surcoat and trousers, but I'll take a stick to you before God and witnesses."

This time Kyle twisted free and retreated, bumping into Kiera, who'd come closer and whose hand was cold as ice on his neck when she stopped him.

"You don't need to pretend, Kyle," she assured him. "I'm sorry you fell and that you didn't hear God's voice. Don't worry. We shared Rapture; we'll share the quest for the Siege of Shadows, too. I wouldn't go without you. You don't have to make up tales about dead wizards to get yourself included."

"I'm not," Kyle insisted and headed for the window, where no one was standing because the casement was open and letting in the frigid air. He pulled it shut. Reflection showed Kiera and Josaf and Taslim, all scowling, all angry for their own reasons. God's mercy, there wasn't anything Kyle could say that would satisfy them all, or buy him the quiet he desperately wanted.

<<If *that's* all you want . . . Stand up straight, Hart-lord. Tell them to look at the surface of the glass, not through it. And keep your eyes open so I can work.>>

The talisman was shimmering again. Maybe the wizard was seeding his thoughts, but Kyle was ready to try anything. The runelight hurt; he wasn't certain he could keep his eyes open, but he'd try.

"Look at the surface of the glass. Watch. He says he'll do something, God knows what."

Josaf's reflection shifted from anger to anxiety. "You've gone mad. Lost your wits entirely."

But Josaf looked at the glass and so did everyone else. A white pinprick grew in the left eye of Kyle's reflection. He flinched, but didn't blink, then jewel-box colors swirled over the glass and he gaped with the rest. Josaf made prayer's Hollow Sphere as the wizard's image congealed in the colors. A woman screamed, a body hit the floor. Fearing it had been his sister, Kyle turned and ended the haunting display.

Kiera hadn't fainted. "It's not *fair*!" she shrieked. "You stole him. You stole my guide. I was promised a guide and you stole him. It was *my* Rapture and you stole him! He wasn't yours. You didn't have the *right*. God's pockets, Kyle—answer me!"

He didn't bother. It didn't take nasen'bei to see that he'd never bungled anything quite as spectacularly as he'd bungled this evening. Everyone—Josaf, the caretaker, the caretaker's wife sitting on the floor, Kiera's maid, Enobred, Renard, and the lodge's least varlet— had something to say to him. He retreated into himself, as he'd always done after he bungled. Experience had taught him it was better to endure in silence than make matters worse with excuses. The babble in the hall blended with the babble his memory churned up from his other disasters: *Kyle's let the chickens loose. Kyle's broken Cook's best bowl. Kyle fell off the roof. Kyle stole his sister's Rapture. Kyle's got a wizard stuck inside his left eye.*

There'd be scolding, maybe a thrashing, then he'd be ignored again. Eventually the trouble would be behind him, forgotten until the next time. All he had to do was stand firm, like a tree, and wait.

<<Wait for what, Hart-lord?>> Taslim blocked Kyle's retreat. <<None of these fools can solve our problem. You're not a blundering child and I'm not a chicken or a bowl. And—by the almighty bolt—I'd not have chosen that sister of yours.>>

"Leave me alone!"

That earned him another round of sharp-voiced concern and a slap from Kiera. He pushed her away. Not hard. Not near as hard as he could have pushed, but she staggered into Josaf and Josaf gathered her protectively into his arms. The hall was silent, with everyone staring at him. They thought he'd gone mad. Maybe he had, talking to a haunt.

<<Bite your tongue when you speak to me, Hart-lord, and they won't hear you. Your thoughts are clear enough. You don't have to open your mouth.>>

<<Ah, that's how he does it . . .>>

<<Close, Hart-lord. You'll have to figure the rest on your own. We're not friends, remember? Your choice; you can always change your mind. I find it remarkable, though, that you cower before these fools but you aren't afraid to roar at me.>>

<<I have to roar at you, otherwise I'd be at your mercy, which I don't trust.>>

Kyle heard his own voice inside his head and realized he'd imagined himself standing in one part of his mind while Taslim stood in another—

<<In nasen'bei,>> the wizard suggested. <<We're both in nasen'bei, though you seem to be here by accident. You did say you were accident prone, didn't you? You're in a very dangerous position, Hart-lord. They think you're dangerously mad; I know you're not, but you're going to have to do some fast roaring, if you don't want them to prevail. What do you want, Hart-lord? Them and madness—locked away in a windowless room someplace—or me and the Siege of Shadows?>>

<<I want you out of my head.>>

<<I haven't the strength. You haven't the skill. You need help, Hart-lord. If not me, some other wizard. Do you know another wizard?>>

He knew the lords Entellen and Drewlen, the lady Shotaille, and the lord magister himself, Marrek Brun, or he knew of them. They were the king's wizards and they traveled with him throughout the kingdom. They'd be at the Chegnon winter court. Kyle had seen them the last year he'd fostered at Chegnon—three dour men and a sour crone—but he'd never met them, never talked to them. He shuddered at the thought of asking them for help.

<<It's a start, Hart-lord. Tell these fools you want to go to Chegnon. Tell them you need the king's wizards. Look straight at them and speak like a man; they'll listen. They fear you now, but they love you more.>>

Kyle made his decision, then asked, <<What about you, Taslim? Do you want their help? Why didn't you go to them first?>>

<<Questions without friendship, Hart-lord? I warned you: no more gifts. Do what you want, or be done unto by fools. It's all the same to me. I *will* look upon the face of God from the Siege of Shadows. I've waited a millennium and I will succeed.>>

In an awkward, wordless way Kyle thought that Taslim was as dangerous an enemy as a man could have, but one who told the truth, when it suited him. The advice was good, whether it came from a friend or an enemy. He'd have to be very careful, more careful than he'd ever been before. He'd have to find a way to keep his thoughts to himself—

<<You can try.>>

And he'd have to go to Chegnon.

"We've done what we came to do," Kyle said aloud and found, as Taslim predicted, that he commanded the hall's attention. "The Harbinger was the fulfillment of the Rapture I shared with my sister. She's heard God's voice; the Renzi priests can best advise her." The words were his own—Taslim didn't know that he and Kiera shared deception, not Rapture—at least Taslim didn't know until Kyle thought about it, which was too late for words. But the words were having an effect. Panic was in retreat. Even Kiera's face was calm again. "For myself, I've run afoul of a wizard and I believe that only the king's wizards can help me, the sooner, the better. We'll return to Roc Dainis quickly, tomorrow morning, if possible."

They listened and they agreed, for their own reasons perhaps, but no one argued. Josaf said he was himself again, which was a palpable lie—and what the others wanted to hear. The lodge folk departed, whispering among themselves; they'd certainly be relieved to have him gone. Kiera left, too, reluctant and suspicious, but without the rage he'd seen when she slapped him.

If anyone had been transformed tonight, that someone was Kiera. He hadn't recognized her.

"Come, lad. Come to bed."

Josaf took his arm and led him like a child to the attached bedchamber. Taslim came too, floating just out of reach whether Kyle's eyes were open or shut.

"He's real. I swear it," Kyle whispered as the old man loosened Father's surcoat. "I see him wherever I look."

"You've hit your head, lad. You're not yourself. You've given us all a good scare when we didn't need it, but you'll rest now and be yourself in the morning. I'll wake you here, beside your bed."

Chapter Five

Kyle didn't know how long Josaf stayed with him, but it was a long time. By hearth light, and sunlight, whenever Kyle opened his eyes he saw the old man sitting beside the bed, tilted in the stool so his back rested against the plastered wall. Kyle saw the haunt, too, the wizard Taslim, whether his eyes were open or shut. His mind throbbed inside his skull. He couldn't get out of bed.

The caretaker's wife brought food, the smells of which made Kyle vomit, which turned his throbbing head into a dark, red agony. When it was clear he couldn't eat, the caretaker's wife brought him a variety of herb teas that didn't unsettle his stomach. He drank them, to ease Josaf's mind, until he heard someone say that the herbs would help him sleep.

He didn't know how long he'd lain in the great bed; he didn't know when he'd decided he could never sleep again. Taslim could make Kyle wish he were dead while he lay on the linen, exhausted, keeping himself awake with the pain in his head and the bite of his own fingernails in the flesh of his palms. But, so long as Kyle didn't succumb to sleep, Taslim couldn't reshape his thoughts.

They thought he slept. Even Josaf, who knew him as well as anyone, thought he was asleep when he lay motionless inside his pain, conserving the strength of his body and mind. Josaf would hold his hand for long, silent stretches of time. Sometimes the old man stroked his hair. It seemed to Kyle that every strand pricked his scalp like a hot needle. He'd almost scream when the stroking began, but gradually Josaf's touch would soothe the pain and he'd have to fight sleep with all his strength until Josaf tired.

Somewhere between one throb and the next, Kyle lost his battle. He slept, and awoke with dawn light fingering the blankets he'd drawn tight around his head.

"Captain, the milk's frozen and the bread won't rise," a woman complained, somewhere nearby. "It's three days now he's lain like that, and it's never been so cold in these parts. The sky's all hid in clouds—"

Kyle could hear ice clattering on the window and a shrill wind whipping against the walls. He believed what she said about the cold and about how long he'd been in bed. He was ashamed that he'd broken his own faith and slept who knew how long after swearing he wouldn't. But his thoughts, as far as he could determine, were his own and he wondered if, perhaps, he'd been ill. Delirium could account for the strange images haunting his memory.

"Sure to tell, Captain, what we saw was the sun falling. There's no break to the cold. The sun's not coming back, this time. We're all going to die, starving if we don't freeze first."

Not delirium, not if the woman had seen what he remembered.

Kyle hooked a finger through his blanket cocoon, enlarging his window on the world. He saw blankets heaped around him, the bed curtains partly opened, and Josaf sitting on the tilted stool.

Nothing else.

<<Fools, Hart-lord. While I drifted in nasen'bei, Alberon's gone nave to chops for fools!>>

Not delirium, not at all. The wizard's voice reverberated inside Kyle's skull, awakening his headache. He sank into the eiderdown mattress, eyes closed and lips pressed tightly together until the urge to groan had passed.

"Whatever shall we do, Captain? The young lord's no good for us." The caretaker's wife was the woman talking to Josaf; Kyle finally recognized her voice.

<<Tell the ninny to lay another log on the hearth and set it ablaze. By the almighty bolt— it's *winter!* What does she expect? Songbirds and southern breezes?>>

"Lay another log or two on the fire, good wife." Josaf didn't suffer fools gently either, but his voice wasn't as harsh as the voice in Kyle's head.

Kyle wasn't surprised that Josaf and the wizard agreed with each other. The worst thing about having a wizard haunting his vision— Well, not the absolute worst thing, which was the headache, but the second-worst thing was that the wizard was wise beneath his arrogance and ambition.

<<I was accounted wise in my day,>> the haunt agreed. <<And I've nurtured *my* wisdom while the kingdom's gone to fools!>>

Taslim's wisdom was the third worst thing, Kyle corrected himself. The first was still the headache, but the second was being spied upon. He was trying to keep his thoughts to himself, but the effort fed the headache. Maybe the spying was worse than the throbbing; his head wouldn't ache so badly if the haunt didn't spy on him.

"Oh—mistress, come quick! Mincey's done dropped the goose eggs and broke every one!"

Another voice entered the room, a kitchen girl, young and agitated, by the sound of her voice. The goose girl's accident was the sort of blunder Kyle readily understood, but hardly enough to justify the furor that successfully sucked both Josaf and the caretaker's wife down the bedchamber's back stairs to the kitchen.

<<The Harbinger,>> Taslim explained. <<Your dear sister's not the only one who thinks the world's come to an end. One night with fire in the sky and they're all seeing doom and omens. God knows what they'd be seeing if the Harbinger had blazed among the stars for a month, the way it did last time.>>

It was the most plainly useful thing Taslim had said, and Kyle was almost grateful for the insight.

<<Then, I almost thank you, Hart-lord. Since you're thinking about getting up, you might as well do it now. They'll be back soon enough and I've gathered from your abundant anxieties that you don't like being fussed over.>>

The haunt hovered where Josaf had sat. He'd exchanged his purple robe for snug, black moleskins and a fitted surcoat with a high, braided collar and crimson slashing at the shoulders, elbows, and wrists. The court garments were nothing Kyle would have been comfortable wearing, but they'd been quite dashing when Prince Gravais had worn them at the winter court two years ago. Taslim had ransacked his memory. God knew what else the haunt had pilfered; Kyle didn't, couldn't.

He got out of bed slowly, measuring his movements through

the corners of his eyes, rather than looking straight ahead where the wizard appeared to be. Kyle didn't need to see his trousers hanging on the bedpost once he'd gotten a side-angle glimpse of them, likewise his shirt and boots. Combing his hair would have been a problem, if he'd been the sort who preened before a looking glass.

Kyle never preened, but he did have to shave, or allow someone else to perform that manly chore for him. He preferred shaving himself and ran an assessing hand over his raspy chin before staring at necessaries sitting on a stand near the hearth. He didn't think he wanted to hold sharp steel against his own throat. No one would care how he looked here at the lodge. It would be different at home or, especially, at Chegnon.

He picked up the hand glass and held it out at an angle.

The haunt faced Kyle from the hand glass and Kyle realized with a start that this was the first time he'd looked in a mirror, the first time Taslim might actually be able to see *his* face. He sensed disappointment, his own as much as the wizard's.

<<You're not what I hoped for, Hart-lord, but that's hardly your fault. I wish you no ill will or pain. I won't harm a hair on your head, your cheek, or your downy chin. If you wish to shave it off at the roots, by all means do.>>

Taslim slid from the silvered glass, leaving Kyle to stare at his own reflection. He'd never wondered what he might look like in a stranger's eyes: shaggy, dirt-brown hair with a mind of its own; a rounded face with a squared-off chin; ordinary brown eyes; an unremarkable nose; and a mouth that was too full, too soft to command respect.

Maybe he'd grow a beard . . .

<<Do you think it would help?>> the haunt asked as he floated back between Kyle and his reflection.

He'd been teased his whole life, at home and in fosterage, and he'd learned—the hard way—that steadfast calm was the best defense against mockery. It was easy for Kyle to be calm; when he wasn't actively fighting the haunt, his headache faded. And, for all his silky venom, Taslim didn't frighten him half as much as the late-night bullies of his early fosterage years.

<<As long as it didn't leave me looking like you.>> He grinned at the mirror, then headed down to the kitchen.

The kitchen was a mistake. Its noise and heat were too much after all his time in the cold, quiet bedchamber. His appearance midway down the open stairs was instantly more important than the unfortunate Mincey and her broken eggs. Cook wanted to feed him everything she had on the hearth. Josaf wanted him back upstairs, immediately. Kiera wanted him to tell *someone* to close the shutters on the hall windows, shutters which had been left purposefully open for her solstice visions.

Belatedly, Josaf asked Kyle how he felt. He said he was tired, achy, and not hungry; all of which were true. Then Josaf asked, "And the other?" meaning his haunt.

Kyle closed his hands over the banister. Every face was upturned toward him, every pair of eyes watched his every move, waited for him to say something to reassure them. And, in their midst, wearing the crown prince's clothes, was Taslim, arms folded and smug.

"Gone," Kyle lied. The haunt's eyebrows rose. Sparks glittered in his talisman. "Vanished while I slept." Kyle's hands shook; he clutched the banister desperately tight. "You were right. I was seeing things, imagining things, because I'd hit my head."

<<By the bolt, Hart-lord, I'm no mote of your overwrought imagination! I *showed* myself to them. They *saw* me.>>

But Kyle understood the minds of kitchen folk, whether in the lodge or in the rocs where he'd been fostered. He'd been too clumsy, too shy to serve at the high table, as the other boys did. For ten years he'd labored in the kitchen, stirring, scrubbing, talking, listening. They wanted to believe him; the haunt itself had convinced him of that.

<<Fools! You and them together. I'm not going to vanish, Hart-lord.>>

Kyle didn't expect the haunt to disappear, but the household relaxed. Lies bought time, and who knew what might happen before his lies were unmasked? Kyle had learned to value a moment's peace, regardless of the future cost.

Josaf started up the stairs, telling him he was pale and trembling, which he was, and that he should go back to bed, which sounded like a good idea.

Kyle spent another two days in the big bed, fighting Taslim's influence, fighting headaches, fighting the sleep he feared above all else. He hadn't caught himself wanting anything he hadn't wanted before, or any change in his notions of what was right or wrong. But he didn't imagine he'd know if he had changed, and the haunt was always pushing. Whenever he lost his battle against sleep, he dreamt of a vast cavern, of a narrow, shining archway, and a golden throne: the Siege of Shadows.

It called to him; he awoke drenched in sweat.

"It's a dream," he whispered urgently while he recalled where he was, who he was, and that this was the fifth night he'd spent at the lodge. "The Siege is his imagination, not mine. I'm not going."

His skull felt as if an iron spike had been driven through it: a good sign. When his head hurt this badly, when he couldn't see or hear the haunt, then his thoughts seemed safely to be his own.

"Are you awake?" Kiera's voice, soft and full of implication: She'd sat beside him while he slept and he'd spoken more than once while he dreamt.

"Yes."

He sat up slowly, rearranging the blankets as he shifted his weight. Even with a crackling fire in the hearth, the room was cold. The wind still whipped the walls, driving ice against the windows. Such light as there was came from the fire or through cracks in the shutters. The sun hadn't fallen, but it wasn't shining brightly, or warmly.

"There's broth on the hearthstones. Want some?"

Kiera smiled as she stood. There was something ominous about her smile, but for the first time in days, Kyle was hungry. He nodded and she brought him a steaming bowl.

She waited until he had a mouthful of hot liquid before saying, "You lied, Kyle Dainis. Taslim didn't vanish, not of his own will. You drove him out. You stole him, then you destroyed him."

"I didn't steal him," Kyle croaked, having swallowed the broth before it cooled.

"He was supposed to be mine. It was my Rapture, Kyle. I let you share it, but stealing's not sharing. I heard God's voice calling me when the Harbinger roared into the Eigela. The Siege of Shadows is *mine*, and Taslim was supposed to be my guide. But you couldn't abide that, so you stole him and then, because you can't hear God and you never want adventure, you destroyed him."

"I didn't steal him," he repeated. Kyle hadn't destroyed the haunt, either, but he was careful not to mention that.

"I heard you. You said he was coming for me and that you got in his way. I've always been your friend, Kyle. I've spoken for you when you wouldn't speak for yourself. Is this how you repay me: destroying my Rapture?"

"No, Kiera, it wasn't like that. Something rose out of the hearth. I was spellbound; I couldn't move to save myself." His headache suddenly intensified. He couldn't see Kiera or the chamber, only a vaguely man-shaped glow where the haunt tried to explode into his consciousness. "He'd have changed your thoughts and swallowed you whole."

"He was supposed to be my guide. He wouldn't have harmed me, Kyle!" she shouted. "I wouldn't have fought him!"

"Please, Kiera, my head hurts."

"As well it should. Just punishment for what you've done. Stew in your own juices for a while, Kyle Dainis," she snarled as she walked away from the bed. "A hurting head is the least of what you deserve for what you've done to me."

Kyle knotted a blanket between his fists. "I'm sorry, Ki. I'm sorry that your adventure's gone so poorly. I'll talk to Father. I'll persuade him that you must come when I go to Chegnon—"

"Why talk of Chegnon now, Kyle? He's gone. What purpose is there?"

He swallowed hard and cursed himself soundly. "No purpose. My memory—I must have hit my head harder than I'd thought. I'm sorry."

"It's not enough, Kyle," Kiera said, slamming the heavy door behind her.

<<Lightning strike, that one's got the earmarks of a shrew.>>

Kyle's hand caught a blanket's corner tassel. He twisted it around his fingers, as if it could armor him against the wizard's scorn. In truth, his only defense was his determination that he *could* exile the haunt—if he were willing to pay the price.

His headache worsened instantly. Pain shot down his neck and arms. His gut soured and stayed sour the rest of the day. When Josaf brought his dinner, Kyle tumbled out of bed and crawled to the ash bucket. Josaf said something that got lost between the heaves and gasps, but the old man had had the sense to take the platter away.

Sleep remained Kyle's greatest enemy. After a millennium of waiting, the haunt apparently didn't need more sleep. Kyle chewed his lip until it bled and kept himself awake through another night. Morbid thoughts swam in his mind: How long *could* a man stay awake? Sleep wasn't like air or food or water, but everyone alive had to sleep. Could a man die if he went too long without dreaming?

Would he die? Kyle's body said he would, and sooner rather than later—if he didn't get the help he needed from the king's wizards. But he couldn't get to Chegnon without unsaying the lie he'd told on the kitchen stairs, the lie that had set the household at ease and estranged him from his twin.

Even if Kyle unsaid the lie, it wouldn't restore Kiera's affection, because he vowed he'd die before he'd let the haunt torment her. So, one way or another, sleeping or waking, he was going to die: the biggest blunder of his life. If he had any choice—if any choices remained for Kyle Dainis, Hart-lord—he'd choose to die at home, at Roc Dainis, in his own little room, his own familiar bed.

Please God, give me the strength—

<<By the bolt, Hart-lord, don't waste your time in prayer. Set out for the Siege of Shadows. We'll have the road to ourselves. We can be there before the king's wizards or any priest or mother's son gets the notion to follow the Harbinger's call. You'll have God's own strength then.>>

With a groan, Kyle thrust the haunt from his mind. His lips were swollen; he gnawed on his thumb instead.

The wind began to die, though the steady rustle of ice against the shutters continued until dawn. Seedy and barely able to stand, Kyle made his way to a tiny, oval, unshuttered window at the top of the stairs. He breathed on the rimed glass until the frost melted and he could swipe the moisture away with a shaky hand.

Taslim glowered on the glass surface. Moaning, Kyle beat

his head on the wall. When he looked up again, he could see through the glass. Sunlight danced on a thick blanket of snow.

He managed to get himself dressed, then, with one hand always touching the wall, made his way through the kitchen and into the garden. Virgin snow crunched beneath the thick soles of his house boots. His nostrils froze when he inhaled. The headache vanished and the haunt didn't appear in its place. Despite exhaustion, Kyle felt like himself when he squatted to collect a handful of snow. The sparkling flakes compacted into a fist-sized ball that left a tidy, white mark on the wall where he threw it.

"Bake journey bread today," he told Cook when he reentered the kitchen. "My sister and I are going home."

"I comes down early, my lord, soon as I heard the wind die. There's a score of loaves already in the oven, more rising in the bowls, and a sack of fruited flour ready to travel with you. I knowed you'd be thinking of home, my lord. 'Tain't no good memories you've got now, but you come back when the weather's good, like your kin always done."

Kyle returned her smile, then pressure mounted behind his left eye: the haunt, clamoring for his attention, wielding headache like a fiery whip.

"Thank you, Cook," Kyle said with a quivering voice.

The stairway from the kitchen to his bedchamber was about twenty paces ahead. He thought he could get that far before the haunt forced himself into his mind. He got halfway, then paused. His vision had blurred. The redoubtable cook was a splotch of russets and brown.

"Tell my sister—please?"

"As you wish, my lord. Are you well, my lord? Has that damned haunt returned to trouble you?"

"No," Kyle insisted. His hand found the banister just as the world went black and red and other, less natural, colors. "It's nothing. I'm a bit light-headed, that's all. I didn't sleep well."

"And didn't eat your supper, neither. Let me fix you something special, my lord?"

Kyle's confidence that he could survive long enough to die at Roc Dainis crashed against the thought of food. With his jaw clenched, he bolted for the bedchamber. When the door was shut and braced by his weight against it, he allowed himself to slide down slowly, until his rump rested against his heels, with his chin on his knees.

Another agonizing clamor struck behind his left eye.

"Leave me alone!" Kyle warned, but withdrew his will even as he spoke.

The wizard manifested himself and the pain ebbed. Impeccably groomed—wearing different garments that Kyle had last seen on the prince's back—Taslim hovered near the bed, an arm's length above the floor.

"We're leaving. I'm going home to die."

<<My, but you're in a good mood this morning. No wonder I had so much trouble getting your attention.>>

The wizard tidied his surcoat, flicking invisible motes from the sleeves, as if he'd been locked away in a dusty closet all this time. Kyle had seen similar dramatics, mostly from Kiera, and was unimpressed. The wizard shed his pretense and his fine clothes with a shrug that left him wearing the twins of Kyle's shirt and trousers.

<<I merely wanted to say that I'm grateful we're leaving here and that my talents—such as they are in my confinement—are at your service as we travel.>>

"That's *all*? I don't believe you," Kyle said aloud.

For the first time, the haunt seemed bewildered. <<Why not? Because I am not charmed by your sister? Because if I must be confined in an untutored mind, I prefer yours to hers? You are a constant source of surprise, Hart-lord.>>

As was Taslim himself. Kyle had the haunt marked as arrogant, but not as a liar or deceiver. If he was right, then Taslim had no notion of the agony he caused. The lessons Kyle had learned in the practice arenas returned: A warrior could turn his injuries to advantages, if he controlled his enemy's knowledge of them.

<<Enemies?>> The haunt cocked his head after plucking that one word from the aether. <<Are we back to that, Hart-lord?>>

"Had we ever left?"

Blinking his eyes—this work of pushing the haunt out of his mind was becoming easier, if no less painful—Kyle made Taslim vanish from his mind.

There was little for Kyle to do as preparations were made for the return journey to Roc Dainis. He dressed in his warmest clothes, struggled vainly to eat the huge breakfast Cook heaped in front of him, and made decisions while others did the work. Being lord-of-all instead of a laboring hart-lord had its pleasurable moments.

And Kyle was grateful for every one of them when, at midday, he entered the courtyard where the traveling party gathered. Men from the lodge had exchanged Kiera's carriage for an enclosed sleigh that had languished for God knew how many years in the stable. They'd repaired and polished every brass bell. The not-quite-musical sound was enough to make Kyle wish he were somewhere else. He was weaving on his feet when his horse was brought up and Josaf gave him a discreet boost into the saddle.

"Are you sure you're well enough for this, lad?"

Lad, not lord—the distinction lent Kyle the strength for a vigorous nod.

The horses were eager after their confinement in the lodge stable. Kyle steadied his mount with calm words and many pats against its winter-shaggy coat. In turn, the animal steadied him.

His meticulous preparations were bearing a second harvest. Every saddle pack was crammed with food and other essentials from the lodge's overstocked larders: flint-and-steel firestarters, gloves and foot bindings, small pots of Lady Irina's gooey salve that protected a man's skin from the raw air. There was even more food in the sleigh with Kiera and Lille, and an abundance of blankets as well, in the unlikely event that they were forced to make their own shelter along the road. An unlikely event because Kyle knew the way to every dwelling larger than a charcoal gatherer's hovel between the lodge and the roc, and because the locked box beneath the sleigh driver's bench held enough gold deyas and silver crettigs to board them comfortably at any inn along the way until the spring thaw.

Not that they'd need the box tonight. A cloister of Mellian hermits lay an afternoon's ride away. They hadn't needed the cloister's austere guest house on their way up, but Kyle had visited it in autumn. He'd given the Mellians four sacks of grain to be held in reserve until spring and a barrel of lowland cider to use whenever they wished. Josaf said he'd made a good impression on the prior. He was as confident of their welcome as he ever was of anything.

Kiera was among the last to appear in the courtyard. She was bright and cheerful, a yellow-haired snowflower wrapped in fur and vermillion. Now that they were leaving, she had kind words for everyone, including her brother, before she and her maid climbed into the sleigh. There was a third young woman with them, Mincey, a slip of a kitchen drudge—too slight and frail for life up here in the Spure, to whom Kiera had promised a warmer, better life. Men from both the lodge and Roc Dainis gave the harness one last examination, then all eyes turned toward Kyle. The hart-lord of Dainis blinked once and gave the order to start.

"Stay out of my sight," he whispered to Taslim, whose presence hovered painfully on the verge of sight and consciousness. The words were—he hoped—lost in the tramp of hooves and the clatter of bells and harness as they left the lodge courtyard.

<<Let me help you, Hart-lord. I can see better with your eyes than you do yourself, hear better with your ears, smell better with your nose.>>

Kyle gulped and the haunt was gone on a wave of nausea, replaced by throbbing temples.

Experienced foresters, Josaf foremost among them, took turns breaking through the fresh snow in front of the sleigh. Kyle rode behind the sleigh, just ahead of Renard and Enobred, who with the other junior men held the lead ropes of their remounts and pack animals. Kyle's place was not a place of honor, no more than his hart-lord's place in the supper progressions had been, but it did mean that his horse wasn't likely to go anywhere it wasn't supposed to go. He could close his eyes against the snow glare, which worsened an already splitting headache.

Once, foolishly, Kyle relaxed and slipped into an almost-sleep that was filled with images of power, pleasure, and—above all—a golden throne at the nether end of a slender golden bridge through darkness.

How easy it would be. There were steps carved into that arch, visible to anyone with the courage—the foreknowledge—to see them. The journey to the throne was made of a hundred simple steps. Then he'd see God's face; he'd receive God's power. Of course, he'd summon Taslim as soon as he had the power. A millennium's waiting had made Taslim wiser than any seventeen year old could hope to be. He'd cede God's power straightaway.

Kyle shuddered free of the haunt's influence, hearing the echo of his own startled yelp as he did.

"I told you to stay out of my sight."

<<Did you *see* me, Hart-lord? I honor my word. Friends might honor the spirit of each other's wishes, but we're not friends. Your decision, not mine—had you forgotten? Would you like to reconsider?>>

"Never."

Kyle clenched his teeth and drove the haunt from his mind. He caught sight of the wizard's shocked expression just before he vanished and the headache returned full force.

No one seemed to have noticed him nodding off or talking to himself. That was good, in a way, but it also accented his insignificance. Trembling from exhaustion, cold, and fears he couldn't name, Kyle found himself lonelier than ever. The forest through which he'd ridden many times before became unfamiliar and vaguely menacing. The fellowship among the foresters in front of the sleigh and among the varlets behind him excluded him—as he excluded the haunt.

Tears seeped from a painful left eye. He daubed them with a gloved finger and smeared his mother's salve. It stung mightily and blurred what was left of his vision.

<<Problems, Hart-lord?>>

"Go away."

<<Turn this cavalcade around. Take us to the Eigela. Ascend the Siege of Shadows. Set me free and you'll never see me again!>>

Kyle swore that he'd never succumb to an enemy who craved God's power and had no scruples for getting it. As long as his will held out, the haunt could only hurt him, and—somehow—he'd die before his will gave out.

The snow-clad trees glowed in the last light of sunset when the foresters shouted that they'd spotted the basalt pillar of the Mellians' road stone. Kyle's knees were shaky when he dismounted in the cloister's yard, but so were every other man's. No one had cause to notice that he clung an extra moment to the saddle leather, waiting for his vision to clear enough to see the door where Josaf waited with the Mellian prior.

The cloister was typically Mellian: austere, primitive, uncommonly quiet for a community of thirty men. The hermits dwelt in cells, scarcely talking to one another, never to outsiders, except for the prior. With brusque courtesy and very few words, that gaunt, bearded man showed them to their quarters for the night: two straw-strewn chambers. Kiera and

Lille would have the smaller room to themselves. The men, all of them, would crowd into the other, normally the guests' stable. Their horses were sheltered, catch as catch can, with the hermits' livestock and in the lee of the guest house.

Supper arrived in the form of a steaming kettle from the cloister kitchen and a basket of loaves baked from coarse, dark flour, but sweetened with fruits and honey. Even Kiera ate heartily and without complaint before she and Lille retired to the small chamber. The men sopped up the last of the soup with the last of the bread, then set about cleaning every piece of horse harness and checking it, too, for the day's damage. Kyle did more than his share of the cleaning and checking. He'd learned that lesson before he entered fosterage, but he worked in silence. He'd forced down a bowl of the Mellians' meatless soup—his body craved fuel after a cold afternoon's riding. It sat like stones in his gut and he feared he'd vomit if he spoke or moved quickly.

When the lanterns were blown out and the fire reduced to embers, Kyle took a piece of straw from his pallet and shoved its sharper end beneath a fingernail. It was a trick he'd learned in fosterage: Pain could keep a boy awake through a boring verger ceremony. But it wasn't long before his fingertip was sticky with blood and his eyelids were as heavy as a blacksmith's anvil.

<<Relax, Hart-lord. Get some sleep, will you? You've got a long day tomorrow.>>

Taslim was a floating presence in Kyle's nighttime vision. He blinked; the haunt refused to vanish. He squeezed his eyes shut and shivered in agony.

<<Don't trust you . . .>> Kyle shaped the words with his mind—though that hurt more than speaking aloud. He was afraid someone would overhear him talking to himself and guess that he was talking to his haunt. It was an idle fear; the chamber echoed with snores and it wasn't likely that anything short of a scream would have drawn a reaction. <<*Can't* trust you.>>

<<Your choice, Hart-lord,>> the haunt purred. <<Sweet dreams.>>

Chapter Six

Kyle woke up.

Certain proof that, despite his determination to remain awake and thereby keep the haunt's influence in check, he'd allowed his mind to fall quiet. The doors of his memory had swung open for Taslim. Kyle had nearly won; at least he thought he remembered lying in his blankets, staring at black nothing for the great part of the night. But he couldn't be confident of anything, not after he'd fallen asleep.

<<I did *nothing*!>> Taslim protested, a face—nothing more this morning.

Every nerve in Kyle snapped at the sound of a voice inside his head that was not his own. He began to shiver, though not from cold. He was pleasantly warm, having built himself a fortress of straw and blankets during the night: a fortress he didn't remember building. The last thing he remembered was a bloody fingertip.

A flick of his thumb confirmed that the straw was missing.

Then Kyle remembered the haunt's final words: *Sweet dreams.* He didn't remember dreaming, though he must have. Priestly physicians and philosophers agreed that dreams were the proper activity of a sleeping mind. They said dreams purged the soul of undigestible thoughts. A man needed sleep the same way he needed a chamber pot. Physicians and philosophers so rarely agreed on anything; when they did, surely they agreed on the truth.

So he must have dreamt. He simply couldn't remember his dreams, the sweet dreams the haunt had promised.

<<Do you usually remember your dreams, Hart-lord?>>

The question froze Kyle from the inside out. He clutched the topmost blanket close with both hands and grew no warmer.

<<You put something in my dreams, didn't you?>> He didn't dare speak aloud, and endured the pain his mind's voice brought. <<You've made me change my mind. I won't go, I tell you. I won't—do you understand? I'm not going to the Eigela. I'm not going to sit in a golden chair that doesn't exist. No matter how much you tempt me. And I won't let you tempt my sister, either. No matter what you make me think, or want, or think that I want.>>

<<You've lost your wits, Hart-lord.>>

<<Only if you stole them while I was sleeping. You took my dreams and left what I can't remember in their place. You've made me think things that make no sense.>>

<<By the bolt, Hart-lord, you're doing *that* yourself.>>

A shadow fell on the blankets, blocking the light that reached Kyle's eyes. It wrenched his attention into the world outside his mind. He pushed the blankets back and saw that the light came through an open door, along with the jangling sounds of men hitching horses to the sleigh. Not only had he fallen into a dreamless sleep, but he'd stayed asleep after everyone had waked and started work. It was doubly embarrassing, doubly frightening.

"You're well enough to come with?" Enobred, the younger of Josaf's sheep and the shadow who'd drawn Kyle out of his thoughts, asked with a worried voice and a mouth that gaped in the middle of the haunt's forehead.

Without thought, Kyle thrashed the air with his fist. "Go away," he snarled, sweeping the image aside.

He imagined stone-and-mortar walls, like those of the guest house, and an iron-hinged door, like the one that opened into the cloister yard. His imaginary door swung on creaky hinges and shut with a resounding thud, imprisoning the haunt. It was a great surprise to Kyle, who hadn't considered his imagination's power within his own mind; but it was almost certainly a greater surprise to Taslim.

The haunt shouted: <<Release me, Hart-lord. Let me out or I'll boil the marrow in your bones!>>

But did those dire threats come from the wizard, or was everything—wall, door, and wizard—the product of Kyle's too vivid imagination? If it were his own imagination, why hadn't Taslim said he'd make Kyle's skull pound like the midsummer drum? Since that was what he was already doing.

Unless Taslim truly didn't comprehend the pain he caused. Kyle had considered that a possibility yesterday; today it seemed a certainty.

"You're not well." Enobred drew Kyle's attention again. "I'll fetch Josaf?"

"I'm well enough," Kyle insisted, but his efforts to spring out of the blankets fell short when his gut spasmed and he sank to his knees in the straw.

"I'll fetch Josaf," Enobred repeated. This time it wasn't a question.

Kyle swallowed bile and forced himself to his feet. "It's nothing. Maybe something I ate last night—nothing more than that."

"Josaf should know," the young varlet stared out the door, to where, presumably, Josaf worked with the other men.

If Josaf learned that his disaster-prone hart-lord had been talking nonsense and weaving on his feet like a storm-tossed sailor, then Josaf would insist that they stay here. Kyle desperately wanted to get back to Roc Dainis. He wanted to present himself and his haunting problem to his family. He'd be embarrassed and ashamed, but he'd be safe, too.

"*I'm* your lord, Enobred, not Josaf. I'll tell Josaf what he needs to be told. There a long, hard journey between us and home, and I mean to get a long, hard part of it behind us today. Understand?"

"But, Kyle—" The common-born varlet took liberty with his name, as if they were boon-friends. In better circumstances, it might have worked.

"*Lord* Kyle. Lord Kyle says: Tell Josaf nothing."

"Yes, Lord Kyle," Enobred whispered as he bowed his head and retreated, a varlet's sullen acknowledgment of rank over wisdom.

"Pack my bundles carefully and see that Rawne's brought up for me. I think I'll ride him today. Saddle him yourself."

"He's been brought up already, Lord Kyle. You asked so yesterday." Enobred's expression slid from insolence to despair. "You don't remember. You're not well, Lord Kyle. Please, Lord Kyle—let me fetch Josaf?"

"That pot of supper the hermits sent set poorly with me, that's all. I'm not one for a supper without meat. I guess it's a lucky thing I had no priests' talent." Over the years and with much practice, Kyle had learned he could disarm many opponents by belittling himself more thoroughly than others dared, and by doing it with laughter. Accordingly, he flashed his broadest, silliest grin.

But he'd learned his lessons before solstice night a week ago when Enobred had stood with Kiera, Josaf, and the others in the lodge hall and had looked at a frosted windowpane to see a wizardly haunt hovering at his side. God alone knew—if God cared—what Enobred saw now, but the young man retreated another half pace and wrapped his arms tightly over his chest. To redeem the situation before it became irredeemable, Kyle spread his hands palms up, a gesture of innocence and ignorance in Alberon and everywhere else.

"That pig swill churned my gut all night," he explained. "You'd feel like vomiting, too—"

"But I don't, Lord Kyle. You're the only one who's suffered. Josaf has to be told. Maybe it were poison!"

"By the almighty bolt, it wasn't poison! Listen, Enobred: You'll pack my bundles and you'll keep my affairs to yourself. You won't talk to your friend, Renard, and you won't talk to Josaf. And if he asks, you tell him that I slept well and I'm eager to be home as quick as is safe. That's the truth. I'm not telling you to lie to Josaf, Enobred."

But Enobred shook his head slowly, massively. "You've changed. You're not who you were, swearing by lightning and such. It's that thing, that haunt—"

Kyle raked his hair. How had Taslim's oath found its way to his tongue? He closed his eyes. The iron-hinged door loomed in his mind's eye. Dark liquid seeped between its planks, surging with each headache throb. An ominous sign: The haunt *did* influence his imagination.

Whatever good his night's sleep might have done evaporated with a shudder. Something real dwelt behind his left eye, giving him a headache and wreaking havoc with every thought and memory. More than ever, Kyle wanted the walls of Roc Dainis around him and the sad-stern voice of his father telling him exactly what had to be done to untangle a hart-lord from his latest disaster.

Roc Dainis was at least six days distant, six days farther than Kyle feared he could go without sleep or surrender. Hopelessness twisted his gut; he couldn't eat, either. He wanted to hide in his blankets, but before he could attempt that foolish retreat, Kiera swept out of her chamber wearing Lille's homespun gown and with her hair still bound in the loose braid women wore during the night.

"How can I *possibly* shut my boxes before I know where we'll stop this evening? Tell this varlet that I'm not ready to travel, and won't be *until* I know where we'll stop!"

Josaf was behind her, and Renard, who balanced an open leather-covered box in his arms, was behind Josaf. The box overflowed with ribbons, lace, and all other manner of ladies' ornaments. Lille, a serious and practical girl, waited silently in the doorway with her hands protectively draped over little Mincey's shoulders.

"I . . . I don't know . . ."

"Kyle, you've memorized every step of the journey, I know you have. You *must* know. Will it be a common inn? Another cloister? Or will you *please* settle me among our peers, where I need to make a good impression. It seems to me that Roc Houle might be in reach."

Roc Houle. Flennon Houle. God have mercy—the last face Kyle wanted to see blending with his haunt was Flen's. But Kiera was right, too. The sturdy sleigh moved better over the snow than their carriage had moved over the frozen ground. Without the time they'd lost for repairs on the trek up to the lodge, Lanbellis might well be in reach on the way down and it would be a good place to spend the night. If he were lucky—Kyle heard mocking laughter between his ears that had nothing to do with his haunt and everything to do with his entire life—Flen might still be hunting boars.

"We'll try for Roc Houle," he told his twin. "No promises, though. And no chance at all if you waste the morning tying ribbons in your hair. If your plain self isn't enough for Flen, then he's not worth dazzling with silk or jewels."

He expected an argument and got a hug instead.

"You don't know what you're talking about, little brother, but you're sweet and kind, all the same." Kiera stood on tiptoe to kiss his cheek and drew back quickly, all trace of frivolity replaced with concern. "You're afire, Kyle," she said. She held the back of her hand against his cheek, then against his forehead.

That got Josaf's attention more surely than anything Enobred might have tattled. The old varlet surged; Kyle dodged.

"It's nothing. I told Enobred; supper sat like swill in my gut. You know me and food. It's passing already. I'll be fine before Kiera's finished dressing."

It was a bald, naked lie and Kyle could only pray he had the strength to survive it. *Roc Houle*, he told himself firmly, not caring if Taslim on the far side of a bleeding door were either real or listening. *I can make it as far as Roc Houle. I can last that long. I* can *last*. Then, realizing that they were staring at him again, he said aloud, "I need air. Cold air will do me good. Has Rawne been brought up?"

"Yes, Lord Kyle," Enobred said quickly. "I told you that before." By his tone, the varlet implied that a healthy man—an unhaunted man—would have remembered.

A particularly violent throb shot down Kyle's spine. He wanted to whimper like a whipped dog, but he scooped up his cloak and furled it around his shoulders on his way out of the guest house. The cold air did clear his lungs and freeze the aches.

Rawne waited in the courtyard, saddled, as Enobred had promised, but with his bridle looped over the saddle until they were ready to leave. The dark brown horse was bound to the rear of the sleigh by a rope that disappeared, along with his head, in a bucket filled—to judge by the steady munching sound Kyle heard several steps away—with a satisfying depth of grain.

The horse's ears flickered at his footsteps. His head rose when Kyle called his name. Forgotten grain dribbled from his nose as he ambled forward, straining the soft rope to its limit. Rawne was Kyle's special horse, and Rawne knew it. He expected a carrot or some other treat whenever he saw Kyle, and he nuzzled hands, sleeves, and the fullness of Kyle's shirt before blowing a cloudy horse sigh into the wintry air. With a shake of his mane, Rawne accepted a scratch beneath his forelock as a tolerable substitute for a carrot.

Yesterday, Kyle had ridden one of his father's horses while Rawne relearned his footing and balance on snow. He'd let Rawne rest tomorrow, too; winter travel was hard on the animals. But today he'd ride high on a friend's strong back—leaving Taslim behind that bloody door, no matter how vicious the pounding.

Kyle scooped grain out of the bucket and held his hand flat as Rawne nibbled down every last grain.

He'd expected Father to give him a horse when he came home from fosterage. Most youths received such a gift and, with three older sons, Father knew what was expected. Kyle hadn't expected Rawne. He'd been speechless when grooms brought a young horse up from the stable at a trot, muscles rippling under a glossy, dark brown coat. Rawne had all the qualities a verge-lord looked for in a stud horse; it was hard to believe that Father didn't have Rawne in his own pasture with his own mares. It was beyond belief that such an animal would be given to him, the last son, with no prospects or needs.

Then the grooms had led Rawne in a circle, giving Kyle a view of his gift both coming and going, right side and left. He'd understood everything in a heartbeat: No verge-lord would breed a walleyed stallion. Sky-colored eyes were held unacceptable by anyone with enough standing to be picky about his horses. Walleyed horses were supposedly blind in their odd eyes and moonstruck. Ride one, the lords and hostlers said, and you'd wind up in a ditch every time. Never mind that Rawne could see both sides of a road and was surefooted, calm, and even tempered.

Breed a walleyed stud, those same men said, and the foal would be spavined before it was weaned. Rawne couldn't refute that prejudice. He'd been gelded. Even so, he couldn't be sold, couldn't be *given* away, except to a hart-lord son who'd be grateful for what he got—if he were wise—and not waste time thinking about what he'd never have.

Kyle had been grateful, sincerely grateful, but, just now, with those mismatched eyes on him, expectantly and full of trust, it seemed he'd missed an omen that spring day: Rawne's walleye, the eye that had transformed his horse's destiny, was his left eye.

And Kyle's left eye was the haunted one.

He brushed a gentle hand around Rawne's fateful eye. Horses didn't think as men did. Rawne was a happy horse, sniffing out treats, taking his rider on long summer rambles through the Renzi Valley, getting a ten-fingered scratch all along the length of an eternally itchy nose. Rawne didn't know what he'd lost or why he'd lost it.

Kyle didn't either, not truly. He wrapped his arms around Rawne's neck and hid his face in the shaggy mane, wishing he did. He would have stood beside his horse for the rest of the morning, the rest of the day . . . the rest of his life, but a few moments were all he had. The ranking man in any company of travelers gave the orders that got the others moving. Kyle was *Lord* Dainis again, for another day, inspecting harness, giving thanks, saying good-bye to the prior, and greeting Kiera with a smile as she joined them.

Several ribbons of green silk, a few shades lighter than the wool of her second-best cloak, fluttered attractively around Kiera's neck and shoulders. She hadn't heeded his advice, but she hadn't delayed their departure either, and was as pleasant as she'd been since the solstice.

"Maybe we should stay an extra day or two at Roc Houle?" she suggested, taking his hand for support as she climbed into the blanket-lined sleigh. "At least until you're feeling better. You really should ride in here with me, you know, while you're sick."

Kyle shrugged, careful not to disrupt the delicate balance within his skull. His headache lingered beneath each cold breath and, with it, the still bleeding imaginary door and the anger of his haunt.

"We'll see. I'm not sick, Ki—just tired."

She scowled and he feared he'd managed to say the wrong words again, until she swept his hair aside with gentle fingers against his forehead. "Fevered's more than tired," she whispered. "You take care of yourself, riding out in the cold all day."

"I can take care of myself."

"Put some of Mother's salve on your face."

"I will," he promised wearily, releasing her hand and turning away.

He wouldn't, Kiera thought, watching her brother join the horsemen who'd break the trail. She considered running after him with another reminder, but the sleigh's driver appeared, to help Lille and Mincey into the sleigh, so she sat down on the forward-facing bench and began wrapping herself in blankets.

Kiera still cared about her brother. In odd moments she admitted that his plight—fevered and haunted by an ancient wizard—was no conscious fault of his. She had, after all, been the one to suggest this adventure after his Rapture failed. He had merely stumbled—as he so often did—between the hearth and herself as the Harbinger's fall to the Eigela lit up the solstice sky.

She couldn't *forgive* that stumble. The wizard belonged to her, as surely as Roc Dainis belonged to Father. But she could continue to fret over Kyle's welfare, as she'd always done, and chide him for his dreamy forgetfulness. He didn't seem to understand the clear-cut difference between loving *him,* and the righteous indignation she felt for what he'd done to her dreams.

Her women understood. At least Lille understood. Lille had been her personal maid since she turned eight. They were the best of friends and confidants, sometimes . . . most of the time. Lille knew when to leave Kiera alone, when to huddle in the blankets with Mincey tucked against her side. Even Mincey understood it was a good time to be quiet.

Men rarely understood anything. Even Father, the wisest, most powerful man Kiera knew, was blind to the little things that held the Verge of Renzi together. Mother said that was to be expected: Men were raised to stand on mountaintops with their eyes fixed vigilantly on the horizon. They could hardly be expected to notice the busy valley beneath their feet, the realm where women worked and ruled. Which would have been all well and good, *if* there'd been a mountaintop for every man in Alberon.

Mother said that there was, that every man was lord over his own family, their fortune and their fate. It didn't matter if they dwelt in a verge-lord's shadow, for even a verge-lord dwelt in the shadow of the king. Mother made a pretty picture, with a place for everyone, but watching Kyle blunder his way through the rituals of leave-taking, Kiera once again judged it an inaccurate picture. Kyle was a man who had no family in a valley below him, no fortune, no fate to call his own. With no aptitude for the priesthood, or for the battlefield, there was precious little for him to do, and no reason to wonder that he did it poorly.

Men needed meaning and purpose in their lives.

Kiera sat bolt upright as the driver cracked his whip and the sleigh lurched forward with a jangle of harness bells and the creak of iron runners cutting through the snow. She smiled and waved at the Mellian servants until the sleigh was through the gate and the view on either side was trees, trees, and more trees, all beautifully shrouded with snow, but mind-dulling, just the same.

"My lady, Renard says Kyle cried out in his sleep last night."

Lille had been chasing Renard since they both left their valley homes to serve the Dainis. She'd finally caught him on solstice night, when the Harbinger fell. The newfound lovers had been inseparable, at least when their time was their own. There'd be a marriage in the spring, a simple dawn-light ceremony, a dowry paid in chickens, fishnets, and feather pillows.

Another young man would climb his mountain. Another young woman would take charge of the realm her new husband kept safe.

Kiera didn't like thinking about the freedom Lille had to find herself a husband. And she didn't want to hear about her twin's haunted dreams. "It's a wonder Renard heard anything at all," she countered, more sharply than she'd intended. "You were gone until dawn!"

Lille's cheeks flushed and inside the sleigh the only sound was that of the runners slicing snow. Kiera sat back, staring out the little window. She was angry with herself for snarling at Lille, who truly was more friend than servant, and for begrudging that friend's happiness—even though she'd always thought Lille was too good for the likes of Renard Fisherson, who truly was the son of a fisherman. Lille was pretty and clever and Kiera had taught her noble manners. Renard was kind, as big and strong as an ox, and no cleverer.

But every time Kiera suggested that Lille flirt with one of the swains who visited Roc Dainis with Flennon Houle—young men not so well born as Flen or her own brothers, of course, but better born than Renard—Lille only laughed and said Renard would be good enough for her once she caught his eye. If Kiera pressed her argument, Lille would pout—the way Kiera had taught her—and say she'd rather marry a man she knew and, besides, their fathers had been talking marriage for years, just like Lord Dainis and Lord Houle.

Kiera shook her head again, clearing her thoughts. She shivered beneath her fur-trimmed blankets. When all the day's eggs were counted, there was love in one basket and fathers in another. Lille was lucky that she loved Renard because, from a father's mountaintop, dowries and alliances were more important than a daughter's happiness.

Or a son's.

Kyle's face flickered briefly in Kiera's thoughts and was quickly replaced by Flennon Houle. The Dainis needed timber from the Houle forests. The Houle needed pig-iron from the Renzi mines. Marriage would keep the annual trade simple, as it had been since Grandfather's time. She and Flen were betrothed. In a very real sense they'd been betrothed since before they were born: the first Dainis daughter and the first Houle son. Flen had grown up loving her, which flattered her, which was not quite the same as loving him.

If she'd fallen in love with someone else, Father might have broken the betrothal. But Father had been very, very careful not to let her meet anyone who might tempt her. He called her a princess, but he never let her see a prince. Time and time again, she'd wanted to cry, to rage, to argue, but she bit her lip instead, curtseyed and thanked her lord father for his praise. And he, man of his mountaintop, never suspected her bitterness. He'd hug her and say that Flennon Houle was a fine young man, as fine as a royal prince.

Of course, Flen had been underfoot at Roc Dainis much of the last three years, since his fosterage ended. He'd made a good impression with Father; probably he got lectured by *his* father before every visit. Flen gave her gifts, most recently a little white dog that walked on its hind legs and balanced a little red ball on its nose. She loved the dog more than she'd ever love Flennon Houle. And she'd hoped—desperately hoped—that her solstice adventure would lead to someone more exciting.

Kiera removed a mitten to pat the ribbons wound through her hair. With her Rapture hopes shattered and her adventure headed toward a dismal end, it was time to stop dreaming of what might have been. She put her mitten back on, pulled a shutter over the little window, and wedged herself into a corner with her feet tucked under her gown so she could rest her chin on her knees.

Time passed with the noisy swaying of the sleigh. Her mind became as numb as her fingers. Thoughts came and vanished, without leaving a trace in her memory, until there were shouts and bone-jarring jolts as the driver reined the horses to a merciless halt.

Lille and Mincey were thrown from their bench, screaming. Kiera thrust both legs out of the blankets; one struck the floor, the other braced against the sleigh's far side. Her right hand grabbed Lille, while her left found a hold on the window shutter. The little wooden panel tore out its hinges, but Lille wasn't hurt, and neither was Mincey, who was squashed between them.

"What's wrong?" Kiera shouted, wrestling at once with tangled blankets, frightened women, and a bent door latch.

Outside, men were shouting, running. The sleigh bounced as the driver leapt off, but the view through the open window was empty road and more snow-covered trees. Kiera cursed and gave the door a solid kick. The latch popped; the door banged wide.

"What's wrong?" she repeated, ignoring the squeals of Lille and Mincey. Sweeping her skirt and cloak into the crook of her left arm, she jumped down into the snow.

The commotion was on the other side of the sleigh. Kiera slipped and stumbled through drifts as high as her waist, determined to see what was happening. A heavy arm fell across her shoulder before she'd cleared the back of the sleigh.

"Stand clear," an unfamiliar voice urged, politely, but very firmly. "The haunt's got him."

"Haunt?"

"He cried out as it took him, my lady. Best you stay back, my lady."

He took her arm at the elbow and tried to push her back the way she'd come. They got one step before Kiera pivoted under his grip and broke free.

"Don't you tell me what to do about my own brother!"

Kiera's defiance wouldn't have impressed old Josaf, but her would-be captor was just a Renzi forester and he let his arms fall limp to his sides.

The Dainismen had formed themselves into a line across the road, their horses behind them and Kyle somewhere in front of them. Using her gathered skirt and cloak as a battering ram, Kiera shouldered between two of them. She saw Rawne first, a few paces away, empty saddled, like all the horses, but spooked and trembling. Then she saw a long, dark shape, half on the road and half off it.

"Kyle!"

He didn't move, not when she called his name the first time, nor the second, nor when she dropped to her knees at his side.

Her brother lay on his stomach. Fearing the worst and scarcely able to breathe herself, Kiera tried to turn him onto his back.

"Help me!" she shouted, and when that brought no one out of the crowd, she added, "God's arse pockets! Someone come over here and help me!" not caring a whit that she'd sworn like a common journeyman.

"It's the haunt, my lady. It's taken him for fair now."

That from Josaf, who should have known better. Kiera was so angry that she didn't need anyone's help to move him. Shedding her mittens, she got her hands under one shoulder and shoved. Kyle groaned as he rolled. The certainty that he was alive kept Kiera from fainting when she saw blood in the snow, blood flowing from his nose and mouth.

The men had heard him groan. They called on her to heed her own safety and leave him where he lay.

"This is *Kyle*, you oat-brain oafs! *Kyle*, my brother, your friend—your lord!"

Kyle coughed once and began to gag. Now that she had him on his back, his blood was seeping down his throat, choking him. Kiera lifted his head into her lap. She needed cloth to wipe away the blood, but her mittens were somewhere under her skirt and the hem of her cloak was tangled beneath her brother.

"He's hurt!"

A vagrant wind twined Kiera's ribbons around her face. She caught the silk strands and yanked them free. Once swabbed, Kyle's wounds didn't appear as bad as they'd seemed. He had smeared Mother's salve on his face and it had spread his blood wider than it would otherwise have flowed. But he didn't respond to her touch and his eyes remained closed.

"Can't you see that he's *hurt*? Don't any of you care?"

Kiera meant to sound like her resourceful mother, not a frightened sister, but her shrill terror got Josaf moving and once Josaf moved, the others followed. They got their larger, stronger hands under Kyle's sprawled limbs.

"Careful!"

They were careful, now that she'd chided them. They lifted Kyle gently. Even so, he groaned again and his eyes fluttered. His left eye—nasen'bei, where the haunt laid claim to him—was stained with blood like the snow. Protectively, Kiera cupped her hand over it before anyone else saw. His lashes brushed against her palm as the eye closed and stayed closed.

"What do you want done with him, my lady?" Josaf asked for himself and the other anxious men.

As if there were a question or a choice! "Put him in the sleigh and mount up! We're going to Roc Houle as fast as we can ride."

If Kiera's wishes had had wings, the sleigh would have soared over the forest and come to a swift, safe landing outside the great hall of Roc Houle.

If Kiera's wishes had had any power at all, the haunt who'd turned her brother's eye blood-red would have been banished back to the ashes and smoke from which he'd risen.

But Kiera's wishes moved nothing—not the haunt, not the sleigh. She sat with one arm wrapped around Kyle and the other clinging to the open window, trying to steady them both as the driver held the horses to the fastest pace the treacherous road allowed.

Kyle was alive. Kiera consoled herself with that thought. He'd broken no long bones in his fall and he moved freely now and again, as any sleeper might, if that sleeper's bed were a swaying sleigh.

Once he mumbled something that might have been her name and stared at her through those terrible, mismatched eyes. She straightened the sweat-drenched hair slicked against his forehead—no need to remove a mitten now to feel his fever—and told him that he was safe. Everything would be all right, if he could just hold out until they reached Roc Houle.

Then Kyle began thrashing. He grabbed the door latch. Kiera needed all her strength, and the help of her frightened women, to keep the door shut and them all inside the sleigh. After that, she ordered Lille to remove her long, embroidered belt and, with whispered apologies, bound Kyle's wrists. He struggled against the restraint and swore oaths she didn't understand.

But the tears he shed were clear as the purest water.

Kiera held him tight and, curse for curse, matched the red-eyed haunt throughout an eternal afternoon.

Chapter Seven

There had been darkness, filled with jumbled, hazy images of faces Kyle almost recognized, in places that might have been familiar.

Now there was light, the muted light of dawn, all lavender and gold, falling on picture tapestries that he knew as well as he knew himself.

A breath Kyle had held for some unknown time escaped. He shrank a little and made himself comfortable beneath the blankets. Everything hinted that a strange, nightmare-filled moment in his life was over. Beyond the tapestries, a rooster crowed challenge to the sun. It was a singular call, with an extra warble, and it came from a singularly bold bird, with singularly gaudy plumage and a fierce temper, who was lord of the coop behind the kitchen at Roc Dainis.

Tears escaped after the sigh. Kyle blotted them quickly. He was seventeen and well past the age when he could safely cry, even tears of joy on finding himself home. He'd awoken on a cot in the great hall, rather than his own bed, and he had a sense that he'd been very ill, but none of that mattered. The fever had broken. His head didn't hurt. His vision was sharp. He was himself again, whole and alone—

No.

Kyle rolled onto his side, clenching his fists. He moaned, and this time didn't wipe away the tears that followed.

Not alone.

Taslim was with him. The throbbing pain fell upon him like an angry rain when he squeezed his eyes shut and pounded the top of his skull with his fists.

<<Easy, Hart-lord.>>

The wizard's talisman shone in the distance of Kyle's mind. More gentle, dawn-colored light glowed in its iron-bound crystals. Misty tendrils reached across the aether. Kyle heard himself whimpering in expectation of agony, but the mist soothed when it arrived.

He feared it all the more.

"Leave me alone!" He imagined fire to dispel the mist and burned with a fever of his own creation.

<<Easy, Kyle,>> Taslim pleaded. The mist expanded until it surrounded Kyle's fire, absorbing the heat and pain without quenching the flames. <<There's nothing to be gained from hurting yourself. I *am* beyond your reach. You cannot harm me. I swear to you: I believed we were equally armored in our enmity. You hid your pain well, Hart-lord, until you couldn't hide it at all.>>

Truth moved through every word the wizard uttered. Kyle swallowed his rage and the imaginary fire it fueled. The mist vanished. His mind was dark and quiet—unnaturally quiet—because he was not, would not be and could not be, alone. There was a new pain that owed nothing to nasen'bei or its haunting wizard. It was the gnawing, empty ache of hopelessness.

<<Why?>> The silent words no longer throbbed between his ears.

<<Why you?>> The haunt enlarged Kyle's question. <<Because the spells I cast flowed through the blood of my son and his sons. We are kin, you and I. A strand of mothers and fathers a millennium long runs unbroken from me to you.>>

Curiosity got the better of Kyle, as it usually did. He opened his left eye and saw Taslim—wearing the prince's clothes—sitting on the cushions near his feet, cradling a lightning-stoked talisman in his lap. With his right eye Kyle saw only the cushions and the hearth. Holding his breath, Kyle opened both eyes. The hearth was visible behind Taslim as if the haunt were painted on glass.

<<I suppose I *am* a haunt,>> Taslim said with an ingratiating smile. <<If I concede that, will you tell me when your head aches, or any other part of you turns toward illness? I believe I would recognize the omens—if I felt them again. But you are a clever young man, Hart-lord, devious in your simplicity. I do not put it past you to find another way.>>

Kyle returned the smile. The pain had gone, except for those sparks of friendship he'd felt from the beginning, and those weren't painful.

<<You will tell me?>>

<<I don't want to go to your Siege of Shadows,>> Kyle countered. <<I want to live my own life.>>

<<You will.>>

<<Live my own life, or want to go on a fool's quest? I *feel* you, Taslim. You're always pushing. Always dangling that damned cavern and its damned gold arch to its damned Siege of Shadows in the verge of my imagination. As if what you wanted were the only thing worth having in this world. I can't trust you. I can hardly trust myself.>>

Taslim lowered his head. Their eyes no longer met—if it could be said that they'd ever met, with the haunt dwelling inside his left eye. Nonetheless, the wizard seemed shamed, and Kyle pressed his point.

<<So, I'm right. You are always looking to twist my desires around to yours.>>

<<The Siege is the doorway to God, Hart-lord. Whoever succeeds will look upon a god's face and become a god himself. How can you *not* want it? Where is your man's ambition, Hart-lord? Is there nothing you wish for? Are you so burdened by this family of yours that you—>>

Kyle heaved the blankets forward. <<Leave my family out of this!>> They passed harmlessly through the wizard.

<<Your kin surround you, Hart-lord. They smother you with their kindness. They treat you like a child or, worse, a favored pet. Seek the Siege of Shadows and gain your freedom.>>

<<No,>> Kyle insisted, and swung his legs over the bedside, through the wizard's image, because that was the rudest thing he could imagine doing. <<Never. And if I should discover that I've changed my mind, why—I'll know it's your meddling and change it back to my own proper thoughts.>> He stood up and began to pace slowly on wobbly legs.

Somewhat surprisingly, the haunt remained on the bed, a peripheral profile shaking its head.

<<I've waited a millennium, Hart-lord. I want to ascend . . . I want to look upon God's face more than you can imagine—and I *will* persuade you, but only as one man may honorably

persuade another. Your dreams are your own, Kyle. Your wishes and heart's desires, also.>>

Taslim spun his talisman, drawing a rune-shaped ray of light from its crystals. For a moment, Kyle was transfixed by the light, then the light was gone and with it a portion of the pressure he'd felt since the Harbinger fell.

<<You admit it, then: You've been trying to influence me in dishonorable ways.>>

<<We hadn't discussed the matter. There was neither honor nor dishonor to it. Now I've given my word, honorably, and you may trust it.>>

They stared at each other, Taslim with his hands around a quiescent crystal and Kyle examining the verges of his mind, much as he would run his tongue over his teeth after being toppled in the practice arena.

<<Never,>> he concluded. <<You're still pushing against me. I can't trust a man who lies when he talks about honor.>>

<<Lies? Lies. Lies!>> the wizard sputtered; his talisman sparked. <<I've given you my *word*, Hart-lord. The word of a freelance wizard. Have you any notion what that means?>>

Kyle shook his head. <<I feel you. I know what that means, and that's enough to know that you're lying.>>

Taslim's face turned red. The sparks flying from his talisman grew bright and more numerous. Kyle braced himself for another blazing headache, or worse. He begged a defensive thought from his imagination, but nothing happened, either in his mind or on the bed beside him.

<<You know nothing of magic, do you?>> Taslim asked after a credible imitation of a heartfelt sigh. His face was its usual color again.

<<I told you that at the start. I know nothing of magic; I have no talent for it. I *don't* lie.>>

<<Yes. Of course. Oh, come now, Hart-lord. You've lied about me. And all this whirling about in your head: God knows, *that's* not magic.>>

For once, caution overcame curiosity before Kyle demanded that the wizard explain himself. Taslim had a way with words that stood their meaning upside down. Kyle had already learned that when the battleground was within his mind, his imagination was as potent as the wizard's talisman. If that was magic, then he didn't need explanations.

<<I'm not without substance, Hart-lord. I'm trapped in

nasen'bei—your nasen'bei—with no one to summon me out. Of course, you feel my presence. How not?>>

He had a sudden realization that the pressure was primarily around his left eye. With the realization came an urge, such as he might have to scratch an awkward itch. Kyle closed the irritated eye, bent a knuckle, raised a hand—

<<Don't touch your eye!>> Taslim shouted loudly enough that Kyle's ears picked up the echo. <<Do you want to hurt yourself?>>

Sheepishly—like Enobred or Renard when Josaf scolded them—Kyle lowered his hand. <<Nasen'bei—>>

<<Is as real as this hall or your thumb, which I strongly advise you to keep away from your eye.>>

A table stood not far from the cot where Kyle had awakened, and among the objects atop it was a silver plate such as the Bydian priests used in their rites of passage. Had he seemed so close to death these last . . . these last what? Days? Weeks? A month? It was still winter: There was a fire in the hearth and the floor was numbing cold beneath his feet as Kyle stood with the plate in his hands. The Renzi Bydians were careless with the vessels they acquired with their Dainis largesse. The plate was dented and splotched with tarnish. He could scarcely make out his left eye's blurred reflection, much less see through it into nasen'bei.

<<Don't be a fool, Hart-lord. You can't see me, except as I appear.>>

The plate clattered to the floor as Kyle spun around. Taslim's voice had seemed to come from outside his head . . . from the bed, where he still sat with his talisman.

<<I don't— Before, wherever I looked, whatever I heard— How?>>

<<Magic, Hart-lord. Wizardry.>> Taslim brandished the talisman, which glowed with amber light. <<As I neither eat nor sleep and you've spent the last two weeks either delirious or sleeping, I've passed my time mastering my confinement. The silent speech is easier now, isn't it?>>

<<Mastering your confinement?>>

<<Stop repeating what others say to you, Hart-lord, unless it pleases you to be mistaken for a fool's cap.>>

<<I want to see you as you truly are, inside me.>>

<<Your heart is truly inside your ribs. Would you want to see it?>>

Kyle's hands and knees had begun to tremble. He'd been too long in bed—two weeks, if Taslim didn't lie—to argue successfully with a haunt. Giving his full attention to moving his legs and feet, he made his way back to the bed.

<<If I saw my heart, I'd die. Would I die if I saw you as you truly are?>> he asked when he was sitting again, but without looking at the wizard.

A faint breeze caressed his neck: an illusion of an arm, an illusion of sympathy, yet he did not shrug free.

<<A millennium is a very long time, Kyle. The world has changed. Wizardry has changed. The spells I cast so long ago have changed in ways I never anticipated. You were very sick. They feared for your life, and rightly so. I would not have you so sick again, for both our sakes. I could do nothing to help you.>>

Ignoring what the wizard said—because if he'd listened, he would have believed the urge to friendship sparked in both directions—Kyle asked, instead, <<What kind of spells did you cast? What were you hoping for?>>

<<Another wizard, what else?>> Taslim laughed bitterly. <<A peer who'd summon me from nasen'bei with a new body and another chance to visit the Siege of Shadows!>>

<<And you got me. No wonder you're angry. I'm sorry.>>

Taslim gave another strangled laugh. <<Honor—you'll remember this, Hart-lord: I am a man of honor, however much honor has changed along with wizardry and the kingdom. Honor compels me to tell you that you have nothing to be sorry for.>>

<<And you? Are you sorry?>>

There was a third bark of laughter and a spark-filled breeze that swirled before Kyle's eyes.

<<Judge for yourself, Hart-lord.>>

He was alone in the mountains. Not the tree-covered mountains surrounding the lodge, where food, fire, and shelter could be had by anyone with the right skills. But barren, rocky mountains—black-rock mountains—where nothing lived and cold winds snapped the ragged sleeves of his robe against his wrists—

(Robe?

Leggings for warmth and comfort, Hart-lord, but always a robe. I was a freelance wizard, and proud.)

And cold. And desperate.

The wind was enough to flatten a man against the mountain, but something far more powerful was shaking the mountains themselves. A black boulder the size of a man's torso crashed down not three paces from where he stood. Animal terror dropped him into a crouch and brought his arms up around his head.

Then the wind died, replaced by a stagnant, bitter-smelling force that lifted his hair from his neck.

Kyle felt a heart that was not his own skip a beat and restart in a blood panic. He felt the tension, the terror, in his arms and legs as the wizard crawled to a jagged brink and peered down first, into a bottomless chasm, then up, toward a seething, bruised sky.

He knew why the mountain cracked and crumbled. Bolts of lightning that beggared his imagination were hammering it apart while he watched. His trembling knees grew strong again. His trembling hand steadied itself against warm iron, cold crystal: a talisman.

(No, I've seen enough.

Courage, Hart-lord. You know *I survived.)*

The ragged sleeve fell back when he raised his arm and the talisman high above his head, daring the thunderbolts to touch his iron, to enter his crystals.

Kyle knew how magic worked: The iron spikes atop the Bydian monastery attracted lightning for the priests, who collected it in seasonal rituals then parceled it out according to God's wisdom. But freelance wizards collected their own lightning. They braved the fiercest storms with their little talismans held high. They did battle with the almighty bolt that gave Alberon's magic its reality and strength. Braving the storms was risky, especially for an inexperienced wizard. The hand Kyle saw above his head was a young man's hand, by definition an inexperienced wizard.

Beyond the talisman, the swirling clouds were as black as the chasm below. The clouds gaped, revealing the storm's high heart, pulsing with scarlet hatred. Terror compressed his ribs—Taslim's terror, palpable after a millennium of memory—but his hand was steady as the storm's malevolent soul shaped and hurled a bolt.

Wizards died when lightning grounded itself in their talismans. Taslim died, and Kyle died with him. The tides of his body froze. His soul soared free to do battle with the storm, to experience a battle that had taken place almost a thousand years earlier. Taslim fought with will alone, confronting an enemy that was surely the ancestor of all nightmares.

Freelance wizards they called themselves: men and women with piercing eyes, ruthless minds, arrogant manners. It took courage to call lightning. Fools' courage, a lesser measure of bravery than what a cohort mercenary carried into battle; at least, that was what Kyle had been taught as he learned the way of the sword and the lance. And Kyle had believed that, until he felt Taslim lock his will around the bolt and draw it—screaming, struggling, and lashing out with talons of white-hot fire—into his talisman.

He'd never look askance at a wizard again.

As soon as the bolt was iron-bound, before Kyle's heart resumed its beat, Taslim shouted out the runes of a spell. Kyle recognized a few—*bul*, that was life; *syrk* for death; *ennas* for time itself—but the grammar of wizardry went deeper than pronunciation. Resonances had to be established in the lightning-stoked crystals. The runes embossed on the talisman's iron bands glowed orange.

And burned.

Kyle felt the sweat on Taslim's brow and felt his flesh char as the talisman grew hotter still. A millennium removed from the moment, Kyle's will wasn't strong enough. Had the body been his own, he would have let the talisman fall into the chasm. Not Taslim. The wizard clung on with smoldering fingers and shouted more runes.

Above, the malevolent storm gathered fire and fury for another bolt. Through Taslim's eyes, Kyle watched lightning kindle. Through Taslim's memory he knew that they were helpless: the talisman could not consume another bolt, even if Taslim had the will to subdue it, which he didn't. But Taslim had the will to finish his rune casting. He shouted *onda*, whose meaning Kyle didn't know, as the bolt began its descent from the cloud's heart. Wind to equal that of the storm roared out of the talisman—out of the wizard himself, out of the formless aether of Kyle's mind. It met the bolt a hair's breadth above the talisman's iron tip.

Kyle's scream reverberated through the Roc Dainis rafters

and broke the bond between him and Taslim's memories. When his throat was empty, he looked down at his hand, which was whole and unharmed. He looked at Taslim, who radiated a calm pride in his accomplishments.

A man appeared in the hall's inner doorway, drawn, no doubt, by Kyle's scream. Their eyes met, but the man didn't cross the threshold. He was gone before Kyle could call him back. Another blunder—Kyle could imagine the message racing toward his parents: "My lord, my lady, he awoke screaming." In a matter of moments, he'd be inundated with concern and questions.

Before that, though, Kyle had a few of his own.

<<Was that the spell that put you in the hearth at the lodge waiting for me on solstice night?>>

<<It was the spell to keep my soul bound to life until the Harbinger returned. That lodge hadn't been built when I stood in the Eigela. I had no thought whom I'd find myself confronting when the time came. Certainly not you, not twins.>> Taslim shook his head. <<More the pity, more the fool. I had time for will, time for faith, but no time at all for thought.>>

<<Faith? You're no priest.>>

A bark of friendly laughter followed. <<You confuse faith with religion, Hart-lord. Priests have both; wizards believe in themselves. And, by the almighty bolt, I *believed* that day.>>

<<You used two mighty bolts to keep yourself alive until the Harbinger returned, because you believed it would return and you believed you'd be drawn to me—a descendant of yours, that is—when it did?>>

<<Clever, Hart-lord, and close on the mark. I cannot say that I was alive, only that my soul was bound to life. I paid heed to the world for a generation or two—long enough to believe that I would have kin waiting when the Harbinger returned.>>

Kyle followed the haunt's unfocused stare into the distance. He felt a chill breeze twine around him.

<<It would be easier to face down a thousand bolts at once than to live a thousand years, Hart-lord. I drifted wherever time and wind would take me, until time, wind, and the runes brought me back—back to that lodge, oh, say three seasons before you were born. You were conceived in that chamber. Did you know that, Hart-lord?>>

Kyle answered with averted eyes and a furious blush. He almost didn't hear Taslim say, <<I made a dream that night, a dream to call you back when the Harbinger appeared.>>

<<No,>> Kyle countered, soft and slow. <<No.>> The Dainis were a secular family, served by orthodox Bydian priests. Kyle didn't think much about religion, and when he did, his thoughts hadn't changed since his nursery days: <<Rapture comes from God, the one true and hidden God who spoke to King Eigela II.>>

<<As may be,>> Taslim agreed. <<But *I* made a dream that night to call a child back to the chamber where it was conceived while the Harbinger blazed across the sky.>>

And that image had certainly appeared in Kiera's Rapture dream, but, again: <<No. No, it makes no sense. Why that chamber? With all your wizardry, why couldn't you have found us here at home? If we'd had carriage trouble and been a day later, we'd have been too late and all your planning and rune casting would have failed. You're lying, Taslim. There has to be a better explanation.>>

Another chill breeze caressed Kyle's shoulder as the wizard sighed. <<I wish there were, Hart-lord. I *expected* the Harbinger; I expected a wizard. I got your mother and father, in front of the hearth. Lightning strike, that *wasn't* what I expected, Hart-lord, I swear to you. I made the dream because there was nothing else I could do. Once I was drawn to that room, I . . . I couldn't leave. I couldn't drift on the winds of time the way I'd been doing since I cast the first spell.

<<I told you that faith was involved, Hart-lord. So, I had faith—even when I found myself drawn to an *occupied* chamber, as it were. I made do, surely you can understand that; you've done it often enough yourself. I could believe that, after a millennium of waiting, my bolt had fallen short, or I could believe that your father's wouldn't, and have faith that my spells were still moving toward fruition.>>

The wizard fell silent, waiting for Kyle speak, but there was nothing Kyle could say. He was in shock; his thoughts were frozen, mortified.

<<I still have faith in my spells and in my bloodline,>> Taslim continued. <<I never *saw* my son, Hart-lord, not with my own eyes. I didn't suspect I *had* a son before I came to the Siege of Shadows. I don't exactly remember who his mother was; most likely she wouldn't have remembered me, either,

considering . . . Well, you know how such things go for younger sons, don't you?>>

Kyle nodded, hurriedly—lest Taslim decide to explain more fully. There was a very remote chance that he, too, might have a son, or a daughter, growing up unacknowledged in Chegnon town. He wasn't naive, he wasn't a virgin, but he wouldn't forget her face or her name: Lacey.

<<Pretty,>> Taslim offered his opinion of the memory image, just before Kyle made it dissolve in boiling embarrassment.

He tried to change the subject, saying, <<I didn't have your dream,>> while striving *not* to remember another face he'd never forget. <<Your faith's misplaced.>>

<<Yours, perhaps, but not mine. I know—>>

But before the wizard could complete his thought, commotion filled the stairwell leading to the inner doorway where the man had appeared and disappeared. Kiera led the household parade with her hair still in night braids and an old cloak hastily wrapped over her linen. She smiled and seemed glad that he was sitting up, but she didn't cross the threshold. Nor did Muredoch, who was right behind her, washed and dressed and most likely hard at work when the message arrived. In less than a heartbeat, Father was there, too, with his beard half-trimmed and a barber's cloth clutched in his hand. Josaf trailed Father and Menager Cook's piercing voice rose from the stairwell, then stopped short in mid-tirade.

In Roc Dainis, Menager Cook stood down for only two people, and Kyle could already see his father. He ran a hand through his hair, another along the seams of his nightshirt, and stood up, a bit unsteadily, as the crowd parted and Lady Irina entered the great hall of Roc Dainis. In Kyle's memory, his mother had never raised her voice or broken into an undignified run—but she did both the moment she saw him standing beside the cot.

"Let me look at you!"

Mother was a head shorter than Father; more than a head shorter than Kyle. He bent down to receive and return her embrace before she pushed him away again.

"Let me see that eye—"

He sat down on the cot and stared at the rafters while she examined his left eye.

"Is *he* gone?"

There could be no doubt whom she meant. "My head doesn't hurt anymore," Kyle said. "We're at peace, I think—"

Mother clamped her hands over his jaw before he could finish. She tilted his head at an uncomfortable angle. Kyle could have freed himself, could have kept talking, but with his mother sometimes it was wisest—easiest—to do everything her way.

"My lord?" Mother called Father. "Look at this, my lord. Tell me what you think."

Father might be lord to everyone in the valley, but he did what Mother wanted. Without thought or will, Kyle stiffened when Lord Dainis' stronger, coarser hands replaced his mother's and his father's blue eyes filled his vision. They'd never been so close to each other. Muredoch played with his son, Pancel, and perhaps Father had roughhoused with Muredoch long ago, but in Kyle's lifetime there'd been arm's length lectures, the back of his right hand, and a very occasional slap on the back for a job well done. Father didn't *play* with anyone, anything; that was for children, not men.

Kyle gulped with astonishment when Father ruffled his hair before releasing him—certainly that had never happened before.

"I see nothing, dear lady." Father's hand settled on Kyle's shoulder. "Perhaps there's nothing to worry about after all."

There was an ominous ring to those words. Kyle strained his eyes looking from face to face, seeking clues. Kiera sat where Taslim had sat. She grinned when she caught him looking at her and seemed inordinately pleased with herself. Taslim had vanished—completely. The nasen'bei pressure was gone, and for the first time since the solstice, Kyle felt alone.

"Is something wrong, son?"

The hand on Kyle's shoulder tightened. He looked up into grave, scowling concern. "Nothing, my lord father," he said, which was the truth, though it felt like a lie.

"You aren't—under duress?"

Father used meaningful words. In tacit recognition that survival was more important than honor, tradition allowed that an otherwise honorable man's oath wasn't binding, if he'd given it under duress.

"I'm not compelled, my lord father," he answered formally, firmly, then added, "The headaches are gone. Taslim says they won't come back." And he regretted the addition before his mouth was closed.

Lord Dainis' hand was gentle as it pressed against his brow, holding his left eye open for another close examination. "We'll talk after you've had something to eat and time to rest."

He ruffled Kyle's hair again. The gesture was meant to be reassuring, but Kyle found it almost as disconcerting as Taslim's initial appearance had been. He glanced at his mother. Her face was paler than it had been when Varos related his Rapture dream. He looked at Kiera, whose confident smile had faded to thin-lipped worry.

"If it pleases you, Father, we can talk now. I'm not tired or hungry. I'd rather know what I've done, my lord, and what you plan to do."

That look of concern on his father's face grew more pronounced. Kyle caught himself straining his thoughts as well as his eyes, trying to find Taslim.

"The priests came while you were ill, Kyle. They tried—" Father crumpled his beard and looked to his wife, who nodded. "This haunt— This wizard who burst into your eye—"

Kiera, alone of the assembled household, dared to interrupt: "The Bydians tried to get him out, Kyle. But you were fevered and couldn't help and they were afraid to apply compulsion. That's what they want to do now."

<<Taslim?>> Kyle cast the name frantically into the aether. <<Taslim—what happened?>>

No answer, except from Kiera, who sidled closer and put her arm around his waist.

"He made you sick, Kyle. It was that haunt all along and us who didn't understand. When I saw your poor eye, then I knew the truth. Why you were acting so strange. You were trying to protect me; I know you were. I got you home as best I could. Lord Houle lent us more men and horses, and a bigger sleigh. Flen set the pace. We made it home in three days, Kyle, and I know you don't remember a moment of them. But your eye was the color of blood and that haunt waged war for your soul. He *has* to be called out, the sooner the better."

Kyle tried to put everyone, everything else out of his thoughts. "What of the Harbinger? The Siege of Shadows and your—" He caught his mistake. "*Our* Rapture? Don't you—" The eyes of his family were on him. He looked for the right words and found that the fever had weakened his mind more than his body. "You don't . . . ?" he stammered, no clearer than before.

Kiera took his hands between hers. "The priests say everything will be all right. I've talked to them. They understand what's happened. They know what has to be done."

<<Taslim?>> Kyle asked the empty aether.

His sister was right: He didn't remember the journey from Roc Houle to Roc Dainis. He did remember wanting to be home where wiser minds could take the wizard's measure. Taslim had been different this morning, but that didn't change anything. A man couldn't trust—couldn't be friends with—someone who'd invaded his mind and threatened his will . . . and then disappeared, just when he was needed most.

<<Taslim? What is this about? Can these priests summon you? Is that what you want?>> He didn't put words around his last question: Has Kiera convinced the priests that you belong to her? but it was in the forefront of his mind, where the wizard could have easily found it, easily refuted it.

But Taslim was gone. He'd said that nothing short of a powerful summoning could separate them, but Taslim cut the truth into thin slices and never served his secrets whole. When nothing emerged from the shadows of his mind, Kyle turned back to Kiera.

"Don't worry, Kyle," she assured him. "Our priests are stronger than any old haunt. As soon as you're strong enough, you can help them summon it out and send it back where haunts belong."

"No," Kyle murmured. He wanted Taslim gone, but not sent to whatever hell the priests undoubtedly had in mind for him.

"Do you want to go on this fool's quest, son?" Lord Dainis weighed back into the conversation.

Kyle shook his head. "No."

"Then, when you're ready—when you've eaten and rested and feel able to help the priests—we'll put a stop to this nightmare of yours. We all want our Kyle back again, just the way you were before this happened."

He wasn't sure that was what he wanted, but he said, "Call the priests now. I'm as ready as I'll ever be."

Lord Dainis dispatched a messenger to the Bydian monastery. Menager Cook sent another down to her domain.

"There's time to eat," she said, giving Kyle's cheek a bruising pinch. "Eggs with green herbs, just the way you like them."

Kyle preferred his eggs parboiled with creamy, yellow cheese, but one didn't say such things to Menager Cook, any more than one winced in the grip of her affection or rubbed one's cheek afterward. Clothes appeared without him asking for them; he had to dress in front of an audience, as if he were a child without modesty, rather than a man with some claim to privacy.

For a heartbeat, while he stamped into his boots, Kyle thought he heard Taslim scolding him for meekness among fools and warning him that his family put more pressure against his will than he had. Hoping that Taslim was returning, he hung back as the household trooped toward Menager Cook's kitchen.

<<Taslim? Talk to me, Taslim. Do you want our priests to summon you? Should I help them?>>

"Lagging as usual." Muredoch's hand came out of nowhere and nearly knocked Kyle off balance as he headed slowly for the door. "Do you want the priests to summon this haunt out of your head?"

"It's the right thing to do, isn't it?"

"You tell me, Kyle. You're the one who's got to put up with him. Kiera says he's power-mad and bound to destroy you. Kiera also says you stole him and that he really belongs to her." Muredoch's jovial tone, fairly invited Kyle to offer his own opinion.

"I could live with him, I think. Even with the headaches, if they came back. I could get used to it, somehow. But not Kiera. You can't let that happen, Muredoch."

Muredoch chuckled. "Don't teach your grandmother to steal sheep, little brother. She hasn't suggested that, yet—not while Flen's here . . . again, or is that still? He doesn't want a rival he can't see. By all accounts, this haunt of yours cut quite a figure in the looking glass."

"It was a window," Kyle corrected, absently—he'd thought he heard Taslim laughing.

But nothing more came out of the aether. He headed downstairs behind his brother and into a swirl of aromas which reminded him that whether the eggs were herbed or parboiled, it had been two weeks since his last remembered meal.

He ate heartily, seated beside Muredoch, who talked endlessly about a plan to double the number of sheep in the valley's higher meadows. It was the last thing Kyle wanted to talk about, but he was Muredoch's steward. A sense of duty kept him listening and answering questions until a red-cheeked messenger announced that the priests were at the gate.

Lord Dainis rose from his chair, Lady Irina and Kiera, too, and the others. Kyle and Muredoch were the only ones left sitting. They stood up together. Swallowing the lump in his throat, Kyle realized how skillfully Muredoch had kept his thoughts away from priests, wizards, and the impending rite. *I'm your brother, not your lord*, Muredoch had said scarcely two months ago. *I don't want to see you like Uncle*. Had that been a subtle criticism of another lord's handling of another younger brother?

Muredoch's hand was never far from Kyle's arm as the household filed back to the great hall. Kyle didn't need its support, in part because he knew it was available, in greater part because he was calm and confident: He'd made the right decision when he entered his brother's service. The Siege of Shadows meant nothing to him; the wizard, Taslim, also, meant nothing.

Three priests were already waiting in the great hall. One wore a deep green robe, girdled at the waist with a belt made from nails and other bits of metal. The other two were acolytes in drab workman's clothes and as brawny as any blacksmith. Those two busied themselves around the cot—removing the blankets, and replacing them with an uncomfortable-looking bolster—and an intimidating array of vials, a palm-sized pair of iron tongs, and a crystal vessel that resembled Taslim's talisman except that it was open at the top and suspended above a blue-flamed lamp.

"Exorcism is a mighty ritual that purges the faithful soul of demons. It returns them to *obol*, the hell of endless night," the green-robed priest began without warning. His voice was deep and his heavy brows were enough to scare any demon.

Kyle's confidence evaporated. "Taslim's not a demon," he murmured—to the floor, because he didn't dare meet those priestly eyes. "He's a wizard. He needs to be summoned out of nasen'bei, not sent to hell."

"A myth, child," the priest corrected, guiding Kyle firmly toward the cot. "A lie to the innocent. Nasen'bei is another name for hell. What dwells there may cloak itself in beauty and promises, but, in truth, it is only and always a demon. It is a threat to your soul and your family until we exorcise it."

"No," Kyle whispered as the priest gave him a shove and he stumbled backward against the cot.

The acolytes each grabbed an arm. Silken ropes, soft, but strong, were wound around his wrists.

"No!" he shouted the denial this time and yanked his right arm free. "He's done me no harm!"

"You were the image of death when your sister and Lord Flennon brought you into this hall."

Kyle clawed unsuccessfully at the left-side silk; the acolytes had it knotted before he could slip free of the loop. He put up a fight to keep his right arm free, but he was weak, and the match was over from its start.

"You can't do this. I *won't* help!"

"Then you will go to hell with the demon!"

"It's for your own good," Mother assured him. "Do what they say. The rite is quick and painless."

He threw his weight against the right-side rope, then the left. Neither gave. He scooted forward, planting his feet on the floor; he was strong enough to haul the cot with him as he stood, and use it as a weapon. Or, he'd been strong enough before Taslim made him ill.

<<Taslim! Help me! Help yourself!>> But, perhaps, that was what Taslim was already doing, why he'd disappeared.

One acolyte levered Kyle backward, onto the cot, while the other used a third length of rope around his ankles. Kyle wasn't tightly bound, or cruelly bound, but he was the priests' prisoner all the same. He appealed to his family, who simply repeated that the rite was for his own good.

"Help them, Kyle," Kiera urged, "and it will only last a moment."

"Listen to your sister," the deep-voiced priest added.

The acolytes seized him at the head and shoulders, bending him back farther, until it was them and the ropes that steadied him. Iron tongs pressed against his left eye, forcing him to stare at the rafters while, beyond his sight, glass vials clanked.

Kyle almost begged for help—surely Muredoch— But no. Kyle clenched his teeth. He wouldn't beg and he wouldn't gibber with fear. He'd already seen their faces. This was just another of his calamities, the biggest yet, but not likely the last. They weren't to blame; he'd wanted to come here where they'd take care of him. If there was blame, it was his, for expecting something different.

The clanking stopped and the priest's unyielding face appeared above him. Bitter smoke curled away from the heated crystal as the priest traced patterns above Kyle's watering eye. Muttering syllables from the same runic language Taslim had used on the black mountain, the priest upended the crystal. Kyle saw red drops falling slowly toward his eye. They landed like liquid fire, blinding him instantly.

Kyle heard his father telling him not to fight and heard his own screams as he ignored that sound advice. Another moment and he was deaf as well as blind.

Kyle found himself on his hands and knees in the black mountains. He called Taslim; there was still no response. The mountains were quiet, not thundering as they'd been earlier, when he'd visited the wizard's memories of another time. They weren't ringing with sword sounds, either.

He recalled something from his forgotten Rapture: There'd been fighting, an ambush—several of them. The shattered face had appeared after the last one. But now the mountains were quiet and he recognized nothing.

His wrists and ankles ached; he remembered the priests and their exorcism rite. The sky here was gray, not dark. Wherever he was, it wasn't obol. Had the priests driven him into his own Rapture or to the Eigela, where Taslim cast his spells? Maybe it didn't matter. Maybe magic was like shooting a long-distance arrow: You were grateful to hit the butts and didn't worry about the bull's-eye.

He called Taslim's name again, and heard moaning in the jagged rocks nearby.

"Taslim?" he said, walking toward the sound, then stopping short.

The shattered, bleeding demon face belonged to the slender warrior who lay at Kyle's feet. There were other bodies in the rocks, none of them moving. There was blood on his own hands, and on his sword, which lay where he'd left it, where he'd found himself.

He heard another moan, but the striped lips hadn't moved. A mask, he realized, and knelt to remove it: an act of mercy as well as curiosity.

<<Hurry, Hart-lord!>>

<<Taslim!>>

Kyle left the masked warrior where he lay. He scanned the black mountainside, looking for the wizard. Nothing moved, save for a dark speck high in the gray sky.

<<Hurry! Save yourself. It's all coming down!>>

The mountain had shuddered before Kyle made sense of Taslim's warning. A dark cloud swelled unnaturally fast and hid the largest mountaintop. He didn't know how Taslim's memories and his own Rapture could overlap, but they had, and every fiber of his body wanted to take the wizard's advice.

Then the mask moaned for a third time. God knew how bad the warrior's wounds were. He might be a heartbeat from death, or merely stunned, as Kyle had been moments ago. Either way, a man didn't leave a wounded man behind to die, no matter how great the danger to them both; at least, not if he was the man on his feet and had a mote of strength left in his arms.

Silver hair as long as his arm flowed down from the mask when Kyle lifted the warrior. It startled him, and he dropped to one knee to keep his balance. Once the mountain began to shudder again, and shudder without stopping, it would have been safer to stay on his knees, but Kyle didn't have time for safety. With Taslim nattering between his ears, he started down the mountain. Boulders crashed all around him. His ankles ached and his arms grew numb, but Kyle kept going, looking one step ahead, no farther, then another, and another.

"Come back, Kyle. Please, Kyle . . .?"

His ankles still ached, his arms were still numb, but he wasn't carrying a masked and wounded warrior down a mountain. He was lying on his back, listening to his sister call his name.

"Kyle Dainis—wake up!"

Someone shook his arm hard enough to hurt. He opened his

eyes and saw Muredoch as well as Mother and Kiera standing over him. Father was shouting:

"Go to your superior. Go to your superior's superior. Tell them whatever you want, but don't forget to tell them that you're a goddamned blunderer!"

"The boy wouldn't help!" the green-robed priest's unforgettable voice shot back. "He believes the lies the demon's told him. At the last moment, he carried his haunt to shelter. It will take a miracle to separate them now."

"Then, on your damned knees and start praying!"

The shouting match ended with the sound of cloth tearing. The three faces above him looked toward the sound, but Kyle looked inward.

<<Taslim?>>

<<Hart-lord?>>

<<It is true?>>

<<Is what true?>>

<<Are you a demon? Was it you that I carried? Are we inseparable?>>

<<No, to the first. No, to the second. I don't know, to the third. The damned priest was stronger than I anticipated. Summoning might still work, if your king's wizards are a damn sight more powerful than any wizard I ever knew. On my honor, Hart-lord, it's my belief we'll need the power of the Siege, if we're to see each other again.>>

Kyle realized, then, that he could hear his haunt, but couldn't see him.

<<Where have you gone? You're still in that nasen'bei place? You're still inside my left eye?>>

<<I think not, Hart-lord.>> For the first time Kyle heard a frosty edge of fear in the cocky wizard's voice. <<It *is* dark here, very dark. I can't move, not as I could. I'm trapped, Hart-lord, quite thoroughly trapped.>>

Obol, the green-robed priest had said, the hell of endless dark, the hell where he intended to send Taslim. Kyle's private thought slipped away; he hoped it wouldn't reach Taslim, but it did.

<<No,>> the wizard replied, more dread than denial.

<<A summoning, Taslim. You said a summoning might still work.>>

While Kyle tried to calm his haunt, more shouting erupted in the great hall, and—unmistakably—the slick sound of swords being drawn from their scabbards. Leaving Taslim to fend for himself a moment, Kyle stood up and saw two unbelievable sights: His father, Lord Dainis, restrained by the two acolytes and the green-robed priest staring down the length of three drawn swords: Josaf's, Muredoch's, and Flennon Houle's.

"I need a wizard's summoning," Kyle announced, drawing their attention. "The king's wizards, they're at Chegnon." He hoped Taslim could hear his spoken words.

Swords were lowered. Acolytes stood aside. Grown men restored themselves to their dignity.

Lord Dainis asked: "Is that the wizard's judgment, Kyle?"

"Wizard!" the priest spat. "Demon. Deceiver! You're all damned. Damned, I say, for listening to him!"

"Be quiet! Does the wizard say a summoning will undo this?"

"I say it," Kyle said, astonished by his own determination. "I intend to go to Chegnon."

Lord Dainis walked past the priest as if he didn't exist. He embraced Kyle tightly, then pushed him aside to address the household. "Send word to Chegnon. Tell our king that Lord Dainis and his sons are coming to see his wizards."

Chapter Eight

Kiera stood at the casement window of her room. With her cheek pressed against the cornerstones, she could see a narrow strip of the road that wound up from the valley floor to the roc. Hours ago, at least it seemed like hours ago, she'd seen four long-robed priests hiking to the roc, exactly as they'd done yesterday morning.

Yesterday morning—the morning after priests from the Bydian monastery had botched Kyle's exorcism—Father had refused to open the gate. Kiera knew what Father had told the priests:

My son is well, no thanks to you. The haunt does not trouble him, no thanks to you. We leave for Chegnon on the Nonesday tide. We'll see the king's wizards there, and competent *priests, if we need them.*

But yesterday evening Kiera had also heard, from the same authority who'd brought her Father's message—a footman friend of Renard's—a message passed by him to Renard, then from Renard to Lille, and from Lille to her, saying that the priests had not come to the roc looking for Kyle. They'd asked to see and speak to her, Lady Kiera; they had *questions*.

After hearing that, she could have gone to Father, but she'd gone straight to bed instead. She'd curled tight around her pillows, eyes wide open and thoughts in turmoil, until dawn dragged her out again. This morning, she'd thought waiting for the priests to appear on the road had been the most trying moments of her life, only to discover that waiting for them to reappear was infinitely harder. Every sound that wasn't immediately recognizable—the crackle of the fire in her hearth, the pop of Lille's needle as it pierced the tightened silk she was embroidering, the gasps of her own, infrequent breaths—struck Kiera's ears as a varlet approaching her door with a summons.

Her mind called her fears groundless; Father wasn't likely to surrender his princess to the priests, not today when he hadn't surrendered her yesterday, not when he'd called them damned, blundering fools to their faces, not when the roc was bustling with preparations for Kyle's sea trek to Chegnon that would begin two days from now, on Nonesday. But Kiera's clever mind couldn't unlock Kiera's fears, because Father didn't know that his princess had lied to the priests when they asked their questions the first time, while Kyle was sick.

The priests might know she'd lied . . . The priests almost certainly knew, or else they wouldn't have asked for her. There was nothing more that she could tell them, except the truth.

"My lady," Lille called from her stitching stool. "My lady, come away from there. You'll catch your death from the cold and I can see your face turning rough and red from here."

Kiera stood straight and felt her cheek, which was cold to the touch and puckered from contact with the black stone. She stroked the skin gently, always in the same direction, toward her ears—lest crow's-feet form at the corners of her eyes or anywhere else. But she couldn't see the road when she was standing, properly, and just this once, beauty wasn't Kiera's most pressing concern. She compromised, tucking her fingers between her cheek and the cold, hard stone.

The narrow strip of road that Kiera could see was empty. Did that mean the priests were still cooling their heels at the roc's gate? Or had Lille distracted her long enough to miss them marching downhill, back to their monastery?

"My lady?" Lille persisted, rising from the stool and joining Kiera at the window. "What are you—"

As luck, both good and bad, would have it, Lille's curiosity was the charm to bring the four priests into Kiera's sight again.

"God'a'mercy," Lille swore. She was taller than her mistress and, standing on tiptoe, could see over the top of Kiera's head. "Oh, my lady—they came back. Do you suppose . . . ?"

Kiera nodded her head and sidestepped away from the window. Flen's most recent present, the little white dog whom she'd named Princess, crowded her ankles until she scooped it up and carried it with her to the cushioned chair beside her embroidery, where it wanted to play with the silk skeins dangling from the frame.

"What else could it be?" she said softly. "They're suspicious. They don't believe what I told them about the Harbinger."

"Oh," Lille said, flat and undecipherable, as she latched the winter shutter over the window and returned to her stool. She picked up her hoop and took a few silent stitches before asking, "There's no reason that the priests should be suspicious, is there, my lady? They asked you what you saw when you looked out that window at the lodge, and you told them. What could be more simple than that, my lady?"

Lille was clever, too clever sometimes, but not this time. Kiera gently pushed Princess from her lap. She'd kept secrets before, from Lille and everyone else, but lying to the Bydians wasn't like anything she'd done in the past. The priests themselves would say that lying to them was lying to God—except God already knew, because she'd lied about God.

"I told them what I saw, Lille," Kiera confessed. "But not what I heard."

"We all said that it sounded like a hundred trees being felled at the same time. It was the same here, the same at Roc Houle. Just because you didn't—"

"I heard *God*, Lille," Kiera said abruptly.

Once again, Lille set aside her needlework. "But you said—"

"I know what I said," Kiera snarled. "I've *never* said I'd heard God's voice, not to you, not to the priests, not to anyone! Kyle said it, *after* we all saw his haunt. Kyle said I needed to talk to the priests." She seized a skein of precious silk and began shredding it into hair-fine filaments. "Or his haunt said it. Or they said it together. I *said* Kyle had stolen my guide to the Siege of Shadows—because my Rapture was looking out the window and his Rapture was looking at me!"

There were so many lies now, so many more than ever before. Looking at Lille's face, Kiera could see that her own maid, her friend and confidant, didn't know what to believe. Lille went pale, then tucked her head, busying herself with her needlework, taking rapid, tight stitches that would have to be clipped out later. Looking down at her own hands, Kiera saw that she'd ruined a crettig's worth of sky-blue silk, and she made her hands lie still in her lap.

She didn't see a way out of the tangled web she'd woven—except the truth, which was what she'd just told Lille: God's voice had filled her mind while she stared out of the lodge window. *Come, my child,* God had said in a thunder-rumble voice. *Follow the Harbinger . . . Face me in the Siege of Shadows.* God's words hadn't made any sense, until Kyle, or Kyle's haunt, had explained them, but God had spoken to her, not her twin.

She'd wondered, naturally, how Kyle knew the secrets of *her* Rapture, then the haunt—the wizard whom Kyle named Taslim—had appeared in a window glass reflection and everything had been clear, for a moment, at least. If God wanted her to go to the Siege of Shadows, it was only proper that God would provide her with a handsome, mysterious guide. Even later, right up until that moment on the Spure road when her twin collapsed in the snow, Kiera's thrusting thought had been to reclaim Taslim.

By then, a week had passed since the solstice; God's voice had begun to fade into memory. The Siege of Shadows had never been more than words echoing in her head. A quest—if that's what God expected—wasn't part of *her* future. She'd had her journey adventure without enjoying it very much. It was a matter of noble principle: Taslim was rightfully hers, so Kiera wanted him. She hadn't any idea what she'd *do* with him once she had him.

Of course, when she saw what Taslim had done to her little brother, she'd known *immediately* what she wanted to do with her handsome guide: Banish him. Accordingly, she'd seen no need to tell the priests about what she'd heard when she saw the Harbinger. In a way, she hadn't so much lied to the Bydians as she'd failed to tell them things they would surely have found *interesting*. And without anything interesting to seize their attention, both priests and family had agreed with her suggestion that the haunt should simply be banished. She'd been scared, like the rest of the Dainis household, when Kyle lay so long in the great hall, so stiff and so still but, otherwise, everything had been moving forward, just the way she intended.

Kyle woke up, well and willing to submit to the rite of exorcism. But the Bydians sent Ferra Dorcelt—Ferra *Damnation* Dorcelt—up to perform the rite!

God's pockets! It was the Bydians' fault that two mornings ago everything had taken a swift, irreversible turn toward catastrophe. Ferra Dorcelt had to start preaching about his favorite subject: damnation and obol, the hell of endless night. Naturally, Kyle panicked. Poor Kyle wouldn't hurt anything, not even the haunt who'd tried to kill him!

Kiera was deep in frustration and injustice when Lille drew her out again.

"My lady, you're distressed; I know you are. Talk to me, my lady. Don't let the words build up inside where they'll make you sick. Let them out, one by one. If that doesn't help, perhaps—well, Lady Irina's very wise where priests are concerned.

Kiera's heart skipped a beat. Mother was wonderful, Mother was wise, and in her heart of hearts, Mother wasn't Dainis. Lady Irina was a merchant magnate's daughter: She believed in God; she trusted priests; and her faith was measured in debts and profits. Once Father and Muredoch left for Chegnon with Kyle, Mother would be in command of the roc. And Mother would never send the priests away; that would be a debt and, merchant's daughter that she was, Mother wouldn't tolerate a debt.

"I can't stay here," Kiera said, tearing into the silk again. "Mother will let the Bydians inside. I've got to go to Chegnon with Father, Lille. Help me think of a way to persuade him."

Deep wrinkles appeared across Lille's brow. Her mouth tightened into a disapproving frown. With considerable dismay, Kiera realized that her own maid distrusted her purpose. "It's not what you think," she countered quickly. "This has nothing to do with the Gray Prince. Prince Gravais is the furthest thought from my mind. I can't stay here, that's all. I *can't* talk to the priests."

Lille's arch skepticism faded without disappearing entirely. "Why not? What did God say that makes His priests in Alberon your enemies?"

What, indeed? Kiera twisted uncomfortably in her chair and wound up staring at the shuttered window rather than Lille. When Ferra Dorcelt threatened Kyle and the haunt with damnation in obol, the hell of eternal night, *she'd* been the one whose vision had gone dark for a heartbeat—as dark as eternal night, except for one thin gold line, as bright and long as eternity itself. While Kyle screamed and Ferra Dorcelt shouted his exorcising runes, Kiera had heard God's voice again, repeating the same words she'd heard solstice night in the lodge: *Come, my child. Follow the Harbinger . . . Face me in the Siege of Shadows.*

She could still hear that thunder-rumble voice, not as memory, but a distant, constant presence in her mind calling her to what everyone, including Kiera herself, agreed was a fool's quest. Except . . . except when she thought about priests or, worse, when she thought of Ferra Damnation's dark hell.

Then, God's voice grew louder, angrier:

Come alone, my child. She could hear His orders even now, in the silence of her sewing room, because she'd been thinking about priests and damnation. *Leave the unbelievers behind.*

"They may know that I've lied, but they won't believe me when I tell the truth."

"Tell me first, my lady," Lille suggested. "Let's see if I believe you."

"God calls me His child. He calls me to the Siege of Shadows."

Lille rolled her eyes. "My lady, that's no different than what we've all said, what your brother said after we saw his haunt in the window glass. Where is the great lie that makes holy men and women into your enemies, my lady?"

Kiera sighed softly and conceded defeat within herself. How could she possibly explain? It wasn't that God spoke to her, or that He was speaking to her at this very moment, or even what God said. It was *how* God spoke, the awing echo of His voice in her thoughts, the empty and dry wind that seemed, somehow, to surround those heavy words. When Kiera spoke God's words with her own voice, they became meaningless babble. If she told the absolute truth, if she said that God's voice rose out of darkness, that would be heresy.

Or it would be heresy if anyone believed her. The very charm that Kiera had nurtured for as long as she could remember meant that no one—not even Lille—believed her when she said something important.

Kiera tossed her shredded silk skein to Princess, who pounced on it as if it were a ferocious beast and she, a mighty hunter. With her tail erect and silly, little growls emerging from her throat, the white dog carried her prize to the farthest corner of the sewing room, where she sat down to guard it against all comers.

Lille laughed at Princess' antics, and Kiera laughed with her. But Kiera's thoughts were less amused, seeing herself not in a mirror but in a corner, guarding a treasure only she valued, from loving enemies who could sweep her aside with a single hand.

"I'm going to Chegnon, Lille. It doesn't matter who believes me, or why, just that, somehow, I'm going to be on that boat with Father and the others. The only question is, Are you with me or against me?"

"Oh—with you, my lady," Lille answered without hesitation. "But how will you manage?"

"I don't know yet," Kiera admitted as she picked up her neglected needle. "I'll think of something. One battle at a time; that's the only way to win a war." She plunged the steel sliver through the cloth and laid another line of color into the design—the Impaled Boar of the Houle over the tri-blue Dainis crest—she was embroidering for her wedding. "One man at a time," she added as she pulled the thread taut.

Come rain or sunshine, whether the household was calm or in an uproar of preparations for a winter journey, Father spent the first hours of every evening in the muniment chamber above the armory. The chamber was a square, forbidding place with walls thicker than Kiera's arms were long and iron bars on its tiny windows. Father kept the double-locked chest of Dainis gold and jewels in the muniment chamber, securely chained to a ring hammered into one of the black Eigela stones. The family chronicle was kept on its own velvet-upholstered pedestal in an interior corner, and scores of parchment deeds and charters, each scroll with a tangled mane of testament ribbons and lead-bead seals, rested on sturdy shelves that could have borne far heavier burdens.

Father's worktable, with roaring lions and other ferocious beasts carved into its legs, stood between the locked chest and the chamber's one, heavy door. Two candleholders stood on the table; both of them were made of metal and were massive enough to have stood for maces in the armory below. They cast conflicting shadows over Father's face as he examined the day's entries, a black-feather quill poised in his hand above the creamy parchment.

Kiera paused at the open door. This afternoon, while she planned what she'd say to persuade Father to bring her to

Chegnon, the notion of cornering him in the muniment chamber had seemed an inspiration. The chamber was their special place in Roc Dainis, largely because no one else in the household, not even Mother, dared disturb Lord Dainis while he tended the family's business. So, when Father was late for supper and the food laid out in the great hall was growing cold, Mother would send her to the armory and up the corkscrew stairway.

Father was always glad to see her, his princess. He never scolded her for interrupting him. Sometimes he'd cover his ink pot and set down his quill immediately, but more often he'd invite her around to his side of the table and show her what a verge-lord did to warrant the king's faith in him: the countless trades, in coin and kind, that kept the Renzi Valley safe and prosperous. She knew things about the Dainis affairs that no one—maybe not even Father himself—suspected she did.

But none of them would help her right now.

"Father?" Kiera whispered from the far side of the threshold.

A moment passed; she feared her voice hadn't carried and was about to try again. Then the quill twitched in his fingers. Her heart pounded and a hard lump formed in her throat while she waited for him to finish.

"Kiera," he said warmly. "Princess. What brings you here? Is it that time already?"

"No, Father, I came—"

Her voice was weak and breathless and, of course, Father noticed at once: "What's the matter, Princess? Are you ill?"

She shook her head. "No, Father—"

"Nonsense. You're distraught. Your face betrays you. Is it our departure for Chegnon? Have you come to plead your cause? I've told you before, Princess: The king's court is no place for a proper lady."

And what, Kiera thought angrily to herself, did that make Mother, whom Father had met, loved, and married, all at the king's court nearly thirty years ago? Not a proper lady, she supposed. Polite wisdom said a proper lady needed three seasons to whelp her second infant, but God would deliver her first whenever He chose. Mother and Father got married at midwinter; God chose to give them Muredoch before the next year's harvest.

God's pockets! Did Mother and Father both think she was a

dithering fool? She could count as well as any shepherd. It was one thing for a verge-lord's son to go prospecting at the royal court and marry a magnate's daughter; that put a huge dowry in gold and jewels in the muniment chest. But a verge-lord's *daughter*? Oh, no—*she* was destined for other things, and God forbid if she wanted a taste of gaiety first!

She had no choice, Kiera reminded herself. She loved her mother and father more than life itself, but they'd left her no choice. They wouldn't listen to honesty, so she'd mastered a deviousness they would hear.

"I know, Father," Kiera said, meeting his eyes. "It was a hard lesson"—the best deceptions were built on honest foundations—"but I've learned it. I'm a betrothed woman now, Father. I'm much too busy sewing for my new life to have time for the frivolous whirl of Chegnon. Truly I am, Father. I don't want to go anywhere."

She sat on the edge of the worktable and gave a demure little sigh as she bowed her head and delicately wrung her hands.

"But I am"—a careful pause, as if searching for the right word were painful —"I am *anxious*—especially for my brother."

Father grunted noncommittally. There were at least a hundred good reasons for the family to be anxious and a thousand more that existed only in Kyle's imagination. If she wanted Father's cooperation, she'd have to get more specific.

"Suppose something goes wrong." Kiera kept her head bowed, her eyes low, and her fingers laced. "After all, our Bydian priests said *nothing* could go wrong, and look what happened. Now Kyle says he wants to treat with the king's wizards." She shivered. "I wouldn't want to even see King Otanazar's four wizards, much less treat with them. But, *suppose* something does go wrong, Father—"

It was time to raise her head and meet those blue eyes again.

"I know *you'll* be there, and Muredoch, and Josaf—and Josaf was there at the lodge with us when everything went awry. Josaf's a good witness, an excellent witness—to everything that *he* saw. I'd trust him over me, of course. But"— another pause while she drew a sigh up from the soles of her feet—"Kyle and I were alone when it all happened. I told the priests everything; at least, I've thought I did. I've gone over and over it in my mind—I've hardly slept since Ferra Dorcelt left. I keep asking myself: Was there something I left out?

Something I could have said differently, more clearly? *Anything* that might have changed what happened?"

Father put his strong, hard hand over hers. "You can unveil all the world's mysteries to a goat, and it's still a goat the next morning. Dorcelt's a bungler, and a fool to boot. If there's blame in the family, it's mine, not yours, Princess. Dorcelt's blown his loose bellows since he came to Renzi. I should have flung the gate closed when he showed up. But what's done is done and nothing for you to worry about."

"But I do worry, Father," Kiera said quickly, taking full advantage of the opening he'd given her. "I'm worried sick, and you haven't yet left. I fear I'll go mad for worrying once you're gone."

He squeezed her hand gently and smiled. "Have a little faith still in your lord father."

"I have all the faith in you that does not belong to God, my lord, but I will worry. What if I should remember something? What if it were the *very* thing the wizards needed to set my brother free of his haunt? What if it were the very missing thing that causes the wizards to fail and Kyle to be lost forever?"

"What if, what if, and what if again. We have Kyle's own word that wizards are what he needs to be rid of that haunt, and—sure enough, Princess—it's his haunt, not yours. Put him and it out of your mind and tend to your sewing while we're gone."

Kiera's breath caught in her throat. She was losing; escape from Roc Dainis was slipping through her fingers. "How can you ask that, my lord?" she rebutted, more fire in her voice than despair—which would have cost her any victory with Mother, but was sometimes the best way with Father. "How can I tend to my sewing? How can I even *think* about my own dear future, knowing that my brother might have none? I should be a poor daughter, indeed, if I put Kyle's misfortune out of my mind. God's pockets—" The oath slipped out. Father's eyes widened and she was duly embarrassed by her own carelessness. "Forgive me, my lord," she said quickly, trying to regain her advantage. "I'm sorry I overspoke myself, but, *Father,* where would *I* be if my brother hadn't stood between me and the lodge hearth? Would it have been me lying in the great hall, still as death, with a bloody eye?"

Father withdrew the hand that had comforted her. "Enough!"

he scolded. "The truth is not a stalking horse, Kiera. You cannot twist it to your liking, first one way, then another. Either your brother stole from you or he saved you; it cannot be both. And neither will get you to Chegnon, you have my word on it!"

"I don't *want* to go to Chegnon, Father," Kiera said calmly, mildly, in the face of her father's growing anger. "I don't *want* to treat with wizards *or* priests. I didn't come here because I *wanted* something. I came because I'm worried—No, I'm more than worried; I'm frightened, because . . . because . . ."

Suddenly, Kiera knew precisely what she needed to say to bring Father around to her way of thinking:

"Because I *did* think Kyle had done wrong on solstice night. I *did* think he'd interfered with my destiny, and then, on the Spure road, I learned that I was wrong. I didn't lie, Father, and I didn't use the truth for a stalking horse; I was wrong and I don't want to be wrong again, not when Kyle's life might hang in the balance. I couldn't live with myself, if I'm not there when the wizards banish his haunt. I'd be so guilt-ridden that I'd be foredoomed to failure as a wife and mother. I don't *want* to go to Chegnon with you, but I *must,* for my brother's life and for the Dainis honor—"

"Enough!" Father shouted. He made a fist and pounded it heavily on the table beside her. "I'll hear no more of this nonsense, Princess—"

Kiera leapt to her feet. "How can you not hear more, when you haven't listened to one word I've said!" she shouted. "You talk to me, but you don't listen to yourself and you *never* listen to me. You call me 'Princess,' then you get angry when I dare to dream of a prince! I wish I'd never been born; I wish *you'd* never been born. I wish lightning would strike the roc, right now, and make me an orphan, so I could do what I want. My maid has more freedom than me—"

Moving faster than her eye could follow, Father rose from his chair and gave Kiera an open-handed slap on the cheek. She rocked back on her heels, stunned and silent with shock. It wasn't the pain; Father hadn't hit her particularly hard—she'd seen him knock a wayward fosterling or brother off his feet with a backhanded clout. But he'd never struck her before.

Of course, she'd never lost her composure before. No right-thinking person *ever* shouted at a verge-lord—but when her inspired words produced a disaster, rather than victory, Kiera had stopped thinking and had said exactly what she was thinking, without regard for the consequences.

God's pockets—*the consequences!*

The muniment chamber was dead silent. Kiera's ill-chosen words didn't echo off the walls; yet they remained with her, a bitter taste on her tongue, a sour note in her ears, a chasm between her and her father. This—not Rapture—was childhood's end. A lifetime's memories melted in the glare of blue-eyed fury.

"Father?" she whispered, then flinched when he reached for her.

"Kiera—"

Father's fingers touched her right arm, then her left. His hands drew her close and held her tightly. Kiera hugged her father as he hugged her. The chasm was bridged, but it did not close, not even when Father tucked her head beneath his chin and rocked her ever so slightly, from one foot to the other.

Neither of them spoke. Kiera couldn't guess what her father might be thinking. For herself, she'd learned the difference between regret and apology: She regretted—oh, God, how she regretted—what she'd said, but she wouldn't—couldn't—apologize for speaking the truth. And, without an apology, she could only dread what Father would do and say once this moment of grace had ended.

She wouldn't cry, no matter what punishment he dealt out. Kiera promised herself that when the rocking and the hugging stopped and he held her at arm's length.

"Sometimes," Father began, utterly without the hardness, the retribution, that she'd expected. "Sometimes you remind me so much of your mother that I see her face on your shoulders."

Kiera's cheek smarted when he touched it with soothing thumb strokes that went the wrong way—not that she was going to say anything.

"If it means so much to you, Princess," he continued, still using the eke-name that stung more than her cheek, "then gather your things together. We leave for Chegnon on the Nonesday tide."

Kiera had no time to savor her victory or calculate its costs. Even with Mother's help, there was hardly enough time to prepare for her first visit to Alberon's royal court. Her own gowns weren't grand enough to wear before the king . . . or prince. After supper, Mother opened her own wardrobe and unwrapped gowns that hadn't been worn in ten years, or twenty, or thirty: jewel-colored velvets so stiff with gold embroidery that they could almost stand by themselves. Kiera tried them all, then picked out her favorites.

As soon as the sun rose the next morning, every needle in Roc Dainis was hard at work, taking in one seam, letting out another, adding a bit of lace to hide a place where the velvet nap had rubbed away. Kiera did less than her share of the stitching. She needed more than jewel-colored gowns, she needed jewels, too, and shoes and gloves and an ivory casket filled with ceramic pots of cosmetic colors.

"A little goes a long way," Mother said, using black powder and a bit of polished shell to draw a fine line on Kiera's eyelids. "Better to use none at all—same advice my mother gave me. I give it to you, along with the pots. Be careful, my daughter. It's not the king's court I fear, but the queen's. The Baldescare . . ." Mother shook her head. "Give an old man a young wife and you get trouble back, no matter if the man's the king. And if the wife's Baldescare—" She didn't complete the thought, but went back to the beginning: "Be careful. *Listen* to your father. I won't ask how you persuaded him to this foolishness, but leave your boldness behind now. Stay out of trouble; stay with your brothers."

Kiera nodded, though most of her attention was on her reflection in Mother's mirror. Two lines of black powder, a few smudges of color, and she was a different person: older and elegant, a true princess. There was silver powder in one of the pots Mother had opened; Kiera wanted to know what it was for and imagined it in a circle around her eyes. But before she could ask, Lille ran into the room, red-faced and breathless.

Flennon Houle was almost ready to leave for Lanbellis. The borrowed sleigh was harnessed behind borrowed horses, his men were mounted, and he himself was waiting outside the great hall, hoping she'd come down before he departed.

Her betrothed! God's pockets! She'd promised to say goodbye. Mother's lips were thin, pale lines of disapproval that no cosmetics could hide.

"I'm coming," Kiera said, setting the mirror aside as she

stood. "Let me borrow your cloak, Lille. There isn't time to get mine."

Lille unclasped her plain wool garment and Kiera skipped down the stairs, with it in her arms, leaving her mother and her maid behind.

"My lord!" she called as she came outside, as if they were already married. "Wait, my lord! Don't leave yet!" She started down the outer stairs as fast as ice and her felt-soled house boots would allow.

Flen broke off the conversation he was having with his men. "Never, my lady," he replied and started up the stairs to meet her.

His greeting was—as always—an enthusiastic embrace that lifted Kiera up and swept her off her feet. Surefooted and smiling, he carried her to the bottom of the stairs and a bit farther—around the corner to the winter-bare garden, where, out of sight of his men, he set her down on a stone bench someone—most likely Flen himself—had swept clean of snow earlier.

Flen was a strong young man, and a handsome one as well, with blond hair that was paler and straighter than hers. His beard, oddly enough, was much darker than his hair. He kept it trimmed close to his jaw and—though she'd *never* complain—it scratched a bit when he kissed her.

It was not a halfhearted pecking kiss on the cheek or forehead, such as she got from her brothers, but a lover's kiss, moist and warm, through parted lips that made her pulse race and her mind empty. She'd been shocked the first time he'd taken the liberty, after Father announced their betrothal. And he shocked her further when he put his hand on her breast. She expected that now, even leaned back a little in his arms, letting him support her—as he so easily could—while she closed her eyes and let her fingers rove through his hair.

Prince Gray's hair was the color of goldwood leaves in autumn—or so Kyle admitted when she'd pressed him for a detailed portrait of the heir to Alberon's throne. Her twin swore he couldn't remember if the prince's hair were wavy or straight and, of course, he didn't know how it felt—whether it was silkier than Flen's. The prince was taller than Flen, because Kyle was taller than Flen and the prince was taller than Kyle, according to Kyle. Beyond that, Kyle was useless: He didn't know what color eyes the prince had, or how broad his shoulders were, or *anything* about the shape of his legs.

Surely, though, every part of the prince was magnificent, after all—even Kyle agreed Prince Gravais was the most handsome man in the kingdom.

And by this time tomorrow she'd be on her way to Chegnon to see *him* and be seen in return.

"You take my breath away," Flen said as their lips finally parted.

He *was* breathing strangely.

"You look . . . different," he said after another moment, and traced the curve of her cheekbone where Mother had smudged the reddest powder.

"Mother's given me her colors. I must look my best when I meet the pr—*king*. What do you think? Do I look more beautiful this way?"

Flen's eyes narrowed and his brow wrinkled, and she was afraid he'd heard what she'd almost said.

"You're beautiful when you smile, my ladylove. Your eyes. Your lips. Everything else is dross."

When it came to words, Flen was clumsier than Kyle, but there was no doubting his honesty—or his love. A woman could do far worse than Flennon Houle, Praverge of Lanbellis. Kiera stretched her neck to kiss him again, and was surprised when he pulled away sooner than before.

"I'm afraid I'll lose you," he said, not with anger, but with a wistfulness that left her feeling ashamed. "My father expects me back with the men and the sleigh, else I'd go with you, to keep you safe. The king's court's all paint and lies—no place for a wildflower beauty."

She kissed his hand when he caressed her chin—because kissing him meant she didn't have to look into his eyes. "It's for Kyle. A debt I owe him because of the haunt. Once that's done with, we'll sail for home, and there'll be no more shadows between us." The words that she'd rehearsed with such passion last night when her arms were wrapped around her pillow, rang hollow in her own ears now; God knew what they sounded like to Flen.

"No man could have a nobler sister. You do your family great honor, my ladylove. I can't believe my own good fortune, that you should be the bride my father chose for me."

Without words, Kiera closed her eyes and shook her head. She felt him moving beside her, but had no notion what he was about until he took her hand and pressed a small, hard, and round object against her palm.

"Here—take this with you. Keep it close to your heart and think of my love."

It was his signet ring, carved onyx and gold, and she did not want it. But he stood up as soon as he'd given it to her, and two of his men had come around the corner to join them, and there was no time to return it.

The sky was a greenish shade of gray, the sea was a greenish shade of gray, and in the pit of his churning stomach, Kyle was certain that he was also a greenish shade of gray. Two days out from Renzi harbor, they'd rounded the tip of Ulver early this morning. With God's will—and a steady wind at their back—they'd put into Chegnon harbor tomorrow evening.

There were three ways to travel from Roc Dainis to Chegnon: valley to valley, south, then north, along the Inland Road; across the Spure on trails blazed by mountain goats and foresters; or sailing the rough waters along Alberon's rocky coast in a verge-lord's broad-beamed packet boat. If anyone had asked him—which they hadn't—Kyle would have preferred to follow the goats, even in the depths of winter. As it was, he sagged amidships, clinging to a bit of rope he'd knotted around the rail before the boat left Renzi harbor.

Kyle reckoned he'd survive, just as he'd survived all the ghastly packet voyages of his fosterage. The boats tied up in the nearest valley harbor before sundown. He ate a light supper ashore, and slept there, too. Father had conceded that after their first night out, when Kyle had kept everyone awake staggering from his bed to the bilge hole.

By day, Kyle shrouded himself in blankets to keep warm and an old sail to keep dry. He hung onto his rope—leaning out over the sea whenever he needed to—and waited patiently for the day to end. It could have been worse. The sea was calm, for winter, and Taslim had sunk so deep into the priest-wrought darkness that for hours at a time Kyle could forget why he was so miserable.

He was in such a thoughtless drowse when Kiera appeared—rosy-cheeked and smiling—at his side.

"Are you feeling any better?"

It was a foolish question and he had no intention of answering it, but as luck would have it—his luck, at any rate—the ship chose that moment to buck a crosswind. His gut went one way, he went another, and they would both have drowned if he'd lost his white-knuckled grip on the rope. Kiera, of course, had been born with sea legs. She just stood before him, swaying, *swaying*, with the boat, never losing her balance and making him very, very ill.

Thank God, the sea was only one lurch away.

"Can I get you anything?" she asked when he'd hauled himself inboard again. "Water? Mint tea?"

Kyle shook his head, slowly.

"Can we talk—*privately*?"

He grunted, which was about the limit of his conversation under the circumstances.

"I've decided to forgive you."

Another grunt, but this time the sound had nothing to do with his gut. "What do you want, Ki?"

"What makes you think I *want* anything? I've gotten what I wanted: passage to Chegnon. No thanks to you, but—I forgive you for that."

"Why?" he countered, rude and abrupt, though the simple truth was that a dose of indignation had done wonders for his stomach.

"You promised that you'd make certain I was included—you were lying at the time. You'd said that you'd driven your haunt away and, of course, you were lying. But I forgive you for that, too. No one had any idea how sick you were. You don't even remember giving me your word, do you?"

"No," Kyle agreed, taking advantage of the opportunity she'd provided. Now that she'd mentioned it, he did remember giving her guilty assurances from his bed in the lodge, but he'd never have recalled them without help.

"I'm going to let you make amends."

Staying with one-word responses, Kyle said, "How?" though he had a strong suspicion of what she wanted.

"Once we get to Chegnon, I want you to introduce me to the prince—and not just 'Your Highness, may I present my *beautiful* sister, Kiera?' I want to pass an afternoon, at least, with him."

Kyle had several reasons to balk at her demand, not the least of which was that he'd never said a word directly to Prince Gravais. "Talk to Muredoch," he suggested instead, foolishly hoping to get out of this without an argument, without agreeing to something he'd surely regret. "He and the prince are the same age. They were friends, I think, when Muredoch fostered."

Kiera made the sour face he'd expected. "Muredoch will remind me that I'm a betrothed woman; he already has. He'll tell me to stay in my room unless I'm needed—that's why I'm here, little brother, why Father agreed. If you run into trouble with the king's wizards, *I'll* be near to tell them what I remember of that night."

"There won't be trouble, Ki."

"That's what you *always* say. I'm here for you; you can trust me. My question is, Can I trust you?"

He sagged against the rope and the rail. "You are betrothed, Kiera. Flen has a right to expect—"

"Flen understands," Kiera said, just a bit too quickly.

His twin didn't love her future husband, not the way Flen loved her. It almost made Kyle feel sorry for the swaggering, but smitten, praverge. Kyle didn't like admitting it, even silently to himself, but Flennon Houle would be better off without his sister for a wife.

"But I have to know," Kiera continued, and Kyle wondered exactly what she'd said to make Father agree to this. If he could see through her wiles, how had Father succumbed to them?

"I have to know, before I'm married and there's no turning back at all, if Flen's the man I'm fated to marry. And you *have* to help. It's only fair."

Kyle didn't think fairness had anything to do with Kiera's intentions. "No." He was going to explain, but the boat began to buck the wind. Clinging to his rope, Kyle realized a single word was answer enough.

"No?" Kiera shot back as the sail luffed suddenly.

Seamen erupted all around them—shouting, hauling ropes, working frantically to recapture the wind before it tore the noisily flapping canvas. The boat pitched and yawed—the steepest movement they'd had since the voyage began in Renzi harbor—and Kiera, who had no notion how truly treacherous a ship's deck could be beneath her feet, tumbled forward. Kyle grabbed her before she was in any real danger of going overboard, but she'd taken a fright and he held her, instead of his rope, until she and the boat were steady again.

"Help me meet the prince, Kyle," she whispered in his ear.

"That's all. You don't have to do more. I understand: Flen's your friend and you don't want to see anything come between us. I'll help you, I swear it, whatever you want, whatever I can do, but help me meet him? Please? Get me out of whatever room Father and Muredoch lock me in? Say that you need me with you. Let me share your freedom to go where you will and talk to whomever you wish. I'll do the rest. And if he looks past me or if he's a boor, I'll return home and marry Flen with an open, willing heart."

Whether he agreed or disagreed, Kyle knew there'd be no honor in his answer, so he said nothing.

"Please, Kyle? Please, little brother? It's not so very much—I swear I'll help you, just swear to help me?"

She smoothed his hair as she withdrew from his arms and knelt on the deck beside him. Her voice remained soft and pleading, but her thoughts had changed direction, like the wind, and Kyle grew wary in his silence.

"I've forgiven you for everything, Kyle. I won't tell anyone how you forgot your own Rapture dream, or that your haunt is truly my haunt. I'll stand aside. Banish him, give him to the wizards, do whatever you like with him, Kyle; I won't say a word, I swear it. I set my own Rapture aside—everything God said when the Harbinger fell on solstice night. It means nothing to me—I swear it—I'll forget it, just as you've forgotten yours, only *help me meet the prince*?"

Kyle met his sister's stare—odd, how his gut held steady when he had something else to concentrate on. What harm could there be, if he did what she wanted and if she'd keep her oath?

"Swear on your honor?" he asked. He couldn't ask for a stronger sword-oath; women didn't bear swords.

Kiera slipped a hand beneath her cloak and dug deep into her bodice. She produced a ring much too large for her fingers: a man's signet ring, *Flen's* praverge ring with the seal of heir of Houle carved in onyx.

"On my honor and on this ring: I'll help you every way I can. I'll say nothing of my Rapture, or yours. I'll marry Flen with an open heart when I go back to Renzi."

He closed her fingers over the ring and squeezed. "All right, my honor, too: I'll do what I can."

Chapter Nine

A fire burned in the hearth of a quiet room in the northwest tower of Roc Chegnon, and though a sleety wind could be heard through the walls, the room itself was comfortable enough that a man—in this instance Prince Gravais Maradze—could shed his boots without worrying that his feet would turn blue. The remnants of a cold supper sat on a low table beside him, along with a flask of ruby-red burnwine. Burnwine was the drink of choice on nights like this, when a sudden winter storm had swept in from the sea.

While Prince Gravais topped off his goblet, a brassy fanfare echoed up the stairwell, masking for a moment the clatter of the sleet. The procession had begun: The king's roast boar was making its entrance into the king's great hall for the king's pleasure and the king's supper. Briefly the prince considered pulling on his boots and taking his seat at the high table. Roast boar—roast anything that was still hot from the spit—would be more appetizing than the cold leather steeped in sludge that the cooks had sent up for his supper. He could almost taste the succulent juices on his tongue; he swallowed, then sighed. His head slid down the velvet upholstery of his chair until his chin butted his breastbone and it was impossible to sip from the goblet that he twirled between his fingers.

The prince had supped with the court three nights past. Boar or no boar, he wasn't ready to endure that company again.

It wasn't that Prince Gravais—Gray to his friends and in his own thoughts—wished to avoid his father. Prince and king got along well. Quite well, considering that King Otanazar—fourth of his name, tenth of the Maradze lineage, lord of the

Spure, and sovereign king of Alberon—stubbornly refused, in the manner of kings everywhere since the dawn of time, to share royal authority with his acknowledged, full-grown heir. Remarkably well, considering that Queen Ezrae, the king's fourth wife, was a treacherous minx several years younger than Gray himself.

Eight years ago, when Ezrae Baldescare first came to court on the arm of her uncle, the Ultramontaine priest Ilsassan, she'd been a tiny, timid creature of unspoiled beauty and gentle manners. Gray pitied her, befriended her, and tried to persuade her to climb into his bed. She preferred a king to a prince and a marriage contract to the loose arrangement he'd had in mind. But he forgave her that, even as she wormed her way into his father's heart and a crown of her own. What harm, he'd foolishly thought, could come from such a doe-like woman?

Three half brothers crowding the Chegnon nursery and nipping at his heels: That was the harm.

Ezrae shed her meekness with her maidenhead. With the support of her uncle, who never returned to a life of scholarly contemplation in his monastery, Ezrae had become a sharp-toothed she-wolf standing over her children's cradles. Between them, uncle and niece, the Baldescare never missed an opportunity to proclaim Gray's failings to anyone who'd listen. That, so far, did not include his father, the king, or the more important of the kingdom's verge-lords. Still, Gray didn't see the queen without sensing that he'd been measured for his coffin.

With the Bitch and her uncle holding forth at the king's high table every evening, a prince could readily develop a taste for leathery meat in cold sauce, no matter how confident he remained of his father's favor.

If anything happened in the hall, Gray would learn of it by midnight. He had his own eyes and ears down there. Some of his retainers served the roast, others got to eat while it was still hot, but all of them were well paid for their loyalty and information. King Otanazar was tight with his power, but not with his purse. Gray paid his household retainers well and his spies better.

Gray was the son of the only woman his father had ever loved—the Bitch notwithstanding. He had no memories of Queen Terye, his mother; she'd died giving birth to him. Father said Gray need only look in a mirror to see his mother's eyes or the shape of her face. Gray's education in the peculiar craft of royalty had been thorough and sometimes painful, but he'd never lived a day without his father's affection. For twenty-two years, until the Bitch whelped her first prince, he'd had no rivals; he still didn't.

King Otanazar was aware of the Baldescare's relentless campaign against his eldest son. He was aware, too, of the growing crop of toddlers in the royal nursery, and as proud of his prowess as only a man nearing the end of the sixth decade of his life could be. *I leave them all to you, Gray, my son,* Otanazar Maradze told the prince on countless occasions, most recently at the end of this afternoon's council. *They are your brothers. Use them. Watch them and use them up in Alberon's service. But remember, my most beloved son, if the likes of Ferra Ilsassan and my queen can bring you down, then you never deserved my throne, or my love.*

Your will is my will, Sire, the most beloved son had replied, as he always did, without voicing the words that lingered in the back of his throat: Use them for what, Sire? Use them how, Sire? When my royal father finds no use for me!

Gray kept a tight rein on his temper around his father and listened carefully to everything the old man said. King Otanazar IV had ruled Alberon long enough to become wise; his advice contained the truth, among other things. Gray paid his eyes and ears around the king more than he paid all his other spies together. The Baldescare were nasty nuisances, but if his father ever turned against him, Gray knew his corpse wouldn't need a coffin.

The prince wasn't alone in his tower chamber this miserable winter night. Three others were with him. Gray trusted one of them, Lockwood, Lord Marelet, with his life and secrets. Of the other two, one was a known spy. The blind minstrel who'd played lullabies beside his cradle and soothed Gray's nerves ever since, he'd sold his soul to Queen Ezrae after the birth of her second son. A known spy—a spy who was loyal to his money—could be as useful as a true friend, and his fingers still charmed the sweetest tones from the strings of a harp or lute. The prince showered gifts and calculated indiscretions into the man's predictable path.

The third person in the prince's cozy chamber was a brown-haired wench from the Chegnon kitchen. She might be someone's spy, or she might not. At the moment, she was fast asleep with Lockwood's thigh for a pillow and his arm for a blanket.

Gray was willing to wager that the woman curled up beneath his friend's arm was no more than she appeared to be: a hard-worked servant, properly awed by the noble might of her masters, and safe within her simple honor. But, even if he were wrong, she was no threat to him. When she'd appeared at his door, weighed down by his supper, her exhaustion had been as real as the dark hollows beneath her eyes. She'd fallen asleep moments after Lockwood invited her into his embrace.

Both he and Lockwood had cut a wide swathe through the womenfolk of Chegnon, both the roc and the town that had grown up around it. Their reputations, however, were often overstated by kitchen wenches who knew that, more often than not, the only thing they got after serving the prince's private supper was a welcome nap.

So long as she didn't snore, the wench could stay where she was for the evening, because the prince wasn't going anywhere.

Lockwood was set for the night, as well. He sprawled across the hearth in a flagrant violation of the protocols against relaxing in the royal presence. Gray watched him as he idly fingered a lock of the woman's hair, tracing the curve of her cheek with the feathery tuft. She smiled and snuggled deeper. Lockwood shifted his legs to accommodate her, rearranging both the dagger and the iron-wrapped crystal he wore on his belt.

Their eyes met.

"My lord, are you troubled," Lockwood asked, his arm draped protectively over the wench's shoulder. He addressed his friend with formal politeness because the prince was scowling, and a wise man, especially if he was of uncertain ancestry and largely dependent on that prince's largesse, took no chances.

"I'm bored, Locky. Bored silly," Gray replied, banishing formality with a twisted grin. "The winter court is duller than usual this season. There's nothing at all to keep me from curling up like a bear waiting for spring. The Baldescare wolves are howling old tunes and Lord Drallin of Bercelen. . ." Gray took a deep breath, pinched the bridge of his nose and pursed his lips before delivering a devastating imitation of the Baldescare's staunchest ally among the verge-lords. "A petition, Sire, to raise the portage duties at Bercelen harbor, in expectation of Stercian pilgrims returning to the Siege of Shadows. A petition, Sire, to endow an Ultramontaine monastery in the valley with the duty proceeds, in expectation of heresy and riot among the peasants. God's pockets!" The Prince ended his imitation with an explosive oath. "There's a red streak in the sky the night before the winter solstice and the Ultramontaines are in an uproar. Pilgrims returning to the Siege of Shadows, *ha!* Heresy among the Bercelen farmers, *ha!* Why? Is there one living soul—aside from a fire-breathing Ultramontaine, who shall remain nameless, and his dupes—who *believes* what happened had anything to do with the Debacle? Perhaps they think my sire's gone senile when all he's trying to do is keep from laughing."

"It was rich," Lockwood agreed.

He loved the Baldescare no more than the prince, but something had indeed happened a few weeks ago. Neither he, nor the lord magister, Marrek Brun, the most powerful among the king's four wizards, nor any other wizard, knew precisely what, but once the snow melted and the mud hardened, the freelance wizards of Alberon would endeavor to find out—and find out *before* the hidebound priests of Alberon. He'd talked with Magister Marrek already, suggesting himself and the prince as worthy candidates, but he hadn't talked to the prince, no more than Marrek had talked to the king. With Baldescare ears all around the throne, royalty was necessarily isolated, even from its friends.

"Especially rich," he continued after a moment's pause, "when your royal father tucked Drallin's petition scrolls beneath the cushions."

The corners of Gray's mouth lifted. " 'We'll take this under proper advisement, my worthy lord,' " he drawled, another perfect imitation, this time of King Otanazar's gravelly voice. "Under advisement and into the fire the moment council ended. He burned the raggy things when we were alone afterward." Gray shot a glance at the minstrel, who plucked another chord from his lute without missing a note. "God love us, I could almost wish the Bitch were safely delivered. The Baldescare are sheep without their Bitch to lead them."

Lockwood winked at Gray. "The Ultramontaine augerists say she carries a boy." Baiting the queen's spy was a game they played often. It was a dangerous game, but those were the only games worth playing. "Five whelps in seven years of marriage. Three sons living, one at the threshold, and only a puling girl-child buried and mourned. Our queen's a paragon of fertility; too bad she's losing her teeth. She lost one just last week. That's why she's taken to her bed. Lady Shotaille cast her own stones; *she* says this will be the queen's last. Then we'll see how long the Baldescare thrive, when their Bitch is barren and toothless."

They both looked at the minstrel, whose milky white eyes betrayed nothing as his fingers skipped over the strings. Unable to get a rise out of the spy, Gray sank into a morose examination of his wine goblet, particularly the angled sword across a blazing sun etched on its side.

The prince's armed-sun crest had been everywhere that day, nine years ago, when King Otanázar set a golden coronet on his son's head and invested him as heir to Alberon's throne. A few months later, Ezrae Baldescare came to court, and since then the armed sun was rarely seen, except in this room.

Lockwood's friend had the look of royalty, the look of a king—as the wizard himself would never have. Gray's hair, worn fashionably long, was a few shades darker than the fire. His slate-colored eyes could be hard or soft or sparkling with mischief, depending on his mood. His limbs were lean, but not spindly; his hands were long and elegant, but strong. If Alberon's crowned prince had a weakness, it was his beard, which was sparse and sallow. He razored away the unmanly fringe as fast as it appeared.

Some years back, a cleanly shaven face had been briefly fashionable—until the nobles discovered they lacked either Gray's shapely chin or his steady hand with the razor.

Lockwood resisted fashion's temptations. His black hair was wiry and reluctantly confined in a leather-bound club at the nape of his neck. His beard, as black as his hair, came in thick and fast. It challenged the finest steel in Alberon, and usually won. He stood nearly a head shorter than his friend, but he was—they had settled the issue countless times—the stronger man.

When he pulled on his trousers each morning, Lockwood asked himself the same question: Where, in all Alberon, had his mother found his father? He'd never know the answer. His mother had been a cloistered Mellian priest who died before his eyes were old enough to fix her face in his memory. The maternal face he did remember belonged to Lady Sabelle, the king's first queen, who'd retired to the cloister when her two half-grown sons died one after the other and her womb could not quicken another.

Queen Sabelle examined many verger daughters before she chose her successor, and when Queen Terye died in the birthing straw, Lady Sabelle opened her heart to the motherless prince—as she'd opened her heart to a priest's orphaned bastard. Lockwood's earliest memories were of a straight-backed, silver-haired woman who prayed most of the day, wrote letters most of the night, yet still found time to teach him his letters.

"Four is enough. One was too many," the prince muttered, their game forgotten. "My father need not plow his furrows so deep or so often. I'm quite able to fulfill my responsibilities to the Maradze dynasty."

"Marriage, Gray?" Lockwood asked, adding a ribald chuckle. "Now, that would give the Baldescare something to chew on."

"Worry my sire even more," his friend said archly. "I'd have dower lands and dower men in my command. I'd be a prince to reckon with, not a damned ornamental rose-lord tripping over toddlers in the hallways. I depend on him for everything. " Gray's chair creaked as he swiveled about to stare at the blind minstrel. "I have no fear of my father, and he has no fear of me, but, God's pockets, Locky, I'd have the kingdom see my mettle before I ascend the throne."

Lockwood took note of the prince's stare: The game was on again. "Bother Alberon, my lord. You mean the Baldescare. Tell me, what will you do with them?"

"Winnow them, one by one, uncles, aunts, nephews, and cousins. Some to the front lines of the mercenaries, some to the cloister, the rest to the headsman."

"The Bitch herself?"

"The block, my friend. The block."

Lockwood rolled his eyes upward in mock prayer, and the minstrel eased into the wordless refrain of his ballad, skipping the noisier verse entirely. Let those words find their way back to the queen's ear and boredom would be the very least of their problems.

"And what of those three, maybe four, little half brothers in leading strings?"

Mischief vanished from Gray's eyes. The little princes were pawns in the Baldescare games. They were too young to pay a price for their birth. Nyan, the eldest, was a sturdy seven-year-old with bright red hair who looked to Gray for a father's affection. An honorable man—a king worthy of his throne—could not send Nyan to the block or sew him into a sack and drown him like an unwanted kitten.

But he'd have to do something with them.

"I'll raise them with my own bastards," Gray announced with a solemn voice and a grinning mouth.

Let the minstrel take that tidbit to his Bitch mistress. Gray had sired no bastards, so far as Lockwood knew, but that was the problem with bastards: A man didn't always know when he'd gotten one. Women were canny creatures, playing their own games to confound men, and there were witches in every town or village who sold come-hither potions that could undo any man's precautions.

"I'll bring them up to love me as their king and father," Gray concluded.

"The love of orphans, bought up or brought up, is a chancy thing," Lockwood bantered, forgetting until the words were out that he was an orphan bought and brought by the king.

"Is it now, Locky? Should I be weighing your purse each day?"

Lockwood swallowed hard and shook his head.

He remembered the day Lady Sabelle had summoned him to her cloister cell. He'd been old enough to feel honored that the great lady wanted to see him, old enough to feel shame when her women stripped off his clothes. They'd stood him on the sloped writing table, where the erstwhile queen had given him an inspection more appropriate for a plucked chicken than a living boy.

His neck grew warm recalling it and he reminded himself, then as now, that the lady had done nothing improper: He was a priest's bastard, a fatherless orphan, and who knew which of his parents' sins he might have inherited? Once the lady was satisfied that he was wholesome, her women had dressed him again in unpatched clothes, clothes that were not his own. Would he like to leave the cloister? the lady had asked.

Lockwood had inherited someone's suspicion, or caught it in the dusty stable corners where he slept. It would depend, he'd answered calmly, on where he was to be sent after he left.

Lady Sabelle's eyes had sparkled when she laughed. Why, to the king's court, to be Prince Gravais' boon-friend, she'd said and, not waiting for him to answer yea or nay, she'd shaped his destiny with a single clap of her hands.

He had no regrets. An orphan's life within a Mellian cloister wasn't anything to regret leaving, and an orphan bastard's was worse. But "boon-friend" was just a royal rendering of "whipping boy." He'd taken the prince's punishment. God knew, Gray had deserved every stroke Lockwood received instead, and the royal tutors were every bit as enthusiastic with the switch as the cloister folk had been. Older now, and a bit wiser, Lockwood understood that his pain had never been of consequence. It was all meant for Gray, who had to witness every bitter stroke. The tutors had been teaching their future king about nothing less than justice and mercy.

Fortunately for Lockwood, the rambunctious prince had been a quick pupil. Confronted with an unpalatable choice—amend his behavior or watch his boon-friend pay the price of it—Gray had appealed his decision to a higher authority: the sovereign king of Alberon, his father. Dressed in his finest clothes—and with Lockwood trailing anxiously behind him—Gray took his place in the common petitioners' line, hoping to catch King Otanazar's eye as he made his daily progress from bedchamber to throne hall. The king had treated his son no differently from the way he treated everyone else, ignoring him for several days before he accepted the by then wrinkled parchment scrap on which Gray had written his plea.

Looking back, it seemed to have been no less a game than the one Lockwood and the prince were currently playing with the Bitch's blind minstrel. The king had made a show of reading the words that had, almost certainly, been reduced to smudges. With royal gravity, King Otanazar had called for his crown and his scepter, declaring to one and all that Prince Gravais had challenged the king's prerogatives with his plea. Thus armed with the symbols of his power, the king had led a solemn procession to the throne hall. Lockwood had followed Gray, a bit behind, a bit to one side of the pleader's carpet, where Gray repeated his memorized petition in a voice that trembled despite his obvious efforts to control it.

Until I'm anointed my father's heir and wear a crown of Alberon in my own right, my person is not sacred. It is not mete or just that a boon-friend take my punishment for me. And it's not fair, either.

King Otanazar had stroked his steely beard and rubbed his brow. He'd stared intently at the huge smoky crystal mounted in his scepter's heart. One by one, he'd called his high officials to his side: the chancellor, who happened to be one of Gray's tutors; the war marshal, who wielded the willow switch with the enthusiasm of a drunken ox drover; the wizard quartet—Unamete was still the magister wizard then, and Marrek one of her assistants—priests; and all the verge-lords who happened to be present that day. God knew what had been said up there by the throne, if they'd even discussed Gray's petition or if they'd discussed something else entirely. Gray had blinked nervously as he waited on the carpet, his clenched fists planted on his hips, the way they still were whenever he was unsure of himself. For his part, Lockwood clearly remembered wishing he were dead.

The gems in the king's crown and the crystal in his scepter had begun to glow as the high officials retreated. The throne itself had risen slowly above its dais—the king's own wizardry, engendered in his anointed person and more potent than ordinary lightning wizardry—or so Lockwood had thought. He knew better now: Unamete made the stones glow; a water pump had raised the throne. But it had been magic that day when King Otanazar IV had granted his son's request before he'd focused his awful stare on Lockwood himself:

Since the prince may take his own beatings now, this bastard serves no useful purpose. Throw him out. Get rid of him.

The words he'd feared, but expected, since he'd arrived at court. Lockwood hadn't blamed Gray. His friend—they *were* inseparable friends from the start, Lady Sabelle had God's gift for matchmaking—was a prince; and princes, anointed or not, didn't understand how the world worked for the rest of mortal mankind.

Of course, that had been another part of the day's lesson.

Forgetting the carpet, the hovering throne, and the shimmering jewels, Gray had launched himself at his father's knees with wailing despair.

Locky's my boon-friend, my only friend. You can't send him away!

Lockwood truly did not know what the king had whispered next: It was one of the few secrets Gray would never share. But in Alberon, while a man was king, his word and wish were law. Still, a man who didn't understand justice and mercy wouldn't remain king for long.

And that had been the final lesson of the day.

Promises had been whispered, bargains were made, and Lockwood, numb below his neck, had been called to the carpet. King and prince had spoken with one voice to ennoble a priest's bastard boy, giving him a token fief: the Mellian cloister where he'd been born. (He suspected Lady Sabelle's foresight, but he'd never dared ask.) Ennobled was not the same as nobly born; a made man could never completely remove the stains of his very cloudy, very common ancestry, but when Lockwood stepped off the carpet, he was no longer an orphan. He'd become the vassal of his boon-friend, Prince Gravais Maradze.

His fief was larger now and he'd earned the talisman that hung from his belt with his own hard work and talent (and some judicious tutoring from his friend, who was a quicker scholar than he'd ever be.) But Lockwood remained Gray's vassal. He had neither regrets nor illusions. Friendship was a sturdy bridge between them, but it would always be a bridge across an unfathomed chasm, for all that Gray seemed to believe that solid ground lay between them.

"There's nothing in my purse that needs weighing, now or ever," Lockwood said, his thoughts still weaving through memory. He caressed the face resting on his thigh rather than look at his friend.

He looked up when Gray nudged him with his toes and looked at a mildly obscene gesture that was meant to cheer him out of morose or philosophic thoughts. So he cheered up, visibly, if not completely, convinced as ever that Gray could be as blind as the Bitch's minstrel when he chose. And cherishing their friendship all the more. He pointed at the minstrel who—no doubt coincidentally—was sipping warm tea and resting his voice.

Let him think I can be bought, he mouthed broadly.

"Ah . . . ," Gray mouthed in reply, nodding slowly, doubting that the Bitch would take the bait and then, for a heartbeat, doubting his doubt. The annals were full of kings and princes betrayed by their favorites.

He knew his history. The walls of this chamber were lined with his books of Alberon's history, Stercia's history, Pelipulay's, and every other kingdom around the Sea of Prayse—most in their proper languages, which he'd learned from the court ambassadors. He studied everything that washed up at his feet and remembered others' mistakes, in the hope of avoiding their misfortune.

He knew royalty attracted lackeys and fools the way campfires attracted moths.

Damn the Bitch and her uncle!

A prince needed a minstrel more than he needed a gullible spy and he needed a friend he never doubted most of all. Worse than the thought of Locky's betrayal was the one that showed him countless nights with no choice save a raucous supper court or a silent room. And he was about to say just that and wreck the game he'd started, but the sound of hurried footsteps on the tower stairs made him swallow his words.

The three of them craned their heads toward the chamber's outer door.

"Your Highness, my lord prince?" a breathless varlet in the king's crimson said between gasps once the door was open. He held out a scroll sealed with blue wax and a tricolor blue braided ribbon.

Lockwood started to rise. Gray gestured for him to stay put, allowing the woman to continue her nap. "Bring it here," he said to the varlet who hesitated before delivering the scroll directly into royal hands.

Gray tugged on the ribbon, dislodging the wax, and tearing the vellum. Without thought, he held the vellum at an angle, so only he could see the words, and read it without the least reaction flickering across his face: another hard-learned lesson from his royal education.

"Your Highness, my lord prince, will there be a reply? Should I summon a scribe? Vellum and ink?"

"No." Gray let the scroll re-form loosely around his fingers before tossing it and the wax-clotted ribbon into the fire. "Go to the kitchen instead. Tell them I want hot mulled wine prepared and hearty delicacies. Tell them, if they can't deliver it warm, then send the cook himself to tend my hearth."

The varlet bowed from the waist. "Yes, Your Highness, my lord prince. As you will it, Your Highness." He retreated with cautious, backward steps until his back bumped the doorjamb, then he turned and bolted down the stairs.

"Guests, trouble, or both?" Lockwood asked when the footfalls had faded.

"Guests. A surprise. Muredoch Dainis, his father, and the twins have tied up in the harbor. They've come to Chegnon with a petition for your folk, the magister and his cohort."

"Wizardry? Whatever for? Does Owl-eyes say why?"

They all had eke-names, even a prince and his boon-companion who traveled with the court, not the fosterling pack. Gravais had become, naturally enough, Gray; Lockwood became Locky; and Muredoch Dainis had been tagged Owl-eyes well before Gray met him. The names set a bond between the youths of a generation; old men remembered the companions of their childhood. Years melted from memory.

Owl-eyes—but never think that Muredoch Dainis was wide-eyed with surprise or shock, Gray reminded himself, unless you'd caught him red-handed in a prank. God's pockets, it would be good to see him again.

"The twins," Gray answered after his moment's reflection. "Lately turned seventeen. A boy, whose name I can't remember, and Lady Kiera, who's never been to court before."

Lockwood nodded. "A surprise indeed. Talent for wizardry's never run in that bloodline. The boy—I barely remember his face. Dreamer, wasn't that what they called him? Spent all his time in the kitchen. If he'd had any bent for lightning, someone would have spotted it, us or them."

Lockwood meant wizards or priests. A bent for lightning usually showed up early and turned either toward the priesthood or away from it. Priests said the bent for lightning was a gift of God, an obligation to serve God. They scoured the valleys looking for novices. Sometimes the priests turned over a stone that didn't belong to them. The lord magister, Marrek, and high priests, like Ilsassan Baldescare, swore there were no mistakes; that priests were priests and wizards were wizards from the start. But Lockwood swore there were priests whose lightning took a freelance bend, not a priestly one. Lockwood thought Ferra Baldescare might be such a miscast priest, as if it would take a wizard to hate wizardry as much as Ilsassan Baldescare did.

Not that the wizards—the declared, open wizards—cared if they had powerful enemies in the priesthood. A man or woman who called lightning out of an angry storm wasn't afraid of anyone, especially chanting priests who hid in their crypts, letting the iron-sheathed steeples of their monasteries do all the dangerous work. Wizards didn't look for likely apprentices. Having the bent wasn't enough, they said. And, maybe, they were right. Every spring, when the first mighty storms formed over the valleys, youngsters got themselves killed by lightning. The ones that didn't—the ones like Lockwood—eventually became wizards . . . or miscast priests.

"Maybe Lady Kiera tried living in the Renzi monasteries but didn't fit, so now her father's bringing her to you," Gray suggested.

"Me?" Lockwood laughed softly and stroked the wench's hair, lest she awaken. "Lady Shotaille, perhaps but not me, not knowing with whom I keep company."

Gray shared his friend's amusement. "True enough. If Lord Dainis heard half the tales about Owl-eyes and us . . . if he believed half of what he heard. No doubt he swore he'd keep his precious daughter safe from prying eyes."

Lockwood's eyes narrowed and he moistened his lips before saying, "I don't imagine it was your *eyes* that had him worried, Gray."

The prince chortled and the minstrel took that as permission to begin a bawdy song about a not-so-innocent maiden and the prince she contrived to marry.

Chapter Ten

Kyle was soaked to the skin and freezing by the time the Dainis boat tied up at the wharf reserved for verge-lords visiting Roc Chegnon. Runners were dispatched to the roc stables with orders to return with a carriage for the women and horses for the men. But runners could hardly be expected to run in such miserable weather. The Dainis party found itself facing an uncertain wait until transportation arrived, and a choice between remaining on the unheated boat or standing on the sleet-slicked wooden wharf.

It wasn't long before even Kiera agreed that walking to the roc would be preferrable to staying where they were. If they crossed path with the runners, the carriage, and the horses, so much the better, but if not, they'd be warm and dry in the king's guest quarters and the carriage could bring their baggage up behind them.

As it happened, they met no one at all on their way to the roc and the majordomo who hailed them in the barbican was surprised to see them.

"My lord Dainis, when you hadn't arrived by sundown," the liveried official apologized, "we assumed you'd gone to shelter from this cursed weather. The king is halfway through his supper—"

Father interrupted the majordomo before he went further in his litany of excuses. "We have more need of warm rooms and dry clothes than hot supper. We'll take rooms in the town if the roc is so filled with peers that royal hospitality is unavailable."

The man bowed from the waist. "Never, Lord Dainis. Be assured, King Otanazar welcomes you, favors you, and extends his largesse. How many chambers do you wish? Have you more men on the wharf? What do you need, my lord Dainis; it shall be provided."

"Tower quarters for myself, with inner chamber for my daughter and her maid."

Kyle caught the dismay on Kiera's face. Had she thought she'd have an outer chamber, with its own door to let her come and go as she willed? The Dainis didn't feud with other vergelords; they had no sworn enemies who'd look at another man's daughter and see only a tempting hostage. But Roc Chegnon was a place where feuds began and Kyle wouldn't have suggested another chamber, even if Father had deigned to ask him.

The fosterlings, thrown together without regard for verger alliances, were sacrosanct in their dormitories, but otherwise kinfolk stuck together when they visited the king's court. Kyle expected inner chambers for himself and Muredoch. He was mildly surprised when Muredoch announced that he would quarter with his old friend, Prince Gravais, and totally unprepared when Father asked him, "Where will you quarter? With one of us, or alone?"

There were solitary chambers throughout the sprawling roc, everything from little out-of-the-way chambers like his Roc Dainis bedchamber, to sumptuous lairs suitable for those with amorous reputations. While he served in fosterage, Kyle had heard the rumors about what went on in the score of private chambers royalty kept ready for its most cherished guests, though, of course, he'd never crossed their thresholds himself and imagined no reason to do so now.

"With you, my lord, if you please," he answered so softly that his father had to ask him to repeat himself.

"Very well," Father agreed curtly before giving orders to the majordomo.

Another royal steward had appeared while their quarters were being decided. He had a message for Muredoch: "His Highness, Prince Gravais, bids you join him for a late supper and wine before his hearth."

Muredoch accepted the invitation, then asked his brother: "Will you join me, Kyle? My word the prince won't mind and the floor won't move."

Kyle hesitated, mostly from surprise, giving Kiera enough time to squeeze his wrist surreptitiously with her icy fingers, which made him hesitate all the more. He'd regretted his oath-promise to help her lay a tempting trail before the prince, regretted it as soon as the words were out of his mouth. But after five days on a ship, especially this last, long day when the storm had blown up and he'd heaved his gut raw, he had no desire to see anyone: king, prince, or his own beloved family.

"My thanks," he said to Muredoch. "But I stand with Father: Dry blankets and a warm hearth will satisfy me tonight. I mean to be in bed and asleep before my clothes hit the floor."

Kiera dug five fingernails into his flesh. He caught her glowering from the corner of his left eye.

Your oath, she mouthed silently and squeezed harder.

Kyle couldn't free himself without risking Father's attention, and Father was already annoyed with him for mumbling. She had some cause for anger: His reluctance to act immediately on the oath he'd sworn sentenced her to a night in her chamber. Once Muredoch had departed, she released him, but made certain he saw how disappointed, sad, and angry she was as they followed Father and the majordomo deep into Roc Chegnon.

His twin's face haunted Kyle as he, Josaf, Enobed, and Renard were escorted to the paired chambers that were to be their quarters. A passage door connected his varlets' antechamber to the similar chamber where Father's varlets would live and work, but there was also an outer door in the antechamber—the precious prize that had eluded Kiera. Kyle could come and go as he wished, without Father's permission, or his knowledge. But he'd spoken the truth when he'd said all he wanted was a bed.

He didn't wait for his baggage to be brought up from the harbor. He didn't wait for Josaf to help him pull off his stiff, wet boots or for one of Josaf's sheep to slide a bedwarmer between the blankets. They were still in the antechamber, talking with their roc counterparts, when he wrestled free of cloak, boots, trousers, and the rest.

He fell asleep with his arm for a pillow and his feet dangling over the bedside. And woke up in much the same position a good many hours later. His arms and legs had cramped during the night. Kyle stretched cautiously, glancing around the room as he did.

For a moment the reasons for his being here at Chegnon, the miserable journey, and even Taslim's no-longer-urgent presence in the pit of memory, yielded to a different thought:

"What a difference a few years makes," he marveled aloud.

The last time he'd been at the Chegnon winter court was two years ago, when he'd been fifteen and part of the fosterling herd that attended royalty wherever it happened to wander. At that time, he'd slept on the floor in a drafty dormitory between the roc kitchen and its stables. An appropriate location: fosterlings were little more than varlets, perhaps a little less. When a fosterling finished serving at the high table or cleaning the feet of the king's horses, he was most likely late for weapons practice in the lower bailey or weapons care in the armory.

But this time Kyle was seventeen, a man and worthy of a place of his own. Fringed carpets cushioned the floor beneath his bare feet. Vivid tapestries cut the winter drafts to bearable levels. There was a glass-pane window to let in the daylight; lanterns set into the walls and branched candlesticks beside the furniture to chase away nighttime shadows. A mannerly, well-constructed fire crackled in the hearth. A kettle hung on the spit; from the rising steam, he could tell there was hot water for washing and shaving and making himself presentable.

The remnants of his fosterling wardrobe as well as new shirts and trousers hastily cut and sewn at Roc Dainis had been unpacked and were neatly folded on the carved wood shelves of an open wardrobe. Court clothes, the formal and uncomfortable garments generations of kings had decreed proper when a nobleman pled his cause before them, lay waiting on a groom's bench.

All the thoughts Kyle had resisted moments earlier became an angry mob in his mind.

<<Taslim?>> he called through the rising doubt and anxiety. <<Taslim?>>

The darkness that had been the wizard's prison since the botched exorcism didn't release him. In truth, every day since that day it had been harder to find him. Each night it seemed that Taslim faded deeper into Kyle's memory. He couldn't forget the wizard's face, no more than he could forget the face of his grandmother, or any of those who had died while he continued to live, or his brothers who might never return from their stint with the Gray Wolves. But like all those faces, including Varos' and Angrist's, Taslim's face was less a portrait than disjointed impressions: the wild, dark hair and ludicrous conical hat of solstice night, menacing pressure inside his skull, the corded veins of a young man's hand as lightning struck his talisman.

A slender golden arch that leapt from the core of his being into the void.

<<Taslim?>>

Kyle would have those images through his life, no matter if the wizard himself never reappeared and this whole journey from Roc Dainis to Chegnon were a fool's chase. He'd remember them alongside the snippets of his Rapture: the shattered face in isolation, the black mountains he and Taslim shared, and the moment when he'd lifted the battered warrior.

Suddenly disoriented, Kyle stumbled and sat down heavily on the mattress. For a heartbeat, he'd felt the broken-masked warrior's weight in his arms again. It came to Kyle, as he sat on the bed in a handsome Roc Chegnon chamber, that the wizard had won: His own Rapture haunted him now. He'd ride north with Rawne as soon as the seasons changed. He'd ride into the black Eigela mountains. He'd be searching for the warrior of his Rapture, but if he found the warrior, like as not, the way the dreamy images played out in his memory, he'd find the Siege of Shadows, too.

<<Taslim?>>

"So, you are awake." Not the wizard, but Josaf peeking around the antechamber door as he opened it. "I thought I heard you stirring, talking to yourself. Feeling better? Breakfast now, or after you're dressed?"

Josaf hadn't had a queasy moment the entire time they were on the water from Renzi harbor. Yesterday, when the storm had laid low a few of the seamen, the old man had stood emergency duty on the deck with the sail's sheet rope clenched in his steady fist. Josaf was patient with Kyle's temperamental gut, which had settled during the night but soured the moment food was mentioned, but Josaf didn't know the meaning of nausea.

"Never," Kyle muttered, burying his face in his hands.

A callused hand parted his hair and kneaded his neck. "Try not to fret so, lad," Josaf advised as he went to work on taut and knotted muscles. "You're no way at fault in this, my lord. King Otanazar's fair and just; he'll see what's fair and what's not. Don't you worry."

But it wasn't the king who stirred Kyle's deepest worry.

<<Taslim?>> He strained the darkness in his mind seeking some trace of the wizard. The only thing worse than begging the king's four wizards to separate him and Taslim would be

finding the words to tell them and Father that his haunt had already disappeared. <<Taslim?>>

<<Yes, Hart-lord?>>

The words drifted into Kyle's consciousness from a faint and distant place. Since the priests, Taslim could scarcely make himself heard, much less engender a blinding headache. He was no more real in Kyle's mind than a dream. God alone knew where Taslim was; Taslim himself certainly didn't. He'd said he was trapped in darkness—obol, the Bydian hell of endless dark, those were the wizard's repeated words—and sinking further with each breath Kyle took.

<<We're here, Taslim. We arrived at Chegnon last night, in a storm. I'll see the king today, I think; maybe the wizards, too. Father's had supper with the king.>> Kyle paused, thinking of the invitation he'd turned down. Kiera wasn't the only one he'd disappointed. <<I'm sorry. I was tired and cold when we got here. All I wanted to do was sleep. I didn't think; I am sorry, Taslim. I— We— You— It could be over now, if I hadn't thought of myself first.>>

<<No apologies, Hart-lord. I was the one who told you to take care of yourself before me. The passage was hard for you and supper's no time to be asking a king for favors, if the wine still flows the way I remember.>>

Taslim had become far more charitable and solicitous since his exile began in the Roc Dainis great hall. Kyle pitied him, and found himself distrusting both himself and the wizard.

<<It will be soon now, in any case,>> he thought to the darkness. <<I'll talk to the king. The king will talk to his wizards. They'll summon you and you'll be free of me.>>

<<Or lost forever.>>

<<Don't say such things. You'll stand a better chance of returning to your Siege of Shadows without me.>>

<<Don't lie, Hart-lord. I may be reduced to a shadow in the night, but I hear your inner thoughts and I know a lie when the wind blows it past me.>>

Kyle lapsed into his own silent darkness. If the wizard could hear his inner thoughts, then he knew about the masked warrior. If the wizard could recognize a lie, then he knew that now, as the last grains of sand flowed through the narrow waist of an imaginary hourglass, Kyle did not look forward to being alone again.

"Are you going to wash yourself, or is that something else you never intend to do again?"

At the sound of Josaf's irritation, Kyle shuddered out of his meandering thoughts. From the old man's tone, it seemed that it hadn't been the first time that Josaf asked the question. God knew, Kyle's thoughts had always tended to wander. Dreamer, they called him, and he'd earned the eke-name. In his more expansive moments, Josaf said he never heard anything until it was said for the second time. But this time, he hadn't merely missed a word or two: The kettle had been unslung from the hearth spit and Renard stood beside it, vigorously stropping a razor.

Taslim wasn't the only one sinking into darkness; he was, too, whenever he communicated with the exiled wizard. For both their sakes, the king's wizards were their only recourse—

Something clamped down on Kyle's shoulder. It shook him hard enough to rattle his teeth and rouse those warrior reflexes he wasn't supposed to have. Faster than thought, Kyle cocked an arm and slashed sideways, meeting solid resistance, and overcoming it. He realized what he'd done the instant before Josaf hit the carpet, rump-first and feet splayed wide in front of him.

Muttering curses about his own absentmindedness, Kyle leapt to the old man's side and got him back on his feet. "Did I hurt you? I didn't mean to. I'm sorry. My thoughts wandered again, as soon as you'd called them back . . ."

Josaf shed Kyle's support, straightened his clothes and gingerly took a step that Kyle had the sense not to notice.

"Don't apologize," Josaf said after a second, more confident step. "It's that cursed wizard haunting you again. I don't mind telling you, lad: I'll be glad when this day's done, that demon's gone, and you're yourself again."

A sudden chill wrapped around Kyle's shoulders, but he hurried to the washbasin and plunged his hands into the hot water before his wayward imagination swept him away again. He scrubbed away the sea-spray grime, then Josaf wielded the razor that removed a week's worth of scruffy whiskers. At the very end, and before Kyle could object, Josaf rinsed his raw face with cold, stinging, flower-scented water.

"What was that for?" Kyle demanded, swiping his chin with a towel.

"Never hurts to make a good impression before the king." Josaf snatched the cloth before Kyle could blot away the scent.

The water chilled him as it dried. He didn't dare touch his

face, so he chafed himself along the forearms instead. "The king's a man. He won't care how I smell."

"I've heard tell that your plight has piqued Queen Ezrae's interest. Word is that she's dressed for the first time in a week and means to sit in council in the dragon chamber. You may be certain that *she'll* notice. There's a woman among the wizards, too. Women always notice, lad, and women always influence the men around them."

Kyle warded off the shirt Renard offered. He shivered in earnest then, thinking of the Baldescare queen, and the wizards, and—especially—the dragon chamber of Roc Chegnon. On the ship he'd tried not to think about the moment when he'd stand before the king, asking for wizardly intervention, but when he had, he'd imagined it happening in the vast throne hall amid tapestries and stained-glass windows, chandeliers and scores of courtiers plying their trade in the alcoves. It had been a comforting, but futile, bit of dreaming. There was nothing about his plight, from the wizard haunting his memory to the Siege of Shadows itself, that King Otanazar would wish to discuss in a public chamber where half the kingdom might overhear.

But the dragon chamber! Kyle had never crossed its notorious threshold, but he and every fosterling knew exactly where it was. Late at night in the dormitory, the oldest boys told the tales that had been passed down through the generations: When Roc Chegnon was built by mortal hands, King Eigela II had commissioned a windowless chamber where his council would meet to discuss the kingdom's most serious affairs. When the verge-lord of Sandrisan learned of the king's plan, he offered Sandrisan's most precious relic: a slab of black stone in which a Hesse wizard had imprisoned a fearsome, winged monster. The dragon would not stir, both Lord Sandrisan and the fosterling storytellers assured their audiences, unless a lie was uttered it its presence; then it came to life and the liar was consumed.

Though Kyle's mature self doubted those dormitory tales, he couldn't shake the dread that settled around him like a pall. There were so many lies woven into his life. He couldn't tell the truth without also telling a lie.

It was just as well that he'd forgone breakfast.

"Put your shirt on, lad," Josaf chided. "I tell you again, you're in no way at fault in this—provided you finish dressing and hie yourself out of here before the king's hair turns snowy white from waiting."

"*Waiting?*" Kyle's voice shattered into a boyish squeak—an indignity he thought he'd outgrown a year ago. Making God's Hollow Sphere surreptitiously with his hands, he swallowed hard and tried again: "Our king is waiting for me?"

Josaf draped the shirt over Kyle's still-cupped hands. "The summons came with your breakfast."

"Oh, God."

"Along with royal assurance that you were not to be awakened or hurried. It seems that someone recalls the Sea of Prayse unsettles you."

"Oh, God," Kyle repeated, fumbling with the shirt. He needed to examine it twice before he recognized front from back and pulled it over his head. "Oh, *God*."

"There's nothing to worry about," Josaf insisted.

There was tugging and smoothing to make the shirt behave, though it was brand-new linen and fit perfectly. Josaf lifted his hair from beneath the collar, an oddly gentle and reassuring sensation. Then the old man straightened the sleeves and tied the cuffs above Kyle's wrists with a double knot that wouldn't loosen during the day and would almost certainly require assistance when it came time to take the shirt off in the evening.

"Here, lad, give me your other arm."

As if he were still a child who couldn't be trusted to stay inside his clothes or to get out of them without help. A child, or some witless fool who didn't know where his imagination ended and the world began.

"You're making yourself sick for no reason at all."

Maybe thoughts of the dragon chamber had stiffened Kyle's spine, or perhaps he'd simply wallowed long enough in his own misery. He didn't know which, or whether something else had suddenly snapped within him. But he was tired of words that hid the truth. Springing off the groom's bench, he wrested his arm from his varlet.

"You haven't got any notion of my reasons, Josaf. Not you, or Father, or the king, or anyone. You didn't have my Rapture and you haven't had a stranger in your every thought since solstice."

Kyle tied the cuff with a simple knot, made between his free hand and his teeth, the way every fosterling learned early on his path to manhood. Except, he'd strayed from that path, looped back to childhood, where the people he loved did everything for him, because the people he loved all agreed that he couldn't do anything right for himself.

"God's pockets!" He borrowed Kiera's oath and her possessive notions: "Taslim is *my* problem! He waited a millennium for me to come along, and now *I've* had to decide what's right to do with him, and I've faced the consequences when everything goes wrong. I let the family talk me into an exorcism. I let Taslim talk me into coming to Chegnon to meet with the king and his wizards. I've let everyone else meddle with my problem, and I've gotten no better than I deserve: My back's in a corner and I'm scared. All right—but it's *my* back that's in the corner, Josaf, not yours. So, don't go patting me on the head like some stable-yard dog and telling me otherwise."

Blood pulsed in Kyle's temple. His hands were clenched and his breath came hard, as it did in the practice arenas. Josaf was dumbstruck: mouth wide open and eyes even wider. Kyle imagined himself through the old man's eyes and saw a half-dressed dolt with damp hair tangled before his eyes.

Most likely his cheeks were red, too. His face felt warm, and he usually blushed whenever he got excited.

"Just leave me alone," he concluded wearily. "I'll manage to get myself dressed, somehow, and get to the dragon chamber without breaking my neck—which wouldn't be such a bad idea, when you think about it, so I won't do it, you can be sure of that." He turned away, rubbing his forehead with fingers that shook with anger, fear, or who-knew-what. "Leave me alone, please," he asked softly after another moment had passed and he hadn't heard footsteps moving toward the door. "I don't know what I'm saying, or why. Don't listen to me."

He heard footsteps: one man, then a second, crossing the room and going out the door. A third man crossed the chamber, but didn't leave. Kyle waited for several moments, willing Josaf to follow his sheep, before he conceded defeat with sagging shoulders and a turn of his head.

"Josaf—I *can* take care of myself."

Josaf nodded. "My eyes are going," he said after a pause, and Kyle considered the chance that he was not the only witless fool in the bedchamber, then Josaf put his hand on the door. "Sometimes I think I see my old friend, your grandfather, standing where you stand, wearing your clothes." He departed, pulling the door shut behind him.

Kyle pulled on his trousers and went on a hunt for his belt.

He hadn't known his grandfather, but by all accounts Pancel Dainis had been a large, earthy man, considered generous and wise—but with a temper to match his vigor. There were chips in the Roc Dainis plaster where Lord Pancel had hurled something at the nearest wall, and an old, thin scar across Father's forehead from the time when some*thing* had been some*one*.

With all the trouble he got himself into, Kyle reckoned he was lucky that his grandfather had been dead by the time he and Kiera were born. If he'd had to cross his grandfather's path very often, he'd surely be a patchwork of scars. Father threatened beatings, but rarely delivered them, and then only with his hand or belt.

Still, Josaf had meant the comparison as a compliment, because—like the rest of those still living who'd known Pancel Dainis, including Father with his scar—Josaf claimed his heart had wept blood the day the old lord died, and that the wound had never healed.

Kyle found his belt and the other garments a nobleman was expected to wear at court, regardless whether he was a vergelord, a fosterling pouring wine at supper, or a man with a wizard stuck far behind his left eye. Fosterlings never had body servants to help get them dressed in a hurry, but they'd had one another. Kyle regretted sending Josaf away. By the time he'd armored himself with two quilted surcoats—one sleeveless, the other with slashing to reveal the lacy ruffles of shirt below—a cockeyed hat with a brace of feathers drooping over the brim, a pair of false buckles for his otherwise plain boots, and most of the trinkets he'd acquired in seventeen years of gift-giving holidays, he'd worked himself into a fine sweat.

Scowling at his imperfect reflection in the looking glass above the hearth, Kyle tugged the hat toward one ear, then the other, before giving up on it completely. Some men—his father, brothers, and future brother-by-marriage among them—looked their best in court clothes. Kyle felt awkward, foolish, and above all else, uncomfortable. That was probably what kings intended. Of course, court clothes were ordinary clothes for the king and those who dwelt near him. Perhaps King Otanazar would feel foolish with just one surcoat or a shirt unadorned by lace—

Kyle caught his thoughts before they ran completely away. He took a final swipe at the hat and headed for the door, and whatever lay beyond it.

A royal servant had joined his varlets in the antechamber. The young man in Maradze crimson swapped jokes with Enobred and Renard, sharing the breakfast Kyle had declined to eat. He jumped to his feet when Kyle entered the chamber.

"Kyle, Hart-lord Dainis, His Royal Highness, King Otanazar the Fourth commands your presence, at your earliest convenience, in the dragon chamber, where matters of deepest urgency may be discussed."

They were the same age, Kyle and the king's messenger. Considering the amount of time Kyle spent among the Roc Chegnon servants, they should have known each other, but the man in crimson stared straight at Kyle without a hint of recognition. For his part, Kyle thrashed his memory trying to match the face before him with two-year-old memories. An awkward moment lengthened until Kyle recalled a stableboy with matching green eyes and a similar sharp chin.

"Hawk?"

"Hawkans, my lord. Whenever you're ready. I've become a man and serve the king now."

"Don't you remember me, Hawk?" Kyle asked, though that wasn't the question truly crowding his mind.

Although Hawk must have recognized or remembered him, he'd chosen to disregard the many long hours they'd worked together mucking out the royal stalls. It was prudence, no doubt, on Hawk's part: A servant's reputation wouldn't be enhanced by association with a haunted hart-lord. But the snub hurt. Had anyone asked, Kyle would have counted Hawk among his friends.

"I'm ready," he conceded, risking a glance at Josaf, who did not seem pleased.

"Then, we're away." Hawkans took a step toward the outer door, then stopped short and spun around, catching Kyle off guard. The mischievous smile Kyle remembered was back. "God's pockets, Dreamer—you've grown a head taller and you *still* can't wear a hat!" He seized the hat near its feather and gave it a slantwise yank. "There," he said with smug satisfaction. "I'm not taking a lopsided hart-lord before the king."

Kyle backed away like an ornery colt. He scowled and shook his head, but not vigorously enough to disturb Hawk's handiwork. Josaf seemed relieved and the two sheep hid their faces, choking on not-quite-silent laughter.

"Be damned, all of you!"

He opened the outer door himself. Looking right, then left, Kyle realized he hadn't been paying attention when the major-domo led them up from the barbican last night. Chegnon was a maze of towers and corridors, but it was a maze he knew as well as he knew Roc Dainis or the other rocs where he'd fostered. Peering out the nearest window, he matched what he saw with what he remembered of the roc's innards and set off for the dragon chamber at the fastest walk his long legs could manage.

The shorter Hawk had to run to keep pace and didn't catch up until Kyle had entered the wide, statue-flanked corridor that was the Alberon king's official domain. Heedless of the guards posted on either side of the council door, Hawk put on one last burst of speed and dropped to one knee in front of Kyle.

"T'weren't no disrespect, Dreamer—my lord—back there with the hat. You won't say how I touched you. You won't tell the king, will you, my lord?"

"Do you think our king would listen to a hart-lord who can't put his hat on straight?" He tried to sound lighthearted as he motioned for Hawk to rise. He heard bitterness instead.

"His Royal Highness will sure be listening to you, my lord," Hawk assured him without rising from his knee. "There's been talk of nothing else since Lord Dainis' message arrived saying you needed the king's wizards without saying exactly what you needed them for. We all seen that Harbinger burning down the sky on solstice night. When it didn't strike down in Chegnon harbor, we knew it'd only be time before someone came looking for priests or wizards. Sure we was expecting someone down from Sandrisan or Bercelen, not Renzi, but we knowed why you'd come soon as the message arrived. Your men said a demon's taken up haunting you—"

"Wizard," Kyle corrected, seeing no reason to deny the truth, and gesturing once again for Hawk to stand. "A wizard, Hawk. A very ancient wizard who belongs with his own kind, not me."

Hawk shaped his hands into a Hollow Sphere as he stood. "As may be," he said, then, looking at his hands as if he'd not felt them form the warding gesture, he lowered them to his sides. "But you're changed, that's true enough."

"I've grown. So have you. It's almost two years since we've seen each other. Taslim hasn't transformed me."

That was true enough. He'd fought so hard to keep Taslim from influencing him that he'd transformed himself instead. Once he'd told the occasional wild tale to hide the truth about his mishaps. Now he told far more subtle lies, and told them far more frequently. He told another:

"Wish me luck in there, Hawk?" He held out his hand. "One stable mucker to another?"

"Luck, my lord? Not likely you'd be needing my luck. Times've changed, you be a lord *and* wizard now and I be past the stables. If you'd be needing it, I'd be willing to dole it out, but it's not fitting that we lay about as we did, my lord. Times've changed. Be changing again on the other side of that door, so I'll be thanking you, and keeping my luck for myself, if'n I need it."

Kyle watched in silence as Hawk raced down the statuary hall, measuring the changes as the footfalls faded. He'd never had many friends, but that had seemed a choice he'd made—he was shy and awkward around his peers, and his inferiors, too. Now it had become a judgment: a stableboy, a one-time companion in hard, dirty work, felt entitled to spurn his hand.

<<Taslim?>> he inquired of the darkness. <<Taslim?>>

The dragon chamber guards were watching him closely, having observed the incongruous exchange between a verger Hart-lord and a royal servant. They exchanged quick glances and regripped their serviceable spears. Like Hawk, they were common men with common fears; King Otanazar wouldn't entrust his personal safety to men he didn't own outright. The king might have given orders to let Kyle sleep as long as he wished, but the king didn't trust him. No one would—not truly—while a *demon* haunted his thoughts.

<<Taslim?>>

Nothing emerged from the darkness, no image, no voice, not even a half-formed impression.

Kyle met the armed men's stares as he approached the double doors. He gave the half nod of a nobleman to a commoner: the gesture he'd seen his father give a thousand times but never tried himself.

I know who I am. Let me pass unchallenged.

The man on the right stood aside. The one on the left triggered the latch before he did the same. But they'd both hesitated for the narrowest of moments. Another man might not have noticed any lag at all. Kyle noticed because he himself had hesitated before striding between them.

Chapter Eleven

A sense of interrupted conversation hung in air as Kyle entered the dragon chamber. His back was to the long side wall. He faced a horseshoe table that opened toward the short side, where a fire crackled in a man-high hearth and a white star set in the black stone showed a petitioner where to stand before the king. Bodies shifted in their dark wooden chairs, each straining for a better look. Those mortal sounds ceased with the closing of the guarded door. The quiet crackle of seasoned wood in the hearth and the soft moan of wind over the roof tiles were all Kyle heard as the king and his councilors gave him a thorough study.

With his head tucked down—he did *not* want to look at the beast that gave the chamber its name—Kyle walked to the white star. He took note of the men and women he faced. There was King Otanazar, of course, seated at the horseshoe's toe: a broad-shouldered man with faded, fire-colored hair. The king held a silver goblet in his right hand and, by his demeanor alone, turned the simple object into a scepter. His eyes were dark and piercing beneath heavy brows, but they told Kyle nothing of the royal opinions or expectations.

Prince Gravais sat at his father's right hand. He, too, held a goblet, but lightly, spinning its stem between his fingers. The prince was the first to acknowledge Kyle's anxious glance, tilting the goblet in a small gesture of courtesy and greeting. Kyle's own father and brother sat farther to the king's right. Father's face was pale and grim; it did not brighten when Kyle forced a smile. Kyle was filled with foreboding that was mitigated only slightly by Muredoch's hooked-thumb salute: an old fosterling signal to stand fast.

Kyle hooked his own thumb in reply and gave a glance to the left side of the table. As Josaf had promised, Queen Ezrae sat beside her husband. She was a tiny woman, about as delicate as the finest steel-blade dagger. To her left was Ilsassan Baldescare: the king's advisor whenever God mattered, the queen's uncle—her lover and father, too, if the unsavory rumors Kyle had heard in the royal kitchens and elsewhere in his fosterage were as truthful as they were persistent. Ferra Baldescare was a high priest of the Ultramontaine order: no plain Bydian or Mellian robes for him. He dressed in bright colors, shot with threads of gold and woven into satin and velvet brocade. King Otanazar might go uncrowned in this, his private chamber; but not so Baldescare, who wore a jewel-encrusted fillet that boldly declared the favor he'd found in his order's eyes, if not in the Hidden God's.

Farther down on the Baldescare side of the horseshoe, though hardly their allies, were the king's four wizards. They each wore black and, like the Bydian priest who had officiated at Kyle's Rapture, they concealed their faces and hands beneath layers of gauze. The magister, Lord Marrek Brun, was the most distinctive of the quartet. His smoldering talisman—no larger than the others, but bound with more iron and ominously brighter—sat on the table in front of him. He wore a black conical hat with a black tassel dangling from its tip, a hat that reminded Kyle of Taslim of solstice night. Kyle couldn't be certain which of the other three wizards was Lady Shotaille and which two were the lords Entellen and Drewlen, though he was aware that all three were staring at him.

On either side of the table, between Prince Gravais and Muredoch on the right and the Baldescare and the wizards on the left, sat other men with studiously impassive faces. These were the kingdom's officers: the war marshal and justiciar, the chancellor of the royal treasure, and the lords equerry, chamberlain, and steward. They'd been verge-lords once, before they resigned their titles to their heirs in order to serve Alberon. The king's wish was always above the kingdom's law, but with these six men present in the dragon chamber, the king's wish *was* law, without appeal or recourse.

Kyle slowly raised his head and looked above King Otanazar, at a ferocious head thrusting out of the black stone wall. Larger than the largest horse that Kyle had ever seen, the dragon's head was a glossy rust color. Its mouth gaped, revealing that it possessed not only a raptor's sharp-edged beak, but an inner jaw lined with countless fangs, all of which shimmered iridescent in the flickering hearth light.

There were more predatory carvings on the walls of Roc Dainis; the Hesse had a taste for the grotesque in their enduring art. But the dragon wasn't a statue. It was a creature confined by magic no living wizard could reproduce—or undo.

Its red eyes leaked fire. A serpentine body raised ridges in the black stone. Staring at them, Kyle half-expected the coils to shift when he blinked. Forelimbs and hindlimbs surged out of the stone. Each bore a skeletal paw and six menacing talons. Only the wings looked counterfeit. Delicate web tracings in red and gold, they appeared to have been painted on the stone and seemed too small to lift the massive body the stone imprisoned.

But one flaw wasn't enough to dispel the dragon's threat. Men entered the dragon chamber; ghosts came out. There wasn't a nerve in Kyle's body that doubted the dragon's ability to slay him where he stood. Gulping down a second wave of terror, he concentrated on the king who began to speak when their eyes met.

"Begin, Kyle Dainis, Hart-lord of Dainis. The kingdom listens."

"Your Royal Highness, King Otanazar Maradze, fourth of your lineage, Lord of the Spure, Sovereign King of Alberon. Gracious and just—"

King Otanazar shoved his goblet aside. Empty-handed, he hunched over the table, leaning on powerful forearms, drumming his fingers on the dark wood. "We can dispense with the formalities, hart-lord. I had a long conversation with Lord Dainis, your father."

That might explain Father's expression, but not in any optimistic way.

"He has a father's understandable desire to protect his youngest child and a verge-lord's equally understandable inclination to befuddle this court. I found his explanation of events unsatisfactory. I expect you to perform better, hart-lord. Let's begin at the beginning: What brought you to Roc Chegnon?"

Kyle hesitated: Where was the beginning? Was Taslim the beginning? Or Rapture? His Rapture, now that he remembered it? Or his twin's? His Rapture seemed more honest, but Kiera's was the true reason he'd been at the lodge when the Harbinger fell. In this chamber the price of deceit was death, and the beginning, whatever it was, wasn't what had *brought* him to Roc Chegnon.

"Your Royal Highness, a boat—my lord father's packet boat."

Discreet chuckles flitted around the horseshoe. The king smiled as he laid his hands flat on the table. Kyle had told the truth; the dragon hadn't broken out of its prison. But there were other ways to die in this chamber, shame foremost among them.

"Very well, hart-lord," King Otanazar said benignly, the worst tone a king's voice could have. "Tell us in your own words, your own way, what do you want from us?"

Kyle remained transfixed by the red eyes, paralyzed by the ambiguity inherent in mortal existence: That which was most believable was not always that which was absolutely true.

King Otanazar began to drum his fingers again. "Come now, hart-lord. Was it your decision to await Rapture in your family's crypt?"

"Yes, Your Royal Highness." That, at least, was a question he could answer emphatically without fearing the dragon's retribution. "Mine and mine alone. I have a twin sister, Your Royal Highness; Roc Dainis has only one Rapture chamber. We agreed that she would sleep there, and I'd sleep in the crypt."

The words had tumbled out of Kyle's mouth before he'd remembered the rooftop conversation he and Kiera had had before the celebration began. They hadn't *agreed.* Kiera had offered him the Rapture chamber, had suggested that anywhere would be better than the crypt, even the roof.

He couldn't breathe or swallow or raise his eyes to meet death with noble courage as the dragon burst free to destroy him because he hadn't told the truth. His heart pounded rapidly, painfully, once, twice . . . ten times.

The dragon hadn't taken him. There were limits, then, to its power, its insight. It didn't know what he hadn't remembered. It couldn't see into his heart, right now, while his thoughts were measuring truth against deception, the way he'd done after countless other catastrophes.

The ultimate truth *was* belief.

Kyle let his breath out confidently.

"Our valley Bydians escorted me there and I fell asleep. There was a storm, and the rain came in to wake me up, but not before I'd had my Rapture." So far, all true *and* believable. He couldn't make a Hollow Sphere with his hands, not here where the entreaty would rouse suspicions. He made it in his mind instead, in the way he'd learned to keep secrets from Taslim when the wizard had been closer to his thoughts and he'd had more to hide. "I dreamt I was in our family's hunting lodge in the Spure, in winter. I looked toward a window. My sister was standing in front of me. We were watching a sunset—or so we thought, because, Your Royal Highness, the next morning we discovered that we'd had the same Rapture dream."

Father lectured that nothing a man said would be believable if he mumbled or stared at his feet while saying it, so Kyle spoke clearly and looked straight at the king. He thought of Kiera standing by the window and of the Harbinger hurtling through the sky. It was a true memory; it had happened, but for a moment Kyle convinced himself that it had, indeed, happened twice: once in Rapture, once in life. He held his breath, waiting to see if anyone else believed.

Moments became an eternity. Bodies shifted. Ferra Baldescare whispered in his niece's ear. King Otanazar retrieved his goblet.

"We know that, hart-lord," the king said, passing the goblet repeatedly from one blunt-fingered hand to the other. "We know how you and your sister went to the Dainis lodge. We saw that damned fiery thing ourselves. What we want to know—in your own words, hart-lord—is what has happened since that haunt attached itself to you. What has it done? What does it want? Where has it been all this time?" The king paused, considered, and spoke again, more rapidly: "Tell us what you've learned about it, hart-lord. How do you live with such a thing? What are your own thoughts about it—if the demon leaves you any."

Before Kyle could begin to answer the king's questions, or protest that his thoughts were still very much his own, Magister Marrek Brun raised an objection:

"Your Royal Highness, my lord—you presume conclusions before the question is finished. We have been told this Taslim is a wizard, and so he should remain. A wizard is in no way a demon."

Ferra Baldescare rose partway from his chair and brandished a fist down the table. "A wizard is a thrice-damned blasphemer and heretic if he can't grasp the difference between himself and a demon."

"Ferra!" the king shouted, a voice that no one in Alberon dared ignore. "Peace and patience!" he added in a tone that admitted precious little of either virtue.

The Ultramontaine priest unclenched his fist and reseated himself, smoothing his luxurious robe. "Always presuming, of course"—his voice a treacherous undercurrent as he scooted his chair forward again—"that there is a difference between any faceless wizard and the least conniving demon."

"Ferra!" The narrow stem of the goblet creased and buckled in the king's fist. "Need I remind you, Ferra, that you are here as the queen's advisor, and not in council."

"As *your* soul's advisor, surely, Your Royal Highness, my son," the priest shot back without hesitation or humility.

"Our souls are not under question or assault, Ferra."

"Who presumes now?" Baldescare pointed an unwavering finger at King Otanazar: an act of supreme confidence or ultimate foolishness. "He who watches not his own feet, falls hardest."

The dragon's smoldering eyes were less menacing than King Otanazar's, until Alberon's monarch blinked and all sign of his displeasure vanished. Calmly, the king straightened the soft metal stem of his goblet and pushed it toward the war marshal, who filled it from a frosted ewer. Baldescare had lowered his accusing hand, but his expression had lost none of its doomsaying wrath.

Kyle was enthralled by the naked exercise of power and defiance between the king and the priest.

King Otanazar sipped wine. "We are here to examine the hart-lord, at his own request, I believe, and to offer our aid, if he makes a compelling statement, if we see fit, if it falls within our purview. Nothing more, Ferra; nothing less. If this displeases you, depart, before your displeasure consumes you."

"I am not displeased, Your Royal Highness," the priest said, as calm as the king. "My ears await the boy's best words."

Kyle bristled. He stood straighter, taller, and tried to catch the priest's elusive eye. He might be a lowly hart-lord, but he wasn't a boy.

"Indeed, my lord husband," the queen said. "Tell him to

speak his piece. We would all hear this tale he has to tell: Why God and a wizard chose him—of all unlikely people in Alberon—to be the Harbinger's messenger. We were told he was a boy with imagination and droll wit to embellish his lies; so far, all we've had is that a boat brought him to Chegnon!"

The look Kyle caught from Queen Ezrae reminded him of Kiera, on solstice night, when she first thought he'd stolen Taslim from her. Kyle couldn't imagine what he might have stolen from the queen, but the similarity was too striking to ignore. As was her use of the word "droll"—the word with which Father described him, at least according to Kiera. Was it possible, even likely, that Father had used the word to describe him last night at the King's supper—with the queen and her uncle in attendance?

Not for the first time this morning, Kyle rued his decision to hide in his bed last night. He should have stayed with Father, or gone to supper with Muredoch and the prince. At the very least he should have arisen earlier. These people—the most powerful folk in the kingdom—had sat too long under the dragon's malevolent eye with nothing to do but talk about him.

As long as they weren't displeased with him. That was most important, and far from assured. He looked across to Muredoch, who seemed the only certain ally he had in this chamber. Muredoch's thumb was no longer hooked in warning. He'd laid his middle finger over his forefinger and tucked his thumb up against his palm: Lay low. Lay quiet. There's a storm brewing above you. Don't draw attention to yourself.

That was hard to do when the king started asking him questions again. Kyle stuck close to the truth when he could, but it wasn't the imprisoned dragon he worried about, it was the queen and her uncle.

King Otanazar wasn't interested in souls of millennial wizards. With inquiry after inquiry, he wanted to know about the Harbinger, because he'd seen it himself, along with the rest of Alberon. Kyle thought that Kiera could have told the king more had she been in the chamber with him now; the fireball had been part of her Rapture, not his, and she'd been looking out the window while he was crushing embers on the floor planks. But he kept that thought to himself and the dragon seemed no wiser for the deception.

"Your Royal Highness, it seemed that a great star was falling from heaven," he said, and not for the first time. "I looked away before it crashed—that was how I first saw the wizard," he explained, omitting much without telling any great lies.

The king nodded slowly, the councilors also, and from the corner of his eye Kyle saw that Father was satisfied with his answer. Predictably, Ferra Baldescare was not.

"Saw, hart-lord?" the priest interjected. "Saw for how long? Long enough to have a thought for your soul's sake? Long enough to concoct this tale of heresy and demons? This is not a cozy roc in a wayward valley, boy. Your lies will get you nothing here, whatever they may have gotten you at home. Tell the truth, boy, before God, before it's too late!"

Religious fervor couldn't account for the Ultramontaine priest's hostility. There was something more, but Kyle couldn't quite grasp it. In fosterage, he'd mastered the art of deflecting anger. He'd had no close friends, but he hadn't been disliked. Ignored, overlooked, and judged insignificant, perhaps, but even Flennon Houle *liked* him, in a pet dog sort of way. No one had ever sneered the way Ferra Baldescare did, waving his hand when King Otanazar chided the priest for interrupting.

Kyle tried to defend himself from the priest's accusations. "Your Royal Highness, I was transfixed: I couldn't move my arms or legs. There was a terrible, painful, burning light, then there was nothing. I fell unconscious and when I opened my eyes again, Taslim was within me."

"A demon! Lies or demons!" Ferra Baldescare interrupted yet again. "Our God doesn't involve himself in the tricks of this boy's fervent imagination. His is a tale not worth the hearing, Your Royal Highness. He talks of a Harbinger when any fool who reads could tell you that we're seven years short of the millennium or that the Harbinger—if it should return—should blaze brighter than the sun for a whole *month*, not a single moment of a single night. He's made this tale up, Your Royal Highness. He's had nothing to do with any true Harbinger that might yet return, nothing to do with the Veshkait Siege of Shadows."

The priest rose from his chair. His voice trembled with credible passion as he addressed the king: "Your Royal Highness, this is *heresy*. Most dangerous heresy to seduce the common sorts away from the high path of righteousness. The lessons of the past are clear, Your Royal Highness. Don't let these lightning lovers blind you with their charlatanry. Give thanks that it is not Eigela of Sandrisan who stands before you spouting tales of Rapture, but a lying Dainis hart-lord. Give thanks and take precautions, Your Royal Highness, for the millennium *will* come, and who knows what will come with it? Any talk of Harbingers and Shadow Sieges must be silenced. If some foreign fool does set foot on our soil, he must be sent home before he destroys himself and *us* on his fool's quest. Our God has scarce forgiven us for the last time: We are not loved, Your Royal Highness, and our rocs shelter fools. You must demonstrate to fools that you won't make the mistakes that King Euben made."

Then Ferra Baldescare swung around and leveled an accusing finger between Kyle's eyes.

"Hear me, my king and you, too, hart-lord of Dainis: The Hidden God of Alberon will not be mocked! Make an example of this fool, my king. Cut out his tongue. Put out his eyes."

Kyle was horror-struck. He would have fallen, but as his world shattered around him, his mind and body separated. He remained standing even as his thoughts whirled in a blind panic.

"Place him in an oarless boat and have him towed from one valley harbor to the next, so all the vergers may witness the price of heresy!"

"My son's done nothing wrong!" That was Father, hammering his fist on the table, refusing to honor the Ultramontaine priest with either his name or title.

"The boy's told tales all his life!" Ferra Baldescare retorted. "You, yourself, admitted you cannot distinguish his truths from his lies. You call it imagination, but it's only lies, Verge-lord, until now; now he speaks heresy and that's my concern, not yours. The boy's a heretic and a liar—"

"The only lies I hear are those that slide off a priest's oiled tongue!" Father shouted. "I listened once to a damned fool priest who nearly killed my son exorcising a demon who doesn't exist. I'll sheathe my sword in the bowels of the next priest who lays hands on him!"

Such exaltation as Kyle might have felt on hearing his father defend him was dashed by the seriousness of the charges flying through the dragon chamber. He'd imagined the king's wizards refusing to help him and he'd imagined something going wrong if they agreed, but he'd never for a moment considered that the Baldescare might accuse him of heresy and thereby endanger all his kin.

And they were all in danger when the Ultramontaine priest said, "Stay hands, Verge-lord, lest you stake your precious Dainis to the tide's judgment."

The threat was real: Priestly courts couldn't impose physical punishment, but they claimed the right to expose men, women, and even children to God's justice by tying them to stakes pounded into low-tide mud and leaving them there for a night and a day. All the nobles of Alberon, including the king, disputed the priests' right, especially when they, themselves, would be affected. But looking at King Otanazar's impassive face, Kyle had no faith that the king would stand with the Dainis against Ferra Baldescare.

That didn't stop Father, who grabbed his wine goblet faster than Muredoch could stop him and threatened to hurl it at the priest. Fear and excitement greater than he'd ever known pounded in Kyle's veins. Then Father lowered his hand: Wine spilled over the goblet's rim as he set it unsteadily on the table.

"You're wise, Verge-lord," the priest purred triumphantly. "Purged of its heretics, your little family will prosper in its little roc above its little valley."

Why? Kyle asked himself. What had he done— What had his family done to earn the destroying hatred of the Baldescare? It seemed a inopportune moment to pray to God. Kyle raised his eyes to the dragon, instead, and shouted curses from his heart.

"Lord Dainis *is* a wise man. He turns to his king rather than his queen's priest." A hitherto unheard voice made itself heard: Prince Gravais, who studied the Baldescare with hooded eyes.

Ferra Baldescare's lips tightened into a sour line; the king folded his hands beneath the table; and Kyle got a clearer understanding of the battle lines. The Gray Prince stood between the Baldescare and the throne, between them and the fruition of their ambitions. King Otanazar was content to let his son stand his ground alone.

Which Gray did quite well, even slouched in his chair, still toying with his goblet.

"You've confused yourself, Ferra. This isn't an Ultramontaine inquisition. This isn't even a meeting of the king's justice—to which neither you nor your charming niece would be invited. This is merely a meeting of the king's council, in its private chamber. We're here to listen and learn and, perhaps, to dispense royal aid. You're here—Well, yes, Ferra, *do* tell us why you're here. Who invited *you*? Not I, I'm sure. I'm sure I would remember inviting *you*. Not my royal father . . ." His voice trailed off, waiting for the priest to reply.

"A millennium ago the prophecies of Veshkai nearly brought Alberon to ruin," Ferra Baldescare answered with as much respect as he'd shown since Kyle entered the dragon chamber, for all that he omitted the prince's honorifics. "In the aftermath, the Ultramontaine order—my order—summoned a synod which declared that the prophecies were false, the pilgrims misguided. No god had sent the Harbinger, not the one Hidden God, not the imposter Veshkai. There was no Siege of Shadows—"

"And that which we all saw in the solstice sky was not truly there?" the prince interrupted and concluded.

"A fireball. A warning. An omen, if you will, of what stands before us today. We must take a stand against heresy, or it will consume us. Make an example of this hart-lord; let him be a warning to one and all. False prophecy and heresy cannot be tolerated; they must be rooted out for the preservation of the kingdom."

The priest seemed genuinely distraught. But, with a disdainful grimace, the prince straightened in his chair.

"Come now, Ferra. Everyone in the roc was looking out the windows on solstice night. Everyone wondered what the fireball was. By morning, the word 'Harbinger' was making the rounds. I said it; your niece said it—before witnesses? Did she tell her children? Are they heretics, too?"

"Nonsense!" the priest snarled, losing his calm demeanor and returning to his former vitriol. "The circumstances are entirely different."

But before the prince could demand to know the differences, or the priest could recite them, King Otanazar stirred.

"There's an easy way to resolve this: The hart-lord's come to see my wizards, so let my wizards see him. Let them do their work. God's arse pockets, if I wanted theology or family bickering, I'd have summoned the council to my bedchamber, where I can sleep in comfort."

Oaths and ribald humor didn't disguise the fact that the king had finally taken command. Both prince and priest settled in their chairs as Lord Marrek Brun rose from his.

"We have already begun our investigation," the lord magister said. "The chronicle of Magister Bashertain, begun in the fifth year of King Euben the Fourth's reign, recounts not only the tumult of the Debacle years, but also the names of those who petitioned for the right to make a talisman during those years. In the tenth year of the chronicle—two thousand five hundred and twenty-six years after the coming of the Hesse—Bashertain received a petition from a youth calling himself Taslim of Fawlen. Now in that time Fawlen was . . ."

Kyle didn't need the magister's help to identify Fawlen. Fawlen Brook was one of several headwaters for the Renzi Valley River. The fast-running brook supported several seasonal sawmills which, in turn, supported one of the inns Kyle had visited during his autumn preparations for the solstice trek to the lodge. It took no great leap of imagination to imagine that there'd been sawmills and inns along the brook a thousand years ago—although the appellation implied that Taslim himself was not of noble birth and that Kyle's own ancestry might be both more complicated and less legitimate than he'd been led to believe by the family chronicle.

Another mention of Taslim's name by Lord Marrek brought Kyle's attention back to the dragon chamber. "Taslim, as he calls himself, will answer the summons, and then the entire matter will be completely clarified. Are you amenable, hart-lord?"

Once again, Kyle's wandering thoughts had betrayed him. He answered the lord magister with a mute and mortified stare. Alberon's most potent wizard reached for the talisman hanging from his belt.

"Lord Kyle appears suspicious," Prince Gravais observed, intervening before wizardry seized the moment. "One can hardly blame him: A verge-kin nobleman comes before the council, as is his right, seeking royal aid, also his right, and is subjected to Ultramontaine accusations and interrogation. Will you take *my* word, Lord Kyle, that no harm will come to you if you allow the lord magister to summon your wizard to a seat of consciousness?"

Kyle pieced it together: The wizards wanted to question Taslim and wanted his consent before they cast their spells. He asked if this would be the summoning he'd requested—the separation for all time between Taslim and himself.

"Not yet," the magister said soberly through his gauze veil. "Many questions remain before we'll know if such a summoning can be attempted. The sooner we have answers to our questions, the sooner we'll have an answer for your question."

It seemed reasonable, if Taslim were willing. Kyle cast the wizard's name into the darkness at the back of his mind. Nothing echoed back, neither yea nor nay, nor the slightest sigh. Had Taslim overheard Ferra Baldescare's hostile questions and retreated so far into his prison that he couldn't be found again?

"I'm willing," Kyle stammered, then remembered his courtly manners. "Your Royal Highness, my lord magister and all my other lords here gathered, I'm willing, but I'm not certain—"

"Give the man a chair!" someone called—one of the high officials, because Kyle didn't recognize the voice. "Be damned if I could hold my feet while staring into one of those infernal things."

"Give him a goblet, too. He's pale enough for two," another man added.

Kyle refused the wine, but was grateful for the lord magister's chair which the lord chamberlain brought around for him—as if he were king instead of a man just escaped from boyhood and scared out of his wits.

"It's simple enough, lad," Lord Marrek Brun explained once Kyle was sitting. "You'll trade places with your haunt, in a sense. We'll talk to him, learn a bit more about him, then summon you back to your rightful place in the seat of your own consciousness."

The wizard held up his talisman and Kyle locked his knuckles around the chair's wooden armrests. He heard the first few syllables of the summoning spell and watched their associated runes begin to glow on the iron bands that wrapped around the sparkling crystal. But after another moment, a breeze seemed to whirl around him. No, it was more like the sea when the tide turned, making him queasy as it carried him away from the shore.

A counter current swirled, pushing him safely away from Taslim's dark prison. The magister's wizardry was a success: Kyle remained aware of himself and the chamber around him, but his body heeded a different consciousness. His shoulders rose slightly and moved forward. His hands relaxed and gave up their death grip on the chair. A smile formed on his lips—not his smile, but Taslim's smile.

"Lord Magister Marrek, I am Taslim of Fawlen. It is my pleasure to answer your summons and your questions."

Kyle listened carefully. Under Taslim's care, his own voice was confident and mature and accented. Not only had Alberon's script changed over the course of a millennium, so had its speech. The words were recognizable, though filled with sounds that had, apparently, been forgotten, while missing some sounds a living ear expected. Overall, Taslim's words were sharper, prouder. Kyle's always wandering thoughts wondered why. Had Alberon's language changed because of the Debacle? Or was something—

<<Perhaps yes, perhaps no, Hart-lord,>> Taslim chided. <<Restrain yourself.>>

The wizard's accent disappeared when neither voice nor ears played a part in the conversation. And again, Kyle wondered why.

<<How should *I* know, Hart-lord? We can discuss it later, but not now. We're not precisely among friends here. *I* held *my* peace; now it's your turn.>>

<<Sorry,>> Kyle replied and tried to think small, quiet, insignificant thoughts as Taslim rapidly answered the magister's onslaught of questions about the wizards of a millennium past and the wizardry they practiced. The exchanges grew more arcane, less intelligible, but Taslim was succeeding. Kyle looked out through a stranger's eyes and watched as Lord Marrek relaxed, then set aside the bulky Bashertain chronicle to ask the questions his own curiosity raised.

"My spells endured," Taslim said at last. "My grandchildren were scattered throughout Alberon. They'd keep my lineage alive. I was assured that a child would be conceived at the right, fateful moment. I cast my final spell: a touchstone to connect me again with that child through his Rapture—"

"Heresy! Blasphemy!" Ferra Baldescare erupted. "Rapture is a divine gift. God cannot be mocked by a petty wizard's lightning and runes!"

"All the better!" Taslim shouted back.

Kyle's body rose from the chair, but it had been too long since Taslim had commanded flesh. They were falling until

Kyle intervened, guiding his arms and legs into balance again. Taslim noticed; the aether echoed with triumphant laughter and reminders that Kyle had succumbed to the very usurpation he'd feared so much at the lodge. Then, in an instant, the laughter and the reminders were gone.

"All the better!" Taslim repeated, though his words still hung in the air. "If God cannot be mocked with wizardry, then what I offer is prophecy, not heresy or blasphemy. *God* allowed me to bind my soul to Alberon until the Harbinger returned and the Siege of Shadows reopened. *God* called me to the hart-lord and *God* calls me back to the Siege of Shadows. The Hidden God wants to be seen. He wants to share his power and He wants me to show the way, because I know the way. I've seen the Siege of Shadows!"

While his eyes flitted from one increasingly thoughtful face to the next, Kyle contemplated the peculiar holes in Taslim's story. He said he'd seen the Siege of Shadows, but he never claimed to have seen God, not the Stercian Veshkai or Alberon's nameless Hidden God. Taslim said he knew the way to the Siege, but he didn't know the way back, at least not a way a living man could take.

Kyle felt all his old familiar suspicions of Taslim's tight-fisted handling of the truth, but he held them close. He hoped that Lord Marrek, King Otanazar, or even Ferra Baldescare would come to the same uncertain conclusions, but they didn't know Taslim as he did. They didn't know about the black mountains he'd seen both in his own Rapture and Taslim's last mortal memories.

The enrapt men and women in the dragon chamber heard exactly what Taslim of Fawlen intended for them to hear. Knowing smiles and plotting smiles formed all around the horseshoe table, even—Kyle suspected—beneath the wizards' swathing.

The first to speak was Ferra Baldescare. "Yes," he mused as he stroked his beard. "Prophecy must be considered. Prophecy, false prophecy, and heresy. The three orders will convene a synod—"

"Including the members of this council," King Otanazar warned. "This is a *royal* matter."

"Of course, Your Royal Highness," Ferra Baldescare agreed, smiling. "But there is the matter of this boy's soul—"

"The hart-lord's soul is his own," Taslim shot back. "As is every other part of him."

Which wasn't altogether true at that exact moment, as Taslim resisted and rejected Kyle's attempts to regain control of his body.

"I am a *wizard*, Priest, not a crazed heretic, not a demon that exists only in your imagination. Wizardry drew me to nasen'-bei, which any wizard will tell you—prove to you—has nothing to do with a man's soul, nothing do to with demons. It's the between place, threshold of wizardry, where the wind always blows."

The lord magister's black-wrapped hand fell lightly on Kyle's arm. "But, by grace of a meddling priest, you no longer dwell in nasen'bei. Is that not true, Taslim of Fawlen? Is that not why you came to us—to be drawn out of the eternal dark of obol, to make cause against meddling priests? To return to us, your peers?"

Lord Marrek Brun was saying the words both Kyle and Taslim had wanted to hear, but the hand wasn't right and the tone wasn't right, and Kyle wanted to warn Taslim not to accept the offer.

<<Don't try to teach your grandmother to steal sheep,>> the wizard said. <<But what of the Siege, Hart-lord? I *will* return to the Siege. Are you prepared for that, Hart-lord? Have you changed your mind?>>

"Let me summon you out of darkness, Taslim of Fawlen. Lead me to the Siege of Shadows," the lord magister said before Kyle could respond to Taslim's questions.

"I think not, Worthy Magister," Taslim said with a slit-eyed smile, the feel of which Kyle wanted to remember for his own use. "God drew me to this young hart-lord. God's priests have hammered me deep and I do not think they would countenance my departure, especially to another wizard. In my day, wizards wouldn't gainsay God and His priests. Do you?"

Ferra Baldescare grumbled and scowled. Lord Marrek raised an already glowing talisman. Kyle felt the tide winds change, pulling him back to the center of his being. For a moment, in a place that existed only in his mind—or nasen'bei, or nowhere at all—he stood face-to-face with another young man, who was cocky and confident, as a hart-lord would never be, and who held out his hand.

<<Trust me, Kyle Dainis,>> the wizard said. His eyes

sparkled in the strengthening wind; the talisman below his waist did not. <<Together, we can outwit these fools.>>

Kyle had a hand—not his body's hand, of course, but a hand of his own imagining—which hung at his side. It was his decision, he told himself: The fulfillment of his own Rapture lay in Taslim's mountains. And if his curiosity took him a little further, to Taslim's Siege of Shadows . . .

An instant had passed before Kyle extended his hand and an instant was too long. Taslim's image shattered before their fingers met. Kyle was himself again, alone in his body as Taslim hurtled, screaming, through darkness. All eyes were on him.

"He's gone, Your Royal Highnesses, my lords," Kyle said. He considered sitting in the chair again, reconsidered, and remained standing.

"Forever?" King Otanazar demanded.

"No, Your Royal Highness." He looked at the cloth-obscured face of the lord magister. "He can be summoned again, I think, but not without wizardry."

"Or ritual," Baldescare added. "As the boy holds the wizard, so we priests should hold the boy—until a proper determination can be made."

The lord magister, naturally, objected, and King Otanazar told them both to be quiet. "There is much to consider. You may each talk with him, with his haunt. Wizards in the forenoon; priests until supper. I will listen to your recommendations in three days' time. Until then, the Dainis—all the Dainis—will remain *my* guests in Chegnon, enjoying *my* hospitality and *my* protection."

Kyle sat down heavily. They were prisoners, or they might just as well be, for three days—then who knew what might happen?

Chapter Twelve

It was Kiera's first day at Roc Chegnon and a sense of foreboding had replaced excitement. Father was gone before she woke up. The Dainismen he'd left behind had disappeared midmorning, after men from the royal guard banged on the outer door. Deep within their nested chambers, Kiera hadn't been able to hear every word exchanged between the king's men and the Dainismen, but those she did hear—"outrage," "demand," and "arrest" among them—convinced her to hide herself and Lille behind the bed until all was quiet again.

They'd been alone since, without Dainismen or royal guards to keep watch over them. Kiera considered venturing out of the Dainis quarters. But caution prevailed—if only because she wanted to speak with her father as soon as he returned from the dragon chamber where he'd gone to meet with the king and Kyle. Not that *Father* had told her that. He'd left her behind twice already: before dawn this morning and last night while she was eating a cold supper.

The only way Kiera knew where her kin might be was through *Renard*—Lille's Renard—who'd come calling between Father's departure and the king's men's arrival. He described how a royal messenger had come to summon Kyle to the king's notorious privy chamber and how Kyle had looked when he departed. It seemed reasonable to suppose that Father and Muredoch would have received a similar summons, but neither she nor Renard knew for certain. Father had ordered his varlets not to answer her questions about his whereabouts or anything else.

Until the Dainismen disappeared, Kiera had intended to

confront her father and insist that it wasn't fair to bring her to Chegnon then leave her trapped inside a bedchamber. But as morning faded and they were still alone, *fair* had begun to seem less important than *safe*. By midafternoon, though, all either she or Lille thought of was *food*.

"Follow your nose," Kiera told her maid.

"I'm fearful," Lille complained, retreating from the outer door like a balky horse.

Kiera opened the door and, taking her maid by the arm, pulled her toward it. "Nonsense. No one pays attention to a lady's maid. Just keep your head down and no one will notice you."

"And if they do?"

"Demand to be brought here. You're a Dainiswoman; you're not responsible for yourself—No, better yet: *Appeal to the Gray Prince!*"

"Oh, my lady," Lille objected with a horrified gasp. "I can't do *that*."

"You won't have to, *if* you find the kitchen and hurry back here with a basket of bread."

Kiera got the necessary leverage on Lille's arm and shoved her maid out the door. It was all true: People of importance didn't notice servants, and if they did, it was only to trace them back to their masters and mistresses. If anything was amiss, Father would surely agree that it was wiser to send Lille in search of food, rather than go herself. And Father surely wouldn't expect her to go hungry all day.

Kiera found it strange—strange and a bit frightening—to be all alone in a Chegnon bedchamber, not knowing what was happening to her father or brothers or any of the twelve Dainismen they'd brought with them. From her window she could see the barbican where men wearing armor and carrying spears guarded the iron-spiked gate. They'd been there when they arrived and again when she first woke up. Guards were part of the royal court, but Kiera couldn't look at them without worrying—a little.

Dutifully, she set up her embroidery by the hearth. She stitched a few strands of silk, then ripped them out again and sat, staring at the fire, until she heard the outer door latch move. Hoping it was Father, she took an extra moment to tidy her hair and clothes. By the time she was ready, Lille had wrestled the door shut and a heavy basket of bread and cheese onto the nearest table.

"Oh, my lady. There's trouble for sure. I saw no sign of Renard or the others, and I must've walked every corridor before I found the kitchen. They gave me the food I asked for, but there was no gossip—none at all, my lady—to catch my ears while I waited. And—God'a'mercy—there's a mean-looking cur come to stand outside our door! He looked me over, up and down, as I came along, and said I'd not be going out again without *his* leave."

Kiera cracked the door wide enough to confirm Lille's opinion, then closed it and shot the bolt to protect them both from the man outside.

"God's pockets! I had more freedom at home!" she complained as she hauled the basket to the bedchamber. She shoved her embroidery frame aside with one foot, spilling an array of carefully sorted silk onto the rough wood floor. "My own father not only doesn't trust me, he doesn't trust the good Dainismen who came with us! He's set a stranger outside our door. I tell you, Lille, it's not to be tolerated. It's not at all to be tolerated! Keeping me locked up. Keeping me in the dark while God-knows-what is happening to my own kinfolk. I should be with them, Lille. I should be with Kyle. Whatever he's going through, I should be with him. We've shared everything up to now."

"Yes, my lady."

Lille spread a cloth over a table and set out the plates of food she'd brought up from the kitchen. "Renard said he'd find Kyle and stay with him no matter what happened, my lady. And he'd do just that. It must be that they're all still with the king, my lady. And the king's *wizards*!" She shuddered dramatically as she lit a lamp with an ember from the hearth. "God'a'mercy on him, my lady. God'a'mercy."

Through Alberon's countryside—and Kiera knew that Roc Dainis stood deep in the countryside—commonfolk turned to God and the priests when they needed magic's aid, not to ragtag itinerant wizards who went out alone in the wildest storms, luring thunderbolts to their talismans and giving little heed to the laws of God or man. Lille's dread of wizards was as real as her compassion for Kyle—and, in silent truth, Kiera felt much the same way. She'd grown up in the countryside; she couldn't help but share its beliefs. She was concerned about Kyle, but her concern paled when she thought about her isolation.

"I gave my word," she muttered, breaking her bread with enough force to send golden crust flakes flying into the fire. Word or not, she still intended to beguile the Gray Prince, and she expected Kyle to help her, which meant she expected him to have *his* problems resolved in time for supper.

"My lady?" Lille tossed the ember back into the fire and knelt at Kiera's feet. "Don't you worry, my lady. Lord Kyle'll be all right."

Kiera glanced away guiltily, wishing she had her twin's imagination. She knew better than to tell anyone that she wasn't worried about her brother half as much as she was annoyed with him for not worrying enough about her.

She scolded Lille instead. "God's pockets, you're such a goose, Lille. The king's wizards do what the king tells them to do, and the king's a God-fearing man who'll see through that Taslim haunt in the blink of an eye. He's ordered Taslim banished by now, I'm sure of it. My brother's free and fit and doing whatever men do when they've got nothing better to occupy their time. He's completely forgotten that I'm alone and trapped in this chamber without him."

"Not alone, my lady." Lille tipped her head toward Father's chamber and the outer door beyond it. "Renard will come, my lady, as quick as he can. Just like he came before. He'll tell us what happened in the dragon chamber." Lille shivered as the words crossed her lips and clutched Kiera's skirt in her fists. "Never you worry, my lady. Lord Dainis won't let anything happen to you or your brother."

Kiera set aside her bread and smoothed Lille's hair. "I could send you out to look for him," she mused. "For Renard, I mean. Or Enobred. Or any Dainisman who might know what's happening."

Lille raised fearful eyes. "No, my lady—if you please: Don't send me out again. This Chegnon's too big a place for the likes of me. I got lost more times than I could count. The cook had mercy on me and sent me partway back with another girl—I heard what goes on here. There's too many people here, my lady, with too many thoughts. Lord Dainis is a wise to set a mean-looking man outside our door. Renard will come—"

"Renard. Renard!" Kiera made the varlet's name a curse

and freed herself from Lille's grasp. Now she *was* getting worried . . . about *everything*. These chambers seemed twice as dark and isolated as before and the guard outside seemed ominously unjust. "I'll go myself."

"My lady—*no*. It's too dangerous for you."

"I'm not afraid," Kiera insisted, and tucked a little knife from the food basket under the snug hem of her sleeve. "I'll find Kyle or Father, or—" She caught herself before she added the prince's name. Truly, this was no time to be thinking about the Gray Prince, not with real worries clamoring in her mind—though nothing would set her heart at rest better than a timely encounter with His Highness.

"Or what, my lady?"

"I don't know what, Lille—but I won't stay mewed up like a molting hawk."

Kiera stalked to the outer entrance, threw the bolt, and flung open the door. Her unwanted guardian came to attention with a slink of chain mail and the powerful thump of his spear butt striking the floor. Staring straight ahead, Kiera got a good view of the nicks in his greased mail. She took a step back.

"I'm going to find my father, Lord Dainis," she announced, because no one could object to an unwed woman searching for her father.

"My lady, my orders are that you're not to leave these chambers. Send your woman instead; I've got no orders regarding her."

The guard had jagged, blackened scars above a grizzled beard, and hard, black eyes above the matching scars. *Black Lightning*, Kiera thought as she clenched her teeth to meet his glower without flinching. Not a respectable cohort like the Gray Wolves where her brothers and ancestors laid claim to noble glory, but a common, hardscrabble lot drawn from the lowest scrapings of Alberonese society. She'd never expected to see a Black Lightning veteran in the royal roc. Lord Dainis ran such men off his land, or he would have, if they'd dared to show their faces in the Renzi Valley.

He'd never commission one to guard his door.

Never.

And Kiera's half-grown worry blossomed into full-grown fear.

In her mind's eye, she measured the width of the corridor

against the shaft of his spear. She managed one stride toward the spiral stairs before the iron spearhead blocked her way.

"Orders, my lady," he explained without a trace of emotion in his voice.

Weapons were part of a roc's daily life. As a little girl, Kiera had proudly carried her father's sword to the practice field where he instructed the Renzi Valley fosterlings. Later, under Mother's careful watch, she'd learned to clean and stitch the wounds that were as much a part of practice as they were of battle itself. She knew a razor edge when she saw it, reckoned the mortal damage it could do, and swallowed hard before turning around.

"Lord Dainis will rescind your orders when I find him. You needn't fear his wrath."

"Queen's orders, my lady, not the lord's, and not to be rescinded."

Kiera nodded slowly. She'd never been to court, that was true enough, but she wasn't ignorant, no matter what her family thought. She listened whenever she heard someone chattering about the queen and her Baldescare relatives, and she'd seen the furrows appear on Father's forehead whenever those names were mentioned.

Alberon's queen and the prince of her dreams were mostly to be found on opposite sides of any question. But she hadn't considered—not until she turned away from those hard, Black Lightning eyes—that Father's reasons for keeping her hidden at Roc Dainis might have less to do with her prince than with his stepmother. Prince Gravais stood alone between the queen's young brood and Alberon's throne, but once the prince married, every child he sired—especially every son—would strengthen his position while weakening the Baldescare's.

The Dainis lineage had never lacked for sons—or daughters to whelp sons for other men.

Kiera retreated until her hip struck the doorjamb. "Why would our queen order *me* confined to these chambers?"

"Not for me to answer questions, my lady," he said, returning his spear to its place at his side.

"Am I under suspicion?" Kiera demanded, and regretted her words immediately. Of course she was under suspicion. Overlooking Prince Gravais, a possible marriage, and inconvenient heirs to a throne the Baldescare considered theirs, her Rapture had foreseen the opening of the Siege of Shadows and her twin brother was haunted by an ancient wizard.

If Kyle's encounter in the dragon chamber had gone badly . . .

"Where is my brother, Lord Kyle Dainis? What happened in the dragon chamber this morning?"

Chain mail slinked as the guard shrugged. "Not for me to know or say, my lady. My orders are to stand here, with you inside."

"My father won't stand for this. I want to speak to my father. Where is he? Tell me where my father is!"

"Wait for him to come to you, my lady," he replied, more threat than advice.

And with those words lying heavy in her mind, Kiera completed her retreat. She pushed the outer door shut, firmly but quietly, and shoved the bolt across. Then she stood with her forehead resting against the cold, rough metal.

Lille's arms circled her and drew her back to the bedchamber.

"How bad, my lady? How bad?"

"That beast stands for the *queen*, not Father, and he won't let me leave. Queen's orders. Oh, Lille—*she's* against me. I should have listened. I thought only of myself and my prince, but *she's* against him, so she's against me, too. It's not Father at all; it's her . . . She's knows who I am, and what I thought to do. She'll ruin us all however she can; she has to, for her own children's sake. We're all in danger. I've been worried about the king's wizards when I should have been worried about the queen's kin."

Lille sighed and sank onto the bed, bringing Kiera with her. "What's to be done, my lady?"

Kiera freed herself and began to pace. "I don't know. Nothing—maybe. Wait for Father. If he returns—Oh, God'a'mercy, Lille, I didn't like the look in that Black Lightning brute's eyes. The bolt's strong—"

"Renard—"

Kiera made a dismissive, snarling sound. "Queen Ezrae herself stands that horrible man outside my door, Lille. I don't know if my own father can send him away. What good can Renard do? Fall on his knees before the queen? She probably surrounds herself with Black Lightning curs. They'd skewer him."

Those were thoughtless, cruel words, and they terrified Lille. The girl's backbone crumpled and she wailed without dignity. Kiera was ashamed of herself. Past and present, the rocs were home to noble men and women who abused their retainers, but that wasn't how she'd been raised. She was Dainis and, like her parents and her brothers, she was supposed to set an example. Still, this was Chegnon, with layers of royal intrigue and a murderous Black Lightning brute posted outside her door. Kiera hadn't been tempered in so hot a fire, and for a moment, all she could do was stand midway between the bed and the hearth with trembling hands clamped over her ears.

But she *was* Dainis, heart and soul. She wouldn't cower in a borrowed bedchamber, waiting for someone to rescue her. She'd stand tall and comfort her less resolute maidservant.

There had to be a path that would save herself, and her family, *and* take her past the Gray Prince, a path worthy of a woman who dreamed of being Alberon's queen.

"My lady?" Lille whispered. "My lady, what are you thinking with that smile on your face?"

Kiera ignored Lille a moment, then said, "I'll go to the queen myself. I'll bait the bear in her den, where she least expects it. I'll charm her and disarm her by myself!"

"Kiera!"

In Lille's astonishment, Kiera momentarily saw her mother's presence in the Chegnon bedchamber. She stiffened, then relaxed: Lady Irina would understand. Lady Irina would put that common, scarred man in his proper place. Mother would hie herself to whatever chamber the queen called her own and demand an accounting. And, of course, Mother would expect no less from her only daughter.

"I can do it," Kiera announced. "Maybe I won't completely persuade her, but I'll show her I'm not to be trifled with."

"Kiera—my lady—please, reconsider. Wait for your lord father to return. Please, I beg you—"

"No. If my enemy were the king, or merely that man standing outside the door, then I'd wait for Father. But this is women's work. I'll lure that man away with me. I'll persuade him to escort me to the queen's chamber; that shouldn't be difficult. Once we're away, you hie yourself in search of Father or any Dainisman you can find—Renard—and you tell him what's happened and what I've done."

Lille swayed where she sat and sniffled before she spoke.

"You shouldn't, my lady. I shouldn't. We'll find ourselves in a world of trouble."

"*You* won't," Kiera corrected. "I'm responsible and I'm prepared. If anyone asks, you're my varlet, and there it ends."

Lille's apprehension was written on her face and pressed by her hands into her wrinkled skirt, but Lille gave her word, however reluctantly, and she was Dainis, too. Her word meant something, which brought Flennon Houle's image to Kiera's mind.

Had her own word been worth less than Lille's when she'd promised to marry Flen? Kiera decided not. The circumstances were very different. Varlets obeyed their noble patrons; noble daughters obeyed—

This wasn't the time for deep philosophies and musings better suited to priests and other useless folk. Kiera grabbed her cloak from the bedpost. Lille arranged it around her like armor.

"Remember: After I've led that guard away, you find the Dainismen."

Lille stabbed herself fitting the enameled broach through the thick cloth of Kiera's cloak. "Do be careful, my lady, if you won't reconsider."

Kiera shrugged the cloak into comfort around her shoulders. She headed for the bolted door. "You do your part, Lille. Don't worry about me. I'll do mine."

And she did, charming the guard—well, convincing him that he might as well escort her to the queen's chamber, since she didn't intend to remain in her chamber and he *truly* did not want to be responsible for tying a verge-lord's daughter to her chair. The precise words weren't terribly important, nor the sighs and fluttering eyelashes, not so long as he walked beside her and neither of them looked back.

Chegnon was bigger than Roc Dainis and built from mismatched parts. There were walls that were far more roughhewn than any at home, and there were galleries lined with man-high, leaded windows that were a wonder to behold. In the galleries, trees unlike any others Kiera had seen or smelled grew in wheeled pots. They bore fragrant pink blossoms and dark red fruits on the same branch.

She tripped on the hem of her skirt trying to get a closer look at them as she strode along beside her Black Lightning companion. He grinned when he caught her arm and kept her on her feet.

It wasn't a friendly smile, and she watched her feet more carefully until they came to a pair of doors inlaid with substantial iron bars and guarded by more Black Lightning. Kiera noticed, with the glance she shot their way before the doors swung open, that they didn't seem surprised to see her or her companion.

She crossed the threshold alone, into a dazzling chamber of white walls, tall windows, gilt-edged mirrors, and plush carpets that cushioned her feet. The doors shut behind her, sealing her in a chamber that could have emerged from one of Kyle's daydreams. In front of her was another door, set into a wall that had been painted not as a wall but as a balcony overlooking a springtime garden. Beside that door there was another guard—a boy of seven or eight dressed in bright satin with jewels in his hair and a tiny spear at his side. A double score of candles shone in the candelabra above her head, though it was brighter than that because of the clear crystals that hung with the candles.

Countless midwinter rainbows formed patterns on the walls, the carpet, and even on her. Kiera shook her cloak, to see if the many-colored splotches would fall to the carpet, or if the colors would cling to her. They did neither, but moved magically across the brocade of her mother's best dress. A bit unnerved, and not quite so certain of herself, Kiera scooted backward, away from the little rainbows, until she felt the doors at her back and heard the boy guard giggle.

Kiera Dainis would not be shamed by a child half her age, and she gave him a scowl that silenced him. He smiled shyly and pointed his spear at the candlelit crystals before opening his door.

There were more wonders in the inner chamber: bright things, glittery things, and colorful things, but mostly there were women's faces that all turned toward her.

"So, *you're* Lord Dainis' only daughter, Kiera," the least bright, glittery, and colorful woman said from the cushioned depths of a daybed.

A long moment passed before Kiera realized that the woman was not unconscionably rude; she was Alberon's queen. Kiera gasped unwittingly and laughter rippled around her. The more polite women hid their faces behind their hands or jeweled feather fans; the rest mocked her openly.

Kiera knew the proper way to address royalty and how to curtsey with deference and grace, but the knowledge fled, burned away by a furious blush that started deep within her old-fashioned dress and quickly stretched to her scalp. Embarrassment had slid toward humiliation before Queen Ezrae extended a pale, delicate hand.

"Come. Sit beside me, child. Tell my why you left your chambers."

Child. The final and completely truthful humiliation was delivered by a woman a mere handful of years older than Kiera was herself. She did feel like a child—a child wearing her mother's clothes—once she'd shed her cloak. After rearranging the queen's silk-and-velvet gown so it would cover a part of hers, she sat down on the ruby-colored cushions.

"Your Royal Highness, my most gracious and great queen." Kiera used the most formal honorific she knew: No one would accuse *her* of childish ignorance. "I seek to learn what happened in the dragon chamber this morning when my brother stood before His Royal Highness, the king, your worthy and glorious husband. I'm very concerned about him—my brother, I mean. And I wanted to find my father—"

Queen Ezrae smiled. The queen had a dazzling smile despite her pallor. "Spare me my titles, child. They're my armor when I walk alone through Chegnon's chambers, but here—thank the Hidden God—I am myself only and 'my lady' to you. I can tell you truly that nothing worth the retelling happened in the dragon chamber this morning; nothing, I'm sure, that you don't already know. Your brother is haunted, by a wizard—so say the wizards—but, in truth, by a demon who threatens his soul and more. The wizards huffed and beat their chests. They have their place; my lord husband gives them a long rope. They questioned your brother and his demon, but nothing was done. They will prepare their case; my cherished uncle will present God's, and in three days all will be decided.

"It was, of course, necessary to question your kin and the Dainismen. The influence your brother bears in his soul cannot be allowed to spread. But no harm will come to anyone. I was sure you knew, else I would have sent word with Geregonal. I know how cruel it can be when you're locked in your chambers while the world whirls on around you. Now that we are friends, my uncle can question you here."

In her head, Kiera wanted to disbelieve Alberon's most influential woman: The queen's smile was too dazzling to be completely trustworthy. And no one in her right mind would send a brute like Geregonal—if that was the Black Lightning veteran's name—with a message meant to reassure a stranger.

In her heart, though, Kiera was beguiled. She basked in the warmth of kindness and the first true sympathy she'd received since that horrible solstice night in the lodge.

She recalled that all the unpleasant tales she'd heard about Queen Ezrae had been told by men, even the best of whom—her father and brothers—were poor judges of a woman's character. Why, they thought she was flighty when she was merely scrambling to stay one step ahead of their blundering. And they thought Queen Ezrae was scheming and malicious when—it was suddenly quite clear to Kiera—the queen was only another woman living in the maze of men's rules.

When you didn't have the full rights of a free man, or a mighty fist to smash through walls, you made your way through the cracks as best you could.

Kiera was good at such woman's work, allowing for her age and for growing up in tucked-away Roc Dainis. Queen Ezrae—

"Are you well, child?"

Kiera's head snapped up and her eyes met the queen's. "No." The queen's weary eyes widened. "No, I'm not." She tried again, but sank further into misunderstanding as the nearest of the queen's maids succumbed to tittering. "That is, I am well; I'm not unwell, my lady. Forgive me, my lady." At least she'd remembered how the queen wanted to be addressed.

"Forgive you for what, child?" Queen Ezrae asked, then laughed herself and dismissed her own question with a wave of her fingers. "Never mind. It's been a long, dull afternoon for all of us, hasn't it? But you've come and we can get to know each other, can't we? My lord's court is a whirling place. I don't have many opportunities to talk to someone I don't already know, especially a verge-lord's daughter. It's very different, isn't it, in the countryside? Strangers come seeking your father's hospitality: peddlers with goods to trade, minstrels with the latest ballads, and rumors?"

"No, my lady," Kiera admitted. "It's all very quiet in the

Renzi Valley. Nothing happens. Lord Dainis likes it that way. He took some verger fosterlings when my older brothers were fostered, but no longer. He'd be happy if the world began and ended with Renzi. And Muredoch's the same way. They'll *have* to take verger fosterlings when my nephew turns six, but that's four years—"

"A lifetime when you're, what . . . ?"

"Seventeen, my lady." And betrothed. She wouldn't be at Roc Dainis when little Pancel turned six, but Kiera perceived no need to mention that.

"Of course. You and your brother are twins." The queen gestured and someone began playing a lute. "I've always wondered what it would be like to have brothers and sisters. I have no one, you know, except for my cherished uncle. Growing up, I was the moon to his sun. Still, it would have been more exciting with brothers."

"Mostly they're not around, my lady, and you've got a hall full of fosterlings instead."

"But a twin!"

Kiera's thoughts drifted sideways, to Kyle, who'd sent her letters sealed with great blobs of red wax, as if she were someone important. He'd brought her little treasures from the rocs where he fostered: a pink seashell from Roc Albra, a bicolored feather, and three cloudy glass beads he'd found in the midden of a mysteriously abandoned hall in the forests above Roc Neharet. Nothing valuable—they had no money in their own right—but valued things, all the same.

"Kyle's not like my other brothers," she agreed. "That's why I worry about him."

"And where would any man be if a woman didn't worry about him? My lord husband's the king of Alberon, and he can't decide which bolt of cloth to cut for our yet-to-be-born son's nameday."

Queen Ezrae snapped her fingers and two women scurried close, each with a bolt of gold-figured cloth, one dyed brilliant crimson, the other midnight blue. Kiera marveled at the cloth, and at the queen's calm confidence that she would whelp another prince. Mostly, though, she marveled at the cloth. She reached out to touch the gold threads of the blue cloth when her curiosity became unbearable.

"The blue then? Well, yes—it's one of the Dainis colors,

isn't it? But the court wore midnight the last time. I thought the red. I like bright colors, don't you?"

Kiera nodded and stroked the sleek cloth.

"The red, I've decided, and this midnight for you, child. It suits you. A blind man will smile when you wear it as you walk past." Queen Ezrae tightened a cold hand around Kiera's wrist. "Have your adventures while you can," she said softly, urgently. "That's why you came to Chegnon, isn't it? Turn a few heads before your father marries you into some other man's keeping? Seize your thrills and adventures, child. You'll be worn out and toothless all too soon."

Thoughtlessly, even rudely, Kiera looked at the queen. It was true: Nothing stole a woman's beauty more thoroughly than whelping a child every year. Better to wait a spell in between, Mother said, implying that she and Father had done precisely that. But Muredoch had been born sturdy and their father wasn't a king with a throne weighing on his lineage.

Ezrae—just Ezrae for a moment, without titles or honorifics, brocades or jewelry, or a swarm of doting women around her. Ezrae Baldescare, who'd been Kiera's age when she met King Otanazar, still had a shapely jaw, but her cheeks were sinking. There were lines on her face and spidery red streaks in the whites of her eyes: the lasting scars of a difficult birthing, or so the Roc Dainis women said.

Their eyes met between two heartbeats, long enough for Kiera to be ashamed of what she'd thought. She lowered her head and tried, unsuccessfully, to withdraw her hand.

"Why *did* you come to Chegnon?" the queen asked without warning. "I've heard the tale of Rapture shared with your twin, and how you went together to the Spure for the solstice, and what happened there: He got the haunting—not that I'd want a demon myself, child, but did it seem unfair? Why did your father let you come to Chegnon, only to shut you away once you were here? Did you even know that my lord husband's summons to council this morning included your name?"

Kiera hadn't known, and knowing cut like a knife. She sat still, not daring to speak or move. Queen Ezrae's question was *her* question, which she didn't know if Father would deign to answer, if she found the courage to ask him.

"You can tell me, child. What do you want from damp, dreary, winter-bound Chegnon?"

The question hurt so much that Kiera blurted out the answer—"I wanted to meet the prince"—before she could stop herself. Then she tucked her chin against her breastbone and wished she could run away.

"Nyan?"

That was the name of the queen's eldest son. Surely Queen Ezrae was mocking her, because, surely, the queen knew she wasn't interested in a little boy. She wanted to hide her shame, but she was Dainis, and she had to face it instead. "No, my lady," she admitted softly.

"You mean Gravais? Oh, not Gravais!" the queen laughed again and all her women did the same. "Whatever for, child? Do you want to sleep in *his* bed?"

"No," Kiera insisted, vigorously denying what had lurked in her thoughts since the day she understood that a woman's fate was marriage. "I'm betrothed already, my lady. He's a very good young man. Our lands complement each other. It will be a good match."

"A good match for lands and fathers, perhaps, but what about you, child? Is your swain a better man than my worthless stepson? Does he scheme with his boon-friend, whenever they haven't drunk themselves into a stupor, or whored themselves to the same state? It's a wonder he hasn't been found lying naked in a ditch. God's pockets, child—my own lord husband worries about his heir night and day. But it's Gray's women who suffer most. He's a boar, child. My maids live in terror that he or that uncouth bastard boon-friend of his will fall upon them as they pass through the corridors. I've gone high and low finding husbands for the women they've ruined. Pray God, I don't have to rescue you."

Shock compounded Kiera's shame. She'd never imagined that the prince was anything but a paragon of noble virtue—but she'd been wrong about the queen. Her barely faded blush surged anew, to the amusement of all around her, all save the queen.

"More's the pity, child. Understand that you're not the first. Pray God, I'm wrong, but I doubt you'll be the last. But he won't ruin you, will he? Let him lunge for your skirts, if he dares. You're too clever to get caught, aren't you?"

"Yes, my lady," Kiera agreed, gasping slightly as the queen's grip tightened around her wrist.

"Oh, then—we'll have a fine lark, Kiera. I promise you a fine and wondrous lark, you'll see. We'll keep your father and brothers here at court long enough to turn this midnight cloth into the finest gown you'll ever see. I'll give a festival. It's so dull here in winter; everyone will attend, even Gravais. He'll make a fool of himself; he always does, but he'll be the least of the swains I'll invite for you."

"My lady . . . ," Kiera stammered, thrilled by the thought, but frightened, too. "My gracious and great queen . . . My father . . . I am betrothed. Promised."

"And so was I, once for every finger, but my cherished uncle knew love *and* good fortune when he saw it. He didn't interfere, and neither will Lord Dainis. I promise you that, too."

"I don't know."

"Don't be a goose, Kiera. Of course you know. You're fairly tingling with delight; I can see it in your eyes. You're beautiful in a fresh, valley way, and you know it. You can do better than whatever gawking lad your father's settled on you. You can do better than our prince. Alberon's fortunes are rising, child—thanks to my lord husband and the wars throughout Prayse. Chegnon fairly seethes with exiled princelings and rich merchants. A dower claim on an Alberon valley would put a sparkle in many a man's eye." Queen Ezrae leaned forward until Kiera could feel the other woman's breath against her ears. "You can do better than I did, child: You can have all this without a lout for a stepson, without a pack of verger wolves slandering you, your family—everything you cherish. You can be *happy*, Kiera Dainis. Truly happy."

"Happy," Kiera repeated, considering the cloth spread across her lap, the bright chamber with its tall windows and white plaster walls, so different from any chamber in black-walled Roc Dainis. Life with Flennon Houle in Lanbellis Valley would be little different from the life she had already known. But would it be happy? Was Queen Ezrae's life happy? She seemed to say that it wasn't. Was happiness more important than family?

Kiera pushed the cloth away.

"I should return to my chamber, my lady. I've learned what I sought to know: My brother is well—"

"Don't leave me, Kiera."

The queen refused to let go, leaving Kiera in a quandary. She knew fosterling tricks that would set her free, but she dared not use them, not with royalty, not with someone who, when Kiera met her eye-to-eye, seemed on the verge of tears.

"My family . . . My father, Lord Dainis. He'll come looking for me."

"If he looks for you, child, he'll have no trouble finding you. Geregonal has returned to his post; he'll tell him where you are and that your virtue's safe with me. Stay, Kiera. We hardly know each other. There's so much to talk about. So much to tell you, to show you. Don't you *want* to stay here with me? Did I mock you too harshly when I spoke of Gravais? I didn't mean to. Gray *could* be all that his father prays for in an heir. He's handsome and he can be charming. He needs a woman's guidance to settle him, but he's not inclined to listen to me. Not at all. Do you believe he would listen to you?"

There had to be mockery beneath the queen's question; there would have been if those words had been Kiera's own. But Queen Ezrae let her go.

"You do believe that. You do, indeed," the queen said as she sat back against her pillows.

Kiera sat tall. She stared out the windows at an ominous winter sky, neither lying nor admitting what she held to be the truth. She felt the queen measure her, as Father measured the yearling colts, determining which to keep, which to geld, which to sell.

"You haven't met him yet, child, and your mind's made up. You remind me of me, Kiera Dainis. I wouldn't listen either. I'll deal you the kindness no one dealt to me: I won't turn away from you. If you want that unwholesome lout—if you think you can make a man of him—I'll loan you the clothes and jewels you'll need for the task. And when he hurts you—if he ruins you—I'll still be here. We will be friends, no matter what."

Slowly Kiera relaxed and faced the queen again. Against all odds, she'd won the queen to her cause and won a powerful friend in the bargain. There was simply no other way to interpret the expression on the other woman's face.

"You'll stay, won't you, child?"

Kiera smiled graciously, as befitted a victor, and stayed in the queen's chamber.

Kiera sat on the daybed beside the queen, listening to the lutenist, surrounded by the queen's ladies, most of whom were serving a social fosterage of the sort that had never been discussed at Roc Dainis—though, in another queen's time, it must have provided the opportunity Mother needed to meet Father. Kiera admired the queen's vast wardrobe and selected two gowns from the many Queen Ezrae swore were just the right cut and color to catch the prince's eye at supper. She accepted a goblet of mulled wine—it would have been rude to refuse a friend's hospitality—and another when the first was gone. There might have been a third; she lost count amid the bright colors and gaiety.

The boy guard with his half-sized spear came in to light the candles.

"I must be going," Kiera announced.

The floor wobbled beneath her feet when she stood. The walls spun when she took a step, and she needed to brace her leg against the daybed to keep from falling. Father would be furious, she thought. He was miserly with the household wine and didn't approve of drunkenness. *Look at your uncle*, he'd say to the boys. *Do you want to spend your life like him?*

Kiera thought of herself with Uncle's bright red nose and bleary eyes. The image was very droll. She tottered, giggling uncontrollably. Mirth was contagious, striking the ladies one by one, until even the queen's face was tear-streaked and she pressed her hands over her swollen belly. Kiera lost her balance completely, collapsing on the carpet in an unhurt tangle of her own and borrowed clothes. The ladies laughed that much harder, and Kiera laughed with them.

She heard a crash in the outer room. Probably the boy dropping his spear. That was good for another moment of merriment. Then she heard a voice:

"Where is my daughter?"

Father, loud and angry.

"Kiera? Kiera Dainis, where are you? Show yourself, if you can!"

Father, as loud and angry as he'd been with the priests after Kyle's exorcism.

Kiera had barely regained her feet when the door slammed

open, raining dust from the white plaster and admitting a familiar man with a wild, unfamiliar look on his face.

"Your Royal Highness, please forgive the intrusion," he said with the barest lowering of his head before he advanced toward Kiera. "What of your oaths, daughter? Your promises to do as you were bound? I've a mind to have you whipped! Ask your leave of the queen."

The borrowed gowns slipped through Kiera's hands. She glanced from Father's snarl to the queen, whose face also belonged to a stranger, implacably cold and hard. Disaster threatened from both directions, and though she knew the words that would soothe each of them, she didn't know any that would calm them both at the same time.

"Now!" Father shouted.

"My gracious queen," Kiera said quickly as she sidestepped; no need to aggravate Father further by taking the liberty the queen had given her. "Please give me your leave to depart?"

"Stay," Queen Ezrae countered, swinging her legs over the edge of her daybed without a trace of her earlier weariness. She was shorter than Kiera, with a child's fist and a dragon's blazing eyes. "Lower your hand, Dainis. These are *my* chambers and you'll strike no woman here, not even one of your own!"

Kiera watched with growing horror as her father, shorn of his title, hesitated then lowered his hand. She'd rather have been beaten bloody than see such an air of impotent rage surround him.

"Lady Kiera's become my fast-friend," the queen continued, pointedly giving Kiera the title she'd withheld from her father. "I will not see her harmed for it. I've given her the gowns that befit a beautiful maiden and I expect to see her wearing one with a smile when my lord husband's supper is served this evening. Is that understood?"

Father's lips were as pale as his teeth, which showed when he said, "Yes, Your Royal Highness. Perfectly."

"Then, I give you leave, both of you. Make yourself beautiful, Kiera, and tell me if your father does not keep his word."

Father strode toward the door. "Daughter—"

Kiera scooped up the gowns and without another glance at the queen, or anyone else, or a trace of her earlier wine giddiness, raced ahead of him.

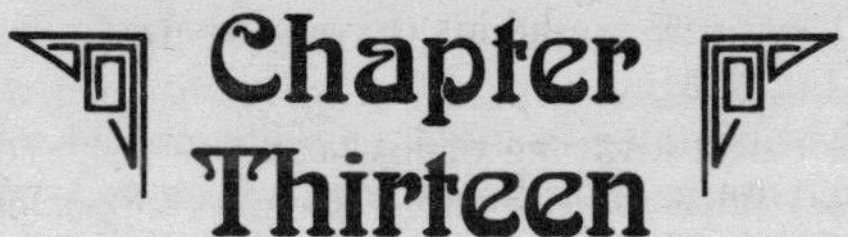

Chapter Thirteen

Kyle had noticed the windswept balcony above the Dainis quarters when he was escorted across the Chegnon bailey after his first grueling encounter with Ferra Baldescare. A meeting that had been mostly the priest telling him that he was damned if he wouldn't damn his demon to hell, and him tempted to agree. Finding the inside path to the promise of solitude he'd spotted had been no great challenge: a loose panel in the antechamber, a rubbish-choked passage, and a door whose hinges had long since gone to rust.

The balcony wasn't like his Roc Dainis bolt-holes: Everyone knew where he was. Josaf had even ordered Enobred and Renard to do the hard work of clearing the passage and rehanging the door the next day while the king's wizards scrutinized him.

After that, whenever his guards brought him back after a session with either the wizards or Baldescare, Kyle had beat a retreat to the balcony without questions. His family seemed to understand that he needed solitude. King Otanazar's chosen interrogators hadn't laid a hand on him—the prince's assurance, confirmed by the king's command, held—but they beat him all the same with inquiries and accusations that left him numb. Then they'd summon Taslim, with wizardry or ritual, and it would begin again.

But that was over now. He'd faced his last interrogator. Tomorrow morning they'd reassemble in the dragon chamber, and his fate—Taslim's fate—would be resolved for once and all.

Kyle gripped the weathered stone of the balcony rail and,

with his head sagging, let the raw wind knife up his sleeves, down his back: true sensations to counterbalance the formless despair of his thoughts.

From the beginning in the dragon chamber, Kyle had answered every question as honestly as he could. A tale spinner knew when to tell the truth and when to tell it simply. He could only hope that honesty had been enough. Tomorrow he'd know.

Death *was* a possibility. Ferra Baldescare had made that very clear. Lord Marrek Brun, who was a bit friendlier, a hair more compassionate, had denied it at first. But not today, not when Kyle had asked his own questions. The wizard had set aside his glowing talisman and admitted that if the Ultramontaine arguments prevailed, King Otanazar would have no other choice.

Midway between his seventeenth and eighteenth birthdays, Kyle hadn't given much thought to his own death. If his life held few bright prospects, at least it had promised the usual length. He'd prayed not to become like Uncle Balwin because he'd reasonably expected to achieve Uncle's middling age.

That seemed unlikely now. Through repeated summonings and unsummonings, the wizards, the priests and Kyle himself had become convinced that he and Taslim were inseparable. With his honesty and meek demeanor, Kyle believed he might have convinced his questioners that he was unswervingly loyal to his king and his God, no threat to either of them. Taslim had done no such thing.

The wizard argued with priests and peers alike. He conceded nothing without a battle and left Kyle aching afterward. Kyle had come to admire his companion's tenacity and obscure sense of honor, but Taslim would never agree to abandon the Siege of Shadows, never concede to another wizard, priest, or even to a king the power he expected to find there.

Taslim was a blasphemer and a heretic. He was a threat to Alberon. There was only one sure way to be rid of Taslim of Fawlen, and that was to be rid of Kyle Dainis.

Men of common birth were put to death by hanging, no matter how high or heinous their crime. Noblemen were above common judgment, but they could be cast adrift, or hanged, or torn limb from limb for high crimes against the crown. When a nobleman saw his punishment catching up with him, usually he chose to die by his own hand, by poison or by falling on his sword.

Or by flinging himself from a high place.

His life would be no great loss. Mother and Kiera would weep. Father would be bitter. Muredoch would lose his steward— No, that wasn't fair. Muredoch wasn't self-serving. Of everyone Kyle knew, only Muredoch might miss him.

Muredoch cared for him, cared about him but—knowing there was another presence haunting his thoughts—could even Muredoch *trust* him? After the last few days, Kyle thought he'd learned where to grab the aether to keep himself separate from his haunt, but he'd never truly trust his own judgment again, no matter how long he lived.

Kyle held his worries in check while a weak and dirty-looking sun slipped behind a horizon-hugging bank of clouds. Winter was half-over, with the dreariest part of the season yet to come: heavy snows, sleety rains, and, finally, endless mud and mire before the land turned green again.

He didn't want to die. He wanted to ride Rawne beneath the white-blooming trees.

Alberon's Hidden God had revealed no more about death than He'd revealed about life. Bydian priests sermonized about a judgment of souls: a winnowing of the worthy from the unworthy. They offered a vague promise of eternal peace for lucky, worthy souls. In the valleys, folk believed souls returned according to the lives they'd led.

Maybe, Kyle wondered, it would be better to try again. Maybe Taslim would find a better match. Muredoch had already sired a son. Surely Angrist and Varos would do the same, if not in Alberon, then in the lands where they served with the Gray Wolves; Taslim might do better with a companion who was not Alberonese. Kiera would have children, too.

Better to start everything anew. The bailey cobblestones were only a moment away—

"Easy, Kyle. Don't even think about it."

Kyle's hand choked the rail. So much for his proud notion that he could control Taslim. <<Go away,>> he thought to the dark aether, then added, <<Serras!>> the sinuous, glowing rune shape with which the wizards summoned Taslim and sent him back again. Kyle wasn't a wizard; there was no reason the rune shape would work for him.

Weight fell around his shoulders. Kyle shuddered and turned, not knowing what to expect, and found his brother.

"Time to come down, Kyle. You'll freeze up here. Your lips are turning blue already."

He hadn't considered the possibility of freezing to death. It had virtue. It was in keeping with the way he'd always done things. No one would know if he'd killed himself deliberately or simply forgotten to come in from the cold . . .

Muredoch's arm tightened and jostled him, awakening his awareness of the raw wind. He shivered. Muredoch pulled him close.

"Let it go, Kyle. It's time for supper."

Supper in the king's great hall, the last place Kyle wanted to be. He hadn't kept anything solid on his stomach since his first breakfast at Chegnon. No wonder he couldn't stop shivering. He was hungry, in a starving beast's way.

Kiera would be at the king's supper. Somehow Kiera had fallen under the queen's wing. Father had told him how, but Father had been livid at the time and Kyle remembered his mood better than his words. It had something to do with Black Lightning guards and the queen's jewels; he didn't understand. Whatever, Kiera and Father were openly, loudly, at odds, with his name as their weapon of choice: *Have a care for Kyle's fate. Do something for Kyle before it's too late.*

But it was Muredoch who'd brought his cloak up to the balcony and who draped it around him.

"I'd rather not go to supper," Kyle said, fumbling with the clasp.

Muredoch didn't offer to help, didn't seem to notice the trouble he had steadying his hands—even when he stabbed his thumb hard enough to draw blood. If there were any thought on the other side of dying, he'd miss Muredoch, miss getting to know Muredoch better.

"King Otanazar passes judgment tomorrow morning in the dragon chamber." Kyle got the words out without stumbling over them. "I don't want to spend tonight listening to Father and Kiera bait each other on my account."

"Me, neither," Muredoch agreed. "That's why when Gray invited me to supper in his chambers, I accepted for both of us." He clapped Kyle soundly between the shoulders.

Surprised and stiff, Kyle lurched forward, belly over the rail. A chunk of weathered stone broke away. He grabbed it, instead of the solid stone from which it had broken. Kyle was in no serious danger of toppling to the bailey, but if he had been, Muredoch's sure hold on his neck would have saved him.

"Try to put it out of your mind, Kyle."

Kyle let the broken stone fall. He raked one hand through his hair and left it poised over his face. "I'm frightened," he confessed through his splayed fingers. "What's to become of me? Where will I be this time tomorrow? On a raft at sea?"

With a long sigh, Muredoch hugged him with both arms before saying, in a soft voice, "You'll be banished, we think; to Roc Dainis, we hope, with a guard of priests and wizards together. That's what Gray says. He's talked to the king; we haven't. It won't be worse, Kyle; Gray won't stand for it. If King Otanazar has to choose between Gray and the Bitch, my fortune's on Gray. Baldescare won't push for what he can't get. You'll be isolated and watched—because it's that wizard haunt who nobody trusts and nobody knows how to remove. But you'll be home, with your family around you. I'm still counting on you to be my steward, Kyle."

Kyle lowered his hand. "But what will you do with a cohort of wizards and priests?" He tried to laugh, though his own ears heard only a poor excuse for humor.

"Let them debate each other; that's what they do best. I need you and don't give a damn about them. Now, come on. You're cold, I'm cold, and our supper's getting cold waiting for us.

Kyle let himself be guided toward the door, but not without one last glance at the gloomy twilight and the broken rail. Muredoch's faith—Muredoch's *love*—was the light that kept him walking forward. But if Muredoch's faith were misplaced . . . If, in the unknowable future, Kyle brought dishonor and disgrace—more dishonor, more disgrace—to his family . . . ?

This was the moment to redeem himself with two strides and a leap. He wouldn't survive the fall. The Dainis name would be freed from the damage he might do to it. Taslim would cast another spell. He'd be free—

<<Easy, Hart-lord. That's no answer for either of us. Whatever you think of me, Hart-lord, you're all I've got. Without the power of the Siege, there's nothing in Alberon that can separate us. I'll die with you, Hart-lord.>>

Kyle remembered *serras*, and realized the rune shape had

wrought magic for him, with the dark aether of his mind. <<You've been spying on me. You were listening.>>

<<I can always *hear* you, Hart-lord. Getting you to listen has been my problem. Your brother's right. He's a good man, Hart-lord. Listen to him, if you won't listen to me. Tomorrow might be worse, but it might be better. We'll never know if you give up now.>>

Muredoch tugged and Kyle followed him into the passageway.

Prince Gravais maintained his household in a part of Chegnon that Kyle knew by reputation, not experience. Fosterling names were called to serve the prince, but his had never been among them, even when he'd been fifteen—a veritable verge-lord in the dormitories. At fifteen he'd still been a hart-lord, still taken his customary place at the end of every line. He expected nothing and was never disappointed.

Even now, Kyle wasn't in the prince's chambers on his own account, but Muredoch's. Muredoch would be a verge-lord when the Gray Prince was King Gravais III. It was no great surprise that Muredoch was welcomed here, but some surprise when the lithe, elegant (how long before those gray and russet garments appeared on Taslim?) prince sprang out of his chair to embrace Muredoch with the hearty greeting of close companions. Lockwood, too, the prince's boon-friend, clapped arms around Kyle's brother, calling him Owl-eyes and bidding him to take his own, now-vacant chair.

Kyle took a backward stride to exclude himself before the friendly trio did it for him.

"Your wine, Lord Kyle." A towheaded fosterling of twelve or thirteen offered him a goblet.

"Thank you," he replied, taking it carefully. He was surprised that the youth knew his name, then reminded himself that he'd become notorious since the solstice. Gossip burned hot in the dormitories.

"Will there be anything else, Lord Kyle?"

He shook his head vigorously and wine sloshed out of the goblet, to their mutual embarrassment, which Kyle made worse by blotting the wine with a sleeve, when he knew it was the fosterling's task to fetch a rag.

"What's your name?" Kyle asked when he faced a choice between joining Muredoch and their hosts or staying where he was.

"Henrik Minatare, Lord Kyle." The boy grinned, then added, "I'm a hart-lord, too. I'm bound for the prince's service. I'm serving you tonight. I've never served another hart-lord."

Kyle took a too-large gulp. His throat burned and his eyes threatened to leak. Trying not to cough or sputter, he dismissed Henrik with a nod and edged along the wall until he reached a corner a good arm's length away from anything breakable and eased himself into insignificance on the floor.

Another hart-lord, yet bound for royal service, not ignored or shunted aside. Dainis sons stayed home or joined the Gray Wolves; they weren't courtiers attached to royalty like so many adornments. That's what Father had said to Varos on one of those rare occasions when all four brothers were home together. Kyle couldn't remember what Varos had said or done to merit Father's sarcasm, only that *he'd* accepted the judgment forever, without question.

"Another cup, Lord Kyle?"

He looked from a goblet he didn't remember draining to Henrik's earnest face. He felt foolish tucked into a corner, too foolish to stand up again. "Yes," he said, when he'd planned to say no.

"Watered or burnt, my lord?"

Burnt? No wonder his throat tingled and he felt warm from the inside out. The prince was serving burnwine to his guests. There was burnwine at Roc Dainis. It was a man's drink, a cold winter night's drink. Uncle drank it all the time, Father, too—though nowhere near as much. Mother never touched it and Muredoch hadn't either, at least not when Father was around.

"Watered or burnt, my lord?" Henrik repeated.

"Watered," Kyle answered from habit, then changed his mind. "Burnt." Tomorrow, King Otanazar might sentence him to death. Tonight he should be old enough to drink burnwine.

Henrik returned with the refilled goblet and a platter heaped with more food than Kyle had eaten since he arrived at Chegnon.

"There's more, if you want it, Lord Kyle," the boy explained, clearly misinterpreting Kyle's astonishment.

"This will be more than enough, I'm sure."

But Kyle found his long-lost appetite in the corner of Prince Gravais' chamber. The meat was cold, but tender and delicately spiced. The bread was still warm within its thick, chewy crust. Morsel by morsel, Kyle ate his way across the platter. Henrik quickly offered to fetch more of whatever he fancied, but Kyle decided not to press his luck. With the goblet standing nearby and a bread crust balanced in his lap, Kyle leaned back and listened to the prince tell tales about the Baldescare.

Ten years ago, no one outside of Bercelen had heard of the Baldescare uncle and niece. They were minor vassals of Lord Drallin, who was, himself, a minor verge-lord—like Father, if the truth were told. Then suddenly they were everywhere: at the height of the Ultramontaine hierarchy, at the king's court, and in the king's bed. In the kitchens, where Kyle had heard more rumors than he'd ever passed along to his sister, the cooks and their helpers called Ferra Ilsassan Baldescare a common panderer who'd traded his beautiful niece for influence, as if that—and that alone—explained the Baldescare rise.

From where he sat, Kyle could understand why the prince and the Baldescare were engaged in a barely submerged war for King Otanazar's ear. It was much harder to understand why the Baldescare were out to destroy the Dainis: Ferra Baldescare had all but promised Kyle that the Ultramontaines would recommend execution. The queen had suborned Kiera; Kyle could only dread what *that* would lead to. And together the queen and her uncle had made Father look foolish before the king, which hurt most of all.

But why?

The Dainis didn't threaten the Baldescare's cozy alliance with King Otanazar. Even Taslim and the Siege of Shadows shouldn't threaten an Ultramontaine priest—not if that priest truly believed Taslim lied. Which, in turn, most likely meant that the priest was lying a bit himself.

And then, from the depths of a burnwine haze, Kyle noticed the map of Alberon that Prince Gravais had hung above the hearth. There was Sandrisan in the northeast, Ulver in the south, and Bercelen in the northwest. Bercelen that hid in the shadow of the Eigela. Bercelen that had grown wealthy during the Debacle, and where a minor vassal might well have been counting down the last years of the millennium until the Harbinger brought another round of rich pilgrims to Alberon's shore.

Taslim's Harbinger was seven years early and it had burned

across the sky for a single night. Surely, the Baldescare had hoped for something better.

To listen to Prince Gravais, though, Baldescare ambition often outran their cleverness. Though the queen and her uncle apparently spent their waking moments in a never-ending succession of plots to bring themselves closer to the throne, the plots were easily foiled. Their poisons smoked and stank. Their assassins got lost, or tripped at the last moment and gutted themselves. And the scandalous rumors they attempted to spread about the prince were too outrageous for anyone to believe.

"If they weren't so damned determined to disgrace me, they could do better at it," the prince concluded with a wry smile.

Lockwood laughed heartily. Muredoch and the fosterlings followed where the black-haired wizard led, but Kyle sipped his burnwine in silence.

Plots and conspiracies couldn't be amusing until they were safely thwarted. The warmth and safety he'd felt in this corner was a royal illusion. The men who served the Gray Prince lived exciting, even dangerous, lives. It was just as well that they were ennobled men, like Lockwood, or hart-lords, like Henrik.

Like himself?

Briefly Kyle imagined another life. Very briefly. There was no point imagining what could never happen. Muredoch would have released him from his stewardship; that wouldn't have been the problem. But no hard-pressed prince could afford the services of a wizard-haunted man with powerful enemies. But as imagination faded, Kyle recalled those fosterage moments when he might have attracted the notice of the prince as young Henrik had. He'd always hung back, never stepped forward, shouting his own name. He'd made himself seem smaller than he was, less significant than even a hart-lord needed to seem.

Twirling a once-again empty goblet between his palms, Kyle stared at the hearth flames until his eyes began to water.

<<Is it you, Taslim? Are you making me see things differently now?>>

The wizard stirred. *Serras* still held him out of his dark exile; his face flickered in the fire. <<How could I make anything different, Hart-lord? I've been away a thousand years. I assure you, this is all new to me. *All* different, if you please.>>

<<That's not what I meant. I've never *thought* about myself

before—about what I didn't do, instead of what I did. Are you pushing me . . . again?>>

In the hearth, a log split apart with a geyser of flame and a shower of sparks. Taslim claimed the priests had stripped him of his power during the exorcism. His talisman was dark, he said; he had no magic left—except coincidence. Kyle jerked his feet back and wrapped his arms around his knees.

<<Blame me for everything, will you?>> Taslim complained. <<May I remind you, Hart-lord: We've been badgered by wizards and priests these last three days. Alberon's illustrious, but lazy and perniciously amused, king holds our lives in his hands. Your father and sister need dosing with their own medicines. And *I'm* pushing you? *I'm* making you see things differently? *I* beg to differ, Hart-lord.>>

<<Something's changed. Suddenly nothing fits together the way it did before. I think of you when that happens.>>

<<Think of yourself—now that *would* be different,>> the wizard said lightly, then repeated himself, slow and sober. <<Think of yourself. The king, the wizards and priests, your family, they've pushed until you changed. You don't believe them anymore. You aren't the first to believe the worst about yourself.>>

Kyle bristled and, as he'd done on solstice night, assaulted the wizard with his most inglorious blunders, adding in his newfound recollections of the opportunities he'd let slip by. His breath caught in his throat. He fought tears that owed nothing to the heat or smoke.

<<Regrets, Hart-lord, not failures or blunders. You can't fail until you try, and you can't regret until you've imagined something better.>>

Closing his eyes and fists, Kyle envisioned *serras*, the glimmering rune shape of summoning. Then he quenched it. The truth hurt—God, it hurt—but truth was no reason to send Taslim back to darkness. He could endure regret, if that's what the hurt was, and his haunt's mockery together.

Yet the laughter Kyle heard in his mind and in the chamber around him was without barbs or slights. It was the eruption of good humor he'd seen often enough around the dormitories but never shared, never quite understood. It was the sound of friendships he'd never tried to make, and riding that wind of realization, there came another twinge of regret.

More gentle laughter followed. <<A little more burnwine,

Hart-lord, and you might think your life was worth living. Imagine what else you'd miss if you'd jumped off that balcony.>>

It was the burnwine. It had to be the burnwine. Kyle had drunk himself dizzy on watered wine more times than he hoped anyone else knew, and it had never been like this. The ordeals of the last few days had been banished by warmth and contentment. The colors and textures of the prince's chamber were so bright, so sharp, that they seemed alive. Every word of every conversation—the prince telling his stories, the fosterlings whispering by the sideboard—rang in his ears.

Kyle's fingers, almost in another world at the end of his arms, moved with wills of their own, overshooting the goblet, which was full again, for the fourth—or was it the fifth?—time. The stemmed glass tottered against his thigh, soaking his dark trousers with cool, but thankfully unnoticeable, moisture. Lunging with more luck than skill, Kyle caught the goblet before it broke on the floor.

Mortified by his clumsiness, he straightened his back against the wall and, concentrating hard, raised the goblet to his lips. Two fiery swallows later, he set an empty goblet between himself and the wall, where Henrik couldn't see it. Then he waited for the chamber to stop spinning.

"Never did get them back." Muredoch leaned back, laughing mightily. His goblet listed between two fingers of his off-weapon hand.

"But did you try, Owl-eyes, did you try?" the prince challenged, equally cheerful.

Watching them, Kyle wondered why he felt embarrassed. He'd always known Muredoch's eke-name, though he didn't consider using it himself. However much burnwine his brother had drunk, what was left stayed inside his tilted goblet. The prince's fingers were steady as a sword when he pointed them between Muredoch's eyes.

"Every night, Gray—while the moon was full. That wench and her night-sisters led me on a merry chase." A musing smile formed on Muredoch's—Owl-eyes'—face as he stared at something only he remembered. "Goddamn, she had teeth like a wolf, and wasn't afraid to use them on a man's bare skin."

"Has your lady wife noticed the scars? Or does she think they're hers?" Bastard-born Lockwood had no awe of his noble companions, and made them laugh with his sly remarks.

Kyle stared fixedly at the hearth.

He'd never imagined that a member of his own family, and upright, respectable—*stuffy*—verge-lord-to-be Muredoch at that, frequented Alberon's brothels, where the night-sisters plied their ancient trade. Then again, he'd never imagined Muredoch giddy on wine, or heard him swear. Such things simply weren't done at Roc Dainis.

Or was it simply that he'd never dared do them?

His own trysts had been furtive encounters beneath stairways and other not-quite-private places. They'd been rare enough by fosterling standards, but far too frequent for a hart-lord son of his family.

Or so he'd thought.

"Doesn't run very deep in the Dainis blood, does it?" Lockwood asked in his dry, deep voice.

Kyle knew they were talking about him, staring at him while he stared at the fire. He willed himself not to move and, especially, not to blush.

"Oh, I wouldn't say that," the prince said slowly. "Your sister's got fire; I'll wager she's got teeth, too. She shows them every time she smiles at me. No wonder you've kept her locked away, Owl-eyes."

"She's betrothed, my prince." That from Muredoch, who no longer sounded giddy.

"Betrothals mean nothing, my friend. Ask the queen, if you don't believe me. Your sister has."

"Princes marry outside," Muredoch countered, meaning Alberon's queens were frequently foreign princesses.

"Not always," the prince said softly. "My mother was Neharet."

"Damn your eyes, Gray! There's a difference! Turn your fool head another way. She knows nothing of court life—"

"She's learning fast."

"She's become the Bitch's pawn, and you damn well know it."

"She's turned heads everywhere she's walked. She's beautiful and on the prowl like a cat in heat, and you damn well know that."

"Touch her, Gray, and I swear you'll never touch another. She's a child."

That was Kiera his brother and the prince were talking about, and treason, too. Kyle held his breath.

"She's playing with fire, Owl-eyes. Her fingers are going to get burnt."

"Leave her alone!"

"I will, Owl-eyes. I have all along, though she does tempt me. Take her home, my friend. Marry her off, *pray* she forgets what the Bitch's taught her."

The air in the chamber was thick enough to chew. Kyle slid his hand down his leg to his boot, where he sheathed his knife when he wore court clothes.

"No need to squabble." Lockwood broke the heavy silence. "Another day, another night, and the Dainis, one and all, will be on their boat headed for Renzi. We've one night. Why spoil it?"

"Why, indeed?" Prince Gravais shrugged off the tension and leaned forward, extending his hand toward Muredoch—

Who hesitated before clasping it.

A pair of fosterlings rushed forward to fill their goblets for a toast of friendship rescued and restored. Kyle let his breath out with a sigh and wished his own goblet wasn't empty. He couldn't take his eyes away from his brother and the prince, still flushed with fading anger, as they linked arms and drank.

How, he wondered, could they remain friends? How could they forgive or trust again, when they'd threatened each other with death and ruin?

How did any friendship survive the imperfections of its friends?

Kyle half-expected to hear Taslim then, but his wizard was silent. It was the prince's wizard who had him under scrutiny.

Lockwood had been observing Kyle Dainis since the young man arrived, some two steps behind his brother, and made his wall-wise scramble for the chamber's most secluded corner. The hart-lord hadn't joined their conversation, hadn't spoken at all, except to the fosterling who brought his food and kept his goblet full—too full, judging by the youth's high color and the deliberateness of his movements.

Muredoch had ignored his brother, and that after insisting that Kyle be included in this private supper among friends. That slight could have been no more than fraternal habit; the casual cruelties practiced by family against family was something no orphan could understand. But Owl-eyes might not be slighting his youngest brother at all. Kyle gave off shyness like fires gave off heat, and he'd borne the brunt of royal, religious, and wizardly suspicion for three long days. Having known and liked Muredoch Dainis for the better part of two decades, Lockwood assumed that whatever habits Owl-eyes had, they were compassionate.

Then, with one ear cocked for his friends' conversation, Lockwood asked himself if Gray had noticed Kyle at all and decided that he probably had. Gray was an observant man beneath his easygoing, center-of-everything demeanor, and compassionate. He was expert at sifting through the fosterlings to forge the practical alliances on which he'd rely when he became king. He'd done it with Owl-eyes and he'd done it with Lockwood himself, who'd done his fair share of crouching in corners when he first came to court.

Still, the Dainis hart-lord was the least conspicuous man Lockwood had seen. According to what he'd been able to learn in the last few days, Kyle had been that way all his life. His name appeared on the roster; he'd served the court three separate times during his fosterage. Each time the majordomos had noted that Kyle Dainis was absentminded, a bit clumsy, occasionally deceitful, and accident prone, but not one of them remembered the boy when Lockwood made inquiries.

That had changed, of course. Half of Alberon already knew that the youngest son of Nustrum, Lord Dainis, was haunted by a millennial wizard. The other half would learn after the spring thaw, when men and rumors traveled more freely. Nothing could be more unpleasant for a shadows-loving youth than the knowledge that all Alberon was talking about him. It wasn't the end of the world; Lockwood himself had survived the scrutiny, the embarrassment.

These days he joked with his friend the prince and other high-born men and hid his secrets so well that he almost forgot he had them—until he'd seen Kyle staring at the fire with his head cocked to one side.

Taslim of Fawlen: ancient, crotchety, arrogant, and giving advice—no doubt—to the hart-lord.

It was very interesting to watch. Since the Renzi Bydians had exorcised Taslim from nasen'bei, consigning him to hell's antechambers, the wizards swore that there could be only one mind or the other inside that honey-haired skull. Without another wizard or priest's aid, Kyle Dainis supposedly lacked the wit and skill to perform a simple summoning; Taslim of Fawlen swore *he* lacked the power. That was what Lord Marrek had told Lockwood, but what Lockwood saw with his own eyes made more sense.

Notwithstanding the roster notes, the prejudice of a magister wizard, or the Bydian-wrought constraints on Taslim of Fawlen, Kyle Dainis was as clever as he was lonely. It took a solid measure of cleverness to be as insignificant as the hart-lord managed to be in an intimate chamber. Cleverness and loneliness had been enough once before.

In Lockwood's experience, strange things got drawn to nasen'bei. Not noisy things claiming to be ancient wizards, but catlike things with aqua eyes, impossibly soft fur, and a glowing purr that had made one clever, lonely boy's cloistered world seem safer than it truly was.

And still did. The catlike haunt he named Havoc was never far from the center of Lockwood's thoughts, never shy when he needed a talisman for doubts, instead of lightning.

Wizards didn't draw attention to their nasen'bei companions, but a haunted wizard usually recognized his peers. Priests called such hauntings demons and would have mounted an inquisition against every wizard in Alberon, if there weren't a few miscast priests with demons of their own.

Lord Marrek Brun had a haunt. Lockwood had gotten a glimpse of the magister's dark, shambling bearlike haunt the very first time he cast a firelight spell in the bedchamber he'd shared with Gray. The next day Lord Marrek, as ominous as his haunt, had cornered Lockwood on his way to the practice ground. After that, Lord Marrek was his mentor. At the rate he was mastering his craft, he'd be a magister by the time he was forty, a decade earlier than Marrek himself.

But unless Kyle Dainis had hidden his talent the way he hid everything else, his ability to use the runes was inexplicable. The door to nasen'bei didn't swing open by accident, and without the wind that blew across that threshold, magic did not happen. If Kyle Dainis had harnessed magic without attracting anyone's attention, then he was what Ilsassan Baldescare claimed he was: an unconstrained wizard with the power to lure the faithful off the Hidden God's difficult path to righteousness.

Gray had taken a risk when he interceded on the hart-lord's

behalf. Tomorrow, Ferra Baldescare would have the support of his priestly peers and the secular members of the council when he demanded that Kyle Dainis be paraded and then executed. Gray had spent a year's worth of favors to broker an agreement that would seal the Dainis—*all* the Dainis, except their daughter—in Renzi for a generation instead.

Muredoch knew the price of his brother's life. He was Gray's friend and an eager participant in the negotiations, but Owl-eyes was no more a courtier than old Nustrum. He'd taken with a quiet grace that verged on relief, the knowledge that this would be his last face-to-face meeting with royalty. Lockwood could only hope that the rest of the Dainis took it half as well.

Not that Gray and Owl-eyes seemed concerned about anything. They'd gotten themselves deep into a discussion of stallions, brood mares, and the proper proportion of each on a working stud. Horses were an obsession Lockwood didn't share with his boon-friend; he'd cleaned too many stalls before Lady Sabelle plucked him up. He didn't think Alberon needed more horses, especially larger horses.

Gray knew how Lockwood felt and wouldn't mind if he struck up a conversation elsewhere. He tipped his goblet toward the fosterling who'd been serving him. After taking a sip from the refilled goblet, he joined the hart-lord in his hearthside corner, hitting the floor a bit harder, a bit sooner than he'd anticipated.

"Good wine," he began. "Good idea to start on the floor. Can't fall off the floor."

Kyle's head came up only enough to stare past his toes, into the fire. "No, my lord," he answered, as polite and deferential as any fosterling, never mind that they were both so close to the bottom of the cadency that there was no need for titles between them.

Lockwood wanted to say: Cheer up, lad—weather permitting, you'll be on your way home this time tomorrow. But Gray had sworn him and Muredoch to silence. It was possible that Owl-eyes had broken his oath; Gray would understand. Kyle might be acting—if so, he was a damned good actor. The hart-lord's shoulders sagged under burdens no man should have to bear, even for a night.

If Kyle had been a few years younger, Lockwood would have tousled his hair. Men could cling to such shreds of boyhood play within their families or among their friends. Kyle was past seventeen, a grown man by men's reckoning, but no one's friend. Lockwood wouldn't intrude without an explicit invitation.

So the wizard sat back, sipping his burnwine, and watching the same flames the hart-lord watched. An invitation would come, or it would not.

"They're alike," Kyle finally said, when Lockwood was starting to think about the greater comfort of his chair.

Lockwood glanced over his shoulder at Owl-eyes and Gray, still talking about mares and stallions. "They think Alberon's horses are Alberon's soul. It's not a fatal error, merely a boring one."

One corner of the hart-lord's mouth lifted and fell. "I meant the talismans," he corrected, pointing toward the iron-wrapped crystal Lockwood suspended from his belt. "The one you have and the one—" Kyle's hand fell; he swallowed the name that had surely been on his tongue.

Lockwood swallowed hard as well, trying to imagine the haunting presence of Taslim of Fawlen. He was ready to leave when Kyle spoke again.

"They could be twins." He folded his hands into tight fists and stared blankly at the fire. "I've wondered," he whispered—Lockwood had to lean forward to hear him above a burst of sparks as a log crumbled into embers. "Could I, my lord— Might I look at yours?"

It was a rude, not to mention dangerous, request, one which Lockwood would have denied any other time. But considering what wizard magic had already done to this young man, how it would shape his life, will he or nil he, it was an understandable request. Lockwood slipped his talisman off its silken cord.

Interest flickered in the youth's dark eyes. His lips parted and his hand moved as if something pulled them, then stopped just short of the polished runes emerging from the iron bands.

The talisman was the prime tool of Lockwood's chosen trade; he sometimes forgot that it was an object of fascination and beauty as well. Gray had given a year's allowance to his father's favorite jeweler for its construction—no haphazard binding of stone and metal for the prince's boon-friend. The jeweler got the crystal from Lord Marrek and labored another year cutting it apart, grinding, polishing, and finally reassembling it as a hollow honeycomb set about with finely wrought iron. Firelight danced across the surface of the facets. Isolated flecks of captured lightning—it was too early in the year for thunderstorms—sparkled in its heart.

"Still think they look alike?" Lockwood asked, knowing that every talisman was unique and that his, though richly elegant, lacked the shimmering intricacy a magister's talisman would have. An intricacy he assumed Taslim of Fawlen's talisman had.

Kyle's fingers twitched but hadn't yet touched the crystal. "No, my lord. Although . . . Although I haven't seen his so closely, and since he was pushed into darkness, he says his talisman is dark. Those sparks—they are *lightning,* aren't they? Do they . . . ? Can you feel the lightning still?"

Lockwood snorted a laugh and set his goblet well aside. "Go on, touch it." A liberty he'd allowed no one but Gray and, of course, Lord Marrek. He met Kyle's eyes, which were a battlefield of curiosity against dread. "Go on. You won't be satisfied until you do."

The young man shuddered when one fingertip brushed the crystal. His eyes showed white all around the dark irises. Fine hair stood erect on the back of his hand.

"It's alive," he said in awe, as awe had been in Gray's voice when he'd said exactly the same words. But Gray had pulled his hand back; Kyle didn't. Gray didn't have talent; God knew they'd tried to find some, not wanting anything to come between them. And Kyle Dainis?

The lightning motes were migrating toward the hart-lord's fingers.

"It tingles . . . tickles. It's looking at me."

"In a way," Lockwood agreed, absently. There were no words to explain the feel of captured lightning. No words, either, to describe the tantalizing sensations a man felt when his talisman bridged between living flesh—except to say that the untalented weren't supposed to feel them and Lockwood was grateful they weren't alone. Then, without warning, Kyle's hand relaxed. Two fingers touched the crystal, another two rested on Lockwood's palm.

Wizards learned to master talismanic shock the way they mastered lightning; if they didn't, they died, or went mad. Lockwood resisted the urges, the images, as if they weren't happening. Kyle wasn't as skilled. The hart-lord's breath caught in his throat with a gasp. He lurched blindly toward the hearth. Lockwood snagged the youth with his free hand. For an instant, they were both dazed. For an instant, the familiar walls were gone and he clutched the arm of a lean man with long, black hair and a face no older or wiser than his own.

This was Taslim of Fawlen who'd defied God and death with spells that lasted a thousand years?

Lockwood looked down on the talisman between them. The crystals were dark, as Kyle said. The ironwork was pitted and flaked; there were only a few legible runes emerging from it. A millennium was a very long time for iron. Even so, time alone hadn't destroyed Fawlen's talisman, and neither had the Bydians. It simply wasn't—and had never been—a magister's tool.

Lockwood had questions and sought answers in Fawlen's eyes, but the other wizard's image was fading into the sadder, younger face of the Dainis hart-lord.

Another wave of talismanic shock washed over them, but shock alone couldn't be blamed for the tear that slipped down Kyle's cheek or the need Lockwood felt to brush it dry. Lockwood overcame his desire. He wrapped his fist over his talisman, shoving Kyle away, breaking the bond between them.

Kyle scrambled backward until his spine was flat against the wall. Drawing his knees up, he hugged himself tightly. His frozen expression was one of outrage and despair.

"I'm as shocked as you," Lockwood insisted once he'd found his voice. "They told me you don't have the talent. I wouldn't have let you, otherwise." At least, not if he wasn't prepared for the shock.

The young man shook his head rapidly. "I wouldn't . . . I wouldn't've touched it, if . . . Taslim would've warned me."

Lockwood nodded and kept his thoughts about Taslim of Fawlen to himself. "It's nothing to be ashamed of, Kyle." He looped the talisman around his belt again and reached for his goblet.

"Please, my lord—please leave me alone."

It was a pleading Lockwood was bound to respect. He returned to his chair and another goblet of burnwine that soured in his mouth. Nothing Gray or Owl-eyes had to say could hold his interest. He wasn't like them, able to ignore the young man huddled by the hearth, misery etched yet more deeply on his face. No, he was worse; he stole glance after glance, hoping to see the youth unclench his jaw.

"You've got ants," Gray chided when his constant twitching

had begun to wear on everyone's nerves, including his own. "Go for a walk, Locky. Stick your head outside and cool off."

Lockwood took the advice, which was as much of a command as he ever got from his boon-friend. He considered walking the Chegnon walls until his head cleared. He considered going directly to his chamber and bed. In the end, he made his way across Chegnon to the vine-covered tower where Lord Marrek Brun and the other royal wizards made their residence.

His mentor was waiting.

"You're distraught," Marrek said gently. "Sit down. Calm down. Collect yourself before we discuss anything of substance."

The older man pointed to a chair, but Lockwood preferred to pace. "You lied to me, Marrek. You told me Fawlen was the key to this; Fawlen was the power. Taslim of Fawlen couldn't make water in the rain. It's Kyle Dainis, Marrek. He's got something no one's had before, and you're ripping him apart for your own damned curiosity."

"Sit down, son." Marrek was considerably less polite with his second request. "Fawlen *is* the power. He's corrupted the boy—"

Lockwood spun around on his heel. Warrior as well as wizard, he'd spent as many hours in the practice arena as he had with Marrek. "The boy's a man, Marrek. Full-grown, full-blooded. He gave me the shock of my life a little while ago. Not Taslim of Fawlen, Marrek. Mark me well, Taslim of Fawlen's a man my age, maybe my skill, and a talisman as dark as a new-moon night. He haunts Kyle Dainis, but he's no damn magister."

"No, you listen—"

"I *saw* him, Marrek. His hand and mine on the same talisman. He's clever. He's passionate, and maybe he's arrogant—"

"Not like anyone we know, then. Are you certain you didn't see your own reflection, son?"

"Marrek!"

Lockwood advanced without a thought for the consequences. Marrek made a wardsign, a wizardly version of the Hollow Sphere, but more reliable and more effective. The gnarled talisman beside him flared and Lockwood had no alternative but to sit in the other chair, fighting for his next breath.

"Kyle Dainis is no threat to anyone," he insisted, when he could speak again. "Neither is Taslim of Fawlen, I'll wager. If he's been to this Siege of Shadows, he came away with nothing to show for it."

"He came away, son; that's enough. He's no ordinary haunting; you know that." The magister touched his left eye, a tacit admission of nasen'bei secrets. "He survived, and whatever fell from the sky at the solstice is the same thing that kept his spirit intact for a millennium—whether he knows it or not. If he was a novice when he cast his spells, then all the more reason to find out how he managed it. This isn't about the Hidden God, son, or the Siege of Shadows. There's a mighty source of magic in the Eigela, and Taslim of Fawlen's going to lead you to it."

Lockwood bolted upright in his chair. "What? Gray said—"

"The prince doesn't know everything. The king's made his decision. Prince Gravais will lead a cohort into the Eigela as soon as the ground's fit for travel. You're going, too: the prince's boon-friend, my eyes and ears. Just like before: Whatever you find, whatever you learn, you bring back here. We don't want Baldescare and his Ultramontaine flock poking their noses where they don't belong, do we?"

Lockwood slouched unhappily. Everything fit together now, in the complex, nigh onto deceitful way in which royal affairs usually fit together.

"Why the lies, Marrek? Lies to me and Gray. If you wouldn't trust us—trust me—from the start, why now? Why let Kyle Dainis—who's never hurt anybody and needs a mentor more than I ever did—why let him think his life's in jeopardy?"

"If we'd been wrong, he or his haunt would have been flushed out. One thing remains absolutely true, son: Those two are inseparable. You must have seen that. If anything happens to Kyle Dainis, it happens to Taslim of Fawlen, too. One way or the other, they'll protect each other. As for you, we've always trusted you. You won't betray us, son, will you?"

"No," Lockwood admitted. He'd never *betray* Lord Marrek Brun. When the time came—if it ever did—he'd kill his own snakes.

"Don't be so glum about it. You and your boon-friend will return from the Eigela as the heroes of Alberon. The Baldescare will never touch you again. What more can you ask?"

"Kyle Dainis. I can ask: What becomes of Kyle Dainis? What becomes of Taslim of Fawlen?"

"What about them, son? I trust you to do what must be done, whatever it might be."

Lockwood stared at the lantern on the table between them. He owed his mentor as much as he owed his prince—but did he owe anyone Kyle Dainis? More important: Was he ready to abandon the hart-lord to the likes of his own mentor?

"Thank you, my lord," he said flatly. "Your faith will not be misplaced. When the time comes, I'll do what I must."

The corridors and stairwells of Chegnon were quiet as Muredoch escorted Kyle back to the Dainis chambers. Most of the ensconced torches had been quenched at midnight. The only pools of light were around the drowsy guards on duty outside important chambers, including guest chambers. Winter air poured though open arrow-slit windows. The howls of a lonely dog rose from a distant courtyard. Closer at hand, muffled conversations and the sounds of passion leaked through the occasional door as they passed.

Because he was suffering from too much burnwine and too many hours basking in the hearth-fire's heat, everything seemed strange to Kyle. He leaned on his brother more than once as they navigated the tight, spiral stairway that was the final passage of their journey.

The moments when he'd touched Lockwood and his talisman were disordered and fading in his mind. Taslim had retreated into darkness, driven there, Kyle supposed, by either Lockwood's wizardry or his own dignity. What must Taslim think—if Taslim had shared the thoughts, the sensations, when his hand touched Lockwood's? He'd never felt *that* for a woman, let alone a man. Lockwood could say there was nothing to be ashamed of, which could only mean that Lockwood didn't know.

Maybe it would have been better if he'd leapt off the balcony earlier. There'd be no leaping now. It was all Kyle could do to shuffle along, dragging his feet as they started down the last corridor. Maybe he'd stumble, fall, and break his neck—

They stopped short, and Muredoch kept a solid grip on Kyle's shirt. He didn't come close to falling.

"Merciful God," Muredoch said bitterly. "They're still at it."

Kyle listened and heard them, too—Father and Kiera, both shouting, neither listening. The words were indistinct, but the subject wasn't hard to guess.

"There's another door," Kyle said, fighting with his tongue, which had grown too large for his mouth. "I can go straight to my own chamber."

"They're *in* your chamber, Kyle-lad."

"Damn," he muttered, influenced, no doubt, by the burn-wine.

He tried to walk away, but Muredoch wouldn't let him.

"Let me do the talking. You head straight for Josaf and, Kyle, drink *whatever* he tells you to drink, or you're truly going to wish you'd died today when you wake up tomorrow."

"Yes, my lord," Kyle said, and began to giggle, which made the walls spin.

He was still reeling when the guards opened the door and Muredoch steered him inside.

"Kyle! I've got the most wonderful news!"

Kiera threw herself into a vigorous embrace that would have left both of them on the floor, if Muredoch hadn't wedged his weight and strength between them.

"It can wait until morning—"

"No, it can't, Muredoch. Queen Ezrae's heard my plea. She and her uncle have prevailed over the king's wizards! Kyle's safe—*and* there'll be a trek to the Eigela to find the Siege of Shadows. The Gray Prince will lead it, and Kyle and I are both going. The queen's promised! She's providing me an escort from her own guard, so there's nothing for you to object to!"

"You're *not* going," Father roared.

"It's Rapture. It's ordained and can't be denied. And it's not for you to decide: I'm of age. I don't belong to anyone. The queen's provided for me. I don't need you. God's pockets! I don't need anyone!"

Kyle staggered. His brother's hand had slipped from his arm, probably from the shock of listening to Kiera. There was nothing to keep the chamber from swinging like a bell. He tried to catch his balance by grabbing hold of the nearest object, a tapestry. It tore loose from the wall, condemning Kyle to a graceless tumble that knocked over chairs, tables, and God alone knew what else on his way down.

Some things never changed.

Chapter Fourteen

Kyle was stone sober as he made his way to the dragon chamber the next morning.

It had taken Renard and Enobred together to get him to his bed after his inglorious collapse. He would have gratefully passed out from the burnwine and embarrassment, but Josaf kept him awake long enough to drink a pitcher of water and gag down a ladle filled with deep green, shockingly bitter muck. The bitter taste still clung to Kyle's tongue, but otherwise he was in better health than he deserved: clearheaded, clear-eyed, he entered the chamber where his life's fate would be revealed.

He stood alone—there'd be no chair this time—at the open end of the table, praying that his knees wouldn't fail him, that the dragon wouldn't come to life and consume him. As before, King Otanazar filled his massive seat at the horseshoe's toe. Prince Gravais sat to the king's right, the queen to his left. The wizards attended, swaddled in their linen gauze, and the high officers, wearing somber colors as befitted the occasion. Ferra Ilsassan Baldescare led a phalanx of priests into the chamber after Kyle had taken his position. There were Ultramontaines in finery, Mellians in austerity, and Bydians in simplicity, but their faces were the same: grim and resolute.

Kyle doubted the conflicting assurances he'd gotten from Muredoch and Kiera. He caught his brother's eye as the rest of his family came in behind the priests. Muredoch gave him a thumbs-up sign to say that all was well, then Muredoch's attention—and his own—was drawn to the queen, who invited

Kiera to sit beside her. An invitation which Kiera boldly accepted.

Kiera had bedecked herself in borrowed jewels and brocade better suited to a festive supper than the king's judgment. Her cheeks were flushed with excitement, though she had the good sense—considering where she chose to sit—not to flirt with the prince. She grinned and winked whenever Kyle looked at her.

The lord magister spoke first and directly to the king, never glancing in Kyle's direction.

"We cannot determine the absolute truth of the matter, Your Highness. Something haunts the boy. It purports to be Taslim of Fawlen, and we find no reason to believe it is not that wizard who was presumed dead nearly a millennium ago. We cannot account for his spells, nor can he, at least not to our satisfaction. Both he and the Dainis hart-lord answer truthfully, yet we cannot completely believe them. Still, Your Highness, we all saw *something* on the solstice. Perhaps the Harbinger, perhaps not. Perhaps the Stercian Siege of Shadows has returned and another Debacle looms.

"A trek to the Eigela seems in order, Your Highness, if we are to have complete answers. We suggest a cohort, led by your eldest son, departing as soon as possible, with Taslim of Fawlen as its guide. Whatever fell into the Eigela, it would not be wise to let it fall into untrusted hands."

Ferra Baldescare rose. He and the magister exchanged glances that Kyle couldn't see, then the wizard sat, and the priest spoke to the king:

"Not wise, indeed, Your Highness. In this matter, the orders and the wizards speak with one voice. Whatever God has placed in the Eigela must not slip away. By all means, assemble a cohort with such resources as only the crown can provide—the best men, the best horses, the best of all that Alberon possesses—including the leadership of His Highness, Prince Gravais Maradze, if Your Royal Highness deems him the best man. And the Dainis twins. Let them not be left behind. Their Rapture lies at the heart of this mystery. The boy's haunt may well be our best guide, but Lady Kiera Dainis . . ."

Kyle gulped angrily to hear himself referred to as "the boy" while his sister got her name and title.

" . . . heard God's voice as the fireball passed overhead. We do not confront the Debacle's return. It was not the Harbinger that streaked across our sky. It is not the heretic Siege of Shadows that calls to this devout young woman, but God Himself. Her Rapture is God's blessing. The orders will provide her with her own escort within whatever cohort the crown provides. We tolerate the abiding interest of the kingdom's wizards, but God guides Lady Kiera Dainis, not a wizard demon."

The priest bowed to the swathed wizards.

"We, too, are tolerant where Alberon's destiny is concerned," Lord Marrek Brun said benignly, without rising from his chair. "By all means, add whomever you wish. Lockwood, Lord Marelet, will ride beside his boon-friend, and with him we are content."

So it was as Kiera promised: a compromise, tense and no more than convenient, had been negotiated between traditional rivals. The high officials raised a few objections—they, apparently, had not been included in the bargaining. The war marshal suggested that he, not the unproven prince, should lead the cohort.

King Otanazar stroked his beard and appeared to give the marshal's proposal a moment's serious thought before deciding that the cohort must have the royal heir leading it. In short order, Kyle heard himself reprieved, on the condition that he—and Taslim—join the prince's cohort. Further, the Dainis would provide half the men, half the horses, half of everything the journey would require—which clearly surprised Father and left him scowling. Kiera, though, was all smiles and pride: Where Father and Muredoch had had only promises from the prince, she'd had the truth from the queen. The prince seemed as surprised as Father, though far more pleased with his own father's decisions.

Alone and virtually ignored, Kyle took a deep breath, then sighed. There'd been no talk of banishment or exile, not a hint about executions or setting examples. He couldn't have hoped for better, yet his neck remained as tight as it had been when he entered the dragon chamber.

Taslim emerged from his mind's dark places.

<<You *have* changed, Hart-lord.>>

And he had, though perhaps not as Taslim had first proposed yesterday on the balcony. Kyle's sense of himself hadn't changed—not that he could measure. But he'd lost his faith in the great folk who determined his fate.

<<They've all got their own reasons for this, Taslim,>> he

told the darkness once they'd left the dragon chamber. <<I don't trust anyone, except Muredoch, and he's not coming with us.>>

<<We have our own reasons, and each other, Hart-lord. We don't need your brother, good man that he is. We don't need any of them, Hart-lord, except for safety while we travel. We know where we're going, and we know what we'll do once we get there.>>

<<Do we?>> Kyle shot back images of thunderstruck peaks and a pillar of soot rising out of the lodge hearth.

<<We do, Hart-lord. Trust me.>>

Kyle didn't reply and the matter didn't come up again, not that day, or the next, when Father and Muredoch departed for Roc Dainis to assemble provisions for the cohort. They left Kyle and Kiera, Enobred and Lille behind. Josaf and Renard would return with horses and a baggage train.

Kiera and Lille lost no time leaving their chamber. Men from the queen's guard carried their baggage into the queen's household. Father's last words to Kyle had been an admonition to keep an eye out for his sister, so he bound himself in fancy court clothes and went to visit her—once and once only. He felt so unwelcome amid the flamboyant furnishing and the Black Lightning veterans that not even the thought of disappointing Father could have driven him back.

He saw his twin each evening at the king's supper, unless she dined privately with Queen Ezrae, whose pregnancy was not as easy as her earlier ones had been. Kyle preferred the nights he didn't see Kiera. She'd always sought attention and blossomed in it, but away from their parents and laced into borrowed—he hoped—gowns that showed off a no-longer-childish figure, she'd become the boldest of the queen's over-bold ladies. Once the supper tables were cleared and the minstrels struck up their instruments for dancing, there wasn't a handsome lad who was safe from her charms.

Except Prince Gravais.

Perhaps the Gray Prince had taken Muredoch's warning to heart. Perhaps he'd seen too much of women and couldn't be amused or attracted by Kiera's artless flirting. Either way, try as she might—and Kyle was shamed by her efforts—she couldn't draw him to her side.

For his part, Kyle kept company with himself—easier to do now that he was neither a fosterling in service, nor surrounded by his family, nor subject to daily interrogations by suspicious wizards and priests, who seemed, indeed, to have forgotten his existence.

Kyle allowed Taslim to keep the freedom he'd gained on the balcony. It seemed only fair, since King Otanazar had done as much for him, and Kyle didn't have a jailer's temperament. More to the point—he wasn't certain he could duplicate the singular sleight of wizardry that had made the *serras* rune effective. The wizard hadn't betrayed Kyle's trust, any more than Kyle would betray his king's. After a week or two living alone in the Chegnon guest quarters with only Enobred for company, talking to Taslim was like talking to himself, and listening, Kyle heard a friend.

A bright, dry morning—unusual for coastal Alberon in the waning days of winter—found Kyle lingering in his chamber, dressed for the practice arena, and looking down from the balcony on an active bailey where a veritable army of fosterlings and varlets assembled a baggage train of oxcarts, and harried grooms grappled with the reins of a score of winter-shy horses.

<<King Otanazar departs on his spring progress,>> he informed Taslim, in case the wizard wasn't paying attention.

<<Some things *never* change. There was a curse in my time: May royalty visit your hall in spring and stay until winter.>>

The wizard was right, at least about the traditions of the royal court. Every year the court arrived at Chegnon shortly before the winter solstice. They sheltered within the ancient fortress for the frigid, inhospitable season, eating, drinking, and heaping waste into equally ancient middens. Then, as the three months of winter drew to a close, the ground thawed. The lower chambers flooded, vast mires appeared in the baileys, and, inevitably—but always without warning—the middens of Chegnon began to belch.

Kyle had seen it happen before and very definitely smelled it before.

Once the middens began to seethe, the king knew it was time to visit a Hesse-built roc where the sewers were less exciting. Fosterlings worked alongside common varlets, packing everything the court needed when it traveled. After the king was gone, the fosterlings worked harder still, hauling, scouring, digging, and—following the shouted oaths of their taskmasters—working the winter fat off their lazy bones.

<<Lightning strike,>> Taslim complained, fending off Kyle's aromatic memories. <<Be damned, if you didn't *enjoy* yourself in the pits!>>

Kyle chuckled; there was no one else around, no reason to restrain his humor. But his mood sank as quickly as it had risen—very much like the middens.

On the advice of her physicians, Queen Ezrae wasn't departing with the king. The noxious vapors that seeped through every window, every door, no matter how tightly it was shut, had been judged less harmful than the prospect of a springtime journey. Prince Gravais was staying at Chegnon also—once the king was safely departed, the kitchens and stables would devote themselves to preparations for his cohort. But in the meantime, there'd be no King Otanazar to keep his wife from his son's throat.

And no chance at all that Kyle would be able to lure Kiera away from the Baldescare habits before Josaf and the Dainismen arrived from home.

When Kyle thought of the cohort, he didn't think of the Siege of Shadows, or even of his masked and silver-haired warrior. He thought of Josaf and Renard and Rawne, all of whom should have arrived from Roc Dainis by now. The view from the balcony included a narrow slice of the Chegnon quays, which he watched more closely than the preparations going on below. A handful of ships had floated past on morning tide. There'd been none flying the tri-blue Dainis banner.

<<Our quest,>> Taslim murmured. <<With them or without them. It doesn't matter, Hart-lord. Don't weary yourself worrying.>>

Taslim didn't care about old men or walleyed horses. In this they disagreed without hope of reconciliation. A wall of Kyle's devising grew between them; he'd become adept at preserving his privacy without exiling the wizard. And he had other ways to deal with the worries that remained. His cloak and a worn, quilted tunic hung on pegs by the door. He grabbed the tunic and departed.

The practice arena in Chegnon's upper bailey was every bit as noisy as the assembling baggage train in the lower one. Any man with the right to bear steel could come to the arena to hone his craft or settle a score, and today it seemed that every man had. The men-at-arms who would accompany the king were taking a last moment to check their weapons and skills before they left. A passel of young fosterlings, excluded by their age and strength from the strenuous task of loading the oxcarts, were being drilled by a bored armsmaster whose sharp tongue and heavy hand Kyle remembered well from his own days here. Another passel of older boys, also exempt from the oxcarts, was paired off in half-time exercises: parry, feint, and thrust, again and again until the moves were as natural and thoughtless as breathing.

Kyle let himself into the arena's outer circle, where men warmed up, cooled down, and generally stayed out of one another's way. There were racks near the inner gate, one each for hauberks, helms, and weapons. He picked up the last armory sword—heavier than the weapon he'd left behind in his chamber—then staked a claim to an unused stretch of gravelly sand.

He swung the sword freely. Its balance was wretched, but no worse than he'd expected from a sword every other man had rejected—his own reward for lingering in his chamber. Kyle's arm was as strong as it had been for his last fosterage practice, more limber, and, he thought, a bit faster. He would have been disappointed otherwise. He'd been coming to this place twice a day, every day, since Father left. By himself and with whomever would spar with him, he'd raised a fine crop of bruises recalling his fosterage lessons. Since neither the king nor the prince had given him responsibilities regarding the cohort, the least Kyle thought he could do was turn himself into a reliable man-at-arms.

Not that he'd be needed. Between the men they expected from Roc Dainis and those Prince Gravais had personally selected from the Chegnon garrison, they'd be well protected. And they might need protection from the men the queen had picked to guard Kiera. There were four of them, all Black Lightning veterans of the Kolish wars. Their captain, Geregonal, was a rare piece of work whom Kyle wouldn't trust for water in the rain.

The queen's men came to the arena every day, too. Kyle had sparred with each of them; a man could learn from men he didn't trust. He'd mastered a few sleighting tricks he hoped he'd never have to use and wouldn't find unnerving if he had to face. But he preferred a more honest match. Once his muscles were warmed and loose, he armored himself and entered the inner circle, hoping someone other than the Black Lightning veterans would notice him.

"Dreamer!"

Kyle turned and found his remembered armsmaster beckoning to him.

"Let's show these white-livered whelps what a man can do if he sets his mind to it."

He could endure his eke-name when it came with an invitation like that—as it had never done in fosterage. They sparred at half-time, while the younger boys watched, then, on the armsmaster's signal, they moved to battle pace. Kyle parried and feinted, thrust and slashed, until they'd both begun to swing wide from exhaustion. The armsmaster called a halt. Kyle sank to one knee, catching his breath.

"Demon's the best thing to happen to you, Dreamer," the master said between his gasps. "Had it ten years ago, and I'd've made a fighting man out of you."

Kyle grunted. Ten years ago, ten *months* ago, he'd had no reason to fight, except to protect himself from bullies, and that didn't require skill or subtlety. Now there was Kiera, who'd gotten herself surrounded by guttersnipes, and Taslim, who'd die if he got himself slain, and a silver-haired warrior whose shattered face haunted his dreams.

The armsmaster had his breath. He threw an arm around Kyle's shoulder as Kyle stood up, and turned him away from the fosterling passel.

"You put on a good display, Dreamer. The lads might have learned a thing or two, but defending yourself's not enough. You can't drop an enemy from exhaustion. Comes a time, you've got to kill."

Kyle wrested free. He thanked the master for his time and walked away. Killing was the ultimate purpose of everything he did here, but it wasn't his purpose. Not yet.

<<Not ever,>> Taslim interrupted, a profile in princely clothes glimpsed from the corner of Kyle's right eye. <<Let the steel skulls do the work of getting us to the Siege. That's what lords and princes and sword-swinging warriors are good for: protecting, defending, and spilling some poor fool's blood on the ground.>>

<<I'm a lord, Taslim. A hart-lord. It's what I'm good for.>>

<<Listen to me, Hart-lord. If you've got to protect something, protect me by staying out of harm's way! Don't go looking for trouble.>>

<<There won't be trouble, not if I'm prepared for it. Haven't you grasped the truth of me yet? The disasters I'm ready for never happen. It's only the ones I'm not ready for that happen. The more I practice, the safer we all are.>>

<<Promises, promises, Hart-lord.>>

A gust of humor flowed across Kyle's thoughts. When it was gone, the wizard had retreated and Kyle's vision was clear again. He slapped the flat of his sword against his palm, looking for another partner. The older fosterlings had moved on while he sparred with the armsmaster, as had Geregonal and his cronies. Prince Gravais, his personal armsmaster, and some of the men who'd accompany them to the Eigela arrived to take their place. Kyle retreated to the fence between the inner and outer arena, prepared to watch and learn a bit himself.

The masters who taught Alberon's verger fosterlings were all good men, but those who sparred with the Gray Prince were the best that gold could buy. Still—as Kyle had just been reminded—without the right spirit, neither money nor masters would make a difference. Gray didn't squander his father's gold. He sparred with a good blade—no battered armory swords for the king's heir—and he was the equal of any master in the arena, including his own. He'd never have to be told why men fought.

Kyle watched in awe as the tall, red-haired man ran through his attacks—Alberonese, Kolish, Jivernaise, and a handful Kyle never saw except when the prince came to the arena. He was piecing together one of the nameless forms when the prince called a halt.

"Dreamer—give me your arm?"

Kyle's head came up along with his sword. The prince gestured for his partner to stand aside.

"May as well know what I'm traveling with, eh? Battle pace or half?"

"Battle," Kyle replied airily. The prince would learn quickly enough.

When the prince said "At hazard!" Kyle brought his weapon up in the traditional Alberonese way: facing his opponent in a three-quarter stance, sword tip extended in an invisible line from his heart, arm tucked close to his side, and the hilt at hip height. The Gray Prince answered with a Kolish stance: weapon pointed straight up in front of him. Geregonal used that stance, and Geregonal's battle face was grimmer than the prince's. Kyle had beaten aside the Black Lightning captain's attack, then disarmed him. He didn't expect to have the same luck with the bright-eyed, smiling prince.

But he did beat the first attack, and parried the ripostes that followed his own unsuccessful attacks. The prince shed his smile; his attacks came at a blisteringly fast pace. Kyle beat the ones he couldn't parry, taking their brunt with the strength of his arm. He sallied thrusts of his own that never came near their intended targets or distracted the prince long enough for an effective riposte.

Still, Kyle had lasted far longer than he'd expected before he got hooked on a feint and Prince Gravais attacked under his guard.

Gray cried "Halt!" with his sword tip touching the lacing of Kyle's hauberk. Kyle stepped back, dragging his sword through the sand.

"You caught me. I knew it, then it was too late. Thank God you don't have to rely on me, Your Highness."

"Gray," the prince corrected. "We're all equal here in the sand."

Kyle's sense of shame grew. Arena equality was the first lesson a fosterling learned. It was the justification for the eke-names they gave one another. He wiped his sweaty face on a bit of sleeve extending beyond the hauberk's mail sleeve—as if that would wipe away his embarrassment, too.

"God's pockets, Dreamer, you worry too much. There's nothing wrong with your right arm." Gray kneaded the muscles of his own forearm. "Swinging a blade against you is like striking a stone wall. If you can get a blow—flat, edge, tip, or the back of your hand—whatever you hit is going down."

"I can't get a blow. I'm no warrior. I don't have the right spirit." Kyle prayed that Taslim wasn't listening, and knew that his prayer would go unanswered. "The armsmasters still say so. I wasn't recommended to the cohorts."

"You're no captain, if that's what you mean. And that's what the masters are looking for. A hot-tempered fosterling who'll lead a charge of common foot soldiers. At least that's what everyone hopes. The crypts are full of arena bravos who pissed in their boots. We let our captains go abroad in search of gold and glory; we keep our sensible men at home where we need them."

Kyle had emotional calluses against insults and criticism, but very few for praise. He took Gray's hand reluctantly when it was offered, and couldn't meet the prince's eyes. "I'm sorry, Your . . . *Gray*."

"God'a'mercy—you're one sorry man, Dreamer."

The prince's efforts to set Kyle at ease came to nothing. "I blunder. I always do. I'll cause problems, no matter how hard I try not to. I have accidents, Gray. If Taslim could go with you—with Lockwood—well, your cohort would be safer. You could leave now, and not have to wait—"

"Is that it?" Gray interrupted with a frown. "You're worried about your Dainismen? I can't tell you not to, not after saying you're a sensible man. I'll wager they're coming by land, not sea, and this time of year, you can find yourself in a week-long quagmire. Give them another week, maybe two, before you start worrying, Dreamer."

"You're right: at least a week, maybe two." Kyle spoke to his toes, as if he were standing in front of his father.

"Get your mind on pleasanter things; join Locky and me for supper. With my sire gone and the Bitch in bed, Chegnon will be quiet as a crypt tonight."

Kyle managed a nod. He sensed that this was one of those opportunities to advance himself that he'd failed to grasp in the past. There had to be something he could say—something more than Yes, Gray, or Thank you very much, Gray, but something that would forge a lasting bond between them. But his tale-spinning tongue failed him.

He was never at a loss for words with Kiera or Taslim. They'd both know what to say right now, though he flushed anew when he thought of his sister, and Taslim offered advice only when it suited him.

"Thank you very—"

"Heads up!" Gray cut him off with a gesture toward the outer circle gate.

"God's pockets," Kyle swore softly as his twin strode up the path.

Kiera had scrounged a sword from who-knew-where, and a boy's mail shirt from the same source. She had used her own linen laces, instead of leather thongs, to bind the shirt around her and hitched up her skirt with a length of bright blue cloth.

Then she'd imitated the quilted breeches some of the men wore by wrapping her legs in bed linen.

Weapons clanged and curses erupted all around the arena as the men took note of their visitor. There was laughter, some of it bawdy, the larger portion embarrassed. All eyes turned toward the prince and Kyle, toward whom Kiera walked once she'd cleared the gates. Arena equality had its limits. No common-born man-at-arms, gentleman, or lord wanted to tell a verge-lord's daughter to go back where she belonged. They gladly left that chore for their royal prince and the daughter's haunted brother.

Gray moistened his lips—to keep from laughing out loud, Kyle suspected. Then he gave Kyle a glance that said, You first.

"Kiera—" he began.

"Teach me to defend myself," she demanded before he could finish. She looked directly at Gray, not him.

It wasn't an entirely unreasonable request. Some women did know how to fight with a sword, and before they reached the Eigela, they'd have to cross large tracts where the king's law existed mostly in the breach. They'd be traveling with enough force to discourage most beasts and outlaws, but if worse came to worst, Kiera could find herself alone. Kyle was pleased that she'd come to him, not Geregonal, with her request. Except, she hadn't come to him; she'd come to the prince, who wasn't interested.

"That's a family man's task," he said quickly, sidestepping behind Kyle. "I'm off to the stables to count the horses the king's left us." He clapped Kyle on the shoulder before continuing his retreat.

Fists cocked against her hips, Kiera watched him go in silence, then she pursed her lips and blew strands of hair away from her nose.

"Well, do you want to learn something?" Kyle asked the back of her head. "Or did you have something else in mind?"

"God's pockets!" she swore as she turned. "You're as thick as stone sometimes. Since Muredoch and Father left, I can't get close enough to him to say two words together. You could have helped me just now, Kyle. You *could* have said you weren't good enough to teach me anything."

Several thoughts sprang to Kyle's mind: the warning Muredoch had given Gray and the way Kiera had attached herself to

Gray's enemy, the queen, foremost among them. He wasn't sure where Kiera was keeping her confidences, though—or, he was almost certain she was confiding in the queen—and he didn't want to start more trouble than he could handle. He left the easy retorts unspoken and said, instead, "But I am good enough, Ki. Gray just said so, and it would have been foolish of me to say otherwise. He says I'm sensible and I'm good. What about you, Ki—can you learn from me, or does it have to be someone royal?"

Kiera narrowed her eyes, shook her head.

"By the bolt, Kiera, you've changed. You're a stranger to me. You march out here in men's clothes, brazen as a bell. When you're not bold, you're rude. I don't know you since you turned to the queen."

"Oh, yes—blame everything on the queen. Don't bother to say thank you to me, or to her. She's the one who interceded for you, little brother—Dreamer—after I interceded with her. She got down on her knees before her uncle and her husband. On her *knees*! In her condition! Do you have any idea where you'd be right now, if I hadn't 'turned to the queen'?"

The question sent shivers down Kyle's back and returned his thoughts to the dragon chamber, where everyone had been smiling, but the smiles of the Baldescare, uncle and niece, had been the broadest.

"I don't trust them," he murmured, unaware he'd spoke aloud, until Kiera said, "But *you* trust Prince Gravais. *I* certainly don't."

Then why chase him so shamelessly? Kyle almost asked, but he'd begun to learn how to avoid unwinnable arguments. "Look, Ki," he said with a sigh. "Do you want to learn anything or not?"

Kiera's sigh was dramatic. Her lips quivered. Her eyelashes fluttered. Kyle assumed she meant yes.

The younger fosterlings had finished their lessons for the day. They were filing out of the arena, depositing their wooden weapons in a heap by the outer circle racks. Kyle called, "Fosterling! Bring me your sword!"—marking the first time he'd exercised a noble adult's right to command any fosterling. He took the practice weapon from the boy, then held it out, hilt first, to his sister. "Put that thing down and take this."

She obeyed reluctantly, complaining, "It's wood," and "It's heavy!"

"Bravo! First lesson: practice is worse than fighting." God have mercy, he'd heard that phrase ten thousand times if he'd heard it once and never imagined that he'd hear himself saying it. "Now, angle your wrist like this." He set Kiera's hand in the proper attitude. "Straighten your arm and elbow, out from the shoulder, and start counting: One, two, three . . ."

"Ky-yle!" She made a grating melody of his name and dropped her arm. "What's gotten into you—as if I didn't know! I don't want to play statues. Teach me something, or I'm leaving."

Kyle yanked her arm into the proper position. "One. Two."

"This is stupid!" She threw the stick weapon at his feet.

"Pick it up."

"You pick it up."

"Pick it up, or get out of here and get out of those rags."

Kiera took a step toward him, then kicked the sword against the fence. They had the undivided attention of everyone in the arena and a good many of those outside it as well.

"You tell me who's changed more, Kyle? If I've changed, at least that's my own doing. You've given yourself to a demon! I truly don't know who you are anymore—if you're still my little brother or some scheming wizard. We made promises, Kyle Dainis, before we got here. I swore to help you, and you swore to help me! I did my part. I helped you when no one else could or would. If I've changed, Kyle, I changed for you. Ferra Baldescare wanted you *dead*, Kyle—not just dead, but sailed up and down the coast in a cage first. Do you understand that? It wasn't easy to persuade the queen to change his mind, and then she had to persuade King Otanazar that someone should go to the Eigela.

"You owe me, Kyle. Do you hear? You *owe* me. I saved you—God knows why—and I'm going to save the Gray Prince, if I can. If you'll honor your word and *help* me."

He retrieved the practice sword by its tip. The wood-grain pattern occupied his eyes while he considered Kiera's assertions.

<<Don't believe her, Hart-lord. Whatever she's done, she's done for her own reasons. Owe her, and you'll never get free. Cut her loose. Leave her to the queen. Let that bolt go to ground where it will.>>

Taslim's unsought advice was worth listening to, but Kyle offered the hilt one last time. "This is the way I learned and

I'm sure it's the way the prince learned," he said evenly. "Everything depends on your arm. We've both got to know how strong it is."

Kiera snarled, but she took the hilt and extended her arm, angled at the wrist, straight at the elbow and shoulder.

"One. Two. Three . . ." She counted to twenty before her arm began to tremble, and held on gamely until she reached thirty-five. "My whole arm's numb. I can't feel my fingers."

The weapon thumped into the sand. Kyle took her hand and gave it a vigorous massage. When she could flex her fingers again, he told her to retrieve the sword.

"We'll skip over the truly boring part—you don't have five years to waste."

Kiera cocked her head and smiled. It was a feeble smile, but the most he'd seen since they arrived at Chegnon of the sister he thought he knew.

"Practice pace. Half-pace, you know what that means. You saw it at Roc Dainis with the Renzi fosterlings. Face-to-face. You do *exactly* what I do."

Kyle raised his weapon. Kiera scampered backward. "You've got a *real* sword!"

He subjected the battered armory blade to scrutiny. "Not hardly."

This time Kiera's smile was momentarily wider and truer before it faded. "But, shouldn't they be the same? I might get hurt."

"I'm the one who's going to get hurt, Ki. And I'd rather have bruises than gashes. Come on. Raise your sword when I say 'Hazard.' All right. Now, count with me, move with me."

They went through the simplest moves. Kiera laughed the first time their weapons touched, and she lost her grip on the hilt. She didn't make the same mistake the second time.

There were women whose strength was the equal of any man's—Menager Cook sprang to mind. Kiera would never be among them. Her slender bones couldn't have supported the muscle a warrior needed, even if she'd had the height and length of arm. But she was game. Kyle looked at her bright, narrowed eyes and knew his twin had the warrior spirit. At half-pace and with a wooden sword, she was determined to win.

At best, he was determined not to lose. That was enough when she began to hedge the rules—speeding up her strokes and hitting as hard as she could. Kyle stepped into the next attack, parried with an angled blade, trapping hers, then pushing up and out, until Kiera lost her balance. She staggered back a step, losing her weapon, before she thumped down hard on the sharp edges of her rusty mail shirt.

Kyle bit his lip. He knew how she felt: At least one rivet popped when you fell like that. At least one sprung link found a way through your tunic and into your skin. Eventually you learned how to roll as you fell, but first you learned how to sit on a punctured and bruised butt.

It wasn't funny at all when it happened to him, but it was when it happened to someone else. And, truth to tell, it was especially funny when it happened to Kiera, who expected life to cushion her falls no matter how foolishly she behaved. Kyle wasn't proud of himself, but it did his heart good to see her sprawl-legged in the sand, gasping and gaping.

"Come on up," he said, offering her his free hand.

She scowled and planted her hands in the coarse sand instead. It didn't work; he'd known it wouldn't. She wasn't prepared for the weight of the shirt: Her hands slipped and she landed hard again, this time with a little yelp.

Kyle didn't offer help a second time, just snatched her wrist and yanked her to her feet.

"I would've gotten up myself," she grumbled, though she was still breathing hard and preferred to lean against him rather than move away.

"It's no disgrace, Ki. Everyone takes a hand up after a fall. Mail's heavy. And hard." A solitary laugh escaped; Kiera smiled, before she turned her head away. "You could visit the stables and ask a hostler to smear some horse lineament on it."

"I'd sooner *die*."

"I could have a jar sent to the queen's chambers."

"That, little brother, would be even *worse*."

Then, unmindful of the mail they both wore, she hugged him tightly. Kyle draped his free arm around her and rested his chin on the top of her head. Thinking about things that couldn't be, he wished they were both back at Roc Dainis and that Rapture hadn't happen. He wasn't looking at anything in particular, until he saw a tall, red-haired man standing near the tower tunnel that connected Chegnon's upper and lower baileys.

Prince Gravais hadn't gone to the stable. He'd been watching the arena, watching *them*, because he hurried into the tunnel as soon as their eyes met.

Kyle was angry; he didn't like to be watched, didn't like the judgment he saw in faces afterward. He was angry for Kiera, too, knowing how much worse she'd feel if she knew the prince had watched her fall—for all that Kyle didn't approve of her flirting with him.

A few men made snide comments a moment later when he helped his twin from the arena. They fell silent, though, when he glanced their way.

"Look at them," the queen of Alberon said from her place beside a window in her most private bedchamber.

The midden stench was overwhelming, even through the scented cloth she held to her face. Chegnon was the last place she wanted to be. If the only risk had been to the child in her belly, she would have followed her husband to Roc Albra. But she'd be risking her own life if she traveled—or so her physicians said, and Ezrae believed them. This pregnancy had sapped her to the bone. It was all she could do to stand and walk across the carpets.

"The famous Dainis twins!" she continued. "Put bells around their necks and they'll lead each other to the slaughter block."

Her uncle joined her at the window, her cherished uncle, Ferra Ilsassan Baldescare. He brushed her curls aside and caressed her neck. Ezrae pressed the cloth tight against her lips. She admired her uncle; he'd been her first mentor, and her best. She loathed him for the liberties he'd taken ever since.

She never *cherished* him.

"I think they're rather sweet, in their simple, rustic way," he whispered in her ear, before he kissed it. "Brother and sister have reconciled. They face their dreams and the Eigela together. Why, I could almost feel a tear welling up in my eye."

"Fools," Ezrae spat and twisted out of her uncle's grasp.

And not just the Dainis twins. She'd been a fool for the last ten years. But her uncle was a greater fool for thinking the next ten would be the same. The soft cushions of her daybed beckoned. Ezrae heaped her bloated self gracelessly atop them.

"Useful fools," Uncle said, following her, sitting at the end of the daybed, where he began to massage her swollen feet. "You said so yourself, my dear. You persuaded me to encourage them. Are you changing your mind? I'd not be pleased."

His grip shifted, bringing a sharp pain to her ankle, a pain that wasn't accidental.

"You'll be pleased," Ezrae replied wearily and he relented.

She loosened the side lacing of her gown. This would be her last pregnancy. The king and her uncle—any man, every man—could amuse themselves in the stables after this. She'd done her duty, and then some, to the old men of her life: husbands, kings, uncles, and priests. She'd live her own life from now on—and she smiled to herself, recalling that little Kiera Dainis had said almost the same thing.

"A smile?" Uncle inquired.

"The girl tells me everything. She believes I'm her dearest friend."

"Aren't you?"

"God have mercy! The dew sparkles in her eyes; the wind whistles between her ears. My dogs are cleverer."

"But you've given Geregonal orders to keep her alive until Gray is dead."

Every muscle in Ezrae's body snapped taut—a discomforting sensation in her current condition. Geregonal had orders, a purse of her own gold, and much more. A cold stab of betrayal and heartbreak shot through her, and she would have screamed, if she'd been alone.

"How much did you have to pay him to learn that?" she asked instead, expertly concealing her distress, and having the great satisfaction of seeing her uncle blink with surprise.

"Exactly thirty-seven gold deyas. Exactly one more than you paid him."

Blood money. Her own blood. Ezrae hadn't thought she needed to *buy* Geregonal. She thought what she'd given him was far more precious, far more *cherished.*

"He lied," she said, as calm as before, at least in her voice. "I only paid him twenty. Men think the world will kneel to their wishes. Women hedge." Because women don't dare trust.

Uncle took a sweetmeat from a nearby tray. He savored the morsel before asking, "And why have you hedged, my dear? Twenty deyas would have bought another four men for Geregonal to throw at Gray."

"Men have a way of getting lost. I hedge because Geregonal's men might not succeed. Gray might slip away, with that bastard wizard's help. If he comes back, the chit will be useful."

"If Gray comes back, my dear, he or his bastard friend is going to have the power of the Siege of Shadows in his hand. And there's no hedge this side of heaven that's going to keep him from the throne."

Ezrae laughed coldly; it healed some of the pain of Geregonal's abandonment. "Why, Uncle—don't tell me *you've* become a believer? All they've got is a web of lies and a boy's imagination. And it is lies, my cherished uncle. Kiera's told me so herself. Her brother had no Rapture at all, while hers was just a sunset in the mountains. They made it all up for *adventure*! There's no Siege of Shadows—not that those two can find."

"Blasphemy, and heresy, too. They may have lied, but Rapture doesn't. *God* doesn't. You heard the demon yourself."

"What? Speak the truth or the king's dragon will burst free to consume you? I heard Marrek Brun and a boy enthralled by wizardry."

"Mind your tongue, daughter dear. It is a dragon."

Ezrae's breath caught in her throat, as it always did when he called her that. It was a lie; it had to be a lie. Her mother had been Uncle's sister; her father, a vassal lord in Bercelen. They died when she was still an infant, but they were real, and they'd had a daughter before they died, a blond, blue-eyed daughter. Unless that daughter had died with them on a shallow lake that summer's day, and she was someone else's blond, blue-eyed daughter, who'd never been near the rushes where Uncle so miraculously found her. Ezrae knew *all* the rumors surrounding her and Uncle, but even she didn't know all the truth.

Alberon's queen couldn't raise her head or meet his eyes. She could hide almost anything behind the mask her face had become, but not the hatred she felt for her uncle . . . her father . . . her lover.

"The boy's possessed by a demon, not Marrek Brun," he went on, blind to her enmity. "I put him to the test, myself, and the demon spoke. Our plans have changed. No matter how rich they are, it won't do to have scores of pilgrims cluttering the

Eigela—because the Siege exists and the Baldescare must have its power."

"How?" Ezrae asked, fascinated despite her loathing. "Either they all die, and we don't have a demon guide, or—as you said—Gray's got the power."

"Oh, they'll die; I trust your Geregonal. They'll all die. The Hidden God will gather them into his bosom—all but the demon. The demon will come to me or rot in hell." Uncle took two sweetmeats from the tray as he stood up. "Rest well, daughter dear. Say your prayers."

Ezrae waited in silence until he was gone and the last door of her chambers had shut tight behind him. So—*now* Uncle thought the Siege of Shadows was real, not a fraud for fleecing pilgrims. *Now* he thought he could take its power for himself. *Now* he thought he had no need for her or her snotlings in the royal nursery.

Now he'd find out how well she'd learned her lessons.

Chapter Fifteen

Five days passed, and five more, each filled with dull gray clouds, misty rains, and no sign of the tri-blue banners Kyle longed to see. When two full weeks had passed with neither message nor men from Roc Dainis appearing at Chegnon's gate, Kyle accepted the prince's invitation to supper. He admitted his concerns while sipping the prince's wine with far more caution than he'd drunk it before.

Prince Gravais laughed, saying a few weeks' delay in their departure for the Eigela made little difference when the northern roads were still streams of mud. Then the prince turned serious and promised to send men south on the inland road to question travelers. He also sent a varlet after a purse of crettigs which Kyle could exchange for seamen's stories in the harbor. With proper thanks, Kyle tied the purse to his belt and enjoyed the prince's company, though he left early, before the burn-wine appeared.

Taslim chided him for worrying about his back when all the important things lay ahead of them in the Eigela. Kyle shrugged. He'd heard all Taslim's jibes before. A full season after the solstice, the wizard was just one more doubting wind in his thoughts.

After telling Enobred to awaken him at dawn, Kyle lay in the dark and tallied the misfortunes that could have befallen Josaf and the others. He fell into a fitful sleep, dreaming of bottomless quagmires and waves crashing over his head. When Enobred called his name, he awoke more relieved than rested and made his way to the harborside without breakfast.

Ships lost themselves in every season of the year, though

there'd been no storms worth remembering since the Dainismen sailed south. In a dreary morning's drizzle, weather-wary sailors took Kyle's crettigs and swore they'd seen no shore wrecks, no riptide flotsam on their way to Chegnon. They told Kyle the sea had been friendly since the last new moon, then, with the superstition common to their ilk, they hawked vigorously into the saltwater, appeasing the vengeful spirits that lurked there.

What man knew tomorrow's storms? Who dared the Sea of Prayse with pride or complacency?

Kyle thanked them all and wished them Godspeed before trudging back to Chegnon's upper bailey, where the arena offered respite from thought. The hour was both early and damp; the inner circle was empty. Oiled cloth remained atop the racks of weapons and armor. Other men—wiser and less haunted men—stayed dry and warm on mornings like this. Without even a shadow for a partner, Kyle feinted with his own anxieties, until one of the prince's gold-paid armsmasters hailed him from the outer circle.

The prince wasn't with the man, but then, princes were wise by birthright and necessarily unhaunted by either doubts or wizards. Gray had better things to do than pass a soggy hour attracting rust in the arena. The prince's master was likewise confident and unhaunted, but the arena was his life. He'd offer a lesson to any man who looked in need of it. He'd taught Kyle a few tricks on other days.

Today, he showed Kyle where to balance his weight when he stood at hazard in the Jivernaise manner, and how to beat aside an attack to that stance with no more than a flick of his wrists and a twist of his blade. The lesson ended with the master thanking Kyle for being a good student and Kyle promising to practice, which he did. He stayed in the arena by himself until sunlight burned through the drizzle and a breeze came up to dry the sweat as it ran down his neck.

He didn't hear the prince approach until the outer gate creaked.

"My men have returned," Gray said, and said no more as he sat down at the grindstone.

Common sense predicted that well-meaning men might withhold good news out of some mysterious notion of humor or friendship, but bad news had to be served hot. Kyle's experience said his prince was well meaning and that the news he was pointedly not sharing was, therefore, not ill-omened. But neither common sense nor experience could keep Kyle's heart from pounding against his ribs as Gray treadled the grindstone and, with great deliberateness, honed a burr from his sword's edge.

Kyle was breathless before the prince was satisfied with the blade. The wheel then slowly whirred to a halt.

"They met a party of priests coming up from Ulver who said the roads are almost dry and there's not a bridge still out on the east coast. Knowing your father and brother, I'll wager your Dainismen and horses will be here in another day or two, at the latest."

Kyle nodded. He should have known Father wouldn't risk good men and horses on rotten roads, not for any son or prince or even the king. The Dainismen would have left Renzi when it was safe to do so. Only a fool would have thought otherwise. A chorus in Kyle's conscience sang about his foolishness.

"A bout?" the prince asked. "Unless you'd rather stand there brooding?"

There was some honor left in Kyle's conscience, some pride—too much for slinking away in shame, if that had been possible, with him inside the inner circle and the prince leaning on the gate.

"I'd like that." Kyle retrieved his sword—his own sword, not an armory reject. "I've been practicing."

The prince grinned and shed his cloak. "I've heard." The cloak had covered a hauberk of blued steel mail, not the sort of garment any man wore for a walk or whim.

Kyle looked beyond the outer circle, where a double handful of men had gathered. His recent master was among them; he winked and held up two fingers. No one had wandered up by accident. No one was here to watch the prince hone his sword. And one man had risked two coins on *him*, Kyle Dainis . . . *Dreamer* Dainis.

"You won't catch me on a feint," Kyle promised, loudly enough for the spectators to hear.

He kept his promise. Hours and days of practice paid off as he repulsed Gray's attacks, one after the other. Any fool could tell that Alberon's crowned prince was a better swordsman, but Kyle had sworn not to play the fool. After a few feints that scarcely broke his defensive rhythm, and intrigued his opponent not at all, he stayed square behind his sword, waiting for a mistake the prince wasn't likely to make.

When his initial flurry of quicksilver attacks met echoing ends against Kyle's stubborn defense, Gray put an extra half step between them and settled into a defensive stance of his own. They circled warily, eyes locked on each other, oblivious of everything else.

Twice again Gray surged; twice Kyle beat him back. Sweat stung Kyle's eyes and his hauberk felt like the weight of the world. Gray dropped his right arm: an apparent invitation, which Kyle declined with a weary shake of his head. Gray closed for the third time, slower and heavy footed, but still a threat. Their blades bound together midway above the hilts. Kyle was too tired to disengage with anything more graceful than a grunting shove that rocked both of them backward.

"Halt." Gray conceded when his back struck the fence.

The bout was over without victory or defeat for either of them. Kyle dropped to one knee. The sword slid from his fingers to the sand. The master had lost his coins.

"I must apologize—"

"God's pockets, Dreamer—*no* apologies!" The prince had sunk to a knee as well. He took a pitcher of water from an eager hand and, after gulping down a few mouthfuls, poured the rest over his head. "I ache from your apologies."

There was another hand, another pitcher at the edge of Kyle's vision. He drank deeply and wondered if young Henrik Minatare, who'd offered it to him, considered it an honor or a disgrace to serve a man who'd neither won nor lost.

"My spirit remains weak."

"If it gets much stronger, they'll have to bury us in the same grave," Gray laughed and offered a hand up.

The prince's remark brought laughter from the crowd. Embarrassed, for reasons he couldn't explain even to himself, Kyle wished to remain where he was, but grabbed Gray's wrist instead—anything else would have taken him from bad to worse.

"You'll dine with me again tonight," Gray said, an order, not a request, as he clapped Kyle soundly between the shoulders.

Stand up straight! Kiera urged silently from her place along the inner circle fence. *Pound him back and tell him you'll be hungry enough to eat an ox. Do something—anything—but don't just stand there with your mouth hanging open!*

Kyle did say something; she saw his lips moving. Prince Gravais heard and laughed, but no one else did, so no one would credit her twin's humor or remember his name. And they would have remembered it: Men who made the Gray Prince cry "halt" were few and far between.

Of course, everyone laughed once the prince laughed, herself included. It was polite to laugh when royalty laughed; more important, it was politic. Kiera had learned that lesson, but Kyle never had and probably never would. Her brother was strong and handsome—there were three well-born women in the queen's household who'd vowed to lure him to their beds, but he'd never looked their way.

He was utterly impolitic.

Ten years of fosterage had rolled off her twin's back like rain off a roof. Kyle knew less about making his way at court than she did. And Prince Gravais—for all his elegant manners and prowess with his sword—was no better. If he had half the sense a woman had in her left little finger, there'd be peace, not strife, in the royal family.

His stepmother, the queen, was only doing what any mother would for her children: protecting their futures and their fortunes. Queen Ezrae knew the Gray Prince would be His Royal Highness, King Gravais III, before her children were grown. She feared for them, if their elder half brother did not love them or, more importantly, provide generously for them. Mothers worried about such things; it was their nature. Lady Irina worried; Kiera would worry herself—unless she married the prince, then she'd explain it all to him, as Mother had explained it to her, as the prince's mother would have surely explained it to him—

If the prince had been raised by his mother, which he hadn't. And neither, for that matter, had the queen. That priestly uncle of hers made Kiera's skin crawl when he looked at her, which he'd done frequently while Kyle's fate hung in the balance. He'd asked her questions, in the privacy of the queen's chambers; he'd asked her to unlace her gown. God alone knew what might have happened if the queen hadn't stormed in at just the right moment. The queen's shortcomings, which *were* numerous, could all be traced back to her uncle.

Without the wisdom of their deceased mothers to guide

them, the prince and the queen were locked in a battle of wills that could only get worse—unless someone wise, bold, and courageous intervened.

Kiera had done her best in the little time she'd had. She'd convinced the queen to offer a festive banquet the night before the Eigela cohort departed Chegnon—whenever that would be, whenever the horses, men, and provisions that Father was sworn to provide finally arrived. There was no assurance that the prince would descend from his tower for the festive event. Kyle might not attend, either.

God knew where Kyle's loyalties lay these days and though the Hidden God *did* still speak with her, He didn't listen and He didn't answer questions.

She was sincerely tempted to march through the inner gate, reach up from her toes, and smash those two handsome heads together until there was room for sense in their manly skulls. They'd listen to her; Kiera was calmly certain of that, because what she had to say was so clearly sensible, but Geregonal wouldn't and Geregonal was watching her, not the prince or her brother.

Try as she might, Kiera couldn't bring herself to like or trust the Black Lightning veteran who was the queen's closest confidant—and *lover*. She'd seen that in the furtive looks they exchanged, the way they contrived to touch hands in the most casual conversation, and the way Queen Ezrae's breath caught ever so slightly in her throat when they did. In her most private heart, Kiera was horrified by the risks her queen took with a common man, and the dishonor she did to Alberon's king, who doted on her. God's pockets! The king's children might not be his, though none of them looked like the glowering Geregonal.

Kiera was devoted to the queen. She could overlook the queen's affairs—she'd keep Queen Ezrae's secrets to the grave—but she couldn't look at Geregonal without being afraid of him. She didn't dare tell the queen that she didn't want Geregonal shadowing her wherever she went, or that she didn't want him and his men as her personal guards. It was a generous gesture and she risked losing the favor she'd so carefully courted.

And she certainly couldn't talk to the Gray Prince while Geregonal was watching.

If Geregonal had his way, she wouldn't talk to her brother

either, but she'd made it quite clear to both him and the queen that the Dainis were a family that *talked* to one another—even when they didn't see eye-to-eye. The Dainis took care of one another and, on their founding ancestor's advice, stayed well away from royal politics.

Queen Ezrae had laughed hard enough to cramp her womb. Kiera still didn't know what the queen had found so amusing, but there'd been no more complaints about her arena lessons—except that Geregonal watched her from the shadows—and there'd be no recrimination after she spoke with her brother about the queen's banquet.

Kyle started out of the arena arm in arm with the prince, all eyes and thoughts for royalty, nothing left for her. God's pockets! After endless years of innocence and ignorance, Kyle would pick *today* to ingratiate himself with the prince!

There was no women's justice. None whatsoever.

Kiera tugged his sleeve as he walked by. He pulled free without a glance. She tugged again, harder, and finally got his attention. His expression—grudge toward her, regret to the prince—wasn't one she wanted to see, but he did drop his arm from Prince Gravais' shoulder.

"I'm sorry," he muttered, predictably.

The prince stopped short. His gaze fell on her and she smiled up at him, damning Geregonal. Answering her with a grin of his own, the Gray Prince tucked his fists on his hips.

"Apology declined, Dreamer," he said after a moment. "Your sister wants her lesson. No honorable man could refuse."

Eyes bright and still smiling, the prince took her unadorned hand—Kyle forbade her jewelry when she came to the arena. The sleeve beneath her clanking mail shirt was coarse linen and stained from previous misadventures here. Yet she did not resist. His breath was warm and moist. Her spine tingled when his thumb brushed her fingers, holding them gently as he raised her hand to his lips.

Kiera thought of Flen, and forgot him instantly. Flen's kisses weren't so exciting and anyway she'd given Renard a letter, along with the praverge ring, to give to Flen. She was going to the Eigela. She'd become part of Alberon's future and couldn't be bound by old promises. Flen would understand.

Kiera held her breath and kept her eyes open so the kiss would etch itself into her memory. And then—without warning and certainly without intent—she *blushed*. Heat flooded her cheeks. Her smile, which she'd practiced until it was reliably demure and mysterious, turned into a broad, silly grin that narrowed her eyes. She couldn't see anything, couldn't feel his lips for her body's furious heat.

"Runs in the family, eh, Dreamer?" the prince asked her brother as he released her hand.

Kyle, naturally, had no answer and Prince Gravais was gone before Kiera collected her wits again. She thumped her head against her brother's mailed chest and groaned.

"I'm mortified. I've made an utter fool of myself." He shed a gauntlet and rested his hand on her hair, his sweaty, leather-stained hand—not that she truly cared. "I'd sooner die than face him again."

"Hush. No one's ever died of a red face. God knows where I'd be otherwise."

"You, maybe, but I've never done anything *so* hideous, not even when you dropped me in the mud the first time I came here."

"Sand, Ki, *sand*. It brushes off much easier than mud. We're very careful with our butts."

He could still make her laugh at the most ridiculous thoughts. Tears seeped from her eyes.

"Are you laughing or crying, Ki?"

"Both," she answered honestly, then, for a moment, it was all crying. "God's velvet pockets, Kyle—I've been trying to get him to notice me since we got here. Borrowed gowns, borrowed jewels, dancing and singing—nothing availed me, nothing at all. I might have been a soot splotch on the wall. But when I wear rags and a shapeless metal shirt, he smiles and lifts my hand! And then *I* melt like some cow-eyed peasant. I've made such a fool of myself." And not with the flaming blush or her outlandish attire—though they were bad enough—but all the other devices she'd borrowed from the queen and the queen's maids. The prince wasn't the only one mocking her. "Do you laugh at me, too?"

Kyle hesitated—for which she wanted to kick him sharply in the shin—and finally said, "No, never *at* you."

"But His Highness thinks I'm a fool, doesn't he? A pretty little fool from some southern valley, who's never been to court before and behaves like the queen's puppet."

Another hesitation. "His Highness thinks you're betrothed,

and you are. Muredoch made certain Gray knew it before he left."

"Damn! Damn Father, Muredoch, the Gray Prince, and *you*!"

"Kiera! Mind your tongue."

The last thing Kiera wanted was a scolding from her little brother. "You could have told me! You could have told me before this!" She wrested away from him, eyeing the canvas-covered heap where the wooden swords were kept. "How long have they been gone? And all that time you've stood aside while I tried to catch his eye. How dare you say you weren't laughing at me. What about *our* oath, Kyle Dainis, the oaths we gave each other!"

She tugged away and threw the canvas aside, not quite aiming at her brother, not caring, either, when a spray of water struck his face. Grabbing the first hilt she saw, Kiera swung it hard enough to make the air sing, then she stood at hazard, the way she'd been taught. Kyle retreated and raised his sword.

It did her good to see that retreat. If she'd learned nothing else on the sand, she'd learned that her little brother was a formidable opponent who didn't need to retreat from anyone. But he was unaware of his presence, even after battling the prince to a draw. He took her anger seriously; she had him on the defensive.

"Well," she demanded, slashing the sword through the air a second time. "What about your oaths? Do you expect me to believe that you simply *forgot* that you were supposed to help me? That my desires were supposed to be your desires?"

"What manner of desires do you have, Kiera?" Kyle still kept his distance. "Do you desire Gray any more than you desire Flennon Houle? Is it that he's a prince—a prince you don't trust, as I recall—and Flen's only a praverge of some southern valley? Is there room for anyone but you in your desires?"

"No," she snarled back, a sweeping, not entirely accurate answer to a question he'd had no right to ask. "I've got to take care of myself first, as best I can. If there's a higher branch, I'll reach for it. I'll pull myself up and you, above all, should be grateful. You're not headed anywhere, hart-lord of Dainis, even with a wizard haunting your thoughts!"

Kiera swung her sword a third time and lunged as she did, for emphasis and a bit of drama. She truly didn't see Kyle move to beat her wood weapon aside. Only, one moment she knew what she was doing, and the next, everything felt unfamiliar as the sword splintered and the hilt bucked in her palm. Looking down, she saw blood on her wrist. Her fingers spasmed, more from shock than pain. The sword fell. She clutched her forearm against her breast and saw a stranger where her brother stood.

"I could have *killed* you," he said and seemed, also, to be saying that such had been his intent. "It's a sword, Kiera, a weapon, for God's sake. I could've killed you, coming at me like that."

There was pain in her arm, in her elbow, but—"I can't feel my fingers! You've cut through my fingers!"

He snarled that he hadn't and twisted her wrist until she could see that he was telling the truth. There was a nasty splinter jutting out of her palm. As long as her little finger, it had broken loose from the sword when it splintered, and gouged the width of her hand before embedding itself at the base of her thumb. Before she could protest, Kyle had dropped his sword and plucked the wood out. Then, he clamped his hand around her wrist and squeezed. The wound bled free and burned.

"You're hurting me!"

Without replying or relenting, Kyle kicked the worthless wood toward the fence. He scooped up his own sword and pulled her toward the gate.

"It's got to bleed out. I'm taking you to the armory. He'll burn it."

Kiera knew what Kyle was talking about. When a wound was too dirty or too tattered to be sewn, Mother sent the men and fosterlings down to the forge. She'd heard the boys wail when the smith laid his hot iron across their bleeding flesh, seen the ugly, meat-colored scabs that took forever to heal into ugly, meat-colored scars.

"You can't! I'll have a *scar!*"

"You should have thought of that before you swung at my face. No more of this, do you hear me? No more swords. No more princes. No more adventures."

He flung the inner gate open, left it swinging, then did the same with the outer gate. They started down the gravel path to the stables, Kyle leading, and her stuck to his hand.

"By the bolt, Ki—I could have killed you!"

He was right to be distraught; it was his fault. He was the one who had the steel sword. He was the one who said he knew what he was doing and that he wouldn't hurt her. *He'd* been wrong. And *she* could have died. She could be dead, at this very moment . . .

"Wait—stop. I can't—" She stumbled. The sky was gray and fading, and so was his face. "I'm going to faint."

She did, and vomited as well, but Kyle never let go of her. He swept her up in his arms while she was still gasping, and ran down the path to the Chegnon forge, shouting for the smith to stoke his fire.

Thank God, the smith took one look at her hand and said there was no need for burning. It was a nasty gouge, but it had already bled white and wanted only a bit of salve and clean linen, both of which he kept in good supply. And—she thanked God a second time—the smith did the bandaging, not her brother. Kyle would have tied the knots too tight. He hadn't said a word to her since he picked her up, and with his lips pulled into pale lines, she was in no hurry to hear his voice.

There was a commotion in the lower bailey as the smith finished his work: shouts and hoof clops that drew everyone's attention. Kiera saw a chance to slip past Kyle. She had one foot in sunlight when he called her back.

"No more foolishness, Ki. No swords, no princes. It's too dangerous."

Kiera was about to say something she knew she'd regret when Enobred raced up, waving his arms.

"Tri-blue! Tri-blue, Kyle—*They're here!* Josaf and Renard and the rest! They're here!"

Kyle's eyes stayed fixed on her for another heartbeat. His brows twitched and his mouth threatened words that he couldn't say, not now with the overdue Dainismen finally arrived. He hesitated another moment, then he was off after Enobred, who, having delivered his message, was on his way back to the lower bailey.

The next two days were a complete tumult as bundle after bundle of provisions for some twenty-five people and their horses were gathered in the lower bailey. There'd be no carriage this time. Kiera would have to ride like the men. Father had sent two geldings for her use—surefooted, placid creatures who wouldn't care what she did with her hands, heels, or reins so long as there was another horse in front of them. The pair were insults to her skills as a rider, and she dearly wanted to beg two spirited mares from the queen's string. But Queen Ezrae had taken to her bed and was avoiding everyone.

Kiera only avoided Kyle, and she avoided him with considerable skill. Their paths crossed constantly, but she was never alone, never able to finish their argument. Lille was always at her side, Renard was usually near Lille, and Kyle never had a chance. The smith's salve worked as well as Mother's—a supply of which she had in a padded leather box that whichever gelding she wasn't riding would carry. Her wrist no longer hurt and it seemed likely that it would heal without a noticeable scar.

She would have forgotten that whole, unfortunate afternoon—if Kyle's expression had softened when he looked at her, if he weren't still watching her with unspoken words hot on his tongue. But he was watching her, and she couldn't forget what they'd said to each other.

Prince Gravais was, by every conceivable measure, several steps above Flennon Houle—which even Flen recognized. Renard had given him her message—he'd been waiting at Roc Dainis when they arrived—and brought back his reply. Flen hoped she'd reconsider when she returned from the Eigela, but in the meantime he accepted his ring and would explain to their fathers that the betrothal was no longer valid. Josaf had brought a separate message for her from Father, which she didn't read, merely tucked in the bottom of Mother's medicine chest. Father couldn't complain if she married the prince, wouldn't complain if she renewed her betrothal vows with Flen.

Another time Kiera would have sought out her brother and discussed it all with him, but not this time. She didn't even invite him to the queen's banquet the night before they set out for the Eigela.

He came, though, and so did the prince. Kyle sat with Josaf and the other Dainismen at the foot of the table where men drank dark ale instead of wine. They jostled one another in animated conversation and seemed to enjoy themselves heartily. Kiera sat on the queen's left. Prince Gravais sat in his father's place, though not in his chair, and little Nyan, the eldest of Queen Ezrae's sons, sat between them.

The boy was irritable, as boys would be when supper didn't start until after bedtime and they'd been laced into uncomfortable clothing. Kiera couldn't help but notice that Nyan minded the Gray Prince better than he minded his mother—of course, his mother mostly ignored him, while Prince Gravais clearly preferred talking to the boy.

But that, in itself, had made the rest of the interminable meal worthwhile.

"He has brotherly affection for your sons, my lady," Kiera assured the queen later.

Queen Ezrae raised her arms. Kiera, Lille, and her other chosen maids for this special evening, loosened the many bows that held her crimson dress together and began to remove it piece by piece: sleeves, robe, skirt, bodice, and linen chemise. Stripped of her finery, the price of the many royal pregnancies could be easily read in Ezrae's hollow neck, protruding ribs, and huge, sagging belly. But it showed most of all when they lifted away her wig with its trailing, golden curls. The queen's hair was thin and lifeless; its once-brilliant gold had turned ash. She looked older than Lady Irina and—though Kiera would never think of saying such a thing aloud to anyone—as if she might not survive this pregnancy.

"My lady mother says that if brothers love each other, then their family is secure," Kiera chattered as she brought forth the queen's nightgown. "She says she never worries about what will become of us—"

The queen's hard eyes bored into hers. "Then, child, your lady mother is either a liar or a fool."

Kiera couldn't breathe for shock. She'd heard Queen Ezrae rage and heard her moan, but she'd never heard such calculated coldness.

"But she is, dear child." The queen smiled, took Kiera's hand—the injured one—and squeezed it until she winced. "No mother can know what will happen to her children tomorrow.

You and Kyle depart for the distant Eigela. A thousand dire fates could befall you along the way."

Queen Ezrae meant to be comforting, Kiera told herself, just as the death grip circling her hand was meant as comfort. The queen was tired; her pregnancy had been uncommonly difficult. She was weary, anxious, and apt to say the wrong thing. But nothing Kiera told herself could banish the sense of malice that lingered in the bedchamber as Lille braided the queen's limp hair and they all assisted her into her bed.

Lille had sensed the same mood. Her eyes were still wide with forbidden knowledge and suspicion when, at last, they were in their own chamber.

"She means us harm," Lille insisted as she lit candles and ransacked their mattresses for loose bits of straw and horsehair. She plaited what she found. "A thousand fates. A thousand *dire* fates. She cast the evil eye on us, my lady. I felt it."

Lille tossed her first straw-and-horsehair ring on the fire—a common warding charm in common houses. She started on a second ring, but Kiera snatched the bits away and tossed them into the ashes.

"Don't be such a goose! Queen Ezrae loves us. She was tired, that's all, worried about her own children. Nothing more."

Lille watched the bits crackle and burn. "Yes, my lady. Nothing at all, my lady."

"Just tell yourself that, again and again, until you believe it."

But later, when the candles had guttered and Kiera couldn't sleep, she heard Lille by the hearth again, whispering words that didn't carry the width of the room. Kiera didn't join Lille. She stayed beneath her blankets, not warm, not safe—and not about to chide her friend when fear had gripped her own heart.

Chapter Sixteen

Three banners preceded Kyle and the other members of Prince Gravais' cohort when they rode through the streets of Chegnon town at the start of their journey. The gold and black of an armed sun on a field of red, the prince's personal device, waved in the middle. A plain black square adorned with two aqua circles and two silver crescents flew to its right: the cryptic symbols with which Lockwood, Lord Marelet, proclaimed his profession and his loyalty. And to the left of the armed sun, the tri-blue chevrons—sky blue, ocean blue and midnight—of the Dainis family, unembellished because neither he nor Kiera was entitled to a personal device.

<<That will change,>> Taslim promised. <<When we return from the Siege.>>

Kyle shook his head and held his thoughts close, determined that neither his wizard's carping nor his sister's aloofness would spoil an otherwise perfect moment.

The folk of Chegnon town were accustomed to banner processions. They gathered in the streets, cheering whoever rode past and waving scraps of red cloth that echoed the royal standard. Prosperous tradesmen bedecked their establishments with cloths that honored the Maradze kings and advertised their wares at the same time. The practice was most true of the gaming houses and taverns and, especially, the brothels.

Laughing night-sisters with painted faces and loose linen gowns draped themselves over balcony rails. They tossed petals and feathers into the air and promised their charms to any man who looked their way—as Kyle was very careful not to do, even when he heard his own name in their chorus.

<<Go ahead,>> Taslim urged. <<What's the harm? Give them a wave and a smile. Give *me* something other than the Bitch and your sister to stir my ancient longings.>>

Kyle blushed—the curse of his existence—and fixed his attention on the furry tips of Rawne's active ears. The air there shimmered, and the equine ears suddenly were moving in a very different, very provocative, way.

<<None of that!>> Kyle blinked and cleared his vision. <<I'm not interested.>>

<<Not interested! By the almighty bolt, Hart-lord, you're a sorry excuse for a man.>>

<<I'm not,>> he insisted, and his ears rang with wizard laughter.

He thought of the moments when Lockwood's talisman had burned his imagination, and he feared Taslim had learned his darkest secrets. Then the lewd illusion returned, exactly as before: dark brown night-sisters swaying beside each other. Kyle grit his teeth and shook his head to banish it again. His movements in the saddle were more than Rawne was prepared to tolerate on the crowded, noisy streets. The gelding pranced sideways on the cobblestones, bumping into Lockwood's raw-boned bay. One look from *that* wizard and Kyle found his thoughts utterly unsettled, but absolutely his own again.

"Problems back there?" Lockwood asked when the balcony distractions were behind them and the horses walked easily again.

"He's not a city horse, my lord." Kyle laid the blame on the innocent.

He wanted to press his heels into Rawne's flanks, but Lockwood spoke before he had the chance:

"Shall I keep my distance, then?" The question came with a slight smile.

"No need, my lord Marelet. He's settled now, and we're almost at the gate."

"I find titles tiresome, my own most of all. We're to be crowded into four tents. There won't be space for lords, barely enough for a highness."

Despite his own misgivings, Kyle relaxed. After that first supper in the prince's chamber, Kyle had kept a healthy distance between himself and the prince's boon-friend, which the wizard hadn't challenged. Indeed, Lockwood treated him with the same rough humor with which he treated everyone. Taslim wouldn't say anything about Lockwood, except that he didn't trust him, which was the pot and the kettle and no consolation at all for Kyle.

"So, what's it to be? Locky? Lockwood? You there with the lightning?"

"Lockwood, I guess," Kyle answered without looking up.

"You guess! Then, I *guess* I'll call you Kyle. Well, Kyle, how many days do you guess we'll need to reach the Eigela and start this search in earnest?"

"Four, if we ride hard and there's no bad weather."

"Fair enough. But we'll have weather, Kyle; wager on it. We're going north and into the Spure. This time of year it could be rain, could be sleet or snow. Then again, look at your sister. She sits her horse well, I grant her that, but I'll wager she's ridden no harder than a warm, sunny day with a hawk on her arm and her own pillow neath her head by sundown. Gray's too much the gracious prince to make a lady ride hard, especially in bad weather."

"No wager, my lord— *Lockwood.* You're right about Kiera, and I've no money of my own," Kyle responded soberly.

"None at all? Lord Dainis sent all this"—Lockwood swept a hand at the horses and baggage—"and not even a tin fent for you to toss at a crossroads beggar? Lightning strike! I was depending on you for a game of odds-and-evens by the fire."

Kyle stared straight ahead. There had to be a purpose in the wizard's banter, but none that he could eke out. "Josaf carries our coin coffer," he explained, more edge in his voice than he'd intended, or was wise with the prince's boon-friend. "I wouldn't ask him to cover an idle wager."

"An idle wager, is it, Kyle? And what other kinds of wagers are there? Never mind, we'll make this the idlest wager under the sun: My silver on both sides. You *can't* lose, Kyle. A crettig a day—how many days until we reach the Eigela?"

"Ten?"

"Say twenty, and you'll be rich."

"Our provisions would be gone. We'll be above the Spure with nothing to eat! The horses can graze, but we'll be hard-pressed."

"Why, we'll hunt—like worthy noblemen, or didn't you notice those bows yonder?" Lockwood pointed at a sheaf of hardwood which Kyle had noticed but mistaken for tent staves. "Of course, that takes time. One rabbit won't feed this lot. But there's big game in the Spure: bear and boar and black elk. Add time to track it, though, and more time to roast it over an open fire, but—by the bolt, Kyle—if the hunting's good and the wood's dry, we'll see the black mountains by summer. What do you say to that?"

"I'd say, my lord, that you must have a reason for telling me this, but I don't guess what it is."

Lockwood sat back in his saddle, a look of surprise and then a smile on his face. "'My lord,' I deserved that. There is a reason, Kyle. Taslim rode hard when he went looking for the Siege—"

Kyle's head snapped around, wondering how Lockwood knew; it was nothing he'd heard Taslim say, even to Lord Marrek.

"A guess, Kyle," Lockwood responded quickly, setting him at ease again. "But no idle wager, either. He wasn't traveling with princes or ladies, and he believed in what he was looking for."

"Prince Gravais doesn't believe we'll find anything?"

Another one of Lockwood's smiles. "Do you?"

Kyle thought of the broken face and quickly banished the thought. He said nothing.

"We'll get to the Eigela, Kyle, and we'll look for the Siege of Shadows. Gray would like nothing better than to come home with something to show for this wandering. When Taslim gets impatient, you tell him that."

"When?"

"Another guess. There's no wizard alive who can pluck the thoughts of another man from his mind. Not me. Not Marrek Brun. And not Taslim of Fawlen—but I *thought* you already knew that. Sometimes your thoughts are as plain as spots on a cow, Kyle; that's your undoing, not wizardry."

"I—"

"You've kept secrets from us all."

"I—" Kyle lost his hold on Rawne's reins. His cheeks grew warm and he tucked his chin while he groped after the reins.

Lockwood leaned forward. He snagged a trailing length of leather and held it beyond Kyle's reach. "Spots on a cow, Kyle. I know you're keeping some, but I don't know what they are. I hope they're not important. Gray's my lord and my boon-friend; there's no secret there. I'll do whatever I can to protect him, whatever I have to do. You understand that?" He offered the rein.

"Yes," Kyle answered, no names or titles.

His flush had subsided in a wave of cold anxiety. He reached for the leather; Lockwood seized his wrist instead. The tingling he'd felt in the prince's chamber returned, though not nearly as strong. When he met Lockwood's stare, he couldn't turn away. He was frightened but there was nothing fearsome in the wizard's dark, steady eyes.

"I wouldn't harm the prince, Lockwood. I wouldn't harm anyone."

"I believe you." Lockwood released his wrist. The tingling ebbed slowly. "Think on this, Kyle. If you have secrets from Fawlen, he may have kept secrets from you. What comes and goes on the wind of nasen'bei is as free as you or I, and just as clever."

The moment for asking questions or sharing confidences came to an abrupt end. They were at the town gate. Not even a royal prince could leave the town without the gatekeeper's knowledge and consent. The paunchy man walked among them, asking their names and squinting up at their eyes when they answered, as if he were the sole judge of righteousness in all Alberon.

"Lockwood," the wizard said when the man got to him. "Wizard. Lord of Marelet." He thrust forth his fist and a heavy, onyx signet ring.

"And you?" he asked Kyle.

"Kyle Dainis, hart-lord of Dainis." He had no ring, nor anything but his word to prove himself.

"And the other?"

"What other?"

"The demon. You speak for him, or can he speak for himself?"

The question took Kyle back to the dragon chamber. He endured a resurgence of all the fears he'd thought he'd laid to rest, and felt them all the stronger because they'd taken him by surprise. His witlessness drew scrutiny that left him all the more unable—unwilling—to speak.

The gatekeeper beckoned to his armed henchmen. The air inside Chegnon town thickened in Kyle's lungs. Lockwood had already ridden ahead. Kyle began to panic.

"What manner of nonsense is this?" Lockwood's voice cut

through the silence as his horse thrust its neck between Kyle and the gatekeeper. "He's given his name; his banner flies beside the armed sun." The wizard was loud and angry; the prince on the far side of the wall turned his horse around. Then Lockwood leaned forward and asked, in an icy whisper, "Who gave you your orders this morning? Tell me, or tell Prince Gravais—"

The gatekeeper retreated. "Pass on," he said before the prince arrived. "Pass on, all of you," and waved the men-at-arms and varlets forward, cutting off the prince.

Lockwood stayed beside Kyle. They'd gone some distance beyond the town before Kyle subdued his fears—and anger—enough to speak.

"I'm grateful," he admitted, simple and stiff, but repressing "my lord" at the last. "With all the attention . . . Sometimes, nothing makes sense."

"If the Siege of Shadows exists," Lockwood replied, "if we return with its secrets mastered, then Alberon will change. There are those who resist change—any change at all—simply because it is change; and there are those who welcome it for the same reason. Between them are those—wizards and priests among them—who welcome change only if it works to their advantage. There's no one who doesn't know the Harbinger flew at solstice-tide, and no one who doesn't have a thought, one way or another, about what we're looking for. You've got enemies, Kyle Dainis, and Fawlen's got enemies. You've got friends, too, good allies—if you don't depend overmuch on them."

Kyle gathered Rawne's reins in one hand and shot a glance at Chegnon's receding walls. "I'm glad to have our enemies behind us."

He expected a reply—at least polite agreement about the best place to keep one's enemies, in keeping with Lockwood's bantering style. He hoped for specific knowledge of who his enemies were; it didn't seem likely that Ferra Baldescare would employ an ordinary gatekeeper to harass him. But he got silence instead, profound and lengthy silence. Lockwood didn't spur his horse away, though. The wizard held pace alongside Rawne, giving nothing away, until Kyle questioned himself.

"I haven't left *our* enemies behind, have I?"

Lockwood faced him from the saddle, but the silence continued.

"*I* don't have enemies—or I wouldn't, except for Taslim. I have friends and allies, but does Taslim? Does he have any dependable allies in this? Any friends?"

"You," Lockwood answered without hesitation.

That wasn't the answer Kyle had hoped to hear. There was a profound emptiness in the darkness of his mind whenever Lockwood was near: Taslim making himself very scarce. Taslim treating Lockwood as not merely untrustworthy, but as an enemy. Lockwood, who knew he, a haunted hart-lord, had secrets and who'd just admitted there were wizards among their enemies. Which wizards? Lord Marrek Brun? Other wizards, not allied with the king? Lockwood himself, who said the prince was both his lord and friend?

Kyle considered asking blunt questions, then reconsidered. Lockwood wasn't the sort who could be intimidated and, whatever stood between the two wizards, Kyle didn't want Lockwood for an open enemy. So Kyle lapsed into his own silence, and after a few moments, Lockwood reined his horse and rode elsewhere in the cohort.

<<Taslim?>>

The emptiness lingered. Wherever Taslim had gone, Kyle's inquiries didn't reach him, or perhaps Taslim's distrust of Lockwood had extended to Kyle himself. They'd never resolved the matter of friendship. They were allies by unusual circumstance: Taslim wanted the Siege of Shadows; Kyle wanted the masked warrior of his Rapture—and both were in the Eigela.

There was more than a single afternoon's pondering in those thoughts, especially when the afternoon and the pondering were interruped by leg cramps. Leg cramps such as he'd never suffered before, but then he'd never spent half the winter sick in bed or marking time at the king's court. Swordwork helped; he didn't want to think how sore he'd be without those hours in the sand. But swordwork wasn't enough, and Kyle had no objections when the prince called for an early halt and the bannermen led the cohort into the noisy, crowded yard of a roadside inn.

When the king and court made their progress through Alberon, they traveled from one roc to the next, exchanging largesse with the verge-lords, but when royalty wanted to move swiftly or without fanfare, they stayed at inns where any man with a pair of fents could buy a crusty loaf of bread and a ladling of hearty soup to pour over it.

Kyle had visited inns before, in fosterage and last autumn when he prepared their way to the lodge, but Kiera had never been inside their wooden palisades. She wriggled, wide-eyed, in the saddle, taking in every detail of the vibrant squalor, and plainly dismayed by the fetlock-deep muck that passed for the inn's courtyard. Her horse slipped and pawed as unfamiliar hostlers scurried through the royal cohort, taking reins and tin coin bribes.

Kyle's purse was empty—as he'd told Lockwood. For Rawne's sake, he could only hope that Josaf would dole out a crettig or two, to be split among all the hostlers. He'd remind Josaf, if he had to, but first he had to dismount himself—no easy task when his back was throbbing and his legs felt like soggy sacks of grain—and then he had to help Kiera. Pain shot past his knees when his feet touched the ground. Certain that it must be worse for Kiera, he shuffled through the muck as quickly as he dared.

Renard spotted him. "I'll fetch her, my lord. Never you mind."

Renard already had Lille in his arms and halfway to the inn's wooden porch. The braggart had ridden around from Renzi with the provisions; his winter knots were distant memories. He could have danced in his saddle at the pace the prince set. But there was no way under heaven that Kyle was going to let Renard carry Kiera, not if he tore his hamstrings getting to her first.

He had Renard beaten, but not Geregonal. The Black Lightning veteran strode in front of him and lifted Kiera out of the saddle, gently as he pleased. Kyle was left standing in the muck, too sore to curse.

A hand fell on his shoulder: Josaf, hale and limber as Renard, and asking for help with the baggage.

"That's a bad thing," the old man said when they were out of earshot. "Black Lightning and your sister. How'd it come to happen?"

There were rivalries between Alberon's mercenary cohorts, bad blood as old as the Praysean wars they fought for others. The Dainis served in the Gray Wolves; they were commanders there before they became vergers at home. The Gray Wolves might agree to fight simply because there were Black Lightning men fighting for the other side. By the king's law, the rivalries were forbidden and forgotten when a veteran came home. It was a good law, a wise law, and observed mostly in the breach.

"He's the captain of the queen's guard, and she sent him and three others to keep her safe."

Josaf's eyebrows rose. "Safe? Since when do the Dainis need the Lightning to keep them safe?"

"There wasn't anything I could do about it, Josaf. Kiera's bound herself to the queen. You saw how it was before Father left; it didn't get better after."

"As may be," Josaf nodded. "But a bad thing all the same. You go along inside, keep an eye on them. The boys and I will take care of the rest."

He'd failed. Father had told him to take care of Kiera, and he'd failed. He hadn't weaned her away from the queen. If anything, he'd driven her deeper into the Baldescare clutches. He hadn't known a way to prevent it, but with another man—a better man—the story would have been different.

<<Remember that, Hart-lord. Your father and brother couldn't stop her from going where she'd go. By your judgment, then, they're no better men than you.>>

Kyle began to berate the wizard for spying, but the prince and Lockwood were walking toward him and Taslim buried himself in darkness. Gray offered him a bed in an upstairs room, which Kyle considered, until he saw the steep stairs. The worst of the leg cramps had already faded, but he didn't want anything between him and his blankets that required lifting his knees.

The inn was as dirty as every other inn that misfortune had brought Kyle to in the past. The chimney smoked, the wenches shrieked. Everyone needed a bath. But the food made up for the rest. Maybe it was that he was tired and sore and out of sorts. Maybe it was that he preferred his meat sliced fresh off the spit, undisguised by spices or sauce. And maybe it was the dark-eyed, curly haired wench who lavished her attention on him and him alone when all the other wenches seemed to have taken aim at the prince and Lockwood. She brought him country ale: dark, sweet, and potent enough to banish the chill of the rain that had begun to fall after sundown.

Kiera and Lille went upstairs as soon as they'd finished eating. A local man appeared to entertain them with ballads that grew more ribald as the hearth fire burned down. Lucky men withdrew to their rooms, if they had them, to the stables or a shadowy corner, if they didn't. This night, Kyle Dainis was a lucky man, with his back eased up against a warm chimney and an arm snugged comfortably around the dark-eyed wench. The doubts he'd nurtured since he'd touched Lockwood's talisman vanished on the tip of her tongue.

She left with the other women when the balladeer departed and the innkeeper snuffed out the lamps. With his mood and body both restored, Kyle spread his blankets on the straw-strewn floor, then pulled his cloak up around his chin. He was asleep when she came back; he thought he was dreaming when she slid in beside him beneath the cloak.

"La, milord," she laughed softly in the singsong patter of wenches who'd known too many men. "You sleep with your boots on and your belt buckled tight."

She seized the tag end of Kyle's belt and jerked it loose. He knew he was awake then, and trapped with his back to the wall.

"I've got nothing to give you, girl," he whispered urgently, earnestly.

"La, milord, I'd not say that."

Her one hand was already under his shirt and the thong that held Kyle's trousers taut beneath his belt was under assault. He caught her wrist and held her—barely—at bay.

"No silver. Not even tin. Nothing at all. I'm not what I seem. I'm just a hart-lord."

"La, milord—you seem like a fine man to me, but you talk too much," she complained as she sealed his lips with first her fingers, then a kiss that left him hoping for more.

Kyle was ashamed of himself, fearful they'd be interrupted, and pleased to be the center of someone's thoughts for a little while. She was gone to her chores before the dawn's light awakened him, and he was pleased by that, too. No one seemed to notice that he had to get dressed even though he hadn't bothered to undress before he lay down.

At least, no one noticed aloud.

Breakfast was porridge and cold leavings from the night before, served by pot boys and the innkeeper's wife. Kyle ate quickly and went outside where the sun was shining and feminine laughter escaped from the hen coop. A voice in his conscience that had nothing to do with Taslim of Fawlen told him to leave well enough alone, but he eased into the coop's shadow.

"La, girl—you owe me another five. I got the tassel from his trousers to prove I done it."

Kyle pressed a hand against his hip. His heart skipped a beat: The little tassel that kept the long leather thong from disappearing into his trouser band was, indeed, missing.

"But was it—"

"La, t'weren't no different from any other man. Naught special about him at all. Naught scary, or haunted."

There was a chorus of disappointed sighs that left Kyle cold in the gut.

"Except, I done it, and you owe me another five."

He heard the clink of coins as he walked away.

<<She was energetic . . . satisfying, in her way, but you didn't think there was *another* reason did you, Hart-lord? By the bolt, did you think she found you *attractive*?>> That from Taslim, along with a chuckle that echoed endlessly between his ears.

He had, of course. He'd dared to think of himself as the equal of other men—perhaps not the prince, but ordinary men. That, more than the wench's enterprising betrayal, was what hurt.

"Damn you!" he shouted, taking a swing at an opponent who wasn't there.

Kyle set the geese squawking and that drew the wenches out of the hen coop: The very last thing he'd wanted to do. She spotted him, called his name—which she knew, though he hadn't learned hers—and came after him. He refused to turn around, refused to run. A weight circled his arm at the stable door. Kyle made a fist, then forced his fingers to uncurl. He didn't hit women; he didn't hit much of anything away from the arena sand, and he wasn't particularly manly there, either. But he had nothing to say and she released him.

"You shouldn't've been there listening, milord."

Of course, everything was always *his* fault.

"What I said wasn't for you to hear, milord."

He sidestepped; she followed.

"La, you were a gentleman, milord—a true, gentle man like

is hard to find anywhere. You were kind and tender. But I couldn't tell them that, milord. They wouldn't've believed me."

"And a lie was worth five fents, bother the truth . . . or me."

"Crettigs, milord," she grinned. "Wouldn't go with a demon for tin, milord. La—that wouldn't've been worth the trouble—but I'd go with you now, for nothing at all."

Kyle let his anger out with a sigh. He still had nothing to say and there wasn't time for the other. She grabbed his hand.

"Half's yours." She dribbled five crettigs into his palm along with the pinched-off tassel. "You're as poor as you said. I know; I looked."

The five silver bits were the first coins Kyle had ever *earned*. He was too astonished to speak or throw them back at her. Then, without warning, she reached up from her toes, wrapped her arms around his neck, and kissed him like a lover.

"You be good, milord," she said as she ran away. "You stay safe."

Kyle was still gaping when he felt a familiar presence in his thoughts: <<I—>>

<<Not a word, Taslim. Not a damned word, or I swear you'll dwell in darkness until we reach the mountains.>>

He expected Taslim to ignore his threats and requests alike, as he usually did. In truth, Kyle wanted an excuse to start an argument. But the wizard faded into mind shadows and Kyle was alone by the stable door with a handful of coins, which he secreted carefully into his belt pouch. He added the tassel to the pouch as well; it was much too precious now to attach to his trousers. He was tying a clumsy knot in the leather thong when a horse nose butted his arm.

A stableboy had spotted him and, remembering the horse he'd ridden, brought Rawne up without being asked. Rawne was glad to see him, hoping for an apple he didn't have and ready for another day's adventure. Kyle scratched the places only fingers could reach, muttered all the endearments he felt for the horse, then handed the reins back to the stableboy.

"Thank you for bringing him up. He's been well cared for, but there's a black-legged dun, Taddy, in the line. I'm riding him today."

The boy stood where he was, leaving Kyle to wonder if he'd heard the sounds of coins flowing and expected a share. But a crettig was too much for one stableboy and one horse, and anyway, Kyle wasn't ready to part with his fortune. He kept the reins and started into the stable, intending to fetch Taddy himself. There was an awkward moment as the boy crowded forward. Rawne protested loudly and tossed his head.

"I'll get him, milord. 'S my work here, and not yours."

Kyle was tempted to backhand the boy,. but he could no more do that than he'd been able to remain angry with the wench. He surrendered the reins and thumped Rawne on the flank as the boy led him past.

"Tomorrow, friend," he promised. "But I'm in no mood for a good horse today."

That was an injustice. Taddy, the other gelding Father had sent up from Roc Dainis for his use, was a good animal, better than Rawne in some ways. When Taddy stretched into his trot, his rider could sip wine without spilling a drop. What Taddy was, was too clever by half for a horse. He had his own idea of how to get from any here to every there. Kyle would have his argument with the stable boy, with Taslim, anJ with himself all from Taddy's back and he'd land on his butt if he let his attention wander too far. There'd be no place in his thoughts for a curly haired girl—which was exactly the way he wanted it.

And the way it was, from the moment he mounted until the slanting rays of the late afternoon sun pointed the cohort to another inn. This time Kyle accepted the prince's offer of an upstairs bed and he went up alone after supper. Someone came scratching late at night, when everything was quiet, but five crettigs was enough, more than enough. He pulled his cloak over his ears.

There was rain the next day, and the day after that. No sleet or snow, not on the inland road, though who knew what was happening in the Spure or the high plain between the Spure and the Eigela?

Rain made the road treacherous and Kiera miserable. She didn't complain—Kyle was proud of her stiff back and silence—but the hardest traveling she'd done was to the lodge and back at the solstice, and that had been sitting under cover both ways.

Kiera didn't ask, but they stayed an extra day at a Bercelen inn, the last inn before they headed into the Spure for the high plain and the Eigela beyond it. They'd been on the inland road for six days then, and Josaf unlocked the Dainis coffer to send a big wooden tub up to her room and twenty buckets of hot water to fill it with. Kyle and the other men made do in a steam house behind the kitchen.

After that, they were riding trails up and through the Spure forests. As Lockwood had warned, the prince called a halt early in each afternoon to give them time to hunt for their supper. No more than five men would take their bows and spears among the trees. The rest raised the tents, tended the fire, or accompanied the prince on a royal visit to some woodsman's homestead.

The folk of the Bercelen Spure were a different breed from those who lived at the Dainis lodge. They weren't sawyers trading with the valleys, monks seeking seclusion for their prayers, or gamekeepers working for the verge-lords. The Bercelen foresters had little use for the amenities of valley life or a verge-lord's law. Alberon's kings claimed these forests for their own, but the foresters had little use for the king, or a prince, either. When pressed, they said their ancestors had sworn oaths to the immortal queen of the Hesse and had never been released.

They viewed Gray with ill-concealed suspicions. The cohort could buy flour and staples from the homestead, but only for hard coins, never royal promises.

After two days of such visits, Kyle preferred to take a bow into the woods with the hunters—unless the hunters were Geregonal and his men; then he preferred to remain in camp. He fell into the habits of his fosterage days: tending pots with varlets, avoiding his peers. Kiera glowered at him; that was half the reason he stayed away from the prince's fire. The prince didn't seem to mind and Lockwood said it was a wise man who knew what he wanted from life.

Taslim fumed—which made Kyle sneeze violently—but Taslim kept his distance. Kyle guessed the wizard was satisfied that they were headed toward the Siege of Shadows, however slowly. And Taslim was gone altogether whenever Lockwood was about.

A week and a half out of Chegnon, the forest gave way to the alpine meadows and evergreen copses of the high plain. Riding along a ridgeway late one morning, they got their first glimpse of the Eigela: blackened saw-teeth on the northern horizon, capped with snow. Taslim clamored for Kyle to squint out of one eye then the other, which was enough to alert Lockwood.

Kyle muttered under his breath that it was his usual luck to find himself between rival wizards, and kept a firm grip on Rawne's reins. The brown gelding liked Lockwood's raw-boned horse about as much as Taslim liked Lockwood.

"No sense hurrying," Lockwood said casually, as if the weather were the only interesting sight on the horizon. "It's still winter there."

It might be winter in the Eigela, but it was unseasonable summer on the rolling high plain. The air was thick. There was a blackness behind them, to the southwest, as well as the saw-tooth black up ahead—haze or smoke, possibly, but more likely a sea storm crashing through Bercelen. If the cohort were lucky, the storm would exhaust itself long before it reached them. But they had Kyle Dainis riding with them, and luck would be in short supply.

The heat was not truly oppressive—not like the last weeks of summer—but it wrapped close around them. Kyle shed his cloak and loosened his shirt. Rawne had sweated himself as dark as the clouds, and despite Kyle's best efforts to control him, he took a vicious nip at Lockwood's bay. The bay trumpeted and showed his teeth. The wizard wisely reined him away before another too casual word could be said.

The cohort strung itself out along a trail that was nothing more than a different shade of green across the meadow. With wildflowers blooming all around them, the land should have seemed beautiful. Instead it seemed unnatural and full of menace.

By afternoon they were buffeted by gusts of southwesterly wind that stayed low to the ground and struck the trees from below. It didn't take priestly weather-wards to know that a bad storm was coming, and that it would get worse for every moment it was delayed. The cohort was irritable and getting sourer by the step—except for Lockwood, who saw the promise of the year's first lightning and rode to the next hilltop for a better view.

<<What about you?>> Kyle asked Taslim. <<Are you going to want to stand out in the storm?>>

<<And risk your fool head?>> the wizard snapped; the weather affected him, wherever he was. <<Talk sense, Hartlord. You're no wizard. You'd get yourself struck and cindered—same as that arrogant bastard if he thinks he can just

snap his fingers and catch a bolt the way he did in Chegnon. The Siege is open.>>

The grassy swell where Lockwood awaited them was crescent-shaped and deeper on its inner curve. It opened to the north. The wizard said it would give them some shelter from the wind and the lightning. Gray took his advice; no one understood storms better than a freelance wizard.

Gray called an early halt. His captain, a Soaring Eagle veteran by the name of Jahn Golight, paced out the lines where the four tents and the horses would be staked. The varlets, Renard and Enobred among them, hurried to lay a weatherproof hearth and get a fire started in it.

They'd passed no homesteads this day. There'd be no backtracked royal visits to sullen subjects, which pleased everyone who would have had to ride with the prince. Gray said there'd be no hunting, either. They had enough cold meat from the forests to see them through the night, through two nights if it came to that. But they were stockpiling for the Eigela, where both firewood and game would be sparse.

Geregonal said he'd seen fresh tracks at the last stream they'd crossed.

"I'll take my men back, Your Highness, if you've no objection."

"Keep an eye overhead," Gray advised. "Go to ground if you need to. We'll wait for your return."

"I trust you will, Your Highness." Geregonal smiled. "Keep an eye overhead yourself, Your Highness."

Chapter Seventeen

Josaf was the oldest man in the Eigela cohort. A captain in the Gray Wolves in his youth, he'd held a similar rank in Lord Pancel Dainis' personal guard before stepping down to the less strenuous duties of a varlet. He'd been setting field camps since his own boyhood and, by common consent, he'd forgotten more than most men knew about living off the land. The prince's captain, Jahn Golight, was a generation younger than Josaf, but old enough to recognize the value of experience when he saw it and to make good use of it.

Since the cohort had left the inland road, Jahn had set Josaf in charge of camp making and the varlets, while he and other men-at-arms escorted the prince to whatever homesteads he'd chosen to visit. With a storm brewing, and the prince staying put for a change, Captain Golight propped his back against a half-grown tree and let Josaf give the orders.

The varlets' first attempt to raise a tent met with disaster. A wind gust took the tent for a sail and carried it across the meadow. None of the men-at-arms offered to help. Lockwood, the prince, and the women thought the sight of eight young men chasing a runaway tent was high comedy. But Kyle took no pleasure sitting, much less laughing, while others struggled to do what had to be done. He was still close to his fosterage; he understood the humiliating power of grown men's laughter, and he was, if nothing else, accustomed to Josaf's orders.

Kyle caught up with the varlets as they caught up with the vagrant tent. He held the center pole while they tied ropes and hammered stakes into the ground. Then he collected stones for the weather shield around the hearth and was prepared to take an axe down to the nearby stream in search of firewood when Renard drew him aside.

"It's not right," the young Dainisman said. "You're noble: a verger. You're not one of us. You don't belong doing our work."

Kyle leaned the long-handled axe against his leg. It balanced momentarily against the buckles of his sword scabbard, then fell flat. The sound was a counterpoint to Renard's complaint: If a man had a sword, he didn't have room for a firewood axe.

"But, I've always worked alongside you and Enobred. Josaf orders the three of us like sheep."

"Not the three of us, not *always*. Only since you came back. Maybe you spent fosterage in a kitchen; that doesn't mean you belong there. You're not one of us, Kyle."

"You call me Kyle."

"Aye—and that's wrong, too. You make yourself part of our lives and work; but we're not part of yours. You come when you please and go when you please."

They were both angry. Renard's face was drawn into a sneer; Kyle felt his face do the same.

"You needed *help*."

"We don't need *your* help, milord."

Renard reached for the axe. Fighting over a weapon—and the axe was a weapon, for all it wasn't taught by masters in the arena—was possibly the greatest mistake two men could make, but Kyle planted his foot on the haft anyway. He gave Renard a shove that sent him sprawling.

"Leave us what's ours, milord. We don't want your help. We don't want *you*."

Renard crawled for the axe. Kyle shifted his full weight to the haft and poised his other foot over the varlet's knuckles. Their eyes met and Renard withdrew.

"Then, do it yourself, milord. Chop until your hands are bloody. We won't work beside you."

Kyle snatched up the axe. "As pleases you," he snarled and headed for the line of packhorses.

Renard would reconsider. Enobred, at least, would join him, Kyle thought. He cared less what the Chegnon varlets did, but surely the Dainismen . . . Kyle peered over the horse's withers. Renard had an arm around Enobred and together they were talking with *their* peers, the Chegnon varlets.

It was the weather—the low, malicious wind—Kyle told himself as he led the horse to a streamside grove where winter-felled trees were numerous. Once the storm passed, they'd be friends again.

Kyle tied the horse to a sturdy branch, discarded his sword and shirt, selected his target, and took his first swing.

Had they ever been friends, or had he come and gone from their lives as he pleased?

Wood chips flew. Kyle dismembered the fallen tree and picked one stout log to be the firebreak. He lashed it behind the horse and drove the animal to the fire pit. Wrestling the heavy log into place, however, was men's work—two men by any reasonable reckoning, but no one offered to help. Kyle was too proud in his anger to ask. His hair was plastered against his skull, his eyes stung from sweat salt, and he'd scraped his forearms raw before he had the log where it belonged.

He went back to the streamside grove for another load. There was grass tinder and kindling near the fire pit; someone else could *start* the fire. Kyle threw his strength into each swing, splitting enough wood to fuel two fires before his aching arms demanded a rest. Sagging against the trunk of a living tree, he noticed a thin stream of smoke rising from the otherwise untended hearth. Heartened by this vaguely conciliatory gesture, he set about binding the fresh-cut wood into sheaves on the horse's back. He had a length of rope around the last sheaf when shouting erupted in the camp.

Kyle finished tying a knot before he looked up.

Of all the mistakes he'd made in his life, that was the worst.

Strangers—

Men—

With weapons drawn—

Lying about the camp—

No arena practice had prepared him for the sight of slashing swords and the screams of defenseless men as they fell.

<<Run, Hart-lord! Take this nag and *run!* They haven't seen you.>>

Kyle couldn't run. Kiera was up there. The prince was up there. Josaf—

God have mercy, Josaf's silver hair was unmistakable. Josaf had his sword, and Josaf was besieged.

<<Run, you fool! Run. You're no warrior.>>

His sword was on the ground, in its scabbard, a stride away—

<<I won't let you throw your life away, Hart-lord! I won't let you *die*!>>

Kyle's feet became stone. His legs had the strength of straw. He couldn't reach his sword. He could reach the horse, that was all: reach the horse, sweep the sheaves from its back, and ride away.

Run away.

"No!" he shouted, loud enough to be heard in the camp.

He took the single stride and retrieved his scabbard. Another stride, this one toward the camp, and the sword was free. By the third, he was running. From the corner of his eye Kyle saw a man aim an arrow at him, slow and very clear. He saw the arrow flying, saw where he and it would meet. He surged and dodged; the arrow caressed his shoulder with steel and feathers, then they went their separate ways.

Men were down and bleeding. Some writhed, some lay still. Kyle refused to recognize faces. There were only two he had to find: Kiera and Josaf.

Geregonal had returned. He and his men formed a wall around Kiera's golden hair. That left Josaf, skilled with his weapon, but slowed by age and backed against a tent. By God's mercy, Josaf got his sword under his enemy's while Kyle was still four strides away. The silver-haired varlet blocked the cut that would have taken his life at the neck.

Josaf's enemy had a dagger in his off-weapon hand. With his back to the tent ropes, Josaf could neither retreat farther nor defend himself against the thrusting dagger.

Kyle screamed; sometimes distraction bought time.

But not this time.

The dagger bit to its hilt in Josaf's left flank. Its tip—God have mercy, surely the tip burst the old man's heart. And Josaf's enemy, forewarned by Kyle's scream, left the dagger in the wound as Josaf collapsed. With his sword before him, the outlaw spun around to deflect Kyle's outraged stroke.

Kyle wanted the death of the man who'd slain Josaf. Holding the hilt with both hands, he dealt slashing cuts that would have been fatal, had they landed. But a raging, grieving heart wasn't enough to make Kyle a killer. After a few bone-rattling exchanges, the outlaw had his enemy measured. He retreated; Kyle followed.

Kyle felt the trap before he saw another outlaw on his left. His rage was blunted by fear as he sought a defensive angle between them.

Then there was only one outlaw. The second man was gone and the fear was on the face of the man who'd slain Josaf as a sword sang between him and Kyle. Blood spurted from the murderer's neck as he crumpled to the ground.

"*Kill* them, Dreamer! Don't play with them!" Gray shouted before he departed.

Kyle wiped his face. Blood and sweat clotted quickly in the gusting wind. Tears, as well.

<<Stay down. Stay out of sight. Get behind the tent—get *inside* it.>>

Kyle lashed out with his sword and his mind: <<Damn you!>> He found Taslim's presence. <<You made me cower. He's dead because of you. *Dead!* Damn you to darkness. Serras! Serras! SERRAS!>>

The wizard dissolved from his consciousness and there was darkness.

The sounds of battle subsided. Clutching his sword, Kyle dared to look around him. Men had fallen; men still fought. The cohort was winning, but at a terrible cost. Three of the varlets had been slain where they sat. A fourth—*Renard,* God have mercy—lay groaning beside them. Four men-at-arms were down, not counting Josaf.

God have mercy.

Kyle's greatest grief, greatest horror, flowed toward Josaf. He would have given anything if Josaf had moved. There was nothing as still and silent as a warm yet lifeless body. He'd seen death in the stables and at the hunt. He'd seen the dying in their beds and shrouded in a crypt. But he'd never seen sudden, bloody death steal the life from a friend's eyes. His vision blurred with a sorrow he couldn't permit, not while the clash of steel still echoed in the air.

"Damn you!"

The words rang from one side of the camp to the other. They expressed Kyle's sentiments, but they hadn't come from him. He turned and watched as a pair of outlaws made their escape on horses they'd cut from the lines.

Lockwood ran to the top of the crescent hill, brandishing his talisman instead of a sword. The runes of the wizard's spell were lost in the wind; the talisman flashed with a blinding light. Instinctively, Kyle raised a hand to shield himself. He heard Lockwood shout, but when he lowered his hand, the look he saw on the wizard's face was failure.

The skirmish was over. The remaining outlaw ambushers were either dead or dying. Kyle looked down at his unbloodied sword, then dropped it. Lille broke through the cordon the Black Lightning had set around the women. She ran straight to Renard's side. Kiera followed, Mother's medicine chest already in her arms; she hesitated long enough for their eyes to meet. Her look said she'd seen Josaf fall and knew the old man was dead.

Renard wasn't. Renard might live, if Lille didn't drown him with her tears.

Kiera lowered her head and kept going. Kyle understood. She was Dainis; she knew what to do now, when men's lives were at stake. Her misbehavior in the king's court no longer mattered. He should have joined her, should have gone to help the living, but he made his way to the tent where Josaf lay.

Kneeling, he smoothed the horror, the shock, and agony from the old man's face as he closed his eyes. Prayers for the dead came mindlessly from his mouth: traditional pleas that God show himself at last to a devout worshipper. Not that Josaf had been devout, not that Kyle was devout himself. Prayers were all the living could give the dead.

Blood seeped from Josaf's wound when Kyle removed the knife. He cupped a hand to catch the dark red liquid before it disappeared into the ground, and pressed his palm against Josaf to stanch the flow.

It wouldn't stop.

He couldn't stop it.

His own body wouldn't support him. The sobs began as he crumpled forward.

"My fault. My fault. I did this."

Prince Gravais surveyed the wreckage of his cohort: himself, Lockwood, the Dainis twins, Jahn Golight, the queen's captain and his men—who'd dutifully protected Lady Kiera and drawn no attacks while doing so—two varlets, three men-at-arms; he named them in his mind. They were moving about, unwounded. Of the rest who'd ridden out from Chegnon, four varlets and five men-at-arms were on the ground. With—Gray counted the unfamiliar bodies—five outlaws among them. And at least two had escaped, despite Lockwood's wizardly efforts.

The southeast horizon was a towering charcoal wall above their sheltering slope. Thunder crashed in the distance as Locky jogged toward him. Gray knew what his friend would say.

"Another hour. Another hour and I could have had them."

In the midst of death, Gray smiled, having guessed his boon-friend's words correctly. He knew Lockwood had been watching the clouds since sunrise, waiting impatiently for the season's first storm to replenish his talisman. Priests in their steepled monasteries stored the lightning strikes of generations, but freelance wizards had only what they harvested. By spring, every wizard in Alberon was depleted.

Gray wouldn't complain. The talisman at Lockwood's belt was dead black; he hadn't held anything in reserve. But he hadn't succeeded, either.

"They've got to ride through that storm, Locky. Maybe lightning will get them yet."

The wizard grimaced. "Damn Spure-folk. I'll wager they've gone to ground in one of those homesteads you visited yesterday. Won't be a soul around who remembers seeing them."

Gray shook his head. Lockwood was a good wizard, a better friend, and relentlessly suspicious of common-born men, like himself. Sometimes Gray paid heed to those suspicions, but not today.

"Look at them," he advised, extending his hand toward the nearest outlaw corpse. "Look at their clothes, their boots. You won't find hard-soled boots up here. Those were lowlanders, valley men, waiting for a chance to catch us napping."

Lockwood cursed. "Then they carried their grudge a damn long way, or someone else's gold."

That thought had crossed Gray's mind. While the wizard joined Jahn in tending their wounded—runes and lightning weren't the only healcraft Lockwood knew—Gray nudged an outlaw's corpse onto its back and squatted down to cut through a purse thong. He wasn't the only man ransacking corpses. The queen's man, Geregonal, was moving among the dead as well. Geregonal was a captain of snakes and a snake himself, but when it came to outlaws and ambushers, the

Black Lightning knew more than the rest of Alberon's cohorts combined.

"Finding anything, Captain?"

"Nothing, Your Highness," Geregonal replied without looking up. "These here're nameless men and scum. Feed 'em to the crows and be done with it. There's none but their mothers who'll mourn."

Gray nodded and cut the thong beneath his knife's edge. The purse was heavier than he'd expected. Brim-filled with fents, he guessed, and guessed wrong. There were fents, of course, a good smattering of them, and in their midst a bright gold deya, so fresh a bit of wax still clung to his father's profile—an odd coin to find so new, so far from his father's mint, and in an outlaw's purse.

The wind on Gray's face was warm. The wind that blew suddenly around his heart was not.

"Geregonal!"

The scarred captain looked at him and at the purse he held in his hand, then he bolted for the loose horses which his three men were so conveniently collecting. In a heartbeat, Gray's suspicion became certainty.

"Stop him!"

He surged after the captain, his knife still clutched in his hand. Gray's legs were long and lean; he could outrun most men, but he couldn't make up the ground between himself and the queen's captain. Geregonal's luck held; he leapt cleanly onto a good horse's back. Clinging to a handful of mane and a halter rope, Geregonal spurred the animal's flanks ruthlessly. Gray shouted and waved his arms, hoping to make the animal rear, but it had taken a thorough fright and bolted from the camp with the Black Lightning captain secure on its back.

Geregonal's three men did not intend to remain behind once their captain fled. They each had a horse and had quickly loosed the other mounts again. Gray set his eye on the best of the held horses and was closing on the man who held him when a whistle distracted him. Between one stride and the next, Gray saw a loose horse—the hart-lord's walleyed brown—stop short. But Gray saw no more as he grabbed onto a traitor's shirt and hauled him off his horse.

The mongrel made a fight of it, landing a few punches, a few kicks, before the prince got the better of him. By then it was too late: The damned horse had run off. Lockwood had come to the same conclusions, and had had better luck dropping his man, but the horse Gray's friend confronted was a tall one; short and brawny Lockwood wasn't going to bound to its bare back in this lifetime.

Gray pushed his friend aside. "Give me a leg up," he commanded and was astride in another heartbeat, looking down on Lockwood and Kyle Dainis, who'd finally put that strong right arm of his to good use. The third of Geregonal's traitors had a bloody face. "After me!" Gray told the hart-lord.

But Kyle would have to catch another horse before he could obey. His well-trained gelding was already in pursuit with a Dainis varlet on his back. The varlet's horse was better than Geregonal's but any horse Kyle could find was likely to be better than the beast Gray swatted and kicked into a reluctant gallop. The prince hoped the varlet could hold the captain once he'd outrun the captain's horse.

God might judge otherwise, but Geregonal's flight was all the confession that Gray needed. God might judge him a fool for not having seen the danger sooner. The Bitch hadn't been interested in Kiera Dainis' welfare; she'd wanted *him* dead far from home. This time he'd underestimated her and she'd nearly gotten what she'd wanted.

Gray hammered his mount with his heels and cursed the pride that inhibited him from wearing spurs. The horse tossed its head and gave him a bit more speed. Briefly, Gray hoped the two ambushers who'd fled from Lockwood might have waited for Geregonal to join them, but that was an ill wish. The Dainis varlet would need a lifetime of luck against Geregonal alone; he couldn't prevail against three desperate men.

In the end, though, when he caught up with them, Gray reckoned that the varlet probably could have handled three desperate men with ease. Geregonal lay facedown, one wrist and both ankles bound together with a lead rope and a shepherd's knot. The unbound arm was broken. Geregonal's sweated horse was tied to a branch and the walleyed brown grazed nearby.

"Enobred Hake'son, Your Highness." The varlet dropped to one knee as Gray slid to the ground.

A prince never escaped being royal. "Rise up, Enobred Hake'son. You've done right well. Let me get a look at you."

Enobred had bloody knuckles and a bloody nose, and the

open-faced intelligence Gray had come to associate with the Renzi Valley.

"Why, Your Highness?" the varlet wanted to know as they started back to the camp.

"He'll tell us before he dies," Gray replied.

"Prince Gravais Maradze's justice!" Geregonal sneered from the back of Gray's horse where they had him sitting backward with his feet tied together beneath the animal's belly. "What crime have I committed that you dare claim my life?"

"You ran."

"Because I knew, when you called my name, that you were about to blame me for what happened and I'd already guessed the nature of *your* justice. Rightly guessed."

Gray held up the purse he'd removed from Geregonal's belt. "Found nothing on them, did you? I found gold, Captain, fresh-minted gold. Yours and what you took from the bodies."

"Coin of the realm to care for me and my men. Your father's good gold that he gives to every man in his service, lest we be reduced to chancy charity."

"My father's gold that my stepmother gave you!"

"Which your father, the king, approves. No more, no less. Her Royal Highness, the queen, will warrant my justice, I rest assured."

Gray let the conversation fade. He'd already made up his mind to execute Geregonal. He was his father's heir, with a crown of his own by right as well as courtesy, and he could order a man's death. There'd be an inquiry when they returned to the valleys; there always was for summary justice. He'd owe fines to the Bitch and to Geregonal's kin, if there were any, both of which he'd gladly pay. There'd be cold satisfaction for this day's disaster, but Geregonal wouldn't tell him anything he hadn't guessed. The man, snake that he was, was worth what the Baldescare paid him.

Geregonal might keep his secrets, but his men did not. The three of them were bound on their knees by the fire when Gray led the little procession into the tattered camp. They'd already confessed everything they knew, but then they'd faced Lockwood and Lockwood's talisman, which Lockwood hadn't told them was as dead as a summer hearth until the storm broke. They begged for mercy as Lockwood related that they'd met with the outlaws several times since leaving the inland road and that the ambush—as these three understood it—was meant to kill Gray and as many of the cohort as possible, but that they'd been ordered to keep Kiera Dainis from harm.

"Why?" Gray asked, letting his voice hint at a mercy he didn't intend to show, whatever their reply. "Why protect Lady Kiera Dainis?"

The trio didn't know, or perhaps, even at the brink of execution, they feared their captain more than they hoped for royal mercy. Geregonal's orders to them had been to protect the girl, and the captain rightly damned any prince of Alberon who executed a veteran for obeying orders.

Jahn and his uninjured men led Geregonal's horse beneath a tree and slung a rope over a branch. They would have put a sack over his head, but the captain declined that nicety.

"Watch me die, all of you. Take careful note how Alberon's crowned prince deals out justice to those who follow their orders." Geregonal twisted around on the horse's back until he found Kiera Dainis watching from the safe distance of the tents. "You, girl," he shouted. "Mind your back, girl. If you live to see my lady, the queen, again, bear witness of my death, or may God damn you to hell."

Gray looked at the Dainis woman. Jahn and the others, even those men who'd die next, craned their heads her way. She was a pale, trembling contrast to the storm behind her.

There was lightning in the bruised clouds now. The wind was mean and steady, whipping the lady's gown and hair, hiding her face. Gray had known Muredoch Dainis for years. He respected Muredoch's father, had come to think well of Muredoch's earnest, youngest brother—but what of Muredoch's sister?

He'd kept the minx at arm's length partly at Muredoch's request, mostly because he knew his weaknesses where women were concerned. She had the right charms—when she wasn't in thrall to the Bitch—to turn his head. He hadn't wanted an amorous distraction right now. Had his reluctance driven her into his stepmother's waiting arms? Did Lady Kiera know the secrets Geregonal would take to hell?

Lady Kiera stood mute until their eyes met. She saw suspicion—Gray didn't try to hide it—and panicked. Covering her face, she ran to the tent where Lockwood still watched their wounded. Gray promised himself that he'd talk to her and untie the bonds that bound her to the queen, but he wouldn't fall into Geregonal's baited trap.

"Let him hang!" he commanded his captain, who swatted the horse's rump.

It was over quickly enough, but not before large drops of icy rain pelted them from the clouds. Geregonal's men were reprieved. In Alberon, no miscreant had to die in lightning; that honor was reserved for wizards. Gray passed Lockwood coming out of the wounded's tent.

"Have a care on your mountaintop," he said with a bark of forced laughter to cover the dread he felt whenever his friend braved the storm's teeth.

Lockwood's hand closed over his. "Always," he promised, grinning fiercely and eager to be off: a wizard in pursuit of his power.

Lightning lit the air around them, followed immediately by thunder loud enough to be felt. They didn't say good-bye or good luck, just took an extra moment to drink down the sight of each other, knowing it might be for the last time. Then they went separately: Lockwood over the hillcrest, Gray inside the tent, following Jahn Golight.

They had three wounded in the tent: two men-at-arms, with bone-deep gashes on their limbs, and the Dainis varlet, Renard, who was by far the worst off. Lady Kiera Dainis sat beside the boy's head, mopping his brow and keeping an eye on the bandage they'd bound tightly from his hips to his breast. The lady's maid looked more haggard than the varlet; Gray recalled they were betrothed. He'd argued against them both coming. He'd been right, but he'd given in.

Gray signaled Jahn Golight who'd been talking to the men-at-arms. They met at the centerpost, the only place under canvas where the prince could stand erect.

"How goes it?"

"My men can ride tomorrow, Your Highness."

"And the varlet?"

Jahn grimaced. "Mercy if he dies tonight, Your Highness. The women sewed him up right pretty, but he's gut-cut and his flesh will rot before long."

"Locky agreed?"

Another grimace. It was an uncommon veteran who'd take

his hurts to a priest, and a precious rare one who'd let a wizard look sideways at him. Jahn Golight was as common as they came. "After the storm, he said. *Bah!* Mercy if he dies aforehand—begging your pardon, of course—but there's no good comes of wizards and wounds."

"We'll see." Gray would sooner trust Lockwood's runes than all the priests and wives' potions in Alberon, but mostly wizards were a sick man's last resort, and mostly there was nothing a wizard could do for them. "Our dead?"

"Under canvas, Your Highness. We'll bury them all tomorrow, while the ground's soft—"

Gray cut his captain short. "Ours. Take the others down to the tree where Geregonal hangs. We're undermanned. We'll bury our own and be gone. Let the outlaw wolves have the outlaw men."

Jahn frowned. "Your will, Your Highness." The captain, like most veterans, had a near religious aversion to leaving a man unburied, but he'd follow orders. "You say the truth," Jahn continued, "when you say we're undermanned."

"I can count, Captain, and add and subtract. You think we should be twelve men by tomorrow morning; I say we'll be nine. My father will not be impressed either way. What else?"

"Geregonal's men, Your Highness. Respectfully, you should reconsider. With him gone, I think they'll take your orders."

"You *think*, Captain?"

Another thunder crack came then, and wind that strained the tent's ropes. Jahn grabbed Gray's arm and pulled him down before lightning came to him instead of Lockwood. Sheets of rain whipped the canvas that served as the tent's door.

"Pray God your wizard-friend draws the worst of this away and swallows it whole," Jahn said, taking his own advice as he made a hollow sphere with his hands.

When lightning flashed, Lockwood shielded his face, the same as any other man. The last thing he wanted was a storm battle this close to the camp. He'd set his sight on another hillock at the meadow's far end. His quest of the moment was getting there alive.

Priests said a thunderstorm was no different from other

storms, which was another reason that wizards despised priests. They cowered in their crypts while their iron-clad steeples did the dangerous work of drawing down the bolts. They'd never seen lightning spawned, or wrested it from a cloud's black heart.

Storms knew when a wizard stalked them. The bolts that sizzled the grass around him and turned the air bitter owed nothing to chance. Lockwood ran when he dared and threw himself on the ground whenever his curly hair began to straighten. He was drenched, muddy, and ready to fight a war when he gained the hilltop.

And surprised to find that he wasn't alone.

"Lightning strike—and it will, Kyle—what are you doing here?"

The hart-lord sat on the crest, chin resting on his knees. Maybe God knew what the young man hoped to accomplish. A wizard of Lockwood's experience could only foresee disaster and assume that Taslim foresaw the same.

"Get back to the camp, Kyle. At least get away from this hill. Your wizard's sand in a storm's eye."

Kyle raised his head. His eyes appeared swollen; he might have been crying. It was impossible to be certain in the rain and sharp shadows of another lightning bolt.

"Josaf's dead."

"I know. I'm sorry." He got down on one knee. "I saw it. You did your best. Another step, another heartbeat, who knows? But it's not your fault, Kyle. Josaf knew that. You can be sure Josaf knew that."

"It's my fault." There were tears; Lockwood could see them through the rain. "I listened to Taslim and Taslim held me back. Now we're going to die here together. It's only right, Lockwood. My just punishment and his."

The storm knew where they were. It was gathering strength to hurl a bolt down on them both, on all three of them. Lockwood held the hart-lord close while his mind made a wind to hide them until the bolt was grounded. He felt Kyle's despair and saw the truth as Kyle saw it.

"We'll talk, Kyle," he shouted after thunder had left their ears ringing. "Get back to the camp. Lie low. There are other ways—"

"You can't bring him back!"

"This isn't justice, Kyle."

Lockwood covered the young man's eyes as another bolt struck the ground. Fool's fire shimmered in the air around them. If he couldn't get Kyle to leave, the storm would have them both. He held Kyle at arm's length and shook him until his teeth chattered.

"You don't want to die, Kyle. Look at me! You don't want to die!"

"Taslim tried to make me do what he wanted. I won't let you, either. You can't make me run. I'm ready to die."

Lockwood got to his feet, dragging Kyle with him. "Be damned, if you are—but *I'm* not! Get out of here!"

He hooked his foot behind Kyle's ankle and gave him a shove that sent him tumbling backward down the hill. There wasn't time to see what Kyle did at the bottom. The storm had cocked its fist for another lightning punch. Lockwood yanked his talisman from his belt and held it overhead.

"Here!" he screamed, making himself the target. "Right here!"

The crystal was obsidian dark, as it had not been since that summer's day years ago when he first dared a storm's fury. This moment was as dangerous as that had been: He had no reserve to draw upon as time congealed around him. Lockwood saw a face in the cloud overhead—the face the coward priests never saw—hideous with hate. Jagged streaks of intense white webbed the cloud, burst through the gaping mouth.

Lockwood bared his teeth as the bolt seared toward him. He turned the talisman at the last instant, not as a shield, but as a trap. The bolt lifted him off the ground. His blood boiled and his heart stopped.

Then started.

Time flowed around him again. Thunder roared in furious frustration. The iron-wrapped crystal shone like the sun.

"Sparks!" he sneered. "Is that the best you've got? My belches are brighter than this!"

He lifted his talisman and, once again, time froze.

Chapter Eighteen

Kyle lay on his back in the cold, wet grass when lightning reached down from the storm to engulf Lockwood in fire and fury. Kyle knew what wizards did—everyone knew that: they went out into Alberon's most spectacular storms and lured the thunderbolts into their talismans. It was likely that he knew more about wizards and lightning than anyone who wasn't a wizard: He'd felt the exhilaration and terror of raw wizardry before the exorcism at Roc Dainis, when he'd moved through Taslim's memories.

That was memory and he'd known that Taslim survived. Kyle had no such foreknowledge as seemingly solid light encased Lockwood, leaving only the upraised talisman as a mote of pure darkness in the white radiance.

No one could survive that.

No one, not even a wizard.

Run. Run for your life!

He didn't know if the command came from within himself, or from Taslim, or from Lockwood. Moments ago, Kyle had been ready to sacrifice himself; now he obeyed. The grass was slick, treacherous; he didn't count the slips or falls as he scrambled for the camp. He counted the bolts—three, four in quick, deafening succession. They struck the ground as stones struck a quiet pond, sending out waves that struck his back hard enough to knock him down again and again.

Kyle kept going, crawling up the crescent-shaped hill on cold-numbed hands and knees. When he had, at last, a wall of dirt at his back, he curled up in a ball and screamed. No one heard; the sound was swallowed by another crack of thunder and sheets of wind-driven rain.

A man could drown while standing in such a storm; Kyle felt the risk while he sat. Lightning revealed their tents still standing. He sprinted for the nearest one, skidded across its muddy threshold. One stride into the tent, Kyle stumbled over a man's outstretched leg. He apologized, as was his custom, and crawled more carefully toward the center of the tent. No one moved to help him, or to get out of his way, then lightning struck with a bright curtain that endured long enough for his eyes to adjust to it.

"God have mercy!"

He was among the corpses, their limbs already grown stiff, their faces shining in the rain that dripped steadily through the tent's seams.

God have mercy . . .

Kyle mouthed the words; his voice had frozen. His attention was inexorably drawn toward that which he didn't want to see: Josaf with little pools of water over his eyes and, between the fingers of the hands someone had folded peacefully across his breast.

Thunder cracked above the tent. Light ceased abruptly and Kyle was blind. He couldn't breathe, couldn't think—except that he had to get out of the tent. Which he did, gasping and thrashing into the rain.

There were living men in the next tent he entered: six men sitting in a circle around a little, smoky fire. Every face turned toward him knew that Prince Gravais had forbidden fire inside the tents, and forbidden drink as well. There were common-born men, Enobred among them, and Kyle was noble with the right—possibly the obligation—to enforce the prince's commands.

They made no effort to smother the fire or hide the uncorked brownware jug that hung by an ear from one man's motionless hand. Heavy silence filled the tent between thunder claps.

Kyle shivered, and gritted his teeth to keep them from chattering. Fire was the most precious thing he could imagine at that moment. Laid and fed by men, it gave off a ruddy light that stood against both lightning and darkness. It hissed, it smoked and clung to life only because the men gave it their care. He wanted to warm himself, inside and out, in this company, but Enobred sat among them, staring at his hands. Kyle couldn't see Enobred without thinking of Renard, who'd scorned him for intruding into common lives.

Priests said God determined a man's ultimate fate, and not the man himself—so what had happened to Renard couldn't be a hart-lord's fault. *If* Kyle believed what priests said.

He wanted to stay, but he wouldn't intrude, wouldn't beg. They could welcome him, or he'd leave. Another shiver shook his body. He was ready to abandon them when Enobred raised his head.

"We're waking the ones who died. Waking Josaf. Will you speak for him first, Kyle?"

Enobred's face, hollow-eyed, slack-jawed, above slumped shoulders, told the day's story: a mentor dead, a friend dying. If Josaf had been Enobred's mentor. If Enobred and Renard were friends as well as companions in varletry. Kyle thought of them as Josaf's sheep: Enobred Hake'son and Renard Fisherson. One was older, the other younger, but he didn't know either of them.

Renard had been just to upbraid him.

"I was too late," Kyle whispered. "I took too long getting to him." He would have left, if he hadn't been so soaked, so cold that his legs refused to carry him.

One of the men, an older man and a royal sergeant by the red chevrons visible through the dirt and shadows of his surcoat, scuttled sideways. Kyle remembered that his name was Gedd Brant, and he made room between Enobred and himself in the firelit circle.

"You can't know," the veteran who held the jug insisted. "It's fate, not mistakes, that makes men die, not your mistakes, not mine." He held up the jug.

Kyle found it much easier to make his legs move toward warmth and life. When thunder hammered them again, he thanked Darvet—he thought that was the veteran's name and no one corrected him—took the jug by both ears and drank deep. It was burnwine. Not the subtly potent burnwine that the prince served, but liquid fire that loosed the tears from his eyes. He took a second pull to end the agony of the first. A hand closed over his, Enobred's hand, cold and trembling. Kyle surrendered the jug. The thunder abated.

"You knew him best," Enobred said before he drank. "He said we were the sons he'd never had, but you were his favorite. We stood in your shadow."

Then Kyle hadn't known Josaf. He'd been the bane of Josaf's existence: clumsy, dreamy, accident-prone. Surely Josaf had despaired every time he'd seen him coming toward him. Lightning lit up the canvas again; thunder shook the rain onto their heads. Kyle remembered Josaf half-smiling, shaking his head, telling him not to worry.

"Let it *go*, Locky!" a man on Kyle's right said, Ilowy, a Dainisman from the deep valley. Kyle didn't know him well, and Ilowy didn't know the ennobled wizard. But that didn't stop Ilowy from offering his opinion. He brandished a fist at the storm and the wizard, too. "You've made your point. Now, let it go and give us peace."

"Wake him, Kyle," Enobred urged, wiping burnwine from his chin and passing the jug along. "Send him off well, so God knows who's coming. You've got the gift for it."

Kyle felt Enobred staring. He kept his vision fixed on the shifting flames and took a deep breath. "I remember Josaf Dainisman first when I was still in the nursery. His hair was mostly dark then. I remember he had a temper that other men feared."

"God'a'mercy, that he did," Enobred agreed. "Took a stick to us, he did, most every day."

"One day he took me to the stables. He put me up on a horse's bare back. I was taller than him, taller than anything . . ."

Kyle hadn't thought of that day in years, but it was bright as fresh paint now. He'd been more afraid of his father's arms-master than he'd been of the horse. Josaf did have a terrible temper, at least in those days. He'd mellowed as his hair silvered, but to the end he had a strong wrist when it came to a switch. Kyle had been thrashed by his father, Josaf, and just about everyone else who'd had a hand raising him. Father and the others would walk away in anger afterward, but Josaf would stay.

Done's done, Josaf said, time and time again, as he dried Kyle's tears, tended the bruises, and pierced the anger before it festered. *Put it behind you, lad. There's always tomorrow.*

But after today, there'd be no tomorrow, not with Josaf. Kyle didn't try to hide the tears that came naturally as he waked the man who'd done all the fatherly things Father hadn't seen fit to do. Today, not Rapture night last summer, was the last day of his childhood. Childhood habits died with Josaf: the habit of thinking that he hadn't mattered to anyone.

They took turns waking the dead. The pain—grief and mourning—didn't truly fade as they reminisced between thunderbolts. But it changed. It became a mortal pain, bearable by mortal men, rather than immortal, like the dead themselves, who were gone now, and would remain that way forever.

Silver light surrounded Lockwood at the top of his hill. It began in the scorched, flattened grass at his feet and rose to the clouds. Night had come to the meadow. The sky, visible in patches near the horizon, was darker than the exhausted storm.

The wizard was drunk with power. His talisman could contain nothing more. He held up his naked hands to ward off the storm's last scraggly bolts, and deflected them into the shimmery mist. Not since the first time he'd called down the lightning had he been the only wizard harvesting a mighty storm, and that first time he'd still been too young, too frightened to appreciate his accomplishment.

These days, wherever the king's court happened to be when a storm broke, Lord Marrek Brun took the first bolt and the choicest ones thereafter. The other wizards of the council took their share. Lockwood hadn't starved, but there wasn't much left once those four sated themselves. Such were the perils of being Gray's boon-friend, and he'd endured them without complaint.

But now Lockwood was sated. He'd gone from a talisman as black and empty as the day Gray had given it to him, to a miniature sun. Then, for the sheer joy of it, he'd set the hilltop shimmering. Anything he could imagine was within his grasp.

He could keep that Dainis varlet alive another night or a year. It wouldn't be healing; wizards scorned the arcane discipline of priestly physicians. There were as many mysteries in the growth of a single strand of hair as there were in the mightiest spell, and as hair grew quite nicely without magical interference, wizards practiced pure magic. When they tended the ailing or injured, wizards imparted vigor to exhausted bodies, weary minds. Lockwood had also mastered the straightforward medicine of the countryside commonfolk—partly because it worked and mostly because his practice of it annoyed not only the priests, but his fellow wizards alike.

Restoring the Dainisman would come later, with lightning from his talisman; the young man was alive and would remain that way until midnight, at least. Lockwood knew that after he probed the camp with the rune shapes of life and knowledge. The lightning he held shimmering around him couldn't be moved, not even as far as the camp. If he didn't use it on the hilltop, it would dissipate with the dawn, which would be wasteful. And the waste of lightning was unthinkable to any self-respecting wizard.

A nasen'bei summoning was possible, and no more dangerous than wrestling with the storm itself had been. Lockwood could have summoned his aqua-eyed haunt, seen it with living eyes, frolicked with it in the rain. But once he saw it with his body's eyes and touched it with his hands, his lifetime companion would be fixed in his memory, which was a poor trade for the wonder of his imagination. He'd have lost more than he gained.

Lockwood considered casting a summons net blindly into nasen'bei, hauling in whatever might be lurking in the nearer netherness. Such reckless curiosity wasn't necessarily unwise in a wizard who expected to be a magister within another decade, but it didn't, in the end, appeal to him. His curiosity had already attached itself to Kyle Dainis, a likeable youth with, Lockwood suspected, a less-than-likeable wizard for a nasen'bei companion.

Kyle had wanted to die a short while ago because Kyle believed he and his haunt were responsible for one of today's deaths. Kyle Dainis was the sort who'd blame himself for any tragedy, but if Taslim of Fawlen *had* meddled with the young man's honor . . .

It was high time for *someone* to confront Taslim of Fawlen. Lockwood adjusted his belt and pushed back his sleeves, like a laborer about to pick up a shovel or axe. He braced his feet solidly in the grass and shouted into the light:

"Fawlen. Taslim of Fawlen! I, Lockwood, Lord Marelet, summon you to this place, this time. Answer my summons!"

He raised his hands once more, not as high as he'd raised them during the storm, but high enough to call the wind and make the light swirl as he added the runes that would make his wizardry happen. A tidal pull swelled in the dark of night, the depths of nasen'bei. Marrek had said Kyle's companion dwelt beyond the reach of ordinary wizardry, and Marrek, as usual, was right. But the storm had left Lockwood capable of extraordinary things.

"Come, Taslim of Fawlen. Come to the light. Come without fear."

There were no lies. He could summon Taslim, but he couldn't harm the haunting wizard, couldn't hold him, either. Whatever form the wizard took, that form would dissipate at dawn with the shimmering mist, and Taslim himself would return to whatever hole the priests had consigned him.

"Come *now*!" Lockwood shouted, and got a dying bolt from the storm instead.

The bolt distracted him for less than a heartbeat, but that was enough for Taslim. Lockwood watched closely as the swirling light tightened, giving form and semblance to his summoning: an older man with a steely beard and a robe of sumptuous brocade, trimmed with plush sable. Marrek in his winter solstice panoply could not have made a grander entrance, and for that reason alone, Lockwood disbelieved.

"As you were and are, Fawlen," he ordered, setting the semblance of cloth and fur in motion with the wind of his wizardry.

That which would be Taslim of Fawlen showed white-rimmed eyes like a panicked horse. It clutched its beard and robe, as if to defy its summoner's wish.

"I'll have the truth from you," Lockwood advised. He gestured with two fingers of his right hand and softly whispered another rune. The swirling wind intensified and, with a sigh, the haunt reshaped itself into a slight-boned man with black hair and narrow, delicate features.

"Better."

It was not quite the face Lockwood had glimpsed when Kyle Dainis touched his talisman, but it was close enough that he allowed the splendid robes to remain.

"That was wastefully done." Those were the first words Taslim spoke as he tidied his sembled garments, before he met Lockwood's eyes.

"My choice."

"A waste, nonetheless. You cannot hold me, Marelet; I will return to my exile with the light. You'd have to sit in the Siege of Shadows before you could summon me *and* hold me to any form."

Lockwood twirled a whisker or two between his fingers. He'd half-expected Taslim to bargain with him for precisely that event: him on the Siege, separating Taslim from the hart-lord, and half-expected to agree. "The thought had crossed my mind, Fawlen." Outright lies were risky between wizards; misdirection and outright bluff were more useful. "If the Siege of Shadows does truly exist."

"It does, novice, truly it does."

Marrek and the other wizards of the council had judged Fawlen to be arrogant, disdainful, and contemptuous when they'd heard him speaking with Kyle's voice. Lockwood wondered how they'd describe the man if they could hear him now. With his clipped syllables and nasal vowels it seemed unlikely that the wizard could have said good morning without turning it into an insult. If everyone in Alberon had sounded like Taslim of Fawlen a millennium ago, it was no wonder the rest of Prayse still took offense. Lockwood reined in his own ready temper and resolved to listen only to what Fawlen said and not how he said it.

"I'd think you'd want a wizard to sit on the Siege and summon you."

Fawlen smiled, showing teeth that glinted lightning. "Not you, novice. No sense to be summoned by a fool who'd be destroyed before he finished his summoning."

"You underestimate me, Fawlen."

"You killed beside your boon-friend, novice. Death stains your soul. God will destroy you when you meet His eyes—if you believe in God. If not, the Siege itself will consume you."

Interesting. Conviction grew in Lockwood's mind that Kyle had good reason to be sitting on the hill when the storm began: Fawlen needed to keep the hart-lord alive, but more than that, Fawlen needed to keep him from killing anyone if they were both to survive the Siege of Shadows. Fawlen would have stopped at nothing to keep the hart-lord from drawing his sword. It was only a guess at the moment, but Lockwood vowed silently that he'd get the truth one way or another.

"Aye, it might," Lockwood drawled, measuring and remeasuring the man in front of him, as he'd do if there'd been a sword in his hand rather than a talisman on his belt. "I've hunted with Gray, and killed my supper more than once. It would seem, then, that God is doomed to remain Hidden. Anyone who's ever eaten from a joint of meat has death on his soul. By the bolt—any creature who's left its mother's teat has eaten death, unless you say there's no life in grass."

Fawlen's eyebrows arched above his too elegant nose as he

took the bait. "You cut too fine, novice. It's the death of men that matters. You went cohorting with your friend the prince. You fought beside him, killed beside him. The Siege of Shadows doesn't forgive that."

Those years with the Soaring Eagle cohort were not Lockwood's most cherished memories. He rarely talked about them, seldom even thought about them, and certainly hadn't done either in Kyle's presence. Yet he had marched with the cohort, and as a warrior, not a wizard. He'd carried a sword, not seeking glory on his own behalf, but to defend Gray. His boon-friend was fearless in battle; he needed someone strong and single-minded at his back.

Pelipulay was deep in war and the Eagle served wherever Pelipulay sent them. They'd skirmished regularly. Gray garnered the glory a prince should have before he ruled, but Lockwood had slain more of the enemy. Fawlen had passed through the nasen'bei wind of Lockwood's wizardry before he appeared in the mist; it wasn't entirely surprising that he'd snagged a notion or two out of Lockwood's memory during the passage.

"Do you know why I summoned you?" Lockwood asked, rather than wonder what else Fawlen might have gleaned.

"I assume: Because you could? Is there some grander reason? Ambition? Deceit? You think you can outwit me, that's clear. You think the power of the Siege of Shadows is something you can steal for your masters at the king's court. That's why you're here, isn't it?"

Lockwood folded his arms and shook his head dramatically, satisfied that he had Fawlen's measure now, and the upper hand between them. "I've come for my friend and my prince. For loyalty, if you will—if loyalty has meaning for you—and I've summoned you for loyalty, too. Kyle Dainis has my friend's protection and mine as well. We'll see no harm comes to him—"

"Then set yourself at ease. I protect the hart-lord, too. He's at no risk."

"He was sitting here when I came to harvest the storm—"

"Fool!" Fawlen interrupted Lockwood for the second time. "He can't harvest storms for me."

"He wasn't trying to, Fawlen; he was trying to get himself killed, hoping you'd die with him. He blames you for Josaf's death; blames himself because you held him back when he would have put himself in harm's way for the old man."

Lockwood paused, waiting for Fawlen to make some haughty, inadequate excuse for himself, but the wizard stood silent, his face frozen between shock and disbelief.

"What don't you understand?" Lockwood asked, grinning broadly at the other wizard's distress. "Are you going to say you didn't restrain him? Damn straight, Kyle's at no risk while you reach through nasen'bei to hold his heart. He'd be no use to you, would he, if he'd killed the man who killed his friend. If God didn't destroy him, the Siege itself would."

"The man was old. He had only a few years left, no matter what. He died with his sword in his hand, not decrepit in his bed. That's what they all want. Surely the hart-lord—Surely Kyle saw that, understood that."

Lockwood flung open his arms. The other wizard staggered backward, lost his footing, then fell to the ground with an audible and satisfying groan.

"Did you lose your soul while you waited for the Harbinger to return, or had you already lost it, Fawlen?" he demanded. "Did you know where and when the old man wished to die? Had you asked him? I scarcely knew Kyle Dainis' name before all this began, but even I could see the bond—the love and loyalty—between them. Protect him! You've damn near destroyed him!"

"No." Fawlen offered an all-inclusive denial without trying to stand up. "No. He hides everything from me."

From which very interesting remark Lockwood inferred that Fawlen didn't know Kyle's every thought and had not known where Kyle sat earlier. "I'll have to send a generous donation to those blundering priests in the Renzi Valley; they've done Kyle more good than they intended."

That brought Fawlen to his feet with a snarl. "Damn those priests. It's them that's left me with no choice but to put Kyle himself on the Siege. I'd have suffered your Magister Marrek or one of the others, and outwitted them, too. I'd suffer *you*. But those priests have as good as buried me, Marelet. I dwell in no part of nasen'bei that you'd recognize. I believe in their damn hells now."

"I won't weep for you and I'll double my donation."

Fawlen gripped Lockwood's wrists with substantial hands. "Fool! Listen to me, answer me: When did you first look into nasen'bei?"

Inevitably, irresistibly, Lockwood thought of Havoc, his

aqua-eyed haunt. He couldn't remember his age, maybe four, maybe five. Certainly before Lady Sabelle sent him to court.

"Kyle's not a wizard. He wasn't born a wizard. Not like you or me," Fawlen continued when Lockwood didn't answer his questions. "He sees me, but he doesn't see nasen'bei. I didn't know at first. If you're going to damn me, damn me for that. I tried to bend his will; he fought back through nasen'bei, so I tried harder. But he wasn't fighting through nasen'bei. I don't know what he does or how he does it. Maybe everyone who isn't a wizard has a mind as labyrinthine as his—but I doubt it. I damn near killed him before I understood how wrong I was. We'd just made peace when those damn priests came along."

Lockwood was still inclined to make a substantial contribution to the Renzi Bydians, but he believed Fawlen, too. More than the ability to shape runes or capture lightning, the connection to nasen'bei was the essence of wizardry in Alberon and elsewhere around the Sea of Prayse. Kyle Dainis broke all the rules.

"It doesn't excuse anything," Lockwood said after a moment's thought. "You held him back for your own reasons, in defiance of his will, and now his friend's dead. You've broken his heart, his spirit."

Fawlen released him. "Would you have done differently—from my place?"

"I can't imagine your place, and wouldn't if I could," Lockwood countered bluntly, refusing to answer Fawlen's question. Then, even more bluntly, he added: "I'd have given my life to save Gray; still would. But I'd sacrifice anyone else to keep us both alive. *Anyone.*" Their friendship had been that way from the beginning, though he'd never put it into words before.

"And what would you tell him, your friend and prince, afterward?"

"I don't know. I'd talk to him until he listened. We've been boon-friends since we were boys; it's different."

They both looked across the misty meadow at the camp. The storm had been reduced to wisps drifting toward the Eigela. Stars shone and the moon threw down its light on the tents.

"Walk the meadow with me," Fawlen said.

"The power's here where the bolts came down. It can't be transferred. You know that."

"I know what I've been told, Marelet, but I've never tried it myself. Have you?"

They walked down the hillside, slowly at first, then gathering speed and confidence. For Lockwood, there was the unique exhilaration of carrying lightning in his heart, not his talisman, of doing something for the first time, of doing something others said couldn't be done. What Fawlen felt remained a mystery. Lockwood didn't ask and the other wizard didn't volunteer. He supposed, though, they felt the same. Marrek hit close to the mark: He and Fawlen were much the same—which didn't inspire Lockwood to declarations of friendship.

Lockwood left Fawlen atop the crescent-shaped hill with the promise that he'd send Kyle to him. Fawlen didn't object; he was wizard enough to know that there'd be more questions than either of them wanted to answer if they both walked among the tents.

The dead were in the dark, silent tent. The injured were visible in a second, with the women hovering over them. The young Dainisman's soft moans reminded Lockwood that he had work to do this night. The prisoners, Geregonal's stalwarts, were in a third tent, guarded by the soaking wet Jahn Golight and the prince himself. Gray beckoned; Lockwood gestured back with two upstretched fingers, meaning there were two things he had to do. With a nod and a wave, Gray accepted the conditions, the way Lockwood accepted Gray's obligations.

Kyle was ready to leave the wake when Lockwood entered the tent. He was grateful for the beckoning that gave him an excuse to breathe cool, misty air after the smoke of the fire and the fumes of a second burnwine jug. He wasn't ready for Lockwood to take him by the arm and point him at the hillcrest.

"He's waiting to talk to you."

"He?" Kyle asked and heard a tremor in his voice. As much as he wished he'd saved Josaf's life, or at least said good-bye, he wasn't eager to face Josaf's ghost.

"Fawlen."

Kyle's free hand went to his throat. He had less interest in talking to Taslim than to Josaf's ghost, but as soon as Lockwood said the wizard's name, Kyle realized the wizard wasn't with him. "What have you done?" he asked on an inward breath.

"The storm gave me the power to summon him into a semblance of his own form. Not forever, only until dawn. I said I'd send you up to talk to him."

Kyle pulled his arm free and refused to take another step. "I won't be pushed around, my lord. You stopped me from doing something foolish, and I'm grateful. But I'm not talking to him, not listening to him ever again. My mind's made up. What he did was wrong and nothing you or he can say will make it different, or undo what's been done."

"I agree," Lockwood said and took his arm again. "But you tell him that when you can see him with both eyes and listen to his reply with both ears."

He trusted Lockwood as, in a curious way, he trusted Taslim. "He's truly up there?"

"Not truly, but I've summoned him, and he's substantial until dawn. I'll go up with you, if you're worried—"

"No, I'm safe enough with him."

A thousand and one curious thoughts competed in Kyle's mind as he climbed the hill, but what he found at the top was simply Taslim of Fawlen, dressed in clean, drab clothes and looking very much as he'd looked on the solstice and every time since. Yet different, too. The grass bent where he stood. A moonlight shadow flared away from him. But mostly it was his face that was different: less bold, more like a man who'd made mistakes in his life.

"No apologies, Hart-lord. I admit restraining you and regret that I didn't do it better. I did it for me, for your getting me to the Siege of Shadows. I regret nothing; I'd do it again in a heartbeat. But if I'd been standing before you, as I am now, and able to take myself to the Siege, I'd have done the same thing. I'd been alone for a millennium, Hart-lord, then I had you. No man's life is worth more to me now."

It was not what Kyle had expected, not what Lockwood had led him to expect, and he was furious with them both. "My life belongs to me, no one else. No wizard. *I* choose what my life is worth."

Kyle spun around in the wet grass, by habit expecting

Taslim to move with him, offering a self-serving argument. But Fawlen remained behind. He could hear Taslim sigh, hear the grass squish, and feel the weight of a hand on his shoulder.

"I won't lie to you, Hart-lord. I have regrets, true regrets. I regret that Josaf is dead. I would rather that he were alive; I would rather that all the men who rode out with us were still alive. I grieve for Josaf because you grieve for him, and you wouldn't grieve for an inconsequential man. That much I can offer you, Hart-lord: regrets and grieving, but no false apologies. Will you accept?"

He didn't then, but Taslim was persistent, asking question after question about Josaf, Kyle's early years at Roc Dainis, the years he spent in fosterage, and his year at home since then. Sitting in the wet grass while the moon coursed overhead (and remarkably comfortable, for all that—he suspected wizardry, he suspected Lockwood, though the prince's boon-friend was nowhere to be seen), Kyle retold the stories he'd told around the fire and added new ones from memory. He sobbed more than once and wished Taslim would disappear, but Taslim asked more questions in a voice that grew gradually softer, with an accent that grew less grating.

By the time the moon had set and the eastern horizon had begun to glow, Kyle didn't mind when the wizard took his hand.

"It's time," Taslim said, nodding toward the glow. He squeezed Kyle's hand once, then stood, clearly intending to walk away before Lockwood's spell ended. "Josaf was a good man, especially to you and for you. He made you the man that I've come to cherish. I regret his death, and I grieve with you, whatever you believe of me. But I still won't apologize for what I did and, Hart-lord, with all that you've told me about him, I don't believe that Josaf would ask me to."

Kyle stared at the grass. "It was wrong."

"It was treachery; that was the wrong. The rest was reaction, each of us—you, Josaf, the Gray Prince, Lockwood, even me—doing the best we could to preserve the lives we cared about. Josaf and I got what we wanted: you alive and unharmed."

"It was wrong!"

But there was no answer. The rays of sunlight had appeared in the east. Taslim was once again a faint and familiar presence in the darkness at the back of Kyle's memory.

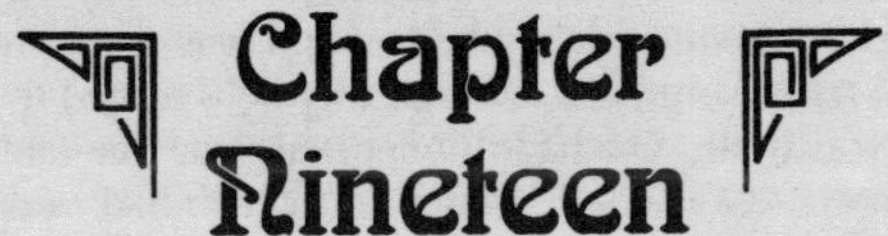

Chapter Nineteen

For two days the men had dug graves in the open meadow beyond their hill-sheltered camp. Working with the small tools they'd brought with them, they'd wrested boulders, some half the size of a man, from the ground. Stripped to the waist, Prince Gravais—Gray—had labored alongside his men, getting as dirty and sweat-stained as Enobred or the other varlets, without ever looking the least bit common.

At least in Kiera's eyes.

And Kiera's eyes had been on the prince. She'd been trying to talk to him since the Deadly Betrayal. There were words she needed to say, explanations mostly, to allay whatever suspicions Geregonal's misconduct had cast across *her* character. But Gray proved even more elusive in the meadows than he'd been at Chegnon. Unless Kiera stooped to following him into the tall grass—which she wasn't quite ready to do—it proved impossible to separate him from his men.

Of course, Kiera could have said her piece moments ago, at sunset.

The prince had called everyone together for the burials. She'd stood with the survivors (excepting Renard and Lille, who nursed him with loving diligence), hands folded and eyes properly downcast, while the bodies were lowered, dirt shoveled, and excavated boulders rolled atop the graves to discourage scavengers. Respect, Gray had said; his eyes were dark and sad as he eulogized the dead—even Josaf, whom he'd hardly known, and Geregonal and the outlaws who didn't deserve anyone's respect.

After he was finished speaking, Gray had asked each of

them to add their own solemn thoughts while the sky turned bloody above them. Kyle spoke last and was surprisingly eloquent, but more surprising was the way he'd turned toward her when he was done. She hadn't expected that. She had nothing to say, except "Godspeed," which other men had said already. The meadow chilled quickly as the sun sank. She'd left her cloak in her tent and her feet were tired from standing.

Kyle was disappointed; she'd seen that clearly in the dimming light when he strode past her without a smile or kind word. Well, Kyle had made mistakes, too, serious ones. Mistakes at least as serious as hers with the queen. Kyle *had* warned her—once—and now Kyle expected her to acknowledge an error in front of God, the dead, and everyone else.

Where were his admissions of guilt? One warning, one and one only, when he *knew* she was headstrong. If he'd persisted, she would have listened. She wasn't unreasonable, but Mother, Father, and the rest of the family—Kyle included—had been so discouraging over the years that she'd had to become headstrong.

Where was Kyle's admission that he'd let her down—again?

She'd repair the damage, no thanks to her brother and with no help from him either, as soon as she got her private moments with the prince. While the men dug graves, she'd racked her soul for the right words, the necessary gestures that would permit Gray to understand how she'd stumbled into Queen Ezrae's clutches, how appalled she was by Geregonal's Deadly Betrayal, how glad she was that the Black Lightning captain was dead, and how desperate she was to prove herself to her beloved prince.

He'd understand; she wouldn't let him go until he did. They'd become friends, allies against the queen, and they'd be more than that. He'd understand that she could offer him more than that wizardly boon-friend of his, especially after she'd conquered the Siege of Shadows . . .

Kiera stopped short while she absorbed that startling revelation. Although she'd anticipated her conversation with the prince in a thousand different ways, until this very moment she'd always assumed Kyle and *his* wizard (who should, of course, have been *hers*) would wield whatever powers the Siege of Shadows bestowed. She'd even begun to prepare the persuasions she might need to use on her brother if he balked at the notion of vengeance (and he probably would; Kyle had no taste for vengeance). But this revelation made everything so much simpler: She'd ascend to the Siege herself.

God had called her, after all, as the Harbinger fell, before Kyle interfered. She looked north, toward the Eigela, where jagged, black peaks lost themselves in deepening twilight, and suffered another revelation: A sunset glow lingered above one small section of the not too distant mountains.

The Siege of Shadows!

No one else had noticed it as they walked through the meadow: none of the men—not that wizard, Lockwood, or her own brother. God *had* called her and God still called her. She didn't need the guide Kyle had stolen, not anymore. She could follow that glow to the Siege herself.

God had called her, Kiera Dainis, to look upon His face and take His power into her own being. Debts would be paid, and everything would be made right.

"My lady?"

Lille had come looking for her when the first men returned to camp. Lille, tear-streaked and haggard, whispering, whimpering, and tugging on Kiera's sleeve. God's pockets! Did the girl have to cry *all* the time?

"My lady? Can you hurry, please?" Another tug, another sniffle.

"Yes, Lille." Kiera turned her thoughts from the glow she alone was worthy to see. *But not for long,* she promised herself and *I'm coming, as fast as I can*, for God. And, finally, for Lille: "What's wrong?"

"It's past time, my lady. You said sunset."

The dressing on Renard's wound. She'd merely repeated Lady Irina's wisdom that wounds should be cleaned and dressed with the sun, and everyone assumed she was a priest-physician. Which, Kiera supposed, she was, when the only other possibility was Lockwood, standing beside the tent.

"Lady Kiera," he said oh-so-politely as she approached.

He and Lille were both so excruciatingly polite and had been since the Deadly Betrayal. They blamed her, of course. They wouldn't *say* anything, but she could see reproach in their eyes when she looked at them. So she didn't look, just pushed the cloth back and entered the tent.

"How goes it with you, Renard?" Lockwood asked, as gruff

and common as any varlet, but that's what he was: common-born and a bastard, too.

Renard managed a smile and raised one hand in greeting. "Better, my lord. Wi' God's grace and your wizardry, I'll be on my feet in no time."

Biting her lip, Kiera grabbed a pad of washed linen from the pile she and Lille had made. He'd thank God and the wizard, but not a word for the women who sat with him day and night—waiting for him to die, if anyone had the courage to speak the truth. And until Renard did die, they were stranded in this meadow, far from the Siege of Shadows, because Gray was adamant that the party not be split further.

She knelt beside Renard, opposite Lille, removing the stitches that held the dressing to a similar linen pad they'd laid beneath him when Jahn and Enobred first carried him into the tent. When that was done, Lockwood held Renard's arms, lest the pain of lifting the old dressing make him thrash and reopen the wound. Renard did stiffen and gasp when Lille dribbled warm water on the stained linen, but it came away easily—as it had not yesterday—and today his flesh was pink, not red, around the wound. The wound itself—a sword gash across his gut—was still terrible to look at.

"Easy now, lad," Lockwood said, changing places with Lille. He unhooked his talisman and held the sparkling crystal just above Renard's torn flesh. "Close your eyes and try to relax. Another few days and you'll be on your feet."

God's pockets—the lies men told each other! Yet she could not take her eyes off the talisman when Lockwood whispered his runes. Tiny threads of light spun down from the crystal, disappearing into the wound. Renard moaned, but it was a sound of release, not pain, and he did look better when Lockwood sat back.

"Thank you, my lord," Renard mumbled, his eyelids fluttering.

Lockwood said it was natural that Renard should sleep afterward, but what did any wizard know about natural? Everything a wizard did, from capturing lightning in a talisman to invigorating a fatally injured man, was unnatural. For Renard Fisherson, natural should have been a grave.

"Will we be able to travel tomorrow?" Kiera asked.

"Not tomorrow, dear lady." There was an edge to his politeness now, as he headed out of the tent: weariness, perhaps finally the truth.

Lille said nothing when they were alone, laying a fresh dressing over the wound, then stitching it tightly to the cloth beneath Renard's back. Kiera preferred silence to sobs or stiff politeness. She helped Lille rearrange the blankets around Renard and, without breaking the silence, left the tent herself.

Pots simmered near the fire, reminding Kiera that she'd eaten only a crust of bread since morning. Men had gathered for the day's hot meal, her brother and Lockwood among them—but not, she realized as she completed her head count, Gray. He wasn't with the horses, or anywhere else that Kiera could see from the lee of the crescent hill. She waited a moment, expecting him to emerge from the shadows. When he didn't, she got her dark cloak and pulled its hood over her bright gold hair. Gray hadn't been ahead of her when she returned to the camp and there was a chance—a good chance, she hoped—that he was still being respectful to the dead.

There'd never be a better time or place.

The moon hadn't risen. The rosy glow of the Siege of Shadows dominated the horizon—her private horizon—but it lent no light to the meadow. Kiera wasn't eager to go stumbling among the fresh graves, but she'd do whatever she needed to get her moments with Gray. A heavy dew had fallen early on grass, which was already higher than her knees. Her gown and cloak were soaked through and her feet were numb by the time she reached the grave mounds.

A special quiet hung in the damp air. Alberonese didn't need priests to hallow the graves of their dead; the respect of ordinary people was sufficient, just as the prince had said. The sounds of camp seemed farther away than they were, as if the serene and peaceful sleep of the dead in their graves had enchanted the ground above them. In the faint starlight, a man could be a boulder or a boulder could be a man.

Kiera opened her mouth, thinking to call out Gray's name, but an unexpected awareness that she demeaned the dead by seeking him here, in their resting place, held the words in her throat.

Was it truly possible that she, Kiera Dainis, could demean the dead? Didn't she have good reasons—pure and noble reasons—for speaking privately with Alberon's prince and eliminating any suspicions he might hold—all in error—of her loyalty? She wasn't Kyle, blundering from one disaster to the next. She thought about what she did, and did nothing until she'd convinced herself that her intentions were noble. And her intentions *had* been noble; even though men had died, they'd died in treachery she could not have foreseen.

What had she foreseen?

Kiera's boldness deserted her between two heartbeats, leaving her with a single thought: *What am I doing here?* Not merely here in the twilight meadow, seeing shadows everywhere and smelling the scents of fresh-turned dirt and death, but here, so far from Roc Dainis, so far from the life she'd once cherished. Uncle Balwin sprinkled his cohort tales with phrases like *My whole life unveiled before my eyes*. She hadn't believed that, no more than she'd believed anything Uncle said. But her life did crowd her thoughts—at least the past several months of it.

Her own voice and her own words became a memory chorus: a litany of disdain directed mostly at her twin. It was so easy to blame Kyle; he'd always been so good-natured about his blunders, and now he was haunted by a wizard.

Her wizard.

As if Kiera didn't know, in her own heart, that she claimed Taslim of Fawlen only because she didn't have him. Kyle had never stood between her and her desires. She'd dragged him back and forth across Alberon, from Roc Dainis to the lodge, from Roc Dainis to Chegnon, from Chegnon to the Eigela. She'd pushed when he couldn't be pulled, pulled when he couldn't be pushed, starting that morning in his bedchamber when she'd teased him about his modesty.

If Taslim of Fawlen haunted Kyle, instead of her, that wasn't Kyle's fault. Nor was it his desire. Kiera had only to remember him in the sleigh, sick and shaking with his poor eye the color of fresh blood . . .

How could she have forgotten that? Because she had forgotten it. The priests binding him to the table before they attempted exorcism; she forgotten that, too. And him standing pale, but brave, in the dragon chamber.

Where had all those memories been when she scolded him and blamed him for every little thing?

When she wasn't blaming someone else.

Lille's face rose beside Kyle's in her mind's eye. Maybe Lille *did* blame her for what had happened to Renard, and maybe she was right. Lille was entitled to sit beside Renard with tears trickling across her cheeks and her nose all red and swollen. Renard was Lille's life, her future—and no future without Lockwood's wizardry.

Did that mean Kiera was wrong about Lockwood? Lockwood was Gray's boon-friend, Kyle's friend, but he simply didn't *belong*. Kiera wouldn't let him intrude into her reverie, but he burst into her thoughts anyway, shrouded in layers of her jealousy and standing between her and those she'd sought to bend and influence.

The patterns of her own acts since Rapture night were painfully clear. Kiera shut her eyes, tucked her head, and held her hands over her ears. Nothing quenched the force of her neglected conscience as it shredded all the wonderful phrases and gestures she'd prepared for Gray—Prince Gravais. She had been wrong—not misguided or mistaken—in a hundred little ways and just as many large ones. At every crossroads, she'd chosen her own path, and it was not one of noble intentions.

She wanted Gray to forgive her—

No. With only the dead as witnesses, Kiera looked deep within herself and saw that she didn't *want* to be forgiven; to be forgiven meant that she had been wrong, and in the rage and heat of her conscience, the thought that she'd been wrong all these months was too potent. What Kiera *wanted* was the assurance that the only errors she'd ever made were these horrible thoughts she was having right now. The thoughts that her intentions had not been noble and that she had wronged the very people she loved most.

She needed to hear Gray tell her that she was too beautiful, too kind, too good, and too pure of heart to need his, or anyone's, forgiveness. And she'd hear those words eventually, if she got Gray alone; that was the most harrowing indictment from her conscience. She was beautiful, but she wasn't kind, good, or pure of heart. She was simply skilled in the same cajoling arts that Queen Ezrae had practiced on her.

Weighed down by guilt, Kiera lowered her hands from her ears and whispered: "I've been cruel. I've been cruel to Lille, cruel to Kyle, cruel to everyone, and all because—"

"Lady Kiera?"

Unheard, Gray had come up behind her. His hands gently

covered her shoulders as his voice—scarcely more than a whisper—breathed into her ears.

"You seem distressed, dear lady. May I help you?"

Kiera turned in his circling grasp. She slid her arms inside his cloak and leaned against his chest. His heartbeat—the ever accurate measure of a man's thoughts and passion—sounded steadily in her ear.

"I have such *doubts,* Your Highness." There was the slightest quiver in her voice, then she pressed herself tighter against him. His heart beat faster. "So much has happened around me; I no longer trust my own thoughts. I'd talk to my maid or my brother—but their hearts are more troubled than my own, and I wouldn't think to bother them."

"Talk to me, Lady Kiera. A prince learns to listen before he learns anything else."

She tilted her head and looked at the stars, not him; Flen said she was irresistible with starlight in her eyes. "I fear it's all foolishness, Your Highness. Surely you have more important things to do."

"None, Lady Kiera. Come, sit beside me and tell me your troubles. The dead won't mind."

Kiera hugged him tight. "I feel so much safer now."

The sounds that roused Lockwood from a midnight sleep were ones he'd hoped never to hear again: panicked alarms, the clash of steel on steel, horses squealing, hoofbeats near and far. He had one hand on his boots, the other tossing blankets, before he was fully awake. Nearby he heard a thump, followed by a groan. The moon was up; there was enough light to see a hulking shadow on the far side of the tent.

He got free of the blanket and held a boot by the toe, having no other weapon to hand. "Gray?" His friend had not been in the tent when he pulled the blankets over his head. He'd missed supper completely; so had Kiera Dainis.

"Kyle."

Lockwood's relief was tempered by concern when he kicked the pallet where Gray should have been and disturbed blankets only. "Damn."

"Hurry. Here."

A sword and scabbard came his way through the charcoal

darkness. Lockwood missed his catch and they clattered to the ground. He stomped into his boots, grabbed the weaponry, and left the tent a few paces behind his younger companion. The three-quarter moon showed that commotion came from two places: the horse line and the tent where they'd confined Geregonal's men.

A man needed no special cleverness to tie the pieces together: Geregonal's men had overpowered their solitary guard and broken free. Even with the moon, there was no point in pursuit. Night could hide a thousand men in its shadows and always gave advantage to the pursued, not the pursuer, regardless of justice. A man could do no more than remember that he'd heard the clash of steel and hope that he wouldn't be digging another friend's grave after sunrise.

They were all clever men and all hurrying toward either the horses or the prisoners' tent. Lockwood lagged a few paces behind, not for cowardice—he was eager to put his sword to use—but to cast his glance around, sorting out the commotion and making decisions. At least two men with the horses were shouting that they were unhurt and demanding a measure of peace for their animals. The flow of activity swung entirely toward the prisoners' tent, where such assurances weren't forthcoming. Yet Lockwood still lagged, scanning the hillcrest, where, at last, Gray's unmistakable coppery hair appeared.

A breath the wizard hadn't known he was holding escaped with a sigh.

No wizardry there, nothing Lockwood had done with a talisman, or with the aqua-eyed haunt who'd sighed with him and purred now, sharing his relief. Only a boon-friend's anxiety and nearly a lifetime of learning Gray's habits.

Lockwood hailed the prince, who acknowledged him with an upraised arm and a hand pointing toward the prisoners' tent, where they should meet. There were more shouted greetings from the men, who'd heard Lockwood shout Gray's name. Then there was a heartbeat of absolute silence as another head cleared the crest: Kiera Dainis, with her cloak pulled tight around her shoulders and her golden hair loose on her neck.

Their eyes met, at once and willfully. For a moment, Lockwood had no thoughts except distrust and anger, leavened with what he knew was jealousy. And he knew everything he felt was reciprocated.

"Damn," he swore for the second time.

God alone knew what they'd been doing all night outside the camp. Likely they'd been talking, nothing that should have stoked his own dark suspicions this way—

"Locky!"

Gray's shout wrenched Lockwood from his distraction. Turning away from Kiera, he ran toward the knot of men outside the prisoners' tent.

Dazed and reeling, Jahn Golight sat up with another man's help. Blood circled one eye and ran down into his beard, but the captain was more indignant than injured.

"Me own knife! Me own damned knife held against me ribs!" he sputtered in rustic grammar and immediately began to repeat himself.

There was another man on the ground as well: one of Geregonal's men, taller than Gray, but older, and simple. Geregonal's cousin, or so he claimed, and Geregonal had never bothered to correct him. By Lockwood's measure, that captain's sole redeeming virtue was his unhesitating acceptance of this cousin's devotion. Now the simple man struggled between two men-at-arms. His wrists were tightly bound behind his back, and his face was as bloodied as Jahn Golight's, except where tears had washed it clean.

It bothered Lockwood to think the prince's men—men like himself—had made their own judgments and meted out a summary punishment to a terrified, simple-witted man who knew no more about right and wrong than an ox. But it must have bothered Gray more, because the prince ordered his men-at-arms to stand back, then drew his own boot knife to cut the weeping man's bonds before asking Golight, "What happened here?"

"Damn me for a fool, Yer Highness! They caught me wi' me noggin against the post and me eyes damn well shuttered. They'd me knife 'fore I was awake and struck me noggin 'fore I'd gotten it back."

"This one, too?" Gray asked, pointing at the simpleton who'd used his freedom to curl tight over his knees, hands on his face, while he continued to sob loudly.

"Didn't see a-one of them, but, Yer Highness, t'weren't me what tied him."

Manifestly ill at ease—neither Lockwood nor his prince had had extensive conversation with simpletons—Gray knelt and laid a hand on the weeping man's shoulder. "What happened here, man?" he asked. "Where did your friends—"

The sobs turned to wails as the tear-streaked face rose. "Friends? No *friends* now. No Captain—" His breath caught, his eyes widened, as if in mortal terror, and his face disappeared behind his hands again. "No Captain. The Captain's kilt. No more Captain. No more."

Gray stood, his hands against his hips as he straightened. "No answers here, that's for certain," he muttered. "They've bolted, that's all. How many horses gone?"

"Two, Your Highness."

Gray shook his head. "Back to Chegnon. Back to their allies. Back to the Bitch, unless they circle around and bite us again. Damn." He stared at the rumpled felt cap atop the simpleton's head.

There was no cruelty in Alberon's crown prince—Lockwood was certain of that. Lightning strike—that was the problem: He'd disarmed Geregonal's men when they wouldn't swear allegiance to him and kept them under guard, but he hadn't bound them. The guards suffered more in the night air than the prisoners did under canvas. No, there wasn't cruelty, but frustration, despair? This jaunt was supposed to make Gray's reputation, and what had he to show for it: an eruption of grave mounds? They'd captured none of their ambushers, hung Geregonal, lost two of Geregonal's three men, and were left with only this poor creature to show for their diligence. None of these were accomplishments that Lockwood would have cared to recite to his father, whoever he was, much less the king of Alberon.

But Jahn Golight had gathered his own wits while Lockwood's had wandered. "By Your Highness' leave," he said clearly, shedding the accent of his childhood and the support of the men around him. "There's answers to be had from him."

Gray drew back, nostrils flared with indignation; he wouldn't stand for cruelty done in his name. He *wasn't* cruel.

And neither was Jahn Golight, *Captain* Jahn Golight. "On your feet, cousin," he ordered, much as Geregonal had done before he swung from a rope.

Sniveling, wiping his nose on a ragged and very dirty sleeve, the man pushed himself upright.

"You were with two other men—" Tears began to flow

again, but Jahn stoppered them with a captain's snarl. "You're on duty; *I'm* your captain now."

No magic could match the glow of awe that spread over the simpleton's face as he swiped his cap from his hair and held it respectfully at his waist. "Captain?" he whispered. "Captain?" He was all innocence and hope that made Lockwood avert his own eyes.

"You were with two other men. They're gone now; left you behind, they did. Left you to tell what happened."

Crumpling the cap until it disappeared in his huge fists, the simpleton began to nod and then to tell his story—from the beginning.

His name, he said, was Usheff, and Geregonal—*Captain* Geregonal—had found him in Jiverne, in a village the Black Lightning had razed on orders of the Kolish king. "The Captain saved my life, so I gave it back to him," Usheff explained, a simple act that had sustained him for—Lockwood racked his memory for the dates of the campaigns Geregonal had bragged about—over twenty years.

Loyal, Gray had said of Geregonal; loyal to a fault, to the death.

Once he'd begun, Usheff unraveled his tale exactly as it was in his mind, digressions and main thrust with equal care. Lockwood couldn't let his attention wander; Gray wouldn't, and Gray would want to talk when this was ended. And better that Gray talk to him than to that Dainis chit, who hadn't gone to her own tent but hovered here, where blood had flowed and women had no need to hover.

Usheff didn't like the queen—a good mark for the simpleton's good sense. The queen kept the captain on night duty, away from the barracks where Usheff dwelt with men who were not his friends. What kind of night duty? Lockwood wondered, and noted that Gray's eyes had narrowed as well. Usheff didn't know about gold, except that it was bright and he'd seen more of it prior to their Chegnon departure than he'd ever seen—which only confirmed the suspicions they'd had when they'd found gold on the corpses after the ambush.

Usheff didn't like Prince Gravais, either, because Prince Gravais had put Geregonal to death; like every sword, loyalty could cut both ways. No rights or wrongs or justice. Geregonal was Usheff's friend, Usheff's protector, and without him, Usheff, by his own admission and slipping back into tears, was a lost soul with no one to tell him what to do, no one to praise him when he did it correctly.

"Enough o'that, Usheff," Jahn insisted. "I'm your captain, now. I'll be telling you what and when, never you worry about His Highness."

Once again, that magical brightening of Usheff's face—and so artfully wrought that Lockwood was compelled to wonder if consoling simpletons, binding their loyalty, wasn't part of every cohort captain's wherewithal. But Golight had gotten Usheff talking again before Lockwood found an answer to his own question.

Usheff didn't consider that he'd been left behind by a pair of men who didn't want to be troubled with him. By Usheff's few bright lights, he'd been the one who made the choice.

"'Tweren't no captain," he explained. "Was always Usheff do this, Usheff do that, and they weren't no captains to be giving Usheff orders like that. Wouldn't answer questions, neither. Wouldn't say where we was bound. Not the Lightning. They'd say that a-much." Then, shaking his head in Gray's silent way, he added, "The *queen*."

Gray raked his hair. "Do we believe him?" His hands dropped from his hips.

"You wouldn't lie to me, Usheff?" Golight asked.

The simpleton raised his cap to his chin and, wide-eyed again, shook his head vigorously from side to side. He was a child, truly; no more than a child, with a child's understanding of the world despite his age. Children could lie and did lie, but when Usheff's head said he wasn't lying, it could only be the truth.

Golight pressed for knowledge. "Did they say they were going to Queen Ezrae?"

Usheff lowered his cap, still shaking his head. "Scared, they was. And arguing. Scared of her if'n they told her what happened to the Captain, scared if'n they didn't."

"So, they argued about where they would go, what they would do if they got away."

Like a wind-blown pendulum, Usheff's head began to nod. "Got to move fast, they said. Move quick—" His whole body began to sway. "Too fast for Usheff. Too quick. No, Captain."

Jahn Golight had more questions, but Usheff had reached the limit of his answers and there was nothing more to be learned.

"I don't reckon he knows any more, Your Highness."

"It's enough, Captain. Thank you. Thank both of you." Gray held out his hand; Usheff shied and Gray withdrew the gesture. "Let's get some sleep, if we can," he said loud enough for everyone to hear. "God knows we've had enough excitement for one night."

The men took their leave quickly, agreeing silently with their prince, until there were only four of them—Gray, Lockwood, Jahn Golight, and Usheff—standing together. The moon stood a few spans above the western treetops. Dawn was still a few night hours away.

"Walk awhile?" Lockwood asked softly.

Gray's chin twitched, all the affirmation Lockwood needed to stay, but Gray wasn't done with Golight.

"What about him, Captain?" he asked softly, tilting his head toward Usheff, who'd made no move toward his tent, or anywhere else. "He'll take looking after, won't he?"

Jahn Golight shrugged, then nodded. "A mite, that's for certain. But Geregonal—damn his soul—never had a complaint of him that I heard. A strong back beneath a simple mind's no fault in any cohort, Your Highness. I'll look after him, Your Highness. Never you worry about it." He turned to Usheff. "Go on inside."

"Alone?"

Not a man with forty-some years creasing his face, but a child inside, afraid of the dark, utterly unaware that another man might well be afraid of him.

"I'll be along," Golight assured Usheff. "You make a bed ready for me."

That glowing smile spread across Usheff's face again. "Yes, Captain!" and he disappeared into the tent.

"You're sure?" Gray asked hesitantly.

"Don't try hanging me, Your Highness," Golight answered with a friendly grin. "Don't think he'll take well to your hanging another captain."

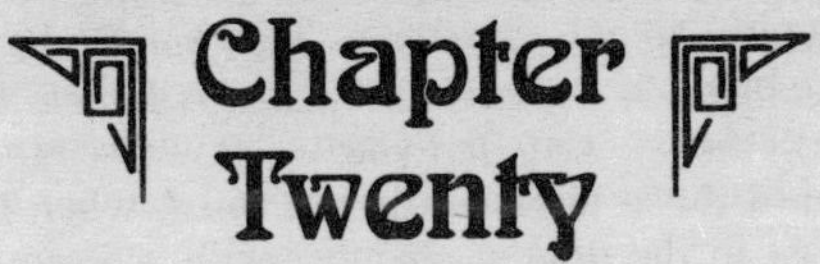

Chapter Twenty

The captain's parting words rang in Gray's ears; he almost didn't hear Golight tell Usheff to "Spread your own blankets out there, by the post . . . Aye, that's a good lad. Give your eyes a rest now. Don't you worry about His Highness out there; he won't hurt you—or me."

Gray had known Jahn Golight since he was a boy hefting his first scaled-down sword, and Golight was his first arms-master. It shouldn't have been such a surprise that Golight showed an expert touch with the simpleton; he'd been patient enough with a princeling who never wanted to start at the beginning of anything. Still, it was a stranger's voice he heard assuring Usheff that *His Highness* was nothing to be afraid of and a stranger who'd joked about hanging.

As crown prince of Alberon, Gray had had the right to hang a man since he'd turned seventeen, some ten years back, but Geregonal's death marked the first time he'd used it. The man had connived against Alberon; he'd committed treason. Gray thought he should feel proud, having defended the Maradze throne; instead, listening to Golight, Gray felt as if he'd lost a friend.

Cherish your friends, my son, his father had said in a thousand remembered conversations. *Princes make few enough in their lives. Kings make none at all.*

Jahn Golight had been a friend. Now, no matter that he jested, no matter that his words were meant to reassure a child-like creature older in years than them both, fear frosted their friendship. Fear that could never melt away.

Of course, they fear us! His father's deep, hearty laughter.

Why else pay our dues and taxes? Life's a frightening thing, my son, and they're the lucky ones. They bundle all their fears together, sit them on a gilded throne and call them King of Alberon. That's me, my son; and you, *when you're ready.*

He'd heard those wise words just once, when the two of them had sat in the dragon chamber with a scrap of creased parchment lying on the table between them. The parchment recorded that there'd been a rebellion in Kol. Merchants, peasants, and a potent handful of renegade nobles had risen against a brother monarch, paraded him naked through the streets of his capital, then crushed him beneath his own monuments. King Irkatul—that was the late monarch's name—was a cruel and rapacious man whom Gray's father had roundly cursed many times. The man who usurped his throne, Bakur Ironfist, now King Bakur, had brought peace to Kol and Jiverne as well. He'd sent the Black Lightning back to Alberon, after forty years continuous service.

Geregonal was Black Lightning. He'd been among those who'd returned, rootless and unvictorious, to an Alberon they scarcely knew, hardly liked. Perhaps that was why now—of all times—Gray recalled that quiet afternoon in the dragon chamber. Perhaps it wasn't right to judge King Bakur by the troublesome veterans he'd ordered out of his kingdom. Bakur was a good king for Kol, but he'd never sit secure on his throne, not considering how he'd come to it, and he'd never have the fellowship of his brother monarchs around the sea of Prayse.

Fear's a mighty, small thing for a king, my son. Too little, and your loyal subjects think they can do as they like. Too much, and they think they can do without you; they start looking for someone else to eat their fears. A man like Ironfist, he's the most dangerous of all, giving men the idea that they can pick a better *king for themselves than the king their god gave them.*

Eat their fears. Gray hadn't been all that young—fourteen or fifteen, old enough to know better—but he'd been very suspicious of his supper for days after that conversation and haunted by the nightmare of him and his father naked in the streets of Chegnon town. The images came back, violent and vibrant, as if he'd thought about them every day, when he hadn't in years. Reflexively, Gray tugged the bands of his shirt. The chill on his skin came from his imagination.

Gray remembered how he'd beaten the nightmares: a

promise to himself that fear would have no part of *his* reign. He'd rule with respect and caution, neither fearing his Alberonese subjects, nor having them fear him. It was a boy's promise, one he'd never make now that he was older, wiser, one that he'd forgotten long ago. There had to be a bit of fear between the kingdom and the throne, but he'd never reckoned on fear between a prince and his friends.

"Gray?"

Lockwood—the friend Lady Sabelle had given him, because he had no family, save his father (or hadn't any when Lockwood arrived and Ezrae Baldescare was still a child in leading strings), the friend he thought he'd have until the end of his life. They feared *for* each, but did even Lockwood fear him? Lockwood wasn't just a friend; Lockwood was a wizard—bound to be a magister in a decade, about when Gray expected to ascend Alberon's throne. Aside from another magister or a lethal lightning bolt, what would Lockwood fear?

A thoroughly mortal, occasionally foolish monarch?

"Gray?"

"I'm listening," Gray replied, thinking his final thoughts on the matter and concluding that, just possibly, Lockwood was the one man who'd never fear him.

"Did you hear yourself say men should sleep now? Do you think that advice might be worth listening to?"

The prince chuckled softly, revelling in the warmth and humor. "What do *I* know about such things, Locky? Walk with me awhile?"

"I'd have thought you'd walked enough earlier."

That wasn't fear in his friend's voice; it was more like jealousy. Lockwood had his preferences, his prejudices—like any man—but they'd never clouded his judgment before—if they were clouding it now.

Gray looked where Lockwood stared and saw the girl, Kiera Dainis, standing by their tent. Of course, it was her brother's tent, too. Like billeted with like: the three noblemen together, the captain and sergeants, the women and their patient . . . The men and varlets slept on the ground. Kyle was already inside, visible as a silhouette on the canvas.

"Grab a torch. We'll walk along the stream. I've had enough of graves for one night."

Lockwood headed toward the fire. The setting moon glinted

off the girl's eyes as she looked at him. Expecting an invitation? Expecting him to choose her over Lockwood? Nonsense—except that Lockwood had believed it possible.

God's pockets! She was a pretty thing and she'd stopped just short of throwing herself at his feet. No, the truth—at least to himself—*she* hadn't stopped. He'd taken a man's honorable pity on a woman—a *child*—who'd surely never smelled death in the air. He'd tried to eat her fears for her and she'd insinuated herself into his arms, tucked her soft, soft hair against his neck, and told him that her betrothed had sent a letter with her father's men and supplies: She was released from her betrothal.

Muredoch must be ecstatic—if he or Lord Dainis even knew what their beloved Kiera had done.

For Gray himself, ecstasy was the last thought in his mind as he listened to her talk about Queen Ezrae. God knew, Kiera Dainis wasn't a match for the Bitch of Baldescare. He didn't hold her responsible for the Bitch's treachery. Or blame her for tumbling into love—or into the idea of love—with him. He'd grown accustomed to ladies of impeccable breeding, with or without their families' consent, falling like leaves on his path.

Accustomed, and bored.

Lord Dainis' only daughter had her charms. She was twice as lively and clever as the other noble daughters he knew. She was fiercely, if sometimes foolishly, protective of those she cared for—most notably her twin brother, but a royal prince, too, if Gray could believe the tale she spun to account for her alliance with the Bitch. He supposed he could believe. At least he could believe that she believed the words that had poured out of her mouth. And that was why he'd hold her at arm's length and then some until this adventure was safely over.

Or simply over. With graves on the far side of the hillcrest, safe was a fleeting wish.

Light rose to Gray's left: Lockwood returning with a rag-and-pitch torch. With the last of his night-attuned vision, Gray watched the Dainis girl turn away with a sweep of skirt.

"Did she get what she wanted?" Lockwood asked bluntly.

"No," he replied, in the same tone. "She got what she asked for, not what she wanted." He started walking toward the trees. Kiera Dainis, her charms and complications weren't the reason he wanted to talk with his friend. "Where do you think Gereg-onal's men tonight are headed?"

"Chegnon, where else? But before we sink further into despair, my friend—I don't think they'll get there."

"That last storm has turned you into a seer?" Gray meant to jest, but the words were flat.

Lockwood laughed. "Not yet; you'll be the first to know if it does. But you took their coins with their weapons when they wouldn't swear. They've got what they took from Golight, two horses, and no food. It won't be enough."

"Not for honest men. They'll rob, maybe kill."

"They're outsiders. They don't know this land. They'll get caught."

"You're quite certain for a wizard who's not a seer. Other, less talented, men might think it wiser to assume they'd reach Chegnon and the Bitch's ear."

"Very well, our pigeons fly home to Chegnon. What then? What's the worst that can happen?"

"They tell the Bitch that I've hanged her midnight lover."

"And?"

"She and her uncle set themselves to my ruin."

"They've set themselves to that task before. King Otanazar doesn't listen to their words when he hears their voices."

"I've always been there to defend myself."

"By the bolt! You're thinking of turning tail and running back to Chegnon, aren't you?"

"This whole journey's been a farce from its first suggestion. You and yours have reasons, my father has reasons, the Baldescare have their reasons, but no one expected anything to come of it—"

"The Baldescare expected all of us to die. It's what they paid for," Lockwood interrupted, suddenly very serious. "Run back, empty-handed and scared, and they'll have gotten the second-best thing: a prince who's lost his nerve. God save the king."

The jibe struck too close. "Don't ride me, Locky," Gray warned. "You don't know everything."

"It seems I don't know you."

Cherish your friends, Father said. Where would he be without Lockwood, who dared to treat a prince as if he were any other man? A friend who would stand fast against a royal rage:

"Men have *died*, Lockwood," he snarled. "Men I led to their deaths. Men I killed!"

"The Baldescare killed those men," Lockwood replied, loud enough to be heard back among the tents, but a friend who would challenge him would challenge the whole world. "Don't blame yourself, unless you'd dishonor them."

Gray strode to the torch's limit where he stood, back to Lockwood, staring into darkness that was not dark enough. "What if more men die, my friend, on this fool's quest? What if *you* died?"

"I'd haunt you until you finished it—*and* the damned Baldescare."

A shiver raced down Gray's spine; Death, the old women claimed, taking the measure for his shroud. He shook it off and returned to the light. "You know what's up there, don't you, *friend*? The worthy magister, Lord Marrek Brun, knows and he's sent you as his spy. What else, Locky? What else that I don't know, that I should know, that you've known from the beginning?"

Lockwood shook his head slowly. "Nothing. No and nothing to all of it, especially the last. Lord Marrek questions me—you know that. He'd like to think he owns me; he'd like to fly, too. He gets what I give him and you know what I give him. Neither one of us *knows* what awaits in the Eigela. *Something*, yes, I do believe that much. Strange things dwell in nasen'bei, but nothing half so strange as a time-stranded wizard."

"Stranger than a cat with aqua eyes?" Gray asked, effectively ending serious conversation. Neither of them could mention the purring haunt without both of them remembering Lockwood's countless, futile attempts to share nasen'bei with his friend. And the remembering was certain to raise a smile.

"Stranger," Lockwood agreed, with that smile creasing his beard.

They talked of other things then, until the torch sputtered and it was time to return to the tents. The night guard—the Dainisman varlet Enobred—hailed their approach with proper diligence as he huddled beneath a blanket. A borrowed sword lay unsheathed on the ground in front of him. A prince could ask no more of his men, but a score of varlets wouldn't help if another ambush came riding up.

But a prince couldn't say that. A prince assured his men that they did their duty and that he was proud of them. The varlet shrugged off the blanket and sat up straight.

"Stay warm, man—that's an order."

"Yes, Your Highness! Yes, indeed!" The youth struggled with the cloth which, now that he sat straight, no longer stretched easily between his rump and his shoulders.

Gray and Lockwood continued toward their quiet tent.

"We'll pull up stakes tomorrow and get a good league under our belts before sundown," Gray said, giving a last glance at the hill and thinking of the graves beyond it. "It will be good to be gone from this deathly place."

"Not tomorrow," Lockwood said as he ducked through the opening.

"What? Now you're playing the slackard!"

"With cause. With cause. I'd like to see that injured young man, Renard Fisherson, with another day's rest and such help as I can give him before we move him."

"God strike me for a fool," Gray swore as the flap fell behind him. He was too tall for the tent. It would have been easier to crawl—easier, but completely undignified. He cricked his neck instead and fumbled through the darkness in search of his blankets. "*Can* we move him? Will he survive it? I tell you true: I hadn't expected him to last this long."

"And I'll tell you the same. But he's young and wants to live. I'll pass my talisman over him more often tomorrow. He can't ride; we'll have to rig one of the tents as a horse-drawn litter. It will be slow traveling, but—yes, I think he'll survive," Lockwood said, followed by a grunt and a curse as he stumbled in the dark.

"Slow traveling," Gray repeated, possibilities glimmering in his thoughts. He forgot where he was and put his head into the cross beam. The whole tent swayed and threatened to collapse. "We'll be our own scouts then, riding ahead and behind, keeping an eye on the land." He braced the cross beam until the swaying stopped, then released it cautiously. "There's nothing wizardry can do to help us, is there? No way to see around the next bend or listen above the trees?"

The tent stayed erect. Gray sat down and began removing his boots. Close by, Lockwood was doing the same. Behind them, young Kyle Dainis slept quietly.

"Well?" Gray asked when his toes were free and wriggling. "Can you help?"

"What you want is transference—to place one's self in another body—and congruence—to make use of those other senses. They're both difficult, dangerous—especially the transference. I've done them, with Lord Marrek as a touchstone. Without him . . . How important is it?"

"Not that important. I'd hoped you could just whisper a couple of runes and turn a tree into a sentry. You've done so well with the varlet."

"Flatterer. Renard *wants* to live; a tree doesn't want to be your sentry. You need some lesser creature with a mind you can dominate and another wizard to call you back if you get lost."

"Enough. I'm convinced it was a fool's question. Go to sleep. You'll have your day with the varlet, I'll have mine scouting ahead."

Gray found his own blankets and threw them lengthwise to his feet. It was well past the spring equinox. The nights would be mild along Alberon's coast, but up here, approaching the Eigela, the midnight ground still felt like the stones of winter. Men huddled together for warmth, back to back or cheek by jowl, and even modest Kyle Dainis, who kept so much to himself while he was awake, would join them long before dawn.

Kyle slid his hands away from his ears. He'd tried mightly not to hear a private conversation between the prince and the wizard. It hadn't worked. They rarely whispered to each other, but talked as if there were no one else billeted in their tent or as if he were a varlet himself and not worthy of consideration.

These nights in the prince's tent took his mind back to fosterage, where it seemed everyone but him had a confidant. He'd had his imagination, composing long letters to his twin that he never sent, or even wrote, until the dormitory was at last quiet and he slipped, all unknowing, from imagination to dreams. The other fosterlings had teased him for his shyness, his accidents, his clumsiness, and countless other failings. They'd called him Dreamer and worse. He'd told himself he didn't care about them or friendship.

And it hadn't been a lie. At least, he'd felt no lack of friendship or knowledge of loneliness until he'd returned to Chegnon. There, tucked away by himself in a too big room with no chores to do, he couldn't fill all his empty hours with imaginary letters; Kiera had become a stranger. Listening to the prince and Lockwood, whether their conversation was joking, as it usually was, or serious, as it had been this night, Kyle felt the thorns of envy.

He'd had to cover his ears. He wanted nothing more than to join their conversation.

<<So? Talk to me instead.>>

Kyle held his breath and his thoughts.

<<We'll talk about the Lord of Marelet, a lightning-mighty wizard with damn cold feet.>>

Taslim. Kyle did have Taslim, and a nagging suspicion that he'd never have envied anyone's friendship, if he hadn't looked up at the wrong time. He kept a firm hold on his thoughts now, almost without a conscious effort, the same as he kept a firm seat in Rawne's saddle. Taslim's voice was a whisper he could ignore as easily as he ignored the men breathing nearby. The wizard's face appeared only if he consciously summoned the image from the darkness behind his own memory. Kyle hoped the practice and discipline of keeping his own self and Taslim rigidly separate would serve him well once they neared the Eigela and Taslim became their only guide—

<<Listen to me, Hart-lord! Answer me! Talk to me, Hart-lord.>>

A notion came to Kyle, sharp and sudden as a thrusting sword: Taslim of Fawlen had been alone for a millennium. For a thousand years the wizard had dwelt in twilight, cut off from conversation, companionship, and all other simple, mortal pleasures.

Kyle felt the twilight as a dense fog. His senses were keen, but twilight held him in a shroud. If he'd screamed his throat bloody, the sound would not have reached his ears. He knew in an instant it wasn't his own notion, but Taslim's, and guessed as the moment lengthened that it was nothing the wizard had forced into his mind, but something that had escaped Taslim's thoughts by mistake. A millennium *was* eternity if Kyle could trust the impressions he now had of Taslim's memories: an unchanging, suffocating gray eternity interrupted by the pure emptiness of madness and the despair of discovering that madness was not, itself, eternal. Nor was imagination. A man could find his imagination's limit; he could think every thought twice over and the fog never thinned.

<<Damn you, Hart-lord! Damn you to the dark.>>

The gray twilight fog had lifted briefly and not long ago—that was when Taslim had run rampant through Kyle's thoughts. But the natural lights of day and night had not endured. Blundering priests had tried to cast Taslim out of Kyle's mind, to cast him back into the fog without a strand of wizardry to pull him back. If it had been mortal death the priests had promised, Taslim might have succumbed, but facing that fog again, he'd made a frantic, mindless defense—

And trapped himself in darkness. For a millennium Taslim hadn't felt himself moving; now he couldn't move at all. For a millennium his senses had been sharp, but empty. Now, without Kyle's aid, he was blind and numb and deaf to everything except the echo of Kyle's thoughts, the sound of Kyle's voice, and—inexplicably—the voice of his nemesis, Lockwood of Marelet.

<<Talk to me, Hart-lord!>>

Kyle felt the dark as he'd felt the fog: at one remove. It was real, but it was not his; it belonged to Taslim, who was—the knowledge had been with Kyle from those first horrid moments—not an ancient wizard, but a man only a few years older than himself, trapped first in eternal fog, now in endless dark. Kyle felt the dark as Taslim felt it: a tight prison around every remembered muscle or joint, a seal over his eyes, his mouth, his nose.

A living tomb.

<<For pity's sake, Hart-lord, *talk to me!*>>

<<Serras!>> Kyle shouted within himself, recalling the lustrous rune shape of summoning. <<Serras! Serras! Serras!>> He let out a breath, and Taslim with it.

The wizard's face was unrecognizable: parchment stretched over a hollow, eyeless skull, unnatural and unnerving to behold until, like water poured into a cup, substance flowed between skin and bone. Familiar black hair, black eyes, and a neatly trimmed black beard all appeared in their proper place.

<<I thought—I thought I'd left you free. I thought . . .>> But he had not thought, merely assumed that Taslim was free because Lockwood had given him form for a night.

<<I have no wizardry, no lightning essence to sustain myself, Hart-lord. I sink. I fade.>>

<<But I saw you the other night. You were not—>> The skull appeared beside Taslim's restored visage.

<<You saw what Marelet summoned. How he and I agreed I should appear.>>

<<And now? How are you? *Which* are you?>>

The Taslim of flesh and the Taslim of bone turned toward each other, and away again. <<I have no wizardry, Hart-lord.>>

Kyle felt a brush of shame across the surface of his thoughts, then wariness, which lingered. <<Are you . . . dying, Taslim?>>

The wariness intensified. <<Does it matter to you, Hart-lord?>>

<<Yes,>> without hesitation.

<<Then, I am not dying. I cannot die.>>

Wariness was a pervasive presence in Kyle's mind, which his own wariness made thicker as he tried guess what other meaning might lie beneath the wizard's words. <<What did you want to talk about?>>

<<Remind the Lord of Marelet that there is another wizard who would help him and his prince.>>

That seemed a safe enough request. <<I'll do that,>> Kyle agreed. <<Anything else? Should I try to stay awake all night?>>

<<By the Almighty Bolt, Hart-lord, whatever for?>>

<<You're blind otherwise, deaf and numb.>>

<<Nonsense, Hart-lord. What gave you that idea?>>

<<You did,>> but Kyle snared his thoughts as they formed and held them where he was nearly certain Taslim could not find them, blind or not, deaf or not. He lay on his back, staring up at the tent canvas that he couldn't see and a pair of heads, one fleshed, the other bone, that seemed to hover just out of reach. His mind was quiet—Taslim had taught him that trick, or, rather, he'd learned it as his primary defense.

<<It's night, Hart-lord. Pitch-black night. There's nothing to see. Close your eyes and go to sleep.>>

Kyle blinked—sooner or later a man *had* to shut his eyes. Both heads vanished.

A cold draft, which he hadn't noticed while Taslim held his attention, attacked his feet. Another penetrated his blankets, chilling his flank. The prince and Lockwood had fallen into the regular rhythms of sleep. They were real; they were warm.

Kyle scrunched his blankets and wormed toward them, stopping as soon as he felt a scratch of wool against his exposed knuckles.

It was the prince's blanket he'd felt, or so Kyle told himself as he tucked his hands against his chest and closed his eyes. Perhaps it was, then, before he fell asleep, but it was Lockwood's thick, curly hair that greeted his eyes when he opened them again. He tried to wriggle away unnoticed, but their blankets were thoroughly tangled and—worst chance of all—Kyle's efforts disturbed the wizard, who awoke with outflung arms and a mighty yawn.

A brawny forearm slammed into Kyle's upper lip before he could dodge sideways, before his own sleepy mind understood that he should dodge. He was surprised, hurt, and embarrassed when he tasted blood. With his slept-in shirtsleeve pressed against his swelling lip, Kyle scrambled frantically to his feet. He hunched over at the rear of the tent, free hand up to guard his face and what was left of his dignity.

"Lightning strike! My apologies. I'd no sense you were so near."

Lockwood extended his arm, which, this time, Kyle dodged easily.

"Damn, Kyle—it was an accident."

Not boy, or Dreamer, or even hart-lord, but his name, as if it had been simply an accident, a rare one that wasn't his fault. Kyle straightened until his head brushed the canvas, then lowered his hand. There was a sizeable damp patch on his sleeve, which was already dirty.

"Got you good."

"It's nothing," Kyle replied. He probed his lip, wincing when the salty oils of his fingertip touched the bleeding places. "I'll survive."

"I hope so. Gray'll have me strung up otherwise. Come here, into the light. I seem to have become our physician. Let me have a look at you."

Kyle stayed where he was. "It's nothing, truly nothing."

"It's a damned awful way to wake up, at the very least. Let me do *something*, Kyle. I'd give you my shirt, but it would be too short in the sleeves."

"There is something. . . Last night, I heard—I wasn't meaning to listen, Lord Lockwood, but I did hear you talking with His Highness."

Lockwood scowled and his whole manner became guarded. "You don't want to go on to the Eigela, is that it? You want to go back to Chegnon, too? I can understand that, I suppose," but there was no understanding on his face.

"No, I've accepted that I must go up into the Eigela, for Taslim. . . for you and all your kind." There was no change in Lockwood's expression. "Last night you told the prince it would take two wizards to keep us safe."

"I don't recall saying that, Kyle."

All the doubts Kyle had harbored since the solstice returned. He doubted the loneliness and anguish he'd felt on Taslim's behalf. He doubted the reality of the overheard conversation that had begun them. He doubted everything about Taslim, and he doubted everything about himself. Given a clear path to the tent opening, he'd have run away from *this* folly. But the path to the door was blocked by a brawny man whose reputation as a fighter was as well known as his wizardry.

"Well, Kyle. I haven't got a day for guessing games. Out with it. You said you wanted something. It's not a return to Chegnon, but it involves two wizards: me, and Taslim?" Lockwood's expression changed then, becoming thoughtful behind an intense stare. "Is it guessing, Kyle? Is it something you *can't* say directly. Give me a sign, man."

He would have. Kyle wished to God he could have done or said something to justify Lockwood's sober scrutiny, but: "Taslim says he'll help. He said I should tell you that there's another wizard who'd help you."

Lockwood held a finger against his lips: a sign for silence, hardly what Kyle expected. "God love it, Dreamer—you *were* dreaming last night! Damn! They're burning the porridge. Pull on your boots and make haste, or we won't get anything but charred dregs for breakfast."

Kyle did as he was told, the safest course through strangeness, but he wasn't surprised when Lockwood seized him around the shoulder and whispered in his ear:

"Saddle your horse, ride north. Get out of sight of the camp. I'll join you."

Danger loomed everywhere, but nowhere more than in the darkest recesses of Kyle's thoughts. He'd been a fool to think he could pass messages between the wizards safely, a fool to think he could trust either of them. But he nodded obediently, all the same, and dared to ask a whispered question: "What have I done wrong, Lord Wizard?"

"Wrong? Why, nothing wrong. But—Kyle, I need to be certain; you understand that, don't you? I'll have to talk to your—to Taslim. I won't do it here, though. I wouldn't ask that of you, not here, where you'd be watched. And if it's nothing—well, no sense letting the world know, is there?"

Everything seemed honest: the slight scowl on the wizard's face, the hint of exasperation amid his concern, the way his grip tightened, then relaxed. Kyle wanted to believe that there was no harm in Lockwood's intentions.

He'd learn the truth soon enough. A man could spend only so many moments choking down a bowl of scalded porridge or cleaning Rawne's healthy hooves. Lockwood had disappeared into the tent where they nursed Renard. The prince, he heard, had ridden off with Jahn Golight and yesterday's bread.

"Will ye be scouting the way ahead?" asked the man Golight had assigned to tend the horses as they tightened the saddle girth.

"I suppose so."

"Eh?"

"Yes, I'll be doing just that. Lord Marelet may ride out after me," Kyle said, and feared he'd said the wrong thing when the man gave a too hard tug on the stirrup leather.

"The wizard, eh?" he said, making the Hollow Sphere as he came around under Rawne's neck. "Sooner you get where you're bound and come back alone." He cupped his hands below the nearside stirrup, giving Kyle a boost into the saddle. "Ye've forgotten your sword, lord. No scouting off without it. The prince took his and wore mail besides. Mind you stay here, I'll fetch it for you."

"No need," Kyle called uselessly to the man's back.

So he rode toward the Eigela with the weight of steel against his thigh and his own foolishness around his shoulders. Rawne was fresh and eager to stretch himself in the cool morning of what promised to be a beautiful day once the sun burnt off the mist. It wasn't fair to hold the gelding to a tight walk simply because his rider was glum. Kyle leaned forward in the saddle, giving Rawne permission to choose his own path, his own pace through one tree-studded meadow after another.

They went farther than they had to. The camp, with its fresh grave mounds, wasn't merely out of sight, it was out of thought. Kyle considered retracing their steps to a nearer place that was more in keeping with Lockwood's instructions. They stopped on a ridge that offered the best view of the brooding, black Eigela he'd yet seen.

<<Do you recognize them?>> he asked the equally black presence at the back of his mind.

<<All mountains look alike to me, Hart-lord.>>

"God have mercy," Kyle said aloud, startling Rawne. "Don't you *know* where we're going, which mountaintop shelters the Siege?"

<<I know it, Hart-lord. I will know it. But it can't be seen from a distance. You'll understand when we get there.>>

The unspoken words were meant to reassure him, but didn't. Kyle rode Rawne back to a stream verge and slipped the bit out of his mouth so he could graze contentedly while Kyle sat with his back to the hidden mountains.

Lockwood arrived after midmorning, a sword at his side, too, and a parcel of cold meat as well. He tossed the parcel to Kyle before he dismounted and turned his horse loose beside Rawne.

"Slip his bit," Kyle advised, then, recognizing a man who had no insight or interest in horse habits, got up to do it himself. "Sorry that I made you ride farther than you would have liked."

"I'm used to it," Lockwood laughed. "Gray would as soon have been born a horse as a prince. But, tell me now, what exactly is your companion offering?"

Kyle answered as best he could, though there was no sure way to answer except for Lockwood to get out his talisman and utter the runic syllables—*serras* and others that touched Kyle's mind without leaving tracks in his memory. He was prepared to be shunted aside, as he had been when Lord Marrek Brun did the summoning, but Lockwood was either more skilled, or less skilled, than the king's magister.

When the runes were faded and the summoning accomplished, he and Taslim could both speak, each with Kyle's voice, and each could gesture with his hands, his face. It was very awkward. It would have been impossible if Kyle had had anything useful to contribute to a conversation about transference, congruence, substance, possession, vision, and other wizardly matters. Still, it was infinitely better than the dreamy helplessness he'd felt in Chegnon.

At least until he understood that the wizards intended to fling one of them—Taslim—into the body and mind of a bird.

"A hawk." Taslim was quite specific. "Excellent vision, strong flight, and a mind attuned to hunting and prey will serve our purpose best. It's no great feat of wizardry. Not in times past. Not to say what it's become in these times."

After years of never questioning his fate, seldom raising his voice or cursing, Kyle's voice was naturally soft and polite. It was not a good voice for Taslim's irony, worse for his abiding arrogance. Or, perhaps, it was the best possible voice, cloaking everything Taslim said with a calm confidence that held the attention of the wizard with a working talisman and won his approval.

Kyle scanned the sky and the trees for a suitable target. A handful of dark specks circled the clear blue sky, but at such a height that Kyle could not be certain if they were hawks or bustards, which Taslim adamantly insisted were not at all acceptable.

"A hawk, Hart-lord, a hunter, not a carrion eater. By the Almighty Bolt, a hawk."

He spied a flash of russet descending into the trees at the meadow's edge. "There—a small kestrel! I'm sure of—!"

"Small?" Taslim again took control of Kyle's tongue.

Kyle took control back. "A *male* bird—I can't imagine you wanting a ladybird!—and probably too young to have a mate this year." He shuddered—Taslim's reaction, not his own—then laughed, which was his.

The kestrel rose out of the tree, its wings brilliant in the sunlight. Kyle held his breath twice over, but the bird didn't soar. It settled instead on a naked branch of a nearer tree.

"Making our work easier for us." Lockwood said what they were all thinking. He slipped the glimmering talisman off his belt. "Ready?"

"Yes," Taslim said eagerly and placed Kyle's hands against the crystal.

The sensations—the talismanic shock—lanced Kyle, but he left his hands where Taslim had placed them and kept his eyes open, fixed on the preening kestrel, while Lockwood uttered a series of runes, most of which Kyle did not recognize. In the heartbeat silence following the last rune, the talisman released its captive lightning.

He wanted to cry out as it coursed into his palms, past his wrists, along his arms, his shoulders, his neck. He felt, rather than saw, the flash as it breached his skull. There should have been pain—every nerve was jangled—but there was light and lightness, as if his feet no longer needed the ground. Kyle was free, floating above his body, then he was alone within himself.

The kestrel took flight.

"Too soon!" Lockwood gasped on an inward breath. He jerked the talisman from Kyle's hands and raised it high above his head. "Come around," he shouted. "Come around, you damned arrogant fool!"

Lockwood's arms remained extended long enough for Kyle to understand that something was very wrong, but he said nothing until those arms hung limp at Lockwood's side. The kestrel had vanished and, except for the swishing of the horses' tails as they grazed, the meadow was silent.

"Where is he, Lockwood?" Kyle asked. "I can't feel him. He's gone. The dark place in my thoughts where I find him is empty."

The wizard's face was pale above his black beard. "Gone," he whispered, a more final sound in Lockwood's voice than it had been in Kyle's.

"With the kestrel?"

"As God wills, I pray so," Lockwood said, a very uncommon statement for a wizard, then he spun around suddenly and hurled an imaginary rock into the stream. Kyle thought it was a rock; it came from Lockwood's imagination. He couldn't be certain. "I believed him! I believed him!"

"About what?" Kyle asked, fearing he already knew the answer.

Lockwood's arms fell against Kyle's, not to offer comfort, but to list against another man's strength. "He knew all the formularies. They haven't changed in a thousand years, Kyle. Wizardry expands, but it rarely changes. He knew more than me. He could recite more than I've bothered to memorize—"

"Lockwood!"

"He's gone, Kyle. I don't know if he caught that kestrel before it flew, or shot clean past. I don't know if he imposed his will on the creature, or it on him. He's *gone*, that's all I know.

I could sense him for a heartbeat after the bird began to fly, then nothing. Nothing at all, Kyle."

"What would happen if he didn't catch the kestrel? He'd come back to me, wouldn't he. He'd come back to that nasen'bei place? Like he did after you summoned him?"

Lockwood shook his shaggy, black head. "Should," he agreed without evident conviction. "Should. Who knows with him? I called. You saw me, Kyle; I called to him and nothing came back. Pray he caught the bird and he's so full of himself that he's gone to spy out everything from the Inland road to the Siege itself. Pray that, Kyle; else we've lost your wizard."

The words struck Kyle's ears like fists in his gut. The wound of Josaf's death, so recently closed, burst open. His shoulders heaved forward around the shorter wizard and they supported each other a moment.

"I believed him." Lockwood returned to his earlier exclamation. "God forgive me, Kyle Dainis: I did truly believe him." Then, pushing himself away from Kyle without completely withdrawing his strength. "I let him persuade me that he could do something I knew, in my heart and mind, that he couldn't."

Kyle slipped out of Lockwood's grasp. "He wasn't a great wizard, was he?"

"Barely a wizard at all, Kyle. He'd read all the scrolls and memorized them—for another wizard's convenience, most likely a magister, like Marrek. They had such a thousand years ago. But wizardry's not in the runes, it's in the mind. It's practice, just like the arena."

"And the right spirit," Kyle added, thinking of the arena and the warrior spirit he did not possess.

"An excess of spirit for Taslim of Fawlen. He could have asked for help. I could have guided him, steadied him until the transference was secure. I could have forced him to accept my help—but that would have proven our standing one to the other."

"Not Taslim."

"Not Taslim," Lockwood agreed.

They went on that way, a reluctant requiem for a man—Taslim was a man; his failings demonstrated that—who was more to blame for this disaster than either of them. Though that was little comfort as the sun crept past its zenith. Several times Kyle thought he saw the russet flash of a kestrel's wings.

Lockwood offered his talisman as a lure, but the bird—if it was their kestrel, their wizard—never came.

"I have to return to the camp. Renard. If we're to leave tomorrow. . ."

They'd never know.

"He'd be with the trees, wouldn't he? If he's not with the kestrel. That's not such a terrible place," Kyle said, more faith than conviction.

"I'll come back," Lockwood said, though Kyle hadn't said he was staying here. He didn't need to. "Call his name. Call his name with your voice and with your thoughts. I'll come back. I'll try to think of something else."

The wizard fumbled with his horse's bit. Kyle fed it expertly into the animal's mouth, then handed the reins to Lockwood.

"You didn't like him. Don't like him."

Lockwood shrugged, but didn't deny the assertion. "You were bound through nasen'bei," he said as he swung himself into the saddle. "That's enough. I'll come back."

That promise sustained Kyle throughout the longest, emptiest afternoon of his life. He mounted Rawne and rode the verge of the meadow, shouting Taslim's name beneath each tree. There was nothing his imagination could conjure that would replace the cynicism, danger, and mystery that had been Taslim of Fawlen. From Rawne's saddle, he made his way to the topmost branches of one of the bigger trees. He called until his throat was sore, his head was throbbing.

The kestrel flew overhead once—Kyle was certain it was the kestrel they'd seen in the morning—but it paid him no heed, flying deeper into the trees. He thought of following afoot or astride Rawne. That would have been utter foolishness: He didn't know these woods. He'd get lost himself, or Lockwood would get lost trying to find him. One error would compound another, as so often happened when things went wrong for him.

Kyle was beside the stream, calling Taslim with his mind, when Lockwood returned. Prince Gravais rode with him. The prince sat in the grass beside Kyle while Lockwood wrought wizardry in the center of the meadow. Lightning flashed without a cloud in the sky; thunder, too. Waves of undulating grass flowed outward from the place where Lockwood stood in grim concentration, to the stream where Kyle and the prince sat.

Gray sat stiffly; Kyle, whose gut was ever-sensitive, was not so lucky. Arms folded around his waist, he doubled over until his forehead rested on the ground. He was able to stand when the sensations ceased, and look straight at Lockwood, who still stood by himself in the meadow.

A great flock of songbirds had answered the summons, a handful of ravens as well, but no kestrels. No hawks of any kind.

Then Kyle understood why Lockwood had brought the prince. Only a royal command could get him on Rawne's back, pointed south to the camp. Lockwood never could have persuaded him away from the place where he'd lost his wizard. They would have come to blows and Kyle might well have discovered the warrior spirit lurking in the darkness Taslim left behind.

But the prince told him to mount up, and Kyle did. He stopped thinking or feeling the moment his foot touched the stirrup, but he needed neither of those to hold the reins as Rawne kept pace with the other two. Habit, empty habit—devoid of imagination or interest—was sufficient for that, and not even the sight of Renard, pale and thin but sitting next to Lille with the waning sunlight on his smiling face, could change that. Kyle ate his supper because, again, the prince said it was his duty. Once the bowl was empty, he couldn't have said what manner of meat or grain he'd eaten. He shivered, though the night was pleasant. Kiera came forward with his cloak, which she clasped around him.

She spoke to him, but the words were empty, like everything else, and she wasn't the prince, so he didn't have to answer.

"Methinks you needs a dose of what the lord wizard gave me," Renard said. Kyle listened because they were the first words Renard had spoken to him since Josaf died.

"No." Kyle's voice was low and ominous, little like the voice he and Taslim had shared earlier.

Far to the south, as far back, perhaps, as the inland road, there was a storm raging. They could see white-light flashes on that horizon, but there was no thunder, no wind.

"Will it come this way?" the prince asked the wizard.

"Not of its own," Lockwood answered, getting to his feet. "But I can get its attention."

Kyle saw fear on the faces around him as Lockwood followed his own path into darkness. No doubt Lockwood needed more lightning: he'd wrought a miracle for Renard . . . and a disaster for Taslim. Kyle was too attuned to injustice, even in his numbed isolation, to blame Lockwood for Taslim's loss. Both wizards had been constrained by their ingrained characters: Lockwood's was impulsive and generous. Taslim's was secretive, even deceitful. The combination was disastrous.

The notion did occur to Kyle that the fault might justly be his own. He'd had doubts from the beginning. He knew better than anyone alive that Taslim couldn't tell God's simplest truth without wrapping it in mystery. But Kyle was too numbed to blame himself. He sat, ignoring everything, until a great streamer of lightning arced silently overhead, connecting the distant storm with the place where one might safely assume Lockwood had uttered a rune.

No wind came, no thunder, no sense of impending storm in the lightning arcs that continued overhead, but, one by one, Kyle's companions sought the shelter of their tents. It made sense with Renard, who tired quickly and was clearly exhausted by supper, and with Usheff, who had a simpleton's honest terror of the unnatural. In short time there were only three of them around the fire: the prince, Kiera, and Kyle.

Kiera had questions; Kyle knew her well enough to see them brewing behind her eyes. She asked a few of them: What had happened to the wizard? What did his loss mean? Were they pressing forward? Neither Kyle nor the prince had answers they wanted to share, so Kiera, who didn't like to be ignored, wrapped herself in her cloak and departed.

That left Kyle and the prince and the lightning.

"Surely he's harvested enough," Kyle blurted out, surprising himself with both the thought and the sound of his voice. "What is he trying to prove?"

Gray's eyebrows rose. "That he's more powerful than Fawlen, what else?"

Kyle shook his head. "He knew that. He knew that from the start. He said his mistake was believing Taslim, when he knew he shouldn't have."

"Then he wants to prove he's more potent than his mistakes."

They lapsed into silence again. The lightning arcs came less frequently and were weaker when they did: The lowland storm was breaking up. Lockwood would return, without having proved anything, because the dark place in Kyle's mind remained an empty place.

Empty enough that Kyle did not hear anyone approaching until the night guard issued his challenge and Gray rose to greet his friend with open arms.

There was a bird perched on Lockwood's shoulder!

Not a kestrel, but an owl. Kyle knew little about owls: There were little grayish ones who slept in the barn and stable lofts, and great white ones that haunted the tall trees near the lodge. The one on Lockwood's shoulder was too big to be the one, too small to be the other.

"God's pockets!" the prince exalted. "You did it!"

Gray clapped Lockwood's arms enthusiastically. The bird—it seemed young, somehow, without the proper dignity of owls—bated, hovering noisily, unhappily, while the men embraced. It resettled once Gray retreated. Obviously pleased with himself, Lockwood coaxed the owlet onto his wrist and offered it to Kyle.

Kyle met Lockwood's eyes with disbelief then looked into the fire. Did either of them think he wanted a *bird*? Did Lockwood, a wizard himself, think a *bird* could replace what he'd lost?

"I give this kestrel," Lockwood said, very solemn, which was suspicious in and of itself. "*The* kestrel, by the grace of God and manifest lightning."

"Kestrel!" Kyle snarled, angered by the poor, distasteful joke. He raised his head, thinking how good it would feel to teach Lockwood a lesson. "It's not—"

"But it *is,*" Lockwood insisted, and this time solemnity lost ground to a grin. "Take him yourself. Place him close by your ear and listen."

Still distrustful and angry, but above all else unspeakably curious and hopeful, Kyle took the owlet Lockwood named a kestrel first on his fist then on his shoulder. He heard nothing at first, nothing out of the ordinary, then a faint and weary voice calling: <<Hart-lord, Hart-lord, Hart-lord . . . >>

"How?" he asked in wonder, the anger and distrust all shed as if they'd never been.

"Brace yourself," Lockwood warned as sparks swarmed from his talisman to his fingers.

Kyle blinked. He felt the sparks but did not hear the rune

Lockwood spoke to transfer Taslim from the owlet, which bated once again and flew to Lockwood's shoulder.

There was no single word vast enough to contain the shock, the outrage, the all-encompassing embarrassment, the profound shame that radiated from a no longer empty place in Kyle's mind, but <<Owl. . .>>was the only word Taslim had at that very moment, and he used it as best he could while Lockwood—trying hard not to further terrify the innocent bird—kept an almost-straight face, almost-straight back and the prince laughed so hard tears streamed down his face and he dropped to one knee to keep from collapsing completely.

<<An owl! An owl! I've linked myself—my very essence—to an owl!—A baby owl. No. No, it can't be. I'd never do anything that foolish. Never. He tricked me—that's it! Damned Marelet tricked me! He trapped me in that lightning of his and switched the switch. Tell him that. Tell him that, Hart-lord. Tell him he's vile and deceitful.>>

But Kyle was laughing himself now, and unable to tell anyone anything.

<<It was a kestrel. I tell you, Hart-lord: I linked myself with a kestrel. Do you think I don't know the difference between a kestrel and an owl? It was a kestrel. Believe me, Hart-lord—it was a kestrel!>>

Chapter Twenty-one

They named the owl Kestrel. Even Usheff, who scarcely comprehended the difference between one bird and the next and whose laughter was most often provoked by belches, not wordplay, called the big-eyed owl by a hawk's name. In his dark prison even Taslim, whose embarrassment had echoed in Kyle's thoughts, bowed to the inevitable. Kyle reckoned that Kestrel marked how far they'd come from Chegnon. By a purely mortal magic, a wizard's mishap had been transformed into never-fail jest. At least he heard no dread or malice in the laughter.

Despite his name, Kestrel would fly only at dusk and returned in the darkest hours after midnight, no matter Taslim's determination or Lockwood's runes. By day, the adolescent owl clung close Kyle's left side.

Nasen'bei, both wizards said—as if that could explain everything, but it seemed to Kyle that the owl sensed that a part of himself was somewhere else, an elsewhere that was connected to the left side of Kyle's face, the nasen'bei side. Kyle had learned to carry a hawk on a well-protected fist; it was one of those ladylike skills all fosterlings learned, along with forks and pouring wine from a full jug. Now he carried an owl on his shoulder.

At first, he'd expected to lose an earlobe to a nervous owl's beak. He rode Rawne three day's in a row, because he trusted Rawne's temper over Taddy's. The pace they set, with Renard bundled into a tent-canvas litter and dragged behind one of Kiera's placid geldings, was no strain on a healthy animal.

At every step the men had breath for conversation and an

understanding that they wouldn't talk about where they were headed or the graves they'd left behind. They took turns telling tales as the horses picked paths through flowery meadows that had not felt a man's foot since the previous autumn, when highland shepherds turned their flocks toward home. They sang, posed riddles, laid foolish bets, and played guessing games like children on an outing—whatever was necessary to keep their hearts from turning as dark as the Eigela, always visible now above the treetops.

Traveling slow, they also made camp early—for Renard's sake, their prince said, but for the hunters, too. The woods had grown thin. Such game as they found was small: rabbits, squirrels, and other creatures of the scrub. Supper was simmered in pots filled mostly with grain, not roasted on spits as it had been. . . *before*, in the days they no longer discussed.

And when supper was done, when the sun had sunk to the lowlands, when the tents were set for the night and Renard had suffered his last dose of Lockwood's lightning for the day, the cohort gathered around Kyle, wherever he sat. All together, they'd wait for Lockwood to slip his talisman from his belt and for wizardry to bridge the gap between nasen'bei and the little owl.

<<This is embarrassing, Hart-lord,>> Taslim grumbled after supper on the fourth night that Kestrel would fly.

From the Gray Prince to simple Usheff, their companions, except for Lockwood, the women, and Renard, had finished their suppers, swirled their bowls in the nearby stream, and, like pigeons to their cote, returned to the fire. The first two nights, before he'd understood that he'd become the centerpiece of an emerging ritual, Kyle had foolishly sought privacy beyond the camp. He knew better now and stayed where their audience would be comfortable, even if he wasn't.

<<It strips me of all dignity.>>

<<Dignity. What dignity?>> Kyle replied in kind. <<You fly off. You're gone as long as you'd like. You don't sit here through the evening-watch worrying about what trouble you might have found or whether you'll come back at all. You don't have white streaks down your back or have a half-digested mouse land on your leg while you're talking to royalty—*That's* embarrassing, Taslim.>>

<<I ate the blasted mice!>> Taslim countered, complete with the dizzying sensations of the hunt and the less exhilarat-

ing details of the feast afterward. It was enough, as Taslim demonstrated, to make a proud, yet delicate and very civilized, wizard profoundly ill.

Kyle wouldn't tolerate thoughts of little bones cracked by a beak he did not have, or of little legs torn from a still-warm carcass by talons that were no part of him. It was unfortunate that Taslim had had to suffer the feast, but he got to fly, too. An owl swooping through a maze of branches wasn't a hawk soaring halfway to the sun, but it wasn't a footbound mortal, either.

Whatever magic bound him and Taslim together it gave Kyle the *remembering* of flight, and left him longing for the living of it. He didn't ask, though, lest it give Taslim an advantage in their always precariously balanced companionship. But it seemed unnecessarily cruel for Taslim to share nothing more than the gory feast, especially since the wizard knew the weaknesses of Kyle's gut.

Poised between nausea and anger, Kyle resolved he would not be the butt of Taslim's ill-intentioned humor. He set his supper bowl aside and, with a great sweep of his will, banished the gory notions Taslim had scattered through his thoughts.

The owl bated, whistling shrilly, adding another set of talon marks along Kyle's much punctured shoulder, and beating his face with strong wings, stiff feathers. Kyle had only himself to blame: He shouldn't have moved so quickly when he set the bowl aside; he knew better than that.

<<Do it again, Hart-lord.>>

<<Scare Kestrel and spill my supper? Not for all the treasure 'neath the sea. I'll hurt and they'll laugh. Even poor Usheff will call me a fool.>>

The wizard radiated frustration. <<You *are* a fool, Hart-lord. I meant that wind you made just then, it blew clear into nasen'bei, clear to my dark hell. *That's* what set him off. A little more control, Hart-lord, and we wouldn't need damn Marelet's help. Think *onda* as you release your will.>>

Onda, the runic syllable that Lockwood uttered to make transference possible but which Kyle had never been able to remember. *Onda. Onda. Onda.* He promised himself he wouldn't forget. There might come a time when *onda* would be more useful than *serras.* But he'd let his thoughts form in the front of his mind, where Taslim could easily snare them and fill his mind with superior laughter.

<<It takes more than *onda*, Hart-lord; more than *serras,* too, for that matter, unless I'm willing. Or have you decided to learn wizardry?>>

<<No,>> Kyle replied quickly, gathering up his private thoughts again, as he believed he could do, unless he listened to Taslim, who could still make him doubt the sun and the moon. He picked up his bowl, not because he was hungry, but because it gave him someplace to stare that did not stare back. He thought of nothing, a skill that was very much like the day-dreaming he seldom did anymore, a skill that he'd perfected since the solstice.

He raised his head when he heard Lockwood coming out of Renard's tent. Kiera trailed behind him. Lille and Renard stayed under canvas. It was their choice and had nothing to do with him, Kyle knew, but he was grateful just the same.

"Is everyone ready?" Lockwood asked, a slight swagger in his stance as he stood on the verge of the circle, his cloak swirled dramatically around his broad shoulders.

And why shouldn't Lockwood swagger? His talisman was bright with the lightning of yet another storm. Life had been good to the prince's boon-friend and he'd returned the favor. He'd saved Renard from certain death, reclaimed Taslim from the wilds of night (never mind that Taslim would never admit he'd been in danger), and uttered the runes that transferred Taslim to the body of an owl whose nightly wandering kept them unafraid of another ambush.

"Yes," Kyle said. There was no point in saying he could never be ready for the lightning sparks that pierced his left eye's vision, then streamed out again, carrying Taslim's essence into Kestrel. Taslim was ready. Mice notwithstanding, Taslim loved flying, loved freedom. Taslim wouldn't have missed this for the world.

The runes were uttered, *onda* among them—or perhaps not; Kyle heard nothing clearly once the sparks touched his eye. He felt a solitary beat of short, powerful wings against his hair, and then he was alone, watching the darkly luminous after-images of Lockwood's wizardry through leaking eyes while Taslim swooped and disappeared into the dusk.

It was known that his eyes watered in the aftermath of Lockwood's transference wizardry. No one noticed that tonight's tears weren't born in pain or irritation. He felt the aloneness, the emptiness more keenly each time Taslim departed. Piled atop that ache was the more shameful one of envy, and somewhere near the very heart of him, was a sudden, cold thought that once they came to the Siege of Shadows, Taslim would leave him behind, alone, forever. He tucked his chin low and pressed a crooked knuckle against his teeth: a niggling pain to distract him from a larger one.

A hand came down on Kyle's scalp. Short-fingered and strong, he knew whose it was before a word was spoken.

"What's wrong?" Lockwood asked, as Lockwood naturally would.

Kyle shrugged. He shook his head without raising it. "Nothing."

The hand stayed where it had landed. He wished Lockwood wouldn't touch him, considering the memories it roused. But he wouldn't shame the friendship Lockwood offered by wishing aloud.

"I don't think I could get used to it—sparks coming at me like that, and flying away, too. Me, I'd find it harder, not easier, every next time." The wizard's voice was little more than a whisper; anyone sitting an arm's length away wouldn't have heard it. "I'd get so angry I'd want to hit something—*hard*. If I couldn't let my anger show, then I might start thinking my life wasn't worth the living of it. Of course, that's me—a priest's bastard son. You can take me out of the stables, but you can't wash the manure out of me. You're born from better blood."

Once again Kyle shook his head. Bastardy had nothing to do with the anger and hopelessness Lockwood had so accurately described.

"Walk with me awhile," the wizard suggested. "This smoke can't be doing your eyes any good."

The advice was well meant. Kyle sighed and pushed himself upright. Following Lockwood past the horse line to the stream, he expected a lecture to begin with every step he took. He thought he might listen to what Lockwood had to say, thought he might take it to heart, because, despite wizardry and disturbing memories, Lockwood was the sort of man another man could trust when he was far away from everything familiar.

But Lockwood had nothing more to say as they sat on one of the many serpentine rock ridges that grew more frequently than trees in this mountainous soil. The moon had waned to a dangerously sharp crescent, already low on the western horizon. Overhead the sky was pricked with stars of spring: the Calf and the Lamb, the Sower, the Fish, all seeming brighter, closer than they did from the rooftop of Roc Dainis.

Had it been Kiera sitting beside him, Kyle would have named the stars and their patterns for her. She never remembered them from one season to the next. Or, she enjoyed hearing him name them and tell their stories. One or the other, but not both. There were so many things he'd thought he'd known about his twin that he hadn't really known at all.

Kiera was the one matter he dared not bring to Lockwood. She didn't like him; he didn't like her. Since Renard's injury, when they'd been face-to-face with each other several times a day, they'd made that clear to everyone, including him. And neither Kiera nor Lockwood had much liking for Taslim, not the way Kyle himself had after a season of sharing thoughts, memories, and more.

He and Taslim were long past the point where they could talk about friendship—*he* was long past that point. As with Kiera, there were aspects of Taslim that Kyle could not understand, that could drive him to distraction in a single thought. And as with Kiera—maybe because of Kiera—Kyle had simply come to accept the wizard as a part of himself.

Lacing his fingers behind his head, Kyle stretched back on the rock. There was peace in that revelation: Taslim had become a part of him. It didn't matter what the wizard did, or how he did it. Just as Kiera would always be his twin sister—his closest family, with a claim on his heart and honor no matter how foolishly she behaved, or how little they saw of each other after she married—Taslim of Fawlen would always be his nasen'bei companion.

"I'm heading back," Lockwood announced.

Kyle sat up with a jolt. The moon had set, the Fish, too; the Lamb's eye was slipping through the trees. Half a watch, as roc guards measured the night. But he wasn't ready to return to the tents. Taslim and Kestrel wouldn't return until midnight, or later, and they'd find him here as easily as near the fire. Lockwood didn't seem to mind rousing out of a sound sleep to perform a bit of wizardry, but not Kyle. He'd stay awake until the owl returned and nap in the saddle tomorrow.

"Later."

"I count on it," Lockwood laughed and unclasped his cloak.

"Keep warm, Dreamer," he advised as he dropped the cloak in Kyle's lap.

It was a rare cloak that fit only one man, and a rare man who couldn't wear another man's cloak. Kyle clasped the garment and stretched back on the rock again. An owl, much larger than Kestrel to judge by the depth of its call, drew Kyle's attention to his right, to the north, toward the great darkness that was the Eigela by night, and—quite unexpected—toward the shimmering curtain of light above the unseen peaks.

"Aurora," he murmured, as if Kiera were beside him. The heavenly lights were common enough in winter, when it was much too cold to appreciate them. This display of pale blue and silvery violet was a poor relation, like him. He watched it all the same.

"Isn't it beautiful!"

Kiera's voice so startled Kyle that he jumped to his feet and felt the clasp of Lockwood's cloak give way from the strain. The borrowed cloth piled around his ankles. He caught the enameled broach as it slipped down his shirt, but the chain had broken and the sharpened clasp rang once against the rock before it was lost without further sound or glimmer in the night.

"Damn."

"Begging your pardon?"

"I broke the clasp of Lockwood's cloak."

"I brought yours."

She thrust an unwieldy bundle into his arms. He dropped the enameled broach, but—thank God—found it easily again once he'd dealt with Kiera's offering.

"I knew you'd be more comfortable in your own clothes . . ."

Then, she didn't know him any better than he knew her. Kyle didn't care about his clothes at all, and certainly hadn't minded wearing a borrowed cloak. But it wasn't the borrowing that bothered Kiera, it was the man who'd loaned it to him.

"Now I've got two and Lockwood's got none; that hardly seems fair, does it? And I've broken his clasp—lost the pin, too—in the bargain."

"The prince will give him another, I'm sure. The prince dotes on his boon-friend. He has no time or thought for anyone else."

Kyle swallowed the first words that formed on his tongue, and several more thereafter. Kiera could bait him into an unwise discussion of wizards or royalty, but not wizards and royalty together.

"Why did you come looking for me?" he asked, and heard wary resignation in his own voice.

"I saw the sky lights—"

"Auroras."

"Them, too. They're so beautiful tonight, so special above the Eigela. I thought of all the times we looked at them together . . . I thought it would be pleasant—hoped it would—to watch them together again. I've missed talking to you, Kyle."

He felt shame. "I'd thought of you, too, just before you came up and surprised me."

"Aren't they the most beautiful lights—auroras—you've ever seen?

"The most beautiful I could watch without freezing. It's spring, nearing summer, Ki—" Kyle lapsed easily into his patient mentor voice. "The biggest ones come in winter."

"Bigger isn't best. Look at the colors, Kyle. Have you ever seen so many colors at once?"

Kyle stared at the pale blues and violets above the dead darkness of the Eigela peaks. So many colors? Not by his counting. There were folk who could not see all God's colors—Gorren Lond of Roc Wisse in fosterage couldn't tell a rose from its leaf except by shape. But Kyle had always seen the difference, had always—in truth—seen a bit more of everything than his sister.

"I see blue and violet. What do you see?"

In the silence that followed, Kyle wondered what had sprung his twin's curiosity and brought her through the scrub to this isolated rock. He'd reached no conclusions when Kiera broke the silence with a diffident sigh.

"Oh, blues and violets, too. What else is there to see, this time of year?"

Kyle's curiosity slipped toward suspicion, of what, he couldn't yet say, but Kiera must have sensed it.

"I thought Taslim might see the lights differently from you or me."

Taslim again. God have mercy, he'd hoped that they were past Taslim, that his twin had had her fill of magic, wizards, and adventure in the tent changing Renard's bandages day after day. Someday—a good many years' worth of days in the future—perhaps they would sit before a comfortable hearth and find the good memories in this. Someday they'd talk about Taslim and Josaf without either pain or anger brewing in Kyle's gut.

But not tonight.

"Does he?" Kiera reiterated her question with a noticeable edge on her voice.

"I wouldn't know. I don't know what owls see, and Taslim's with Kestrel now. Don't tell me you'd forgotten that, Kiera; I won't believe it. Why did you come up here? What do *you* see?"

There was a sniffle in the darkness. Tears, too, he'd have wagered, if he'd had an owl's eyes to see them; he was just as glad he didn't.

"It was only a question, Kyle," she said with a perfect tremor. "I thought—maybe—when *he* was gone, you'd be more yourself. I only wanted to know about the lights. I can't help it, Kyle. I wonder what it must be like to see the world through a wizard's eyes."

"I don't see the world through his eyes," Kyle replied, harshly at first, then soft. The tears, damn them, worked their predictable magic against his will. He dreaded hurting anyone. "Taslim sees what I see, what Kestrel sees, I suppose. In the beginning he claimed otherwise, but since the priests at Roc Dainis, except when he's flying with Kestrel, I don't think he sees anything at all unless it's what I see, too."

"Oh," Kiera said, and nothing more, not even a sniffle, for several long moments, then: "Will you walk me back to the tents?"

It was a small enough request, one any nobleman ought to grant to any woman, regardless of her birth, especially to a twin sister. But Kiera had come out here by herself, and it seemed to Kyle that she could go back the same way. There wasn't anything lurking in the bushes.

"I want to stay here awhile longer. Go on ahead, if you want."

Kiera didn't want and didn't go. When Kyle sat down again, she sat down beside him, watching whatever it was she saw in the north. The aurora was unseasonable. It was hovering above the Eigela where their journey would end. Twice Kyle thought of the Siege of Shadows. Twice he thought of asking Kiera if the Siege had anything to do with her coming out to the rock. And twice he held his peace.

Aware of his sister, but ignoring her, Kyle closed his left eye and studied the aurora with his right, then shut the right and looked through the left alone. Nagah'bei and nasen'bei, the sight of seeming and the sight of truth, the simple superstitions he thought he'd understood a year ago, before he'd learned otherwise.

Tonight, everything was the same, no matter how he looked or where.

Kiera fidgeted. Kyle heard her draw breath several times, as if to start a conversation. Each time, she sighed and the silence continued, until, with her most dramatic sigh, Kiera got to her feet.

"You don't have to wait for him," she said, raising her cowl so not even her profile was discernable. He didn't need to ask to whom she referred. "Set yourself free, Kyle. Come back with me now and stand up for yourself. Don't let Lockwood shove Taslim back into your soul. We don't need Lockwood. We don't need Taslim, not with the lights to guide us."

Not need Taslim? Not need Lockwood? Rely on the lights? The aurora shone above the whole Eigela. Possibly its unseasonable appearance had something to do with the Siege of Shadows; but as a guide, it would be useless. Kyle could have said that, and more. The words were bursting in his head. He didn't want a fight, though, and for the third time, he held his peace.

Kiera retreated across the rocks. "We don't need wizards, Kyle. We never did."

He almost called her back. Something was amiss. There'd been more to her words from the moment she'd startled him. More, but nothing new: She was still caught up in resentment and jealousy that went back to the solstice and Taslim. Kyle listened to her movements through the brush until he couldn't hear them; then, grappling with two cloaks, he explored the rock on hands and knees, looking for the broken clasp, which wasn't anywhere to be found. With Lockwood's cloak folded carefully in his arms and his own hanging around his shoulders, Kyle retraced the path to the camp by the aurora's fading light.

Midnight had come and gone, to judge by the stars along the treetops. Kestrel would be bringing Taslim back, or the other way around. Kyle assumed it was different when Lockwood's wizardry moved Taslim out of the owl's body, but he didn't ask Taslim questions, not about wizardry anyway.

The camp was quiet, with the fire banked. Captain Golight sat the watch, with Usheff beside him. They exchanged nods and said nothing that might disturb the sleepers. A few of the men had chosen to sleep by themselves, away from the tents. Kyle knew Lockwood wouldn't be among them. The stocky wizard would be sleeping across the threshold, waiting for Kyle to rouse him. Kyle caught himself smiling as he sat down outside the tent, wrapping the extra layer of Lockwood's cloak around him against the still-cooling night, as, surely, Lockwood had appropriated Kyle's blankets for the same purpose. The wizard who would face down a thunderhead swore he couldn't sleep without a roof over his head, even a roof of canvas.

Kyle was dozing when he heard a hoot from an overhead branch. He didn't have to look up. Kestrel's call was unmistakable in his ears: <<Hart-lord, Hart-lord.>> No matter that an owl couldn't make such sounds, that's what he heard and what moved him to reach through the canvas to shake Lockwood's leg.

He returned the cloak and offered his own clasp to replace the broken one. His was hammered iron, as reliable as a well-tempered sword but a paltry thing compared to the bright enamel disk Kyle had laid wordlessly in Lockwood's hand; its chain dangled uselessly over the wizard's thumb. The clasp, of course, was missing. Lockwood said the loss was nothing; that he'd get it fixed when they returned to Chegnon, but Kyle could hear the disappointment lurking beneath the words. Disappointment had a particular tone which he'd heard all his life and which never failed to make his gut churn.

"Ready?" Lockwood asked when Kestrel was settled on Kyle's shoulder and sparks had gathered in the crystal talisman. That resigned, slightly acid tone still tinged the wizard's voice.

The wizardry would hurt, in the simple physical sense of sparks hurtling into Kyle's left eye, just as a thrashing left him bruised and stiff. But the real pain hadn't come from the back of another man's hand or his belt, and wouldn't come from the talisman.

"Ready," he replied, emptying his lungs as the sparks rose

out of the crystal. *God,* he swore to himself. *God, onda, serras, make it quick!*

Kyle rocked back on his heels—the first time that had happened. Kestrel shed a feather swooping to safety. Lockwood seized his shirt and kept Kyle on his feet. The transference had been made. Taslim was back in the dark place, but Taslim was reeling, too.

"You caught me by surprise, Kyle," Lockwood said and Kyle heard more disappointment.

He apologized and had his apology rebuffed when Lockwood released his shirt. "Next time warn me."

Warn Lockwood about what? Kyle wondered but did not ask. Taslim had recovered.

<<Tell him that nothing's happening ahead of us, Hart-lord. A handful of shepherds coming up behind with their flock and dogs. Nothing to worry about. There's no one taking the high road to the Siege. No one at all except us.>>

Kyle repeated Taslim's report, adding, "He seems almost disappointed," which brought comments from Taslim, questions from Lockwood, and more comments from Taslim. Kyle winced, trying to keep a hold on his own thoughts. Both wizards fell silent.

"There's nothing that can't wait until morning," Lockwood said, then: "Get some sleep," which Taslim echoed.

Kyle took the suggestion for a command. He ducked into the tent, snagged a loose blanket from the heap where Lockwood had been resting, and curled up in the farthest corner, boots still laced. Sleep might catch him before dawn—no man could predict the future—but it wasn't nearby. Kyle wasn't complaining. Whenever he'd fallen asleep still smarting from failure, his dreams were troubled and he woke up with a heavier heart than he'd taken to bed. If he lay awake until the dawn birds began to sing, there might be time before they broke camp to return to the rocks. One night's sleep would be a small price to pay, if he could find the broken clasp.

<<Pins, Hart-lord. Pins, everywhere. How is a man supposed to rest after a night hunting shrews and mice when he's surrounded by sharp pins?>>

Taslim took Kyle by surprise. The last several nights Taslim had returned to his prison moments after giving his report.

<<Returned? I do not *return*, Hart-lord; I *sink*. I sink with stones tied around my neck, courtesy of that oh-so-helpful

lump snoring oh-so-loudly at your feet. Lightning strike and turn him black as coal.>>

A rush of curiosity and questions swirled up in Kyle's thoughts. He smothered as many as he could, but a few slipped away.

<<*You* brought me in, Hart-lord. You and the runes you've managed to learn—and me, of course. You couldn't do it quite alone. What did you think your oh-so-helpful friend was talking about?>>

Kyle couldn't contain his astonishment. It sprang forth like weeds in the herb garden, watered by Taslim's laughter. His face burned in the darkness, but there was a measure of pride, too, which outlasted the astonishment.

<<I did wizardry!>>

Taslim harrumphed. <<You greased the wheel,>> and quenched Kyle's triumph with a pointed question: <<What of these haunting pins?>>

Not pins, but a single bronze clasp and a broken chain that flashed with lightning brilliance and left the whole story behind as an afterimage.

<<Hardly your fault, Hart-lord>> Taslim said soothingly; he was generous and compassionate once he'd won. <<Send me to Kestrel again.>>

<<Why?>>

The answer came to Kyle the same way his questions often escaped: in a flood of images that were both more and less than words: If the lost pin was so important to him, then Taslim, using Kestrel's night-tuned eyes, would bring it back, even though the pin had come from Lockwood, Lord of Marelet and right-rotten arrogant bastard, who thought he had some special gift for wizardry and who deserved to lose far more than a bronze clasp. The revelations stopped as abruptly as they'd begun: Taslim inhaling his private thoughts the same way Kyle inhaled his.

For once the laughter echoing between Kyle's ears was his own.

<<Well then, set me free. Lift me to Kestrel. Let me feed on the skulls of vermin.>>

Kyle's laughter stopped. <<Onda? Serras?>> The arcane syllables had no power.

<<You're not the wizard, Hart-lord; you're the power. Let your will flow toward Kestrel—*serras!*>>

There was no glittering talisman to dazzle Kyle's eyes, or sparks to draw his tears, but wind sprang out of the darkness and wizardry began to happen.

<<Wait!>> Kyle gathered the wind into himself. <<How will you come back? Will you come back?>>

<<You'll make the wind blow the other way, Hart-lord, the way you did before. Now, wish me well and let me go.>>

Two wishes merged into the wind with Taslim: *Find the clasp* and *Come back,* then the wishes, the wind, and the wizard were gone. Too late, Kyle considered that he hadn't told Taslim where to look, and that Taslim hadn't asked. Full of confidence, the thought came back to him: Taslim hadn't needed to ask. The wizard had gleaned an image of the rocks from Kyle's anxiety, and Kestrel would find them with his sharp eyes.

<<Stop worrying, Hart-lord!>>

Kyle shuddered violently beneath his cloak and blanket. Taslim was gone; the dark place in his mind was empty. Yet a bond remained, as it had not remained when Lockwood provided the transference power. Though Kyle didn't know where Kestrel was, or what Kestrel saw, he knew Taslim and the owl were flying together and, deeper than sensation, knew that they intended to return.

With that knowledge between him and the darkness, Kyle made a sincere effort not to worry and got as far as removing his boots. His toes were still cold between the blankets when something small and hard thumped against the canvas. Before it had skidded down the angled ceiling, that wind in his mind had begun to swirl. Make it blow the other way, Taslim had said, and with no greater understanding that he could and should, Kyle willed the wind to blow toward him.

<<Not a heartbeat too soon!>> Taslim fell into Kyle's thoughts with a something very like a relieved sigh. <<He's seen a mouse, and what passes for his mind has room for only one hungry thought once that happens.>>

<<You found the clasp?>>

<<Outside. He'll put his big foot on it first step out—By the almighty bolt, Hart-lord, it's lying in the grass, nothing more. He's not going to impale himself!>>

Chapter Twenty-two

Kiera held her horse's rein tight as they rode through yet another wildflower meadow, yet another pleasant mountain spring afternoon. She didn't need to clutch the rein. Her horse was even-tempered, even-gaited and together they held the noble lady's place in the center of the cohort. There was little likelihood that anything would spook her mount, even less that it would bolt. Kiera could have dropped the leather, closed her eyes, and been not one whit less safe or secure than she was with her death grip.

For two days Kiera had ridden one heartbeat removed from panic. Her knuckles were white and aching. She was very familiar with the condition of her travel-battered hands, from swollen knuckles to broken fingernails and skin as rough and wrinkled as leather. Consciously and carefully, she wanted nothing else to capture her eyes' attention: not the riders around her or the ground directly in front her horse's hooves, certainly not the landscape through which they rode, the wildflowers and blooming trees, the mare's-tail clouds in the bright blue sky, the black wall of the Eigela, so close now that she could make out individual crags.

Not so long ago, she'd taken care of her hands, washing them thrice daily in warm buttermilk, shaping her nails with a sharp, little knife; it had a hilt of polished lapis and the Dainis crest etched on its blade. She'd put the knife to another, better use when Lady Irina's scalpel broke after the ambush when Renard was injured and Josaf died. The knife was tucked away in the medicine box now, with nicks along its edge and stains on the metal. It hadn't seemed right to use it on her fingernails again.

Kiera thought her mother would be proud of her daughter's cleverness, her resourcefulness, her bravery. She yearned for her mother's voice, for words of praise . . . and advice. Were Lady Irina riding through these windy meadows, her cheeks would not have turned brown like a farm wife's, her long hair would not have become a rat's nest of tangles that broke off in clumps and broke the teeth of the comb as well. Lady Irina Dainis' hair and skin simply didn't misbehave; Lady Irina was never at a loss, never anything but in command of the world around her.

For two days Kiera had asked herself: What would Mother do? Whom would Mother talk to? What would Mother say to make everything come up right again?

Mother was in the far-off Renzi Valley, where she'd lived since Father had brought her home after their wedding. Mother had grown up in Grandfather's counting house; that was where Mother had learned the world's wisdom. Mother hadn't dreamt of princes or adventures; she'd dreamt of a verge-lord and married him.

Irina Dainis wouldn't have worried about tangled hair, tanned skin, and all the other, far more serious matters weighing so heavily on Kiera's mind. Irina Dainis would never have left the Renzi Valley. *Mother doesn't make mistakes because Mother doesn't do things she hasn't done before. Mother stays where she belongs. She never loses because she never wages a battle she hasn't won before. If I'd stayed home, I'd be like her. If she were here, she'd be the same as me . . . or maybe even worse.*

The realization sent shivers down Kiera's spine: Her last illusions had melted away. Her life was no longer a matter of saying the right words in just the right way to get the right thing done properly: the way *she* wanted. The problems she faced in the shadow of the black Eigela were hers and hers alone. She couldn't turn to anyone for answers. She'd find her answers, if they existed, deep inside herself, which was a landscape far less familiar than these meadows and mountains.

A trill of laughter broke Kiera's thoughts: Lille's laughter as Lille rode beside Renard. Lille's place was at Kiera's side, but Kiera had not insisted, not today, when, with Lockwood's reluctant permission, they'd boosted Renard into a saddle for the first time since the ambush.

Kiera lifted her eyes long enough to catch Renard's stiff and slightly lopsided silhouette as Lille reached across to touch his cheek. Then Kiera tucked her chin against her breastbone. Her chafed, swollen hands swam in her vision. She closed her eyes until the threat of tears ebbed.

The mountain air had not turned Lille ugly. The rawest blasts of winter couldn't have marred Lille's beauty. Lille's man was alive. He'd been returned to her no worse for his brush with death. And Renard was glad to be alive with Lille beside him. The looks that passed between the betrothed lovers excluded everyone else, even Lockwood, who'd brought Renard back from the dead. Whatever she said aloud, within herself Kiera conceded that the wizard had wrought the miracle and returned a happy future to Renard and Lille.

From everything Kiera had learned about wizards, she knew that they cared only about their talismans and the debts they laid on those who sought their aid. Then again, until she'd gone to Chegnon, everything Kiera knew came from the sermons the Renzi Valley priests preached each new moon and full moon in their iron-clad sanctuaries. God, the priests said, didn't *approve* of parsimonious wizards who bartered lightning and magic. By God's will, the only safe reservoir of magic was the crystal grove beneath their steeples. A wizard and his talisman wandering among the innocent doing that which ought to be done by prayer and priests, if it ought to be done at all, was nothing less than an offense against God's order, a disaster waiting for opportunity.

All the tragedies in Alberon's history, including both the arrival of the Hesse and their summary departure, could be laid on some wizard's threshold—according to God's priests. No one spoke for the wizards. They didn't preach, didn't appear to care whether they were hated or feared.

This far into their journey to the Siege of Shadows, Kiera didn't hate or fear Lockwood, lord of Marelet, she simply did not *like* the man, regardless of his magic. He'd looked straight at her when they talked about Renard. That was impolite behavior in a nobleman, but inexcusable insolence from a common bastard. He stood between her and the prince, a toothy watchdog who dared to disapprove of *her*. Of late, and especially since he'd brought Taslim's damned owl back to the camp, Lockwood stood between her and her brother as well.

For those reasons, and more, Kiera Dainis eagerly condemned Lockwood to the dust and ashes priests called hell, even as another part of her acknowledged the good he'd done for Renard and Lille. She didn't have to be consistent; she wasn't God. Kiera had grown up with that assumption: God, like her mother, had all the answers before the rest of Roc Dainis knew there was a question. If Lady Irina had met the arrogant bastard lord of Marelet, she'd have known in a heartbeat whether he belonged in hell—

Another realization shot down Kiera's spine: *Lady Irina Dainis wouldn't judge Lockwood an arrogant bastard.* Lady Irina would have made a friend of the common-born lord—elegantly, of course, as befitted a verge-lord's wife, but sincerely, too. And then, when unanswerable questions, unsolvable problems loomed, Lady Irina Dainis would not have been alone to deal with them.

"No," Kiera murmured, denying her own conclusions, then adding so softly that the words were mere movements of tongue and lips, not spoken at all: "I can't."

She had mocked Lockwood, scorned him and disdained him, damned him. It was—barely—possible that she'd been wrong about him, but that very concession made mending bridges all the more difficult. No, not difficult: impossible.

Her sigh became a shiver in the sunlight. It penetrated Kiera's bones and lingered there. She longed for her cloak, bundled with the tents on the packhorses because she had not thought she'd need it today. Yesterday, she would have asked Lille, Lille would have told Captain Golight, and everyone would have waited until she was warm again. Today, she said nothing, not even a silent plea to God.

Kiera was numb inside when she heard—faintly and without interest—the hails and hoofbeats of a rider coming toward them. She recognized Enobred's voice, recalled that he'd been one of the men sent ahead at midday to choose the night camp and start the fire. It was another ritual of this journey, a measure of the prince's confidence in the reports he got each morning from Kyle, Taslim, and the owl. It was nothing to lift Kiera's spirits. If anything, her gloom increased when she thought of Kyle working his own wizardry.

She'd begun to brood again when Enobred said, enthusiastically: "Yonder, Your Highness, you can see them!" and, like a fool, she obeyed, following his arm's arrow with her eyes.

They'd come to the end of their journey. The Eigela loomed in front of them, like rocks piercing a harbor, like the thrusting walls of Roc Dainis. Kiera let her eyes scale the black peaks to the highest summits where winter snow still shimmered red, gold, and amber. The colors might have been sunset reflections, if the sun had been setting, or if anyone else in the cohort had seen them.

Come quick, child. Face the east and come to the gate. Come in unstained innocence. Leave the tainted ones behind.

The voice roared in Kiera's skull. It pressed outward against her eyes, filling her vision with an aisle of tall, black stones set in pairs. God's entrance into the Eigela, the path to the Siege of Shadows. A woman walked down the aisle. She had golden-blond hair and a vermillion cloak. She walked alone, and when Kiera called her own name, the woman did not turn around.

A small yelp of terror escaped through Kiera's taut lips before her chin dropped against her chest. She could close her eyes and squeeze her hands against her ears, but the voice—the voice of the Siege of Shadows, God's voice—surged past her feeble defenses.

Come, child. Come. I will show you the secrets of eternity, the power of life and death.

Another yelp swelled in Kiera's throat. Her eyes would not close tighter. Her hands could not press harder against her ears. And still the voice pummeled her.

"Kiera!" someone shouted, probably Kyle.

It was hard to hear an ordinary voice. She had become the center of attention, but not by her own choice. For a heartbeat, embarrassment was stronger than God. Kiera found the strength to lower her hands, to straighten her back, to open her eyes—

It's no matter, she tried to say, but her strength ran out on the first word. The world turned gray, then black before she closed her eyes. She couldn't breathe.

"Catch her! She's falling!"

He was correct, whoever he was. An unseen force curled her forward, twisting her feet in the stirrups as the horse's mane brushed against her cheek. She was going to land on her head, with her legs in linen trousers trailing after her, and her skirt covering the wrong half. Kiera would sooner die than surrender her dignity; with the last of her strength she reached for her skirt instead of the ground.

There was a moment, perhaps two, of numb blackness. Then another moment while she collected her wits, then she knew she'd rolled as she'd fallen and wound up facedown in the grass. The terrible voice was silent. Grass tickled her nose as she breathed easily. Her fingers wriggled and bent to her mind's command, her toes within their riding boots, also. But not her arms or legs, because they were tangled in her skirt which still covered all the parts it was meant to.

"Kiera."

Hands of authority and strength grasped her shoulders, turning her gently onto her back. Other hands circled her ankles and tried to ease her legs straight. She'd put too much effort into preserving her dignity to permit *that*, but there was pain in her right ankle when she resisted. Her eyes popped open—she hadn't realized they were still closed. Kyle's hands were the hands at her shoulders; Lockwood's were those at her ankles. The prince stood behind Kyle, and everyone else except Renard and Lille seemed to be hovering nearby. Kiera had been part of similar gatherings around Kyle on the solstice and afterward. She knew what those anxious frowns and worried brows meant—and wanted them gone, at any cost.

"God's pockets, Kyle," she exclaimed, trying desperately to sound like herself. "I've been sitting on a horse's back so long that I forgot where I was. I'm shamed enough as it is. Don't make me feel worse by staring at me like that."

Kyle, bless his heart, obediently sat as far back as his long arms would allow. But the others didn't twitch, and Lockwood, kneeling at her feet, had gone deadly suspicious. Ignoring the discomfort—and it was only discomfort, (she must have bruised her right ankle against the stirrup iron as she tumbled)—Kiera kicked free of the wizard's concern and constraint.

"Let me up!" she insisted, getting a leverage hold at Kyle's elbow and pulling herself up with a jerk. "I can stand on my own—"

But she couldn't. Color drained from the faces and the trees; everything was gray and floating again. She gasped, and got no air for the effort. God's voice hadn't returned, but she was frightened, all the same. Kyle's arm became a lifeline to everything that was safe and familiar.

He drew her in against his chest; color, breath, and life returned. Belatedly she looked at his shirt, which was soft and reasonably clean—trust her brother to shed the stained leather vest he wore to protect his skin from Kestrel's talons before coming to her rescue.

"What's wrong with her?" Kyle asked, and snug in his arms, Kiera cocked an ear for answers.

Lockwood's voice rang first. "She gave herself a scare when she fell. Twisted her ankle. Had the wind knocked out of her. Then the silly goose tried to sit up too fast—"

Kiera flinched deeper into her brother's protection. He was insufferable, talking about her that way.

"How serious, Locky? Can she ride?" That was Prince Gravais, all royal concern, and nothing more.

"Not today. She fell away from the horse—clever girl; I don't think she hit her head. We'll keep an eye on her tonight."

"Does she need your help?"

"No," Kiera whispered.

She couldn't face Lockwood's wizardry; he'd capture her secrets with his talisman's swirling sparks, and God knew what would happen then. *God* knew. Leaning against Kyle's ribs, listening to his heart, she held her breath. Maybe she'd faint again. Neither God nor wizards could hold her responsible for what happened after she fainted. But the time of gray weakness had passed. She breathed when she had to, and heard Lockwood's answer:

"No," he echoed. "I'll wager wizardry's the last thing you want right now, isn't it, dear lady?" He gave her leg a friendly shake before he stood.

Kyle's arms loosened, encouraging her to turn her head, to look at Lockwood and answer him. The wizard was staring at her with eyes as dark as his curly hair and a wry smile twisting his mouth. He was taunting her; he had to be taunting her. But was that because she'd taunted him so many times, or did he already know why she'd fallen off the damned horse?

Lockwood's smile was inverted, becoming one of those anxious scowls, which spread to every face she could see. "You would tell me if you changed your mind." The wizard folded his arms across his chest. "You'd tell someone, wouldn't you, my lady? Your brother? Prince Gravais?"

How could she tell anyone anything while he stood there looking like Father when it was time to cull the herds in autumn? The best animals went into the barn; the others became salted meat and sausage. Which kind did he think she was?

Then his hand dropped toward his talisman and her hand dug into Kyle's forearm.

"Yes," she agreed. "Yes, I'll tell someone."

Lockwood still looked like Father at the slaughter cull. He'd seen the fear in her eyes; he was too shrewd to have missed it. Yet he folded his arms again, gave a curt nod, and retreated.

"How far to the night camp?" Kyle asked. Her little brother got his feet underneath him and lifted her in his arms as he stood. "I'll carry her—if Lockwood says she can't ride."

Kiera could have ridden. Except for a twisted ankle she was completely recovered—so long as she didn't look at the black mountains. But it seemed a wise time to play the helpless maiden, especially when Gray offered to hold her while Kyle remounted his horse. She thanked her prince graciously once she was settled sidewise—not comfortably, but securely—on a pillion behind Kyle's saddle. The smile the prince granted her was as enigmatic as the wizard's.

She wrapped her arms around Kyle's waist when the cohort started moving again and, at his suggestion, slid her leg against his and caught the toe of her boot in the laces of his. Kiera was proud that she'd learned to sit astride a horse when she was a little girl. She'd never been tempted to sit demurely behind someone else. But it was, all-in-all, a very cozy way to ride, especially when she could feel the warmth and muscles of Kyle's calf against hers. She wondered where her not-so-little brother had learned the trick and wondered as well what it would be like if she were riding a-pillion with Prince Gravais instead.

Then Kiera cursed herself for blind foolishness. Too much wishful thinking about Alberon's prince had gotten her into this mess and wasn't apt to get her out of it. She sagged against Kyle's spine thinking of Rapture, and winter, and God's deafening voice.

"I wish we'd never come," she muttered at the back of Kyle's ear. "I wish we'd stayed home. I wish we'd never gone to the lodge, or anywhere else." She took a breath and continued: "I wish we could turn around right now and forget we'd ever heard of the Siege of Shadows—"

Kestrel swooped close, challenging Kiera's right to Kyle's shoulder, reminding her that when the bird was near, Kyle was not alone. She cocked her fist and shooed the owl away, since she could not do anything about the wizard. Kestrel gave a high-pitched screech. Defending his perch, he threatened Kiera's arm with his talons and beat her face with his wings.

"Easy—*all* of you!"

Kyle held out his fist for Kestrel, who landed hard. Kiera felt her brother wince and got a mind's-eye image of him riding along with the owl in front, her behind, and who knew what kind of harassment from Taslim. She thought better of clinging to him and tried to sit up straight: a clear mistake, as the horse shied and the owl bated again.

"Kiera—just hold still, please?"

Kyle held out his arm again, revealing a bloody splotch on his sleeve. But the bird wanted nothing more to do with him and flew silently, in the way of all owls, to Lockwood's shoulder, where, by the sound the bastard-wizard made, it was not expected.

"I'm sorry."

"I know," her brother replied with a weary tone that was not reassuring.

"Tell Taslim I'm sorry, too. I didn't mean to cause trouble for you or for him. He is . . . listening, isn't he?" Kiera phrased her question carefully, as she always did when she wanted a specific answer. Lady Irina called it *herding her menfolk* and said it was the most effective way to keep harmony in the family. Kiera found it useful for learning what she needed to know and getting what she wanted.

She needed to know where Taslim was before she said anything important to her brother and she truly wanted to hear that Taslim was ensconced in the owl and out of earshot. She had reason to hope for the answer she wanted: Kyle no longer needed Lockwood's help to move Taslim between Kestrel and that nasen'bei place where wizards kept their haunts. That meant that Kyle was sometimes alone, sometimes himself.

It also meant that her twin had taken the first dangerous step along the path to wizardry.

The horse took several strides without any answer at all from Kyle. *Still water,* Mother called him and meant that in some ways he seemed a breath short of stagnant, but in others, his currents ran so deep they didn't show on the surface. Neither way could be herded. Kiera took a deep breath.

"He wouldn't fly off with Kestrel just because I was near,

would he?" Another carefully angled question, laden with hope and deception.

"No, he didn't," Kyle finally replied, with words that seemed carefully chosen.

"Tell him I'm sorry I frightened his owl."

Another advantage of herding: It left her with something to say, even when it failed.

They rode in silence the rest of the way to the night camp, which was, as it was supposed to be, near a brook. Brooks meant trees, and even this close to the Eigela, trees hid the black mountains from her eyes, and the other way round, as well. Kiera didn't wait for Kyle to dismount and help her down from the pillion. Her ankle protested the abuse, but it didn't buckle and she was able walk without limping.

It was quiet under the trees—quiet, at least, in the important sense that she couldn't hear God's voice. She was relieved—the voice frightened her as nothing had ever frightened her—yet it was disconcerting to think that an imperfect wall of wood and spring-green leaves could hide anyone from God.

Sitting by herself on the verge of the camp, with everyone else bustling about preparing supper, tending the horses or some other chore, Kiera thought deeply about a god who promised the power of life and death, but couldn't call her through a grove of trees. She got up once and walked cautiously through the grove, pausing behind each tree trunk, listening on bated breath, ready to retreat, but not needing to. When she saw the sunset glow clinging to the highest somber peaks, Kiera stopped and dared go no farther.

No one else could see that northern glow. No one else *admitted* seeing it—any more than Kiera admitted it. But Kyle hadn't mentioned red or gold or amber when she'd asked him herding questions about the aurora. Kyle had stolen her wizard guide—for which crime she no longer blamed him—but Kyle hadn't stolen her Rapture. Kiera was sure of that now, and sure as well that whatever lay at the far end of the stone-guarded aisle she'd seen in her mind's eye was going to change her life in ways neither she nor her imaginative brother could foresee.

She'd wanted adventure. Going to the lodge for the solstice had been an adventure. Trying to capture Prince Gravais' devotion was an adventure Kiera was not ready to abandon. But going through the Eigela to the Siege of Shadows was one too many adventures for her. Kiera hadn't lied to Kyle; she would have gladly turned back.

Lille came looking for her when supper was ready. Kiera said she wasn't hungry, that she wanted to go to bed instead; she should have known better, should have forced herself to eat a first and second bowl of the evening's stew. Lack of appetite and drowsiness were bad signs if you thought someone had hit her head. She knew them herself and would have done exactly what her companions did: sit someone beside her with orders to wake her up every few hours through the night.

Prince Gravais decided she should be wakened by people she knew well and trusted. That ruled out Lockwood, for which Kiera was grateful, and the prince himself, for which she was not. Renard needed his own rest. Enobred, Kyle, and Lille split the vigil. First it was Lille, then poor Enobred, who was completely undone by the whole situation, especially the prospect of laying hands on a lady while she slept.

Kiera tried to cooperate with him, but he was scarcely more comfortable with conversation, so they sat staring past each other by lamplight until he fell asleep. Then Kiera blew out the lamp and pulled the blanket up over her head.

"All right, Ki—Taslim's off hunting mice with Kestrel. What do you want to talk about?"

Kiera threw off the blanket and sat up before she was truly awake. For a moment there was a stranger beside her, propped up on a three-legged camp stool, forearms resting on his knees and the smoky light of a tallow lamp illuminating his face. The flickering shadows made him seem old. His hunched posture emphasized that there was nothing little about him anymore. He wasn't frightening, but he wasn't her brother, either.

"What are you talking about? What are you doing here?"

He sighed, and all Kiera's dreamy confusion dissipated. "This afternoon, Kiera. You fainted off your horse; you never faint. You terrorized Kestrel and then you apologized to Taslim; I couldn't believe a word of it—"

"Did he?"

"No. But now he's gone. What do you want to talk about? I

pointed Enobred toward Jahn. He's asleep there, if he didn't fall on his face first. There's one man awake near the fire, but he won't hear us if we talk softly. That's what you wanted: me, without Taslim, without anyone? What do you want to talk about? Gray?"

He made everything sound so petty. She buried her face behind her hands. Maybe she had hit her head and this was a nightmare; it couldn't be her brother.

"Don't start crying, Ki. I'll listen to anything you have to say. You're my sister, my twin; we're family. I'll sit here until dawn—*if* you don't start crying. I'll leave if you do. I've sworn that to myself."

Kiera lowered her hands, skillfully wiping away the few tears that had already leaked out. Still water—not stagnant, but deep.

"I don't want to go any farther. I'm afraid. Something terrible's going to happen. I know it; I feel it—" The words to describe the red glow, the stone-lined aisle, and the voice of God foundered in her throat.

But something must have struck Kyle's heart; he raked his hair and stared hard at the tallow flame before answering. "I know."

Kyle rubbed his chin. Kiera heard the crackle of whiskers beneath his fingernails. Not little at all.

"Let's not go, Kyle," she pleaded, reaching for his arm. "Right now—let's saddle our horses and head home—" He looked at her as if she'd suddenly grown another head. She released his hand. Her arms drifted slowly back to her lap. "If you *know*, why go on?"

"I know I'm afraid, that's all. I can't run from my fear. Men can't; it's not permitted."

"What do you think will happen?"

He shrugged and looked away. "The Siege of Shadows will give me the power to set Taslim free."

"And then?"

"I don't know," Kyle said, turning toward her again. The look in his eyes hinted that he did know.

"What do you see when you look at the Eigela, Kyle? What do you truly see?"

"Black. Black mountains streaked with ice, going up to a gray sky. A big, black cave some place. Black rocks falling all around me."

Kiera pulled her blanket up to her chin. She believed him, but what he described wasn't part of her vision. "Do you see the red glow? Ever?" Her heartbeat was louder in her ears than her voice, but Kyle heard and shook his head to say no. "Two rows of tall black stones leading into the mountains?"

"No," he said, then—before Kiera could derive any benefit from the relief—he added, "But Taslim has, I think. There's a place with tall stones that he's looking for right now. He calls it the Queen's Gate, and he means the Hesse queen. It's where he entered the Eigela. It's east of where we are now, that's what he remembers. Now that we're here, we'll just continue east until we come to it."

Tears wandered out of Kiera's eyes before she felt them simmering. She swiped at them with a corner of her blanket. That did no good; these weren't her artful tears that came and went by her command. "Don't go . . ."

Kyle eased off the stool to kneel beside Kiera's pallet. "I won't."

She was glad of the arms he offered, but he'd misunderstood her request. "Don't go to the Siege. Please don't go to the Siege of Shadows."

"Ki, I have to."

When she opened her mouth to plead with him again, ghastly sobbing sounds came out.

"You don't have to," Kyle assured her. "There'll be a waiting camp. Renard can't possibly climb through the mountains, nor can the horses. Someone will have to stay at the Queen's Gate until we come back. You can stay with them."

"If . . . you . . . come . . . out," Kiera gasped between sobs.

Kyle hugged her, but he didn't say a word and Kiera's tears flowed like a cold, winter rain.

A good king ate what his army ate, that was what King Otanazar IV had told his son, and that was what Gray did every morning, mopping up whatever was left from supper with hot, mushy pan bread. These last several mornings he'd had breakfast with Lockwood, Kyle Dainis, and a sleepy owl. Gray didn't expect to hear that Taslim of Fawlen or his owl had seen another living soul last night, but after four days' traveling east along the

Eigela foothills, he hoped to hear that Taslim's night journeys had finally brought him to something familiar.

This morning, it seemed, his hopes were to be fulfilled.

"He said it was foggy there, and even Kestrel couldn't fly very far into the fog. But he saw a pair of standing stones before they had to turn back."

Fog. It had been clear as a bell in camp last night, but weather in the Eigela was known to be tricky. Gray didn't complain; Alberon's kings traditionally relied on the treacherous Eigela to seal their northern border.

"How far?" he asked between mouthfuls.

"Late afternoon," Kyle said with a shrug. "The way Kestrel flies, there's more up and down than over. Taslim's never sure about the distances."

"Give the order then. We'll push ourselves. After all we've been through, I admit I'm eager to lay eyes on our quarry."

And push they did, taking fewer, shorter rests and going without their midday meal, but that was as much because the sky had turned gray. Lockwood didn't think there was a storm brewing, and Lockwood had a nose for storms, though he kept fingering his talisman. Gray wasn't taking chances. He kept the cohort together.

"We'll get there with time enough to make a camp," he assured his companions. "We've been smoking meat since we left Chegnon. Tonight we'll eat some of it, if worse comes to worst."

Fresh meat for the stew pot, though, seemed a reasonable hope when they cleared a black-rock ridge and looked across another godforsaken valley, no different from any of the others they'd traversed, except for the double row of black stones strung along its deepest lie.

Kiera Dainis cried out when she saw the stones. Gray thought she might faint again. She'd been uncommonly quiet since her last fainting spell. Ashamed of herself, no doubt. Another time, another place, another verge-lord family, and he'd have taken what she seemed determined to offer him. A month or two from now, when they were back in Chegnon and he'd dealt with the Bitch and Ferra Baldescare, he might reconsider. As Lockwood continually reminded him, verge-lords raised their daughters to pursue a royal prince the way they raised their sons to pursue a rutting stag. Kiera Dainis was far from the worst of her breed, and he would have to think seriously about a wife once he was the one and only heir again.

But for now, Gray couldn't say he objected when she kept to herself and out of the way as he and the men laid out the lines for the camp where most of the men—and both of the women—would stay while he led a select few of them to the Siege of Shadows and back.

If there were a Siege of Shadows.

They'd lost more good men getting this far than Gray cared to count, and he still wasn't convinced they'd find anything. Of course, he hadn't expected they'd find a pair of standing stones, much less the twenty-eight pair he counted as they'd ridden into the valley.

"What do you make of them?" he asked Lockwood when he found the wizard examining one the stones nearest the camp.

"Same stone as the rocs, but that's no surprise, is it? The Hesse existed. If they could build forty-seven rocs, they could plunk fifty-six stones into the ground as they left."

"The Queen's Gate, eh?" Gray ran his fingers along the stone. The stones could have been hewn yesterday. "Tragic Queen Spure, leading the Hesse back to heaven?"

"I think I prefer that explanation."

"Are there others?"

But before Lockwood could answer, the whole camp rang with a woman's screaming.

"Kiera. Damn," Gray swore, and started racing.

The screaming stopped before he was close. Kyle had her wrapped against his chest, her face tucked under his arm, protecting her from another glimpse of what had brought on the screaming.

"Lockwood!" the prince shouted to his shorter-legged friend. "Hurry on! Everyone else—*stay back!*"

"What are they?" Jahn Golight asked; he was one of the four men who'd rushed to the scene and arrived before Gray had. He'd go back, if his prince gave him an order, but he wasn't going to stay back without one.

"*Who* are they?" Gray corrected.

He counted eight, but it was a quick count and there could have been more. They were men, or they'd been men once. Now they were corpses, weathered to the color and texture of last year's straw. Corpses, not skeletons, not decayed; their flesh was dry, but intact. Their hair and their clothes retained natural colors. Two of them sat—sat dead and upright—around a burnt-out fire. The rest lay under blankets.

Lockwood came to a heavy-footed halt at Gray's side.

"By the bolt," the wizard said, taking a stride toward the nearest sitting corpse. "We're not the first." He touched a sleeve. It broke away like flaking plaster. The arm beneath was the same mottled gray and yellow as the hand and face. "Old," he added.

"Before the solstice?" Gray asked. "Before the Harbinger burned up the sky?"

Lockwood nodded slowly. He'd touched a lock of the corpse's dark hair. It had crumbled like the sleeve. He reached for the knife the corpse wore in its boot. The corpse lurched sideways as the wizard worked the blade free. The corpse broke into dusty chunks against the ground.

Gray heard a gasp come from his own lips.

"Very old," Lockwood said when he had the blade in his hand. "Like nothing I've ever seen before." He held out the weapon for Gray's examination. "Have you?"

"It's from before," Kyle Dainis announced. The boy's voice was thick and he was staring at the mountains. "Not the first, but the last. His name was Shallan. Taslim knew him."

"A godforsaken thousand years?" Jahn sputtered. "They'd be dust. They'd be past dust."

But Lockwood was shaking his head, looking at Kyle Dainis. Looking at Taslim of Fawlen. "Before," he said. "The Siege of Shadows opened with the Harbinger, then it closed when you cast your runes. And then it opened again at the solstice and you popped up in a Dainis lodge. What was it, Fawlen—What did you cast? *Bul* or *syrk*? How did they die, Fawlen?"

"It was mercy," the voice that was not quite Kyle's replied.

While they were all absorbing that, there was another sound—another scream, but none that a woman could make, and from high in the Eigela as well. Taslim had a word for that, too—

"Dragon."

Chapter Twenty-three

Dragon.

Gray let the word echo in his ears. No living man credibly claimed to have heard a dragon scream. In Alberon, the most a man could claim was a visit to Chegnon's dragon chamber, where the beast was held in a slab of black Eigela rock. It was an unforgettable sight, as Gray could attest, but Chegnon's dragon was silent. As Gray's childhood years of wonder became buried by adult reason, the dragon had been reduced to a work of art.

Yet when a second malevolent scream reached them, Gray had no doubt that the gaping jaws above his father's lesser throne could have produced the sound. He rubbed his forearm, where once, answering Lockwood's challenge, he'd scaled the wall and slung himself from the dragon's lower jaw. There were two scars—one from the dragon's outer beak, which had gashed him straight, the other small, dark, and round, where an inner fang had pierced him to the bone. He'd hung on while Lockwood counted to ten, and thus won whatever prize they'd set between them. It must have been something he'd wanted badly but he'd be damned if he could remember it now.

He could remember that the dragon's jaw had seemed to move as the count neared ten, that he'd broken the throne's carved wood arm when he'd let go, and that a fetid odor had lurked in his nostrils for days afterward. Lockwood had ribbed him for his lapse of courage. Gray looked aside, wondering if his friend remembered that same afternoon and if his opinion might be changing. But Lockwood's eyes were pointed at the darkening sky.

There was a third scream, and a fourth right after, telling

them that there were two dragons, not one. At least two. A wise man wouldn't assume dragons were solitary, or paired like eagles; he'd assume that when creatures came in pairs, they likely came in greater numbers.

"I like this not, Your Highness," Jahn Golight said, sweeping an open hand to encompass the dragons in the sky and the withered corpses in front of them. "It reeks of wizardry—begging your lord of Marelet's pardon, of course."

Lockwood shrugged out of his trance at the condemnation of his vocation. "I like it no better than you, Captain—and for the same reason."

"We could pull back," Golight suggested, made bold, no doubt, by Lockwood's unexpected support.

And Gray would have liked to oblige; the prospect of another assault on his cohort didn't appeal to him. But the clouds shrouding the Eigela peaks fell as the day's light waned. Already the air around them was thickening with fog. There'd been fog here last night, fog an owl wouldn't fly through. He had to weigh the dangers of staying put in an ill-omened place, against those of moving across unfamiliar ground in that fog.

A wise man, when he'd seen that paired-stone aisle, would have spread his scouts around before he plunged his camp into a clearly unnatural place. A wise man would have remembered he'd been ambushed. A wise man never would have allowed the Bitch to add her men to his cohort.

Gray wasn't feeling wise. He flinched when another scream echoed through the mountains. Lockwood offered him the knife he'd taken from the now-crumbled corpse and a bit of advice: "The beasts didn't harm them while they lived, or afterward. We'll be safe enough here."

"And if you're wrong, Locky?" Gray took the knife.

The blade was short and double-edged, wide near the hilt and with a slightly concave taper to its point. He'd seen its like painted on old, faded murals and carved in the funerary effigies lining Chegnon's crypt of kings, but he'd never held one, or expected to. Alberon had her own iron and coal. She didn't need to trade for a steady supply of virgin steel, but the metal was too precious to waste in nostalgia or keepsakes: An old-fashioned weapon went back to the smith for reforging until there was nothing left but slag for the priests' steeples. The knife Gray held had a freshly honed edge and there wasn't a speck of rust on the blade. Little as he liked the notion, he found himself believing it had belonged to a man named Shallan, a man Taslim of Fawlen had known a millennium ago.

Gray handed the knife back to his friend. He considered the ancient camp in which he stood. Whatever had slain these men had taken them completely by surprise. An unwelcome image filled his mind's eye: himself, Lockwood, and his other companions similarly withered and forgotten for a thousand years. "I suppose there could be worse fates than meeting a dragon."

"And we may meet them before we see home again," Lockwood agreed, rather more easily than Gray had expected. The wizard tucked the knife into the leather cuff of his boot. "But not tonight."

Kyle Dainis joined them, an arm around his sister and her accepting the support. Lady Kiera was still stunned by what she'd seen, which surprised Gray; she'd seen worse after the ambush. Perhaps she saw herself sitting here forever, same as he did. That was an image to crush the boldest spirit and Lady Kiera hadn't recovered her spirit since she'd fallen off her horse.

She'd been her usual willful self when she first stood up again, but by the next morning she'd slipped into an eyes-down quiet from which nothing had roused her. Both Kyle and Lockwood had taken pains to convince Gray that her fall had been a moment's distraction, nothing more, nothing that justified halting their progress a few days while she recovered, which Gray would have readily done.

Her welfare had become a matter of perverse pride to him. Over and above any affection he felt for the Dainis as a family or as individuals, he was determined that he'd have a royal confrontation with the Baldescare and he'd have it with Kiera Dainis standing at his side.

Let them see with their own eyes the price of involving an innocent woman in a royal quarrel. Let them see it; let the king, his father, see it, overdue as it was. Then let royal justice be done.

"No harm will come to you, Lady Kiera," he said to her, thinking well beyond tonight.

She raised her chin against Kyle's chest, then turned hesitantly, as if every movement was preceded by a soul-wrenching choice. Her eyes were red and the expression that formed in them seemed to say a prince's promise had come too late. The dragons screamed again and she disappeared into her brother's shirt.

No king could rule his realm if his lords and their families didn't take his word on faith. No prince could become a king with hollow promises. Gray thought of all the lectures he'd gotten from his father and his mentors, all the advice they'd given him. He couldn't remember a single word they'd said, not with dragons screaming. Instead, he recalled the ill-fated King Irkatul of Kol, and imagined himself walking, not to the headsman's block, but to this desolate spot.

"God have mercy," Gray murmured before he could stop himself, then, having sunk as deep into misery as royal pride would permit, he banished Irkatul from his thoughts. "Kyle, since your friend recognized this place, ask him how long until we're there and back."

Kyle's eyelids fluttered and his face took on the vaguely pained expression it got whenever he and the haunt spoke. Jahn Golight cupped his hands in the Hollow Sphere. Lady Kiera pried herself out of her sanctuary against her brother's chest to stare at him. Gray stood his ground, an arm's length away. Only Lockwood went closer, as Lockwood would.

The young man blinked and was himself again. "Your Highness, Taslim said there'll be a path at the end of these stones. It leads to the Siege, and they walked for three days getting there. He doesn't know about getting back . . ."

Of course not, Gray chided himself. Taslim hadn't come out of these mountains. No one had. God knew what torment the wizard had just inflicted on the hart-lord. Gray should have been more careful with his questions. "I'm sorry, friend—slip of the tongue—"

But Kyle Dainis cocked his head. Brown hair fell across one eye; he looked half his age. Then he managed a lopsided smile. "It will be different this time, Your Highness; he swears it."

No wonder every majordomo or fosterage lord had judged him a youth of no worthy substance. Usheff, who was truly simple-minded, couldn't seem half so witless as Kyle Dainis when Kyle Dainis set his cleverness to that task. Lockwood said Kyle was a rock-solid ally. Gray hoped his boon-friend was right, because by the time a man that knew Kyle Dainis was his enemy, it would be too late.

Gray clapped the younger man soundly on the back—a

blow that did nothing to change his expression. He clapped him a second time and left his arm resting on a broad shoulder. A gentle tug and they walked together, leading Lockwood, Lady Kiera, and Jahn Golight toward the camp where their anxious companions were waiting.

"I don't hold oaths from men I can't see," Gray said and was relieved when Kyle swallowed his artless smile. He turned his attention to Golight. "Mark that, Captain: The wizard says three days. The mountains will give us water this time of year. We'll sleep in our cloaks. See that we carry sufficient food."

"Aye, Your Highness. I been thinking it through. I suggest leaving Gedd Brant as captain in my stead, seeing as we lost Josaf Dainisman. I'd bring Darvet and Paggat with us; they're good men what fought with us in Pelipulay. They've seen magic in battle; it won't panic them, should it come to that. And Ilowy, the Dainismen, he's an unshakable sort. Your permission, Your Highness, that we bring Usheff with us, too. He can carry more than any other man I know, and he'll be better off knowing where I am."

Gray nodded. "My permission, Captain. See to it."

They reached the camp. A fire had been kindled, with pots around it and spits slung over it, but these were left untended as everyone cupped their hands and looked to their prince for an explanation. Or another explanation. Gray quickly realized that Ilowy, the Dainisman his captain wanted to bring into the Eigela, had been telling tales. He'd identified dragons as the source of the overhead screams and suggested encircling the camp with fresh blood.

"For protection, Your Highness. My grammer said the old ones can't cross a bloodline, nor pierce a circle. 'Twere best, Your Highness, as it's too late to move the camp beyond the bones."

Bones instead of stones, blood in circles, an old woman's nostrums, and a bumpkin telling a prince what to do—what he should have done. And wasn't that the same look in Ilowy's eyes that he'd seen in Lady Kiera's? The same look all around the camp? Gray's doubts flowed back to him soaked in anger.

"We're safe where we are—safe without the shedding of blood. We have the lord of Marelet's word and his talisman as surety." He glanced at Lockwood, who, thank God, looked confident and resolute. "By the wizard's reckoning we may be gone six days. Tomorrow morning we'll move the camp to the lee of the ridge. The ladies will be more comfortable there. Gedd Brant will command the camp while Captain Golight's with me and the others: Lord Kyle, Lord Marelet, Usheff, Darvet, and Paggat from the royal guard, and—" Gray looked square at Ilowy, weighing in his own mind the risks of taking him with them against leaving a superstitious tale-spinner behind. "You, Ilowy, you'll be captain among the Dainismen, second to Brant. Mark your responsibilities well, Ilowy; you'll answer to me as well as your lord."

He heard himself making decisions with his mouth, not his head, hardly a wise way for a prince to behave. But the decisions felt right, and there was satisfaction on the faces of the men around him. A dragon screamed while he held their attention. The sound was fainter than the previous ones but the camp tensed and the myriad Hollow Spheres were clenched tight enough to hold water.

"Dragons roost against the cliffs at night—surely your grammer told you *that,* Ilowy, when she told you the rest?" It was petty and foolish: Gray had no idea how dragons slept or when or where. But he'd cut his teeth staring up at his father's throne; he could bluff better than any ten gamblers. The Dainisman hung his head. "Enough, then. Who's tending the supper fire?"

Their food was plain, smoke-dried meat simmered in a thick gruel and sopped up with yesterday's bread crusts. No one went hungry, and on Gray's signal, Golight dug deep in their provisions to produce a crock of Ulver's finest burnwine. All along, Gray had planned for a celebration before they entered the mountains. With grave mounds still fresh in their memories and dragon screams still echoing in the distance, he reckoned his anxious men needed it more than ever. There weren't enough spirits in the jug to dull any man's edge, if both he and Lockwood had misjudged the screaming beasts.

Gray hoped his gesture would cheer his diminished cohort before they divided up. He might well have hoped for a thousand bright stars to pierce the foggy night. His own attempts to hearten them fell flat in his own ears and he chided himself for forgetting that burnwine nurtured melancholy as well as levity.

It was more than simple distance that separated them from their homes. There was no solace in thoughts of the past or the future. Both were equally, and painfully, remote in this unnaturally dark valley that had become unnaturally quiet, as well. No dragons had screamed since they'd finished their supper, but none of the usual night sounds came through the fog.

Conversations started, sputtered, and died, as listeners listened for sounds that weren't there. When the owl took flight from Kyle's shoulders, every spine jerked straight. They scanned the fog, fingered their weapons. Through the long moments that the bird was gone, Gray's breath came in shallow gasps, if it came at all. And when the owl returned with a mouse clutched in its talons, which it proceeded to dismember without modesty or delicacy, he wasn't the only one laughing.

A man had to laugh to dispel the shame of dreading a mouse in the dark. God knew where the vermin had come from—probably their own baggage. A man had to laugh, as well, watching the owl do to its prey what a man suspected a dragon would do to him.

And having laughed, they dared to talk about the dragons. Ilowy offered more of his grandmother's wisdom: A dragon's most dangerous aspect wasn't its teeth, but its iron-tipped tail, which it wielded as a whip. Gray could hardly dispute the claim. His knowledge of the beasts ended where a man would belt his breeches, where the dragon surging from the wall merged with its Eigela stone prison.

Taslim, for all his faults, would have been a more believable authority, but the wizard only spoke through Kyle Dainis and Gray wasn't about to subject that young man to questions. He'd resigned himself to a farm wife's superstitions, when Kyle began speaking:

"They have long, dark-tipped tails," the young man said, staring into the fire. "And a man could be toppled by its lashing. But dragons don't attack with their tails, no more than a cock attacks with his. They're bastards; they scavenge the dead and harry the wounded. They don't attack a whole and healthy man unless he gets between them and their feast. But they've got four talons on each foot and each can gut a man." Kyle paused, moistened his lips, and continued. "They've got both teeth and beak. They spit a foul pitch that inflames whatever it touches and no amount of water can extinguish. They char their prey before they devour it."

Gray could vouch for a dragon's teeth and beak. And the smell, too, now he could identify it: pitch, as Kyle said, charred meat, and the rot of the middens. Once again Gray looked at Lockwood, and this time his boon-friend's chin dropped in a barely perceptible nod of agreement.

"Damned dainty beasties," Captain Golight said with a snorted laugh: a veteran's lifelong defiance of an enemy he thought he couldn't defeat. "Got to cook their meat 'fore they can eat it."

But it fell to simple Usheff to ask questions that demanded answers: "What way do them dragons eat at all, when save for us'ns who come today, there's naught alive here but a mouse? What way do they stay and starve when wings'd take them anywhere?"

Gray made up answers and offered them quickly, as befitted a prince and leader of their cohort: "Dragons are no natural creatures, Usheff. They're the stuff of magic and bound by magic to guard the Siege of Shadows, which legend and our wizard-friend, Taslim, tells us has been shut away from the world of men for a thousand years. That's their place and where they've stayed all this time. They don't get hungry in the way of men or mice or owls or horses."

"Some folk would say they feed in Sandrisan," Gedd Brant said, all unexpected. Gedd was a man of Sandrisan, where the old king's memory was revered along with the Hidden God's. Head bowed and eyes shadowed, Gedd continued: "There's a lay of stones at the far end of the valley, black as these or the roc, though not so tall and not so many, only seventeen: eight by pairs and a straggler on the end. They lay off toward the mountains—or away from 'em, as you please, Your Highness. Rightly, they don't go nowhere, they're just there. We call 'em Eigela's tears and the priests don't take notice when there's a fire burnin' there. That's the Hesse King Eigela, Your Highness, as you might wonder—his tears as he left Alberon for the last time. But it's said our own King Eigela walked the lay before he restored the kingdom. After, too."

"So you and yours think there've been dragons haunting the verge of Sandrisan? Since when, Gedd Brant? The Hesse King Eigela or King Eigela the Second?"

"No stone, Your Highness, no dragon—save I heard sounds like we heard today tendin' the fire. Faint an' far-off, Your Highness, but I matched 'em. Never named 'em dragons afore now, Your Highness. Called 'em the 'dark folk' an' the fires kept 'em out. Like as not, it'd be wise to move the camp, Your Highness, but I reckon to keep a fire burnin' right here while you and yours are after that Siege o' Shadows, Your Highness. Lest you forbid it, but I'd like that not."

"Nor I, Gedd," Gray said.

He had a hope that Fawlen would seize Kyle Dainis' tongue to refute the Sandrisan sergeant as he'd refuted Ilowy. But if Fawlen inside Kyle's mind disagreed with what Gedd Brant was saying, there was no sign of it on Kyle's face. The young man was rapt, with his forearms supporting his chin above his knees as he sat with the owlet preening on his shoulder. Lockwood was just as bad.

Perhaps Gray would have found Gedd's words more entertaining if he hadn't been wondering what else his mentors had left out of their books, what other curious customs endured deep in the valleys.

They had ample wood at hand to keep the fire burning until dawn. It was simple prudence in the wilderness, where wolves, bears, and mountain cats were known to prowl by night. The watchmen were always careful to keep it lit. Gray had no doubt they'd be doubly careful this night. The invigorating effects of the burnwine had worn off. They were all weary. Once one man yawned, they were all yawning, stretching, thinking of their blankets—dragons be damned. Lady Kiera and her woman retired to their tent. Gray doubled the watch and bid them do their best to divide the night evenly, with no stars to help them measure the passage of time, then he wrapped himself in his cloak.

There was no dawn, as there'd been no sunset, only a gradual lightening overhead to an unclouded gray. The bald sky was bright enough to make the prince squint when he scanned the Eigela peaks for dragons, but permitted no shadows to mark the time. Some of the men complained that it took all day to reestablish their camp on the valley ridge. Gray himself thought they were finished before midday.

Either way, Gedd Brant wanted wood to fuel his fire for a month and Jahn Golight wanted to bury the withered corpses Lady Kiera had discovered. Gray privately disagreed with his captain. It seemed sacrilegious to disturb them after a millennium's vigil around their cold fire, but he wasn't a religious man and Jahn had an obsession with burying the dead. He split their able-bodied men between the captain and the sergeant, and regretted his decision soon enough.

Usheff's wail echoed off the mountains. Gedd and his men boiled out of the trees with axes at the ready. Lady Kiera got herself up on one of the horses and rode recklessly down from the ridge camp. For his part, Gray lost his place on the sword he was sharpening and nicked three fingers on—thank God for small blessings—his off-weapon hand. The wounds were still smarting when he joined the others.

Yesterday, a corpse had broken apart when Lockwood examined it; today, the first one Usheff touched disintegrated into a heap of dust. The simpleton thought it was his fault. Gray blamed Jahn Golight, but he kept his anger to himself; there was nothing to be gained by haranguing the grim captain. He calmed and soothed, forgave and reassured, and finally sent them all away by saying, "The lord of Marelet and I will deal honorably and respectfully with these dead. Such unnaturalness is the natural work of wizards."

Bare-chested and still dripping from an interrupted bath in a nearby stream, Lockwood waited quietly until they were alone.

"Your Highness, the right-worthy lord of Marelet," he began with exaggerated courtesy, "unnaturally, but honorably and very respectfully, suggests a broom."

"A broom, my right-worthy lord?" Gray countered, trying to maintain his friend's solemnity. It was a losing fight. The proposal was so macabre, so elegant, so outrageous, and so very Lockwood. He surrendered to laughter.

Lockwood pressed a finger to his lips. "Respectfully—remember?"

Gray did remember. They didn't have a broom, but they had the length of cloth Jahn had intended to use as a shroud. It was easy work and quickly done. They stood for a moment's silence on opposite sides of the grave.

"I can't think of anything to say, Locky. They died a thousand years ago. God have mercy."

"That says it." Lockwood tamped the dirt into the grave. Talisman, sword, or an undersized camp shovel—he handled them all with equal skill. "Come along—let's wash away the dust of the millennium."

Gray stayed put. "What do you make of it, Locky? All of it. Siege of Shadows, dusty corpses, dragons. God's pockets—the way you went after Taslim yesterday. What was that all about? *Bul* and *syrk*; life and death—do you think he had something to do with this?"

Lockwood braced the shovel across the back of his neck and crooked his arms over the handle, much more the common laborer than an ennobled wizard. "It takes life to make life. There's nothing in the runes to stop a wizard from stealing another man's natural life."

"There were only eight men here. Eight men together wouldn't live for a thousand years. He'd have needed, what—a hundred men, two hundred?"

"Eight would do, *if* it could be done. The runes say it can, but the runes say a lot of things. The runes say water can flow uphill and the dead can rise, but no wizard's done it. *Bul* and *syrk* say you can live forever, but no wizard's done that either. The wind won't blow; it can't be done."

"But Fawlen did it. How? The Siege of Shadows?"

Lockwood shrugged the shovel off his shoulders. "If I knew the answer to that—"

"Could you question Fawlen?"

"Maybe he knows something. That's what Marrek and Baldescare think, what they tried to pry out of him . . . and Kyle. Myself, I've *met* Taslim of Fawlen, and whatever he knows, it's not half of what he *doesn't* know."

"So, we climb into the Eigela tomorrow, looking for what: the Siege of Shadows? God? The biggest lightning bolt in creation? I tell you, Locky, listening to Gedd Brant last night, I could almost believe we're following old King Eigela's trail. 'When Alaria spread her crimson cloak and flew, blood-red against the sun . . .' "

"What?"

Gray sighed; he knew where this was going to end. "'The Song of Eigela.' Alaria, Gandrel, and Nezzaran, they were the mortals who opened Alberon to the king's enemies and left when he did."

"Oh—*poetry*. If you say so."

As a scholar, Lockwood had memorized a thousand runic formularies before Marrek let him have his talisman, and a thousand more since, but not a single line of poetry. By almost any other measure, Lockwood was a learned man, but he had a peasant's mundane soul.

A shape in the grass caught Gray's eye. They'd intended to

bury the dead with all their possessions except the knife Lockwood had removed yesterday, and this little coin they'd apparently missed. It was a crettig—silver coins in Alberon had always been called crettigs; the word was an old way of saying "little silver." The metal was untarnished.

"King Euben's crettig. A thousand years," Gray murmured.

"Last I checked, Gray, this was the twenty-second year of your lord father's reign, the three-thousand, seven-hundred, twenty-ninth of Alberon. If you believe the chroniclers, we're creeping toward the end of our fourth millennium. The Stercians claim a fifth."

"The Stercians *always* claim more than the Alberonese. But what do they have for their claim—a sheaf of tales about gods who mated with mortal women and a few old temples where no one worships."

"While we have the Hesse, who weren't gods but who mated with everything, and the rocs they built when they weren't mating."

"You're incorrigible, Locky."

"I'm honest; it's not quite the same thing."

Gray turned away from his friend. He stared at the Eigela. They hadn't heard a dragon scream all day, but he believed they were there, waiting for them. "I see our whole history here: you and me today, the Debacle dead we just buried, King Eigela the man, King Eigela the Hesse. Even Alaria, Gandrel, and Nezzaran and *poetry.* We're all on one path and it leads up into those black mountains."

A hand clamped around his arm and spun him around. "The stream, my prince. You're ripe enough that the smell's affecting your mind." Their eyes met at close distance and Lockwood was immediately sober. "I believe there's something up there. I don't know what it is, but I can feel it."

"Me, also. I'm not sure it's God, not anymore."

"That's the difference between us, Gray"—the merry irreverence had returned to the wizard's face—"I never did."

He let Lockwood take the lead going to the stream.

"Gray, you know what the Stercians think of Alberon, but did you know they say the Eigela were snow-white until the coming of the Hesse?"

"Locky—"

"All right, the Stercians don't mention the Hesse in their

chronicles, they say the 'dark folk,' just like Gedd Brant, and Alaria, Gandrel, and—"

"*Locky!*"

"I swear by lightning!"

"You swear *at* lightning."

"Whatever."

Gray started to laugh again, and this time there was no reason to be discreet.

Seven men set out for the Siege of Shadows the next, gray morning: a wizard, a prince, a hart-lord, a captain, a simpleton, and two men-at-arms. They traveled with what they could carry slung from their shoulders and their waists. Their fervent hope was to be seven hungry men when they returned.

They followed the paired-stone path past undisturbed graves and into a curved and narrowing ravine. Mountain grasses gave way to gravel scree. The standing stones—shorter, thinner, but still thrusting from the rock—guided them until the scree gave way to naked, barren rock.

Their path grew steeper. A man had to measure his steps and mind his balance, but otherwise the path was easy for a single file of climbers, as Taslim had promised. Rock walls rose on both sides of the path. Kyle didn't fear falling; he feared the walls might clash together and squash them.

He knew that would change. Through words and images Taslim had shown him a mountainside trail, but more significantly, since he'd talked with Kiera in her tent—the last time he'd talked to her except in passing and to say good-bye—his dreams had been filled with images from his own forgotten Rapture dream. Soon he'd be keeping back from a sheer edge and scraping his knuckles raw.

There was no rush. Kyle had dreamt and remembered that he had his own notion of dragons: dragons screaming, men screaming, men in flames, men falling to a more merciful death than a dragon would grant them.

And at the end of all his dreams, the face he'd never forgotten, lines of black and white, and smeared with blood. But possibly not inevitable. He knew the men in front of him: Captain Golight leading, then Usheff, Gray, and Lockwood. None of them had the shape or sound of the men Kyle remembered from his Rapture dream. Nor had Rapture hinted that he'd have an owl clamped to his left shoulder, making unhappy *huiw-w-w, huiw-w-w* noises in his ear at every step.

Several times, Kyle tried to persuade Taslim to utter the necessary runes. He couldn't reassure Kestrel the way the wizard could, if the wizard would, and Kyle couldn't afford the distraction of Kestrel's misery, especially after they entered an area where the path was riddled with cracks and flakes of black scree that broke loose with every step. Taslim was adamant; he preferred his nasen'bei prison and the coherence of Kyle's thoughts.

The cracks became a fissure, a barely visible black gash through the black stone, wide enough to swallow a man's foot to the ankle. Kyle lowered his head and watched his feet. He was living his Rapture now.

His mind was empty when Captain Golight let out a yell. Like sheep coming to a halt, they bumped into one another. And like sheep they looked up with dumb astonishment. The ravine had ended. There was sheer mountain on their right, sheer nothing on their left. Kyle held Lockwood's arm while the wizard leaned and looked down.

"There's no end to it," he said after he'd satisfied his curiosity. "It drops forever."

There were other mountains around them . . . endless mountains jumbled one after another. Kyle knew them from his dream; Taslim knew them from before. They were ready to walk again, but their companions remained awestruck. Gray wanted Kestrel to scout ahead, and as there'd be no moving forward until Gray was satisfied, Taslim uttered the runes.

Kestrel didn't want to leave Kyle's shoulder and Kyle didn't want to think what pressure Taslim must have applied to get the owl to spread his wings. It flew left, over the abyss, began to spiral up, and then, with a panicked screech, began to veer and tumble wildly. In a heartbeat, the owl was gone from sight.

"Taslim! Come back!" Kyle shouted, echoing the plea with his thoughts. He grabbed Lockwood's arm and leaned over the brink. Kestrel still screeched and flapped his wings, but he was falling, not flying. "Taslim! Up here! Taslim, I'm up here!"

Lockwood jerked him back against the mountainside. For an instant, the warrior spirit Kyle lacked was in the ascendant and he was prepared to rip his companion's throat with his bare hands. Then the wizard shoved something hard and tingling into his hand: the crystal talisman—with all its intimate associations. But those lasted only for an instant, until Lockwood disappeared, the mountains disappeared, everything disappeared. There was only himself, the bald gray sky above him, around him, below him, and—after a painful heartbeat—Lockwood's reassuring voice:

"Call them again, Kyle, with all your strength."

With Lockwood's talisman growing hot in his hand, he poured his soul a single word—not a name, but the rune *serras.* Wind gusted against his face. He felt wings and talons and then a cold, frightened presence at the back of his mind.

<<There are no mountains,>> Taslim told him. <<There's nothing but nothing out there. It's all illusion.>>

Kyle repeated his wizard's words.

"This is illusion?" Captain Golight retorted, giving the mountain beside him a solid slap.

Kyle believed what he'd seen and felt, or, rather, what he hadn't seen, hadn't felt. He tried to explain, but words failed him.

Lockwood came to his rescue. "Not illusion, Captain, not for you or me or any of us, but for an owl? An owl's not a man. An owl can't be deceived as a man can be deceived. We've entered magic's realm, Captain. We're not climbing in the Eigela. God knows where we are." Lockwood grimaced and then slapped the stone himself. "*God* knows. That's the whole point of it, Captain. God knows. The Siege of Shadows isn't *in* the Eigela, it's *beyond* the Eigela, and that's where we are, Captain: We've passed through the Eigela to God knows where."

Lockwood laughed, but Captain Golight wouldn't share the jest. He checked the knots and buckles on the sack he slung over his shoulders, then started walking. "Sooner there, sooner back. God have mercy on us all."

<<Is Lockwood right?>> Kyle asked when they were walking again.

There was a silence, then a sigh, then, <<Marelet's very clever, very bold. I wouldn't wager against him—ever.>>

Kyle took that for yes, and as much admiration as Taslim could concede for anyone.

They were beyond time, beyond distance. Their path had curved and doglegged so many times, none of them could guess whether their faces pointed north or south. Not that it mattered. There was little conversation—a warning about a loose stone, a curse or two when knuckles rasped against the mountainside—little that needed saying. They walked the steep path, they stopped, they rested, they started walking again. That became the measure of time and distance. Kyle lost himself in an unexpected serenity: They'd gotten this far; the rest was out of his hands.

They'd rested three times, eaten once, and had just negotiated another right-side dogleg when a dragon screamed. Illusion or not, the mountains gave back real echoes in such number that they were looking in different directions when the second scream came. The third scream wasn't a dragon, and by then they were looking in the same place and at a man engulfed in flame, who tumbled down the mountainside ahead of them.

It's happening, Kyle thought as the screams of men and beast continued. He flattened himself against the mountainside. He closed his eyes, but his ears told him when another man had died.

The screaming didn't last long. It was replaced by growls and the crack of long bones and, yes, the aroma of charred meat. Captain Golight had drawn his sword. He kept it out—for all the good it might do—as they continued along.

<<We were alone. You said we were the only ones.>> The thought was both question and statement. <<Who were they?>>

<<I said we were the only ones in *Alberon*. We'll find out who else is here when we get there, if we get there.>>

The wizard was keeping secrets again. Kyle swore he'd tell Lockwood the next time they stopped, and did nothing to keep his intention hidden from Taslim, who didn't rise to the bait. Captain Golight kept them walking longer than he had—prudence when there were enemies about.

Although the place where the dragons had attacked and fed had seemed to be almost directly above them, they came to it before the captain had called a halt. At least they all assumed the grisly place they entered was the same. It seemed easier—safer in some ways—to think magic had rearranged their path rather than that there had been two other cohorts in the mountains and two dragon attacks.

The path had widened into what might have been called

bailey-verge, if the mountains that surrounded it in a horseshoe shape had been walls instead. And there was another path entering the bailey-verge—or the remains of a path. A massive rock slide obscured it now. The slide had taken the other men by surprise: The mangled lower half of a corpse protruded from it. Or perhaps the man had already been dead.

"We didn't hear no rock slide," Darvet muttered. "I don't like this."

Neither statement seemed worthy of argument.

The verge was large enough that all seven of them could gather around a mangled corpse. Dragons were, as Taslim had warned them, scavengers. The remains were torn and broken as well as charred. Usheff wept. Paggat, their other man-at-arms, managed to reach the rock-slide rubble before he vomited. But there was more to be read from these deaths. Dragons hadn't killed this man, an arrow had. It had pierced the man's skull just below his ear, either a terrible accident or a damned good shot.

<<A damn good shot, Hart-lord,>> Taslim offered his opinion a heartbeat before the captain and the prince said much the same thing. <<There was a fight here before the dragons. A fight to the death won by soft-hearted victors. Count our blessings.>>

Kyle heard and vowed to remember, but Taslim's cryptic comments didn't claim his mind's forefront. It had been hard to discern at first, between the blood and the mangling, but now he was certain: The corpse was manlike, but it was not a man, not as men lived around the sea of Prayse. The ear was too narrow, the fingers were too long between the knuckles—and the teeth were too narrow, too long, and too sharp.

<<What are they?>> he demanded.

<<The same as us, Hart-lord: men seeking the Siege of Shadows.>>

Captain Golight knelt down, drew his knife, and delicately turned the corpse's head so the other ear was exposed.

"*Accuree*," Usheff named them.

"Nightling," the captain translated, but he couldn't explain how a Jivernaise legend had gotten ahead of them.

Two of the other corpses resembled the nightling; the rest, including the one protruding from the rock-slide rubble, seemed to have been men shaped like themselves. *Seemed.* There were unfamiliar things—strange clothing, strange weapons—that made all of them uneasy.

Worse, the gray sky had darkened.

"We'll camp here," Gray announced through gritted teeth. "Move the bodies. Make a fire."

There was wood scattered among the corpses, sticking out of the rubble. Perhaps one or both of the other groups had been carrying it. Perhaps it had been here all along, though they'd seen no trees since they'd entered the mountains. Perhaps God had put it there for the survivors.

Kyle didn't know, couldn't know, and after a moment's hesitation, didn't care. A fire would go a long way toward dispelling anxiety. He helped to haul the corpses to one side of the verge and gathered wood for a fire on the other side.

When it was kindled and they were sitting as secure as they could be, with swords at their sides and the one bow they'd salvaged, along with a handful of arrows, beside Darvet, their best archer, the questions began. Taslim insisted he knew nothing about nightlings. He did not, in fact, believe the corpses they'd put on the bottom of the pile had anything to do with Jivernaise superstitions.

<<There were stranger-looking men in these mountains a thousand years ago,>> the wizard said, and Kyle repeated aloud. "And we were strange to them, I'm sure. They blocked our path to the Siege; we blocked theirs. We couldn't turn back, so we fought and they died, until we reached the Siege itself."

Captain Golight spat into the fire. "Been in battles like that. Hold the bridge. Take the castle. Been times it was easy. Been times it turned into a bloodbath: man against man an' God against all."

"God's a fool," Lockwood suggested. "And so are we."

They argued that awhile, then ate, and kept their ears pricked for dragons—or so they said. Kyle knew he was listening for other sounds, man-shaped sounds.

<<Remember,>> Taslim whispered. <<Stay back. Let the others bloody their hands. Keep yours clean—or it's all been for nothing.>>

Kyle seethed with resentment because Taslim's words were true now. There'd been too many sacrifices; what he wanted—what he thought was right—no longer mattered.

<<I'll set you free. I'll do whatever has to be done. But no

more, Taslim. I'll have nothing from a god that demands *this*.>>

<<You'll reconsider, once you see how much there is to be done. How much we can do. Turn your back on God, if you want, but not on God's power. Together we can conquer God's temptation.>>

The golden archway to the Siege loomed in Kyle's mind as it had not since the priests had performed their exorcism. There was no pressure, no pain, only temptation, which Kyle resisted by retreating into his own thoughts. He imagined he was back in the Renzi Valley, riding Rawne through the fields on a bright summer day.

"Ware away!"

Darvet's shout dragged him back to the fire. There were sounds through the darkness, along their own path. Kyle reached for his sword, but he stayed back while the others moved forward with weapons and brands from the fire. He didn't see what they saw, only heard the prince shout:

"Hold fire!"

Lockwood ran toward him. "It's your sister, Kyle. Hurry!"

Chapter Twenty-four

The men parted as Kyle approached, giving him a clear view of Kiera clinging to Prince Gravais. Her hair was stiff and tangled, as if she'd walked against the wind. As if, because they'd encountered no wind and it was inconceivable that she'd followed any other path. It was barely conceivable that she'd followed them at all.

"Kiera . . . ," Kyle said gently.

Her right sleeve was tattered and bloody where she'd rasped herself against the mountainside.

There was isinglass in the black rock, the sharp bits that had bloodied Kyle's knuckles in Rapture and in life. By firelight, isinglass sparkled like stars. Here a man could see the difference between mountainside and nothing at all. Kyle imagined what the path had been like for Kiera, all alone as the light faded, dogleg turns, right and left, and bodies falling forever.

"Kiera . . . " Carefully, tenderly, he took his sister from the prince's keeping. She accepted the change without seeming to notice it. "Kiera—Kiera, look at me, please?"

He hooked a finger under her chin and raised it easily. Again, he said her name. She blinked and stared past him as if he were part of the darkness. Compassion wanted to reassure her that, whatever the reason she'd come, she was safe beside him, but compassion hesitated. Her eyes were huge in the firelight. Looking into them, Kyle had the sense that he was looking through a tunnel. She blinked again; he saw a shape in the distance: an arc of gold rising, disappearing into the dark.

"The Siege . . . The Siege of Shadows . . ."

<<Let her go, Hart-lord,>> Taslim advised from his own dark place. <<Bad enough she's come, but worse to follow.>>

<<No,>> Kyle argued, then, to Kiera: "Ki, come back. Come away from there. Don't listen. You can fight it; you can win."

Kiera blinked. The golden arc vanished, her pupils shrank, and her stare became purest malice.

<<Let her go, Hart-lord!>> the wizard begged.

There was a war for the muscles of his arms, a small and desperate war. Kyle won an easy, meaningless victory between heartbeats. Kiera's expression didn't change; she didn't want his arms around her, his face before her eyes. She wanted Gray—her prince—and she took him as Kyle released her.

Be wary, he mouthed to Gray over the top of her head. The prince tipped his head, acknowledging the warning, accepting it.

"She's cold as the grave, Kyle. If you have an extra shirt, she needs it," Gray said as he guided Kiera to the fire. "If not, open my pack; I have one. Locky?"

Lockwood shook his head. "My cloak if she needs it, nothing more. Not yet, maybe not at all. She's not herself, Gray."

Lockwood's warning was no more or less than Kyle's own had been, yet Kyle's hands were shaking when he knelt down beside his pack. <<What's wrong with her?>> he demanded, fumbling with the knots. And when there was no immediate answer, he made the wind he used to propel Taslim into Kestrel and larded it with every rune shape he remembered. White light exploded in his skull. It wasn't painful, not as he remembered pain, but it left him dazzled and blinded.

<<Not here, Hart-lord,>> Taslim scolded. <<By the Almighty Bolt! Not here, not now. Did you see *nothing* when you looked into her eyes?>>

He answered with an image: Kiera's face moments ago, a golden arc glowing in the depth of her huge, black eyes. Another image echoed, identical in every significant way, yet subtly different. It was the image of the Siege of Shadows that Taslim had thrown at him so many times in the early days after the solstice. Kyle didn't know now if he'd remembered it or if it came from the wizard.

<<She's been *called*, Hart-lord. God prefers her. God knows why . . . and so do we all.>>

The knots gave way and his pack opened. <<How?>> Kyle demanded.

<<How would I know, Hart-lord? Jealousy? Ambition? I didn't put it there, Hart-lord. Keeping secrets runs in the blood.>>

<<But you'd know all about that, wouldn't you?>> Kyle yanked his second shirt out of the pack—he hadn't expected to change shirts in the mountains, but Josaf had taught him that a man might unexpectedly need clean cloth, so he carried an extra one. <<You're our great-grandfather. We're like *you*!>>

He seethed with anger, wanting to lash out even as he drew the shirt gently over Kiera's head. She didn't help, didn't hinder. Kyle brushed her hair with his hands, trying to calm the wildness from it and her. She'd lost the ribbon that bound one of her plaits. He undid the other, intending to braid them together. If he could restore her appearance, perhaps she, too, would be restored. But Kyle hadn't braided anyone's hair since they left the nursery. His fingers had forgotten the art.

The prince, who'd undoubtedly had more recent experience, gestured Kyle aside. Gray did a better job controlling and confining the thick tresses than Kyle could have hoped; that did nothing for his simmering anger, his growing uneasiness. Kiera surrendered herself to the movements of royal hands. When Gray was finished, she spoke her first words:

"I'm hungry."

The voice was Kyle's sister's, as were the movements with which she broke the bread he offered. But Kiera remained a stranger, ignoring him as she ignored everyone but Gray, and ignoring Gray when he asked, "Why did you follow us, Lady Kiera?"

When she was done eating, Kiera announced that she was tired and, with no other by-your-leave, wrapped herself in Gray's cloak. To all appearances, she was asleep as soon as she was settled. Usheff muttered Jivernaise prayers. The rest of them kept their prayers, if they had any—and Kyle no longer did—to themselves, but they'd all been unnerved, even Lockwood. The stocky wizard shook his head and waved Kyle away before Kyle could ask any questions.

<<So, the brash soul admits a limit. Marelet recognizes that

there's something more powerful than him, something he doesn't dare challenge,>> Taslim retorted when Kyle had chosen the patch of stone where he'd try to sleep.

But Taslim's irritating smugness couldn't conceal the sense that he was frightened or that he'd hoped Lockwood hadn't lost his confidence. Kyle was trying without much success to argue the reasons for that fear out of his companion when Captain Golight touched his shoulder.

"His Highness says ye'll take a third watch tonight, after himself and the lord wizard. Like as not, ye won't be the only man awake, but ye'll be the man on watch."

Kyle nodded to the captain, and a second time to Gray, who sat the first watch with an unsheathed sword on his knees. A man couldn't help but notice that the prince's post gave him a better view of Kiera than it gave of the path. A brother couldn't help but rage inwardly, nor could he deny that the prince was wise. He stretched out with half an eye for the prince, the rest for his twin.

A month out of Chegnon, he was used to sleeping on hard ground, but there was no ground as hard as rock. He didn't expect to close his eyes, didn't think he had, until he heard his name whispered and felt someone shaking his shoulder.

"Your turn, Kyle." Lockwood offered him a hand, which he gratefully took.

Grinding unfinished, forgotten dreams from his eyes, Kyle asked, "How goes the night?"

"Quiet as the grave."

Kyle scowled and the grinning wizard took a backward step.

"It's quiet, Kyle Dainis. Simply quiet. Everyone's sleeping the sleep of the innocent. We'll see what dawn brings."

"Dawn." He shook his head; there'd be no dawn here. "Do you . . . Do you think she'll be herself?"

"I have hope," Lockwood answered, but his face belied the words. "If she's biddable, we mean to send her back with Paggat and orders to move the camp farther away. It's a risk, and Paggat knows it, but the man had no love of this when we began. He left Chegnon on orders, and walked between the stones yesterday for the same reason. He's a good man, but he'll be braver getting your sister out of these mountains than he'll be climbing higher."

<<Useless,>> Taslim interjected.

Kyle was inclined to agree, though he kept his opinion to

himself. Whatever had drawn Kiera yesterday wasn't likely to let her leave. Knowing something of her fears, he wanted Kiera out of the Eigela for her own sake, but he had little hope and no desire to argue the matter with a man he trusted. Instead, Kyle wished Lockwood the best sleep he could find on the unyielding stone.

Feeding the fire a stick at a time was the only way to measure time, unless one counted Captain Jahn's snores. There was enough wood to keep Kyle busy until the end of his watch, but nothing to keep his thoughts from wandering.

Nothing except Taslim.

<<That's enough, Hart-lord,>> the wizard interjected whenever he gave a passing thought to his sister, the Siege, or the future.

So he thought about the past, about fosterage and Flennon Houle, who loved Kiera and who'd be a fool if he married her now . . .

<<That's enough, Hart-lord.>>

. . . About Roc Dainis and his family, whom he missed, especially Muredoch. Nothing seemed to surprise or unsettle Muredoch. Kyle wished he'd confided more in his eldest brother. He wished he knew what Varos had dreamt. Muredoch knew and Muredoch had told him he didn't need to tell the truth about his Rapture . . .

<<That's enough, Hart-lord.>>

. . . About lying in the sun on a summer day or racing Rawne through a Renzi meadow, chasing butterflies or birds. Maybe a kestrel . . .

<<hart-lord!>>

Hours, or what felt like hours, had passed. With no notion of east or west, Kyle scanned the entire horizon hoping for a break in the darkness. He fed another stick to the fire and watched it burn. There was a pattern to its flames: an arc—

<<That's—>>

A sound drew their attention. Kiera was sitting up with her face hidden behind her hands. Her head bobbed in the firelight. Kyle took a step toward her.

<<Your sword, Hart-lord. Don't forget your sword!>>

He hadn't forgotten it; he'd left it behind. If he needed weapons, there was a knife on his belt, another in his boot. If knives weren't enough, a sword wouldn't help.

"Kiera?" His hand touched her hair. "Kiera, talk to me, let me help you—"

She raised her head slowly. Lockwood had been wrong. Kiera, at least, had not slept the sleep of the innocent. Her cheeks glistened with tears; her lips were dark with blood. Through her fingers, the flickering firelight cast shifting shadows on her face. In memory, Kyle saw another face, the shattered face of his Rapture dream. The faces weren't the same: one, soft, feminine, living, and familiar; the other, harsh and far less familiar than the nightling corpses. But both faces filled his soul with despair. With a sob of his own, he lowered her arms, wiped her bloody palms on his sleeve.

"Oh . . . Kiera . . ."

More tears, another sob that was also a cough as fresh blood escaped the corner of her mouth. But it was his sister who looked at him through eyes that were wide with understandable terror, not unnatural magic. Her hands slid free, reached for his face. Taslim screamed a warning, which Kyle ignored. He didn't flinch when her fingers touched his chin, then traced the rough line of his jaw—he'd grown his first beard—and around his eyes.

Kiera made a sound deep in her throat. A single word: "help" or "home." Kyle guessed; he couldn't be sure. She wouldn't, or couldn't, open her mouth.

"I'll try. I swear—"

"Kyle . . . ?" Another voice, soft yet commanding, stopped Kyle's oath before he could finish it. He looked up at Prince Gravais.

"Your Highness, we've got to get her down from these mountains."

"I know. Soon. Paggat will take her once there's light enough. Pray God they've got the fortitude to reach the valley stones before dark."

The first shading from black to charcoal differentiated the peaks from the sky. Once begun, morning light came as quickly as night had come before. Men stretched and yawned and complained as they levered themselves off their rocky beds. Lockwood was the last to awaken. The other men had kept their distance, but not Lockwood, who crouched next to Kyle and frowned when he saw the blood.

"She'll leave. She'll go down the path with Paggat. I know she will," Kyle whispered. "The Siege calls to her because she saw the Harbinger in her Rapture dream, but she doesn't want to go."

"It doesn't call to you, hart-lord? Didn't you share the same Rapture dream? Or was that a story to entice foolish wizards, priests, and kings?" Gray demanded. He'd followed Lockwood, overheard a remark not meant for his ears, and was suddenly very much a prince. "Which one of you dreamt of the Siege of Shadows, hart-lord? Which one of you leads the race?"

Kyle looked nowhere but at his sister. Three seasons had passed since they turned seventeen, since Kiera burst into his bedroom complaining that she'd dreamt of a sunset. But he'd told the first lie when he said that he hadn't dreamt.

"Kiera," he said softly, hoping she could hear and would respond. "We went too far."

Fresh tears flowed over her cheeks. Kyle swiped them with his thumbs, then stood up to face the prince. A last downward glance showed that Kiera had hidden her face again.

"Your Highness, neither of us dreamt of the Siege of Shadows. Kiera dreamt she saw the Harbinger through a window at our family's hunting lodge. Her Rapture was the dream Taslim made a thousand years ago near here, near the Siege of Shadows. Taslim came to me by mistake—"

<<Wrong, Hart-lord! If you must confess, confess the truth. I planned for a wizard; I didn't consider twins. That was the mistake; the *only* mistake. My dream went astray, not me!>>

Kyle shook his head and the prince said, "It would appear Fawlen disagrees."

"He's wrong, Your Highness. It was all a mistake. All lies. Kiera wanted adventure, first to the lodge, then to Chegnon, then the lies had life of their own. I was told I'd be executed, then exiled, then that I was coming here, and my sister with me. If there is a race, Your Highness, we don't lead it. We should never have left Chegnon, Your Highness. We should all return to the valley—"

<<Impossible!>>

"We should," Kyle repeated softly, "but we can't. Not all of us; I have to go forward. I have to face the Siege of Shadows. Kiera should go back, Your Highness, if she can, and you and the others."

"Did you dream on Rapture night, Kyle?" Lockwood asked, before the prince said anything.

Not "hart-lord," in anger, but "Kyle." Not *what* had he dreamt, but had he dreamt at all. A wealth of implications there, and no time to consider them.

"I thought that I hadn't. There was a face . . ." Kyle saw it again in his mind's eye; Taslim saw it, too, but said nothing. "Not like ours. Like those over there." He pointed across the verge where the corpses lay. "Only more different. Black and white, with holes for eyes. It was broken, with cracks that seeped blood."

"A mask?" Lockwood asked.

He nodded. "A mask. Yes. I saw it again when the priests tried to separate Taslim and me. I heard dragons and saw men dying, but Taslim—" Kyle shrugged. "It's hard to always know the difference between his memories and my dreams. He has been all the way up these mountains. He's seen the Siege."

"But in your Rapture dream, you didn't see the Siege, didn't ascend; and you haven't since?" That was the prince, no less demanding than before.

"No, Your Highness. I'm sure of that, but I believe Taslim: It's ahead of us, and I can sit in it."

"And turn your wizard loose?"

"Yes, Your Highness."

"Then what?"

"I don't know," Kyle admitted, forgetting Gray's titles. "Once I've set Taslim free, I'll have no use for the Siege. I mean to leave its gifts behind—"

<<We can change the world, Hart-lord, we can make it better. *This* will not happen again—>>

"Taslim disagrees, of course. But the power will be mine, and I can leave it behind. I will leave it behind. No one can stop me." He said the last while looking from the prince to Lockwood and back again.

"And the mask?" Lockwood asked, as if he'd perceived neither Kyle's warning nor his threat.

"I don't know where it fits. It could change everything, or not. I don't know. It's Rapture."

Gray cursed under his breath. "Rapture! What's the use of it? You don't know. I don't know. No one knows. I tell you—and God, if He's listening—Rapture's a jest, a damned jest He plays on us!"

"Jest yourself quietly, Gray," Lockwood said: a command, not a warning. "You're disturbing the lady."

Kiera rocked from side to side. Fresh tracks of blood marked her chin as her lips worked. It seemed she bit them bloody to keep words unsaid. Kyle bent down to wipe the blood away again, but she reached past him, to Gray, and, reluctantly, Kyle stepped aside.

In the natural course of their lives, brothers surrendered their sisters—even their twin sisters—to the love and protection of another man. By any measure, Prince Gravais was a good man, good for Alberon and good for Kiera, the man in whose arms she felt safe. Kyle wanted her to feel safe—to *be* safe—as much as he wanted anything, but that didn't make it easier to see Gray lift Kiera to her feet and hold her with a gentle passion that was forbidden to him as both brother and lowly hart-lord.

"I've waited ten years for the red-haired woman who'd be my queen and the mother of my children, my heirs." Gray continued talking to Lockwood as he caressed Kiera's hair. "I've walked away from a woman more than once, because she wasn't the one. And I'm lucky compared to the twins, here. Goddamn, Locky, Rapture's God's a poor jest on all Alberon."

Lockwood lowered his head and sucked his teeth. "It would be, I suppose," he said, slowly meeting Gray's glower again, "if all Alberon dreamt. But it doesn't. There are dreams and there are pretty stories. *I* didn't dream, Gray, I told a pretty story."

The prince's hand dropped to his side. His eyes widened, his nostrils flared. Kyle thought of himself and Muredoch. His breath caught in his throat and he wouldn't have traded places with the wizard for all the treasure in the world.

"You knew—" Gray got no farther.

"I *never* said *she* had red hair. I said she was beautiful. I said your children had red hair."

"But you knew."

"Of course I knew! I knew as soon as you opened your mouth. What was I supposed to do—run up to your father—*your* father, my king—and say 'He's wrong *and* he's lying, Your Royal Highness; I know because I lied three years ago and now he's got my story wrong!' By the bolt, I thought I was the only one ever who had to tell a tale instead of a dream the next morning—until I heard you."

"You could have said something after."

"Consider this as 'after,' Gray. If I'd thought I was going to wind up here, I'd have said something before. You'd think—wouldn't you—that if you were going to wind up on a wild chase like this, God would've warned you."

There was a silence, which Paggat broke.

"He warned me, Your Highness, milord," the blond veteran said softly. "I saw myself in this place, all black mountains and gray sky. But, by my soul, milord, I done the same as you the next day. I didn't tell no one the truth. I told them a story."

"Is there more that you can tell us, Paggat? More that we don't know?" Gray asked.

The man shook his head, then said, "Death and dying, Your Highness."

"Whose, man?" Gray pressed "Mine? Somebody else's?"

"Mine, Your Highness," Paggat said, and they all fell silent.

Wizards told stories, princes and common foot soldiers, too. But when Kyle let Kiera weave him into her Rapture, the story had brought them all here. Men had died: Josaf, others. Men *would* die—

<<Easy, Hart-lord. You're seeing this wrong way out. Paggat's got nothing to do with us, but he's here—>>

<<He's going to *die*!>> Kyle buffeted Taslim with thoughts of death and, before the wizard recovered, turned to the prince. "Please, Your Highness, say it's all my fault and let me be the one to fix it. I'll go on alone. But take Kiera far away from here." He dropped to one knee, bowed his head, and held out his hands, palms up. It was the most solemn entreaty one man could make of another, a complete surrender of honor in exchange for a promise.

"Rise, Kyle, there's no need for this." The prince shed Kiera gently and brushed Kyle's hands aside. "My mind was made up about Lady Kiera before you took the watch, before any of this."

Kyle drew in his arms, but did not rise. "Your Highness, there were lies. Even in the dragon chamber, there were lies and men have died because of them."

"As God wills, Kyle, when this is over, we will sit down at a counting board to measure our blunders, but not before. We came as friends; an oath now would be dishonor to us both. Get up!"

He started to rise on his own, but Gray seized his arm and pulled him up fast.

"No more of this, Kyle, understood?"

Kyle did, and stepped out of earshot as Gray once again put his arms around Kiera and whispered to her. She shook her head no several times before nodding a hesitant assent.

"Paggat, what say you now—ahead with us, or back with the lady?"

"Your Highness, God willing, I'll see her out of these cursed black mountains by sundown." The towheaded Paggat dropped to his knee before Gray and had his oath accepted with a hand clasp. "The sooner we're gone, Your Highness, the better. If the lady's ready . . . ?"

Kiera still wouldn't speak, but for her answer she took a step toward the downside path.

Paggat's sword was already slung below his waist. His bulging pack was ready where he'd slept. He snatched it up one-handed and threw it over his shoulder. With the other hand he kept an easy grip on Kiera's wrist, leading her across the verge. Paggat craned his head around when he set his foot on the downward path, flashing them all a confident salute and smile. Kiera never looked back. They were both gone from sight and sound in a handful of moments.

"Well, my men," the prince said, clapping his hands for their attention. "No sense standing here. Sooner gone, sooner back. Break camp."

Lockwood took his place behind Gray as they continued up the black mountain. The pace was easy enough and the pack no strain to carry. He'd been as strong as most men before Lady Sabelle's whim plucked him out of a monastery stable, a trait he assumed he owed to his nameless father. Between them, he and Usheff could carry all the gear—not that he planned to volunteer his shoulders anytime soon. While other men had to mind their feet and their breathing, he could let his thoughts wander.

They wandered to his stomach first, and he retrieved a withered stick of smoke-dried meat from the hem of his shirt. Tearing off a sizeable chunk with his teeth, Lockwood set about the lengthy, not entirely unpleasant task of chewing the homemade leather into submission. With his appetite thus assuaged, his thoughts roamed a bit further . . .

Kyle Dainis intended to free himself from Fawlen, then

turn his back on whatever power the Siege of Shadows offered. That was hardly what Magister Marrek wanted, but the magister was trailing after King Otanazar, not trekking through the Eigela, if they were still in the Eigela. Magister Marrek hadn't seen dragons or Jivernaise nightlings or Kiera Dainis' bloody lips. Marrek didn't know about Kyle's true Rapture or poor Paggat's. Moreover, in the end, Magister Marrek would only know what Lockwood and the others chose to tell him.

As wizards went, Lockwood knew he was brash and vulgar, but also talented and damned hardworking. He reveled in lightning's dangers and delighted in taunting his enemies. Fawlen and he had at least that much in common. He liked power for its own sake and, knowing his weakness, was careful to earn what he used. The Siege didn't tempt him; there were bound to be strings attached somewhere.

Kyle's idea of leaving the power behind struck him as the best he'd heard since Marrek first told him he was joining a fool's cohort. Lockwood decided to give Kyle whatever help he could, then tore off another chunk of meat.

He had no illusions about their path. There was nothing natural about these mountains. The black rock beneath his feet and at his right side wasn't real. The chasm on his left might be as deep as it appeared, or it might not. He wasn't about to try his luck walking on air, but he wasn't surprised, either, when the chasm closed up and they found themselves in a rubble-bottomed ravine some six paces wide. Its walls towered, but they were jagged, not sheer. The wizard sensed that the mountains could spawn deadly rocks at any moment.

The ravine cut left and right according to a mad god's whim and came to an end in a steep rampart rising some twenty-five or thirty feet, just enough to be inconvenient. By what they could see from the bottom, it seemed that there was another verge at the top and a left-side mountain path beyond it. Jahn Golight heaved a rock at the slide and swore mightily when it loosened enough debris to cripple a man.

"One man at a time," the captain decreed. "First man takes a rope, to steady the others. Usheff!"

Usheff had the rope, and a willingness to be the first up the rampart, but Jahn wouldn't send a man who didn't understand danger into that danger. The captain took the coil over one shoulder and started up the slope himself. Golight hadn't clambered far when there was a thump farther up the rampart, and rock shifted all around him.

Another stone hurtled down the rampart. The captain backslid to solid ground, cursing man and nature, neither of which was to blame. Lockwood looked up quickly enough to see a silhouette disappear into the jagged shadows.

"Enemy atop!" he shouted and raced for shelter as a barrage flew at them.

He caught a rock on the thigh. It hurt, but did no serious harm. He limped a few paces and dove behind the nearest boulder. A scream behind him announced that someone else hadn't been so lucky.

Gray—

But Gray was shouting orders. The dropped man was Darvet, their archer with the scavenged bow, their best recourse against an enemy they couldn't close with.

Well, maybe their *second best* recourse. A wizard learned a few recourses that weren't in magisterial scrolls, if he skirmished with the cohorts.

The enemy atop the rampart lobbed more stones at Darvet, striking the defenseless man. It was an outrage; and Lockwood wanted to answer it in kind. Massacres started this way, when the enemies stopped thinking of one another as men. Of course, after yesterday, Lockwood didn't think they faced *men.*

Gray darted out of shelter. Another volley came down the rampart, half aimed at Gray, half at Darvet. Gray scrambled out of harm's way, but Darvet took another pounding. One stone barely missed the archer's skull. The Alberonese had gained something, though: Lockwood had fixed the location of an enemy, and the precarious tooth of rock hanging over him.

He reached for his talisman, and stroked his fingertips over the crystal facets, awakening his lightning. The runes forged into the iron veins between the crystals grew warm.

Myas, he thought, directing the essence to a jagged rune at the bottom of the talisman. There was a sting, like the prick of a sharp, hot needle, when he passed his forefinger over it. He thought *tyras*, and held his thumb against the cup-shaped rune at the talisman's top. Then he shouted his boon-friend's name.

"Make it quick. I've got a noisy, nasty surprise for our friends up there."

"Knew I could count on you. Captain, run with me."

"Get ready," Lockwood advised.

There were three aspects of wizardry: gathering the lightning essence and sealing it in a talisman; mastering the shapes and names of the runes, and what could be done with them; and, last but not least, summoning the wind from nasen'bei to carry the spell away from the wizard's fingertips. Lockwood peered deep into himself.

A pair of glowing blue-green eyes awaited him, and below those familiar eyes, a snoutful of teeth that he'd never seen before.

<<Not what you'd call a good idea, Havoc?>>

The haunt's eyes brightened, and so did its teeth.

<<I've got friends out there, you know that. They need what I can do for them. Move aside.>>

Lockwood thought of his haunt as a cat sinking down on its haunches, ears back and tail lashing, but that was only habit. Before today, he'd seen no part of it except its eyes. Unlike Fawlen, it didn't talk, but somehow he knew what it was thinking.

<<Yes, I know someone's watching. Some*thing's* watching and it doesn't like haunts or wizards. We'll have to take our chances: burn our bridges before we cross them and hope there's another upstream. Move aside, let the wind flow.>>

The teeth disappeared. A sweet, musky scent wafted through Lockwood's nostrils, a rumbling purr filled his ears, and elsewhere he felt a soft, plush darkness against his nerves. The blue-green eyes remained, hovering in the place wizards called nasen'bei. It was a different nasen'bei than Lockwood had seen before, but nasen'bei was different every time he looked at it. And on a day when Havoc had bared its teeth for the first time, Lockwood wasn't really surprised that nasen'bei matched the Siege mountains.

Wind came when he summoned it and spiraled down his arm to the waiting spell.

"On three, Gray. One."

He pointed his windswept, tingling arm at the hanging rock where he wanted *myas* and *tyras*, lightning and thunder, to strike. Aiming was a habit born of too many hours' practice at the butts, but wizardry was habit, too, and Lockwood refused to vary his habits when lives were at stake.

"Two."

His fingers came together in the wind that carried the spell away.

"Three!"

There was a flash of light on the cliff above the rampart as Gray and Jahn began their scramble to carry Darvet to shelter. An instant later, maybe less, a sound, like a quarryman's mallet shattering stone, deafened them all. Lockwood saw the lightning-struck rock tumble and saw Darvet rescued. He celebrated his success by clapping fist against palm.

All Alberonese wizards used the *myas* and *tyras* talisman runes to capture their lightning; it had been his singular inspiration to use them to expel a bolt instead. *Wasteful*, Magister Marrek, called it: *childish*, *puerile*. Wizards weren't storm clouds; give a wizard all the lightning essence imaginable and he'd produce a piddling bolt. Lockwood didn't argue with his mentor, and didn't bother explaining what a well-aimed piddling bolt could do in close quarters, or what a piddling drain it was on his talisman.

Grinning to himself, he fingered the crystal talisman again. The way to nasen'bei was clear this time. Havoc was purring; Havoc *loved* to hurl bolts. Its musky scent flew with the nasen'bei wind as he loosed bolt after bolt—six in all—in the verge at the top of the rampart.

The air above their enemies turned gray with dust that roiled down the rampart, choking them as well. Gray ordered them back until it settled. Darvet was conscious by the time they moved again. The archer was battered and light-headed, but his worst injury was a broken arm. The captain would have broken the scavenged bow to splint it, but Gray restrained him.

"We'll see what we find topside before we go ruining our only bow."

It was just the three of them—he, Gray, and the captain—who worked their way up the ravine, boulder by boulder, to the rampart's base. They'd left the other three behind, but they needn't have. The bolts or falling rock might have slain an enemy or two, but it was *tyras* that did the most damage. With hard walls to confine it, thunder wasn't sound, it was death.

Knowing what they'd find, and with an untroubled conscience, Lockwood cleared the rampart first. There were eight bodies scattered across a verge little different from the one where they'd camped last night. Seven had blood seeping from their mouths, noses, and ears. The eighth had been crushed by rock. There were no indications that any of them had moved after they'd fallen. Their blood was layered with fine, gray dust.

"Search them," Gray ordered, and Lockwood nudged a lifeless arm with his toe.

They weren't men, weren't as manlike as yesterday's nightlings. They were no taller than half-grown boys, but as brawny as Lockwood or Usheff. Their skulls were misshapen: too round, too broad, with the usual features subtly misplaced. But it was their sixth finger, a second thumb opposite the first one, that told the tale.

Lockwood drew a dagger from the corpse's belt sheath. The hilt was small for his hand, but long compared to the blade and slightly curved. The steel looked decent, but as a knife it was useless in a man's hand. Lockwood added it to his growing collection of odd weapons removed from odder bodies: the withered corpses, Usheff's nightlings, and now these two-thumbed folk.

Their swords were as bad, but the shorter scabbards made acceptable splints for Darvet's arm. Lockwood continued his examination of the corpses while Jahn did the bandaging, but Gray found the day's prize: a parchment map. Although the lettering was unreadable, it seemed likely that the black marks in the map's center represented the Eigela, as a single red line signaled the path, and what appeared to be the mouth of a cave marked their destination. Beyond the map's Eigela, however, were lines, letters, and blotches of color that bore no relation to the known lands of Prayse.

"No Alberon," Gray mused. "No Bardisk. God have mercy, Locky, what have we climbed into?"

Lockwood took the map out of his friend's hands, rolled it, and tucked it in his pack. "I'm starting to think there's a damn good reason our so-called God hides his face. He doesn't want us to know what he looks like."

"You think God looks like this?" Gray gestured at the corpse on whom he'd found the map.

"No more than he looks like us, Gray. No more than I think he's a god."

"Hesse?"

"Be damned if I know. I've got a lifetime of questions, and we haven't reached the damned Siege! First thing I'm going to do when this is over is blow the dust off the oldest chronicles I can find in Alberon, Stercia—wherever I can find them. Then I'm going to start reading." Lockwood laughed—of the two of them, Gray was the scholar, not him—but it wasn't the jest he made it out to be.

"Pardon, lords," Kyle Dainis, polite as ever, bid for their attention, "Taslim . . ." The young man swallowed hard and started over. "Taslim says we can't wait any longer. We've got to move away from here, no matter what."

"I wasn't aware we were waiting for anything," Gray countered. "And what matter—"

Gray's question answered itself with an all-too-familiar scream. Four dragons were close enough that no one who'd been in Chegnon's dragon chamber could doubt that the creature in the stone and the ones overhead were related—and nothing one man or six wanted to confront on a narrow ledge. The verge, though wider and deeper, was no better. If they didn't find themselves trapped against the black stone, they'd find themselves attacked from behind.

"Back to the ravine," Gray shouted.

Back where there were boulders for shelter and where huge wings might be a hindrance.

But Kyle shouted, "No!" and made for the upslope side of the verge. "We can't go back. We'll be trapped on the wrong side!"

The wrong side of what? Lockwood wondered, then he remembered yesterday's rock slide, and then there was no time to wonder about or remember anything as the dragons plummeted from the sky, talons forward.

Syrk, the death rune, was the best spell, when there was a clear target. Lockwood drew enough essence out through the arrow-shaped rune to send searing pain up his arm past his shoulder; any more and he'd have risked his own death. The nasen'bei wind carried it true to the breast of a scaly beast, where, by all that was just or holy, a dragon's heart ought to beat.

Lockwood's spell found its target. The dragon lurched from the impact, clashing the wrist talons of its wings together, screaming, spitting a venom that, as Fawlen had promised, burst into flames. The stench was enough to drive Lockwood back against the stone but, worse, the dragon righted itself. With no visible damage on its *syrk*-struck breast, it came after

Lockwood with double jaws gaping and talons poised to tear him apart.

There were other runes, some thirty of them, forged into the iron of Lockwood's talisman. None of them leapt instantly into his mind. *Syrk* had failed. *Myas* and *tyras* were as likely to blast him and his friends as they were to affect a dragon. He warded off a gout of flaming venom with nothing more than nasen'bei wind. There was a neglected rune for wind near the bottom of his talisman; he put it to quick use on behalf of them all, but, to a man, their backs were soon against the black rock. Swords were useless, and the scavenged bow, if any one had had the presence of mind to use it, wouldn't likely succeed where *syrk* had failed.

Kyle's warning notwithstanding, their best hope—their only hope—lay in the ravine and the chance that the dragons wouldn't follow them into a more confined space. Fawlen had said the creatures were scavengers who preferred a corpse to a kill, though Lockwood had had his doubts about Fawlen's honesty long before this.

Gray, with Darvet defenseless behind him and Lockwood's windy wizardry supporting him, had worked his way around to the top of the ravine. Lockwood and Kyle were following the same route, but Golight and Usheff were standing firm near the upslope path from the verge. The screams of four dragons drowned the shouts of men no matter how desperate or angry. They were reduced to gestures, equally desperate and angry, in a futile attempt to surmount Jahn Golight's sheer stubbornness. The captain wouldn't take one step toward the ravine. He and Usheff were doomed.

"Damn you, Golight!" Lockwood shouted as another blast of wind shot off his hand to keep them alive for another few heartbeats. The captain had earned his death, but Usheff's only crime was loyalty.

Lockwood was still buffeting dragons when something brushed his arm. He outscreamed the dragons, then spun around with wizardry glowing on his fingertips. It was Gray, back from the ravine, with Kyle and Darvet and—lightning strike him dead—Kiera and Paggat behind them. His heart skipped a beat in shock and missed another handful in pure confusion.

Gray clouted Lockwood hard, bringing the wizard back to his senses, then shoved him around so he could see the dragons, wings touching on the far side of the verge, drawing their serpentine necks back for a final strike against the captain and Usheff. The wizard raised his arm. The repressed wind spell came off his hand badly. Twisted and spun like a windscrew, it had no speed behind it and there was no guessing where the nasen'bei wind would take it. There'd be no time for a second spell, either.

His wizardry had failed. He'd failed—unless he could do something magic could not.

Without the intervention of thought, Lockwood squared his shoulders and took one long, powerful stride toward the dragons. There was a fist, though, tangled in his hair, and another man's determination holding him back. He swung wide with a forearm that had, on past occasions, battered through doors. This time it accomplished nothing.

A dragon opened its mouth . . .

And the miscast, whirling spell slammed into one of the dragons—which of the four, Lockwood, couldn't say. They lurched one against the other, talons scratching rock; wings, necks, and tails tangling. The flailing mass overbalanced itself and with screams and flames disappeared over the edge.

"You did it, Locky!" an exuberant Gray bellowed in his ear. "What took you so long?"

Lockwood stared down at his hand. Opportunity and accident: two of the four pillars of wizardry. How *had* he held his fingers? His wrist? Was position important, or was it the time the spell had spent aging on his fingertips? Memory and practice: the other two pillars—

"Locky! Move it! Fawlen claims there'll be more."

With one final glance down, Lockwood headed across the verge. He grabbed his pack, which he hadn't remembered dropping, and fell in behind Paggat.

Paggat?

Paggat and Kiera Dainis should have been halfway to the valley, not in front of him. There was no time for questions. Dragons screamed behind them amid the roar of a rock slide. Jahn Golight at the front of their line doubled the pace. He kept them moving until panic had become exhaustion, and still they climbed until they came to another verge. Beside them, as they entered it, there was a path rising out of a ravine that could have been the twin of the one where they'd walked and fought earlier.

"We're going about in circles!" Darvet wailed. He was pale around his bruises, and sweating. There was a fresh bloodstain on the bandage cloth binding his splints.

Safe or not, they had to rest, for all their sakes, but Darvet's most of all. Gray gave the order to make camp. Lockwood joined Kyle and Usheff in clambering down the rampart to collect firewood providentially scattered in the ravine.

"What does Fawlen say about this?" Lockwood demanded, brandishing an arm's length of seasoned hardwood.

"He says the mountains aren't the test."

Of course it was Kyle Dainis who answered the question, sincere and earnest Kyle, who nowise deserved the aimless anger Lockwood felt. He hurled the wood at the rock and succeeded only in scaring the owl—which hadn't budged from the younger man's shoulder since yesterday afternoon—into a swooping, panicked flight down the ravine. Kyle started after it; Lockwood restrained him.

"Keep close. It'll fly back. It's not as frightened as it was."

"I think it's had all the scare scared out of it. I have."

"Me, too—when I saw Paggat and your sister. Should've known she'd change her mind and drag him back."

Kyle shrugged. "Don't know, but he was leading Kiera when I first saw them in the ravine."

"Surprised you, too?"

"Yes—but it shouldn't have."

Lockwood cocked his head and Kyle continued:

"Taslim. He was worried about the dragons, but he was *waiting* for something else. Them, I think." Kyle's eyelids fluttered and the muscles of his jaw clenched, but he kept talking. "Taslim knows more than he's told me. It's a game with him. Even now, with everything at stake."

Kestrel returned to Kyle's shoulders, where it preened its feathers.

There was a way to get some answers. It wouldn't be pretty or fair, especially for the owl, but if Fawlen truly wanted to get to the Siege of Shadows, the owl would survive. Lockwood decided to wait until they were back in the verge and had the fire started before doing what needed to be done. The delay gave him that much more incentive.

Paggat had already sworn to the prince, and now swore to Lockwood and Kyle as they approached him, that the path he and Kiera followed came to an end not in the paired-stone valley or in a ravine but—

"Flat into the side of the mountain, Your Highness, milords. Bang-up, just like walls at a corner. And then coming back, we don't come to our old camp. No, not at all, just path and path until we come to that ravine and heard the fighting. Dragons and men who aren't men. Kill or be killed 'cause there's no way down! No way out! We're going to die in here, your lordships. Die like those poor sods by the stones! Just the way I seen it in my dream."

Lockwood dumped the firewood at his feet. His fingers caressed his talisman, drawing its essence. Then, while Paggat swore his frustration and fear, the wizard seized Kyle by the chin and whispered the runes. Kestrel screeched and the nasen'bei wind knocked Kyle to the ground despite Lockwood's honest efforts to hold him upright. Firewood broke the younger man's fall.

"You let him back," Lockwood warned, "and I'll drop you both over the brink. Understand?"

"What's the use? He can't answer you except through me."

"He'll make Kestrel talk, if he wants to. He's a clever bird."

Lockwood ran his fingers over his talisman again, collecting *onda* by itself. *Onda,* quickening, the rune that was to all other runes what salt was to meat, and by itself what salt was to an open wound. He held his hand where Kestrel could see it and Fawlen fear it. Trailing feathers, Kestrel dodged behind Kyle.

"Remember what I told you: Let him back and you're both over the brink." There was a flicker of doubt in the young man's eyes. "Damn it, Kyle Dainis, you want answers as much as the rest of us!"

Kyle blinked and the doubt was gone. Fawlen drove the terrified owl toward the rampart; Lockwood loosed his rune spell and the bird crashed into the black rock.

"Had enough?"

Not then, but after two more *onda* encounters, the owl perched on Kyle's shoulder where it, and Fawlen as well, probably felt safest.

"Very well, what don't you know yet, Marelet?"

The voice had the arrogant qualities Lockwood expected from Fawlen, but framed in the harsh edginess of an owl. There were little screeches between the words, but nothing they couldn't understand.

"Where are we? Who are the men we've fought? Where are they from? Why couldn't Lady Kiera and Paggat return to the valley? Do we have a choice whether we go forward, whether we kill or be killed, as Paggat said? What truly is the Siege of Shadows that lies ahead of us?"

"For the Siege, ask her; for the rest: There is no path, Marelet. It's all illusion; you knew that yesterday when you pulled us out of the gray. So what's the wonder that the mountains move? Those men with the odd ears, the ones with the extra thumbs—I've never seen their like before, but I saw stranger folk the first time, and so will you, because Paggat's right: There's no way down. I didn't think there was, but it took this enlightened cohort to prove it. Set one foot on the path to the Siege of Shadows and you've got to go all the way, or die trying. That's what God wants."

The others had gathered around Lockwood and Kyle. Lady Kiera clung to Gray's arm as if it were the only thing that wasn't an illusion. Her mouth was still clenched tight and bloody, but she was listening.

"We found a map," Gray said. "There seemed to be a cave drawn on it. Is that what we're looking for, a cave?"

"Yes, a cave, a cavern as big as the sky, and a sliver of gold arching out through the void to the Siege itself. But don't think you can look on God's face, Prince Gravais Maradze. God's not looking for royalty. God won't take anyone who's wielded the power of life and death."

"What is this god looking for, then? You?" Lockwood asked.

"No. Does that surprise you, Marelet? Remember, I've had a millennium to think about it. God's power is so great, the least flaw in a man's character becomes his destruction. God wants someone who's unfinished, someone the power can mold and strengthen—"

"Someone like Kyle Dainis?" Lockwood interrupted.

"Or Lady Kiera?" Gray whispered after him.

Chapter Twenty-five

"Kiera Dainis?" The owl screeched the words. "*Lady* Kiera? The Siege of Shadows will shape, strengthen, and mold whoever ascends, but there must be something to shape, strengthen, or mold to begin with!"

Kiera turned away. She hid her face against Prince Gravais' chest and pressed her hands over her ears. The gestures accomplished little. Her hands couldn't keep Taslim of Fawlen's mockery from her ears, and closing her eyes only sharpened the image already in her mind: a vicious little man, waving his fists and sneering as he defamed her.

"What would the Siege want with Kiera Dainis? She's had one thought in her entire, coddled life: find an adoring, gullible husband. No—wait, she had a second one: She wanted *adventure*! Lightning strike—I made a mistake. A moment's oversight on my part and the Rapture dream I forged found its way to her empty, little head. She has a vision never meant for her and now she thinks that she's the one who's been chosen to sit in the Siege of Shadows!"

The prince's arm shifted. His hand covered hers, defending her against this unjust onslaught of words. She could still hear Kyle's screeching wizard, but the words lost their sharpest sting as Gray's fingers wove through her disheveled hair and his callused thumb gently traced the curve of her cheek. Even the din of God's voice which had been in her ears since they approached the mountains, was muted by his presence. Slowly—and ready to stop if he twitched or objected in any other way—she slid her arm around his waist, between his shirt and his cloak, where no one would notice.

His arm shifted again, tightening around her as his heart stuttered, then beat faster. For a moment nothing else mattered. There was no wizard, no black mountains, no Siege of Shadows, no God telling her to hurry.

Standing with her cheek against Gray's breast, Kiera had found the perfect romantic passion that bards extolled in their ballads. She felt the soaring excitement she'd prayed for nightly since she was old enough to understand that "love" was more than what she felt for her parents or brothers. "Love" was a worthy man to whom she'd give her beauty, her loyalty, and her honor and who would cherish all that she gave. Flennon Houle was a worthy man, but Prince Gravais was worthier.

There'd been no declarations between them. How could there have been when he'd been a prisoner of Lockwood's deceit: the tale Lockwood had told when he turned seventeen and which had condemned Gray to wait for a woman who didn't exist? How odd, too, and yet how fitting that neither the prince nor Kyle had dreamt on their Rapture nights. Of course, it seemed that Kyle *had* dreamt and it was Lockwood who was dreamless, like her prince. But Kiera didn't want to think about Lockwood; she wanted to think about Gray and this precious moment when their love bloomed.

This precious moment that Taslim of Fawlen threatened with his lies—

"Jealousy, unfettered jealousy. The greedy ambition of a coddled girl-child who thinks the sun has naught to do but shine on her pretty head. By the bolt, would you have *her* ascend to the Siege over her brother? Think hard, Your Highness, before you answer. Remember her at the king's supper, dancing in the queen's shadow, spilling out of a borrowed gown. Remember her standing safe while good men died around her. She ran when Geregonal swung but had nothing to say when good men went to their rest."

Kiera bit her already swollen lips, suppressed her indignation, and—most important—said nothing. Bad things would happen if she opened her mouth; God's voice was muted, but it wasn't silent and she would repeat the terrible things God said about wizards if she unclenched her jaw.

Gray might not understand.

Bad things would happen.

Gray would defend her. He'd forgiven her for Chegnon, assured her that he didn't for one moment think she was Ezrae Baldescare's puppet. And then he'd kissed her, their one and only kiss amid the graves in a moonlit meadow.

His caressing fingers paused in their course. Tension raced in his muscles, and though Gray didn't push her aside, Kiera could feel doubt brewing in his thoughts. She held him tight, bit down harder on her lips, and prayed to no god that Kyle, her twin, who surely knew how his wizard slandered her, would speak quickly in her defense.

But it was Lockwood, wizard, bastard, and lord of Marelet, who spoke.

"You quibble, Fawlen. By your own admission, she'd have had to kill those men herself before she became unworthy in the eyes of the Siege's magister. The lady's no more guilty of Captain Josaf's death than her brother is and, by that measure, no less worthy of ascending."

Lockwood's damning defense insulted her and Kyle alike!

Kiera's rage whirled like a sea storm. In her struggle to contain it, she nearly missed what Lockwood said next.

"I can think of a reason or two to send Kyle Dainis to the Siege instead of his sister, but I can think of a score to send no one at all."

"You've got no choice, Marelet. The only way out of these mountains is through the Siege of Shadows. He *must* ascend, or you'll wither here, like those corpses in between the stones."

"So you say, Fawlen, but that's not enough, not for me, not for Kyle, not anymore. What's up there? What makes *you* think Kyle Dainis is the right man? The more than merely worthy man. What happened the last time—what *truly* happened? Kyle says you're still keeping secrets, Fawlen. Start emptying your conscience, or I'll do it for you."

"You're a fool, Marelet."

"I'm not the only one, Fawlen. Start talking. You got this far, then what?"

The prince's hand fell away from Kiera's cheek. His attention was on Lockwood and after another heartbeat, Kiera's was, too. Remaining within the protective circle of his arms, she turned around and saw the owl—the little brown-and-gray owl—clamped on Kyle's shoulder. Then she saw Lockwood with a ribbon of white fire writhing between his talisman and his hand.

They *were* fools, both of them. They couldn't hear God, of course. God didn't talk to wizards; God spoke only to her, telling her how much He despised wizards' rogue magic. Kiera despised them, too. If God would have destroyed only the two wizards, she would have done nothing to interfere, but Lockwood's wanton wizardry drew God's attention. God's wrath. God despised wizards so much that God would destroy them all, even her, if Lockwood released whatever magic whirled around his hand. She had to stop them . . .

"*Now*, Fawlen," Lockwood said, low and ominous.

. . . But not with spoken words. Kiera was desperate, without a notion of what she could do, and then the owl solved her problem for her. It stretched its wings and fluffed its feathers and told Lockwood to swallow his spell.

"There's no need for threats, Marelet. What do you want to know? We fought three battles as we climbed. We faced men who looked very much like ourselves, men who were covered with fur, and men who were half again taller than us. We saw the dragons and we felt the mountains move, especially at the end, after the last battle.

"There were five of us left—their names don't matter. The path led into a cave, so we made ourselves torches and found ourselves in a cavern the size of the sky with a golden bridge pointed up and out into nothing . . ."

God had shown that bridge to Kiera. It led to the Siege of Shadows, to God Himself, where He wanted her to come, and where she still wasn't certain she wanted to go. She pulled Gray's arms around her and leaned into his strength.

". . . Our lord went out first, sword in hand, as much for balance; we had no sense of danger there. The four of us watched until he'd disappeared, then waited and made more torches. Night—what passes for night—fell. He hadn't returned and there was no hiding our worry. Lady Meerthee—"

"Your mentor? Your master?" Lockwood interrupted.

The owl let out a long, hooting whistle and fluffed its feathers again before admitting, "My mentor *and* master, yes."

A woman, Meerthee was a woman's name. The great Taslim of Fawlen—whose myth had been exploded when he mistook an owl for a hawk—had come to the Eigela as another wizard's apprentice, and a woman's apprentice, at that. At first breath, Kiera took the revelation as yet one more indication that Taslim should have been drawn to her: He was accustomed to serving a noblewoman. With her second breath, she realized that neither the solstice nor Taslim mattered.

"What did Meerthee do?" Lockwood pressed.

Kestrel credibly shrugged his owlish shoulders. "She went after our lord, what else? Her talisman shone awhile, then it disappeared."

"And? You followed her? You ran away to cast your spells?"

By what she knew about Taslim of Fawlen, Kiera expected the owl to bate with great indignation, but it only swayed from side to side, lifting one foot, then the other. When her little hawk did that, it was anxious and Father had taught her to slip a leather hood over its head until it was quiet again. Kyle had no such mercy available for the owl, even if Lockwood had been disposed to permit it.

"She returned," the owl said, sibilant and reluctant. "Wounded and in torment. Her strength failed as she approached the end of the bridge. I . . . I caught her before she collapsed and carried her safely to the verge where we'd waited. As she died, she told us that our lord had been destroyed and that the Siege would destroy anyone with a bloody soul. She told us the mountains were coming down; our lord had been the last. The Siege was closing and we should run. The men ran, leaving me behind—but I knew, even before she told me, that running was useless. She gave me her talisman and told me to wait for the moment when the mountains converged, and what runes to cast when they did. There'd be another time; she wanted me to bring someone back who could ascend the Siege and do what our lord could not.

"She died in my arms. I didn't have to wait long before the mountains began to move. I cast the runes, and then my wait truly began. You know the rest, Marelet."

The owl sidled close to Kyle's neck and pulled its neck into its shoulders before closing its eyes.

"Can I draw him in, Lockwood, my lord?" Kyle asked. "Kestrel's exhausted and so is he."

Lockwood didn't answer—Lockwood could be as arrogant as Taslim when he chose. The wizard simply scratched his wooly beard and stared at the mountains. Kiera wondered if he saw plain, black stone or if he saw the Eigela as she saw them: rife with writhing red and orange streams of light. Serpents, truly, because they reared up like serpents when they flowed near the verge where the cohort had made its camp. There were more every time Kiera looked, and one of them oozing down the rock at her brother's back.

"*Liar!*" Lockwood roared, frightening them all with his voice, and then a second time, when he loosed a rune spell that went wild and crashed into the rock above Kyle's head.

Or maybe the rune hadn't gone wild—because when the white flash of lightning was gone, so was the orange serpent.

"Damn you, Fawlen!" Lockwood swore, and hurled another spell. "Tell the truth for once."

The spell struck rock, but the serpents were retreating and Kiera didn't think it was a coincidence. The prince and the others, though, including Kyle, seemed only to notice the wizard's bolts. Their attention never wandered from the white flashes—

Except to return to Kyle's shoulder when the owl began to speak again.

"What lies, Marelet? Everything I told you is true."

"As may be—but you haven't told me everything. You say Meerthee was dying—why? Was her soul bloody? A lady magister who did her own killing? What do you take me for? The Siege had been drawing pilgrims for five years. What did Meerthee do to make it close? And what did she truly tell you, Fawlen? What did she want you to do that she couldn't do?"

Taslim was surprised. The little owl's eyes grew wider than circles; it truly did look a bit like Muredoch. Lockwood smiled triumphantly, but Kiera was mystified.

"It would be easier, my lord, if he were with me."

"I'm not interested in making it easier for him. I'm interested in what Meerthee told him about the Siege of Shadows before she died—*if* she died."

"She died, Marelet," the owl said, and it seemed, for a moment, that there was a sense of loss around him. "She'd found our lord on the Siege—what was left of him. There were no cohorts then, but there were wars, and our lord had fought in them. The stain of blood's no lie, Marelet. Carry the death of a man to the Siege of Shadows and your blood burns. That's what she told me and you'd do well to believe her."

"I do, Fawlen. I'm not tempted. Did Meerthee sit in the Siege?"

"She didn't say, but I don't imagine she did. She was a wizard, a magister. I imagine she faced God standing on her own two feet."

"And didn't like what she saw?"

"No. It wasn't God."

Kiera felt her eyes go round and wide as the owl's. Not God? *Not God?* The red and orange serpents halted their retreat and oozed back. In the corners of her mind, God's voice became a roar.

"It wasn't anything she could name or describe, but it was nothing that belonged in Alberon, or Stercia, around the Sea of Prayse, or anywhere at all. Nowhere that men would live free as men, not animals. Just hunger, hatred toward wizards, contempt for everything else."

A wizard's judgment. Another damned wizard's judgment.

"The face of the storm?" Lockwood asked, a sincere question.

And a sincere answer: "I didn't ask; she didn't say. She *was* dying, Marelet. My first thought was to save her. Hers was to tell me that she'd tried to draw it down, like a bolt—but she failed. It was consuming her the way it had our lord, but slowly enough that she'd been able to get back to the verge, to me, before she died. She said—" The owl shivered. "She said she could close the Siege, but I would have to come back to . . . *destroy* . . . it."

There was silence on the verge, silence everywhere, except in Kiera's mind, where God's wrath was a howling storm that threatened to overwhelm her. The score of shimmering serpents had become hundreds. They merged into a single, encircling curtain of fire. But if Lockwood felt the danger, the doom surrounding them, he showed no sign of it.

"Is that what you intend to do?" he demanded.

"Meerthee had a moment. I've had a millennium to think and plan. It's not necessary to *destroy* the Siege of Shadows. We don't *destroy* the lightning when we draw it down. We harvest it, hold it, control it, put it to good use. When Kyle ascends—"

The wind and the rage were too much for Kiera to contain another heartbeat. Shoving free of the prince, she advanced toward her brother and the owl. Fingers of flame from the fiery curtain surged toward her. They were God's fingers, and when they touched her, they would transform her: Kiera Dainis would become God.

Kiera Dainis would vanish, disappear . . . die. The part of her that was Kiera Dainis who loved sunlight and flowers, the Gray Prince, and her twin brother shrank in terror from the destiny, the *oblivion* God held before her. But retreat was the worst mistake she could make; it gave God more of her. Already God moved her feet closer to Kyle, her hands closer to the owl. Once the wizards were gone, God would draw her along the path again—there was only one confrontation left, and God was confident that she would survive, that she was the worthy soul He'd been waiting for.

She would ascend the Siege of Shadows and the world would enter a new age—once the wizards were gone: all the wizards, starting with the owl, starting with Taslim of Fawlen, who should have died long, long ago.

The power was hers—or God's, it scarcely mattered—and she wasn't afraid to use it or enjoy it. Kiera swelled with wild joy as the owl beat its wings frantically, breaking feathers in futile attempts to escape. The owl was too frantic for Taslim of Fawlen to make it speak about destroying the Siege of Shadows before Kiera ascended it. It was too frantic for Kyle to draw the wizard out of it—had he been foolish enough to do such a thing.

If Kyle knew what was good for him, he wouldn't try. She knew his secrets—*God* knew his secrets—and he was defenseless against her. His strengths were wasted; he was weak, and the weak deserved whatever the strong gave them. Kyle might not deserve God's wrath now, but he would eventually—the weak were weak. They disappointed; that was their essence. Why should she wait until he disappointed her again, when with God's strength she could destroy him now?

Madness! This is madness! Kiera thought. She could not dispossess God, but she could, with all her will and determination, wrench the madness away from her brother. Taslim of Fawlen wasn't weak, he was a wizard who'd stand against God and for that treason *he* deserved destruction. A single word would have been sufficient, if, with God's help, she could have found the right one. She tried with whispers and shouts. She imagined Kestrel as a smoldering cinder and Taslim of Fawlen as a fading memory.

Nothing worked.

The panicked owl and equally panicked wizard hovered just out of rage's reach, but not out of the reach of Kiera's still-mortal hands. A word would have been more fitting for God, once she was transformed into God. Until then, if her hands were all God had, then her hands would be enough—one feather, bone, and limb at a time.

Kiera lunged for the owl. Feathers brushed her fingers and then were gone. Everything was gone: the owl, Taslim, Kyle. The fiery curtain was extinguished; the black mountains themselves dissolved into a sparkling gray fog. She looked at her hands, at the place where her hands should be, and they were fog.

Kiera blinked. She knew she blinked; she'd felt her eyelids move, experienced an instant of darkness amid the gray, but the gray remained. It obscured everything. Her fingers flexed, straightened, brushed against one another, and remained invisible. Perhaps if she brought them closer to her eyes?

That attempted movement at Kiera's elbows met resistance. There were heavy manacles around her wrists— No, not manacles, *hands,* another pair of hands. They emerged in the gray: brawny, blunt-fingered, and sparsely grown with coarse, dark hair. Lockwood's hands circled her wrists, imprisoning her, yet steadying her as well and restoring her substance to her eyes.

"Where am I?"

The question was her own. God's voice did not penetrate the fog. Her mind was quietly her own, as it hadn't been since she walked the meadow graves with her prince.

"Right where you were, dear lady, but utterly without illusions."

Lockwood's face appeared with his voice. His was a coarse, common face, too broad across the cheeks to be called handsome, and framed with woolly hair and woolly whiskers. His nose was misshapen; he'd broken it at least once. A lopsided smile and eyes so dark that Kiera couldn't tell where the pupils ended and the color began completed the wizard's disreputable appearance. There was nothing at all attractive about the lord of Marelet—except he wasn't part of the gray fog and, with his hold on her wrists, he kept her apart from it as well.

"Rest a moment," he advised. "Collect yourself, *find* yourself."

"What have I done?"

The lopsided smile became a grin that warmed Kiera before she realized the fog was ice.

"You've given Fawlen the scare of his overlong life, for a start. Can you stand? Feet down, head up."

She'd fallen; Kiera remembered that now. She'd stumbled when she'd reached for the owl and fallen into the gray. Her hands were bruised. They hurt. Her knees hurt, too, and her elbow, and her chin.

"Oh . . . *God,*" Kiera murmured, thinking of the damage a bloody, dirty scrape could do to her face.

"Not very likely, dear lady. Come on now, try to stand up."

"I can't see anything—anything but your hands, your face. Everything's gray! *Illusions!*" She recalled the word Lockwood himself had used and began to shiver.

"Aye, dear lady, but solid illusions, if you'll believe in them. Give it a try. On three, dear lady. One . . . Two . . ."

Lockwood started to rise, lifting her with him. The sparkling fog thinned and Kiera could see the dark mass of the mountains, the moving shapes of her brother, Gray, and the other men of their cohort. She couldn't imagine facing them with a bloody chin . . . couldn't imagine facing them after she'd lunged after a little owl like . . . Like what? Like a madwoman? Like a God-possessed madwoman?

What manner of god would drive anyone to tear another living creature apart with her bare hands?

The deepest and worst fears that Kiera had harbored since the winter solstice were confirmed. She shook her head and pulled against Lockwood's hands. The wizard relaxed immediately.

"Another moment, no more. A place without illusions is no place for a highborn lady."

He squeezed her wrists gently as he smiled and made it clear, in this gray, foggy nowhere, that his teasing had no teeth but was meant to cheer her.

An echo passed through Kiera's mind; it held all the hatred she'd felt for wizards, all the harm she'd intended for Taslim of Fawlen, Lockwood, and her own twin brother. Not God's hatred of wizards—though that was a terrible hatred—but her own hatred, which God had inflamed. Kiera sank onto her knees. Her hair fell forward, hiding her face until her forehead rested against his hands.

"Wrong way."

"I wanted you dead. Taslim most, but all wizards. You. My brother. I was ready to slay you all, with or without God."

"That would have been a mistake." Lockwood shifted his hands, freeing one to smooth her hair. "Your brother's not a wizard and neither, dear lady, are you—for which, I must admit, I'm very grateful. You've got a powerful rage, Kiera, but rage isn't enough, not for wizardry."

"God doesn't like wizards," she whispered.

"Whatever made the Siege of Shadows doesn't like us."

"God."

"Not God, dear lady. Certainly not *my* God. I'll have no part of a god who'd kill me for being what I was born to be. I won't even have a part of a god who'd kill Fawlen for being a wizard, when he's not a very good one and there are so many better reasons."

Kiera almost laughed, almost raised her head. Lockwood's hand slid along her jaw. Her chin came up before his thumb touched it. Their eyes met—why had she thought they were dark when they were the most beautiful shade of greenish blue she'd ever seen?

"And I'm not impressed by a god who'd suborn your will as he's so manifestly done, Kiera Dainis."

"God calls me. He called me when the Harbinger fell, then He was quiet, except, sometimes, in my dreams. He called me again when we approached the Eigela. Now I hear Him all the time."

"Now? God calls you, Lady Kiera, even *now*?"

Kiera shook her head. "No—not now. I can't hear him now." It was a measure of the irreverence the prince's friend wore like an old, comfortable shirt that she could hear his words another way, leading to a different question and a different answer: a confession. "God never called me Lady Kiera, or Kiera or any name at all. God calls me 'child.' Come quick, He says, as if I could. Come alone, as if I could. Leave the others behind, as if I could. Come to the Siege, accept His gifts, do whatever He wants . . . He calls me worthy, but I know I'm not the only one He's calling." And the final confession: "I'm frightened, Lockwood. I'm afraid of what will become of me."

"A wise fear, dear lady," he said, which was not what she'd expected, but reassuring all the same because he'd told her she could trust herself.

She noticed his hands again, because she couldn't look at his eyes. They were a laborer's hands, but they were also clean and manicured, as her own were not.

"You've fought a brave fight, Lady Kiera Dainis, and fought it alone until now. A wise warrior knows when he—or she—needs an ally. You don't hear any voices now, do you?"

Since she'd stumbled into this gray fog, Kiera's thoughts had remained her own, her memories, too. She could remember the ordeal of their overland journey and terror of the last few days, especially the dragons and the six-fingered corpses they'd come to feed upon. Without Lockwood's tainted wizardry, they'd all be dead now. When she'd seen the dragons, she'd prayed to God, but it was wizardry that kept them alive.

Prince Gravais' boon-friend was no proper lord, no proper companion for a verge-lord's daughter. He was vulgar and completely lacking the respect bastards should have for their betters. She disliked him and resented his influence over her beloved prince, but he wasn't an evil man. He'd saved them all, without hesitation before or expectation after. He'd reached into the formless gray fog—

No. He couldn't have *reached* into the fog.

"You? This is your making—a place where I can't hear God's voice, where He can't find me."

Lockwood shook his head sadly. "I wish it were that simple, dear lady. Oh, I made this place—the first thing a wizard learns is how to hide from that storm he just called down on his head. If he doesn't learn that right-quick, he doesn't ever learn anything."

The wizard wasn't a jester, but he could make anyone smile, even her, even here. Smiling lifted her head again, high enough that she could see that he wasn't smiling.

"I can hide you so you can't hear the voice of the Siege, but I can't hide you from the Siege, dear lady, and every moment I hold you *here*, our friends *there* are exposed. Once again—can you stand? It won't get any easier."

Kiera believed him, but she had one last thing to say: "I . . . I still don't like you. I know I should: You're Gray's friend, and Kyle's. I know you're a good man, and I should like you. But it's not enough. I'm sorry, truly, I'm sorry—"

"But Lockwood, cock-wood, he's a priest's bastard, born in a cow barn and should've stayed there? Risen too high; forgotten his rightful place? He's insolent; he should be flogged or put to sea in an oarless boat? I've heard it all before, dear lady. Nobody *likes* an upstart between them and the throne. There's scarcely a verge-lord in the kingdom who hasn't wanted a piece of my hide, but not one of them's succeeded. Remember that."

The blue-green gloss had faded from Lockwood's dark eyes, his good humor, too, as if it were a harvest-moon mask. Bitterness hardened his face. He no longer looked common; he reminded her of Geregonal, only shrewder and without the Black Lightning scars, of course.

"You know, Kiera, I think I would have lived a better life in the cow barn. Happier, anyway. I didn't ask to go to court—I wasn't looking for adventure. Tradition says a young prince needs a whipping boy to take his punishment. As I see it, the old queen figured Gray couldn't make enough trouble to kill me, so she sent me off. I'm lord of Marelet now, but I've never been back. I grew where they planted me; common weeds do that. I went from whipping boy to boon-friend. Gray means more to me than life itself. If you're the woman he loves, then I'll accord you the same. But you've been careless with your company, Kiera Dainis: questionable priests, questionable queens, questionable gods. When it comes to Gray, I don't care whether you like me; I don't even care if he loves you."

Kiera gulped and blinked. The fog thinned to a sheer mist. Black mountainside filled her vision again, along with the silhouettes of the people she knew, and beyond them the probing fire-fingers of God. But none of them were as important as Lockwood's final words.

"Does he?" Kiera asked before she thought to censor herself. "Does the prince love me?"

"I like that not," Jahn Golight said, giving a nod in front of him, to where Lockwood and Kiera had knelt, one facing the other, in a shroud of sparkling light.

Lockwood's back had arched suddenly away from the lady. His mouth gaped, his face was toward the sky—what men thought of as the sky elsewhere. Since Lockwood had wrapped himself and Kiera in wizardry, the sky here had swarmed with streams of light in colors a man hoped never to see again.

Gray was more worried about the light than he was about Lockwood. "He's laughing," he told Golight and the others.

Paggat complained, "He don't make no sounds."

"Wizardry," Gray assured them, adding a silent plea that his friend put a stop to it quickly.

There were voices in that swarming light, and if he could hear them, it was likely the men did, too; and just as likely that Locky was the reason they hadn't heard anything before this. Gray didn't fault Lockwood for isolating himself and Kiera in that wizardry cloud he could spin out of his talisman. He'd seen Kiera's eyes as she advanced on her brother and the owl. If Lockwood hadn't acted quickly, there'd have been another death on his conscience.

Another death between him and the Siege of Shadows? The voices said no, he was a prince, he hewed to a different standard than other men, lesser men. God would welcome him with open arms.

The way God had welcomed Fawlen's nameless lord? Or the crown prince of Pelipulay? God had already given Gravais Maradze a keen memory for the names he read in the royal chronicles. The overhead voices couldn't tempt him—not yet.

Damn, Locky, settle it. Get yourself back here *where you're needed!*

He could reach into the sparkling light. He'd get their attention and learn what they were laughing about. Gray wasn't a jealous man, or he hadn't been, but a man had to wonder when he saw his best friend and the woman he'd just begun to love in the throes of uncontrolled gaiety.

It would be different once he had the power of the Siege of Shadows, the power of God to know another man's thoughts—

Lockwood!

Lockwood couldn't hear Gray's thoughts, and neither could Kyle Dainis, but Kyle was the one who came forward, with the owl still clinging to his shoulder, and thrust his hands into the wizard light, one hand on his sister's shoulder, the other on Lockwood's. The sparks spun away in an eyeblink; the resonance of Lockwood's laughter echoed a heartbeat longer—until Kyle pointed at the sky.

"This god's a nasty bastard, isn't he?" Lockwood said as he got to his feet, raising Kiera with him.

She seemed calmer, more herself than she'd been in many days—if Gray could convince himself that he knew Kiera Dainis well enough to know when she was herself. He offered her his hand, her brother did the same, but she preferred to stand by herself. Perhaps if she hadn't had to choose between them . . . ?

"Ah, but so am I," Lockwood finished.

There was a bit of drama in every wizard Gray had known, more than a bit in his boon-friend when he flung his arms wide, baring his breast to the sky. The unholy voices began to fade from Gray's hearing as the unnatural lights drew together, attracted to Lockwood—as lightning was attracted to any wizard. But it wasn't all drama. Gray knew Lockwood well enough to know a real battle took place in the moments before quiet darkness was restored.

"Can you hold?" Gray asked, hiding his concerns beneath a layer of royal presumption and command.

"From now until the end of time. If that's the best he's got, we've got nothing to worry about," Lockwood said, turning toward Gray.

A cold shiver raced down Gray's spine: his friend's eyes were glazed and unfocused. In his heart of hearts he believed Lockwood was blind—and trying to hide both the infirmity and the terror that came with it: A blind wizard was a defenseless wizard in a storm. Matching bravado with bravado, he took a stride and seized Lockwood's still-outflung hand. His knuckles screamed protest when his friend's fingers tightened.

Gray didn't clearly remember life before Lockwood, who was three years older than him. He couldn't remember a time when he'd felt a tremor of fear like the one that passed from Lockwood's hand to his.

"I've got you," he whispered, collapsing his arm and pulling the wizard close. "What else?"

"Nothing. Time. It's passing." A sigh that started in Lockwood's toes split his lips. "It's passing," he repeated and relaxed his grip. "It's all right, now."

"Thank God."

"Which one?"

They arm wrestled a moment—the Chegnon men were used to witnessing the liberties they took with each other—then Gray released Lockwood with a shove. "Damn you, Locky, for scaring me."

"Anytime, Gray," the wizard replied, a breath too slow for conviction.

Their eyes met, which should have been a relief but wasn't. Gray had come too close to losing his indestructible friend to breathe easily. But there was no time for reflection and no way down this black mountain except by going farther up. He was the Crown Prince of Alberon; it was his right—his duty—to lead the way.

"I believe Meerthee was correct," he began. "The power of the Siege of Shadows is nothing the Maradze want in Alberon. If it can be destroyed, I want to destroy it."

A thought came to Gray as he went on to confess the temptation he'd felt from the sky during Lockwood's wizardly preoccupation with Kiera Dainis: He was going to die a prince, like the older half brothers he'd never known. Whether they succeeded in destroying the Siege of Shadows or not, they were all doomed, all as dead as the men they'd already buried. Little Nyan would inherit the throne. His name was Nyan Maradze, but he'd be Baldescare by the time he was crowned; the Bitch and her uncle would see to that. The Maradze were finished, like so many dynasties before them.

Gray's acid thought seared his soul as it sank to the pit of his stomach, collecting fear, resignation, and rage as it fell. He scarcely heard Captain Golight and the others confess similar temptations. There'd be no reign of justice and prosperity associated with his name. There wouldn't even be the personal satisfaction of destroying the goddamned Siege of Shadows himself. To a man, and one chastened woman, they agreed that the dubious honor of confronting the Siege of Shadows belonged to Kyle Dainis, steadfast and sober Kyle Dainis, who'd gone as pale as he'd been in Chegnon's dragon chamber.

"I'll try to destroy it. I'll do my best," the young man said when the discussion drifted his way. "I'll be careful."

"Will *he* help?" Lockwood asked.

The "he" was Fawlen, with whom they no longer spoke directly. The last thing Locky needed—according to Locky, who was hard-pressed by the Siege's hostile magic and still shaken by his brush with blindness—was a feathered, defenseless wizard sitting on someone else's shoulder. He'd given Kyle permission to draw Fawlen in.

Kyle answered, "I think so, maybe. It doesn't matter, does it? I'll do my best, with his help or without it. Maybe I can do as much as Meerthee did, and you can cast Taslim's runes to keep you all. . . . To preserve you until the next time."

Jahn Golight hawked into the fire as soon as Kyle was finished. "No, thank ye kindly, my lords. No runes for me. All's I hope to get out of this is a good death with my sword in my hand."

The common soldiers huddled beside the captain shared that hope—and they might get it. Both Kiera and Taslim had spoken of a third skirmish before they attained the Siege of Shadows. This time they held the verge. They'd have the high ground and they'd lay the ambush. On Gray's order, they broke apart the fire and slept cold—if anyone slept at all, which he doubted—until black night yielded to another charcoal dawn. The red, orange, and yellow streams faded in the growing light, but didn't disappear. Lockwood maintained his vigil, as he had throughout the night.

"It knows where we are," the wizard said, rubbing red-rimmed eyes. "It knows that Lady Kiera no longer listens to its call, and what we mean to do."

"And?" Gray asked, knowing there had to be more.

Lockwood slapped the black rock beside him. "It's all illusion, Gray—this cliff, that path." He pointed at the ravine. "You're wagering that there's someone walking toward us, but the Siege has the dice."

"What are you saying? That we shouldn't stay here? That we should climb instead? We could climb forever or come face-to-face with a wall, as Paggat and Lady Kiera did yesterday. The Siege doesn't just have the dice, Locky, it's got all the rules."

His friend shrugged, then nodded; Kyle did the same.

Gray drew his sword from its scabbard. "We stand here and we pray to the true god, the Hidden God, that we're standing in the right place."

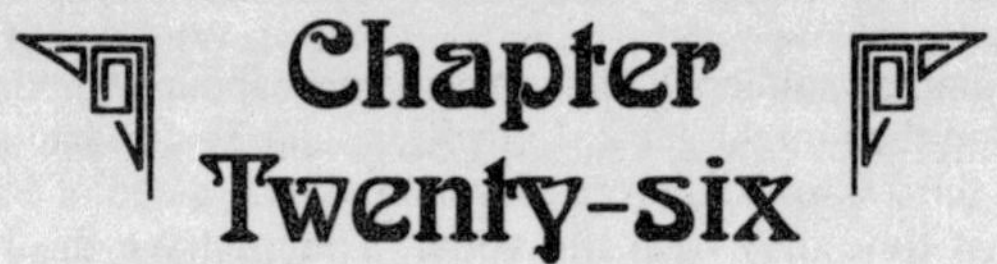

Chapter Twenty-six

Kyle ignored Gray's call for prayer. There were no gods in these mountains, but there was destiny, his destiny: another skirmish, falling rocks, and a bleeding, black-and-white face.

<<Your *destiny* is the Siege of Shadows, not a loser's corpse!>> Taslim protested. The broken mask transformed to darkness and a rising arch. <<Your will is the power. We can conquer it, or destroy it, whatever you decide, Hart-lord, but the Siege of Shadows is your destiny.>>

Kyle countered with the warrior's broken, bicolored face, larger than before, and held it steady despite the wizard's attempts to obliterate it.

"Problems?" Lockwood's voice, Lockwood's crooked knuckle in the corner of his vision, stroking the owl's breast.

"A difference of opinion. Why should that change now? And you?"

The wizard lowered his hand before he shrugged. "Don't worry about me, Kyle."

But it was difficult not to. Lockwood's battle had begun last night when he pulled Kiera back from the brink of madness. While the rest of them huddled under their blankets, the wizard had waged countless skirmishes against malevolent light that slithered down from the sky. And at dawn, when they could see their hands in front of their faces and the fever sweat on Darvet's brow, Lockwood had reached for his talisman again. The iron-bound crystals were still bright and swarming with sparks, but the wizard himself was hollow-eyed and his hand, when he raised it to stroke Kestrel's feathers, trembled with weariness.

"Is there something, anything that I could do—or Taslim?"

<<*Me*?>> his own companion sputtered. <<Why would *I* do anything for Marelet?>>

Taslim needn't have feared; Lockwood shook his head. "Take care of yourselves."

Kyle caught the wizard's hand before it withdrew. They arm wrestled a moment, as Lockwood and the prince had done last night. They'd begun to draw away from each other when a dam burst inside Kyle and he gave into the yearning he'd felt since that night in Gray's Chegnon chamber. Kestrel shrieked—and Taslim did, too. Kyle ignored them both; he embraced the lord of Marelet with his arms and his heart until his lungs cried out for breath.

There was a tear in Lockwood's eye when Kyle straightened his arms—or maybe it was in his own eye, because it was gone after he blinked. He didn't know what to say for himself, so Lockwood said it for him—"Later, friend"—as he bumped a fist gently against Kyle's arm, then walked away.

But Taslim got the last words: <<You have a generous soul, Hart-lord.>> Disgust and admiration were completely intertwined.

The sky had brightened to a lusterless ash-gray. There were no shadows by which a mortal man could measure time's passage, only the rhythms of his body, grown less reliable after a sleepless night. Kyle guessed it was noontide when Paggat let out a yell and pointed at a cluster of black dots high overhead.

"Dragons!" Gray sprang to his feet, one fist thrust into the air. "The trap's sprung! Someone's coming!"

<<He's mad,>> Taslim suggested, as the prince tried to rally them.

<<Speak for yourself. We're all a little mad, I think. Even you.>>

<<True enough.>>

They planned a simple, bloody ambush. The ravine they guarded was shorter and shallower than the one they'd fought in yesterday, but the tactics would be much the same, with them holding the highground. Whoever advanced along the ravine had no retreat, no alternative except the verge where the Alberonese awaited them. Gray had their scavenged bow and a handful of arrows with oddly shaped, but sharp, metal heads; he'd pick off as many of the enemy as he could. Lockwood had his talisman and responsibility for any wizardly folk who might try to do to them what Lockwood had done to the six-fingered folk.

The rest of the men, except for Darvet, who rested in such shelter as they could create for him, had swords and orders to stay down among the boulders until the enemy was in the verge. Kiera had Darvet's sword beside her when she appeared in front of Kyle's rock.

"May I wait with you?"

Kyle shuffled sideways. Kestrel took flight.

"Taslim?"

"Is with me."

Kiera lay the naked sword between them. She knelt down and began twisting her hair into tight plaits. She had one half-finished before she let her breath out in a sigh. "You were right."

"About what?"

"The other night—I heard you talking to Lockwood and Gray. I couldn't say anything then, but you were right. We went too far and now there's no way back. No way at all. I'm so sorry, little brother, so very sorry."

"Don't be."

She sank back on her heels, loose hair spilling over her face and hands. "You're still angry with me. I can't blame you. I've ruined your life. Why should you forgive me?"

"There's nothing to forgive, Ki." He reached out and brushed her tangled hair aside. Her face was as sad as he'd ever seen it, but her eyes were dry; she wasn't crying. He hadn't intended to be so abrupt with her. "This is my Rapture, Ki. This is what I dreamt. I've remembered it, bit by bit as we go. I belong here."

"With me beside you, all covered in dirt and blood and stinking like last month's dirty linen?"

Kyle shook his head. "I don't know about the smell."

<<Liar!>>

<<What's the harm?>> he asked as Kiera succumbed to the bright, cheerful smile he hadn't seen in a long time.

<<The *harm* is, it's not the truth, Hart-lord. You didn't dream about *her*!>>

<<I didn't dream about you, either.>>

Exaltation deafened Kyle's inner ears. <<Ah—the moment of truth, at last, Hart-lord. Rapture is *not* destiny!>>

Kiera caught him smiling to himself. "He—Taslim, he's talking to you? About me?"

"No, he's not," Kyle said firmly, and cast the protesting wizard out of his mind with a question: <<Very well, Taslim—What did *you* dream on your Rapture night?>>

Not that Kyle and his twin had more to say to each other—or, rather, they had a lot to say, but Gray didn't want his cohort chattering and, even if Gray hadn't objected, there wasn't enough time to say it all. It seemed wiser to sit in silence instead. The owl returned to its accustomed perch on Kyle's shoulder and, shortly thereafter, Taslim crept back into his awareness.

<<I dreamt that I could fly, Hart-lord. When I cast Meerthee's spells and set myself adrift in time, I thought that I'd come to my destiny. I was wrong.>>

Kiera had fallen asleep; Kyle was floating toward a nap when a pebble struck the side of his head. He whirled around to see Lockwood pointing toward the ravine and, just as quickly, clamped a hand over Kiera's mouth as she awakened. She gasped beneath his hand when he pointed at the ravine, but collected her nerve with a blink of her eyes.

Moments passed, long and endless. They couldn't see anything but gray sky and black rock, couldn't hear anything but the sound of their own breathing. Kiera clutched the stained hilt of Darvet's sword. Her knuckles turned white and Kyle walked his fingers across them, urging her to relax.

<<Better to let her do all the fighting, Hart-lord. I tell you, it's all for nothing if you use your sword.>>

Kyle stifled Taslim with a whirl of will. He'd heard a sound and then another coming out of the ravine. Rising as tall on his knees as he dared, he could see Gray with an arrow nocked and another clenched between his teeth. On the opposite side of the gap, Lockwood had one hand covering his talisman and the other one shielding his eyes.

The verge was silent, and so was the ravine. Were it not for Gray and Lockwood, Kyle would have thought he'd been mistaken, but those two had fought in Pelipulay. They were veterans, same as Captain Golight, Paggat, and even Usheff, who'd risen to his feet: a great, shaggy bear with a two-handed sword. Kiera started to stand. Kyle seized her arm, holding her down, not to please or aggravate Taslim, but because an ambush was no place for beginners to stick their heads up, especially not when opposition didn't seem to be making mistakes.

He was watching Gray, thinking the ambush would begin with an arrow's flight. He was looking in the wrong place, leaping to the wrong conclusion. The folk in the ravine were wary and they, too, had a wizard. A wall of flame boiled through the gap between Lockwood and the prince. Lockwood countered faster than Kiera could scream: a flash of white light and a thud—as of a door slamming shut at the distant end of a long corridor. The flame was reduced to foul-smelling smoke and pale ash that fell on the black rock like snow.

Gray shot his first arrow and was nocking the next when Lockwood loosed another rune. This spell had the flash and crack of a thunderbolt, followed by the crumbling crash of shattered rock Kyle remembered from yesterday's battle. Lockwood hurled more thunderbolts; Gray shot his remaining arrows, then tossed the bow aside in favor of his sword.

Cut off from retreat by Lockwood's wizardry and the illusory mountains themselves, the enemy charged up to the gap. They were fearsome creatures, tall and lithe, with shaggy hair and grotesque, painted faces, though none bore the swirling black-and-white pattern Kyle recalled from Rapture. Their swords were long and curved slightly toward the tip. Kyle judged them light and ineffective weapons until a warrior with a green-and-yellow face slashed through Captain Golight's arm—cloth, flesh, and bone together.

The captain went down with a silent scream. The green-and-yellow warrior looked for his next victim: Kiera. She froze in panic, but Kyle would have clambered over the boulder to put himself between her and the warrior even if she hadn't. Taslim was nowhere in his thoughts as Kyle raised his sword in the straightforward Alberonese guard stance. He saluted his enemy with a fleeting nod and met a slashing attack like none he'd imagined. Courtesy of his afternoons in the Chegnon arena where he'd encountered style after unfamiliar style, Kyle had learned to think while he fought, getting an arm's length of tempered Alberonese steel wherever it needed to be.

If he couldn't manage a killing counter thrust, it wasn't because he lacked a warrior's spirit or because his thoughts were bound to the Siege of Shadows. The green-and-yellow warrior was a master of his craft. Kyle needed time to uncover the enemy's weakness—just as the enemy probed for his own. He thought he'd spotted a consistent mistake, a moment when the lithe warrior's flank was exposed after each off-side parry. After one more feint to test his assumptions, Kyle was ready to commit himself to a deadly attack.

And damn the Siege of Shadows.

He'd thrust once, beat aside the warrior's off-side parry, and was behind his sword's point when a steel-driven breeze swirled in from his left: Usheff swinging his two-handed sword like a woodsman's axe below the green-and-yellow warrior's ribs.

"You don't fight! You don't kill!" the Jivernaise giant shouted as he yanked his blade free of the corpse. "No blood. No blood on you. Stay back!"

Kyle blinked twice, recovering from the shock of an unfinished attack. He grabbed Kiera and pushed her to the ground behind a rock, but he didn't join her there. He studied the skirmish quickly, looking for an unengaged enemy or a friend in need of help. His cohort companions were evenly matched and holding their own. He edged around to the gap where the enemy's reserve—if they had one—would be waiting for opportunity.

A handful of bodies sprawled in the gap and along the bottom of the ravine. None were moving; none were threats. Kyle turned back to the verge skirmish in time to see Lockwood using his cloak as a diversion against a swift and tall enemy who thought—mistakenly—that he had the advantage. The wizard closed fast enough, kicked faster, and finished the warrior with a thrust from the dagger beneath his cloak.

Their eyes met—Kyle's and the wizard's. Lockwood winked, and then they were both observers, keeping a wary eye on the combat, waiting for opportunity. The Alberonese had won. Only the prince and Paggat were still engaged. Gray called a halt, retreating a pace and opening his arms as he shouted for the blue-faced man in front of him to lay down his sword, but neither the words nor the gestures were meaningful to the lean warrior. The enemy charged, and so did Lockwood—without his sword.

The wizard grabbed the enemy from behind as Gray moved

in to disarm him. But the blue-faced warrior would sooner die than be taken. He threw his sword at Gray—who easily beat it aside—then, before Lockwood could stop him, he drew a dagger from his belt. With an eerie war cry he stabbed once into Lockwood's forearm and a second time into his own gut. Lockwood staggered backward and the blue-faced warrior dropped first to his knees, then onto his face, driving the knife hilt-deep.

That left Paggat and a warrior whose face was as red as blood.

"Make a circle," Gray shouted. "I want him alive. We're *not* murderers!"

Kyle picked up Lockwood's sword and handed it to him as they joined the prince and Usheff in a wary ring around the last combatants. Paggat was bloodied, weary, and ready to step out of the slow-moving duel when Gray's sword made it possible.

"Defend yourselves, if he attacks," Gray advised warily, lowering his guard. He got the warrior's attention and shouted, "Peace," and "Surrender," and "Drop your sword."

Taslim's thoughts impinged on Kyle's; he pushed the wizard away before words formed. He stood on one side of Gray; Lockwood stood on the other. The wizard held his sword steadily, but there was blood on his sleeve and he might not be as fast or strong as he'd need to be if the enemy chose to attack rather than surrender. Kyle didn't want to risk another fatal hesitation.

There was no risk. The red-faced enemy looked at Gray, looked at Lockwood, looked at him, then threw his head back and, with the same warbling war cry as before, reversed his sword in his hands. He plunged the blade into his gut and fell forward.

"Damn!" Gray swore as he threw his sword down.

<<I don't understand,>> Kyle protested. <<Gray offered terms—>>

<<What terms? We ambushed *his* companions. We look as strange to him as he looks to us. And His Highness, the prince, *shouts* at him! Why shout? I don't think he was deaf, Hartlord.>>

The argument was moot. The red-faced warrior was dead, as was every other garishly painted warrior on the verge. Their attention turned to Captain Golight, who'd dragged himself to the cliff side, where he sat, deep in shock, clutching the stump of his arm against his chest.

Kyle wasn't one to blanch at the sight of blood, but a man and his hand separated by a good five paces was another matter. If there'd been no one else to tend the captain, Kyle would have managed, somehow, but with Lockwood and Usheff already moving, he held it no cowardice to give them all the room they needed. He returned to the gap connecting the verge with the ravine.

Rapture wasn't a perfect vision of the future; he'd known that since they entered these mountains. But he'd believed in the black-and-white face, the broken, bleeding mask. These were certainly the folk of his Rapture, but their faces were painted, not masked, and none of those on the verge had the swirling simplicity of his memory.

He stood at the top of the rubble incline. What he saw in the ravine was no different from what he'd seen in the verge—except for one body lying in the shadows near the ravine walls. The warrior's face was turned away from the gap, but his long, silvery hair struck Rapture's chord. Kyle started down the incline without another thought.

<<hart-lord! No! You *can't* go backward. You *can't* follow another path!>>

<<Another secret unveiled at the last?>> Kyle snarled, but he'd stopped.

<<Secret? What secret? Think about it! The dragons come, the paths change, the victors keep climbing and the losers disappear.>>

Kyle started walking again. <<I've got to know.>> He could thwart any attempt Taslim made to seize his thoughts, but he couldn't ignore the maelstrom the wizard roused in the dark recesses of his mind. With another snarl he returned to the verge.

They'd stretched the captain out on the ground. Usheff knelt at his shoulders; Gray stood at his feet holding the torn remnants of a clean shirt. Kiera knelt on his injured side, holding the ends of a tightly twisted cord. The cord circled Golight's stump and kept blood from gushing while Lockwood chanted *myas* repeatedly. A cone of blue-white light sprouted from the crown of his talisman. When he touched the tip to the captain's wound, the man screamed and his flesh began to char.

Golight lost consciousness moments later, making it easier for Lockwood to complete his cautery.

"Bandage it up in the cleanest cloth we've got," he told Kiera when the work was done. "Be better if we had parchment and rendered grease, but it's cloth or nothing."

Kyle waited while the wizard got to his feet. Both he and the prince noticed that Lockwood's arm was still bleeding freely.

"Flesh wound," the wizard said, peeling back his sleeve. He spoke the truth; the stab wound wasn't serious—not compared to the captain's. It went clear through the muscle, missing the bones and tendons, "Not worth the wizardry."

"You're sure?" Gray asked.

Lockwood spat on his arm and rubbed the spittle into the wound. "I'm sure I'm going to be looking hard for the next storm."

The prince grimaced and Kyle did, too. He'd wanted Lockwood to speak the runes that would pull Taslim out of nasen'bei and put him in Kestrel while he went down into the ravine to take a closer look at the silver-haired corpse. Resigned to Taslim's carping, he'd begun his retreat when Lockwood called him.

"No need to go— What's on your mind?"

Kyle turned, said, "Nothing," and continued his retreat.

Next he knew, there was a tug on his sleeve.

"Spots on a cow, Kyle," Lockwood said, handing Kyle a length of bandage. "When something's bothering you, I want to know about it." He held out his bleeding forearm.

"It's nothing, truly." Kyle began folding the cloth into a suitable shape.

The wizard rolled his eyes.

"A selfish thing: I wanted to ask a favor—until I heard what you said about waiting for the next storm. Now—it's nothing, nothing worth asking." He laid the thickest part of the folded cloth against the wound; Lockwood held it in place while Kyle wrapped and tied the ends.

"*I* decide what to do with my lightning, Kyle. You don't have to like it, and neither does Gray. Now, what did you want? *I'll* decide if it's important."

"It's not—"

"Kyle!" the wizard snapped, and seized Kyle's wrist, giving it a twist as he did.

"I wanted to go down into the ravine—alone—and I'd need you to speak the runes." Lockwood released him. Kyle flexed his fingers and wondered how strong the wizard's grip was when his arm wasn't wounded. "I know: It's a selfish thought."

"As may be, but what you need from me isn't the lightning in my talisman. Give me your hand—"

<<hart-lord, this isn't necessary! I won't say a word. I won't *think* a thought . . .>>

But Kyle didn't trust Taslim's promises. He took Lockwood's hand and made the wind blow from nasen'bei to Kestrel. Lockwood whispered the runes and the transference happened without sparks or pain in Kyle's eye. The owl took sulky flight to a shallow ledge well above anyone's reach.

"Don't be long, Kyle," Lockwood advised and clapped Kyle's back to send him on his way.

Kyle didn't plan to be more than a few moments, long enough to look at a face and fix its true image in his memory. Then again, he expected to nudge a corpse onto its back with his toe. What he got was a man who groaned softly as he rolled, a man who wore a broken, bloody, black-and-white mask.

For a heartbeat Kyle was transfixed, then he dropped to one knee and brushed aside the bloodstained strands of silver hair. He leaned closer, listening for another breath.

"Lockwood! Gray—Your Highness! He's alive. There's one down here who's still alive!"

The blood on the mask came from beneath, from cuts it had made when it broke. Otherwise, there were no obvious injuries—no protruding arrows. The warrior of Kyle's Rapture had succumbed to Lockwood's wizardry. Kyle appreciated the irony as he slipped his hands beneath the lean warrior's back: First they'd tried to kill him, now they'd try to save him.

That was the way of war, the way of the battlefield—or so the veterans said.

Silver hair cascaded over Kyle's arm as he stood—an image not from Rapture, but from the exorcism he'd shared with Taslim. His heart skipped a beat, but Taslim wasn't screaming doom in his ears, the mountains weren't falling around him, and he was carrying the warrior up, toward the verge.

Like those from Rapture, the memories from the exorcism were truth and illusion combined.

Gray and Usheff were coming toward him, offering their assistance. He was grateful. Lockwood's wizardry had added another shifty layer of rubble at the bottom of the ravine. The wounded warrior was lean, but still a substantial burden, and Kyle couldn't see his feet as he walked. He was careful, though, as he always was in such straits, looking at the rocks he could see and thinking about nothing else.

The ground shifted as soon as he put a foot on the rubble incline to the verge, and he nearly lost his balance. It shifted a second time with his next step. Kyle stopped and waited for Gray and Usheff.

"Hurry, Kyle! Don't stop!"

That was Gray, no longer walking toward him, but poised on the slope, one arm stretched behind and clinging to Usheff, the other reaching forward. Kestrel flew tight circles above Gray's head. Pebbles rolled past his feet—

—Toward Kyle, who was mystified, until the stones he stood upon shifted beneath him and a fist-sized rock broke loose from the black wall above him. It landed a few paces ahead, dislodging a stream of smaller stones that battered his ankles and chilled his soul.

Hurry, Taslim said, from the exorcism memory, not nasen'bei. *Save yourself. It's all coming down!*

And he could. If he dropped the warrior, he could clasp Gray's arm in a single long stride and be on the verge with his friends in another two. If he dropped the warrior. Kyle couldn't do that. He couldn't save his own life and leave his destiny behind.

Stones and pebbles had begun to flow like water, and though he hadn't moved, the prince's arm was no longer a stride away. In desperation, Kyle churned up the incline, but for every step he took he stayed a step away from safety. More rocks were breaking loose from the walls, bigger rocks that struck close.

And still he carried the wounded warrior in his arms.

"Kyle!" Lockwood shouted. "Drop him, Kyle! You *can't* bring him up!"

The air was thick with magic as illusion faded and the mountains above the ravine turned gray. Risky as it was, and foolish, Lockwood called on nasen'bei and lightning to give him the speed to reach the young man before it was too late. He shoved Gray aside and back to the verge, where the mountains were Eigela black.

Havoc snarled in the wind. The haunt's eyes glowed with their own light and its teeth were bared. It was enraged and frightened, but the bond between them held and Lockwood could feel the warrior's silver hair against his knuckles—

For a moment.

The wind shifted. It blew from below and with a stench worse than the heart of the dankest swamp. He fought for the fingers and hand beneath the silver hair. If he could get any part of Kyle in his grasp, Havoc would anchor them; Havoc would pull them back to the place they'd left.

But the blasting stench grew hot with the promise of fire to come and Havoc would wait no longer. It buried its fangs in Lockwood's arm and brought him back to solid, black ground. For one moment Lockwood could see Kyle Dainis. He saw Kyle pitch forward in a rain of black rock, falling atop the masked warrior of his Rapture.

And then, the flames roared out of the ground, stinking, reeking, and hot enough to melt rock—far more potent than anything Lockwood could counter with a crystal talisman.

"Kyle!"

Lockwood caught Kiera as she lunged blindly at the flames and wrapped her in his arms, so she couldn't see. Heat and smoke and exploding rock drove them away from the gap. They crouched like frightened beasts against the verge's back wall as thunder shook the mountains around them.

The conflagration ended as suddenly as it had begun, and completely. One moment they were in a fiery hell, the next, a cold, dry wind blew up Lockwood's sleeves, down his neck. Raising his head, he had to blink twice before he believed that he wasn't blind again. It was the world around him that had gone dark.

Beneath him, Kiera Dainis shifted and sobbed. Lockwood helped her stand with him.

The whispered words "God have mercy" came from his right, from Gray. "*Stars.*"

Stars, indeed. The darkness was night, with a familiar moon overhead and familiar twinkling patterns in the sky around it.

"Where are we?" Another voice, Captain Golight's, wound-weak and awestruck.

Lockwood looked about. Under the starry sky was black rock—honest rock, with none of the illusions of the past few days. Ribbons of ice twined across the rock, reflecting the moonlight, reminding the wizard of the malevolent streams he'd fought—how long ago?

"The Eigela," Gray said. "We've come back to the Eigela."

They certainly weren't where they'd been. Lockwood walked across pale, crumbling stones, toward the place where—if memory served—the gap had been. There was no gap now, only the black rock of the Eigela. He put his hands against it and pushed. Nothing yielded; the rock here was solid, hard, and ancient. Kiera Dainis had followed him. She flattened herself against the rock and hammered it futilely with her fists as she sobbed her brother's name.

Lockwood touched her arm and she turned slowly to face him.

"Where is he? *Where is he?*"

"Gone, dear lady. Gone. Kyle found his destiny at the last, and it took him away."

Her mouth opened in a silent scream. Lockwood took her in his arms again, holding her tight and swaying gently until her sobs found her voice.

"Paggat's gone, too," Gray whispered when he joined them. "Darvet's got a few more bruises and Usheff's holding onto his captain for dear life."

Lockwood nodded without missing a beat as he rocked Kiera. He considered stepping aside, but Gray's affection was for Kiera, not Kyle, Dainis and, for the moment, she needed someone who'd loved her brother.

"There's no way out of here, Locky. Look around. We're trapped like snakes in a pit."

He did as Gray asked, and agreed with his boon-friend's conclusions. "Look at the ground." The pale rubble all around them wasn't rocks, it was bones: skulls and ribs, long bones and bony chunks from countless hands, feet, and spines. Here and there he could see a darker lump: a boot, perhaps, or a belt, or a bit of cloth.

"God have mercy."

"You keep saying that, Gray. There is no god."

"There's something, Locky. There has to be something."

"And we've found it, the same as every poor sod who came before us."

"Fawlen didn't mention this place."

"Maybe he lied. Maybe he was never here; maybe Meerthee was a better wizard. Maybe, maybe, maybe—it doesn't matter. We're here now."

"Damn."

"We've got the moon, Gray; we'll have the sun. Wait until light."

Gray didn't have to wait that long. As the moon moved in its westerly course, the shadows around them shifted, all save one.

"A cave," he said, pointing north.

Lockwood nodded. The mouth of the cave was nearly as large as the pinnacle that contained it, as if the mountain were merely a hollow shell. "The cavern," his friend said with a long sigh. "Lightning strike. The cavern of the god-be-damned Siege of Shadows."

Between them, Lady Kiera stirred and poked her head out of the shelter they'd made for her with their cloaks and bodies, as Lockwood and Usheff had done on the wizard's other side for Darvet and Captain Golight.

"I want to see it."

Gray caught her cold hand when it appeared through the layers of cloth. "Later, my lady. After the sun's come up and we can see our way."

She didn't argue, but squirmed about until her cheek was against his breast, not Lockwood's, and her face was pointed north. They all shifted after her, a sea change of emotion turning them away from the blank mountains where they'd lost their friends, toward the hollow mountain.

He slept sometime after that—or, his thoughts wound deep and strange enough that it seemed he was dreaming of thrones and gods and the power to govern a kingdom so righteously, so thoroughly that there'd be no place for fear. King Eigela had ruled that way—both King Eigelas had, the Hesse and the mortal man—and while they reigned, Alberon had been the jewel on the shores of the Sea of Prayse. Could King Gravais III rule so well, if he came to Alberon's throne?

The dream turned strange and dark then. The righteous reigns of both King Eigelas had their fill of strange and dark days, days of rebellion and defeat when flames had leapt up the walls of the black rocs—flames the same color as his hair and the hair of his children.

Gray heard their wailing and awoke with a shudder.

The muted gold-and-amber light of dawn touched the yawning crag. A lacy chain of handholds and footrests emerged from the night shadows as the light spread down the mountain.

He could go to the Siege and be back before the others awoke.

"Not alone, Gray," Lockwood whispered before Gray had gotten himself untangled and on his feet. "If you're going to go, we'll go together, all right?"

Lockwood held his crystal talisman in his hand. It caught the light coming off the mountains. For an instant, Gray was blinded by its light, then his was himself again, with wobbly knees and a pounding heart.

"It's the Siege, Locky. It *is* the Siege. It was calling me. God have mercy, we need Kyle Dainis."

They didn't have Kyle Dainis, of course, but they had his owl. Kestrel greeted them when they gathered on the cavern's lower lip. It settled on Lockwood's left shoulder.

"Is it . . . ? Is he . . . ?" Gray asked.

Lockwood urged the bird onto his fist, where he stroked its feathers and raised it up so he could look straight into its eyes. "Truly, Gray, I don't know. Kyle bade me separate them before he went into the ravine."

That was something Gray hadn't known before, not that it mattered, not that there'd been time or reason for Lockwood to say anything before this.

"In all the confusion, I lost sight of the owl. I thought they'd wound up together; they're bound. If Fawlen's here, alone," he stroked Kestrel's feathers with special gentleness, "I pity him, that's all."

"You can't be sure? Didn't you summon him out once before? And yesterday—the day before—whenever, you made him talk."

Lockwood shook his head, then settled the bird back on his left shoulder. "I had bolts to spare, and Kyle Dainis as an anchor. Now I've got neither." He held up his talisman. The crystals glistened with a sparkling swarm, but not so brightly as Gray had seen them. "Golight needs care." He cocked his head away from the cave, toward the bone-strewn pit where the captain and Darvet sat huddled together under Usheff's watchful eye.

There should, however, have been four people down there.

"Where's Lady Kiera?" Gray asked, and knew the answer before he heard her voice behind him.

"Here. I can do it, Gray; I can do what Kyle was going to do. I can set Taslim free and destroy the Siege of Shadows. I know I can."

"My lady." He looked closely at her face, her eyes, fearing what he'd find there, but there was only Kiera Dainis, the one good thing that might yet emerge from his personal debacle. But the danger was high and the risks were higher. "You need not—"

She laughed and took his hand. "Who else, if not me? There's no other way out of that bone pit."

"If the Siege is too strong, if it destroys you, instead of you destroying it—" Then he'd lose the woman he loved, but that wasn't Gray's deepest fear, the fear he couldn't speak aloud. His lady was charming and beautiful, impulsive and naive. If the Siege chose her without destroying her; if she succumbed to its temptations, the Baldescare would be the least of his problems, the least of anyone's problems.

"If the Siege is too strong for me to destroy alone, my lord, then the lord of Marelet will help me, won't you?"

Lockwood seemed surprised by the question, the request. "If I can, dear lady."

They entered the cavern. The golden bridge was there, exactly as Fawlen said it would be, a narrow, gleaming ribbon leaping away from the ledge where they stood and disappearing God knew where, because the inside of the cavern was *not* the inside of the pinnacle. The inside of the world, perhaps, but not the inside of one mountain.

Lockwood suggested that he and Lady Kiera walk the golden bridge together and she agreed, which set Gray's royal Maradze heart at ease as he bid them farewell. But the sight of them on the fathomless brink froze his soul. He could lose them both. No matter that he'd be doomed himself if he did, he'd die knowing he'd lost them first, that he'd led them to their doom.

Gray was almost relieved when the endless bridge swayed wildly under their combined weight and they knew, before they'd taken two steps, that they could not go together. He was relieved again when they did not ask him who should go first.

Lady Kiera unfastened her cloak, slipped off her boots, and unbound her woolen socks. Then, with her skirt hitched up in the crook of her arm, she set a bare foot into the golden light. The bridge held steady beneath her. She flashed a hooked thumb, the fosterling signal to hold fast—but she had brothers, had had a twin brother—and continued confidently on her way.

Lockwood had rejoined Gray before she disappeared from sight.

"Do you trust her, Locky?" he asked.

"Do you?"

"I do."

"Then, so do I."

They watched in silence as she grew smaller and smaller in the distance, until she was a dark moving point on the golden bridge, until she had vanished entirely. Then they waited—him, Lockwood, the owl on Lockwood's shoulder, and the three men below. Gray considered going to the lip and shouting out what had happened, but he could tell them nothing that would truly ease their minds, and more than that, Gray felt that if he broke his vigil, even for a moment, he'd be breaking faith with Lady Kiera.

Moments became minutes and minutes became an eternity. He'd have welcomed conversation, if Lockwood would have started it; the silence was too heavy for him to break. And perhaps it was the same for his boon-friend. Whenever Gray did glance sideways, neither the wizard nor the owl on his shoulder appeared to have moved.

"Lockwood!" Kiera's voice, shrill with fright, echoed through the vast chamber. "Lord Marelet—help me! *Help me quick!*"

They looked at each other and started walking toward the golden bridge.

"I can't do anything—not from here, Gray. I can't find her, can't feel her. I'll have to follow her."

"Quick."

"As quick as I can, you know that."

Lockwood kept his weapons, his talisman, his boots; he shed only his cloak, giving it to Gray. As the cloth spilled from one man's arms to the other's, their hands touched then clasped together.

"Have a care for yourself," Gray whispered, his usual farewell when his boon-friend went out after lightning—the same words he'd spoken when the three of them were together not long ago.

"Always," Lockwood assured him.

But the bright-eyed confidence wasn't there and Gray couldn't let go.

"Come back safe, Locky. Alone, if you must, but come back."

Lockwood nodded and, after a final squeeze that left Gray's fingers numb, set out along the golden bridge, the little owl clinging to his shoulder.

Sitting where the golden bridge touched the cavern ledge, Gray aged a year with each breath as he watched his boon-friend climb Lady Kiera's path into oblivion. He was older than Fawlen—much older—before he saw a dark mote move against the gold. His heart wanted to soar as high as the sun, but he held it in check, and wisely. Though the mote grew steadily larger, it was not large enough to be two people.

Of course, they hadn't journeyed out to the Siege of Shadows together. It was no cause for concern that they would come back separately. No cause for concern that it was Lady Kiera coming toward him. Lockwood would naturally send her first.

And she was smiling radiantly, as she wouldn't be if anything were wrong. At least that's what Gray told himself as she neared the end of the bridge, running toward him with her arms spread wide. He shunted his fears and his doubts aside, catching her easily when she leapt from the bridge to his arms.

Lady Kiera's lips were against his before he could speak, and while they kissed, there was no place in his thoughts for anyone but her. But he had to breathe, and breath brought his boon-friend back to the forefront of his mind.

"Where's Locky?" he asked, only to realize she'd asked the same question, calling him Lord Marelet instead.

"Oh . . . No . . ." she gasped while Gray remained speechless, the point of a sword embedded in his heart. "Oh no."

"You called," he murmured. His lungs were on fire; every word burned. "For help. He went."

Her left arm circled his waist; her right hand touched his neck, holding him close until, small and fragile woman that she was, she was supporting him, because his strength fled.

"He went. He went with the owl. To you. To help you. You called. You called for help."

"He never found me," she whispered, a beautiful, gentle sound in his ear.

The tears began then. He loved Lady Kiera. Somewhere beneath the pain, he was glad she'd come back, but Lockwood was gone. The world was empty; the world was nothing.

"We'll go home," she said. "We'll mourn together."

Gray nodded once, then shook his head and stood straight. "How, my lady? It's no different than before."

"But it is, Gray, my lord, my love. Everything's different. I can take us home."

And the mountain began to move.

Epilogue

Kyle awoke with a splitting headache. Thick fog hung between him and the rest of the world. Some of the fog was due to his headache, but the rest was smoke.

He remembered fire bursting through the rock in front of him. He remembered struggling up a shifting slope, grasping for a hand that was just out of reach. He remembered the face that went with that hand, and then he remembered everything.

"Lockwood! Gray! Kiera! Where are you?"

The fog swallowed his words and any answers. He stumbled in a direction that might—or might not—lead to the verge.

Destiny.

Destiny be damned.

There were bodies underfoot. He had to get close—closer than he wanted—to convince himself that, with the possible exception of one towheaded corpse who might be Paggat, his friends hadn't died on the verge.

And hadn't waited to see what had become of him.

Kyle yelled himself hoarse before conceding that he was alone. Alone with the silver-haired warrior he had rescued.

Night was coming. Kyle found his battered pack, then he cursed and kicked and stumbled his way back to the ravine. The warrior had managed to sit up. Two paces away, he was a hazy silhouette in the fog. At arm's length—

At arm's length and despite a spiderweb of cuts, Kyle would stake his life that the silver-haired warrior was a *woman.*

She said something, not friendly by the tone of it.

"My name is Kyle Dainis, Hart-lord of Dainis," he replied, not imagining that she understood him any better than he'd understood her. But they had to start somewhere. "We're alone—just the two of us. And I think, I think your leg's broken."

Another blast of sharply spoken syllables.

"Kyle Dainis. Kyle. You're going to need my help."

He held out his hand.

She spat on it.

Rapture. Destiny. Standing in the fog with a warrior woman spitting at him. He'd have walked away, if he hadn't believed there was nowhere to go. He sat down against another rock and rooted through his pack until he found his smoked meat and stale flatbread. It wouldn't last forever, no matter how careful he was, so he cut off a good-sized chunk of meat, tore it in two, and tossed the smaller piece to his companion.

She snatched it out of the air, sniffed it a few times, and took a bite. She said another word he didn't understand, but it wasn't as angry-sounding as her other words had been. At least they'd gone from curses to food.

The warrior woman had her own worries, Kyle imagined, her own grief, and the pain of a broken leg. He left her alone; there was truly nothing he could say or do. He was waiting for—hoping for—Kestrel to return. The owl preferred to fly at night, but not through fog.

Still, it couldn't hurt to try. Kyle made the nasen'bei winds blow and filled them with Taslim's name in such blind, mindless repetition that a moment passed before he knew he wasn't alone any longer.

<<Hart-lord! Hart-lord! Where are you?>> Taslim's presence was faint in the wind and grew fainter.

Kyle shouted "Here!" and jumped to his feet. He shouted the runes *"Serras!"* and *"Onda!"* as well, and added them to the nasen'bei wind, but Taslim's presence grew no stronger until a light began to shine at Kyle's feet.

The silver-haired warrior of Kyle's Rapture wasn't only a woman, she was a wizard, with a crystal talisman that burned through the fog.

<<She killed him, Hart-lord! She took the Siege and then killed him! Start running! Save yourself!>>

<<Run where?>> Kyle demanded, and <<Killed who?>> though he knew the answer to that question in the moment he asked it.

<<It's all coming down!>> Taslim screamed, nearer now, and clearer in Kyle's mind; he could feel the owl's exhaustion, the wizard's panic. <<The mountains are moving! Run!>>

<<Run where, Taslim? All along you've said there's no way out!>>

Taslim was in Kyle's mind then, radiating exhaustion, panic, and images Kyle did not want to decipher, but nothing that looked like a way back to Alberon. The thunder was already louder and continuous, and Kyle didn't doubt that mountains were moving. He wasn't a wizard, Taslim wasn't a very good wizard, and the woman sitting at his feet with a talisman couldn't understand a word he said.

<<It's over, Taslim. There's no place to go; no way to get there.>> He said it again, aloud, and felt calmer. He scarcely jumped at all when his silver-haired companion held up her talisman and said something incomprehensible.

<<Who is that, Hart-lord?>>

<<My destiny,>> Kyle replied with heavy irony. <<The face beneath the Rapture mask.>>

She started talking; Kyle paid no attention.

<<Her leg's broken. I think she's a wizard.>>

<<She says she is. She also says you're a fool and if we don't start moving, we're all going to die. Help her, Hart-lord. I think she knows a way out. You can carry her, can't you?>>

He could, and did, one step at a time as the mountains bucked and heaved around them.

A step at a time, just as he had in his dreams, until the fog lifted and, looking up, he saw a midnight sky and not a single familiar star.